THE SHIP WHO
SAVED
THE
WORLDS

THE SHIP WHO
SAVED
THE
WORLDS

ANNE McCAFFREY
JODY LYNN NYE

THE SHIP WHO SAVED THE WORLDS

Copyright © 2003 by Bill Fawcett & Associates. *The Ship Who Won* © 1994 by Bill Fawcett & Associates; *The Ship Errant* © 1996 by Bill Fawcett & Associates.

A Baen Books Original

Baen Publishing Enterprises
P.O. Box 1403
Riverdale, NY 10471
www.baen.com

ISBN: 0-7434-7171-7

Cover art by Carol Heyer *638 3223*

First Megabooks hardcover printing, December 2003

Library of Congress Cataloging-in-Publication Data

McCaffrey, Anne.
 The ship who saved the worlds / by Anne McCaffrey & Jody Lynn Nye.
   p. cm.
"A Baen Books original."
 ISBN 0-7434-7171-7
 1. People with disabilities--Fiction. 2. Interplanetary voyages--Fiction. 3. Life on other planets--Fiction. 4. Space ships--Fiction. 5. Women--Fiction. I. Nye, Jody Lynn, 1957- II. Title.

 PS3563.A255S46 2003
 813'.54--dc22

                                                                    2003020713

Distributed by Simon & Schuster
1230 Avenue of the Americas
New York, NY 10020

Production by Windhaven Press, Auburn, NH
Printed in the United States of America

10 9 8 7 6 5 4 3 2 1

CONTENTS

THE SHIP WHO
SAVED
THE
WORLDS

The Ship Who Won

CHAPTER ONE

The ironbound door at the end of the narrow passageway creaked open. An ancient man peered out and focused wrinkle-lapped eyes on Keff. Keff knew what the old one saw: a mature man, not overly tall, whose wavy brown hair, only just beginning to be shot with gray, was arrayed above a mild yet bull-like brow and deep-set blue eyes. A nose whose craggy shape suggested it may or may not have been broken at some time in the past, and a mouth framed by humor lines added to the impression of one who was tough yet instinctively gentle. He was dressed in a simple tunic but carried a sword at his side with the easy air of someone who knew how to use it. The oldster wore the shapeless garments of one who has ceased to care for any attribute but warmth and convenience. They studied each other for a moment. Keff dipped his head slightly in greeting.

"Is your master at home?"

"I have no master. Get ye gone to whence ye came," the ancient spat, eyes blazing. Keff knew at once that this was no serving man; he'd just insulted the High Wizard Zarelb himself! He straightened his shoulders, going on guard but seeking to look friendly and non-threatening.

"Nay, sir," Keff said. "I must speak to you." Rats crept out of the doorway only inches from his feet and skittered away through the gutters along the walls. A disgusting place, but Keff had his mission to think of.

"Get ye gone," the old man repeated. "I've nothing for you." He tried to close the heavy, planked door. Keff pushed his gauntleted forearm into the narrowing crack and held it open. The old man backed away a pace, his eyes showing fear.

"I know you have the Scroll of Almon," Keff said, keeping his voice gentle. "I need it, good sir, to save the people of Harimm. Please give it to me, sir. I will harm you not."

"Very well, young man," the wizard said. "Since you threaten me, I will cede the scroll."

Keff relaxed slightly, with an inward grin. Then he caught a gleam in the old man's eye, which focused over Keff's shoulder. Spinning on his heel, Keff whipped his narrow sword out of its scabbard. Its lighted point picked out glints in the eyes and off the sword-blades of the three ruffians who had stepped into the street behind him. He was trapped.

One of the ruffians showed blackened stumps of teeth in a broad grin. "Going somewhere, sonny?" he asked.

"I go where duty takes me," Keff said

"Take him, boys!"

His sword on high, the ruffian charged. Keff immediately blocked the man's chop, and riposted, flinging the man's heavy sword away with a clever twist of his slender blade that left the man's chest unguarded and vulnerable. He lunged, seeking his enemy's heart with his blade. Stumbling away with more haste than grace, the man spat, gathered himself, and charged again, this time followed by the other two. Keff turned into a whirlwind, parrying, thrusting, and striking, holding the three men at bay. A near strike by one of his opponents streaked along the wall by his cheek. He jumped away and parried just before an enemy skewered him.

"Yoicks!" he cried, dancing in again. "Have at you!"

He lunged, and the hot point of his epee struck the middle of the chief thug's chest. The body sank to the ground, and vanished.

"There!" Keff shouted, flicking the sword back and forth, leaving a Z etched in white light on the air. "You are not invincible. Surrender or die!"

Keff's renewed energy seemed to confuse the two remaining ruffians, who fought disjointedly, sometimes getting in each other's way while Keff's blade found its mark again and again, sinking its light into arms, shoulders, chests. In a lightning-fast sequence, first one, then the other foe left his guard open a moment too long. With groans, the villains sank to the ground, whereupon they too vanished. Putting the epee back into his belt, Keff turned to confront the ancient wizard, who stood watching the proceedings with a neutral eye.

"In the name of the people of Harimm, I claim the Scroll," Keff said grandly, extending a hand. "Unless you have other surprises for me?'

"Nay, nay." The old man fumbled in the battered leather scrip at his side. From it he took a roll of parchment, yellowed and crackling with age. Keff stared at it with awe. He bowed to the wizard, who gave him a grudging look of respect.

The scroll lifted out of the wizard's hand and floated toward Keff. Hovering in the air, it unrolled slowly. Keff squinted at what was revealed within: spidery tracings in fading brown ink, depicting mountains, roads, and rivers. "A map!" he breathed.

"Hold it," the wizard said, his voice unaccountably changing from a cracked baritone to a pleasant female alto. "We're in range of the comsats." Door, rats, and aged figure vanished, leaving blank walls.

"Oh, spacedust," Keff said, unstrapping his belt and laser epee and throwing himself into the crash seat at the control console. "I was enjoying that. Whew! Good workout!" He pulled his sweaty tunic off over his head, and mopped his face with the tails. The dark curls of hair on his broad chest may have been shot through here and there with white ones, but he was grinning like a boy.

"You nearly got yourself spitted back there," said the disembodied voice of Carialle, simultaneously sending and acknowledging ID signals to the SSS-900. "Watch your back better next time."

"What'd I get for that?" Keff asked.

"No points for unfinished tasks. Maps are always unknowns. You'll have to follow it and see," Carialle said coyly. The image of a gorgeous lady dressed in floating sky blue chiffon and gauze and a pointed hennin appeared briefly on a screen next to her titanium column. The lovely rose-and-cream complected visage smiled down on Keff. "Nice footwork, good sir knight," the Lady Fair said, and vanished. "SSS-900, this is the CK-963 requesting permission to approach and dock—Hello, Simeon!"

"Carialle!" The voice of the station controller came through the box. "Welcome back! Permission granted, babe. And that's SSS-

900-C, now, C for Channa. A lot's happened in the year since you've been away. Keff, are you there?"

Keff leaned in toward the pickup. "Right here, Simeon. We're within half a billion klicks. Should be with you soon."

"It'll be good to have you on board," Simeon said. "We're a little disarrayed right now, to put it mildly, but you didn't come to see me for my housekeeping."

"No, cookie, but you give such good decontam a girl can hardly stay away," Carialle quipped with a naughty chuckle.

"Dragon's teeth, Simeon!" Keff suddenly exclaimed, staring at his scopes. "What happened around here?"

"Well, if you really want to know . . ."

The scout ship threaded its way through an increasingly cluttered maze of junk and debris as they neared the rotating dumbbell shape of Station SSS-900. After viewing Keff's cause for alarm, Carialle put her repulsors on full to avoid the very real possibility of intersecting with one of the floating chunks of metal debris that shared a Trojan point with the station. Skiffs and tugs moved amidst the shattered parts of ships and satellites, scavenging. A pair of battered tugs with scoops on the front, looking ridiculously like gigantic vacuum cleaners, described regular rows as they sieved up microfine spacedust that could hole hulls and vanes of passing ships without ever being detected by the crews inside. The cleanup tugs sent hails as Carialle passed them in a smooth arc, synchronizing herself to the spin of the space station. The north docking ring was being repaired, so with a flick of her controls, Carialle increased thrust and caught up with the south end. Lights began to chase around the lip of one of the docking bays on the ring, and she made for it.

" . . . so that was the last we saw of the pirate Belazir and his bully boys," Simeon finished, sounding weary. "For good, I hope. My shell has been put in a more damage resistant casing and resealed in its pillar. We've spent the last six months healing and picking up the pieces. Still waiting for replacement parts. The insurance company is being sticky and querying every fardling item on the list, but no one's surprised about that. Fleet ships are remaining in the area. We've put in for a permanent patrol, maybe a small garrison."

"You have had a hell of a time," Carialle said, sympathetically.

"Now let's hear the good news," Simeon said, with a sudden surge of energy in his voice. "Where've you been all this time?"

Carialle simulated a trumpet playing a fanfare.

"We're pleased to announce that star GZA-906-M has two planets with oxygen-breathing life," Keff said.

"Congratulations, you two!" Simeon said, sending an audio burst that sounded like thousands of people cheering. He paused, very briefly. "I'm sending a simultaneous message to Xeno and Explorations. They're standing by for a full report with samples and graphs, but me first! I want to hear it all."

Carialle accessed her library files and tight-beamed the star chart and xeno file to Simeon's personal receiving frequency. "This is a precis of what we'll give to Xeno and the benchmarkers," she said. "We'll spare you the boring stuff."

"If there's any bad news," Keff began, "it's that there's no sentient life on planet four, and planet three's is too far down the tech scale to join Central Worlds as a trading partner. But they were glad to see us."

"He thinks," Carialle interrupted, with a snort. "I really never knew what the Beasts Blatisant thought." Keff shot an exasperated glance at her pillar, which she ignored. She clicked through the directory on the file and brought up the profile on the natives of Iricon III.

"Why do you call them the Beasts Blatisant?" Simeon asked, scanning the video of the skinny, hairy hexapedal beings, whose faces resembled those of intelligent grasshoppers.

"Listen to the audio," Carialle said, laughing. "They use a complex form of communication which we have a sociological aversion to understanding. Keff thought I was blowing smoke, so to speak."

"That's not true, Cari," Keff protested. "My initial conclusion," he stressed to Simeon, "was that they had no need for a complex spoken language. They live right in the swamps," Keff said, narrating the video that played off the datahedron. "As you can see, they travel either on all sixes or upright on four with two manipulative limbs. There are numerous predators that eat Beasts, among other things, and the simple spoken language is sufficient to relay information about them. Maintaining life is simple. You can see that fruit and edible vegetables grow in abundance right there in the swamp. The overlay shows which plants are dangerous."

"Not too many," Simeon said, noting the international symbols for poisonous and toxic compounds: a skull and crossbones and a small round face with its tongue out.

"Of course the first berry tried by my knight errant, and I especially stress the errant," Carialle said, "was those raspberry red ones on the left, marked with Mr. Yucky Face."

"Well, the natives were eating them, and their biology isn't that unlike Terran reptiles." Keff grimaced as he admitted, "but the berries gave me fierce stomach cramps. I was rolling all over the place clutching my belly. The Beasts thought it was funny." The video duly showed the hexapods, hooting, standing over a prone and writhing Keff.

"It was, a little," Carialle added, "once I got over being worried that he hadn't eaten something lethal. I told him to wait for the full analysis—"

"That would have taken *hours*," Keff interjected. "Our social interaction was happening in *realtime*."

"Well, you certainly made an impression."

"Did you understand the Beasts Blatisant? How'd the IT program go?" asked Simeon, changing the subject.

IT stood for Intentional Translator, the universal simultaneous language translation program that Keff had started before he graduated from school. IT was in a constant state of being perfected, adding referents and standards from each new alien language recorded by Central Worlds exploration teams. The brawn had more faith in his invention than his brain partner, who never relied on IT more than necessary. Carialle teased Keff mightily over the mistakes the IT made, but all the chaffing was affectionately meant. Brain and brawn had been together fourteen years out of a twenty-five-year mission, and were close and caring friends. For all the badinage she tossed his way, Carialle never let anyone else take the mickey out of her partner within her hearing.

Now she sniffed. "Still flawed, since IT uses only the symbology of alien life-forms already discovered. Even with the addition of the Blaize Modification for sign language, I think that it still fails to *anticipate*. I mean, who the hell knows what referents and standards new alien races will use?"

"Sustained use of a symbol in context suggests that it has meaning," Keff argued. "That's the basis of the program."

"How do you tell the difference between a repeated movement with meaning and one without?" Carialle asked, reviving the old argument. "Supposing a jellyfish's wiggle is sometimes for propulsion and sometimes for dissemination of information? Listen, Simeon, you be the judge."

"All right," the station manager said, amused.

"What if members of a new race have mouths and talk, but impart any information of real importance in some other way? Say, with a couple of sharp poots out the sphincter?"

"It was the berries," Keff said. "Their diet caused the repeating, er, repeats."

"Maybe that . . . habit . . . had some relevance in the beginning of their civilization," Carialle said with acerbity. "However, Simeon, once Keff got the translator working on their verbal language, we found that at first they just parroted back to him anything he said, like a primitive AI pattern, gradually forming sentences, using words of their own and anything they heard him say. It seemed useful at first. We thought they'd learn Standard at light-speed, long before Keff could pick up on the intricacies of their language, but that wasn't what happened."

"They parroted the language right, but they didn't really understand what I was saying," Keff said, alternating his narrative automatically with Carialle's. "No true comprehension."

"In the meantime, the flatulence was bothering him, not only because it seemed to be ubiquitous, but because it seemed to be controllable."

"I didn't know if it was supposed to annoy me, or if it meant something. Then we started studying them more closely."

The video cut from one scene to another of the skinny, hairy aliens diving for ichthyoids and eels, which they captured with their middle pair of limbs. More footage showed them eating voraciously; teaching their young to hunt; questing for smaller food animals and hiding from larger and more dangerous beasties. Not much of the land was dry, and what vegetation grew there was sought after by all the hungry species.

Early tapes showed that, at first, the Beasts seemed to be afraid of Keff, behaving as if they thought he was going to attack them. Over the course of a few days, as he seemed to be neither aggressive nor helpless, they investigated him further. When they dined, he ate a meal from his own supplies beside them.

"Then, keeping my distance, I started asking them questions, putting a clear rising interrogative into my tone of voice that I had heard their young use when asking for instruction. That seemed to please them, even though they were puzzled why an obviously mature being needed what seemed to be survival information. Interspecies communication and cooperation was unknown to them." Keff watched as Carialle skipped through the data to another event. "This was the potlatch. Before it really got started, the Beasts ate kilos of those bean-berries."

"Keff had decided then that they couldn't be too intelligent, doing something like that to themselves. Eating foods that caused them obvious distress for pure ceremony's sake seemed downright dumb."

"I was disappointed. Then the IT started kicking back patterns to me on the Beasts' noises. Then I felt downright dumb." Keff had the good grace to grin at himself.

"And what happened, ah, in the end?" Simeon asked,

Keff grinned sheepishly. "Oh, Carialle was right, of course. The red berries were the key to their formal communication. I had to give points for repetition of, er, body language. So, I programmed the IT to pick up what the Blatisants meant, not just what they said, taking in all movement or sounds to analyze for meaning. It didn't always work right . . ."

"Hah!" Carialle interrupted, in triumph. "He admits it!"

" . . . but soon, I was getting the sense of what they were really communicating. The verbal was little more than protective coloration. The Blatisants do have a natural gift for mimicry. The IT worked fine—well, mostly. The system's just going to require more testing, that's all."

"It always requires more testing," Carialle remarked in a long-suffering voice. "One day we're going to miss something we really need."

Keff was unperturbed. "Maybe IT needs an AI element to test each set of physical movements or gestures for meaning on the spot and relay it to the running glossary. I'm going to use IT on humans next, see if I can refine the quirks that way when I already know what a being is communicating."

"If it works," Simeon said, with rising interest, "and you can read body language, it'll put you far beyond any means of translation that's ever been done. They'll call you a mind-reader. Softshells so seldom say what they mean—but they do express it through their attitudes and gestures. I can think of a thousand practical uses for IT right here in Central Worlds."

"As for the Blatisants, there's no reason not to recommend further investigation to award them ISS status, since it's clear they are sentient and have an ongoing civilization, however primitive," Keff said. "And that's what I'm going to tell the Central Committee in my report. Iricon III's got to go on the list."

"I wish I could be a mouse in the wall," Simeon said, chuckling with mischievous glee, "when an evaluation team has to talk with your Beasts. The whole party's going to sound like a raft of untuned engines. I know CenCom's going to be happy to hear about another race of sentients."

"I know," Keff said, a little sadly, "but it's not *the* race, you know." To Keff and Carialle, the designation meant that most elusive of holy grails, an alien race culturally and technologically advanced enough to meet humanity on its own terms, having independently achieved computer science and space travel.

"If anyone's going to find *the* race, it's likely to be you two," Simeon said with open sincerity.

Carialle closed the last kilometers to the docking bay and shut off her engines as the magnetic grapples pulled her close, and the vacuum seal snugged around the airlock.

"Home again," she sighed.

The lights on the board started flashing as Simeon sent a burst requesting decontamination for the CK-963. Keff pushed back from the monitor panels and went back to his cabin to make certain everything personal was locked down before the decontam crew came on board.

"We're empty on everything, Simeon," Carialle said. "Protein vats are at the low ebb, my nutrients are redlining, fuel cells down. Fill 'er up."

"We're a bit short on some supplies at the moment," Simeon said, "but I'll give you what I can." There was a brief pause, and his voice returned. "I've checked for mail. Keff has two parcels. The manifests are for circuits, and for a 'Rotoflex.' What's that?"

"Hah!" said Keff, pleased. "Exercise equipment. A Rotoflex helps build chest and back muscles without strain on the intercostals."

He flattened his hands over his ribs and breathed deeply to demonstrate.

"All we need is more clang-and-bump deadware on *my deck*," Carialle said with the noise that served her for a sigh.

"Where's your shipment, Carialle?" Keff asked innocently. "I thought you were sending for a body from Moto-Prosthetics."

"Well, you thought wrong," Carialle said, exasperated that he was bringing up their old argument. "I'm happy in my skin, thank you."

"You'd love being mobile, lady fair," Keff said. "All the things you miss staying in one place! You can't imagine. Tell her, Simeon."

"She travels more than I do, Sir Galahad. Forget it."

"Anyone else have messages for us?" Carialle asked.

"Not that I have on record, but I'll put out a query to show you're in dock."

Keff picked his sodden tunic off the console and stood up.

"I'd better go and let the medicals have their poke at me," he said. "Will you take care of the rest of the computer debriefing, my lady Cari, or do you want me to stay and make sure they don't poke in anywhere you don't want them?"

"Nay, good sir knight," Carialle responded, still playing the game. "You have coursed long and far, and deserve reward."

"The only rewards I want," Keff said wistfully, "are a beer that hasn't been frozen for a year, and a little companionship—not that you aren't the perfect companion, lady fair"—he kissed his hand to the titanium column—"but as the prophet said, let there be spaces in your togetherness. If you'll excuse me?"

"Well, don't space yourself too far," Carialle said. Keff grinned. Carialle followed him on her internal cameras to his cabin, where, in deference to those spaces he mentioned, she stopped. She heard the sonic-shower turn on and off, and the hiss of his closet door. He came out of the cabin pulling on a new, dry tunic, his curly hair tousled.

"Ta-ta," Keff said. "I go to confess all and slay a beer or two."

Before the airlock sealed, Carialle had opened up her public memory banks to Simeon, transferring full copies of their datafiles on the Iricon mission. Xeno were on line in seconds, asking her for in-depth, eyewitness commentary on their exploration. Keff, in Medical, was probably answering some of the same questions. Xeno liked subjective accounts as well as mechanical recordings.

At the same time Carialle carried on her conversation with Simeon, she oversaw the decontam crew and loading staff, and relaxed a little herself after what had been an arduous journey. A few days here, and she'd feel ready to go out and knit the galactic spiral into a sweater.

Keff's medical examination, under the capable stethoscope of Dr. Chaundra, took less than fifteen minutes, but the interview with Xeno went on for hours. By the time he had recited from memory everything he thought or observed about the Beasts Blatisant he was wrung out and dry.

"You know, Keff," Darvi, the xenologist, said, shutting down his clipboard terminal on the Beast Blatisant file, "if I didn't know you personally, I'd have to think you were a little nuts, giving alien races silly names like that. Beasts Blatisant. Sea Nymphs. Losels— that was the last one I remember."

"Don't you ever play Myths and Legends, Darvi?" Keff asked, eyes innocent.

"Not in years. Its a kid game, isn't it?"

"No! Nothing wrong with my mind, *nyuk-nyuk*," Keff said, rubbing knuckles on his own pate and pulling a face. The xenologist looked worried for a moment, then relaxed as he realized Keff was teasing him. "Seriously, it's self-defense against boredom. After fourteen years of this job, one gets fardling tired of referring to a species as 'the indigenous race' or 'the inhabitants of Zoocon I.' I'm not an AI drone, and neither is Carialle."

"Well, the names are still silly."

"Humankind is a silly race," Keff said lightly. "I'm just indulging in innocent fun."

He didn't want to get into what he and Carialle considered the serious aspects of the game, the points of honor, the satisfaction of laying successes at the feet of his lady fair. It wasn't as if he and Carialle couldn't tell the difference between play and reality. The game had permeated their life and given it shape and texture, becoming more than a game, *meaning* more. He'd never tell this space-dry plodder about the time five years back that he actually stood vigil throughout a long, lonely night lit by a single candle to earn his knighthood. *I guess you just had to be there,* he thought. "If that's all?" he asked, standing up quickly.

Darvi waved a stylus at him, already engrossed in the files. Keff escaped before the man thought of something else to ask and hurried down the curving hall to the nearest lift.

Keff had learned about Myths and Legends in primary school. A gang of his friends used to get together once a week (more often when they dared and homework permitted) to play after class. Keff liked being able to live out some of his heroic fantasies and, briefly, *be* a knight battling evil and bringing good to all the world. As he grew up and learned that the galaxy was a billion times larger than his one small colony planet, the compulsion to do good grew, as did his private determination that he could make a difference, no matter how minute. He managed not to divulge this compulsion during his psychiatric interviews on his admission to Brawn Training and kept his altruism private. Nonetheless, as a knight of old, Keff performed his assigned tasks with energy and devotion, vowing that no ill or evil would ever be done by him. In a quiet way, he applied the rules of the game to his own life.

As it happened, Carialle also loved M&L, but more for the strategy and research that went into formulating the quests than the adventuring. After they were paired, they had simply fallen into playing the game to while away the long days and months between stars. He could put no finger on a particular moment when they began to make it a lifestyle: Keff the eternal knight errant and Carialle his lady fair. To Keff this was the natural extension of an adolescent interest that had matured along with him.

As soon as he'd heard that the CX-963 was in need of a brawn, his romantic nature required him to apply for the position as Carialle's brawn. He'd heard—who hadn't?—about the devastating space storm and collision that had cost Fanine Takajima-Morrow's life and almost took Carialle's sanity.

She'd had to undergo a long recovery period when the Mutant Minorities (MM) and Society for the Preservation of the Rights of Intelligent Minorities (SPRIM) boffins wondered if she'd ever be willing to go into space again. They rejoiced when she announced that not only was she ready to fly, but ready to interview brawns as well. Keff had wanted that assignment badly. Reading her file had given him an intense *need* to protect Carialle. A ridiculous notion, when he ruefully considered that she had the resources of a brainship at her synapse ends, but her vulnerability had been demonstrated during that storm. The protective aspect of his nature vibrated at the challenge to keep her from any further harm.

Though she seldom talked about it, he suspected she still had nightmares about her ordeal—in those random hours when a brain might drop into dreamtime. She also proved to be the best of partners and companions. He liked her, her interests, her hobbies, didn't mind her faults or her tendency to be right more often than he was. She taught him patience. He taught her to swear in ninety languages as a creative means of dispelling tension. They bolstered one another. The trust between them was as deep as space and felt as ancient and as new at the same time. The fourteen years of their partnership had flown by, literally and figuratively. Within Keff's system of values, to be paired with a brainship was the greatest honor a mere human could be accorded, and he knew it.

The lift slowed to a creaky halt and the doors opened. Keff had been on SSS-900 often enough to turn to port as he hit the corridor, in the direction of the spacer bar he liked to patronize while on station.

Word had gotten around that he was back, probably the helpful Simeon's doing. A dark brown stout already separating from its creamy crown was waiting for him on the polished steel bar. It was the first thing on which he focused.

"Ah!" he cried, moving toward the beer with both hands out. "Come to Keff."

A hand reached into his field of vision and smartly slapped his wrist before he could touch the mug handle. Keff tilted a reproachful eye upward.

"How's your credit?" the bartender asked, then tipped him a wicked wink. She was a woman of his own age with nut-brown hair cut close to her head and the milk-fair skin of the lifelong spacer of European descent. "Just kidding. Drink up, Keff. This one's on the house. It's good to see you."

"Blessings on you and on this establishment, Mariad, and on your brewers, wherever they are," Keff said, and put his nose into the foam and slowly tipped his head back and the glass up. The mug was empty when he set it down. "Ahhhh. Same again, please."

Cheers and applause erupted from the tables and Keff waved in acknowledgment that his feat had been witnessed. A couple of people gave him thumbs up before returning to their conversations and dart games.

"You can always tell a light-year spacer by the way he refuels in port," said one man, coming forward to clasp Keff's hand. His thin, melancholy face was contorted into an odd smile.

Keff stood up and slapped him on the back. "Baran Larrimer! I didn't know you and Shelby were within a million light years of here."

An old friend, Larrimer was half of a brain/brawn team assigned to the Central Worlds defense fleet. Keff suddenly remembered Simeon's briefing about naval support. Larrimer must have known exactly what Keff had been told. The older brawn gave him a tired grimace and nodded at the questioning expression on his face.

"Got to keep our eyes open," he said simply.

"And you are not keeping yours open," said a voice. A tiny arm slipped around Keff's waist and squeezed. He glanced down into a small, heart-shaped face. "Good to see you, Keff."

"Susa Gren!" Keff lifted the young woman clean off the ground in a sweeping hug and set her down for a huge kiss, which she returned with interest. "So you and Marliban are here, too?"

"Courier duty for a trading contingent," Susa said in a low voice, her dark eyes crinkling wryly at the corners. She tilted her head toward a group of hooded aliens sitting isolated around a table in the corner. "Hoping to sell Simeon a load of protector/detectors. They plain forgot that Marl's a brain and could hear every word. The things they said in front of him! Which he quite rightly passed straight on to Simeon, so, dear me, didn't they have a hard time bargaining their wares. I'd half a mind to tell CenCom that those idiots can find their own way home if they won't show a brainship more respect. But," she sighed, "it's paying work."

Marl had only been in service for two—no, it was three years now—and was still too far down in debt to Central Worlds for his shell and education to refuse assignments, especially ones that paid as well as first-class courier work. Susa owed megacredits, too. She had made herself responsible for the debts of her parents, who had borrowed heavily to make an independent go of it on a mining world, and had failed. Fortunately not fatally, but the disaster had left them with only a subsistence allowance. Keff liked the spunky young woman, admired her drive and wit, her springy step and dainty, attractive figure. The two of them had always had an affinity which Carialle had duly noted, commenting a trifle bluntly that the ideal playmate for a brawn was another brawn. Few others could understand the dedication a brawn had for his brainship nor match the lifelong relationship.

"Susa," he said suddenly. "Do you have some time? Can you sit and talk for a while?"

Her eyes twinkled as if she had read his mind. "I've nothing to do and nowhere to go. Marl and I have liberty until those drones want to go home. Buy me a drink?"

Larrimer stood up, tactfully ignoring the increasing aura of intimacy between the other two brawns. He slapped his credit chit down on the bar and beckoned to Mariad.

"Come by if you have a moment, Keff," he said. "Shelby would be glad to see you."

"I will," Keff said, absently swatting a palm toward Larrimer's hand, which caught his in a firm clasp. "Safe going."

He and Susa sat down together in a booth. Mariad delivered a pair of Guinnesses and, with a motherly cluck, sashayed away.

"You're looking well," Susa said, scanning his face with a more than friendly concern. "You have a tan!"

"I got it on our last planetfall," Keff said. "Hasn't had time to fade yet."

"Well, I think you look good with a little color in your face," she declared. Her mouth crooked into a one-sided grin. "How far down does it go?"

Keff waggled his eyebrows at her. "Maybe in a while I'll let you see."

"Any of those deep scratches dangerous?" Carialle asked, swiveling an optical pickup out on a stalk to oversee the techs checking her outsides. The ship lay horizontally to the "dry dock" pier, giving the technicians the maximum expanse of hull to examine.

"Most of 'em are no problem. I'm putting setpatch in the one nearest your fuel lines," the coveralled man said, spreading a gray goo over the place. It hardened slowly, acquiring a silver sheen that blended with the rest of the hull plates. "Don't think it'll split in temperature extremes, ma'am, but it's thinner there, of course. This'll protect you more."

"Many thanks," Carialle said. When the patching compound dried, she tested her new skin for resonance and found its density matched well. In no time she'd forget she had a wrinkle under the dressing. Her audit program also found that the fee for materials was comfortingly low, compared to having the plate removed and hammered, or replaced entirely.

Overhead, a spider-armed crane swung its burden over her bow, dropping snakelike hoses toward her open cargo hull. The crates of xeno material had already been taken away in a specially sealed container. A suited and hooded worker had already cleaned the nooks and niches, making sure no stray native spores had hooked a ride to the Central Worlds. The crane's operator directed the various flexible tubes to the appropriate valves. Fuel was first, and Carialle flipped open her fuel toggle as the stout hose reached it. The narrow tube which fed her protein vats had a numbered filter at its spigot end. Carialle recorded that number in her files in case there were any impurities in the final product. Thankfully, the conduit that fed the carbo-protein sludge to Keff's food synthesizer was opaque. The peristaltic pulse of the thick stuff always made Cari think of quicksand, of sand-colored octopi creeping along an ocean floor, of week-old oatmeal. Her attention diverted momentarily to the dock, where a front-end loader was rolling toward her with a couple of containers, one large and one small, with bar-code tags addressed to Keff. She signaled her okay to the driver to load them in her cargo bay.

Another tech, a short, stout woman wearing thick-soled magnetic boots, approached her airlock and held up a small item. "This is for you from the station-master, Carialle. Permission to come aboard?"

Carialle focused on the datahedron in her fingers and felt a twitch of curiosity.

"Permission granted," she said. The tech clanked her way into the airlock and turned sideways to match the up/down orientation of Carialle's decks, then marched carefully toward the main cabin. "Did he say what it was?"

"No, ma'am. It's a surprise."

"Oh, Simeon!" Carialle exclaimed over the station-master's private channel. "Cats! Thank you!" She scanned the contents of the hedron back and forth. "Almost a realtime week of video footage. Wherever did you get it?"

"From a biologist who breeds domestic felines. He was out here two months ago. The hedron contains compressed videos of his cats and kittens, and he threw in some videos of wild felines he took on a couple of the colony worlds. Thought you'd like it."

"Simeon, it's wonderful. What can I swap you for it?"

The station-masters voice was sheepish. "You don't *need* to swap, Cari, but if you happened to have a spare painting? And I'm quite willing to sweeten the swap."

"Oh, no. I'd be cheating *you*. It isn't as if they're music. They're nothing."

"That isn't true, and you know it. You're a brain's artist."

With little reluctance, Carialle let Simeon tap into her video systems and directed him to the corner of the main cabin where her painting gear was stowed.

To any planetbound home-owner the cabin looked spotless, but to another spacer, it was a magpies' nest. Keff's exercise equipment occupied much of one end of the cabin. At the other, Carialle's specially adapted rack of painting equipment took up a largish section of floor space, not to mention wall space where her finished work hung—the ones she didn't give away or *throw* away. Those few permitted to see Carl's paintings were apt to call them "masterpieces," but she disclaimed that.

Not having a softshell body with hands to manage the mechanics of the art, she had had customized gear built to achieve the desired effect. The canvases she used were very thin, porous blocks of cells that she could flood individually with paint, like pixels on a computer screen, until it oozed together. The results almost resembled brush strokes. With the advance of technological subtleties, partly thanks to Moto-Prosthetics, Carialle had designed arms that could hold actual fiber brushes and airbrushes, to apply paints to the surface of the canvases over the base work.

What had started as therapy after her narrow escape from death had become a successful and rewarding hobby. An occasional sale of a picture helped to fill the larder or the fuel tank when bonuses were scarce, and the odd gift of an unlooked-for screen-canvas did much to placate occasionally fratchety bureaucrats. The sophisticated servo arms pulled one microfiber canvas after another out of the enameled, cabinet-mounted rack to show Simeon, who appreciated all and made sensible comments about several.

"That one's available," Carialle said, mechanical hands turning over a night-black spacescape, a full-color sketch of a small nocturnal animal, and a study of a crystalline mineral deposit embedded in a meteor. "This one I gave Keff. This one I'm keeping. This one's not finished. Hmm. These two are available. So's this one."

Much of what Carialle rendered wouldn't be visible to the unenhanced eyes of a softshell artist, but the sensory apparatus available to a shellperson gave color and light to scenes that would otherwise seem to the naked eye to be only black with white pinpoints of stars.

"That's good." Simeon directed her camera to a spacescape of a battered scout ship traveling against the distant cloudlike mist of an ion storm that partially overlaid the corona of a star like a veil. The canvas itself wasn't rectangular in shape, but had a gentle irregular outline that complimented the subject.

"Um," Carialle said. Her eye, on tight microscopic adjustment, picked up flaws in some individual cells of paint. They were red instead of carmine, and the shading wasn't subtle enough. "It's not finished yet."

"You mean you're not through fiddling with it. Give over, girl. I like it."

"It's yours, then," Carialle said with an audible sigh of resignation. The servo picked it out of the rack and headed for the airlock on its small track-treads. Carialle activated a camera on the outside of her hull to spot a technician in the landing bay. "Barkley, would you mind taking something for the station-master?" she said, putting her voice on speaker.

"Sure wouldn't, Carialle," the mech-tech said, with a brilliant smile at the visible camera. The servo met her edge of the dock, and handed the painting to her.

"You've got talent, gal," Simeon said, still sharing her video system as she watched the tech leave the bay. "Thank you. I'll treasure it."

"Its nothing," Carialle said modestly. "Just a hobby."

"Fardles. Say, I've got a good idea. Why don't you do a gallery showing next time you're in port? We have plenty of traders and bigwigs coming through who would pay good credit for original art. Not to mention the added cachet that it's painted by a brainship."

"We-ell . . ." Carialle said, considering.

"I'll give you free space near the concessions for the first week, so you're not losing anything on the cost of location. If you feel shy about showing off, you can do it by invitation only, but I warn you, word will spread."

"You've persuaded me," Carialle said.

"My intentions are purely honorable," Simeon replied gallantly. "Frag it!" he exclaimed. The speed of transmission on his frequency increased to a microsquirt. "You're as loaded and ready as you're going to get, Carialle. Put it together and scram off this station. The Inspector General wants a meeting with you in fifteen minutes. He just told me to route a message through to you. I'm delaying it as long as I dare."

"Oh, no!" Carialle said at the same speed. "I have no intention of letting Dr. Sennet 'I am a psychologist' Maxwell-Corey pick through my brains every single fardling time I make stationfall. I'm cured, damn it! I don't need constant monitoring."

"You'd better scoot now, Cari. My walls-with-ears have heard rumors that he thinks your 'obsession' with things like Myths and Legends makes your sanity highly suspect. When he hears the latest report—your Beasts Blatisant—you're going to be in for another long psychological profile session, and Keff along with you. Even Maxwell-Corey has to justify his job to someone."

"Damn him! We haven't finished loading my supplies! I only have half a vat of nutrients, and most of the stuff Keff ordered is still in your stores."

"Sorry, honey. It'll still be here when you come back. I can send you a squirt after he's gone."

Carialle considered swiftly whether it was worth calling in a complaint to SPRIM over the Inspector General and his obsessive desire to prove her unfit for service. He was witch-hunting, of that she was sure, and she wasn't going to be the witch involved. Wasn't it bad enough that he insisted on making her relive a sixteen-year-old tragedy every time they met? One day there was going to be a big battle, but she didn't feel like taking him on yet.

Simeon was right. The CK-963 was through with decontamination and repairs. Only half a second had passed during their conversation. Simeon could hold up the IG's missive only a few minutes before the delay would cause the obstreperous Maxwell-Corey to demand an inquiry.

"Open up for me, Simeon. I've got to find Keff."

"No problem," the station-master said. "I know where he went."

"Keff," said the wall over his head. "Emergency transmission from Carialle."

Keff tilted his head up lazily. "I'm busy, Simeon. Privacy." Susa's hand reached up, tangled in his hair, and pulled it down again. He breathed in the young woman's scent, moved his hands in delightful counterpoint under her body, one down from the curve of her shoulder, pushing the thin cloth of her ship-suit down; one upward, caressing her buttocks and delicate waist. She locked her legs with his, started her free hand toward his waistband, feeling for the fastening.

"Emergency *priority* transmission from Carialle," Simeon repeated.

Reluctantly, Keff unlocked his lips from Susa's. Her eyes filled with concern, she nodded. Without moving his head, he said, "All right, Simeon. Put it through."

"Keff," Carialle's voice rang with agitation. "Get down here immediately. We've got to lift ship ASAP."

"Why?" Keff asked irritably. "You couldn't have finished loading already."

"Haven't. Can't wait. Got to go. Get here, stat!"

Sighing, Keff rolled off Susa and petulantly addressed the ceiling. "What about my shore leave? Ladylove, while I like nothing better in the galaxy than being with you ninety-nine percent of the time, there *is* that one percent when we poor shell-less ones need—"

Carialle cut him off. "Keff, the Inspector General's on station."

"What?" Keff sat up.

"He's demanding another meeting, and you know what that means. We've got to get as far away from here as we can, right away."

Keff was already struggling back into his ship-suit. "Are we refueled? How much supplies are on board?"

Simeon's voice issued from the concealed speaker. "About a third full," he said. "But it's all I can give you right now. I told you supplies were short. Your food's about the same."

"We can't go far on that. About one long run, or two short ones." Keff stood, jamming feet into boots. Susa sat up and began pulling the top of her coverall over her bare shoulders. She shot Keff a look of regret mingled with understanding.

"We'll get missing supplies elsewhere," Carialle promised. "What's the safest vector out of here, Simeon?"

"I'll leave," Susa said, rising from the edge of the bed. She put a delicate hand on his arm. Keff stooped down and kissed her. "The less I hear, the less I have to confess if someone asks me under oath. Safe going, you two." She gave Keff a longing glance under her dark lashes. "Next time."

Just like that, she was gone, no complaints, no recriminations. Keff admired her for that. As usual, Carialle was correct: a brawn's ideal playmate was another brawn. It didn't stop him feeling frustrated over his thwarted sexual encounter, but it was better to spend that energy in a useful manner. Hopping into his right boot, he hurried out into the corridor. Ahead of him, Susa headed for a lift. Keff deliberately turned around, seeking a different route to his ship.

"Keep me out of Maxwell-Corey's way, Simeon." He ran around the curve of the station until he came to another lift. He punched the button, pacing anxiously until the doors opened.

"You're okay on that path," the station-master said, his voice following Keff. The brawn stepped into the empty car, and the doors slid shut behind him. "All right, this just became an express. Brace yourself."

"What about G sector?" Carialle was asking as Keff came aboard the CK-963. All the screens in the main cabin were full of star charts. Keff nodded Carialle's position in the main column and threw himself into his crash couch as he started going down the pre-launch list.

"Okay if you don't head toward Saffron. That's where the Fleet ships last traced Belazir's people. You *don't* want to meet them."

"Fragging well right we don't."

"What about M sector?" Keff said, peering at the chart directly in front of him. "We had good luck there last time."

"Last time you had your clock cleaned by the Losels," Carialle reminded him, not in too much of a hurry to tease. "You call that good luck?"

"There're still a few systems in that area we wanted to check. They fitted the profile for supporting complex life-forms," Keff said, unperturbed. "We would have tried MBA-487-J, except you ran short of fuel hotdogging it and we had to limp back here. Remember, Cari?"

"It could happen any time we run into bad luck," Carialle replied, not eager to discuss her own mistakes. "We're running out of time."

"What about vectoring up over the Central Worlds cluster? Toward galactic 'up'?"

"Maxwell-Corey's going toward DND-922-Z when he leaves here," Simeon said.

Carialle tsk-tsked. "We can't risk having him following our scent."

Keff stared at the overview on the tank. "How about we head out in a completely new direction? See what's out there thataway?"

"What's your advice, Simeon?" Carialle asked, locking down any loose items and sliding her airlock shut with a sharp hiss. Her gauges zoomed as she engaged her own power. Nutrients, fuel, power cells all showed less than half full. She hated lifting off under these circumstances, but she had no choice. The alternative was weeks of interrogation, and possibly being grounded—unfairly!—at the end of it.

"I've got an interesting anomaly you might investigate," Simeon said, downloading a file to Carialle's memory. "Here's a report I received from a freighter captain who made a jump through R sector to get here. His spectroscopes picked up unusual power emanations in the vicinity of RNJ-599-B. We've no records of habitation anywhere around there. Could be interesting."

"G-type stars," Keff noted approvingly. "Yes, I see what he meant. Spectroanalysis, Cari?"

"All the signs are there that RNJ could have generated planets," the brain replied. "What does Exploration say?"

"No one's done any investigation in that part of R sector yet," Simeon said blandly, carefully emotionless.

"No one?" Carialle asked, scrolling through the files. "Hmmm! Oh, yes!"

"So we'll be the first?" Keff said, catching the excitement in Carialle's voice. The burning desire to go somewhere and see something *first*, before any other Central Worlder, overrode the fears of being caught by the Inspector General.

"I can't locate any reference to so much as a robot drone," Carialle said, displaying star maps empty of neon-colored benchmarks or route vectors. Keff beamed.

"And to seek out new worlds, to boldly go . . ."

"Oh, shush," Carialle said severely. "You just want to be the first to leave your footprints in the sand."

"You've got twelve seconds to company," Simeon said. "Don't

tell me where you're going. What I don't know I can't lie about. Go with my blessings, and come back safely. Soon."

"Will do," Keff said, strapping in. "Thanks for everything, Simeon. Cari, ready to—"

The words were hardly out of his mouth before the CK-963 unlatched the docking ring and lit portside thrusters.

✳CHAPTER TWO

The Inspector General's angry voice pounded out of the audio pickup on Simeon's private frequency.

"CK-963, respond!"

"Discovered!" Keff cried, slapping the arm of his couch. The next burst of harsh sound made him yelp with mock alarm. "Catch us if you can, you cockatrice!"

"Hush!" Carialle answered the hail in an innocent voice, purposely made audible for her brawn's sake. "S . . . S-nine . . . dred. H . . . ving trou—" Keff was helpless with laughter. "Pi . . . s repeat mes . . . g?"

"I said get back here! You have an appointment with me as of ten hundred hours prime meridian time, and it is now ten fifteen." Carialle could almost picture his plump, mustachioed face turning red with apoplexy. "How dare you blast out of here without my permission? I want to see you!"

"Sorr . . ." Carialle said, "br . . . long up. Will send back mission reports, General."

"That was clear as a bell, Carialle!" the angry voice hammered at the speaker diaphragm. "There is no static interference on your transmission. You make a one-eighty and get back here. I expect to see you in ninety minutes. Maxwell-Corey out."

"Oops," said Keff, cheerfully. He tilted his head out of his impact couch toward her pillar and winked. His deep-set blue eyes twinkled. "M-C won't believe that last phrase was a fluke of clear space, will he?"

"He'll have to," Carialle said firmly. "I'm not going back to have my cerebellum cased, not a chance. Bureaucratic time-waster! I know I'm fine. You know you're fine. Why do we always have to go bend over and cough every time we make planetfall and explore a new world? I landed, got steam-cleaned and decontaminated, made our report with words and pictures to Xeno and Exploration. I refuse to have another mental going-over just because of my past experiences."

"Good of Simeon to tip us off," Keff said, running down the ship status report on his personal screen. "I hope he won't catch too much flak for it. But look at this! Thirty percent food and fuel?"

"I know," Carialle said contritely, "but what else could I do?"

"Not a blessed, or unblessed thing," Keff agreed. "Frankly, I prefer the odds as opposed to what we'd have to go through to wait for Simeon's next shipments. Full tanks and complete commissary do not, in my book, equate with peace of mind if M-C's about. Eventually we will have to go back, you know."

"Yes, if only to make certain Simeon's coped with the man. Before we do though, I'll just send Simeon a microsquirt to be sure Maxwell-Corey's left for D sector...."

"Or someplace else equally distant from us. It isn't as if we can't hang out in space for a while on iron rations until Sime sends you an all-clear burst," Keff offered bravely, although Carialle could see he didn't look forward to the notion.

"If the IG is sneaky enough..."

"... And he is if anyone deserves that adjective...."

"... to scan message files he'll know when Simeon knows where we are, and he could put a tag on us so no station will supply the 963."

"We shall not come to that sorry pass, my lady fair," Keff said, lapsing into his Sir Galahad pose. "In the meantime, let us fly on toward R sector and whatever may await us there." He made an enthusiastic and elaborate flourish and ended up pointing toward the bow.

Carialle had to laugh.

"Oh, yes," she said. "Now, where were we?" The Wizard was back on the wall, and he spoke in the creaking tenor of an old, old man. "Good sir knight, thou hast fairly won this scroll. Hast anything thou wish to ask me?"

Grinning, Keff buckled on his epee and went to face him.

✳   ✳   ✳

While Keff chased men-at-arms all over her main cabin, Carialle devoted most of her attention to eluding the Inspector General's attempts to follow her vector.

As soon as she cut off Maxwell-Corey's angry message, she detected the launch of a message drone from the SSS-900, undoubtedly containing an official summons. As plenty of traffic was always flying into the station's space, it took no great skill to divert the heat-seeking flyer onto the trail of another outgoing vessel. Nothing, and certainly not an unbrained droid, could outmaneuver a brainship. By the time the mistake was discovered, she'd be out of this sector entirely, and on her way to an unknown quadrant of the galaxy.

Later, when she felt less threatened by him, she'd compose a message complaining of what was really becoming harassing behavior to SPRIM. She'd had that old nuisance on her tail long enough. Running free, in full control of her engines and her faculties, was one of the most important things in her life. Every time that right was threatened, Carialle reacted in a way that probably justified the IG's claim of dangerous excitability.

In the distance, she picked up indications of two small ships following her initial vector. All right, score one up for the IG: he'd known she'd resist his orders and had ordered a couple of scouts to chase her down. That could also mean that he might have even put out an alarm that she was a danger to herself and her brawn, and must be brought back willingly or unwillingly. Would the small scouts have picked up her power emissions? She ought to have been one jump ahead of old Sennet and expected this sort of antic. She ought to have lain quiescent. Oh well. She really couldn't contest the fact that proximity to the IG did put her in a state of confusion. She adjusted her adrenals. Calm down, girl. Calm down. Think!

Quick perusal of her starchart showed the migration of an ion storm only a couple of thousand klicks away. Carialle made for it. She skimmed the storm's margin. Then, letting her computers plot the greatest possible radiation her shields could take without buckling, she slid nimbly over the surface, a surfer riding dangerous waters. The sensation was glorious! Ordinary pilots, unable to feel the pressures on their ships' skins as she did, would hesitate to follow. Nor could their scopes detect her in the wash of ion static. Shortly, Carialle was certain she had shaken off her tails. She turned a sharp perpendicular from the ion storm, and watched its opalescent halos recede behind her as she kicked her engines up to full speed.

Returning to the game, she found Keff studying the floating map holograph over a cold one at the "village pub." He glanced up at her pillar when she hailed him.

"I take it we're free of unwanted company?"

"With a sprinkling of luck and the invincibility of our radiation proof panels," Carialle said, "we've evaded the minions of the evil wizard. Now it's time for a brew." She tested herself for adrenaline fatigue, and allowed herself a brief feed of protein and vitamin B-complex.

Keff tipped his glass up to her. Quick analysis told her that though the golden beverage looked like beer, it was the non-alcoholic electrolyte-replenisher Keff used after workouts. "Here's to your swift feet and clever ways, my lovely, and confusion to our enemies. Er, did my coffee come aboard?"

"Yes, sir," she replied, flashing the image of a saluting marine on the wall, "The storesmaster just had time to break out a little of the good stuff when Simeon passed the word down. I even got you a small quantity of chocolate. Best Demubian." Keff beamed.

"Ah, Cari, now I know the ways you love me. Did you have time to load any of my *special* orders?" he asked, with a quirk of his head.

"Now that you mention it, there were two boxes in the cargo hold with your name on them," Carialle said.

Clang. BUMP! *Clang.* BUMP!

The shining contraption of steel that was the Rotoflex had taken little time to put together, still less to watch the instructional video on how to use it. Keff sat on the leatherette-covered, modified saddle with a stirrup-shaped, metal pulley in each outstretched hand. His broad face red from the effort, Keff slowly brought one fist around until it touched his collarbone, then let it out again. The heavy cables sang as they strained against the resistance coils, and relaxed with a heavy thump when Keff reached full extension. Squeezing his eyes shut, he dragged in the other fist. The tendons on his neck stood out cordlike under his sweat-glistening skin.

"Two hundred and three," he grunted "Uhhh! Two hundred and four. Two . . ."

"Look at me," Carialle said, dropping into the bass octave and adopting the spiel technique of so many tri-vid commercials. "Before I started the muscle-up exercise program I was a forty-four-kilogram weakling. *Now* look at me. You, too, can . . ."

"All right," Keff said, letting go of the hand-weights. They swung in noisy counterpoint until the metal cables retracted into their arms. He arose from the exerciser seat and toweled off with the cloth slung over the end of his weight bench. "I can acknowledge a hint when it's delivered with a sledgehammer. I just wanted to see how much this machine can take."

"Don't you mean how much *you* can take? One day you're going to rupture something," Carialle warned. She noted Keff's heart-beat at over two hundred pulses per minute, but it was dropping rapidly.

"Most accidents happen in the home," Keff said, with a grin.

"I really was sorry I had to interrupt your tryst with Susa," Carialle said for the twentieth time that shift.

"No problem," Keff said, and Carialle could tell that this time he meant it. "It would have been a more pleasant way to get my heart rate up, but this did nicely, thank you." He yawned and rolled his shoulders to ease them, shooting one arm forward, then the other. "I'm for a shower and bed, lady dear."

"Sleep well, knight in shining muscles."

Shortly, the interior was quiet but for the muted sounds of machinery humming and gurgling. The SSS-900 technicians had done their work well, for all they'd been rushed by circumstances to finish. Carialle ran over the systems one at a time, logging in repair or replacement against the appropriate component. That sort of accounting took up little time. Carialle found herself longing for company. A perverse notion since she knew it would be hours now before Keff woke up.

Carialle was not yet so far away from some of the miners' routes that she couldn't have exchanged gossip with other ships in the sector, but she didn't dare open up channels for fear of tipping off Maxwell-Corey to their whereabouts. The enforced isolation of silent running left her plenty of time for her thoughts.

Keff groaned softly in his sleep. Carialle activated the camera just inside his closed door for a brief look, then dimmed the lights and left him alone. The brawn was faceup on his bunk with one arm across his forehead and right eye. The thin thermal cover had been pushed down and was draped modestly across his groin and one leg, which twitched now and again. One of his precious collection of real-books lay open facedown on the nightstand. The tableau was worthy of a painting by the Old Masters of Earth— Hercules resting from his labors. Frustrated from missing his close encounter of the female kind, Keff had exercised himself into a stiff mass of sinews. His muscles were paying him back for the abuse by making his rest uneasy. He'd rise for his next shift aching in every joint, until he worked the stiffness out again. As the years went by it took longer for Keff to limber up, but he kept at it, taking pride in his excellent physical condition.

Softshells were, in Carialle's opinion, funny people. They'd go to such lengths to build up their bodies which then had to be maintained with a significant effort, disproportionate to the long-term effect. They were so unprotected. Even the stress of exercise, which they considered healthy, was damaging to some of them. They strove to accomplish goals which would have perished in a few generations, leaving no trace of their passing. Yet they cheerfully continued to "do" their mite, hoping something would survive to be admired by another generation or species.

Carialle was *very* fond of Keff. She didn't want him anguished or disabled. He had been instrumental in restoring her to a useful existence and while he wasn't Fanine—who could be?—he had many endearing qualities. He had brought her back to wanting to live, and then he had neatly caught her up in his own special goal—to find a species Humanity could freely interact with, make cultural and scientific exchanges, open sociological vistas. She was concerned that his short life span, and the even shorter term of their contract with Central Worlds Exploration, would be insufficient to accomplish the goal they had set for themselves. She would have to continue it on her own one day. What if the beings they sought did not, after all, exist?

Shellpeople had good memories but not infallible ones, she reminded herself. In three hundred, four hundred years, would she even be able to remember Keff? Would she want to, lest the memory be as painful as the anticipation of such loss was now? *If I find them after you're . . . well, I'll make sure they're named after you,* she vowed silently, listening to his quiet breathing. That immortality at least she could offer him.

So far, in light of that lofty goal, the aliens that the CK team had encountered were disappointing. Though interesting to the animal behaviorist and xenobiologist, Losels, Wyverns, Hydrae, and the Rodents of Unusual Size, et cetera ad nauseam, were all non-sentient.

To date, the CK's one reasonable hope of finding an equal or superior species came five years and four months before, when they had intercepted a radio transmission from a race of beings who sounded marvelously civilized and intelligent. As Keff had scrambled to make IT understand them, he and Carialle became excited, thinking that they had found *the* species with whom they could exchange culture and technology. They soon discovered that the inhabitants of Jove II existed in an atmosphere and pressure that made it utterly impractical to establish a physical presence. Pen pals only. Central Worlds would have to limit any interaction to radio contact with these Acid Breathers. Not a total loss, but not the real thing. Not *contact.*

Maybe this time on *this* mission into R sector, there would be something worthwhile, the real gold that didn't turn to sand when rapped on the anvil. That hope lured them farther into unexplored space, away from the *known* galaxy, and communication with friends and other B&B ship partnerships. Carialle chose not to admit to Keff that she was as hooked on First Contact as he was. Not only was there the intellectual and emotional thrill of being the first human team to see something totally new, but also the bogies had less chance of crowding in on her . . . if she looked further and further ahead.

For a shellperson, with advanced data-retrieval capabilities and superfast recall, every memory existed as if it had happened only moments before. Forgetting required a specific effort: the decision to wipe an event out of one's databanks. In some cases, that fine a memory was a curse, forcing Carialle to reexamine over and over again the events leading up to the accident. Again and again she was tormented as the merciless and inexorable sequence pushed its way, still crystal clear, to the surface—as it did once more during this silent running.

Sixteen years ago, on behalf of the Courier Service, she and her first brawn, Fanine, paid a covert call to a small space-repair facility on the edge of Central Worlds space. Spacers who stopped there had complained to CenCom of being fleeced. Huge, sometimes ruinously expensive purchases with seemingly faultless electronic documentation were charged against travelers' personal numbers, often months after they had left SSS-267. Fanine discreetly gathered evidence of a complex system of graft, payoffs and kickbacks, confirming CenCom's suspicions. She had sent out a message to say they had corroborative details and were returning with it.

They never expected sabotage, but they should have—Carialle corrected herself: *she* should have—been paying closer attention to what the dock hands were doing in the final check-over they gave her before the CF-963 departed. Carialle could still remember how the fuel felt as it glugged into her tank: cold, strangely cold, as if it had been chilled in vacuum. She could have refused that load of fuel, should have.

As the ship flew back toward the Central Worlds, the particulate matter diluted in the tanks was kept quiescent by the real fuel. Gradually, her engines sipped away that buffer, finally reaching the compound in the bottom of her tanks. When there was more aggregate than fuel, the charge reached critical mass, and ignited.

Her sensors shut down at the moment of explosion but that moment—10:54:02.351—was etched in her memory. That was the moment when Fanine's life ended and Carialle was cast out to float in darkness.

She became aware first of the bitter cold. Her internal temperature should have been a constant 37° Celsius, and cabin temperature holding at approximately twenty-one. Carialle sent an impulse to adjust the heat but could not find it. Motor functions were at a remove, just out of her reach. She felt as if all her limbs—for a brainship, all the motor synapses—and most horribly, her vision, had been removed. She was blind and helpless. Almost all of her external systems were gone except for a very few sound and skin sensors. She called out soundlessly for Fanine: for an answer that would never come.

Shock numbed the terror at first. She was oddly detached, as if this could not be happening to her. Impassively she reviewed what she *knew*. There had been an explosion. Hull integrity had been breached. She could not communicate with Fanine. Probably Fanine was dead. Carialle had no visual sensing equipment, or no control of it, if it still remained intact. Not being able to see was the worst part. If she could see, she could assess the situation and make an objective judgment. She had sustenance and air recirculation, so the emergency power supply had survived when ship systems were cut, and she retained her store of chemical compounds and enzymes.

First priority was to signal for help. Feeling her way through the damaged net of synapses, she detected the connection for the rescue beacon. Without knowing whether it worked or not, Carialle activated it, then settled in to keep from going mad.

She started by keeping track of the hours by counting seconds. Without a clock, she had no way of knowing how accurate her timekeeping was, but it occupied part of her mind with numbing lines of numbers. She went too quickly through her supply of endorphins and serotonin. Within a few hours she was forced to fall back on stress-management techniques taught to an unwilling Carialle when she was much younger and thought she was immortal by patient instructors who knew better. She sang every song and instrumental musical composition she knew, recited poems from the Middle Ages of Earth forward, translated works of literature from one language into another, cast them in verse, set them to music, meditated, and shouted inside her own skull.

That was because most of her wanted to curl up in a ball in the darkest corner of her mind and whimper. She knew all the stories of brains who suffered sensory deprivation. Tales of hysteria and insanity were the horror stories young shellchildren told one another at night in primary education creches. Like the progression of a fatal disease, they recounted the symptoms. First came fear, then disbelief, then despair. Hallucinations would begin as the brain synapses, desperate for stimulation, fired off random neural patterns that the conscious mind would struggle to translate as rational, and finally, the brain would fall into irrevocable madness. Carialle shuddered as she remembered how the children whispered to each other in supersonic voices that only the computer monitors could pick up that after a while, you'd begin to hear things, and imagine things, and feel things that weren't there.

To her horror, she realized that it was happening to her. Deprived of sight, other than the unchanging starscape, sound, and tactile sensation, memory drive systems failing, freezing in the darkness, she was beginning to feel hammering at her shell, to hear vibrations through her very body. Something was touching her.

Suddenly she knew that it wasn't her imagination. Somebody had responded to her beacon after who-knew-how-long, and was coming to get her. Galvanized, Carialle sent out the command along her comlinks on every frequency, cried out on local audio pick-ups, hoping she was being heard and understood.

"I am here! I am alive!" she shouted, on every frequency. "Help me!"

But the beings on her shell paid no attention. Their movements didn't pause at all. The busy scratching continued.

Her mind, previously drifting perilously toward madness, focused on this single fact, tried to think of ways to alert the beings on the other side of the barrier to her presence. She felt pieces being torn away from her skin, sensor links severed, leaving nerve endings shrieking agony as they died. At first she thought that her "res-cuers" were cutting through a burned, blasted hull to get to her, but the tapping and scraping went on too long. The strangers were performing salvage on her shell, with her still alive within it! This was the ultimate violation; the equivalent of mutilation for trans-plants. She screamed and twitched and tried to call their atten-tion to *her*, but they didn't listen, didn't hear, didn't stop.

Who were they? Any spacefarer from Central Worlds knew the emblem of a brainship. Even land dwellers had at least seen tri-dee images of the protective titanium pillar in which a shellperson was encased. Not to know, to be attempting to open her shell without care for the person inside meant that they must not be from the Central Worlds or any system connected to it. Aliens? Could her attackers be from an extra-central system?

When she was convinced that the salvagers were just about to sever her connections to her food and air recycling system, the scratching stopped. As suddenly as the intrusion had begun, Carialle was alone again. Realizing that she was now on the thin edge of sanity, she forced herself to count, thinking of the shape of each number, tasting it, pretending to feel it and push it onward as she thought, tasted, and pretended to feel the next number, and the next, and the next. She hadn't realized how different numbers *were*, individuals in their own right, varying in many ways each from the other, one after the other.

Three million, six hundred twenty-four thousand, five hundred and eighty three seconds later, an alert military transport pilot recognized the beacon signal. He took her shell into the hold of his craft. He did what he could in the matter of first aid to a shellperson—restored her vision. When he brought her to the nearest space station and technicians were rushed to her aid, she was awash in her own wastes and she couldn't convince anyone that what she was sure had happened—the salvage of her damaged hull by aliens—was a true version of her experiences. There was no evidence that anything had touched her ship after the accident. None of the damage could even be reasonably attributable to anything but the explosion and the impacts made by hurtling space junk. They showed her the twisted shard of metal that was all that had been left of her life-support system. What had saved her was that the open end had been seared shut in the heat of the explosion. Otherwise she would have been exposed directly to vacuum. But the end was smooth, and showed no signs of interference. Because of the accretion of waste they thought that her strange experience must be hallucinatory. Carialle alone knew she hadn't imagined it. There had been someone out there. There had!

The children's tales, thankfully, had not turned out to be true. She had made it to the other side of her ordeal with her mind intact, though a price had to be extracted from her before she was whole again. For a long time, Carialle was terrified of the dark, and she begged not to be left alone. Dr. Dray Perez-Como, her primary care physician, assigned a roster of volunteers to stay with her at all times, and made sure she could see light from whichever of her optical pickups she turned on. She had nightmares all the time about the salvage operation, listening to the sounds of her body being torn apart while she screamed helplessly in the dark. She fought depression with every means of her powerful mind and will, but without a diversion, something that would absorb her waking mind, she seemed to have "dreams" of some sort whenever her concentration was not focused.

One of her therapists suggested to Carialle that she could recreate the "sights" that tormented her by painting the images that tried to take control of her mind. Learning to manipulate brushes, mixing paints—at first she gravitated toward the darkest colors and slathered them on canvas so that not a single centimeter remained "light." Then, gradually, with healing and careful, loving therapy, details emerged: sketchily at first; a swath of dark umber, or a wisp of yellow. In the painstaking, meticulous fashion of any shellperson, her work became more graphic, then she began to experiment with color, character, and dimension. Carialle herself became fascinated with the effect of color, concentrated on delicately shading tones, one into another, sometimes using no more than one fine hair on the brush. In her absorption with the mechanics of the profession, she discovered that she genuinely enjoyed painting. The avocation couldn't change the facts of the tragedy she had suffered, but it gave her a splendid outlet for her fears.

By the time she could deal with those, she became aware of the absence of details; details of her schooling, her early years in Central's main training facility, the training itself as well as the expertise she had once had. She had to rebuild her memory from scratch. Much had been lost. She'd lost vocabulary in the languages she'd once been fluent in, scientific data including formulae and equations, navigation. Ironically, she could recall the details of the accident itself, too vividly for peace of mind. Despite meticulously relearning all the missing details concerning her first brawn, Fanine—all the relevant facts, where their assignments had taken them—these were just facts. No memory of shared experiences, fears, worries, fun, quarrels remained. The absence was shattering.

Ships did mourn the loss of their brawns: even if the brawn lived to retire at a ripe old age for a dirtside refuge. Carialle was *expected* to mourn: encouraged to do so. She was aware only of a vague remorse for surviving a situation that had ended the life of someone else. But she could not remember quite enough about Fanine or their relationship to experience genuine grief. Had they even liked one another? Carialle listened to hedrons of their mission reports and communiques. All of these could be taken one way or the other. The nine years they had spent together had been reduced to strict reportage with no personal involvement that Cari could recall.

As occupational therapy, Carialle took a job routing communication signals coming in to CenCom, a sort of glorified directory-assistance. It was busywork, taking little effort or intellect to do well. The advantage lay in the fact that voices and faces surrounded her.

She was ready for a new ship within two years of her rescue, and thank God for required insurance. As soon as the last synapse connection was hooked up and she was conscious again, Carialle felt an incredible elation: she was whole again, and strong. This was the way she was meant to be: capable of sailing through space, available and eager for important missions. Her destiny was not to answer communication systems or scuttle on a grav-carrier through corridors filled with softshells.

The expenses of the rescue operation and her medical care had been assumed by CenCom since that last mission had been hazardous, but the new CX-963 got quite a shock at the escalation of price in ship hulls. Her insurance had been based on *purchase*, not replacement price. She'd done a preliminary assessment of the cost but erroneously based her figures on those of her original shipself. Her savings vanished in the margin between the two as unseen as a carbon meteor in atmosphere. She'd have no options on missions: she'd have to take any and many, and at once, to begin paying her enlarged debt.

Concurrently her doctors and CenCom urged her to choose a new brawn. After losing her last so spectacularly, Carialle was reluctant to start the procedure; another choice might end in another death. She agreed to see one man who came particularly well recommended, but she couldn't relate at all to him and he left in the shortest possible courteous time. She didn't *have* to have a brawn, did she? Brainships could go on solo missions or on temporary assignments. She might accept one on those terms. Her doctors and CenCom said they'd check into that possibility and left her alone again.

Though there were rarely so many, nine B&B ships were currently on the Regulus CenCom base, either between missions or refitting. She did have the chance to speak with other shellpeople. She was made to feel welcome to join their conference conversations. She knew that they knew her recent history but no one would have brought the subject up unless she did. And she didn't. But she could listen to the amiable, often hilarious, and sometimes brutally frank, conversations of her peers. The refits were five 800s and two 700s with such brilliant careers that Carialle felt unequal to addressing them at all: the eighth was preparing for a long mission, and there was herself. On an open channel, the brainships did have a tendency to brag about their current partner, how he

or she did this and that, and was so good at sports/music/gaming/
dancing, or how silly he or she could be about such and such—
but hadn't they discovered Planet B or Moon C together, or
managed to get germdogs to Colony X and save ninety percent
of the afflicted from horrible deaths? The 800s were fond of reciting
the silly misunderstandings that could occur between brain and
brawn. Within Carialle, a wistfulness began to grow: the sense of
what she, partnerless, was lacking.

When the FC-840 related having to mortgage her hull again to
bail her brawn out of the clutches of a local gambling casino,
Carialle realized with a sense of relief that she'd never have had
that kind of trouble with Fanine. That was the first of the feelings, if not specific memories, that resurfaced, the fact that she
had respected Fanine's good sense. More memories emerged, slowly
at first, but all reassuring ones, all *emphasizing* the fact that she
and Fanine had been *friends* as well as co-workers. Inevitably,
during this process, Carialle became aware that she was lonely.

With that awareness, she announced to CenCom that she would
now be willing to meet with brawns for the purpose of initiating a new partnership. At once she was inundated with applica-
tions, as if everyone had been poised to respond to that willingness.
She wondered just how much the conversations of the other
brainships had been calculated to stir her to that decision. They
had all been keeping an eye on her.

The first day of interviews with prospective partners was hec-
tic, exciting, a whirl of courtship. Deliberately Carialle avoided
meeting any who were physically similar to Fanine, who had been
a tall, rather plain brunet with large hands and feet, or anyone
from Fanine's home planet. Fortunately there were few with either
disqualification. None of the first lot, male or female, quite suited,
although each did give Carialle a characteristic to add to her wish-
list of the perfect brawn.

Keff was her first visitor on the morning of the second day. His
broad, cheerful face and plummy voice appealed to her at once.
He never seemed to stop moving. She followed him with amusement as he explored the cabin, pointing out every admirable detail.
They talked about hobbies. When he insisted that he would want
to bring his personal gym along with him, they got into a silly
quarrel over the softshell obsession with physical fitness. Instead
of being angry at his obduracy in not recognizing her sovereignty

over her own decks, Carialle found herself laughing. Even when he was driving a point home, Keff's manner was engaging, and he was willing to listen to her. She informed CenCom that she was willing to enter a brain/brawn contract. Keff moved aboard at once, and his progressive-resistance gear came with him.

Just how carefully CenCom had orchestrated the affair, Carialle didn't care. CenCom, after all, had been matching brains with brawns for a very long time; they must have the hang of it now. Keff and Carialle complemented one another in so many ways. They shared drive, hope, and intelligence. Even during the interview Keff had managed to reawaken in Carialle the sense of humor which she had thought unlikely to be resuscitated.

In a very few days, as they awaited their first assignment, it was as if she'd never been paired with anyone else but Keff. What he said about spending almost all their time together went double for her. Each of them did pursue his or her private thoughts and interests, but they did their best work together. Keff was like the other half of her soul.

Despite her recent trauma, Carialle was a well-adjusted shell-person as indeed her recovery had proved. She was proud of having the superior capabilities that made it possible to multiplex several tasks at once. She felt sorry for nonshell humans. The enhanced functions available to any shellperson, most especially a brainship, were so far beyond the scope of "normal" humans. She felt lucky to have been born under the circumstances that led to her being enshelled.

Several hundred years before, scientists had tried to find a way to rehabilitate children who were of normal intelligence but whose bodies were useless. By connecting brain synapses to special nodes, the intelligent child could manipulate a shell with extendable pseudopods that would allow it to move, manipulate tools or keyboards. An extension of that principle resulted in the first spaceships totally controlled by encapsulated human beings. Other "shellpeople," trained for multiplexing, ran complicated industrial plants, or space stations, and cities. From the moment a baby was accepted for the life of a shellperson, he or she was conditioned to consider that life preferable to "softshells" who were so limited in abilities and lifespans.

One of the more famous brainships, the HN-832, or the Helva-Niall, had been nicknamed "the ship who sang," having developed a multivoice capability as her hobby. Though she docked in CenCom environs but rarely, Helva's adventures inspired all young shellpeople. Although Carialle was deeply disappointed to discover she had only an average talent for music, she was encouraged to find some other recreational outlet. It had taken a disaster for Carialle to find that painting suited her.

Encapsulated at three months and taught mostly by artificial intelligence programs and other shellpeople, Carialle had no self-image as an ordinary human. While she had pictures of her family and thought they looked like pleasant folks, she felt distinct from them.

Once Carialle had gone beyond the "black" period of her painting, her therapists had asked her to paint a self-portrait. It was a clumsy effort since she knew they wanted a "human" look while Carialle saw herself as a ship so that was what she produced: the conical prow of the graceful and accurately detailed spaceship framed an oval blob with markings that could just barely be considered "features" and blond locks that overlaid certain ordinary ship sensors. Her female sibling had had long blond hair.

After a good deal of conferencing, Dr. Dray and his staff decided that perhaps this was a valid self-image and not a bad one: in fact a meld of fact (the ship) and fiction (her actual facial contours). There were enough shellpeople now, Dr. Dray remarked, so that it was almost expectable that they saw themselves as a separate and distinct species. In fact, Carialle showed a very healthy shellperson attitude in not representing herself with a perfect human body, since it was something she never had and never could have.

Simeon's gift to Carialle was particularly appropriate. Carialle was very fond of cats, with their furry faces and expressive tails, and watched tapes of their sinuous play in odd moments of relaxation. She saw softshells as two distinct and interesting species, some members of which were more attractive than others.

As human beings went, Carialle considered Keff very handsome. In less hurried situations, his boyish curls and the twinkle in his deep-set blue eyes had earned him many a conquest. Carialle knew intellectually that he was good-looking and desirable, but she was not at all consumed with any sensuality toward him, or any other human being. She found humans, male and female, rather badly designed as opposed to some aliens she had met. If Man was the highest achievement of Nature's grand design, then Nature had a sense of humor.

Whereas prosthetics had been the way damaged adults replaced lost limbs or senses, the new Moto-Prosthetics line went further than that by presenting the handicapped with such refined functions that no "physical" handicap remained. For the shellperson, it meant they could "inhabit" functional alter-bodies and experience the full range of human experiences firsthand. That knocked a lot of notions of limitations or restrictions into an archaic cocked hat. Since Keff had first heard about Moto-Prosthetic bodies for brains, he had nagged Carialle to order one. She evaded a direct "no" because she valued Keff, respected his notion that she should have the chance to experience life outside the shell, join him in his projects with an immediacy that she could not enjoy encapsulated. The idea was shudderingly repulsive to her. Maybe if Moto-Prosthetics had been available before her accident, she might have been more receptive to his idea. But to leave the safety of her shell—well, not really leave it, but to seem to leave it—to be vulnerable—though he insisted she review diagrams and manuals that conclusively demonstrated how sturdy and flexible the M-P body was—was anathema. Why Keff felt she should be like other humans, often clumsy, rather delicate, and definitely vulnerable, she couldn't quite decide.

She started Simeon's gift tape to end that unproductive, and somewhat disturbing line of thought. Although Carialle had a library that included tapes of every sort of creature or avian that had been discovered, she most enjoyed the grace of cats, the smooth sinuousness of their musculature. This datahedron started with a huge spotted feline creeping forward, one fluid movement at a time, head and back remaining low and out of sight as if it progressed along under a solid plank. It was invisible to the prong-horned sheep on the other side of the undergrowth. Carialle watched with admiration as the cat twitched, gathered itself, sprang, and immediately stretched out in a full gallop after its prey. She froze the frame, then scrolled it backward slightly to the moment when the beautiful creature leapt forward, appreciating the graceful arc of its back, the stretch of its forelimbs, the elongated power of the hindquarters. She began to consider the composition of the painting she would make: the fleeing sheep was frozen with its silly face wild-eyed and splay-legged ahead of the gorgeous, silken threat behind it.

As she planned out her picture, she ran gravitational analyses, probable radiation effects of a yellow-gold sun, position of blip possibly indicating planet, and a computer model, and made a few idle bets with herself on whether they'd find an alien species, and what it'd look like.

✲CHAPTER THREE

Keff ignored the sharp twigs digging into the belly of his environment suit as he wriggled forward for a better look. Beyond the thin shield of thorny-leafed shrubbery was a marvel, and he couldn't believe what he was seeing. Closing with his target would not, could not, alter what he was viewing at a distance, not unless someone was having fun with optical illusions—but he painfully inched forward anyway. Not a hundred meters away, hewing the hard fields and hauling up root crops, was a work force of bipedal, bilaterally symmetrical beings, heterogeneous with regard to sex, apparently mammalian in character, with superior cranial development. In fact, except for the light pelt of fur covering all but lips, palms, soles, small rings around the eyes, and perhaps the places Keff couldn't see underneath their simple garments, they were remarkably like human beings. *Fuzzy* humans.

"Perfect!" he breathed into his oral pickup, not for the first time since he'd started relaying information to Carialle. "They are absolutely perfect in every way."

"Human-chauvinist," Carialle's voice said softly through the mastoid-bone implant behind his ear. "Just because they're shaped like Homo sapiens doesn't make them any more perfect than any other sentient humanoid or humanlike race we've ever encountered."

"Yes, but think of it," Keff said, watching a female, breasts heavy with milk, carrying her small offspring in a sling on her back while she worked. "So *incredibly* similar to us."

45

"Speak for yourself," Carialle said, with a sniff.

"Well, they are almost exactly like humans."

"Except for the fur, yes, and the hound-dog faces, exactly."

"Their faces aren't really that much like dogs," Keff protested, but as usual, Carialle's artistic eye had pinned down and identified the similarity. It was the manelike ruff of hair around the faces of the mature males that had thrown off his guess. "A suggestion of dog, perhaps, but no more than that last group looked like pigs. I think we've found the grail, Cari."

A gust of cold wind blew through the brush, fluttering the folds of loose cloth at the back of Keff's suit. His ears, nose, and fingers were chilly and growing stiff, but he ignored the discomfort in his delight with the objects of his study. On RNJ-599-B-V they had struck *gold*. Though it would be a long time before the people he was watching would ever meet them on their own terms in space.

Coming in toward the planet, Carialle had unleashed the usual exploratory devices to give them some idea of geography and terrain.

The main continent was in the northern hemisphere of the planet. Except for the polar ice cap, it was divided roughly into four regions by a high, vast mountain range not unlike the European Alps of old Earth. Like the four smaller mountain ranges in each of the quadrants, it had been volcanic at one time, but none of the cones showed any signs of activity.

The team had been on planet for several days already, viewing this and other groups of the natives from different vantage points. Carialle was parked in a gully in the eastern quadrant, four kilometers from Keff's current location, invisible to anyone on foot. It was a reasonable hiding place, she had said, because they hadn't seen any evidence during their approach of technology such as radar or tracking devices. Occasional power fluctuations pinged the needles on Carialle's gauges, but since they seemed to occur at random, they *might* just be natural surges in the planet's magnetic field. But Carialle was skeptical, since the surges were more powerful than one should expect from a magnetic field, and were diffuse and of brief duration, which made it difficult for her to pin the phenomenon down to a location smaller than five degrees of planetary arc. Her professional curiosity was determined to find a logical answer.

Keff was more involved with what he could see with his own eyes—his wonderful aliens. He studied the tool with which the nearest male was chipping at the ground. The heavy metal head, made of a slagged iron/copper alloy, was laboriously holed through in two places, where dowels or nails secured it to the flat meter-and-a-half long handle. Sinew or twine wound around and around making doubly sure that the worker wouldn't lose the hoe face on the back swing. By squeezing his eyelids, Keff activated the telephoto function in his contact lenses and took a closer look. The tools were crude in manufacture but shrewdly designed for most effective use. And yet no technology must exist for repair: the perimeter of the field was littered with pieces of discarded, broken implements. These people might have discovered smelting, but welding was still beyond them. Still, they'd moved from hunter/gatherer to farming and animal husbandry. Small but well-tended small flower and herb gardens bordered the field and the front of a man-high cave mouth.

"They seem to be at the late Bronze or early Iron Age stage of development," Keff murmured. "Speaking anthropologically, this would be the perfect species for a long-term surveillance to see if this society will parallel human development." He parted the undergrowth, keeping well back from the opening in the leaves. "Except for having only three fingers and a thumb on each hand, they've got the right kind of manipulative limbs to attain a high technological level."

"Close enough for government work," Carialle said, reasonably. "I can't see that the lack of one digit would interfere with their ability to make more complex tools, since clearly they're using some already."

"No," Keff said. "I'd be more disappointed if they didn't have thumbs. A new species of humanoid! I can write a paper about them." Keff's breath quickened with his enthusiasm. "Parallel development to Homo sapiens terraneum? Evolution accomplished separately from Earth-born humanity?"

"It's far more likely that they were seeded here thousands of years ago," Carialle suggested, knowing that she'd better dampen his enthusiasm before it got out of hand. "Maybe a forgotten colony?"

"But the physical differences would take eons to evolve," Keff said. The odds against parallel development were staggering, but the notion that they might have found an unknown cousin of their own race strongly appealed to him. "Of course, scientifically speaking, we'd have to consider that possibility, especially in the light of the number of colonial ventures that never sent back a 'safe down' message."

"Yes, we should seriously consider that aspect," Carialle said, but without sarcasm.

By thrusting out the angle of his jawbone, Keff increased the gain on his long-distance microphone to listen in on the natives as they called out to one another. All the inhabitants of this locale were harvesting root produce. If any kind of formal schooling existed for the young, it must be suspended until the crops were brought in. Typical of farm cultures, all life revolved around the cycle of the crops. Humanoids of every age and size were in or around the broad fields, digging up the roots. They seemed to be divided into groups of eight to ten, under the supervision of a crew boss, either male or female, who worked alongside them. No overseer was visible, so everyone apparently knew his or her job and got on with it. Slackers were persuaded by glares and peer pressure to persevere. Keff wondered if workers were chosen for their jobs by skill, or if one inherited certain tasks or crop rows by familial clan.

Well out of the way of the crews, small children minding babies huddled as near as they could to a low cavern entrance from which Carialle had picked up heat source traces, suggesting that entrance led to their habitation. It made sense for the aborigines to live underground, where the constant temperature was approximately 14° C, making it warmer than it was on the surface. Such an accommodation would be simple to heat, with the earth itself as insulation. Only hunger could have driven Keff out to farm or hunt in this cold, day after day.

Keff could not have designed a world more likely to be dependent upon subsistence culture. The days were long, but the temperature did not vary between sunup and sundown. Only the hardiest of people would survive to breed: and the hardiest of plants. It couldn't be easy to raise crops in this stony ground, either. Keff rubbed a pinch of it between his finger and thumb.

"High concentration of silicate clay in that soil," Carialle said, noticing his action. "Makes it tough going, both for the farmer and the crop."

"Needs more sand and more fertilizer," Keff said. "And more

water. When we get to know one another, we can advise them of irrigation and soil enrichment methods. See that flat panlike depression at the head of the field? That's where they pour water brought uphill by hand." A line of crude barrels nestled against the hillside bore out his theory.

Dirt-encrusted roots of various lengths, shapes, and colors piled up in respectable quantity beside the diggers, whose fur quickly assumed the dull dun of the soil.

"It's incredible that they're getting as much of a yield as they are," Keff remarked. "They must have the science of farming knocked into them."

"Survival," Carialle said. "Think what they could do with fertilized soil and steady rainfall. The atmosphere here has less than eight percent humidity. Strange, when you consider they're in the way of prevailing continental winds, between the ocean and that mountain range. There should be plenty of rain, and no need for such toil as *that.*"

Under the direction of a middle-aged male with a light-brown pelt, youngsters working with the digging crews threw piles of the roots onto groundsheets, which were pulled behind shaggy six-legged pack beasts up and down the rows. When each sheet was full, the beast was led away and another took its place.

"So what's the next step in this production line?" Keff asked, shifting slightly to see.

The female led the beast to a square marked out by hand-sized rocks, making sure nothing fell off as she guided the animal over the rock boundary. Once inside, she detached the groundsheet. Turning the beast, she led it back to the field where more folded groundsheets were piled.

"But if they live in the cave, over there," Keff said, in surprise, "why are they leaving the food over here?"

"Maybe the roots need to dry out a little before they can be stored, so they won't rot," Carialle said. "Or maybe they stink. You find out for yourself when we make contact. Here, visitor, eat roots. Good!"

"No, thanks," Keff said.

The six-legged draft animal waited placidly while the young female attached a new sheet to its harness. The beast bore a passing resemblance to a Terran shire horse, except for the six legs and a double dip of its spine over the extra set of shoulder-hips. Under layers of brown dust, its coat was thick and plushy: good protection against the cold wind. Some of the garments and tool pouches worn by the aborigines were undoubtedly manufactured out of such hide. Keff gazed curiously at the creature's feet. Not at all hooflike: each had three stubby toes with blunt claws and a thick sole that looked as tough as stone. The pack beast walked with the same patient gait whether the travois behind it was fully loaded or not.

"Strong," Keff said. "I bet one of those six-legged packs—hmm, six-packs!—could haul you uphill."

Carialle snorted. "I'd like to see it try."

Team leaders called out orders with hand signals, directing workers to new rows. The workers chattered among themselves, shouting cheerfully while they stripped roots and banged them on the ground to loosen some of the clinging soil. Carialle could almost hear Xeno gibbering with joy when they saw the hedrons she was recording for them.

"Funny," Keff said, after a while. "I feel as if I should understand what they're saying. The pace of their conversation is similar to Standard. There's cadence, but measured, not too fast, and it's not inflected like, say, Old Terran Asian."

A thickly furred mother called to her child, playing in a depression of the dusty earth with a handful of other naked tykes. It ignored her and went on with its game, a serious matter of the placement of pebbles. The mother called again, her voice on a rising note of annoyance. When the child turned to look, she repeated her command, punctuating her words with a spiraling gesture of her right hand. The child, eyes wide with alarm, stood up at once and ran over. After getting a smack on the bottom for disobedience, the child listened to instructions, then ran away, past the cave entrance and around the rise of the hill.

"Verrrry interesting," Keff said. "She didn't *say* anything different, but that child certainly paid attention when she made that hand gesture. Somewhere along the line they've evolved a somatic element in their language."

"Or the other way around," Carialle suggested, focusing on the gesture and replaying it in extreme close-up. "How do you know the hand signals didn't come first?"

"I'd have to make a study on it," Keff said seriously, "but I'd speculate because common, everyday symbols are handled with verbal phrases, the hand signals probably came later. I wonder why it evolved that way?"

"Could a percentage of them be partially hearing-impaired or deaf?"

"Not when they have such marked cadence and rhythm in their speech," Keff replied. "I doubt this level of agriculturalist would evolve lipreading. Hmm. I could compare it to the Saxon/Norman juxtaposition on Old Earth. Maybe they've been conquered by another tribe who primarily use sign language for communication. Or it might be the signs come from their religious life, and mama was telling baby that God would be unhappy if he didn't snap to it."

"Ugh. Invisible blackmail."

Keff patted the remote IT unit propped almost underneath his chin. "I want to talk to some of these people and see how long it takes my unit to translate. I'm dying to see what similarities there are between their language structure and Standard's." He started to gather himself up to stand.

"Not so fast," Carialle said, her voice ringing in his mastoid-bone implant. He winced. "When something seems too good to be true, it probably is. I think we need to do more observation."

"Cari, we've watched half a dozen of these groups already. They're all alike, even to the size of the flower gardens. When am I going to get to talk to one of them?"

The brain's voice hinted of uneasiness. "There's something, well, odd and seedy about this place. Have you noticed how old all these artifacts are?"

Keff shrugged. "Usable tools passed down from generation to generation. Not uncommon in a developing civilization."

"I think it's just the opposite. Look at that!"

Coming toward the work party in the field were two furry humanoid males. Between them on a makeshift woven net of rough cords, they carefully bore a hemispherical, shieldlike object full of sloshing liquid. They were led by the excited child who had been sent off by his mother. He shouted triumphantly to the teams of workers who set down their tools and rubbed the dust out of their fur as they came over for a drink. Patiently, each waited his or her turn to use the crude wooden dippers, then went immediately back to the fields.

"Water break," Keff observed, propping his chin on his palm. "Interesting bucket."

"It looks more like a microwave raydome to me, Keff," Carialle said. "Whaddayou know! They're using the remains of a piece of advanced technical equipment to haul water."

"By Saint George and Saint Vidicon, you're right! It does look like a raydome. So the civilization's not evolving, but in the last stages of decline," Keff said, thoughtfully, tapping his cheek with his fingertips. "I wonder if they had a war, eons ago, and the opposing forces blew themselves out of civilization. It's so horribly cold and dry here that we could very well be seeing the survivors of a comet strike."

Carialle ran through her photo maps of the planet taken from space. "No ruins of cities above ground. No signatures of decaying radiation that I saw, except for those sourceless power surges—and by the way, I just felt another one. Could they be from the planet's magnetic disturbance? There are heavy electromagnetic bursts throughout the fabric of the planet, and they don't seem to be coming from anywhere. I suppose they *could* be natural but—it's certainly puzzling. Possibly there was a Pyrrhic victory and both sides declined past survival point so that they ended up back in the Stone Age. Dawn of Furry Mankind, second day."

"Now that you mention it, I do recognize some of the pieces they made their tools out of," Keff said. He watched an adolescent female guiding two six-packs in a tandem yoke pulling a plow over part of the field that had been harvested. "Yours is probably the best explanation, unless they're a hard-line back-to-nature sect doing this on purpose, and I doubt that very much. But that plowshare looks more to me like part of a shuttlecraft fin. Especially if their bucket has a ninety-seven-point resemblance to a raydome. Sad. A viable culture reduced to noble primitives with only vestiges of their civilization."

"That's what we'll call them, then," Carialle said, promptly. "Noble Primitives."

"Seconded. The motion is carried."

Another young female and her docile six-pack dragged a full load of roots toward the stone square. Keff shifted to watch her.

"Hey, the last load of roots is gone! I didn't see anyone move it."

"We weren't paying attention," Carialle said. "The ground's

uneven. There might be a root cellar near that square, with another crew of workers. If you walk over the ground nearby I could do a sounding and find it. If it's unheated that would explain why it's not as easy to pick out as their living quarters."

Keff heard a whirring noise behind him and shifted as silently as he could. "Am I well enough camouflaged?"

"Don't worry, Keff," Carialle said in his ear. "It's just another globe-frog."

"Damn. I hope they don't see me."

Beside the six-packs, one of the few examples of animal life on RNJ were small green amphibioids that meandered over the rocky plains, probably from scarce water source to water source, in clear globular cases full of water. Outside their shells they'd be about a foot long, with delicate limbs and big, flat paws that drove the spheres across dry land. Keff had dubbed them "globe-frogs." The leader was followed by two more. Globe-frogs were curious as cats, and all of them seemed fascinated by Keff.

"Poor things, like living tumbleweeds," Carialle said, sympathetically.

"The intelligent life isn't much better off," Keff said. "It's dry as dust around here."

"Terrible when sentient beings are reduced to mere survival," Carialle agreed.

"Oops," Keff said, in resignation. "They see me. Here they come. Damn it, woman, stop laughing."

"It's your animal magnetism," Carialle said, amused.

The frogs rolled nearer, spreading out into a line; perhaps to get a look at all sides of him, or perhaps as a safety precaution. If he suddenly sprang and attacked, he could only get one. The rumble of their cases on the ground sounded like thunder to him.

"Shoo," Keff said, trying to wave them off before the field workers came over to investigate. He glanced at the workers. Luckily, none were paying attention to the frogs. "Cari, where's the nearest water supply?"

"Back where the raydomeful came from. About two kilometers north northeast."

"Go that way," Keff said, pointing, with his hand bent up close to his body. "Water. You don't want me. Vamoose. Scram." He flicked his fingers. "Go! *Please.*"

The frogs fixed him with their bulbous black eyes and halted their globes about a meter away from him. One of them opened its small mouth to reveal short, sharp teeth and a pale, blue-green tongue. With frantic gestures, Keff beseeched them to move off. The frogs exchanged glances and rolled away, amazingly in the direction he had indicated. A small child playing in a nearby shallow ditch shrieked with delight when it saw the frogs passing and ran after them. The frogs paddled faster, but the tot caught up, and fetched one of the globes a kick that propelled it over the crest of the hill. The others hastily followed, avoiding their gleeful pursuer. The light rumbling died away.

"Whew!" Keff said. "Those frogs nearly blew my cover. I'd better reveal myself now before someone discovers me by accident."

"Not yet! We don't have enough data to prove the Noble Primitives are nonhostile."

"That's a chance we always take, lady fair. Or why else are we here?"

"Look, we know the villagers we've observed do not leave their sites. I haven't been able to tell an inhabitant of one village from the inhabitant of any other. And you sure don't look like any Noble Primitive. I really don't like risking your being attacked. I'm four kilometers away from you so I can't pull your softshell behind out of trouble, you know. My servos would take hours to get to your position."

Keff flexed his muscles and wished he could take a good stretch first. "If I approach them peacefully, they should at least give me a hearing."

"And when you explain that you're from off-planet? Are they ready for an advanced civilization like ours?"

"They have a right to our advantages, to our help in getting themselves back on their feet. Look how wretchedly they live. Think of the raydome, and the other stuff we've seen. They once had a high-tech civilization. Central Worlds can help them. It's our duty to give them a chance to improve their miserable lot, bring them back to this century. They *were* once our equals. They deserve a chance to be so again, Carialle."

"Thou hast a heart as well as a brain, sir knight. Okay."

Before they had settled how to make the approach, shouting broke out on the work site. Keff glanced up. Two big males were standing nose to nose exchanging insults. One male whipped a knife made of a shard of blued metal out of his tool bag; another relic that had been worn to a mere streak from sharpening. The male he was facing retreated and picked up a digging tool with a ground-down end. Yelling, the knife-wielder lunged in at him, knife over his head. The children scattered in every direction, screaming. Before the pikeman could bring up his weapon, the first male had drawn blood. Two crew leaders rushed up to try to pull them apart. The wounded male, red blood turning dark brown as it mixed with the dust in his body-fur, snarled over the peacemaker's head at his foe. With a roar, he shook himself loose.

"I think you missed your chance for a peaceful approach, Keff."

"Um," Keff said. "He who spies and runs away lives to chat another day."

While the combatants circled each other, ringed by a watching crowd, Keff backed away on his hands and knees through the bush. Cursing the pins and needles in his legs, Keff managed to get to his feet and started downhill toward the gully where Carialle was concealed.

Carialle launched gracefully out of the gully and turned into the face of planetary rotation toward another spot on the day-side which her monitors said showed signs of life.

"May as well ring the front doorbell this time," Keff said. "No sense letting them get distracted over something else. If only I'd moved sooner!"

"No sense having a post mortem over it," Carialle said firmly. "You can amaze *these* natives with how much you already know about them."

Reversing to a tail-first position just at the top of atmosphere, Carialle lowered herself gently through the thin clouds and cleaved through a clear sky onto a rocky field in plain sight of the workers. Switching on all her exterior cameras, she laughed, and put the results on monitor for Keff.

"I could paint a gorgeous picture," she said. "Portrait of blinding astonishment."

"Another regional mutation," Keff said, studying the screen. "They're still beautiful, still the same root stock, but their faces look a little like sheep."

"Perfectly suited for open-mouthed goggling," Carialle said promptly. "I wonder what causes such diversity amidst the groups. Radiation? Evolution based on function and lifestyle?"

"Why would they *need* to look like sheep?" Keff said, shrugging out of the crash straps.

"Maybe they were behind the door when ape faces like yours were handed out," Carialle said teasingly, then turned to business. "I'm reading signs of more underground heat sources. One habitation, three entrances. Ambient air temperature, fourteen degrees. This place is *cold*."

"I'll wear a sweater, Mom. Here goes!"

As Keff waited impatiently in the airlock, checking his equipment carriers and biting on the implanted mouth contact to make sure it was functioning properly, Carialle lowered the ramp. Slowly, she opened the airlock. A hundred yards beyond it, Keff saw a crowd of the sheep-faced Noble Primitives gathered at the edge of the crop field, still gaping at the tall silver cylinder.

Taking a deep breath, Keff stepped out onto the ramp, hand raised, palm outward, weaponless. The IT was slung on a strap around his neck so he let his other hand hang loosely at his side.

"Hail, friends!" he called to the aliens huddled on the edge of the dusty field. "I come in peace."

He walked toward the crowd. The Primitives stared at him, the adults' faces expressionless underneath the fur masks, the children openly awestruck. Cautiously, Keff raised his other hand away from his body so they could see it, and smiled.

"They're not afraid of you, Keff," Carialle said, monitoring the Noble Primitives' vital signs. "In fact, they're not even surprised. Now that's odd!"

"Why does one of the mages come to us?" Alteis said, worriedly, as the stranger approached them, showing his teeth. "What have we done wrong? We have kept up with the harvest. All proceeds on schedule. The roots are nearly all harvested. They are of good quality."

Brannel snorted, a sharp breath ruffling the fur on his upper lip, and turned an uncaring shoulder toward the oldster. Old Alteis was so afraid of the mages that he would do himself an injury one day if the overlords were *really* displeased. He stared at the approaching mage. The male was shorter than he, but possessed of a mighty build and an assured, cocky walk. Unusual for a mage, his hands showed that they were not unacquainted with hard work.

The out-thrust of the cleft chin showed that he knew his high place, and yet his dark, peaty blue eyes were full of good humor. Brannel searched his memory, but was certain he had never encountered this overlord before.

"He is one we do not know," Brannel said quickly in an undertone out of the side of his mouth. "Perhaps he is here to tell us he is our new master."

"Klemay is our master," Alteis said, his ruff and mustache indignantly erect on his leathery face.

"But Klemay has not been seen for a month," Brannel said. "I saw the fire in the mountains, I told you. Since then, no power has erupted from Klemay's peak."

"Perhaps this one serves Klemay," Mrana, mate of Alteis, suggested placatingly. Surreptitiously, she brushed the worst of the dust off the face of one of her children. None of them looked their best at harvest time when little effort could be wasted on mere appearance. The overlord must understand that.

"Servers serve," Brannel snorted. "No overlord serves another but those of the Five Points. Klemay was not a high mage."

"Do not speak of things you do not understand," Alteis said, as alarmed as that foolish male ever became. "The mages will hear you."

"The mages are not listening," Brannel said.

Alteis was about to discipline him further, but the overlord was within hearing range now. The stranger came closer and stopped a couple of paces away. All the workers bowed their heads, shooting occasional brief glances at the visitor. Alteis stepped forward to meet him and bowed low.

"What is your will, lord?' he asked.

Instead of answering him directly, the mage picked up the box that hung around his neck and pushed it nearly underneath Alteis's chin. He spoke to the leader at some length. Though Brannel listened carefully, the words meant nothing. Alteis waited, then repeated his words clearly in case the overlord had not understood him. The mage smiled, head tilted to one side, uncomprehending.

"What may I and my fellow workers do to serve you, exalted one?" Brannel asked, coming forward to stand beside Alteis. He, too, bowed low to show respect, although the germ of an idea was beginning to take shape in his mind. He tilted his chin down only the barest respectable fraction so he could study the visitor.

The male fiddled with the small box on his breast, which emitted sounds. He spoke over it, possibly reciting an incantation. That was not unusual; all the overlords Brannel had ever seen talked to themselves sometimes. Many objects of power were ranged about this one's strongly built form. Yet he did not appear to understand the language of the people, nor did he speak it. He hadn't even acknowledged Brannel's use of mage-talk, which had been cleverly inserted into his query.

Puzzled, Brannel wrinkled his forehead. His fellow servers stayed at a respectful distance, showing proper fear and respect to one of the great overlords. They were not puzzled: they had no thoughts of their own to puzzle them or so Brannel opined. So he took as close a look at this puzzling overlord as possible.

The male appeared to be of the pure blood of the Magi, showing all three signs: clear skin, whole hand, and bright eyes. His clothing did not resemble that which overlords wore. Then Brannel arrived at a strange conclusion: this male was *not* an overlord. He could not speak either language, he did not wear garments like an overlord, he did not act like an overlord, and he had clearly not come from the high places of the East. The worker male's curiosity welled up until he could no longer contain the question.

"Who are you?" he asked.

Alteis grabbed him by the ruff and yanked him back into the midst of the crowd of shocked workers.

"How dare you speak to an overlord like that, you young puppy?" he said, almost growling. "Keep your eyes down and your mouth shut!"

"He is not an overlord, Alteis," Brannel said, growing more certain of this every passing moment.

"Nonsense," Fralim said, closing his hand painfully on Brannel's upper arm. Alteis's son was bigger and stronger than he was, but Fralim couldn't see the fur on his own skin. He loomed over Brannel, showing his teeth, but Brannel knew half the ferocity was from fear. "He's got all his fingers, hasn't he? The finger of authority has not been amputated. He can use the objects of power. I ask forgiveness, honored lord," Fralim said, speaking in an abject tone to the stranger.

"He does not speak our language, Fralim," Brannel said clearly. "Nor does he understand the speech of the Magi. All the Magi speak the linga esoterka, which I understand. I will prove it. Master," he said, addressing Keff in mage-talk, "what is thy will?"

The stranger smiled in a friendly fashion and spoke again, holding the box out to him.

The experiment didn't impress Brannel's fellow workers. They continued to glance up at the newcomer with awe and mindless adoration in their eyes, like the herd beasts they so resembled.

"Keff," the stranger said nodding several times and pointing to himself. He shifted his hand toward Brannel. "An dew?"

The others ducked. When the finger of authority was pointed at one of them, it sometimes meant that divine discipline was forthcoming. Brannel tried to hide that he, too, had flinched, but the gesture seemed merely a request for information.

"Brannel," he said, hand over pounding heart. The reply delighted the stranger, who picked up a rock.

"An dwattis zis?" he asked.

"Rock," Brannel said. He approached until he was merely a pace from the overlord. "What is this?" he asked, very daringly, reaching out to touch the mage's tunic sleeve.

"Brannel, no!" Alteis wailed. "You'll die for laying hands on one of them!"

Anything was better than living out his life among morons, Brannel thought in disgust. No bolt of punishment came. Instead, Keff said, "Sliv."

"Sliv," Brannel repeated, considering. It sounded almost like the real word. Ozran was great! he thought in gratitude. Perhaps Keff *was* a mage, but from a distant part of the world.

They began to exchange the words for objects. Keff led Brannel to different parts of the holding, pointing and making his query. Brannel, becoming more interested by the minute, gave him the words and listened carefully to the stranger-words with which Keff identified the same things. Keff was freely offering Brannel a chance to exchange information, to know his words in trade for his own. Language was power, Brannel knew, and power held the key to self-determination.

Behind them, the villagers followed in a huddled group, never daring to come close, but unable to stay away as Brannel claimed the entire, and apparently friendly, attention of a mage. Fralim was muttering to himself. It might have meant trouble, since Fralim saw himself as the heir to village leadership after Alteis, but he

was too much in awe of the seeming-mage and had already forgotten some of what had happened. If Brannel managed to distract him long enough afterward, Fralim would forget forever the
details of his grudge. It would disappear into the grayness of
memory that troubled nearly every server on Ozran. Brannel
decided to take advantage of the situation, and named every single
worker to the mage. Fralim whitened under his fur, but he smiled
back, teeth gritted, when Keff repeated his name.

The stranger-mage asked about every type of root, every kind
of flower and herb in the sheltered garden by the cavern mouth.
Twice, he tried to enter the home-cavern, but stopped when he
saw Brannel pause nervously on the threshold. The worker was
more convinced than he was of anything else in his life that this
mage was not as other mages: he didn't know entry to the home
site between dawn and dusk was forbidden under pain of reprisal.

Toward evening, the prepared food for the villagers appeared
in the stone square, as it did several times every day. Brannel
would have to pretend to eat and just hope that he could control his rumbling guts until he had a chance to assuage his
hunger from his secret cache. He'd worked a long, hard day before
he'd had to stimulate his wits to meet the demands of this
unexpected event.

Muttering began among the crowd at their heels. The children
were hungry, too, and had neither the manners nor the wit to keep
their voices down. Not wishing to incur the wrath of the visiting mage, Alteis and Mrana were discussing whether or not they
dared offer such poor fare to the great one. Should they, or
shouldn't they, interrupt the great one's visit at all by letting mere
workers eat? What to do?

Brannel took care of the problem. Keeping a respectful distance,
he led Keff to the stone square and picked up the lid of one of
the huge covered dishes. With one hand, he made as if to eat from
the steaming tureen of legume stew.

Keff's eyes widened in understanding and he smiled. Though
he waved away offers of food, he encouraged the villagers with
friendly gestures to come forward and eat. Knowing that Alteis was
watching, Brannel was forced to join them. He consumed a few
tiny mouthfuls as slowly as he dared.

Fortunately, he had plenty of interruptions which concealed
his reluctance to eat. Keff questioned him on the names of the

foodstuffs, and what each was made of, pointing to raw vegetables and making an interrogative noise.

"Stewed orange root," Brannel said, pointing out the appropriate
field to the mage. "Grain bread." Some of the grain the plough
animals ate served to demonstrate what kind. "Legume stew. Sliced
tuber fried in bean oil." Beans were unavailable, having been
harvested and gathered in by the mages the month before, so he
used small stones approximately the right size, and pretended to
squeeze them. Keff understood. Brannel knew he did. He was as
excited as the mage when the box began to make some of the right
sounds, as if finding them on its tongue: frot, brot, brat, bret, bread.

"Bread! That's right," Brannel said enthusiastically, as Keff
repeated what the box said. That's right, Magelord: bread!"

Keff slapped Brannel hard on the back The worker jumped and
caught his breath, but it was a gesture of friendliness, not disapproval—as if Keff was just another worker, a neighbor . . . a—a
friend. He tried to smile. The others fell to their knees and covered their heads with their arms, fearing the thunderbolt about
to descend.

"Bread," Keff repeated happily. "I think I've got it."

"Do you?" Carialle asked in his ear. "And does the rain in Spain
fall mainly in the plain?"

"Ozran, I think," Keff said, subvocalizing as the villagers picked
themselves off the ground and came around cautiously to inspect
Brannel who was smiling. Keff himself was wild with glee, but
restraining himself for fear of scaring the natives further. "I can
hardly believe it. I'm making progress faster than I even dared to
hope. There's some Ancient Terran forms in their speech, Carialle,
embedded in the alien forms, of course. I believe the Ozrans had
contact with humankind, maybe millennia ago, significant contact
that altered or added to the functionalism of their language. Are
there any records in the archives for first contact in this sector?"

"I'll put a trace through," Carialle said, initiating the search
sequence and letting it go through an automatic AI program. A
couple of circuits "clicked," and the library program began to hum
quietly to itself.

By means of Keff's contact button, Carialle focused on the antics
of the natives. A few of the females were picking up the spilled
dishes with a cautious eye on Keff, never venturing too close to
him. The large, black-furred male and the elderly salt-and-pepper

male examined a protesting Brannel. The slender male tried without success to wave them off.

"What is wrong with these people?"

"Mm-mm? I don't know. They're looking Brannel over for damages or marks or something. What did they expect to happen when I patted him on the back?"

"I don't know. Bodily contact shouldn't be dangerous. I wish you could get close enough to them so I could read their vital signs and do a chemspec analysis of their skin."

Keff stood at a distance from the villagers, nodding and smiling at any who would meet his eyes, but the moment he took a step toward one, that one moved a step back. "They won't let me, that's obvious. Why are most of them so downright scared of me, but not surprised to see me?"

"Maybe they have legends about deities that look like you," Carialle said with wry humor. "You may be fulfilling some long-awaited prophecy. 'The bare-faced one will come out of the sky and set us free.'"

"No," Keff said, thoughtfully. "I think the reaction is more immediate, more present day. Whatever it is, they're most courteous and absolutely cooperative: an ethnologists dream. I'm making real progress in communications. I think I've found the 'to be' verb, but I'm not sure I'm parsing it correctly yet. Brannel keeps grinning at me when I ask what something 'is.'"

"Keep going," Carialle said encouragingly. "Faint heart never won fair lady. You're all getting along so well there."

With every evidence of annoyance, Brannel fought free of the hands of his comrades. He smoothed his ruffled fur and glared at the others, his aspect one of long suffering. He returned to Keff, his expression saying, "Let's resume the language lesson, and pay no more attention to *those* people."

"I'd love to know what's going on," Keff said out loud in Standard, with a polite smile, "but I'm going to have to learn a lot more before I can ask the right questions about your social situation here."

One of the other Noble Primitives muttered under his breath. Brannel turned on him and hissed out a sharp phrase that needed no translation: even the sound of it was insulting. Keff moved between them to defuse a potential argument, and that made the other Primitive back off sharply. Keff got Brannel's attention and pointed to the raydome water carrier. Listening to prompts from the IT program through his implant, he attempted to put together a whole sentence of pidgin Ozran.

"What are that?" Keff asked. "Eh? Did I get that right?"

From Brannel's merry expression, he hadn't. He grinned, giving the local man his most winsome smile. "Well, *teach* me then, can you?"

Emboldened by Keff's friendly manner, the Noble Primitive laughed, a harsh sound; more of a cackle than a guffaw.

"So," Keff asked, trying again in Ozran, "what are yes?" He whispered an aside to Carialle. "I don't know even how to ask 'what's right?' yet. I must sound like the most amazing idiot."

"What *is* that. What *are* those," Brannel said, with emphasis, picking up one stone in one hand, a handful of stones in the other, and displaying first one and then the other. He had correctly assumed Keff was trying to ask about singular and plural forms and had demonstrated the difference. The others were still staring dumbly, unable to understand what was going on. Keff was elated by his success.

"Incredible. You may have found the only intelligent man on the planet," Carialle said, monitoring as the IT program recorded the correct uses of the verb, and postulated forms and suffixes for other verbs in its file, shuffling the onomatopoeic transliterations down like cards. "Certainly the only one of this bunch who understands abstract questions."

"He's a find," Keff agreed. "A natural linguist. It could have taken me days to elicit what he's offering freely and, I might add, intelligently. It's going to take me more time to figure out that sign language, but if anyone can put me on the right track, it's Brannel."

Having penetrated the mystery of verbal declension, Keff and Brannel sat down together beside the fire and began a basic conversation.

"Do you see how he's trying to use my words, too?" Keff subvocalized to Carialle.

Using informal signs and the growing lexicon in the IT program, Keff asked Brannel about the below ground habitation.

" . . . Heat from . . . earth," Brannel said, patting the ground by his thigh. IT left audio gaps where it lacked sufficient glossary and grammar, but for Keff it was enough to tell him what he wanted to know.

"A geothermal heating system. It's so cold out; why can't you enter now?" Keff said, making a cave by arching his finger and thumb on the ground and walking his other hand on two fingers toward it.

"Not," Brannel said firmly, with a deliberate sign of his left hand. The IT struggled to translate. "Not cave day. We are . . . work . . . day."

"Oh," Carialle said. "A cultural ban to keep the slackers out on the field during working hours. Ask him if he knows what causes the power surges I'm picking up."

Keff relayed the question. The others who were paying attention shot sulky glances toward Brannel. The dun-colored male started to speak, then stopped when an older female let out a whimper of fear. "Not," he said shortly.

"I guess he doesn't know," Keff said to Carialle. "You, sir," he said, going over to address the eldest male, Alteis, who immediately cowered. "Where comes strong heat from sky?" He pantomimed arcs overhead. "What makes strong heat?"

With a yell, one of the small boys—Keff thought it might be the same one who had defied his mother's orders—traced a jagged line in the sky. The he dove into his mother's lap for safety. An adolescent female, Nona, Keff thought her name was, glanced up at him in terror, and quickly averted her eyes to the ground. The others murmured among themselves, but no one looked or spoke.

"Lightning?" Keff asked Alteis softly. "What causes the lightning, sir?"

The oldster with white-shot black fur studied his lips carefully as he spoke, then turned for help to Brannel, who remained stoically silent. Keff repeated his question. The old male nodded solemnly, as if considering an answer, but then his gaze wandered off over Keff's head. When it returned to Keff, there was a blankness in his eyes that showed he hadn't understood a thing, or had already forgotten the question.

"He doesn't know," Keff said with a sigh. "Well, we're back to basics. Where does the food go for storage?" he asked. He gestured at the stone square and held up one of the roots Brannel had used as an example. "Where roots go?"

Brannel shrugged and muttered something. "Not know," IT amplified and relayed. "Roots go, food comes."

"A culture in which food preparation is a sacred mystery?"

Carialle said, with increasing interest. "Now, that's bizarre. If we take that back to Xeno, we'll deserve a bonus."

"Aren't you curious? Didn't you ever try to find out?" Keff asked Brannel.

"Not!" Brannel exclaimed. The bold villager seemed nervous for almost the first time since Keff had arrived. "One curious, all—" He brought his hands together in a thunderclap. "All . . . all," he said, getting up and drawing a circle in the air around an adult male, an adult female, and three children. He pantomimed beating the male, and shoved the food bowls away from the female and children with his foot. Most of the fur-faced humanoids shuddered and one of the children burst into tears.

"All punished for one person's curiosity? But why?" Keff demanded. "By whom?"

For answer Brannel aimed his three-fingered hand at the mountains, with a scornful expression that plainly said that Keff should already know that. Keff peered up at the distant heights.

"Huh?" Carialle said. "Did I miss something?"

"Punishment from the mountains? Is it a sacred tradition associated with the mountains?" Keff asked. "By his body language Brannel holds whatever comes from there in healthy respect, but he doesn't like it."

"Typical of religions," Carialle sniffed. She focused her cameras on the mountain peak in the direction Keff faced and zoomed in for a closer look "Say, there are structures up there, Keff. They're blended in so well I didn't detect them on initial sweep. What are they? Temples? Shrines? Who built them?"

Keff pointed, and turned to Brannel.

"What are . . . ?" he began. His question was abruptly interrupted when a beam of hot light shot from the peak of the tallest mountain in the range to strike directly at Keff's feet. Hot light engulfed him. "Wha—?" he mouthed. His hand dropped to his side, slamming into his leg with the force of a wrecking ball. The air turned fiery in his throat, drying his mouth and turning his tongue to leather. Humming filled his ears. The image of Brannel's face, agape, swam before his eyes, faded to a black shadow on his retinas, then flew upward into a cloudless sky blacker than space.

The bright bolt of light overpowered the aperture of the tiny contact-button camera, but Carialle's external cameras recorded the whole thing. Keff stood rigid for a moment after the beam struck, then slowly, slowly keeled over and slumped to the ground in a heap. His vital-sign monitor shrieked as all activity flatlined. To all appearances he was dead.

"Keff!" Carialle screamed. Her system demanded adrenaline. She fought it, forcing serotonin and endorphins into her bloodstream for calm. It took only milliseconds until she was in control of herself again. She had to be, for Keff's sake.

In the next few milliseconds, her circuits raced through a diagnostic, checking the implants to be sure there was no system failure. ALL showed green.

"Keff," she said, raising the volume in his implant. "Can you hear me?" He gave no answer.

Carialle sent her circuits through a diagnostic, checking the implants to be sure there was no system failure. All showed green except the video of the contact camera, which gradually cleared. Before Carialle could panic further, the contacts began sending again. Keff's vitals returned, thready but true. He was alive! Carialle was overjoyed. But Keff was in danger. Whatever caused that burst of power to strike at his feet like a well-aimed thunderbolt might recur. She had to get him out of there. A bolt like that couldn't be natural, but further analysis must wait. Keff was hurt and needed attention. That was her primary concern. How could she get him back?

The small servos in her ship might be able to pick him up, but were intended for transit over relatively level floors. Fully loaded they wouldn't be able to transport Keff's weight across the rough terrain. For the first time, she wished she had gotten a Moto-Prosthetic body as Keff had been nagging her to do. She longed for two legs and two strong arms.

Hold it! A body was available to her: that of the only intelligent man on the planet. When the bolt had struck, Brannel, with admirably quick reflexes, had flung himself out of the way, rolling over the stony ground to a sheltered place beneath the rise. The other villagers had run hell-for-leather back toward their cavern, but Brannel was still only a few meters away from Keff's body. Carialle read his infrared signal and heartbeat: he was ten meters from Keff's body. She opened a voice-link through IT and routed it via the contact button.

"Brannel," she called, amplifying the small speaker as much as she could without distortion. "Brannel, pick up Keff. Bring Keff home." The IT blanked on the word home. She spun through the vocabulary database looking for an equivalent. "Bring Keff to Keff's cave, Brannel!" Her voice rose toward hysteria. She flattened her tones and increased endorphins and proteins to her nutrients to counter the effects of her agitation.

"Mage Keff?" Brannel asked. He raised his head cautiously from the shelter of his hiding place, fearing another bolt from the mountains. "Keff speaks?"

Keff lay in a heap on the ground, mouth agape, eyes half open with the whites showing. Brannel, knowing that sometimes bolts continued to burn and crackle after the initial lightning, kept a respectful distance.

"Bring Keff to Keff's cave," a disembodied voice pleaded. A female's voice it was, coming from underneath the mage's chin. Some kind of familiar spirit? Brannel rocked back and forth, struggling with ambivalent desires. Keff had been kind to him. He wanted to do the mage's wishes. He also wasn't going to put himself in danger for the sake of one of Them whom the mage-bolts had struck down. Was Keff Klemay's successor and that was why he had come to visit their farm holding? Only his right to succeed Klemay had just been challenged by the bolt.

Across the field, the silver cylinder dropped its ramp, clearly awaiting the arrival of its master. Brannel looked from the prone body at his feet to the mysterious mobile stronghold. Stooping, he stared into Keff's eyes. A pulse twitched faintly there. The mage was still alive, if unconscious.

"Bring Keff to Keff's cave," the voice said again, in a crisp but persuasive tone. "Come, Brannel. Bring Keff."

"All right," Brannel said at last, his curiosity about the silver cylinder overpowering his sense of caution. This would be the first time he had been invited into a mage's stronghold. Who knew what wonders would open up to him within Keff's tower?

Drawing one of the limp arms over his shoulder, Brannel hefted Keff and stood up. After years of hard work, carrying the body of a man smaller than himself wasn't much of an effort. It was also the first time he'd laid hands on a mage. With a guilty thrill, he bore Keff's dead weight toward the silver tower.

At the foot of the ramp, Brannel paused to watch the smooth door withdraw upward with a quiet hiss. He stared up at it, wondering what kind of door opened without hands to push it.

"Come, Brannel," the silky persuasive voice said from the weight on his back.

Brannel obeyed. Under his rough, bare feet, the ramp boomed hollowly. The air smelled different inside. As he set foot over the threshold into the dim, narrow anteroom, lights went on. The walls were smooth, like the surface of unruffled water, meeting the ceiling and walls in perfect corners. Such ideal workmanship aroused Brannel's admiration. But what else would one expect from a mage? he chided himself.

In front of him was a corridor. Narrow bands of bluish light like the sun through clouds illuminated themselves. Along the walls at Brannel's eye level, orange-red bands flickered into life, moving onward until they reached the walls' end. The colored lights returned to the beginning and waited.

"I follow thee. Is that right?" Brannel asked in mage-speak, cautiously stepping into the corridor.

"Come," the disembodied voice said in common Ozran and the sound echoed all around him. Mage Keff was certainly a powerful wizard to have a house that talked.

Carialle was relieved that Brannel hadn't been frightened by a disembodied voice or the sight of an interplanetary ship. He was cautious, but she gave him credit for that. She had the lights guide him to the wall where Keff's weight bench was stored. It slid noiselessly out at knee level before the Noble Primitive who didn't need to be told that that was where he was to lay Keff's body.

"The only intelligent man on the planet," Carialle said quietly to herself.

Brannel straightened up and took a good, long look at the cabin, beginning to turn on his callused heels. As he caught sight of the monitors showing various angles of the crop field outside, and the close-up of his fellow Noble Primitives crouched in a huddle at the cave mouth, he let out a sound close to a derisive laugh.

Carialle turned her internal monitors to concentrate on Keff's vital signs. Respiration had begun again and his eyes twitched under their long-lashed lids.

Brannel started to walk the perimeter of the cabin. He was careful to touch nothing, though occasionally he leaned close and sniffed at a piece of equipment. At Keff's exercise machines, he took a deeper breath and straightened up with a snort and a puzzled look on his face.

"Thank you for your help, Brannel," Carialle said, using the IT through her own speakers. "You can go now. Keff will also thank you later."

Brannel showed no signs of being ready to depart. In fact, he didn't seem to have heard her at all. He was wandering around the main cabin with the light of wonder in his eyes beginning to alter. Carialle didn't like the speculative look on his face. She was grateful enough to the furry male for rescuing Keff to let him have a brief tour of the facilities, but no more than that.

"Thank you, Brannel. Good-bye, Brannel," Carialle said, her tone becoming more pointed. "You can go. Please. Now. Go. Leave!"

Brannel heard the staccato words spoken by the mage's familiar in a much less friendly tone than it had used to coax him inside Keff's stronghold. He didn't want to leave such a fascinating place. Many objects lured him to examine them, many small enough to be concealed in the hand. Some of them might even be objects of power. Surely the great mage would not miss a small one.

He focused on a flattened ovoid of shiny white the size of his hand lying on a narrow shelf below a rack of large stiff squares that looked to be made of wood. Even the quickest glance at the white thing told him that it had the five depressions of an item of power in its surface. His breathing quickened as he reached out to pick it up.

"No!" said the voice. "That's my palette." Out of the wall shot a hand made of black metal and slapped his wrist. Surprised, he dropped the white thing. Before it hit the floor, another black hand jumped away from the wall and caught it. Brannel backed away as the lower hand passed the white object to the upper hand, which replaced it on the shelf.

Thwarted, Brannel looked around for another easily portable item. Showing his long teeth in an ingratiating smile and wondering where the unseen watcher was concealed, he sidled purposefully toward another small device on top of a table studded with sparkling lights. His hand lifted, almost of its own volition, toward his objective.

"Oh, no, you don't," Carialle said firmly, startling him into dropping Keff's pedometer back onto the monitor board. She watched as he swiveled his head around, trying to discover where she was. "Didn't anyone ever tell you shoplifting is rude?"

He backed away, with his hands held ostentatiously behind him.

"You're not going to leave on your own, are you?" Carialle said "Perhaps a little push is in order."

Starring at the far side of the main cabin, Carialle generated complex and sour sonic tones guaranteed to be painful to humanoid ears. The male fell to his knees with his hands over his ears, his sheep's face twisted into a rictus. Carialle turned up the volume and purposefully began to sweep the noise along her array of speakers toward the airlock. Protesting, Brannel was driven, stumbling and crawling, out onto the ramp. As soon as she turned off the noise, he did an abrupt about-face and tried to rush back in. She let loose with a loud burst like a thousand hives of bees and slid the door shut in his face before he could cross the threshold.

"Some people just do not know when to leave," Carialle grumbled as she ordered out a couple of servos to begin first aid on Keff.

Driven out into the open air by the sharp sounds, Brannel hurried away from the flying castle and over the hill. On the other side of the field the others were crouched in a noisy conference, arms waving, probably discussing the strange mage. No one paid any attention to him, which was good. He had much to think about, and he was hungry. He'd been forced to consume some of the woozy food. He hoped he hadn't had enough to dull what he had learned this day.

During his youth, when he had fallen ill with fever, vomiting and headache, he had been unable to eat any of the food provided by the overlords. His parents had an argument that night about whether or not to beg Klemay for medical help. Brannel's mother thought such a request would be approved since Brannel was a sturdy lad and would grow to be a strong worker. His father did not want to ask, fearing punishment for approaching one of the high ones. Brannel overheard the discussion, wondering if he was going to die.

In the morning, the floating eye came from Klemay to oversee the day's work. Brannel's mother did not go running out to abase herself before it. Though he was no better, she seemed to have forgotten all about the urgency of summoning help for him. She settled Brannel, swathed in hides, at the edge of the field, and patted his leg affectionately before beginning her duties. She *had* forgotten her concern of the previous night. So had his father.

Brannel was not resentful. This was the way it had always been with the people. The curious thing was that *he* remembered. Yesterday had not disappeared into an undifferentiated grayness of mist and memory. Everything that he'd heard or seen was as clear to him as if it was still happening. The only thing that was different between yesterday and the day before was that he had not eaten.

Thereafter, he had avoided eating the people's food whenever possible. He experimented with edible native plants that grew down by the river, but lived mostly by stealing raw vegetables and grain from standing crops or from the plough-beasts' mangers. As a result, he grew bigger and stronger than any of his fellows. If his mother remarked upon it at all, when the vague fuzz of memory lifted, she was grateful that she had produced a fine strong big son to work for the overlord. His wits sharpened, and anything he heard he remembered forever. He didn't want to lose the gift by poisoning himself with the people's food. So far, the mages had had no cause to suspect him of being different from the rest of his village. And he was careful *not* to be disobedient or bring himself to their attention. The worst fate he could imagine was losing his clarity of mind

That clear mind now puzzled over Keff: was he or was he not a mage? He possessed objects of power, but he spoke no mage-talk. His house familiar knew none of their language either, but it used the same means that Mage Klemay did to drive him out, as the workers of his cave were driven by hideous noises outside to work every day of their lives. Keff seemed to have power yet he was struck down all unaware by the mage-bolt. Could Keff not have sensed it coming?

Once on the far side of the field, Brannel squeezed between bushes to the slope that led to his hiding place near the river. Observed only by a few green-balls, he ate some raw roots from the supply that he had concealed there in straw two nightfalls before. All the harvests had been good this year. No one had noticed how many basket loads he had removed, or if they had, they didn't remember. Their forgetfulness was to his advantage.

His hunger now satisfied, Brannel made his way back to the cavern, to listen to the remarkable happenings of the day, the new mage, and how the mage had been struck down. No one thought to ask what had happened to this mage and Brannel did not enlighten them. They'd have forgotten in the morning anyway. When night's darkness fell, they all swarmed back into the warm cave. As they found their night places, Alteis looked at his son, his face screwed as he tried to remember something he had intended to ask Brannel, but gave up the effort after a long moment.

✺CHAPTER FOUR

At a casual glance, the council room of the High Mage of the South appeared to be occupied by only one man, Nokias himself, in the thronelike hover-chair in the center, picked out by the slanting rays of the afternoon sun. Plennafrey realized, as she directed her floating spy-eye to gaze around the palatial chamber, that more presence and power was represented there and then than almost anywhere else on Ozran. She was proud to be included in that number allied to Nokias, proud but awed.

Closest to the rear of the hover-chair hung the simple silver globes of his trusted chief servants, ready to serve the High Mage, but also guarding him. They were the eyes in the back of his head, not actual fleshly eyes as Plennafrey had imagined when she was a child. Ranged in random display about the great chamber were the more ornate globe eyes of the mages and magesses. In the darkest corner hovered the sphere belonging to gloomy Howet. Mage-height above all the others flew the spy-eye of Asedow, glaring scornfully down on everyone else. Iranika's red ball drifted near the huge open window that looked out upon the mountain range, seemingly inattentive to the High Mage's discourse. Immediately before Nokias at eye level floated the gleaming metallic pink and gold eye of Potria, an ambitious and dangerous enchantress. As if sensing her regard, Potria's spy-eye turned toward hers, and Plennafrey turned hers just in time to be gazing at High Mage Nokias before the mystical aperture focused.

At home in her fortress sanctuary many klicks distant, Plenna felt her cheeks redden. It would not do to attract attention, nor would her inexperience excuse an open act of discourtesy. That was how mages died. For security, she tightened her fingers and thumb in the five depressions on her belt buckle, her personal object of power, and began to draw from it the weblike framework of a spell that would both protect her and injure or kill anyone who tried to cross its boundaries as well as generate an atmosphere of self-deprecation and effacement. Her magical defenses were as great as any mage's: lack of experience was her weakness. Plennafrey was the most junior of all the mages, the sole survivor of her family. She had taken her father's place only two years ago. Thankfully, Potria appeared not to have taken offense, and the pink-gold spy-eye spun in air to stare at each of its fellows in turn. Plenna directed her blue-green spy-eye to efface itself so as not to arouse further notice, and let the spell stand down, inactive but ready.

"We should move now to take over Klemay's stronghold," Potria's mental voice announced. Musical as a horn call, it had a strong, deep flavor that rumbled with mystic force. On the walls, the mystic art of the ancients quivered slightly, setting the patterns in motion within their deeply carved frames.

"Counsel first, Lady Potria," Nokias said, mildly. He was a lean, ruddy-faced man, not so tall as Plennafrey's late father, but with larger hands and feet out of proportion to his small stature. His light brown eyes, wide and innocent, belied the quick mind behind them. He snapped his long fingers and a servant bearing a tray appeared before him. The fur-face knelt at Nokias's feet and filled the exquisite goblet with sparkling green wine. The High Mage of the South appeared to study the liquid, as if seeking advice within its emerald lights. "My good brother to the east, Ferngal, also has a claim on Klemay's estate. After all, it was his argument with our late brother that led to his property becoming . . . available."

Silence fell in the room as the mages considered that position.

"Klemay's realm lies on the border between East and South," said Asedow's voice from the electric blue sphere. "It belongs not to Ferngal nor to us until one puts a claim on it. Let us make sure the successful claim is ours!"

"Do you hope for such a swift promotion, taking right of leadership like that?" Nokias asked mildly, setting down the half-empty goblet and tapping the base with one great hand. A mental murmur passed between some of the other mages. Plenna knew, as all of them did, how ambitious Asedow was. The man was not yet bold enough nor strong enough to challenge Nokias for the seat of Mage of the South. He had a tendency to charge into situations, not watching his back as carefully as he might. Plennafrey had overheard others saying that it probably wouldn't be long before carrion birds were squabbling over *Asedow's* property.

"Klemay carried a staff of power that drew most strongly from the Core of Ozran," Asedow stated. "Long as your forearm, with a knob on the end that looked like a great red jewel. He could control the lightning with it. I move to take possession of it."

"What you can take, you can keep," Nokias said. The words were spoken quietly, yet they held as much threat as a rumbling volcano. Even then, Asedow did not concede. Unless he *was* baiting Nokias into a challenge, Plenna thought, with a thrill of terror. Not now, when they were facing a challenge from a rival faction! Cautiously, she made her spy-eye dip toward the floor, where it would be out of the way of flying strikes of power. She'd heard of one mage crisped to ash and cinders by a blast sent through his spy-eye.

Nokias was the only one who noticed her cautious deployment and turned a kindly, amused glance in her drone's direction. She felt he could see her through its contracting pupil as she really was: a lass of barely twenty years, with a pixie's pointed chin and large, dark eyes wide with alarm. Ashamed of showing weakness, Plenna bravely levitated her eye to a level just slightly below the level held by the others. Nokias began to study a corner of the ceiling as if meditating on its relevance to the subject at hand.

"There is something stirring in the East," Iranika said in her gravelly mental voice, rose-colored spy-eye bobbing with her efforts to keep it steady. She was an elderly magess who lived at the extreme end of the southern mountain range. Plennafrey had never met her in person, nor was she likely to. The old woman stayed discreetly in her well-guarded fortress lest her aging reflexes fail to stop an assassination attempt. "Twice now I have felt unusual emanations in the ley lines. I suspect connivance, perhaps an upcoming effort by the eastern powers to take over some southern territory."

"I, too, have my suspicions," Nokias said, nodding.

Iranika snorted. "The Mage of the East wants his realm to spread out like sunrise and cover the whole of Ozran. Action is required lest he thinks you weak. Some of you fly on magic-back at once to Klemay's mountain. The power must be seized now! Strange portents are abroad."

"'Some of you' fly to the mountain? You will not be of our number, sister?" Howet rumbled from his corner.

"Nay. I have no need of additional power, as some feel they do," Iranika said, an unsubtle thrust at Asedow, who ignored it since she sided with him to attack. "I have enough. But I don't want Klemay's trove falling into the hands of the East by default."

"One might say the same about yours," Potria said offensively. "Why, I should claim yours now before your chair falls vacant, lest someone move upon it from the West."

"You are welcome to try, girl," Iranika said, turning her eye fully upon Potria's.

"Shall I show you how I'll do it?" Potria asked, her voice ringing in the huge chamber. The pink-gold sphere loomed toward the red. Both levitated toward the ceiling as they threw threats back and forth.

Plenna's eye's-eye view wobbled as she prepared for what looked like another contretemps between the two women. As Asedow yearned for the seat of Mage of the South, Potria craved Iranika's hoard of magical devices. Though Nokias was the senior mage in this quarter, Plennafrey had heard he held the seat only because Iranika didn't want it. She wished she was as secure in her position as the old woman. Plennafrey would have given a great deal to know if old Iranika kept her place by right or by bluff. If one was seen as weakening, one became an almost certain victim of assassination, and one's items of power would be gone even before the carrion birds arrived to circle around the corpse.

To achieve promotion in the hierarchy, a mage or magess must challenge and win against senior enchanters. Such battles were not always fatal, nor were they always magical. Sometimes, such matters were accomplished by suborning a mage's servants to steal artifacts that weakened power to the point where the mage could be overcome by devious means. Kills gave one more status. Plennafrey knew that, but she was reluctant to take lives. Even *thoughts* of theft and murder did not come easily to her, though she was learning them as a plain matter of survival. Another way to get promotion was to acquire magical paraphernalia from a secret cache left by the Ancient Ones or the Old Ones—such things were not unknown—or to take them from a mage no longer using them. Plenna wouldn't get much of Klemay's hoard unless she was bold. She was determined to claim *something* no matter what it cost her.

The items of power that descended from the Ancient Ones to the Old Ones and thence to the mages varied in design, but all had the same property, the ability to draw power from the Core of Ozran, the mystic source. There seemed to be no particular pattern the Ancient Ones followed in creating objects that channeled power: amulets, rings, wands, maces, staves, and objects of mysterious shape that had to be mounted in belts or bracelets to be carried. Plennafrey had even heard of a gauntlet the shape of an animal's head. Nokias bore upon his wrist the Great Ring of Ozran and also possessed amulets of varying and strange shapes. His followers had fewer, but all these artifacts had one feature in common: the five depressions into which one fit one's fingertips when issuing the mental or verbal Words of Command.

"Enough bickering," Nokias said wearily. "Are we agreed then? To take what we can of Klemay's power? What we find shall be shared between us according to seniority." Nokias settled back, the look in his eyes indicating he did not expect a challenge. "And strength."

"Agreed," the voice issued forth from Potria's spy-eye.

"Yes," boomed Howet.

"All right," Asedow agreed sourly.

"Yes." Plenna added her soft murmur, which was almost unheard among the other equally low voices around the great room.

Iranika alone remained silent, having had her say.

"Then the eyes have it," Nokias said, jovially, slapping his huge hands together.

Plennafrey joined in the chorus of groans that echoed through the chamber. That joke was old when the Ancient Ones walked Ozran.

"How shall we do this thing, High Mage?" Potria asked. "Open attack or stealth?"

"Stealth implies we have something to hide," Asedow said at once. "Ancient treasures belong to anyone who can claim and hold them. I say we go in force and challenge Ferngal openly."

"Ah!" Potria cried suddenly. "Ferngal and the Easterlings are on the move at this very moment! I sense a disruption in the lines of power in the debated lands! *Unusual* emanations of power."

"Ferngal would not dare!" Asedow declared.

"Wait," Nokias said, his brows drawn over thoughtful eyes. His gaze grew unfocused. "I sense what you do, Potria. Dyrene"—he raised a hand to one of his minions hovering just behind her masters chair. "You have a spy-eye in the vicinity. Investigate."

"I obey, High Mage," Dyrene's voice said. The young woman was monitoring several eyes at once for Nokias, to keep the High Mage from having to occupy his attention with simple reconnaissance. "Hmm—hmmm! It is not Ferngal, magical ones. There is a silver cylinder in the crop fields among the workers. It is huge, High Mage, as large as a tower. I do not know how it got there! There is a man nearby and . . . I do not know this person."

Iranika cackled to herself. The other spy-eyes spun on hers, pupils dilated to show the fury of their operators.

"You knew about it all the time, old woman," Potria said, accusingly.

"I detected it many hours ago," Iranika said, maddeningly coy. "I told you there had been strange movement in the ley lines, but did you listen? Did you think to check for yourselves? I have been watching. The great silver cylinder fell through the sky with fire at its base. A veritable flying fortress. It is a power object of incredible force. The man who came from within has been consorting with Klemay's peasants."

"He is not tied to the Core of Ozran," Nokias declared after a moment's concentration, "and so he is not a mage. That will make him easy to capture. We will find out who he is and whence he comes. Lend me your eyes, Dyrene. Open to me."

"I obey, lord," the tinny voice said.

Concentrating on his target, the Mage of the South laid his left hand across his right wrist to activate the Great Ring, and raised both hands toward the window. A bolt of crackling, scarlet fire lanced from his fingertips into the sky.

"He falls, High Mage," Dyrene reported

"I must see this stranger for myself," Iranika said. Without asking for leave, her spy-eye rose toward the great window.

"Wait, high ones!" Dyrene called. "A peasant moves the stranger's body. He carries it toward the silver tower." After a moment, when all the spy-eyes hovered around Dyrene's sphere, "It is sealed inside."

Iranika groaned.

"I want this silver cylinder," Asedow said in great excitement. "What forces it would command! High Mage, I claim it!"

"I challenge you, Asedow," Potria shrilled at once. "I claim both the tower and the being."

Other voices raised in the argument: some supporting Potria, some Asedow, while there were even a few clamoring for *their* right to take possession of the new artifacts. Nokias ignored these. Potria and Asedow would be permitted to make the initial attempt. Subsequent challengers would take on the winner, if Nokias himself did not claim liege right to the prizes.

"The challenge is heard and witnessed," Nokias declared, shouting over the din. He raised the hand holding the Great Ring. With a squawk, Plenna sent her spy-eye to take refuge underneath Nokias's floating chair and warded the windows of her mountain home. Humming, scarlet power beams lanced in through Nokias's open window, one from each of the two mages in their mountain strongholds. They struck together in a crashing explosion sealed by the Great Ring. "And the contest begins."

All the eyes flew out of the arching stone casement behind the challengers to have a look at the objects of contention.

"It is bigger than huge," Plennafrey observed, spiraling her eye around and around the silver tower. "How beautiful it is!"

"There are runes inscribed here," Iranika's old voice said. Plennafrey felt the faint pull of the old woman trying to attract attention, and followed the impulse to the red spy-eye floating near the broad base. "Come here and see. I have not seen anything in all my archives which resemble these."

"I spy, with my little eye, an enigma of huge and significant proportions," Nokias said, his golden sphere hovering behind them as they tried to puzzle out the runes.

"It is a marvelous illusion," Howet said, streaking back a distance to take in the whole object. "How do I know this isn't a great trick by Ferngal? Metal and fire—that's no miracle, High Mage. I can build something like this myself."

"It is most original in design," Nokias said.

"Ferngal hasn't the imagination," Potria protested.

"It's lovely," Plenna said, admiring the smooth lines.

Iranika sputtered. "Lovely but useless!"

"How do you know?" Potria snapped.

*   *   *

While her servos were taking care of Keff, Carialle kept vigil on the mountain range to the south. No rain was falling, so where had that lightning, if it *was* lightning, come from? An electrical discharge of that much force had to have a source. She didn't read anything appropriate in that direction, not even a concentration of conductive ore in the mountains that could act as a natural capacitor. The fact that the bolt had fallen so neatly at Keff's feet suggested deliberate action.

The air around her felt ionized, empty, almost brittle. After the bolt had struck, the atmosphere slowly began to return to normal, as if the elements were flowing like water filling in where a stone had hit the surface of a pond.

Her sensors picked up faint rumbling, and the air around her drained again. This time she felt a wind blowing hard toward the mountain range. Suddenly the scarlet bolts struck again, two jagged spears converging on one distant peak. Then, like smithereens scattering from under a blacksmith's hammer, minute particles flew outward from the point of impact toward her.

She focused quickly on the incoming missiles. They were too regular in shape to be shards of rock, and also appeared to be flying under their own power, even increasing in speed. The analysis arrived only seconds before the artifacts did, showing perfect spheres, smooth and vividly colored, with one sector sliced off the front of each to show a lenslike aperture. Strangely, she scanned no mechanisms inside. They appeared to be hollow.

The spheres spiraled around and over her, as if some fantastic juggler was keeping all those balls in the air at once. Carialle became aware of faint, low-frequency transmissions. The spheres were sending data back to some source. She plugged the IT into her external array.

Her first assumption—that the data was meant only for whatever had sent each—changed as she observed the alternating pattern of transmission and the faint responses to the broadcasts from the nontransmitting spheres. They were *talking* to each other. By pinning down the frequency, she was able to hear voices.

Using what vocabulary and grammar Keff had recorded from Brannel and the others, she tried to get a sense of the conversation.

The IT left long, untranslatable gaps in the transcript. The Ozran language was as complex as Standard. Keff had only barely begun to analyze its syntax and amass vocabulary. Carialle recorded everything, whether she understood it or not.

"Darn you, Keff, wake up," she said. This was *his* specialty. He knew how to tweak the IT, to adjust the arcane device to the variables and parameters of language. The snatches of words she did understand tantalized her.

"Come here," one of the colored balls said to the others in a high-pitched voice. ". . . (something) not . . . like (untranslatable)."

". . . (untranslatable) . . . how do . . . know . . ." Carialle heard a deep masculine voice say, followed by a word Brannel had been using to refer to Keff, then another unintelligible sentence.

". . . (untranslatable)."

"How do you know?"

An entire sentence came through in clear translation. Carialle perked up her audio sensors, straining to hear more. She ordered the servo beside the weight bench to nudge Keff's shoulder.

"Keff. Keff, wake up! I need you. You have to hear this. Aargh!" She growled in frustration, the bass notes of her voice vibrating the tannoy diaphragms. "We get a group of uninhibited, fluent native speakers, situated who knows where, and you're taking a nap!"

The strange power arcs that she had sensed when they first landed were stronger now. Did that power support the hollow spheres and make them function? Whoever was running the system was using up massive power like air: free, limitless, and easy. She found it hard to believe it could be the indigenous Noble Primitives. They didn't have anything more technologically advanced than beast harness. Carialle should now look for a separate sect, the "overlords" of this culture.

She scanned her planetary maps for a power source and was thwarted once again by the lack of focus. The lines of force seemed to be everywhere and anywhere, defying analysis. If there had been less electromagnetic activity in the atmosphere, it would have been easier. Its very abundance prevented her from tracing it. Carialle was fascinated but nervous. With Keff hurt, she'd rather study the situation from a safer distance until she could figure out who was controlling things, and what with.

No time to make a pretty takeoff. On command, Carialle's servo robots threw their padded arms across Keff's forehead, neck, chest, hips, and legs, securing him to the weight bench. Carialle started launch procedures. None of the Noble Primitives were outside, so she wouldn't scare them or fry them when she took off. The flying eye-balls would have to shift for themselves. She kicked the engines to launch.

Everything was go and on green. Only she wasn't moving.

Increasing power almost to the red line, she felt the heat of her thrusters as they started to slag the mineral-heavy clay under her landing gear, but she hadn't risen a centimeter.

"What kind of fardling place is this?" Carialle demanded. "What's holding me?" She shut down thrust, then gunned it again, hoping to break free of the invisible bonds. Shut down, thrust! Shut down, thrust! No go. She was trapped. She felt a rising panic and sharply put it down. Reality check: this could not be happening to a ship of her capabilities.

Carialle ran through a complete diagnostic and found every system normal. She found it hard to believe what her systems told her. She could detect no power plant on this planet, certainly not one strong enough to hold her with thrusters on full blast. She should at least have felt a *twitch* as such power cut in. Some incredible alien *force* of unknown potency was holding her surface-bound.

"No," she whispered. "Not again."

Objectively, the concept of such huge, wild power controlled with such ease fascinated the unemotional, calculating part of Carialle's mind. Subjectively, she was frightened. She cut her engines and let them cool.

Rescue from this situation seemed unlikely. Not even Simeon had known their exact destination. Sector R was large and unexplored. Nevertheless, she told herself staunchly, Central Worlds had to be warned about the power anomaly so no one else would make the mistake of setting down on this planet. She readied an emergency drone and prepared it to launch, filling its small memory with all the data she and Keff had already gathered about Ozran. She opened the small drone hatch and launched it. Its jets did not ignite. The invisible force held it as firmly as it did her.

Frequency analysis showed that an uncapsuled mayday was unlikely to penetrate the ambient electromagnetic noise. Even if she could have gotten one in orbit, who was likely to hear it in the next hundred years? She and Keff were on their own.

"Ooooh." A heartfelt groan from the exercise equipment announced Keff's return to consciousness.

"How do you feel?" she asked, switching voice location to the speaker nearest him.

"Horrible." Keff started to sit up but immediately regretted any upward movement. A sharp, seemingly pointed pain like a saw was attempting to remove the rear of his skull. He put a hand to the back of his head, clamped his eyes shut, then opened them as wide as he could, hoping to dispel his fuzzy vision. His eyelids felt thick and gritty. He took a few deep breaths and began to shiver. "Why is it cold in here, Cari? I'm chilled to the bone."

"Ambient temperature of this planet is uncomfortably low for humans," Carialle said, brisk with relief at his recovery.

"Brrr! You're telling me!" Keff slid his legs around and put his feet on the ground. His sight cleared and he realized that he was sitting on his weight bench. Carialle's servos waited respectfully a few paces away. "How did I get in here? The last thing I remember was talking to Brannel out in the field. What's happened?"

"Brannel brought you in, my poor wounded knight. Are you sure you're well enough to comprehend all?" Carialle's voice sounded light and casual, but Keff wasn't fooled. She was very upset.

The first thing to do was to dissolve the headache and restore his energy. Pulling an exercise towel over his shoulders like a cape and moving slowly so as not to jar his head more than necessary, Keff got to the food synthesizer.

"Hangover cure number five, and a high-carb warm-up," he ordered. The synthesizer whirred obediently. He drank what appeared in the hatch and shuddered as it oozed down to his stomach. He burped. "I needed that. And I need some food, too. Warm, high protein.

"While I replenish myself, tell all, fair lady," Keff said. "I can take it." With far more confidence than he felt, he smiled at her central pillar and waited.

"Now, let's see, where were we?" she began in a tone that was firm enough, but his long association with Carialle told him that she was considerably agitated. "You got hit by scarlet lightning. Not, I think, a natural phenomenon, since none of the necessary meteorological conditions existed. There's also the problem with its accuracy, landing right at your feet and knocking you, and you only, unconscious. I *refuse* to entertain coincidence. Someone shot that lightning right at you! I persuaded Brannel to bring you inside."

"You did?" Keff was admiring, knowing how little of the language she would have had to do any persuading.

"After he scooted, and not without persuasion, I add for accuracy's sake, we had a plague of what I would normally class as reconnaissance drones, except they have no perceptible internal mechanisms whatsoever, not even flight or anti-grav gear." Carialle's screens shifted to views of the outside, telephoto and close-angle. Small, colored spheres hovered at some distance, flat apertures all facing the brainship.

"Someone has very pretty eyes," Keff said with interest. "No visible means of support, as you say. Curious." The buzzer sounded on the food hatch, and he retrieved the large, steaming bowl. "Ahhh!"

On the screen, a waveguide graph showing frequency modulation had been added beside the image of each drone. The various sound levels rose and fell in patterns.

"Here's what I picked up on the supersonics."

"Such low frequencies," Keff said, reading the graphs. "They can't be transmitting very sophisticated data."

"They're broadcasting voice signals to one another," Carialle said. "I ran the tapes through IT, and here's what I got." She played the datafile at slightly higher than normal speed to get through it all. Keff's eyebrows went up at the full sentence in clear Standard. He went to the console where Carialle had allowed him to install IT's mainframe and fiddled with the controls.

"Hmm! More vocabulary, verbs, and I dare to suggest we've got a few colloquialisms or ejaculations, though I've no referents to translate them fully. This is a pretty how-de-do, isn't it? Whoever's running these artifacts is undoubtedly responsible for the unexpected power emissions the freighter captain reported to Simeon." He straightened up and cocked his head wryly at Carialle's pillar. "Well, my lady, I don't fancy sneak attacks with high-powered weapons. I'd rather not sit and analyze language in the middle of a war zone. Since we're not armed for this party, why don't we take off, and file a partial report on Ozran to be completed by somebody with better shields?"

Carialle made an exasperated noise. "I would take off in a Jovian second, but we are being held in place by a tractor beam of some kind. I can read neither the source nor the direction the power is coming from. It's completely impossible, but I can't move a centimeter. I've been burning fuel trying to take off over and over—and you know we don't have reserves to spare."

Keff finished his meal and put the crockery into the synthesizers hatch. With food in his belly, he felt himself again. His head had ceased to revolve, and the cold had receded from his bones and muscles.

"That's why I'm your brawn," he said, lightly. "I go and find out these things."

"Sacrificing yourself again, Keff? To pairs of roving eyes?" Carialle tried to sound flip, but Keff wasn't fooled. He smiled winningly at her central pillar. All his protective instincts were awake and functioning.

"You are my lady," he said, with a gallant gesture. "I seek the object of my quest to lay at your feet. In this case, information. Perhaps an Ozran's metabolism only gets a minor shock when touched with this mystical power beam. We don't know that the folk on the other end are hostile."

"*Anything* that ties my tail down is hostile."

"You shall not be held in durance vile while I, your champion, live." Keff picked up the portable IT unit, checked it for damage, and slung it around his chest. "At least I can find Brannel and ask him what hit me."

"Don't be hasty," Carialle urged. On the main screen she displayed her recording of the attack on Keff. "The equation has changed. We've gone suddenly from dealing with indigenous peasantry at no level of technology to an unknown life-form with a higher technology than *we* have. This is what you're up against."

Keff sat back down and concentrated on the screen, running the frames back and forth one at a time, then at speed.

"Good! Now I know what I need to ask about," he said, pointing. "Do you see that? Brannel knew what the lightning was, he knew it was coming, *and* he got out of its way. Look at those reflexes! Hmmm. The bolt came from the mountains to the south. Southwest. I wonder what the terms are for compass directions in Ozran? I can draw him a compass rose in the dust, with planetary sunrise for east . . ."

Carialle interrupted him by filling the main cabin with a siren wail.

"Keff, you're not listening. It might be too dangerous. To unknown powers who can tie up a full-size spaceship, one human male isn't a threat. And they've downed you once already."

"It's not that easy to kill Von Scoyk-Larsens," Keff said, smiling. "They may be surprised I'm still moving around. Or as I said, perhaps they didn't think the red bolt would affect me the way it did. In any case, can you think of a way to get us out of here unless I do?"

Carialle sighed. "Okay, okay, gird your manly loins and join the fray, Sir Galahad! But if you fall down and break both your legs don't come running to me."

"Nay, my lady," Keff said with a grin and a salute to her titanium pillar. "With my shield or upon it. Back soon."

✳️CHAPTER FIVE

Keff walked into the airlock. He twitched down his tunic, checked his equipment, and concentrated on loosening his muscles one at a time until he stood poised and ready on the balls of his feet. With one final deep breath for confidence, he nodded to Carialle's camera and stepped forward.

Regretting more every second that she had been talked into his proposed course of action, Carialle slid open her airlock and dropped the ramp slowly to the ground. As she suspected, the flying eyes drifted closer to see what was going on. She fretted, wondering if they were capable of shooting at Keff. He had no shields, but he was right: if he didn't find the solution, they'd never be able to leave this place.

Keff walked out to the top of the ramp and held out both hands, palms up, to the levitating spheres. "I come in peace," he said.

The spheres surged forward in one great mass, then *flit!*, they disappeared in the direction of the distant mountains.

"That's rung the bell," Keff said, with satisfaction. "Spies of the evil wizard, my lady, cannot stand where good walks."

A whining alarm sounded. Carialle read her monitors.

"Do you feel it? The mean humidity of the immediate atmosphere has dropped. Those arching lines of stray power I felt crisscrossing overhead are strengthening directly above us. Power surge building, building..."

"I feel it," Keff said, licking dry lips. "My nape hair is

standing up. Look!" he shouted, his voice ringing. "Here come our visitors!"

Nothing existed beyond three hundred meters away, but from that distance at point south-southwest, two objects came hurtling out of nonexistence one after the other, gaining dimensionality as they neared Carialle, until she could see them clearly. It took Keff a few long milliseconds more, but he gasped when his eyes caught sight of the new arrivals.

"Not the drones again," Keff said. "It's our wizard!"

"Not *a* wizard," Carialle corrected him. "Two."

Keff nodded as the second one exploded into sight after the first. "They're not Noble Primitives. They're another species entirely." He gawked. "Look at them, Cari! Actual humanoids, just like us!"

Carialle zoomed her lenses in for a good look. For once Keff's wishful thinking had come true. The visitor closest to Carialle's video pickup could have been any middle-aged man on any of the Central Worlds. Unlike the cave-dwelling farmers, the visitor had smooth facial skin with neither pelt, nor beard, nor mustache; and the hands were equipped with four fingers and an opposable thumb.

"Extraordinary. Vital signs, pulse elevated at eighty-five beats per minute, to judge by human standards from the flushed complexion and his expression. He's panting and cursing about something. Respiration between forty and sixty," Carialle reported through Keff's mastoid implant.

"Just like humans in stress!" Keff repeated, beatifically.

"So were Brannel and his people," Carialle replied, overlaying charts on her screen for comparison. "Except for superficial differences in appearance, this male and our Noble Primitives are alike. That's interesting. Did this new species evolve from the first group? If so, why didn't the Noble Primitive line dead-end? They should have ceased to exist when a superior mutation arose. And if the bald-faced ones evolved from the hairy ones, why are there so many different configurations of Noble Primitives like sheep, dogs, cats, and camels?"

"That's something I can ask them," Keff said, now subvocalizing as the first airborne rider neared him. He started to signal to the newcomer.

The barefaced male exhibited the haughty mien of one who expected to be treated as a superior being. He had beautiful, long-fingered hands folded over a slight belly indicative of a sedentary lifestyle and good food. Upright and dignified, he rode in an ornate contraption which resembled a chair with a toboggan runner for a base. In profile, it was an uncial "h" with an extended and flared bottom serif, a chariot without horses. Like the metal globes that had heralded the visitors' arrival, the dark green chair hovered meters above the ground with no visible means of propulsion.

"What is holding that up?" Keff asked. "Skyhooks?"

"Sheer, bloody, pure power," Carialle said. "Though, by the shell that preserves me, I can't see how he's manipulating it. He hasn't moved an extra muscle, but he's maneuvering like a space jockey."

"Psi," Keff said. "They've exhibited teleportation, and now telekinesis. *Super* psi. All the mentat races humankind has encountered in the galaxy rolled *together* aren't as strong as these people. And they're *so* like humans. Hey, friend!" Keff waved an arm.

Paying no attention to Keff, the sledlike throne veered close to Carialle's skin and then spun on its axis to face the pink-gold chariot that followed, making the occupant of that one pull up sharply to avoid a midair collision. She sat up tall in her seat, eyes blazing with blue-green fire, waves of crisp bronze hair almost crackling with fury about her set face. Her slim figure attired in floating robes of ochre and gold chiffon, she seemed an ethereal being, except for her expression of extreme annoyance. She waved her long, thin hands in complex gestures and the man responded sneeringly in kind. Keff's mouth had dropped open.

"More sign language," Carialle said, watching the woman's gestures with a critical eye. "New symbols. IT didn't have them in the glossary before."

"I'm in love," Keff said, dreamily. "Or at least in lust. Who is she?"

"I don't know, but she and that male are angry at each other. They're fighting over something."

"I hope she wins." Keff sighed, making mooncalf eyes at the new arrival. "She sure is beautiful. That's some figure she's got. And that hair! Just the same color as her skin. Wonderful." The female sailed overhead and Keff's eyes lit up as he detected a lingering scent. "And she's wearing the most delicious perfume."

Carialle noted the rise in his circulation and respiration and cleared her throat impatiently.

"Keff! She's an indigenous inhabitant of a planet we happen to be studying. Please disengage fifteen-year-old hormones and re-enable forty-five-year-old brain. We need to figure out who they are so we can free my tail and get off this planet."

"I can't compartmentalize as easily as you can," Keff grumbled. "Can I help it if I appreciate an attractive lady?"

"I'm no more immune to beauty than you are," Carialle reminded him. "But if she's responsible for our troubles, I want to know why. I particularly want to know *how*!"

Across the field, some of the Noble Primitives had emerged from their burrow. Stooping in postures indicative of respect and healthy fear, they scurried toward the floating chairs, halting some distance away. Keff noticed Brannel among them, standing more erect than any of the others. Still defying authority, Keff thought, with wry admiration.

"Do you want to ask him what's going on?" Carialle said through the implant.

"Remember what he said about being punished for curiosity," Keff reminded her. "These are the people he's afraid of. If I single him out, he's in for it. I'll catch him later for a private talk."

The elder, Alteis, approached and bowed low to the two chair-holders. They ignored him, continuing to circle at ten meters, calling out at one another.

"I knew I could not trust you to wait for Nokias to lead us here, Asedow," Potria shouted angrily. "One day, your eagerness to thrust out your hand for power will result in having it cut off at the shoulder."

"You taunt me for breaking the rules when you also didn't wait," Asedow retorted. "Where's Nokias, then?"

"I couldn't let you claim by default," Potria said, "so your action forced me to follow at once. Now that I am here, I restate that I should possess the silver cylinder and the being inside. I will use it with greater responsibility than you."

"The Ancient Ones would laugh at your disingenuousness, Potria," Asedow said, scornfully. "You want them just to keep them from me. I declare," he shouted to the skies, "that I am the legitimate keeper of these artifacts sent down through the ages to me, and by my hope of promotion, I will use them wisely and well."

Potria circled Asedow, trying to get nearer to the great cylinder, but he cut her off again and again. She directed her chair to fly up and over him. He veered upward in a flash, cackling maddeningly. She hated him, hated him for thwarting her. At one time they had been friends, even toyed with the idea of becoming lovers. She had hoped that they could have been allies, taking power from Nokias and that bitch Iranika and ruling the South between them despite the fact that the first laws of the First Mages said only one might lead. She and Asedow could never agree on who that would be. As now, he wouldn't support her claim, and she wouldn't support his. So they were forced to follow archaic laws whose reasoning was laid down thousands of years ago and might never be changed. The two of them were set against one another like mad vermin in a too-small cage. She or Asedow must conquer, must be the clear winner in the final contest. Potria had determined in her deepest heart that she would be the victor.

The rustle in her mystic hearing told her that Asedow was gathering power from the ley lines for an attack. He had but to chase her away or knock her unconscious, and the contest was his. Killing was unnecessary and would only serve to make High Mage Nokias angry by depriving him of a strong subject and ally. Potria began to wind in the threads of power between her fingers, garnering and gathering until she had a web large enough to throw over him. It would contain the force of Asedow's spell and knock him out.

"That one is unworthy," she heard Asedow call out. "Let me win, not her!"

Stretching the smothering web on her thumbs, she spread out her arms wide in the prayer sign, hands upright and palms properly turned in toward her to contain the blessing.

"In the name of Ureth, the Mother World of Paradise, I call all powers to serve me in this battle," she chanted.

Asedow flashed past her in his chariot, throwing his spell. Raising herself, Potria dropped her spread counter-spell on top of him and laughed as his own blast of power caught him. His chair wobbled unsteadily to a halt a hundred meters distant. His cursing was audible and he was very angry. He switched his chair about on its axis. She saw his face, dark with blood as a thundercloud. He panted heavily.

"Thought you would have an easy win, did you?" Potria called, tauntingly. She began to ready an attack of her own. Something not fatal but *appropriate*.

She felt disturbances in the ether. More mages were coming, probably attracted by the buildup of power in this barren, uninteresting place. Potria changed the character of the cantrip she was molding. If she was to have an audience, she would give a good show and make a proper fool of Asedow.

By now, her opponent hovered invisible in a spell-cloud of dark green smoke that roiled and rumbled. Potria fancied she even saw miniature lightnings flash within its depths. He, too, had observed the arrival of more of their magical brethren, and it made him impatient. He struck while his spell was still insufficiently prepared. Potria laughed and raised a single, slim hand, fingers spread. The force bounced off the globe of protection she had wrought about herself, rushed outward, and exploded on contact with the nearest solid object, a tree, setting it ablaze. Some of it rebounded upon Asedow, shaking his chariot so hard that he nearly lost control of it.

Having warded off Asedow's pathetic attack, Potria stole a swift look at the newly arrived mages. They were all minor lights from the East, probably upset that she and Asedow had crossed the border into their putative realm. By convention, they were bound to stay out of the middle of a fairly joined battle, and so they hovered on the sidelines, swearing about the invasion by southern mages. So long as they kept out of her way until she won, she didn't care what they thought of her.

Keff saw the five new arrivals blink into existence, well beyond the battleground. The first two came to such a screeching halt that he wondered if they had hurried to the scene at a dead run and were having trouble braking. The others proceeded with more caution toward the circling combatants.

"The first arrivals remind me of something," Keff said, "but I can't put my finger on what. Great effect, that sudden stop!"

"It looked like Singularity Drive," Carialle said, critically. "Interesting that they've duplicated the effect unprotected and in atmosphere."

"That's big magic," Keff said.

The new five were no sooner at the edge of the field than the magiman and magiwoman let off their latest volley at each other.

Smoke exploded in a plume from the green storm cloud. It was shot along its expanse with lightning and booms of thunder. Enwrapping the magiwoman in its snakelike coils, it closed into a murky sphere with the golden female at its center. Lights flashed inside and Keff heard a scream. Whether it was fury, fear, or pain he couldn't determine.

Suddenly, the sphere broke apart. The smoke dissipated on the evening sky, leaving the female free. Her hair had escaped from its elegant coif and stood out in crackling tendrils. The shoulder of her robe was burned away, showing the tawny flesh beneath. Eyes sparking, she levitated upward, arms gathering and gathering armfuls of nothing to her breast. Her hands chopped forward, and lightning, liquid electricity, flew at her opponent.

The male crossed his forearms before himself in a gesture intended to ward away the attack, but only managed to deflect some of it. Tiny fingers of white heat peppered his legs and the runner of his chair, burning holes in his robe and scorching the vehicle's ornamentation. In order to escape, he had to move away from Carialle toward the open fields, where the lightning ceased to pursue him. Triumphantly, the female sailed in and spiraled around the brainship in a kind of victory lap. In front of the ship, a translucent brick wall built itself up row by row, until it was as tall as Carialle herself.

Keff stared.

"Are they fighting over us?" he asked in disbelief.

Carialle took umbrage at the suggestion. "How dare they?" she said. "This is my ship, not the competition trophy!"

The male did not intend to give up easily. As soon as the cloud of lightning was gone, he headed back toward the ship. Between his hands a blue-white globe was forming. He threw it directly at the brick wall and the enchantress behind it.

The female was insufficiently prepared and the ball caught her in the belly. It knocked her chair back hundreds of meters, past the hovering strangers who hastily shifted out of her way. The illusory wall vanished. With a cry, the female flew in, arching her fingers like a cat's claws. Scarlet fire shot from each one, focusing on the male. His chair bounced up in the air and turned a full loop. Miraculously, he kept his seat. He tried to regain his original position near Carialle.

"They *are* fighting over me. The unmitigated gall of the creatures!"

*　　*　　*

At the first sign of mystic lightning, the workers had judiciously fled to a safe distance from which they avidly watched the battle. Ignoring Alteis's hissed commands to keep his head down, Brannel watched the overlords hungrily, as his eyes had earlier fed on Keff. Maybe this time a miracle would occur and one of them would drop an object of power. In the confusion of battle, it would go unnoticed until he, Brannel, dove for it and made it his own. Mere possession of an object of power might not make one a mage, but he wanted to find out. All his life he had cherished dreams of learning to fly or control lightning.

The odds against his success were immense. The mages were the mages, and the workers were the workers, to live, die, or serve at the whim of their overlords, never permitted to look above their lowly station. Until today, when Mage Keff arrived out of the sky, Brannel had never thought there was a third way of life. The stranger was not a mage by Ozran standards, since the overlords were fighting over him as if he wasn't there; but he was certainly not a worker. He must be something in between, a stepping stone from peasant to power. Brannel knew Keff could help him rise above his lowborn status and gain a place among mages, but how to win his favor and his aid? He had already been of service to Mage Keff. Perhaps he could render other services, provided that Keff survived the contest going on above his head.

Brannel had recognized Magess Potria and Mage Asedow by their colors while his peers were too afraid to lift their heads out of the dust. He'd give his heart and the rest of his fingers to be able to spin spells as they did. In spite of the damage that the combatants were doing to one another, not a tendril of smoke nor a tongue of flame had even come close to Keff, who was watching the battle rage calmly and without fear. Brannel admired the stranger's courage. Keff would be a powerful mentor. Together they would fight the current order, letting worthy ones from the lowest caste ascend to rule as their intelligence merited. That is, if Keff survived the war in which he was one of the prizes.

"A world of wizards, my lady!" Keff chortled gleefully to Carialle. "They're doing magic! No wonder you can't find a power source. There isn't one. This is pure evocation of power from the astral plane of the galaxy."

The beautiful woman zipped past him in her floating chair, hands busy between making signs and spells. He adjusted IT to register all motions and divide them between language and ritual by repeat usage and context. He was also picking up on a second spoken language or dialect. IT had informed him that Brannel had used some of the terms, and Keff wondered at the linguistic shift from one species to the other.

"Magical evocation is hardly scientific, Keff," Carialle reminded him. "They're getting power from somewhere, that's for sure. I can even follow some of the buildup a short way out, but then I lose it in the random emanations."

"It comes from the ether," Keff said, rapt. "It's magic."

"Stop calling it that. We're not playing the game now," Carialle said sharply. "We're witnessing sophisticated manipulation of power, not abracadabra-something-out-of-nothing."

"Look at it logically," Keff said, watching the male lob a hand-sized ball of flame over his head at his opponent. "How else would you explain being able to fly without engines or to appear in midair?"

"Telekinesis."

"And how about knitting lightning between your hands? Or causing smoke and fireballs without fuel? This is the stuff of legends. Magic."

"It's sophisticated legerdemain, I'll grant that much, but there's a logical explanation, too."

Keff laughed. "There is a logical explanation. We've discovered a planet where the laws of magic *are* the laws of science."

"Well, there's physics, anyhow," Carialle said. "Our magimen up there are beginning to fatigue. Their energy levels aren't infinite."

Ripostes and return attacks were slowing down. The magiwoman maintained an expression of grim amusement throughout the conflict, while the magiman couldn't disguise his annoyance.

As if attracted by the conflict, a bunch of globe-frogs appeared out of the brushy undergrowth at the edge of the crop fields. They rolled into the midst of the Noble Primitives, who were huddled into the gap, watching the aerial battle. The indigenes avoided contact with the small creatures by kicking out at them so that the globes turned away. The little group trundled their conveyances laboriously out into the open and paused underneath the sky-borne battle. Keff watched their bright black eyes focus on the combatants. They seemed fascinated.

"Look, Carialle," Keff said, directing his contact-button camera toward them. "Are they attracted by motion, or light? You'd think they'd be afraid of violent beings much larger than themselves."

"Perhaps they are attracted to power, like moths to a candle flame," Carialle said, "although, mind you, I've never seen moths or candles in person. I'm not an expert in animal behaviorism, but I don't think the attraction is unusual. Incautious, to the point of self-destructive, perhaps. Either of our psi-users up there could wipe them out with less power than it would take to hold up those chairs."

The two mages, sailing past, parrying one another's magic bolts and making their own thrusts, ignored the cluster which trailed them around the field. At last the little creatures gave up their hopeless pursuit, and rolled in a group toward Keff and Carialle.

"Your animal magnetism operating again," Carialle noted. The globe-frogs, paddling hard on the inner wall of their spherelike conveyances with their oversize paws, steered over the rocky ground and up the ramp, making for the inside of the ship. "Ooops, wait a minute! You can't come in here. Out!" she said, in full voice on her hatchway speakers. "Scat!"

The frogs ignored her. She tracked them with her internal cameras and directed her servos into the airlock to herd them out the door again. The frogs made a few determined tries to get past the low-built robots. Thwarted, they reversed position inside their globes and paddled the other way.

"Pests," Carialle said. "Is everyone on this planet intent on a free tour of my interior?"

The globe-frogs rolled noisily down the ramp and off the rise toward the underbrush at the opposite end of the clearing. Keff watched them disappear.

"I wonder if they're just attracted to any vibrations or emissions," he said.

"Could be—Heads up!" Carialle trumpeted suddenly. She put her servos into full reverse to get them out of Keff's way. Without waiting to ask why or what, Keff dove sideways into Carialle's hatch and hit the floor. A split second later, he felt a flame-throwerlike blast of heat almost singe his cheek. If he'd remained standing where he was, he'd have gotten a faceful of fire.

"They're out of control! Get in here!" Carialle cried.

Keff complied. The battle had become more serious, and the

magic-users had given up caring where their bolts hit. Another spell flared out of the tips of the woman's fingers at the male, only a dozen meters from Keff.

The brawn tucked and rolled through the inner door. Carialle slid the airlock door shut almost on his heels. Keff heard a whine of stressed metal as something else hit the side of the ship.

"Yow!" Carialle protested. "That blast was cold! *How* are they doing that?"

Keff ran to the central cabin viewscreens and dropped into his crash seat.

"Full view, please, Cari!"

The brain obliged, filling the three surrounding walls with a 270° panorama.

Keff spun his pilot's couch to follow the green contrail across the sky, as the male magician retreated to the far end of the combat zone. He looked frustrated. The last, unsuccessful blast that hit Carialle's flank must have been his. The female, beautiful, powerful, sitting up high in her chair, prepared another attack with busy hands. Her green eyes were dulling, as if she didn't care where her strike might land. The five magimen on the sidelines looked bored and angry, just barely restraining themselves from interfering. The battle would end soon, one way or another.

Even inside the ship, Keff felt the sudden change in the atmosphere. His hair, including his eyebrows and eyelashes and the hair on his arms, crackled with static. Something momentous was imminent. He leaned in toward the central screen.

Out of nothingness, three new arrivals in hover-chairs blinked into the heart of the battle zone. Inadvertently Keff recoiled against the back of his chair.

"Yow! They mean business," Carialle said "No hundred meters of clearance space. Just smack, right into the middle."

The spells the combatants were building dissipated like colored smoke on the wind. Carialle's gauges showed a distinct drop in the electromagnetic fields. The mage and magess dropped their hands stiffly onto their chair arms and glared at the obstacles now hovering between them. If looks could have ignited rocket fuel, the thwarted combatants would have set Carialle's tanks ablaze. Whatever was powering them had been cut off by the three in the center.

"Uh-oh. The Big Mountain Men are here," Keff said flippantly, his face guarded

The newcomers' chairs were bigger and gaudier than any Keff and Carialle had yet seen. A host of smaller seats, containing lesser magicians, popped in to hover at a respectful distance outside the circle. Their presence was ignored by the three males who were obviously about to discipline the combatants.

"Introductions," Keff said monitoring IT. "High and mighty. The lad in the gold is Nokias, the one in black is Ferngal, and the silver one in the middle who looks so nervous is Chaumel. He's a diplomat."

Carialle observed the placatory gestures of the mage in the silver chair. "I don't think that Ferngal and Nokias like each other much."

But Chaumel, nodding and smiling, floated suavely back and forth between the gold and black in his silver chair and managed to persuade them to nod at one another with civility if not friendliness. The lesser magicians promptly polarized into two groups, reflecting their loyalties.

"Compliments to the Big Mountain Men from my pretty lady and her friend." Keff continued, "She's Potria, and he's Asedow. One of the sideliners says they were *something*—bold? cocky?— to come here. Aha, that's what that word Brannel used meant: forbidden! That gives me some roots for some of the other things they're saying. I'll have to backtrack the datahedrons—I think a territorial dispute is going on."

Nokias and Ferngal each spoke at some length. Keff was able to translate a few of the compliments the magimen paid to each other.

"Something about high mountains," he said, running IT over contextual data. "Yes, I think that repeated word must be 'power,' so Ferngal is referring to Nokias as having power as high, I mean, strong as the high mountains and deep as its roots." He laughed. "It's the same pun we have in Standard, Cari. He used the same word Brannel used for the food 'roots.' The farmers and the magicians do use two different dialects, but they're related. It's the cognitive differences I find fascinating. Completely alien to any language in my databanks."

"All this intellectual analysis is very amusing," Carialle said, "but what are they saying? And more to the point, how does it affect *us*?"

She shifted cameras to pick up Potria and Asedow on separate screens. After the speeches by the two principals, the original combatants were allowed their say, which they had with many interruptions from the other and much pointing towards Carialle.

"Those are definitively possessive gestures," Keff said uneasily.

"No one puts a claim on *my ship*," Carialle said firmly. "Which one of them has a tractor beam on me? I want it off."

Keff listened to the translator and shook his head. "Neither one did it, I think. It may be a natural phenomenon."

"Then why isn't it grounding any of those chairs?"

"Cari, we don't know that's what is happening."

"I have a pretty well-developed sense of survival, and that's exactly what it's telling me."

"Well, then, we'll tell them you own your ship, and they can't have it," Keff said, reasonably. "Wait, the diplomat's talking."

The silver-robed magician had his hands raised for attention and spoke to the assemblage at some length, only glancing over his shoulder occasionally. Asedow and Potria stopped shouting at each other, and the other two Big Mountain Men looked thoughtful. Keff tilted his head in amusement.

"Look at that: Chaumel's got them all calmed down. Say, he's coming this way."

The silver chariot left the others and floated toward Carialle, settling delicately a dozen feet from the end of the ramp. The two camps of magicians hovered expectantly over the middle of the field, with expressions that ranged from nervous curiosity to open avarice. The magician rose and walked off the end of the chair's finial to stand beside it. Hands folded over his belly, he bowed to the ship.

"So they can stand," Carialle said. "I gather from the shock on the faces of our Noble Primitives over there that that's unusual. I guess these magicians don't go around on foot very often."

"No, indeed. When you have mystic powers from the astral plane, I suppose auto-ambulatory locomotion is relegated to the peasants."

"He's waiting for something. Does he expect us to signal him? Invite him in for tea?"

Keff peered closely at Chaumel's image. "I think we'd better wait and let him make the first move. Ah! He's coming to pay us a visit. A state visit, my lady."

Chaumel got over his internal debate and, with solemn dignity, made his way to the end of the ramp, every step slow and ponderous. He reached the tip and paused, bowing deeply once again.

"I feel honored," Carialle said. "If I'd'a known he was coming I'd'a baked a cake."

✶CHAPTER SIX

"The initiative is ours now," Keff said. He kept watch on the small screen of his Intentional Translator as it processed all the hedrons Carialle had recorded while he was unconscious and combined it with the dialogue he had garnered from Brannel and the magicians' discussions. The last hedron popped out of the slot, and Keff slapped it into his portable IT unit on the control panel. "That's it. We have a working vocabulary of Ozran. I can talk with him."

"Enough to ask intelligent questions?" Carialle asked. "Enough to negotiate diplomatically for our release, and inform them, 'by the way, folks, we're from another planet'?"

"Nope," Keff said, matter-of-factly. "Enough to ask stupid questions and gather more information. IT will pick up on the answers I get and, I *hope*, translate them from context."

"That IT has never been worth the electrons to blow it up," Carialle said in a flat voice.

"Easy, easy, lady," Keff said, smiling at her pillar.

"Sorry," she said. "I'm letting the situation get to me. I don't like being out of control of my own functions."

"I understand perfectly," Keff said "That's why the sooner I go out and face this fellow the better, whether or not I have a perfect working knowledge of his language."

"If you say something insulting by accident, I don't think you'll survive a second blast of that lightning."

"If they're at all as similar to humans as they look, their curiosity will prevent them killing me until they learn all about me. By then, we'll be friends."

"Good sir knight, you assume them to be equal in courtesy to your good self," Carialle said.

"I must face the enchanter's knight, if only for the sake of chivalry."

"Sir Keff, I don't like you leaving the Castle Strong when there's a dozen enchanters out there capable of flinging bolts of solid power down your gullet, and there's not a thing I can do to protect you."

"The quest *must* continue, Carialle."

"Well . . ." she said, then snorted. "I'm being too protective, aren't I? It isn't exactly first contact if you stay inside and let them pelt away at us. And we'll never get out of here. We have to establish communications. Xeno will die of mortification if we don't, and there go our bonuses."

"That's the spirit," Keff said, buckling on his equipment harness.

Carialle tested her exterior links to IT. "Anything we say will come out in pidgin Ozran. Right?"

Keff paused, looked up at her pillar. "Should you speak at all? Are they ready for the concept of a talking ship?"

"Were we ready for flying chairs?" Carialle countered. "We're at least as strange to them as they are to us."

"I'd rather not have them know you can talk," Keff said thoughtfully.

"But they already know I can speak independently. I talked to Brannel while you were unconscious. Unless he thought you were having an out-of-body experience."

"Supposing Brannel had the nerve to approach our magicians, he wouldn't be able to explain the voice he heard. He was gutsy with me, but you'll notice on the screen that he's staying well out of the way of the chair-riders. They're in charge and he's a mere peon."

"He is scared of them," Carialle agreed. "Remember how he explained punishment came from the mountains when one of his people is too curious. It's no problem for them to dispense punishment. They're endlessly creative when it comes to going on the offensive."

"Contrariwise, I take leave to doubt that any of the magicians would give him a hearing if he did come forward with the information. There's a big crowd of Brannel's folk out there on the perimeter and the wizards haven't so much as glanced their way. No one pays the least attention to the peasants. Your secret is still safe. That's why I want you to keep quiet unless need arises."

"All right," Carialle said at last. "I'll keep mumchance. But, if you're in danger . . . I don't know what I'll do."

"Agreed." And Keff shot her column an approving grin.

"Let's test the system," Carialle said. The small screen to the right of the main computer lit up with a line diagram of Keff's body. He rose and stood before it, holding his arms away from his sides to duplicate the posture.

"Testing," he said. "Mah, may, mee, mo, mu. The quick brown fox jumped over the lazy dog. Maxwell-Corey is a fardling, fossicking, meddling moron." He repeated the phrases in a sub-vocal whisper. Small green lights in the image's cheeks lit up.

"Got you," Carialle's voice said in his ear. Lights for the mastoid implants clicked on, followed by the fiber optic pickups implanted in the skin at the outer corners of his eyes. "I'm not trusting the contact buttons alone. The lightning earlier knocked them out for a while." Heart, respiration, skin tension monitors in his chest cavity and the muscles of his thighs lighted green. The lights flicked out and came on again as Carialle did double backup tests. "You're wired for sound and ready to go. I can see, hear, and just about feel anything that happens to you."

"Good," Keff said, relaxing into parade rest. "Our guest is waiting."

"Here comes the stranger."

Keff's implant translated Asedow's comment as he stepped outside. He assumed the same air of dignity that Chaumel displayed and walked to the bottom of the ramp. He paused, wondering if he should stay there, which gave him a psychological advantage over his visitor who had to look up at him. Or join the fellow on the ground as a mark of courtesy. With a smile, he sidestepped. Chaumel backed up slightly to make room for him. Face-to-face with the silver magician, Keff raised his hand, palm out.

"Greetings," he said. "I am Keff."

The eyewitness report had been correct, Chaumel realized with a start. The stranger was one of them. The oddest thing was that he did not recognize him. There were only a few hundred of the caste on all of Ozran. A family of mages could not conceal a son like this one, grown to mature manhood and in possession of such an incredible power-focus as the silver cylinder.

"Greetings, high one," Chaumel said politely, with the merest dip of a nod. "I am Chaumel. You honor us with your presence."

The man cocked his head, as if listening to something far away, before he responded. Chaumel sensed the faintest hint of power during the pause, and yet, as Nokias had informed him, it did not come from the Core of Ozran. When at last he spoke, the stranger's words were arranged in uneducated sentences, mixed with the odd word of gibberish.

"Welcome," he said. "It is . . . my *honor* meet you."

Chaumel drew back half a pace. The truth was that the stranger did not understand the language. What could possibly explain such an anomaly as a mage who used power that did not come from the core of all and a man of Ozran who did not know the tongue?

The stranger seemed to guess what he was thinking and continued although not ten words in twenty made sense. And the intelligible was unbelievable.

"I come from the stars," Keff said, pointing upward. He gestured behind him at the brainship, flattened his hand out horizontally, then made it tip up and sink heel first toward the ground. "I flew here in the, er, silver house. I come from another world."

" . . . Not . . . here," Chaumel said. IT missed some of the vocabulary but not the sense. He beckoned to Keff, turned his back on the rest of his people.

"You don't want me to talk about it here?" Keff said in a much lower voice.

"No," Chaumel said, with a cautious glance over his shoulder at the other two Big Mountain Men. "Come . . . mountain . . . me." IT rewound the phrase and restated the translation using full context. "Come back to my mountain with me. We'll talk there."

"No, thanks," Keff said, with a shake of his head. "Let's talk here. It's all right. Why don't you ask the others—uh!"

"Keff!" Carialle's voice thudded against his brain. He knew then why all the Noble Primitives were so submissive and eager to avoid trouble. Chaumel had taken a gadget like a skinny flashlight from a sling on his belt and jabbed it into Keff's side. Fire raced from his rib cage up his neck and through his backbone, burning away any control he had over his own muscles. For the second time in as many hours, he collapsed bonelessly to the ground. The difference this time was that he remained conscious of everything going on around him. Directly in front of his eyes, he saw that, under the hem of his ankle-length robe, Chaumel wore black and silver boots. They had very thick soles. Even though the ground under his cheek was dry, dust seemed not to adhere to the black material, which appeared to be some kind of animal hide, maybe skin from a six-pack. He became aware that Carialle was speaking.

" . . . Fardle it, Keff! Why didn't you stay clear of him? I know you're conscious. Can you move at all?"

Chaumel's feet clumped backward and to one side, out from Keff's limited field of vision. Suddenly, the ground shot away. Unable to order his muscles to move, Keff felt his head sag limply to one side. He saw, almost disinterestedly, that he was floating on air. It felt as if he were being carried on a short mattress.

Unceremoniously, Keff was dumped off the invisible mattress onto the footrest of Chaumel's chariot, his head tilted at an uncomfortable upward angle. The magician stepped inside the U formed by Keff's body and sat down on the ornamented throne. The whole contraption rose suddenly into the air.

"Telekinesis," Keff muttered into the dental implant. He found he was slowly regaining control of his body. A finger twitched. A muscle in his right calf contracted. It tingled. Then he was aware that the chair was rising above the fields, saw the upper curve of the underground cavern in which Brannel's people lived, the mountains beyond, very high, higher than he thought.

"Good!" Carialle's relief was audible. "You're still connected. I thought I might lose the links again when he hit you with that device."

"Wand," Keff said. He could move his eyes now, and he fixed them on the silver magician's belt. "Wand."

"It looked like a wand. Acted more like a cattle prod." There was a momentary pause. "No electrical damage. It seems to have affected synaptic response. That is one sophisticated psi device."

"Magic," Keff hissed quietly.

"We'll argue about that later. Can you get free?"

"No," Keff said "Motor responses slowed."

"Blast and damn it, Galahad! I can't come and get you. You're a hundred meters in the air already. All right, I can track you wherever you're going."

Carialle was upset. Keff didn't want her to be upset, but he was all but motionless. He managed to move his head to a slightly more comfortable position, panting with the strain of such a minor accommodation. Empathic and psionic beings in the galaxy had been encountered before, but these people's talents were so much stronger than any other. Keff was awed by a telekinetic power strong enough to carry the chair, Chaumel, and him with no apparent effort. Such strength was beyond known scientific reality.

"Magic," he murmured.

"I do not believe in magic," Carialle said firmly. "Not with all this stray electromagnetic current about."

"Even magic must have physics," Keff argued

"Bah." Carialle began to run through possibilities, some of which bordered a trifle on the magic she denied but *something* which would bring Keff back where he belonged—inside her hull—and both of them off this planet as soon as her paralysis, like Keff's, showed any signs of wearing off.

Brannel hid alone in the bushes at the far end of the field waiting to see if Mage Keff came out again. After offering respect to the magelords, the rest of his folk had taken advantage of the great ones' disinterest in them and rushed home to where it was warm.

The worker male was curious. Perhaps now that the battle was over, the magelords would go away so he could approach Keff on his own. To his dismay, the high ones showed no signs of departing. They awaited the same event he did: the emergence of Magelord Keff. He was awestruck as he watched Chaumel the Silver approach the great tower on foot. The mage waited, eyes on the tight-fitting door, face full of the same anticipation Brannel felt.

Keff did not come. Perhaps Keff was making them all play into his hands. Perhaps he was wiser than the magelords. That would be most satisfyingly ironic.

Instead, when Keff emerged and exchanged words with the mage, he suddenly collapsed. Then he was bundled onto the chariot of Chaumel the Silver and carried away. All Brannel's dreams of freedom and glory died in that instant. All the treasures in the silver tower were now out of his reach and would be forever.

He muttered to himself all the way back to the cave. Fralim caught him, asked him what he was on about.

"We ought to follow and save Magelord Keff."

"Save a mage? You must be mad," Fralim said. "It is night. Come inside and go to sleep. There will be more work in the morning."

Depressed, Brannel turned and followed the chief's son into the warmth.

✳CHAPTER SEVEN

"Why . . . make things more . . . harderest . . . than need?" Chaumel muttered as he steered the chair away from the plain. IT found the root for the missing words and relayed the question to Keff through his ear-link. "Why must you make things more difficult than they need to be? I want to talk . . . in early . . ."

"My apologies, honored one," Keff said haltingly.

He had sufficiently recovered from the bolt to sit up on the end of Chaumel's chair. The magician leaned forward to clasp Keff's shoulder and pulled him back a few inches. Once he looked down, the brawn was grateful for the reassuring contact. From the hundred meters Carialle had last reported, they had ascended to at least two hundred and were still rising. He still had no idea how it was done, but he was beginning to enjoy this unusual ride.

The view was marvelous. The seven-meter square where Brannel and his people laid their gathered crops and the mound under which the home cavern lay had each shrunk to an area smaller than Keff's fingernail. On the flattened hilltop, the brainship was a shining figure like a literary statuette. Nearby, the miniature chairs, each containing a colorfully dressed doll, were rising to disperse.

Keff noticed suddenly that their progress was not unattended. Gold and black eye spheres flanked the silver chair as it rose higher still and began to fly in the direction of the darkening sky. More spheres, in different colors, hung behind like wary sparrows trailing

109

a crow, never getting too close. This had to be the hierarchy again, Keff thought. He doubted this constituted an honor guard since he had gathered that Nokias and Ferngal outranked Chaumel. More on the order of keeping watch on both the Silver Mage and the stranger. Keff grinned and waved at them.

"Hi, Mum," he said.

"It'll take you hours at that rate to reach one of those mountain ranges," Carialle said through the implant. "I'd like to know how long he can fly that thing before he has to refuel or rest, or whatever."

Keff turned to Chaumel.

"Where are we . . ."

Even before the question was completely out of his mouth, the view changed.

" . . . going?"

Keff gaped. They were no longer hanging above Brannel's fields. Between one meter and another the silver chariot had transferred effortlessly to a point above snowcapped mountain peaks. The drop in temperature was so sudden Keff suffered a violent, involuntary shudder before he knew he was cold.

"—Ramjamming fardling flatulating dagnabbing planet!" Carialle's voice, missing from his consciousness for just moments, reasserted itself at full volume. "There you are! You are one hundred and seventy four kilometers northeast from your previous position."

"Lady dear, what language!" Keff gasped out between chatters. "Not at all suitable for *my* lady fair."

"But appropriate! You've been missing a long time. Confound it, I was worried!"

"It only felt like a second to me," Keff said, apologetically.

"Fifty-three hundredths of a second," Carialle said crisply. "Which felt like eons to my processing gear. I had to trace your vital signs through I don't know how many power areas before I found you. Luckily your evil wizard told us you were going to a *mountain*. That did cut down by about fifty percent the terrain I had to sweep."

"We teleported," Keff said, wonderingly. "I . . . teleported! I didn't feel as if I was. It's effortless!"

"I hate it," Carialle replied. "You were off the air while you were in transit. I didn't know where you had gone, or if you were still alive. Confound these people with their unelectronic toys and nonmechanical machines!"

"My . . . mountain home," Chaumel announced, interrupting Keff's subvocal argument. The silver magician pointed downward toward a gabled structure built onto the very crest of the highest peak in the range.

"How lovely," Keff said, hoping one of the expressions he had gleaned from Carialle's tapes of the broadcasting drones was appropriate. By Chaumel's pleased expression, it was.

At first all he could see was the balcony, cantilevered out over a bottomless chasm, smoky purple and black in the light of the setting sun. Set into the mountaintop were tall, arched glass windows, shining with the last highlights of day. They were distinguishable from the blue-white ice cap only because they were flat and smooth. What little could be seen of the rest of the mountain was jagged outthrusts and steep ravines.

"Mighty . . . not . . . from the ground," Chaumel said, pantomiming something trying to come up from underneath and being met above by a fist. IT rewound the comment and translated it in Keff's ear as "This is a mighty stronghold. Nothing can reach us from the ground."

"No, to be sure." Well, that stood to reason. No mage would want to live in a bastion that could be climbed to. Much less accessible if it could be reached only by an aerial route.

The balcony, as they got nearer, was as large as a commercial heliport, with designated landing pads marked out in different colored flush-set paving stones. One square, nearest the tall glass doors, was silver-gray, obviously reserved for the lord of the manor.

The chariot swung in a smooth curve over the pad and set down on it as daintily as a feather. As soon as it landed, the flock of spy-eyes turned and flew away. Chaumel gestured for Keff to get down.

The brawn stepped off the finial onto the dull stone tiles, and found himself dancing to try and keep his balance. The floor was smooth and slick, frictionless as a track-ball surface. Losing his footing, Keff sprawled backward, catching himself with his hands flat behind him, and struggled to an upright position. The feel of the floor disconcerted him. It was heavy with power. He didn't hear it or feel it, but he sensed it. The sensation was extremely unnerving. He rubbed his palms together.

"What's the matter?" Carialle asked. "The view keeps changing. Ah, that's better. Hmm. No, it isn't. What's that dreadful vibration? It feels mechanical."

"Don't know," Keff said subvocally, testing the floor with a cautious hand. Though dry to look at, it felt tacky, almost clammy. "Slippery," he added, with a smile up at his host.

Dark brows drawn into an impatient V, Chaumel gestured for Keff to get up. Very carefully, using his hands, Keff got to his knees, and tentatively, to his feet. Chaumel nodded, turned, and strode through the tall double doors. Walking ding-toed like a waterfowl, Keff followed as quickly as he could, if only to get off the surface.

Each time he put a foot down, the disturbing vibration rattled up his leg into his spine. Keff forced himself to ignore it as he tried to catch up with Chaumel.

The silver magiman nattered on, half to Keff, half to himself. Keff boosted the gain on IT to pick up every word, to play back later.

The glass doors opened out from a grand chamber like a ballroom or a throne room. Ceilings were unusually high, with fantastic ornamentation. Keff stared straight up at a painted and gilded trompe l'oeil fresco of soaring native avians in a cloud-dotted sky. Windows of glass, rock crystal, and colored minerals were set at every level on the wall. There was one skylight cut pielike into the ceiling. Considering that his host and his people flew almost everywhere, Keff wasn't surprised at the attention paid to the upper reaches of the rooms. The magifolk seemed to like light, and living inside a mountain was likely to cause claustrophobia. The walls were hewn out of the natural granite, but the floor everywhere was that disconcerting track-ball surface.

"This (thing) . . . mine . . . old," Chaumel said, gesturing casually at a couple of framed pieces of art displayed on the wall. Keff glanced at the first one to figure out what it represented, and then wished he hadn't. The moire abstract seemed to move by itself in nauseous patterns. Keff hastily glanced away, dashing tears from his eyes and controlling the roil of his stomach.

"Most original," he said, gasping. Chaumel paused briefly in his chattering to beam at Keff's evident perspicacity and pointed out another stomach-twister. Keff carefully kept his gaze aimed below the level of the frames, offering compliments without looking. Staring at the silver magician's heels and the hem of his robe, Keff padded faster to catch up.

They passed over a threshold into an anteroom where several servants were sweeping and dusting. Except when raising their eyes to acknowledge the presence of their master, they also made a point of watching the ground in front of them. It was no consolation to Keff to realize that others had the same reaction to the "artwork."

Chaumel was the only bare-skin Keff saw. The staff appeared to consist solely of fur-skinned Noble Primitives, like Brannel, but instead of having just four fingers on each hand, some had all five.

"The missing links?" Keff asked Carialle. These beings looked like a combination between Chaumel's people and Brannel's. Though their faces were hairy, they did not bear the animal cast to their features that the various villagers had. They looked more humanly diversified. "Do you suppose that the farther you go away from the overlords, the more changes you find in facial structure?" He stopped to study the face of a furry-faced maiden, who reddened under her pelt and dropped her eyes shyly. She twisted her duster between her hands.

"Ahem! A geographical cause isn't logical," Carialle said, "although you might postulate interbreeding between the two races. That would mean that the races are genetically close. Very interesting."

Chaumel, noticing he'd lost his audience, detoured back, directed Keff away from the serving maid and toward a stone archway.

"Will you look at the workmanship in that?" Keff said, admiringly. "Very fine, Chaumel."

"I'm glad you..." the magiman said, moving on through the doorway into a wide corridor. "Now, this... my father..."

"This" proved to be a tapestry woven, Carialle informed Keff after a microscopic peek, of dyed vegetable fibers blended with embroidered colorful figures in six-pack hair.

"Old," she said. "At least four hundred years. And expert craftwork, I might add."

"Lovely," Keff said, making sure the contact button scanned it in full for his Xenology records. "Er, high worker-ship, Chaumel."

His host was delighted, and took him by the arm to show him every item displayed in the long hall.

Chaumel was evidently an enthusiastic collector of objets d'art and, except for the nauseating pictures, had a well-developed appreciation of beauty. Keff had no trouble admiring handsomely made chairs, incidental tables, and pedestals of wood and stone; more tapestries; pieces of scientific equipment that had fallen into disuse and been adapted for other purposes. A primitive chariot, evidently the precursor of the elegant chairs Chaumel and his people used, was enshrined underneath the picture of a bearded man in a silver robe. Chaumel also owned some paintings and representational art executed with great skill that were not only not uncomfortable but a pleasure to behold. Keff exclaimed over everything, recording it, hoping that he was also gathering clues to help free Carialle so they could leave Ozran as soon as possible.

A few of Chaumel's treasures absolutely defied description. Keff would have judged them to be sculpture or statuary, but some of the vertical and horizontal surfaces showed wear, the polished appearance of long use. They were furniture, but for what kind of being?

"What is this, Chaumel?" Keff asked, drawing the magiman's attention to a small grouping arranged in an alcove. He pointed to one item. It looked like a low-set painter's easel from which a pair of hardwood tines rose in a V. "This is very old."

"Ah!" the magiman said, eagerly. ". . . from old, old day-day." IT promptly interpreted into "from ancient days," and recorded the usage.

"I'm getting a reading of between one thousand six hundred and one thousand nine hundred years," Carialle said, confirming Chaumel's statement. The magiman gave Keff a curious look.

"Surely your people didn't use these things," Keff said "Can't sit on them, see?" He made as if to sit down on the narrow horizontal ledge at just above knee level.

Chaumel grinned and shook his head. "Old Ones used . . . sit-lie," he said.

"They weren't humanoid?" Keff asked, and then clarified as the magiman looked confused "Not like you, or me, or your servants?"

"Not, not. Before New Ones, we."

"Then the humanoids were not the native race on this planet," Carialle said excitedly into Keff's implant. "They *are* travelers. They settled here alongside the indigenous beings and shared their culture."

"That would explain the linguistic anomalies," Keff said. "And that awful artwork in the grand hall." Then speaking aloud, he added, "Are there any of the Old Ones left, Chaumel?"

"Not, not. Many days gone. Worked, move from empty land to mountain. Gave us, gave them." Chaumel struggled with a pantomime. "All . . . gone."

"I think I understand. You helped them move out of the valleys, and they gave you . . . what? Then they all died? What caused that? A plague?"

Chaumel suddenly grew wary. He muttered and moved on to the next grouping of artifacts. He paused dramatically before one item displayed on a wooden pedestal. The gray stone object, about fifty centimeters high, resembled an oddly twisted urn with an off-center opening.

"Old-*Old*-Ones," he said with awe, placing his hands possessively on the urn.

"Old Ones—Ancient Ones?" Keff asked, gesturing one step farther back with his hand.

"Yes," Chaumel said. He caressed the stone. Keff moved closer so Carialle could take a reading through the contact button.

"It's even older than the Old Ones' chair, if that's what that was. Much older. Ask if this is a religious artifact. Are the Ancient Ones their gods?" Carialle asked.

"Did you, your father-father, bring Ancient Ones with you to Ozran?" Keff asked.

"Not *our* ancestors," Chaumel said, laying three imaginary objects in a row. "Ozran: Ancient Ones; Old Ones; New Ones, we. Ancient," he added, holding out the wand in his belt.

"Carialle, I think he means that artifact is a leftover from the original culture. It is ancient, but there has been some modification on it, dating a couple thousand years back." Then aloud, he said to Chaumel. "So they passed usable items down. Did the Ancient Ones look like the Old Ones? Were they their ancestors?"

Chaumel shrugged.

"It looks like an entirely different culture, Keff," Carialle said, processing the image and running a schematic overlay of all the pieces in the hall. "There're very few Ancient One artifacts here to judge by, but my reconstruction program suggests different body types for the Ancients and the Old Ones. Similar, though. Both species were upright and had rearward-bending, jointed lower limbs—can't tell how many, but the Old One furniture is built for larger creatures. Not quite as big as humanoids, though."

"It sounds as if one species succeeded after another," Keff said.

"The Old Ones moved in to live with the Ancient Ones, and many generations later after the Ancients died off, the New Ones arrived and cohabited with the Old Ones. They are the third in a series of races to live on this planet: the aborigines, the Old Ones, and the New Ones, or magic-using humanoids."

Carialle snorted. "Doesn't say much for Ozran as a host for life-forms, if two intelligent races in a row died off within a few millennia."

"And the humanoids are reduced to a nontechnological existence," Keff said, only half listening to Chaumel, who was lecturing him with an intent expression on his broad-cheeked face. "Could it have something to do with the force-field holding you down? They got stuck here?"

"Whatever trapped me did it selectively, Keff!" Carialle said. "I'd landed and taken off six times on Ozran already. It was deliberate, and I want to know who and why."

"Another mystery to investigate. But I also want to know why the Old Ones moved up here, away from their source of food," Keff said. "Since they seem to be dependant on what's grown here, that's a sociological anomaly."

"Ah," Carialle said, reading newly translated old data from IT. "The Old Ones didn't move up here with the New Ones' help, Keff. They were up here when the humanoids came. They found Ancient artifacts in the valleys."

"So these New Ones had some predilection for talent when they came here, but their contact with the Old Ones increased it to what we see in them now. Two space-going races, Carialle!" Keff said, greatly excited. "I want to know if we can find out more about the pure alien culture. Later on, let's see if we can trace them back to their original systems. Pity there's so little left: after several hundred years of humanoid rule, it's all mixed up together."

"Isn't the synthesis as rare?" Carialle asked, pointedly.

"In our culture, yes. Makes it obvious where the sign language comes from, too," Keff said. "It's a relic from one of the previous races—useful symbology that helps make the magic work. The Old Ones may never have shared the humanoid language, being the host race, but somehow they made themselves understood to the newcomers. Worth at least a paper to *Galactic Geographic*. Clearly, Chaumel here doesn't know what the Ancients were like."

The magiman, watching Keff talking to himself, heard his name and Keff's question. He shook his head regretfully. "I do not. Much before days of me."

"Where do your people come from?" Keff asked. "What star, where out there?" He gestured up at the sky.

"I do not know that also. Where from do yours come?" Chaumel asked, a keen eye holding Keff's.

The brawn tried to think of a way to explain the Central Worlds with the limited vocabulary at his disposal and raised his hands helplessly.

"Vain hope." Carialle sighed. "I'm still trying to find any records of settlements in this sector. Big zero. If I could get a message out, I could have Central Worlds do a full-scan search of the old records."

"So where do the Noble Primitives fit in, Chaumel?" Keff asked, throwing a friendly arm over the man's shoulder before he could start a lecture on the next objet d'art. He pointed at a male servant wearing a long, white robe, who hurried away, wide-eyed, when he noticed the bare-skinned ones looking at him. "I notice that the servants here have lighter pelts than the people in the farm village." He gestured behind him, hoping that Chaumel would understand he meant where they had just come from. He tweaked a lock of his own hair, rubbing his fingers together to indicate "thin," then ran his fingers down his own face and held out his hand.

"They're handsomer. And some of them have five fingers, like mine." Keff waggled his forefinger. "Why do the ones in the valley have only four?" He bent the finger under his palm.

"Oh," Chaumel said, laughing. He stated something in a friendly, offhanded way that the IT couldn't translate, scissors-chopping his own forefinger with his other hand to demonstrate what he meant. ". . . when of few days—babies. Low mind. . . . no curiosity . . . worker." He made the scissors motion again.

"What?" Carialle shrieked in Keff's ear. "It's not a mutation. It's *mutilation.* There aren't two brands of humanoids, just one, with most of the poor things exploited by a lucky few."

Keff was shocked into silence. Fortunately, Chaumel seemed to expect no reply. Carialle continued to speak in a low voice while Keff nodded and smiled at the magiman.

"Moreover, he's been referring to the Noble Primitives as property. When he mentioned his possessions, IT went back and translated his term for the villagers as 'chattel.' I do not like these people. Evil wizards, indeed!"

"Er, very nice," Keff said in Ozran, for lack of any good reply. Chaumel beamed.

"We care for them, we who commune with the Core of Ozran. We lead our weaker brothers. We guard as they working hard in the valleys to raise food for us all."

"Enslave them, you mean," Carialle sniffed. "And they live up here in comfort while Brannel's people freeze. He looks so warm and friendly—for a slave trader. Look at his eyes. Dead as micro-chips."

"Weaker? Do you mean feeble-minded? The people down in the valleys have strong bodies but, er, they don't seem very bright," Keff said. "These, your servants, are much more intelligent than any of the ones we met." He didn't mention Brannel.

"Ah," Chaumel said, guardedly casual, "the workers eat stupid, not question . . . who know better, overlords."

"You mean you put something in the food to keep them stupid and docile so they won't question their servitude? That's monstrous," Keff said, but he kept smiling.

Chaumel didn't understand the last word. He bowed deeply. "Thank you. Use talent, over many years gone, we give them," he pantomimed over his own wrist and arm, showed it growing thicker, "more skin, hair, grow dense flesh . . ."

IT riffled through a list of synonyms. Keff seized upon one. "Muscles?" he asked. IT repeated Chaumel's last word, evidently satisfied with Keff's definition.

"Yes," Chaumel said. "Good for living . . . cold valleys. Hard work!"

"You mean you can skimp on the central heat if you give them greater endurance," Carialle said, contemptuously. "You blood-sucker."

Chaumel frowned, almost as if he had heard Carialle's tone.

"Hush! Er, I don't know if this is a taboo question, Chaumel," Keff began, rubbing his chin with thumb and forefinger, "but you interbreed with the servant class, too, don't you? Bare-skins with fur-skins, make babies?"

"Not I," the silver magiman explained hastily. "But yes. Some lower . . . mages and magesses have faces with hair. Never make their places as mages of . . . but not everyone is . . . sent for mightiness."

"Destined for greatness," Keff corrected IT. IT repeated the word. "So why are you not great? I mean," he rephrased his statement for tact, "not one of the mages of—IT, put in that phrase he used?"

"Oh, I am good—satisfied to be what I am," Chaumel said, complacently folding his fingers over his well-padded rib cage.

"If they're already being drugged, why amputate their fingers?" Carialle wanted to know.

"What do fingers have to do with the magic?" Keff asked, making a hey-presto gesture.

"Ah," Chaumel said. Taking Keff's arm firmly under his own, he escorted him down the hall to a low door set deeply into the stone walls. Servants passing by showed Keff the whites of their eyes as Chaumel slipped the silver wand out of his belt and pointed at the lock. Some of the fur-skins hurried faster as the red fire lanced laserlike into the keyhole. One or two, wearing the same keen expression as Brannel, peered in as the door opened. Shooting a cold glance to speed the nosy ones on their way, Chaumel urged Keff inside.

The darkness lifted as soon as they stepped over the threshold, a milky glow coming directly from the substance of the walls.

"Cari, is that radioactive?" Keff asked. His whisper was amplified in a ghostly rush of sound by the rough stone.

"No. In fact, I'm getting no readings on the light at all. Strange."

"Magic!"

"Cut that out," Carialle said sulkily. "I say it's a form of energy with which I am unacquainted."

In contrast to all the other chambers Keff had seen in Chaumel's eyrie, this room had a low, unadorned ceiling of rough granite less than an arm's length above their heads. Keff felt as though he needed to stoop to avoid hitting the roof.

Chaumel moved across the floor like a man in a chapel. The furnishings of the narrow room carried out that impression. At the end opposite the door was a molded, silver table not unlike an altar, upon which rested five objects arranged in a circle on an embroidered cloth. Keff tiptoed forward behind Chaumel.

The items themselves were not particularly impressive: a metal bangle about twelve centimeters across, a silver tube, a flattened disk pierced with half-moon shapes all around the edge, a wedge of clear crystal with a piece of dull metal fused to the blunt end, and a hollow cylinder like an empty jelly jar.

"What are they?" Keff asked.

"Objects of power," Chaumel replied. One by one he lifted them and displayed them for Keff. Returning to the bangle, Chaumel turned it over so Keff could see its inner arc. Five depressions about two centimeters apart were molded into its otherwise smooth curve. In turn, he showed the markings on each one. With the last, he inserted the tips of his fingers into the depressions and wielded it away from Keff.

"Ah," Keff said, enlightened. "You need five digits to use these."

"So the amputation is to keep the servers from organizing a palace revolt," Carialle said. "Any uppity server just wouldn't have the physical dexterity to use them."

"Mmm," Keff said. "How old are they?" He moved closer to the altar and bent over the cloth.

"Old, old," Chaumel said, parting the jelly jar.

"Old Ones," Carialle verified, running a scan through Keff's ocular implants. "So is the bangle. The other three are Ancient, with some subsequent modifications by the Old Ones. All of them have five pressure plates incorporated into the design. That's why Brannel tried to take my palette. It has five depressions, just like these items. He probably thought it was a power piece, like these."

"There's coincidence for you: both the alien races here were pentadactyl, like humans. I wonder if that's a recurring trait throughout the galaxy for technologically capable races," Keff said. "Five-fingered hands."

Chaumel certainly seemed proud of his. Setting down the jelly jar, he rubbed his hands together, then flicked invisible dust motes off his nails, taking time to admire both fronts and backs.

"Well, they are shapely hands," Carialle said. "They wouldn't be out of place in Michelangelo's Sistine Chapel frescoes except for the bizarre proportions."

Keff took a good look at Chaumel's hands. For the first time he noticed that the thumbs, which he had noted as being rather long, bore lifelike prostheses, complete with nails and tiny wisps of hair, that made the tips fan out to the same distance as the forefingers. The little fingers were of equal length to the ring fingers, jarring the eye, making the fingers look like a thick fringe cut straight across. Absently conscious of Keff's stare, Chaumel pulled at his little fingers.

"Is he trying to make them longer by doing that?" Carialle asked.

"It's physically impossible, but I suppose telling him that won't make him stop. Superstitions are superstitions."

"That's er, grotesque, Chaumel," Keff said, smiling with what he hoped was an expression of admiration.

"Thank you, Keff." The silver magiman bowed.

"Show me how the objects of power work," Keff said, pointing at the table. "I'd welcome a chance to watch without being the target."

Chaumel was all too happy to oblige.

"Now you see how these are," he said graciously. He chose the ring and the tube, putting his favorite, the wand, back in its belt holster. "This way."

On the way out of the narrow room, Chaumel resumed his monologue. This time it seemed to involve the provenance and ownership of the items.

"We are proud of our toys," Carialle said deprecatingly. "Nothing up my sleeve, alakazam!"

"Whoops!" Keff said, as Chaumel held out his hand and a huge crockery vase appeared on the palm. "Alakazam, indeed!"

With a small smile, Chaumel blew on the crock, sending it flying down the hall as if skidding on ice. He raised the tube, aimed it, and squeezed lightly. The crock froze in place, then, in delayed reaction, it burst apart into a shower of jet-propelled sand, peppering the walls and the two men.

"Marvelous!" Keff said, applauding. He spat out sand. "Bravo! Do it again!"

Obligingly, Chaumel created a wide ceramic platter. "My mother this belonged to. I do not *ever* like this," he said. With a twist of his wrist, it followed the crock. Instead of the tube, the silver magiman operated the ring. With a crack, the platter exploded into fragments. A glass goblet, then a pitcher appeared out of the air. Chaumel set them dancing around one another, then fused them into one piece with a dash of scarlet lightning from his wand. They dropped to the ground, spraying fragments of glass everywhere.

"And what do you do for an encore?" Keff asked, surveying the hall, now littered with debris.

"Hmmph!" Chaumel said. He waved the wand, and three apron-clad domestics appeared, followed by brooms and pails. Leaving the magical items floating on the air, he clapped his hands together.

The servers set hastily to work cleaning up. Chaumel folded his arms together with satisfaction and turned a smug face to Keff.

"I see. You get all the fun, and they do all the nasty bits," Keff said, nodding. "Bravo anyway."

"I was following the energy buildup during that little Wild West show," Carialle said in Keff's ear. "There is no connection between what Chaumel does with his toys, that hum in the floors, and any energy source except a slight response from that random mess in the sky. Geothermal is silent. And before you ask, he hasn't got a generator. Ask him where they get their power from."

"Where do your magical talents come from?" Keff asked the silver magiman. He imitated Potria's spell-casting technique, gathering in armfuls of air and thrusting his hands forward. Chaumel ducked to one side. His face paled, and he stared balefully at Keff.

"I guess it isn't just sign language," Keff said sheepishly. "Genuine functionalism of symbols. Sorry for the breach in etiquette, old fellow. But could the New Ones do that," he started to make the gesture but pointedly held back from finishing it, "when they came to Ozran?"

"Some. Most learned from Old Ones," Chaumel said, not really caring. He flipped the wand into the air. It twirled end over end, then vanished and reappeared in his side-slung holster.

"Flying?" Keff said, imitating the way the silver magiman's chair swooped and turned. "Learned from Old Ones?"

"Yes. Gave learning to us for giving to them."

"Incredible," Keff said, with a whistle. "What I wouldn't give for magic lessons. But where does the power come from?"

Chaumel looked beatific. "From the Core of Ozran," he said, hands raised in a mystical gesture.

"What is that? Is it a physical thing, or a philosophical center?"

"It is the Core," Chaumel said, impatiently, shaking his head at Keff's denseness. The brawn shrugged.

"The Core is the Core," he said. "Of course. Non-sequitur. Chaumel, my ship can't move from where it landed. Does the Core of Ozran have something to do with that?"

"Perhaps, perhaps."

Keff pressed him. "I'd really like an answer to that, Chaumel. It's sort of important to me, in a strange sort of way," he said, shrugging diffidently.

Chaumel irritably shook his head and waved his hands.

"I'll tackle him again later, Cari," Keff said under his breath.

"Now is better . . . What's that sound?" Carialle said, interrupting herself.

Keff looked around. "I didn't hear anything."

But Chaumel had. Like a hunting dog hearing a horn, he turned his head. Keff felt a rise of static, raising the hair on the back of his neck.

"There it is again," Carialle said. "Approximately fifty thousand cycles. Now I'm showing serious power fluctuations where you are. What Chaumel was doing in the hallway was a spit in the ocean compared with this."

Chaumel grabbed Keff's arm and made a spiraling gesture upward with one finger.

"This way, in haste!" Chaumel said, pushing him through the hallway toward the great room and the landing pad beyond. His hand flew above his head, repeating the spiral over and over. "Haste, haste!"

✱CHAPTER EIGHT

Night had fallen over the mountains. The new arrivals seemed to glow with their own ghostlight as they flew through the purple-dark sky toward Chaumel's balcony. Keff, concealed with Chaumel behind a curtain in the tall glass door, recognized Ferngal, Nokias, Potria, and some of the lesser magimen and magiwomen from that afternoon. There were plenty of new faces, including some in chairs as fancy as Chaumel's own.

"The big chaps and their circle of intimates, no doubt. Wish I had a chance to put on my best bib and tucker," Keff murmured to Carialle. To his host, he said, "Shouldn't we go out and greet them, Chaumel?"

"Hutt!" Chaumel said, hurriedly putting a hand to his lips, and raising the wand at his belt in threat to back up his command. Silently, he pantomimed putting one object after another in a row. ". . . (untranslatable) . . ."

"I think I understand you," Keff said, interrupting IT's attempt to locate roots for the phrase. "Order of precedence. Protocol. You're waiting for everyone to land."

Pursing his lips, Chaumel nodded curtly and returned to studying the scene. One at a time, like a flock of enormous migratory birds, the chariots queued up beyond the lip of the landing zone. Some jockeyed for better position, then resumed their places as a sharp word came from one of the occupants of the more elaborate chairs. Keff sensed that adherence to protocol was strictly enforced among the magifolk. Behave or get blasted, he thought.

As soon as the last one was in place, Chaumel threw open the great doors and stood to one side, bowing. Hastily, Keff followed suit. Five of the chairs flew forward and set down all at once in the nearest squares. Their occupants rose and stepped majestically toward them.

"Zolaika, High Magess of the North," Chaumel said, bowing deeply. "I greet you."

"Chaumel," the tiny, old woman of the leaf-green chariot said, with a slight inclination of her head. She sailed regally into the center of the grand hall and stood there, five feet above the ground as if fixed in glass.

"Ilnir, High Mage of the Isles." Chaumel bowed to a lean man in purple with a hooked nose and a domed, bald head. Nokias started forward, but Chaumel held up an apologetic finger. "Ferngal, High Mage of the East, I greet you."

Nokias's face crimsoned in the reflected light from the ballroom. He stepped forward after Ferngal strode past with a smug half-grin on his face. "I had forgotten, brother Chaumel. Forgive my discourtesy."

"Forgive mine, high one," Chaumel said, suavely, holding his hands high and apart. "Ureth help me, but you could never be less than courteous. Be greeted, Nokias, High Mage of the South."

Gravely, the golden magiman entered and took his place at the south point of the center ring. He was followed by Omri of the West, a flamboyantly handsome man dressed fittingly in peacock blue. Chaumel gave him an elaborate salute.

With less ceremony and markedly less deference, Chaumel greeted the rest of the visiting magi.

"He outranks these people," Carialle said in Keff's implant. "He's making it clear they're lucky to get the time of day out of him. I'm not sure where he stands in the society. He's probably not quite of the rank of the first five, but he's got a lot of power."

"And me where he wants us," Keff said in a sour tone.

As Nokias had, a few of the lesser ones were compelled to take an unexpected backseat to some of their fellows. Chaumel was firm as he indicated demotions and ignored those who conceded with bad grace. Keff wondered if the order of precedence was liquid and altered frequently. He saw a few exchanges of hot glares and curt gestures, but no one spoke or swung a wand.

Potria and Asedow had had time to change clothes and freshen up after their battle. Potria undulated off her pink-gold chariot swathed in an opaque gown of a cloth so fine it pulsed at wrists and throat with her heartbeat. Her perfume should have been illegal. Asedow, still in dark green, wore several chains and wristlets of hammered and pierced metal that clanked together as he walked. The two elbowed one another as they approached Chaumel, striving to be admitted first. Chaumel broke the deadlock by bowing over Potria's hand, but waving Asedow through behind her back. Potria smirked for receiving extra attention from the host, but Asedow had preceded her into the hall, dark green robes aswirl. As Carialle and Keff had observed before, Chaumel was a diplomat.

"How does one get promoted?" he asked Chaumel, who bowed the last of the magifolk, a slender girl in a primrose robe, into the ballroom. "What criteria do you use to tell who's on first?"

"I will explain in time," the silver mage said. "Come."

Taking Keff firmly by the upper arm, he went forth to make small talk with his many visitors. He brought Keff to bow to Zolaika who began an incomprehensible conversation with Chaumel literally over Keff's head because the host rose several feet to float on the same level as the lady. Keff stood, staring up at the verbal Ping-Pong match, wishing the IT was faster at simultaneous translation. He heard his name several times, but caught little of the context. Most of it was in the alternate, alien-flavored dialect, peppered with a few hand gestures. Keff only recognized the signs for "help" and "honor."

"I hope you're taking all this down so I can work on it later," he said in a subvocal mutter to Carialle. Hands behind his back, he twisted to survey the rest of the hall.

"With my tongue out," Carialle said "My, you certainly brought out the numbers. Everyone wants a peep at you. What would you be willing to bet that everyone who could reasonably expect admittance is here. I wonder how many are sitting home, trying to think up a good excuse to call?"

"No bet," Keff said cheerfully. "Oh, look, the decorator's been in."

The big room, which had been empty until the guests arrived, was beginning to fill in with appropriate pieces of furniture. Two rows of sconces bearing burning torches appeared at intervals along the walls. Three magifolk chatting near the double doors discovered a couch behind them and sat down. Spider-legged chairs chased mages through the room, only to place themselves in a correct and timely manner, for the mages never once looked behind to see if there was something there to be sat on: a seat was assumed. Fat, ferny plants in huge crockery pots grew up around two magimen who huddled against one wall, talking in furtive undertones.

A wing chair nudged the back of Zolaika's knees while an ottoman insinuated itself lovingly under the old woman's feet. She made herself comfortable as several of the junior magifolk came to pay their respects. A small table with a round, rimmed top appeared in their midst. Several set down their magical items, initiating an apparent truce for the duration.

After kissing Zolaika's hand, Chaumel detached himself from the group and steered Keff toward the next of the high magimen in the room. Engrossed in a conversation, Ilnir barely glanced at Keff, but accorded Chaumel a courteous nod as he made an important point using his wrist-thick magic mace for emphasis. A carved pedestal appeared under Ilnir's elbow and he leaned upon it.

Each of the higher magimen had a number of sycophants, male and female, as escort. Potria, gorgeous in her floating, low-cut peach gown, was among the number surrounding Nokias. Asedow was right beside her. They glared at Chaumel, evidently taking personally the slight done to their chief. As Chaumel and Keff passed by, they raised their voices with the complaint that they had been wrongly prevented from finishing their contest.

Ferngal and Nokias were standing together near the crystal windows beyond their individual circles. The two were exchanging pleasantries with one another, but not really communicating. Keff, boosting the gain of his audio pickup with a pressure of his jaw muscles, actually heard one of them pass a remark about the weather.

Chaumel stopped equidistant between the two high mages. His hand concealed in a fold of his silver robe, he used sharp pokes to direct Keff to bow first to Ferngal, then Nokias. Keff offered a few polite words to each. IT was working overtime processing the small talk it was picking up, but it gave him the necessary polite phrases slowly enough to recite accurately without resorting to IT's speaker.

"I feel like a trained monkey," Keff subvocalized.

As he straightened up, Carialle got a look at his audience. "That's what they think you are, too. They seem surprised that you can actually speak"

Chaumel turned him away from his two important guests and tilted his head conspiratorially close.

"You see, my young friend, I would have preferred to have you all to myself, but I can't refuse access to the preeminent magis when they decide to call at my humble home for an evening. One climbs higher by power . . . (power-plays, IT suggested) managed, as ordered by the instructions left us by our ancestors. Such power-plays determine one's height (rank, IT whispered). Also, deaths. They are most facile at these."

"Deaths?" Keff asked. "You mean, you all move up one when someone dies?"

"Yes, but also when one *makes* a death," Chaumel said, with an uneasy backward glance at the high mages. Keff goggled.

"You mean you move up when you kill someone?"

"Sounds like the promotion lists in the space service to me," Carialle remarked to Keff.

"Ah, but not only that, but through getting more secrets and magical possessions from those, and more. But Ferngal of the East has just, er, discarded . . ."

"Disposed of," Carialle supplied.

" . . . Mage Klemay in a duel, so he has raised/ascended over Mage Nokias of the South. I must incorporate the change of status smoothly, though"—his face took on an exaggerated mask of tragedy—"it pains me to see the embarrassment it causes my friend, Nokias. We attempt to make all in harmony."

Keff thought privately that Chaumel didn't look that uncomfortable. He looked like he was enjoying the discomfiture of the Mage of the South.

"This is a nasty brood. They make a point of scoring off one another," Carialle observed. "The only thing that harmonizes around here is the color-coordinated outfits and chariots. Did you notice? Everyone has a totem color. I wonder if they inherit it, earn it, or just choose it." She giggled in Keff's ear. "And what happens when someone else has the one you want?"

"Another assassination, I'm sure," Keff said, bowing and smiling to one side as Ferngal made for Ilnir's group.

As the black-clad magiman's circle drifted off, Nokias's minions spread out a little, as if grateful for the breathing room. Keff turned to Potria and gave her his most winning smile, but she looked down her nose at him.

"How nice to see you again, my lady," he said in slow but clear Ozran. The lovely bronze woman turned pointedly and looked off in another direction. The puff of gold hair over her right ear obscured her face from him completely. Keff sighed.

"No sale," Carialle said. "You might as well have been talking to her chair. Tsk-tsk, tsk-tsk. Your hormones don't have much sense."

"Thank you for that cold shower, my lady," Keff said half to Potria, half to Carialle. "You're a heartless woman, you are." The brain chuckled in his ear.

"She's not that different from anyone else here. I've never seen such a bundle of tough babies in my life. Stay on your guard. Don't reveal more about us than you have to. We're vulnerable enough as it is. I don't like people who mutilate and enslave thousands, not to mention capturing helpless ships."

"Your mind is like unto my mind lady dear," Keff said lightly. "*That* one doesn't look so tough."

Near the wall, almost hiding in the curtains behind a rose-robed crone was the last magiwoman Chaumel had bowed into the room. IT reminded him her name was Plennafrey. Self-effacing in her simple primrose gown and metallic blue-green shoulder-to-floor sash, her big, dark eyes, pointed chin, and broad cheekbones gave her a gamin look. She glanced toward Keff and immediately turned away. Keff admired her hair, ink-black with rusty highlights, woven into a simple four-strand plait that fell most of the way down her back.

"I feel sorry for her," Keff said. "She looks as though she's out of her depth. She's not mean enough."

Carialle gave him the raspberry. "You always do fall for the naive look," she said. "That's why it's always so easy to lure you into trouble in Myths and Legends."

"Oho, you've admitted it, lady. Now I'll be on guard against you."

"Just you watch it with these people and worry about me later. They're not fish-eating swamp dwellers like the Beasts Blatisant."

Keff had time to nod politely to the tall girl before Chaumel yanked him away to meet the last of the five high magimen. "I know how she feels, Cari. I'm not used to dealing with advanced societies that are more complicated and devious than the one I come from. Give me the half-naked swamp dwellers every time."

"Look at that," Potria said, sourly. "My claim, and Chaumel is parading it around as if he discovered it."

"Mine," Asedow said. "We have not yet settled the question of ownership."

"He has a kind face," Plennafrey offered in a tiny voice. Potria spun in a storm of pink-gold and glared at her.

"You are mad. It is not fully Ozran, so it is no better than a beast, like the peasants."

Remembering her resolution to be bolder no matter how terrified she felt, Plennafrey cleared her throat.

"I am sure he is not a mere thing, Potria. He looks a true man." In fact, she found his looks appealing. His twinkling eyes reminded her of happy days, something she hadn't known since long before her father died. If only she could have such a man in her life, it would no longer be lonely.

Potria turned away, disgusted. "I have been deprived of my rights."

"You have? *I* spoke first." Asedow's eyes glittered.

"I was winning," Potria said, lips curled back from gritted white teeth. She flashed a hand signal under Asedow's nose. He backed off, making a sign of protection. Plenna watched, wild-eyed. Although she knew they wouldn't dare to rejoin their magical battle in here, neither of them was above a knife in the ribs.

Suddenly, she felt a wall of force intrude between the combatants. The thought of a possible incident must also have occurred to Nokias. Asedow and Potria retreated another hand-span apart, continuing to harangue one another. Plenna glanced over at the other groups of mages. They were beginning to stare. Nokias, having been disgraced once already this evening, would be furious if his underlings embarrassed him in front of the whole assemblage.

Asedow was getting louder, his hands flying in the old signs, emphasizing his point. "It is to my honor, and the tower and the beast will come to me!"

Potria's hands waved just as excitedly. "You have no honor. Your mother was a fur-skin with a dray-beast jaw, and your father was drunk when he took her!"

At the murderous look in Asedow's eye, Plenna warded herself and planted her hand firmly over her belt buckle beneath the concealing sash. At least she could help prevent the argument from spreading. With an act of will, she cushioned the air around them so no sound escaped past their small circle. That deadened the shouting, but it didn't prevent others from seeing the pantomime the two were throwing at one another.

"How dare you!" Zolaika's chair swooped in on the pair, knocking them apart with a blast of force which dispelled Plenna's cloud of silence. "You profane the sacred signs in a petty brawl!"

"She seeks to take what is rightfully mine," Asedow bellowed. Freed, his voice threatened to shake down the ceiling.

"High one, I appeal to you," Potria said, turning to the senior magess. "I challenged for the divine objects and I claim them as my property." She pointed at Keff.

Keff was taken aback.

"Now just a minute here," he said, starting forward as he recognized the words. "I'm no one's chattel."

"Hutt!" Zolaika ordered, pointing an irregular, hand-sized form at him. Keff ducked, fearing another bolt of scarlet lightning. Chaumel pulled him back and, keeping a hand firmly on his shoulder, offered a placatory word to Potria.

"She's not the enchantress I thought she was," Keff said sadly to Carialle.

"A regular La Belle Dame Sans Merci," Carialle said. "Treat with courtesy, at a respectable distance."

"Speaking of stating one's rights," Ferngal said as he and the other high magimen moved forward. He folded his long fingers in the air before him and studied them. "May I mention that the objects were found in Klemay's territory, which is now my domain, so I have the prior claim. The tower and the male are mine." He crushed his palms together deliberately.

"But before that, they were in my venue," the old woman in red cried out from her place by the window. Her chair lifted high into the air. "I had seen the silver object and the being near my village when first it fell on Ozran. I claim precedence over you for the find, Ferngal!"

"I am no one's find!" Keff said, breaking away from Chaumel. "I'm a free man. My ship is *my* magical object, no one else's."

"I'm *mine*," Carialle crisply reminded him.

"I'd better keep you a piece of magical esoterica, lady, or they'll kill me without hesitation over a talking ship with its own brain."

La Belle Dame Sans Merci raised a shrill outcry. Chaumel, eager to keep the peace in his own home, flew to the center of the room and raised his hands.

"Mages and magesses and honored guest, the hour is come! Let us dine. We will discuss this situation much more reasonably when we all have had a bite and a sup. Please!" He clapped his hands, and a handful of servants appeared, bearing steaming trays. At a wave of their master's hand they fanned out among the guests, offering tasty-smelling hors d'oeuvres. Keff sniffed appreciatively.

"Don't touch," Carialle cautioned him. "You don't know what's in them."

"I know," Keff said, "but I'm starved. It's been hours since I had that hot meal." He felt his stomach threatening to rumble and compressed his diaphragm to prevent it being heard. He concentrated on looking politely disinterested.

Chaumel clapped his hands, and fur-faced musicians strumming oddly shaped instruments suddenly appeared here and there about the room. They passed among the guests, smiling politely. Chaumel nodded with satisfaction, and signaled again.

More Noble Primitives appeared out of the air, this time with goblets and pitchers of sparkling liquids in jewel colors. A chair hobbled up to Keff and edged its seat sideways toward his legs, as if offering him a chance to sit down.

"No thanks," he said, stepping away a pace. The chair, unperturbed, tottered on toward the next person standing next to him. "Look around, Cari! It's like Merlin's household in *The Sword in the Stone*. I feel a little drunk on glory, Cari. We've discovered a race of magicians. This is the pinnacle of our careers. We could retire tomorrow and they'd talk about us until the end of time."

"Once we get off this rock and go home! I keep telling you, Keff, what they're doing isn't magic. It can't be. Real magic shouldn't require *power*, least of all the kind of power they're sucking out of the surrounding area. Mental power possibly, but not battery-generator type power, which is what is coming along those electromagnetic lines in the air."

"Well, there's invocation of power as well as evocation, drawing it into you for use," Keff said, trying to remember the phrases out of the Myths and Legends rule book.

Carialle seemed to read his mind. "Don't talk about a game! This is real life. This isn't magic. Ah! There it is: proof."

Keff glanced up. Chaumel was bowing to something hovering before him at eye level. It was a box of some kind. It drifted slightly so that the flat side that had been directed at Chaumel was pointing at him. Looking out from behind a glass panel was a man's face, dark-skinned and ancient beyond age. The puckered eyelids compressed as the man peered intently at Keff.

"See? It's a monitor," Carialle said. "A com unit. It's a device, *not* magic, *not* evoked from the person of the user. He's transmitting his image through it, probably because he's too weak to be here in person."

"Maybe the box is just a relic from the old days," Keff said, but his grand theory did have a few holes in it. "Look, there's nothing feeding it."

"You don't need cable to transmit power, Keff. You know that. Even Chaumel isn't magicking the food up himself. He's calling it from somewhere. Probably in the depths of the dungeon, there's a host of fuzzy-faced cooks working their heads off, and furry sommeliers decanting wine. I think he's acting like the teleportative equivalent of a maitre d'."

"All right, I concede that they *might* be technicians. What I want to know is just what they want with us so badly that they have to trap us in place."

"What we appear to be, or at least I appear to be, is a superior technical gizmo. Your girlfriend and her green sidekick at least don't want something this big to get away. The greed, by the way, is not limited to those two. At least eighty percent of the people here experience increased respiration and heartbeat when they look at you and the IT box, and by proxy, me. It's absolutely indecent."

Chaumel went around the room like a zephyr, defusing arguments and urging people to sit down to prepare for the meal. Keff admired his knack of having every detail at his fingertips. Couches with attached tables appeared out of the ether. The guests disported themselves languidly on the velvet covers while the tables adjusted themselves to be in easy range. The canape servers vanished in midstep and the remains of the hors d'oeuvres with them. Napery, silver, and a translucent dinner service appeared on every table followed by one, two, three sparkling crystal goblets, all of different design. White, embroidered napkins opened out and spread themselves on each lap.

Something caught Keff squarely in the belly and behind the knees, making him fold up. A padded seat caught him, lifted him up and forward several feet into the heart of the circle of magifolk, and the tray across his middle clamped firmly down on the other arm of the chair. Under his heels, a broad bar braced itself to give him support. A napkin puffed up, settled like swansdown on his thighs.

"Oh, I'm not hungry," he said to the air. The invisible maitre d' paid no attention to his protest. He was favored with china and crystal, and a small finger bowl on a doily. He picked up a goblet to examine it. Though the glass was wafer-thin, it had been incised delicately with arabesques and intricate interlocking diamonds.

"How beautiful."

"Now that is contemporary. Not bad," Carialle said, with grudging approval. Keff turned the goblet and let it catch the torchlight. He pinged it with a fingernail and listened to the sweet song.

A hairy-faced server bearing an earthen pitcher appeared next to Keff to fill his glass with dark golden wine. Keff smiled at him and sniffed the liquid. It was fragrant, like honey and herbs.

"Don't drink that," Carialle said, after a slight hesitation to assess the readouts from Keff's olfactory implant. "Full of sulfites, and just in case you think the Borgias were a fun family, enough strychnine in it to kill you six times over."

Shocked, Keff pushed the glass away. It vanished and was replaced by an empty one. Another server hovered and poured a cedar-red potation into its bowl. He smiled at the furry-faced female who tipped up the corners of her mouth tentatively before hurrying away to the next person.

"Who put poison in my wine?" Keff whispered, staring around him.

Chaumel glanced over at him with a concerned expression. Keff nodded and smiled to show that everything was all right. The silver magiman nodded back and went on his way from one guest to another.

"I don't know," Carialle said. "It wasn't and *isn't* in the pitcher, but I wasn't quick enough to follow the burst of energy back to its originator. Seems it isn't an unknown incident, though."

All around the room, a Noble Primitive was appearing beside each mage. Full of curiosity, Keff eyed them. Each bore a different cast of features, some more animal than others, so they were undoubtedly from the magimen's home provinces. Asedow's servant did look like a six-pack. The pretty girl's servant was hardly mutated at all, except for something about the eyes that suggested felines. Potria didn't look at her pig-person, but stiff-armed her goblet toward him. Cautiously, the Noble Primitive took a sip. Nothing happened to him, but two other servants nearby fell over on the floor in fits of internal anguish. They vanished and were replaced by others. Whites showing all around the irises of his eyes, the pig-man handed the goblet back to his mistress, and waited, hands clenched, for her nod of approval. Other mages, their first drink satisfactory, held their glasses aloft, calling loudly to the wine servers for refills.

"Food-tasters! There's more in heaven and on earth than is dreamed of in your philosophy, Horatio," Keff said.

"Hmph!" Carialle said. "That's an understatement. I wish you could see what I do. Those languorous poses are just that: poses. I'm recording everything for your benefit, and it's taking approximately eighteen percent of my total memory capacity to absorb it. I'm not merely monitoring three language forms. There is a lot more going on sub rosa. Every one of our magifolk is tensed up so much I don't know how they can swallow. The air is full of power transmissions, odd miniature gravity wells, low-frequency signals, microwaves, you name it."

"Can you trace any of it back? What is it all for?"

"The low-frequency stuff is easy to read. It's chatter. They're sending private messages to one another, forming conspiracies and so on against, as nearly as I can tell, everyone else in the room. The power signals correspond to dirty tricks like the poison in your wine. As for the microwaves, I can't tell what they're for. The transmission is slightly askew to anything I've dealt with before, and I can't intercept it anyway because I'm not on the receiving end."

"Tight point-to-point beam?"

"I wish *I* could transmit something with as little spillover," Carialle admitted. "Somebody is very good at what they're doing."

IT continued to translate, but most of what it reported was small talk, mostly on the taste of the wine and the current berry harvests.

With their chairs bobbing up and down to add emphasis to their discourse, two magiwomen were conversing about architecture. A couple of the magifolk here and there leaned their heads toward one another as if sharing a confidence, but their lips weren't moving. Keff suspected the same kind of transference that the magifolk used to control their eye spheres. He looked up, wondering where all the spy-eyes had gone. That afternoon on the field the air had been thick with them.

Keff contrasted the soup that appeared in huge silver tureens with the swill that Brannel's people had to eat. And he and Cari were still not free to leave the planet. Still, in spite of the shortcomings, he had a feeling of satisfaction.

"This is the race everyone in Exploration has always dreamed of finding," he said, surveying the magifolk. "Our technical equals, Cari. And against all odds, a humanoid race that evolved parallel to our own. They're incredible."

"Incredible when they amputate fingers from babies?" asked Carialle. "And keep a whole segment of the race under their long thumbs with drugged food and drink? If they're our equals, thank you, I'll stay unequal. Besides, they don't appear to be makers, they're users. Chaumel's mighty proud of those techno-toys left to him by the Old Ones and the Ancient Ones, but he doesn't know how to fix 'em. And neither does anyone else. Over there, in the corner."

Keff glanced over as Carialle directed. On the floor lay Chaumel's jelly jar. He gasped.

"Does he know he lost it?"

"He didn't lose it. I saw him drop it there. It doesn't work anymore, so he discarded it. Everybody else has looked at it with burning greed in their eyes and, as soon as they realized it doesn't work anymore, ignored it. They're operators, not engineers."

"They're still tool-using beings with an advanced civilization who have technical advantages, if you must call it that, superior in many ways to ours. If we can bring them into the Central Worlds, I'm sure they'll be able to teach us plenty."

"We already know all about corruption, thank you," Carialle said.

A servant stepped forward, bowed, and presented the tureen to him. Keff sniffed. The soup smelled wonderful. He gave them a tight smile. Another popped into being beside him bearing a large spoon, and ladled some into the bowl on his tray. The rich golden broth was thick with chunks of red and green vegetables and tiny, doughnut-shaped pasta. Keff poked through it with his silver spoon.

"Cari, I'm starved. Is any of this safe to eat? They didn't assign me a food-taster, even if I'd trust one."

"Hold up a bite, and I'll tell you if anyone's spiked it." Keff obliged, pretending he was cooling the soup with his breath. "Nope. Go ahead."

"Ahhhh." Keff raised it all the way to his lips.

His chair jerked sideways in midair. The stream of soup went flying off into the air past his cheek and vanished before it splashed onto his shoulder. He found himself facing Omri.

"Tell me, strange one," said the peacock-clad mage, lounging back on his floating couch, one hand idly spooning up soup and letting it dribble back into his bowl. "Where do you come from?"

"Watch it," Carialle barked.

"From far away, honored sir," Keff said. "A world that circles a sun a long way from here."

"That's impossible."

Keff found himself spun halfway around until he was nose to nose with a woman in brown with night-black eyes.

"There are no other suns. Only ours."

Keff opened his mouth to reply, but before he could get the words out, his chair whirled again.

"Pay no attention to Lacia. She's a revisionist," said Ferngal. His voice was friendly, but his eyes were two dead circles of dark blue slate. Tell me more about this star. What is its name?"

"Calonia," Keff said.

"That leaves them none the wiser," Carialle said.

"That leaves us none the wiser," Chaumel echoed, turning Keff's seat in a flat counterclockwise spin three-quarters around. "How far is it from here, and how long did it take you to get here?" Keff opened his mouth to address Chaumel, but the silver magiman became a blur.

"What power do your people have?" Asedow asked. Whoosh!

"How many are they?" demanded Zolaika. Hard jerk, reverse spin.

"Why did you come here?" asked a plump man in bright yellow. Blur.

"What do you want on Ozran?" Nokias asked. Keff tried to force out an answer.

"Not—" Short jerk sideways.

"How did you obtain possession of the silver tower?" Potria asked.

"It's my sh—" Two half-arcs in violently different directions, until he ended up facing an image of Ferngal that swayed and bobbed.

"Will more of your folk be coming here?" Keff heard. His stomach was beginning to head for his esophagus.

"I . . ." he began, but his chair shifted again, this time to twin images of Ilnir, who gabbled something at him in a hoarse voice that was indistinguishable from the roar in his ears.

"Hey!" Keff protested weakly.

"The Siege Perilous, Galahad," Carialle quipped. "Be strong, be resolute, be brave."

"I'm starting to get motion sick," Keff said. "Even flyer training wasn't like this! I feel like a nardling lazy Susan." The chair twisted until it was facing away from Ilnir. A blurred figure of primrose yellow and teal at the corner of his eye sat up slightly.

Beside Keff's hand, a small glass appeared. It was filled with a sparkling liquid of very pale green. Keff's vision abruptly cleared. Was he being offered another shot of poison? The silver blob that was Chaumel shot a suspicious look at the tall girl, then nodded to Keff. The brawn started to take the ornate cup, when two more tasters abruptly keeled over and let their glasses crash to the ground. Two more servants appeared, always four-fingered fur-faces. Keff regarded the cup suspiciously.

"What about it, Cari? Is it safe to drink?"

"It's a motion sickness drug," Carialle said, after a quick spectroanalysis. Hastily, before he was moved again, Keff gulped down the green liquid. It tasted pleasantly of mint and gently heated his stomach. In no time, Keff felt much better, able to endure this ordeal. He winked at the pretty girl the next time he was whirled past her. She returned him a tentative grin.

The Siege Perilous halted for a moment and Keff realized his soup plate had vanished. In its place was a crescent-shaped basket of fruit and a plate of salad. His fellow diners were also being favored with the next course. Some of them, with bored expressions, waved it away and were instantly served tall, narrow crockery bowls with salt-encrusted rims. Before he spun away again, he watched Zolaika pull something from it and yank apart a nasty-looking crustacean.

"Ugh," Keff said. "No fish course for me."

Thanks to the young woman's potion he felt well enough to eat. While trying to field questions from the magifolk, he picked up one small piece of fruit after another. Carialle tested them for suspicious additives.

"No," Carialle said. "No, no, no, yes—oops, not anymore. No, no, yes!"

Before it could be tainted by long-distance assassins, Keff popped the chunk of fruit in his mouth without looking at it. It burst in a delightful gush of soft flesh and slightly tart juice. His next half-answer was garbled, impeded by berry pulp, but it didn't matter, since he was never allowed to finish a sentence anyway before the next mage greedily snatched him away from his current inquisitor. He swallowed and sought for another wholesome bite.

The basket disappeared out from under his hand and was replaced by the nauseating crock. His fingers splashed into the watery gray sauce. It sent up an overwhelming odor of rotting oil. Keff's stomach, tantalized by the morsel of fruit, almost whimpered. He held his breath until his invisible waiter got the hint and took the crock away. In its place was a succulent-smelling vol au vent covered with a cream gravy.

"No!" said Carialle as he reached for his fork.

"Oh, Cari." His chair revolved, pinning him to the back, and the meat pastry evaporated in a cloud of steam. "Oh, damn."

"Why have you come to Ozran?" Ilnir asked. "You have not answered me."

"I haven't been allowed," Keff said, bracing himself, expecting any moment to be turned to face another magiman. When the chair didn't move, he sat up straighter. "We come to explore. This planet looked interesting, so we landed."

"We?" Ilnir asked. "Are there more of you in your silver tower?"

"Oops," Carialle said.

"Me and my ship," Keff explained hastily. "When you travel alone as I do, you start talking out loud."

"And do you hear answers?" Asedow asked to the general laughter of his fellows. Keff smiled.

"Wouldn't that be something?" Keff answered sweetly. Asedow smirked.

"That man's been zinged and he doesn't even know it," Carialle said.

"Look, I'm no danger to you," Keff said earnestly. "I'd appreciate it if you would release my ship and let me go on my way."

"Oh, not yet," Chaumel said, with a slight smile Keff didn't like at all. "You have only just arrived. Please allow us to show you our hospitality."

"You are too kind," Keff said firmly. "But I must continue on my way."

The spin took him by surprise.

"Why are you in such a hurry to leave?" Zolaika asked, narrowing her eyes at him. The face with the monitor, hovering beside her, looked him up and down and said something in the secondary, more formal dialect. Keff batted the IT unit slung around his chest, which burped out a halting query.

"What tellest thou from us?"

"What will I say about you?" Keff repeated, and thought fast. "Well, that you are an advanced and erudite people with a strong culture that would be interesting to study."

He was slammed sideways by the force of the reverse spin.

"You would send others here?" Ferngal asked.

"Not if you didn't want me to," Keff said. "If you prefer to remain undisturbed, I assure you, you will be." He suffered a fast spin toward Omri.

"We'll remain more undisturbed if you don't go back to make a report at all," the peacock magiman said. A half-whirl this time, and he ended up before Potria.

"Oh, come, friends," she said, with a winning smile. "Why assume ill where none exists? Stranger, you shall enjoy your time here with us, I promise you. To our new friendship." She flicked her fingers. A cup of opal glass materialized in front of her and skimmed across the air to Keff's tray. Keff, surprised and gratified, picked it up and tilted it to her in salute.

"What's in it, Cari?" he subvocalized.

"Yum. It's a nice mugful of mind-wipe," she said. "Stabilized sodium pentothal and a few other goodies guaranteed to make her the apple of your eye." Keff gave the enchantress a smile full of charm and a polite nod, raised the goblet to her once again, and put it down untasted. "Sorry, ma'am. I don't drink."

The bronze woman swept her hand angrily to one side, and the goblet vanished.

"Nice try, peachie," Cari said, triumphantly.

Keff seized a miniature dumpling from the next plate that landed on his tray.

"Yes," Carialle whispered. Keff popped it into his mouth and swallowed. His greed amused the magifolk of the south, whose chairs bobbed up and down in time to their laughter. He smiled kindly at them and decided to turn the tables.

"I am very interested in your society. How are you governed? Who is in charge of decision-making that affects you all?"

That simple question started a philosophical discussion that fast deteriorated into a shouted argument, resulting in the death or discomfort of six more fur-skinned foodtasters. Keff smiled and nodded and tried to follow it all while he swallowed a few bites.

Following Carialle's instructions, he waved away the next two dishes, took a morsel from the third, ignored the next three when Carialle found native trace elements that would upset his digestive tract, and ate several delightful mouthfuls from the last, crisp, hot pastries stuffed with fresh vegetables. Each dish was more succulent and appealing than the one before it.

"I can't get over the variety of magic going on in here," Keff whispered, toying with a souffle that all but defied gravity.

"If it was really magic, they could magic up what you wanted to eat and not just what they want you to have. As for the rest, you know what I think."

"Well, the food is perfect," Keff said stubbornly. "No burnt spots, no failed sauces, no gristle. That sounds like magic."

"Oh, maybe it's food-synths instead," Carialle countered. "If I was working for Chaumel, I'd be terrified of making mistakes and ruining the food. Wouldn't you?"

Keff sighed. "At least I still have my aliens."

"Enough of this tittle-tattle," Chaumel called out, rising. He clapped his hands. The assemblage craned their necks to look at him. "A little entertainment, my friends?" He brought his hands together again.

Between Nokias and Ferngal, a fur-skinned tumbler appeared halfway through a back flip and bounded into the center of the room. Keff's chair automatically backed up until it was between two others, leaving the middle of the circle open. A narrow cable suspended from the ceiling came into being. On it, a male and a female hung ankle to ankle ten meters above the ground. Starting slowly, they revolved faster until they were spinning flat out, parallel to the floor. There was a patter of insincere applause. The rope and acrobats vanished, and the tumbler leaped into the air, turned a double somersault, and landed on one hand. A small animal with an ornamented collar appeared standing on his upturned feet. It did flips on its perch, as the male boosted it into the air with thrusts of his powerful legs. Omri yawned. The male and his pet disappeared to make room for a whole troupe of juvenile tumblers.

Keff heard a gush of wind from the open windows. The night air blew a cloud of dust over the luminescent parapet, but it never reached the open door. Chaumel flashed his wand across in a warding gesture. The dust beat itself against a bellying, invisible barrier and fell to the floor.

"Was that part of the entertainment?" Keff said subvocally.

"Another one of those power drains," Carialle said "Somehow, what they do sucks all the energy, all the cohesive force out of the surrounding ecology. The air outside of Chaumel's little mountain nest is dead, clear to where I am."

"Magic doesn't have to come from somewhere," Keff said.

"Keff, physics! Power is leaching toward your location. Therefore logic suggests it is being drawn in that direction by need."

"Magic doesn't depend on physics. But I concede your point."

"It's true whether or not you believe in it. The concentrated force-fields are weakening everywhere but there."

"Any chance it weakened enough to let you go?"

There was a slight pause. "No."

A prestidigitator and his slender, golden-furred assistant suddenly appeared in midair, floating down toward the floor while performing difficult sleight-of-hand involving fire and silk cloths. They held up hoops, and acrobats bounded out of the walls to fly through them. More acrobats materialized to catch the flyers, then disappeared as soon as they were safely down. Keff watched in fascination, admiring the dramatic timing. Apparently, the spectacle failed to maintain the interest of the other guests. His chair jerked roughly forward toward Lacia, nearly ramming him through the back. The acrobats had to leap swiftly to one side to avoid being run over.

"You are a spy for a faction on the other side of Ozran, aren't you?" she demanded.

"There aren't any other factions on Ozran, madam," Keff said.

"I scanned from space. All habitations are limited to this continent in the northern hemisphere and the archipelago to the southwest."

"You must have come from one of them, then," she said. "Whose spy are you?"

Just like that, the interrogation began all over again. Instead of letting him have time to answer their demands, they seemed to be vying with one another to escalate their accusations of what they suspected him of doing on Ozran. Potria, still angry, didn't bother to speak to him, but occasionally snatched him away from another magifolk just for the pleasure of seeing his gasping discomfort. Asedow joined in the game, tugging Keff away from his rival. Chaumel, too, decided to assert his authority as curator of the curiosity, pulling him away from other magifolk to prevent him answering their questions. In the turmoil, Keff spun around faster and faster, growing more irked by the moment at the magi using him as a pawn. He kept his hands clamped to his chair arms, his teeth gritted tightly as he strove to keep from being sick. Their voices chattered and shrilled like a flock of birds.

"Who are you . . . ?"

"I demand to know . . . !"

"What are you . . . ?"

"Tell me. . . ."

"How do . . . ?"

"Why . . . ?"

"What . . . ?"

Fed up at last, Keff shouted at the featureless mass of color. "Enough of this boorish interrogation. I'm not playing anymore!"

Heedless of the speed at which he was spinning, he pushed away his tray, stepped out from the footrest, and went down, down, down. . . .

✷CHAPTER NINE

Keff fell down and down toward a dark abyss. Frigid winds screamed upward, freezing his face and his hands, which were thrust above his head by his descent. The horizontal blur that was the faces and costumes of the magifolk was replaced by a vertical blur of gray and black and tan. He was falling through a narrow tunnel of rough stone occasionally lit by streaks of garishly colored light. His hands grasped out at nothing; his feet sought for support and found none.

Gargoyle faces leered at him, gibbering. Flying creatures with dozens of clawed feet swooped down to worry his hair and shoulders. Momentum snapped his head back so he was staring up at a point of light far, far above him that swayed with every one of his heartbeats. The movement made him giddy. His stomach squeezed hard against his rib cage. He was in danger of losing what little he had been able to eat. The wind bit at his ears, and his teeth chattered. He forced his mouth closed, sought for control.

"Carialle, help! I'm falling! Where am I?"

The brain's tone was puzzled.

"You haven't moved at all, Keff. You're still in the middle of Chaumel's dining room. Everyone is watching you, and having a good time, I might add. Er, you're staring at the ceiling."

Keff tried to justify her observation with the terrifying sensation of falling, the close stone walls, and the gargoyles, and suddenly all fear fled. He was furious. The abyss was an illusion! It was all an illusion cast to punish him. Damn their manipulation!

"That is enough of this nonsense!" he bellowed.

Abruptly, all sensation stopped. The buzzing he suddenly felt through his feet bothered him, so he moved, and found himself lurching about on the slick floor, struggling for balance. With a yelp, he tripped forward, painfully bruising his palms and knees. He blinked energetically, and the points of light around him became ensconced torches, and the pale oval of Plennafrey's face. She looked concerned. Keff guessed that she was the one who had broken the spell holding his mind enthralled.

"Thank you," he said. His voice sounded hollow in his own ears. He sat back on his haunches and gathered himself to stand up.

He became aware that the other magifolk were glaring at the young woman. Chaumel was angry, Nokias shocked, Potria mute with outrage. Plenna lifted her small chin and stared back unflinchingly at her superiors. Keff wondered how he had ever thought her to be weak. She was magnificent.

"Her heartbeat's up. Respiration, too. She's in trouble with them," Carialle said. "She's the junior member here—I'd say the youngest, too, by a decade—and she spoiled her seniors' fun. Naughty. Oops, more power spikes."

Keff felt insubstantial tendrils of thought trying to insinuate themselves into his mind They were rudely slapped away by a new touch, one that felt/scented lightly of wildflowers. Plennafrey was defending him. Another sally by other minds managed to get an image of bloody, half-eaten corpses burning in a wasteland into his consciousness before they were washed out by fresh, cool air.

"Keff, what's wrong?" Carialle asked. "Adrenaline just kicked up."

"Psychic attacks," he said, through gritted teeth. "Trying to control my mind."

He fought to think of anything but the pictures hammering at his consciousness. He pictured a cold beer, until it dissolved inexorably into a river of green, steaming poison. He switched to the image of dancing in an anti-grav disco with a dozen girls. They became vulpine-winged harpies picking at his flesh as he swung on a gibbet. Keff thought deliberately of exercise, mentally pulling the Rotoflex handles to his chest one at a time, concentrating on the burn of his chest and neck muscles. Such a small focus seemed to bewilder his tormentors as they sought to corrupt that one thought and regain control.

Sooner or later the magifolk would break through, and he would never know the difference between his own consciousness and what they planted in his thoughts. He felt a twinge of despair. Nothing in his long travels had prepared him to defend himself against this kind of power. How much more could he withstand? If they continued, he'd soon be blurting out the story of his life—and his life with Carialle.

Not that—he wouldn't! Angrily, he steeled his will. If he couldn't protect himself, he couldn't guard Carialle. Even at the cost of his own life he must prevent them from finding out about her. Her danger would be worse than his, and worse than what had happened to her that time before they became partners.

The Rotoflex handles of his imagination became knives that he plunged agonizingly again and again into his own breast. He forced his mental self to drop them. They burst into flames that rose up to burn his arms. He could feel the hair crackling on his forearms. Then a soft rain began to fall. The fire died with hisses of disappointment. Keff almost smiled. Plennafrey again.

He was grateful for the young magiwoman's intercession. How long could she hold out against the combined force of her elders? He could almost feel the mental sparks flying between Plennafrey and the others. She was actually holding her own, which was causing consternation and outrage among them. The outwardly calm standoff threatened to turn into worse.

"Small power spikes," Carialle announced. "A jab to the right. Ooh, a counter to the left. A roundhouse punch—what was that?"

Keff felt himself gripped by an invisible force. Slowly, like the rope-dancers, he began to revolve in midair, this time without his chair. He turned faster and faster and faster. What little remained of his original delight at having discovered a race of magicians was fast disappearing in the waves of nausea roiling his long-suffering stomach. He tried to touch the floor, or one of the other mages, but nothing was within reach. Faster, faster, faster he turned, until the room was divided into strata of light and color. Images began to invade his consciousness, accompanied by shrieks tinged with fear and anger, shriveling his nerves. He could feel nothing but pain, and the roaring in his head overwhelmed his other senses.

Keff felt a touch on the arm, and suddenly he was staggering weak-kneed across the slick floor behind Plennafrey. She had abandoned the battle in favor of saving him. Holding his hand firmly, she made for the open doors.

Chaumel's transparent wall proved no barrier. Plennafrey plunged her hand under her sash to her belt, and a hole opened in the wall just before they reached it, letting a cloud of dust whip past them into the room. Coughing, she and Keff dashed out onto the landing pad. Keff remembered what Carialle had said about color coordination and ran after the girl toward the blue-green chair at the extreme edge of the balcony. His feet were unsteady on the humming floor, but he forced himself to cover the distance almost on the young woman's heels.

She threw herself into her chariot, hoisted him in, too. Without ceremony, the chair swept off into the night. Behind him, Keff saw other magifolk running for their chairs. He saw Chaumel shake a fist up at them, and suddenly, the image blanked out.

They emerged into a vast, torchlit, stony cavern that extended off into the distance to both left and right. Plenna paused a split second and turned the chair to the right. Her big, dark eyes were wide open, her head turning to see first one side, then the other as they passed. Keff hung on as the chair skipped up to miss a stalagmite and ducked a low cave mouth. He gasped. The air tasted moist and mineral heavy.

"Where are you?" Carialle's voice exploded in his ear. "Damnation, I hate that!"

"Watch the volume, Cari!"

Sound level much abated, Carialle continued. "You are approximately nine hundred meters directly below your previous location, heading south along a huge system of connected underground caverns. Hmm!"

"What?" he demanded, then bit his tongue as Plennafrey's chair dodged through a narrow pipe and out into a cavern the bottom of which dropped away like the illusionary abyss.

"I'm reading some of those electromagnetic lines down there, not far from you, but not intersecting the tunnel you are currently traveling."

"Where are we going?" he asked the girl.

"Where we will be safe," she said curtly. Her forehead was

wrinkled and she was hunched forward as if straining to push something with her shoulders.

"Is there something wrong?"

"It's the lee lines," she said. "Where we are is weak. I'm drawing on ones very far away. We must reach the strong ones to escape, but Chaumel stops me."

"Lee lines?" Keff said, asking for further explanation. Then a memory struck him and he sent IT running through similar-sounding names in Standard language. It came up with "ley," which it defined as "adjective, archaic, related to mystical power." Very similar, Keff noted, and turned his head to mention it.

The chair bounced, hitting a small outcropping of rock, and Keff felt his rump leave the platform. He gripped the edges until his knuckles whitened. The air whistled in his ears.

"What if you can't reach the strong ley lines?" he shouted.

"We can get most of the way to my stronghold through down here," the girl said, not looking down at him. "It will take longer, but the mountains are hollow below. Oh!"

Ahead of them, the air thickened, and a dozen chariots took shape. These swooped in at Keff and the girl, who took a hair-pin curve in midair and looped back toward the narrow passage. Keff caught a glimpse of Chaumel in the lead, glittering like a star. The silver mage grinned ferociously at them.

Asedow spurred his green chariot faster to beat Chaumel to Plenna's vehicle. He succeeded only in creating a minor traffic jam blocking the neck of stone as Plennafrey disappeared into it. By the time they straightened themselves out, their prey had a head start.

Plennafrey retraced their path through the forest of onyx pillars. Keff leaned back against her knees as she cut a particularly sharp turn to avoid the same outcropping as on the way out. Keff glanced up at her face and found it calm, intense, alert, pale and lovely as a lily. He shook his head, wondering how he had possibly missed noticing her before. He risked a quick glance back.

Far behind them, the magimen in pursuit were coming to grief amidst the stalactite clusters. Keff heard shouts of anger, then warning, and not long after, a crash. Their pursuers were down to eleven.

"The passage widens out beyond the junction where you first appeared," Carialle said, narrating from her soundings of the underground system. "Life-forms ahead."

They swooped under a low overhang that marked the boundary of the next limestone bubble cavern. Keff smelled food and
squinted ahead in the torchlight. The smell of hot food blended
with the cold, wet, limestone scent of the caves. Before them lay
the subterranean kitchens whose existence Carialle had postulated.
Compared to the frosty ambient temperature above, this place was
positively tropical. Keff felt his cheeks reddening from the heat that
washed them. Plennafrey turned slightly pink. Scores of fur-faced
cooks and assistants hurried around like ants, carrying pots and
pans to the huge, multi-burner stoves lined up against the walls
or hauling full platters of cooked food to vast tables that ran down
the center of the chamber.

"Natural gas, geothermal heat," Carialle said. "The catering
service for the nine circles of Hell."

In one corner, discarded like toy dishes in a doll's tea set, were
hundreds of bowls, plates, and platters, sent back untouched from
upstairs by fussy diners.

"What a waste," Keff said as they passed over the trash heap.
The reeking fumes of deteriorating food made his eyes water. He
gasped.

Avoiding a low point in the ceiling, the chariot bore down on
the cooks, who dropped their pans and dishes and dove for cover.
The bottom of the runner struck something soft, but kept going.
Keff glanced behind them and saw the ruins of a tall cake and
the pastry chef's stricken face.

"Sorry!" Keff called.

Behind them, the magimen on their chariots swooped into the
cavern, shouting for Plennafrey to surrender her prize. Bolts of
red fire struck past them, impacting the stone walls with explosive reports. Chunks of stone rained down on the screaming cooks.
Plennafrey jerked the chariot downward, and a lightning stroke
passed over them, shattering a stalactite into bits just before they
reached it. Keff threw his hands up before his face just a split
second too late, and ended up spitting out limestone sand.

"Don't damage anything!" Chaumel yelled. "My kitchen!" Keff
saw him frantically making warding symbols with his hands, sending spells to protect his property.

Plennafrey stole a look over her shoulder and poured on the
speed. She pulled Keff's body back against her legs. He looked up
at her for explanation.

She said, "I need my hands," and immediately began weaving her own enchantments in a series of complex passes. Keff braced himself between the end of the chariot back and the chair legs to keep Plennafrey from bouncing out of her seat.

The cavern narrowed sharply at its far end, forcing them farther and farther toward the floor. Fur-faced Noble Primitives who had been throwing themselves down to get out of their way went entirely flat or slammed into the wall as Plennafrey's chariot flashed by. Females shrieked and males let out hoarse-voiced cries of alarm.

Scarlet fire ricocheted from wall to wall, missing the blue-green chariot by hand-spans. The young magiwoman launched off fist-sized globes of smoky nothingness, flinging them behind her back. Keff, intent on the wall above the cave mouth zooming toward them, heard cries and protests, followed by a series of explosive puffs.

Plennafrey resumed control of her chair just in time to direct them sharply down and into the stone tunnel. This must have been the central corridor of Chaumel's underground complex. Hundreds of Noble Primitives dropped their burdens and dove for cover as he and Plennafrey zoomed through. Skillfully zigzagging, dipping, and rising, she avoided each living being and stone pillar in the long tube.

"She's good on this thing," Keff confided to Carialle. "What a rocket-cycle jockey she'd make."

To right and left, several smaller tunnels offered themselves. Plennafrey glanced at each one as they passed. With the inadequate light of torches, Keff could see no details more than a dozen feet up each one. The magiwoman bit her lip, then banked a turn into the ninth right.

"Keff, not that one!" Carialle said urgently.

"Aha!"

Keff heard Chaumel's crow of victory, and view-halloo cries from the other pursuers. He wondered why they sounded so pleased.

Plenna dodged against the left wall to avoid colliding with a grossly-wheeled wagon pulled by six-packs and piled high with garbage. There was barely enough space for both of them, but somehow the magiwoman made it by. After a short interval, Keff heard a few loud scrapes, and a couple of hard splats, followed by furious and derisive yells. Two more magimen would be abandoning the race as they went home to clean refuse out of their gorgeous robes. Another scrape ended in a sickening-sounding crunch. Keff guessed the magiman on that chariot had misjudged the space between the cart and the wall. That left eight in pursuit. Keff risked a glance. The silver glimmer at the front was Chaumel, and behind him the dark green of Asedow, the pink-gold of Potria, Nokias's gold, and the shadow that was Ferngal were grouped in his wake. More ranged behind them, but he couldn't identify them.

Plennafrey wound her way through the irregular, narrowing corridor, tossing spells over her shoulder to slow her pursuers.

"I would turn around and weave a web to snare them," she said, "but I dare not take my eyes off our path."

"I agree with you wholeheartedly, lady," Keff said. "Keep your eyes on the road. Look, it's lighter up ahead."

A lessening of the gloom before them suggested a larger chamber, with more room to maneuver. Plenna crested the high threshold and let out a moan of dismay. The room widened out into a big cavern, but it was as smooth and featureless as a bubble. Racks and racks of bottles lined the lower half of the walls. No spaces between them suggested any way out.

"A dead end," Keff said, in a flat tone. "We're in Chaumel's wine cellar. No wonder he was gloating."

"I was trying to tell you," Carialle spoke up in a contrite voice. "You weren't listening."

"I'm sorry, Cari. It was a wild ride," Keff said.

Plennafrey turned in a loop that brought Keff's heart up into his throat and made for the narrow entrance, but it was suddenly filled by Chaumel and the rest of the posse. Plennafrey reversed her chair until she was hovering in the center of the room. Eight chairs surrounded her, looking like a hanging jury.

" . . . And it looks like it's over."

"There you are, my friends. You left us too soon," Chaumel said. "Magess Plennafrey, you overreached yourself. You misunderstand how reluctant we are to allow such prizes as this stranger and his tower to be won by the least of our number."

Keff felt Plenna's knees tighten against his back.

"Perhaps he does not want to be anyone's property," she said. "I will leave him his freedom."

"You do not have the right to make that choice, Magess," Nokias said. He stretched out his arms and planted one big hand across the ring that encircled his other wrist. Keff braced himself as red bolts shot out of the bracelet, enveloping him and the floating chair.

An invisible rod collected the bolts, diverting them harmlessly down into nothingness. The astonished look on Nokias's face said that he neither expected Plennafrey to defy him nor to be able to counteract his attack.

"That's what hit you on the plain," Carialle whispered in Keff's ear. "Same frequency. It must have been Nokias. My, he looks surprised."

The other magimen lifted their objects of power, preparing an all-out assault on their errant member.

"Please, friends," Chaumel said, moving between them toward the wary pair in the center. His eyes were glowing with a mad, inner light. "Allow me."

He took the wand from the sleeve on his belt and raised it. Keff glanced up at Plennafrey. The magiwoman, glaring defiance, began to wind up air in her arms.

"I see what she's doing," Carialle said, her voice alarmed. "Keff, tell her not to teleport again. I won't—"

The cavern exploded in a brilliant white flash.

Except for the absence of eight angry magimen, Keff and Plennafrey might not have moved. They were in the center of a globe hewn from the bare rock. Then Keff noticed that the walls were rougher and the ceiling not so high. Plennafrey hastily brought the chair to earth. She sighed a deep breath of relief. Keff seconded it.

He sprang up and offered her his hand. With a small smile, she reached out and took it, allowing him to assist her from the chair.

"My lady, I want to thank you very sincerely for saving my life," Keff said, bowing over their joined hands. When he looked up, Plenna was pink, but whether with pleasure or embarrassment Keff wasn't sure.

"I could not let them treat you like chattel," she said. "I feel you are a true man for all you are not one of us."

"A true man offers homage to a true lady," Keff said, bowing again. Plennafrey freed herself and turned away, clutching her hand against herself shyly. Keff smiled.

"What pretty manners you have," Carialle's voice said. It sounded thin and very far away. "You're forty-five degrees of planetary arc away from your previous location. I just had time to trace you before your power burst dissipated. You're in a small bubble pocket along another one of those long cavern complexes. What is this place?"

"I was just about to ask that." Keff looked around him. "Lady, where are we?"

Unlike Chaumel's wine cellar, this place didn't smell overpoweringly of wet limestone and yeast. The slight mineral scent of the air mixed with a fragrant, powdery perfume. Though large, the room had the sensation of intimacy. A comfortable-looking, overstuffed chair sprawled in the midst of little tables, fat floor pillows, and toy animals. Against one wall, a small bed lay securely tucked up beneath a thick but worn counterpane beside a table of trinkets. Above it, a hanging lamp with a cobalt-blue shade, small and bright like a jewel, glowed comfortingly. Keff knew it to be the private bower of a young lady who had taken her place as an adult but was not quite ready to give up precious childhood treasures.

"It is my . . . place," Plennafrey said IT missed the adjective, but Keff suspected the missing word was "secret" or "private." Seeing the young woman's shy pride, he felt sure no other eyes but his had ever seen this sanctuary. "We are safe here."

"I'm honored," Keff said sincerely, returning his gaze to Plennafrey. She smiled at him, watchful. He glanced down at the bedside shelf, chose a circular frame from which the images of several people projected slightly. He picked it up, brought it close to his eyes for Carialle to analyze.

"Holography," Carialle said at once. "Well, not exactly. Similar effect, but different technique."

Keff turned the frame in his hands. The man standing at the rear was tall and thin, with black hair and serious eyebrows. He had his hands on the shoulders of two boys who resembled him closely. The small girl in the center of the grouping had to be a younger version of Plennafrey. "Your family?"

"Yes."

"Handsome folks. Where do they live?"

She looked away. "They're all dead," she said.

"I am sorry," Keff said.

Plennafrey turned her face back toward him, and her eyes were red, the lashes fringed with tears. She fumbled with the long, metallic sash, lifted it up over her head, and flung it as far across the room as she could. It jangled against the wall and slithered to the floor.

"I hate what that means. I hate being a magess. I would have been so happy if not for . . ." IT tried to translate her speech, and fell back to suggesting roots for the words she used. None of it made much sense to Keff, but Carialle interrupted him.

"I think she killed them, Keff," she said, alarmed. "Didn't Chaumel say that the only way to advance in the ranks was by stealing artifacts and committing murder? You're shut up in a cave with a madwoman. Don't make her angry. Get out of there."

"I don't believe that," Keff said firmly. "They all died, you said? Do you want to tell me about it?" He took both the girl's hands in his. She flinched, trying to pull away, but Keff, with a kind, patient expression, kept a steady, gentle pressure on her wrists. He led her to the overstuffed foot-rest and made her sit down. "Tell me. Your family died, and you inherited the power objects they had, is that right? You don't mean you were actually instrumental in their deaths."

"*I do,*" Plenna said, her nose red. "I did it. My father was a very powerful mage. He . . . ed Nokias himself."

"Rival," IT rapped out crisply. Keff nodded.

"They both wished the position of Mage of the South, but Nokias took it. Losing the office troubled him. Over days and days—time, he went—" Helplessly, she fluttered fingers in the vicinity of her temple, not daring to say the word out loud.

"He went mad," Keff said. Plenna dropped her eyes.

"Yes. He swore he would rival the Ancient Ones. Then he decided having children had diminished his power. He wanted to destroy us to get it back."

"Horrible," Keff said. "He *was* mad. No one in his right mind would ever think of killing his children."

"Don't say that!" Plennafrey begged him. "I loved my father. He had to keep his position. You don't know what it's like on Ozran. Any sign of weakness, and someone else will . . . step in."

"Go on," Keff said gravely. Aided occasionally by IT, Plennafrey continued.

"There is not much to tell. Father tried many rituals to build up his connection with the Core of Ozran and thereby increase his power, but they were always unsuccessful. One day, two years ago, I was studying ley lines, and I felt hostile power stronging up. . . ."

"Building up," interjected IT.

"As I had been taught to do, I defended myself, making power walls. . . ."

"Warding?" Keff asked, listening to IT's dissection of the roots of her phrase.

"Yes, and feeding power back along the lines from which they came. There was more than I had ever felt." The girl's pupils dilated, making her eyes black as she relived the scene. "I was out on our balcony. Then I was surrounded by hot fire. I built up and threw the power away from me as hard as I could. It took all the strength I had. The power rushed back upon its sender. It went past me into our stronghold. I felt an explosion inside our home. That was when I knew what I had done. I ran." Her face was pale and haunted. "The door of my father's sanctum was blown outward. My brothers lay in the hall beyond. All dead. All dead. And all my fault." Tears started running down her cheeks. She dabbed at them with the edge of a yellow sleeve. "Nokias and the others came to the stronghold. They said I had made my first coup. I had achieved the office of magess. I didn't want it. I had force-killed my family."

"But you didn't do it on purpose," Keff said, feeling in his tunic pocket for a handkerchief and extending it to her. "It was an accident."

"I could have let my father succeed. Then he and my brothers might be alive," Plennafrey said. "I should have known." A tear snaked down her cheek. Angrily, she wiped her eye and sat with the cloth crumpled in her fists.

"You fought for your life. That's normal. You shouldn't have to sacrifice yourself for anyone's power grab."

"But he was my father! I respected his will. Is it not like that where you live?" the girl asked.

"No," Keff said with more emphasis than he intended. "No father would do what he did. To us, life is sacred."

Plenna stared at her hands. She gave a little sigh. "I wish I lived there, too."

"I hate this world more than ever," said Carialle, for whom special intervention to save her life had begun before she was born. "Corruption is rewarded, child murder not even blinked at; power is the most important thing, over family, life, sanity. Let's have them put an interdict on this place when we get out of here. They haven't got space travel, so we don't have to worry about them showing up in the Central Worlds for millennia more to come."

"We have to get out of here first," Keff reminded her. "Perhaps we can help them to straighten things out before we go."

Carialle sighed. "Of course you're right, knight in shining armor. Whatever we can do, we should. I simply cannot countenance what this poor girl went through."

Keff turned to Plennafrey. She stared down toward the floor, not seeing it, but thinking of her past.

"Please, Plennafrey," Keff said, imbuing the Ozran phrases with as much persuasive charm in his voice as possible, "I'm new to your world. I want to learn about you and your people. You interest me very much. What is this?" he asked, picking up the nearest unidentifiable gewgaw.

Distracted, she looked up. Keff held the little cylinder up to her, and she smiled.

"It is a music," she said. At her direction, he shook the box back and forth, then set it down. The sides popped open, and a sweet, tinny melody poured out. "I have had that since, oh, since a child."

"Is it old?"

"Oh, a few generations. My father's father's father," she giggled, counting on her fingers, "made it for his wife."

"It's beautiful. And what's this?" Keff got up and reached for a short coiled string and the pendant bauble at the end of it. The opaline substance glittered blue, green, and red in the lamplight.

"It's a plaything," Plennafrey said, with a hint of her natural vitality returning to her face. "It takes some skill to use. No magic. I am very good with it. My brothers were never as skilled."

"Show me," Keff said. She stood up beside him and wound the string around the central core of the pendant. Inserting her forefinger through the loop at the strings end, she cradled the toy, then threw it. It spooled out and smacked back into her palm. She flicked it again, but this time moved her hand so the pendant ricocheted past her head, dove between their knees, then shot back into her hand.

"A yo-yo!" Keff said, delighted

"You have such things?" Plennafrey asked. She smiled up into his face.

Keff grinned. "Oh, yes. This is far nicer than the ones I used to play with. In fact, it's a work of art. Can I try?"

"All right." Plenna peeled the string off her finger and extended the toy to him. He accepted it, his hands cradling hers for just a moment. He did a few straight passes with the yo-yo, then made it fly around the world, then swung it in a trapeze.

"You are very good too," Plenna said, happily. "Will you show me how you did the last thing?"

"It would be my pleasure," Keff told her. He returned the toy to her hands. As his palms touched hers, he felt an almost electric shock. He became aware they were standing very close, their thighs brushing slightly so that he could feel the heat of her body. Her breath caught, then came more quickly. His respiration sped up to match hers. To his delight and astonishment he knew that she was as attracted to him as he was to her. The yo-yo slipped unnoticed to the hassock as he clasped her hands tightly. She smiled at him, her eyes full of trust and wonder. Before she said a word, his arms slid along hers, encompassing her narrow waist, hands flat against her back. She didn't protest, but pressed her slim body to his. He felt her quiver slightly, then she nestled urgently against him, settling her head on his shoulder. Her skin was warm through the thin stuff of her dress, and her flowery, spicy scent tantalized him.

She felt so natural in his arms he had to remind himself that she was an alien being, then he discarded inhibition. If things didn't work out physically, well, they were sharing the intense closeness of people who had been in danger together, a kind of comfort in itself. Yet he let himself believe that all would be as he desired it. There were too many other outward similarities to humanity in Plennafrey's people. With luck, they made love the same way.

Plennafrey had none of the seductive art of the gauze-draped Potria, but he found her genuine responsiveness much more desirable. While her elders were tormenting Keff, it had probably not occurred to her to think of him as anything but an abused "toy."

She was merely being kind to an outsider, or less charitably, to a dumb animal that couldn't defend itself. Now that they were together, intriguing chemistry bubbled up between them. He watched the long fringe of her lashes lift to reveal her large, dark eyes. He admired the long throat and the way her pulse jumped in the small shadow at the hollow inside her collarbone. The corners of her mouth lifted while she, too, stopped to study him.

"What are you thinking?" he asked, looking up at her.

"I am thinking that you are handsome," she said.

"Well, you are very beautiful, lady magess," he whispered, bending down to kiss the curve of her shoulder.

"I hate being a magess," Plennafrey said in a voice that was nearly a sob.

"But I am glad you are a magess," Keff said. "If you hadn't been, I would never have met you, and you are the nicest thing I have seen since I came to Ozran."

He put his hand under her chin, stroked her soft throat with a gentle finger like petting a cat. Almost felinely, Plenna closed her eyes to long slits and let her head drift back, looking like she wanted to purr. She raised her face to his, and her hand crept up the back of his neck to pull his head down to her level. Keff tasted cherries and cinnamon on her lips, delighted to lose himself in her perfume. He deepened the kiss, and Plenna responded with ardor. He bent down to kiss the curve of her shoulder, felt her brush her cheek against his ear.

Suddenly she let go of him and stepped back, looking up at him half-expectantly, half-afraid. Keff gathered up her hands and kissed them, pulled Plenna close, and brushed her lips with soft, feather-light caresses until they opened. She sighed.

"Sight and sound off, please, Cari," Keff whispered Plennafrey nestled her head into the curve of his shoulder, and he kissed her.

Carialle considered for a moment before shutting off the sensory monitors. While in a potentially hostile environment, especially with hostiles in pursuit, it was against Courier Service rules to break off all communications.

The Ozran female let out a wordless cry, and Keff matched it with a heartfelt moan. Carialle weighed the requirement with Keff's right to privacy and decided a limited signal wasn't unreasonable. Such a request was permissible as long as the brain maintained some kind of contact with her brawn partner.

"As you wish, my knight errant," she said, hastily turning off the eye and mouth implants. She monitored transmission of his cardial and pulmonary receivers instead. They were getting a strenuous workout.

✳   ✳   ✳

With her brawn otherwise occupied, Carialle turned her attention to the outside of Ozran. Most of the power and radio signals were still clustered on and inside Chaumel's peak. Each magiman and magiwoman proved to have a slightly different radio frequency which she or he used for communication, so Carialle could distinguish them. The eight remaining hunters who had pursued Keff and his girlfriend down the subterranean passages fanned out again and again across the planetary surface, and regrouped. The search was proving futile. Carialle mentally sent them a raspberry.

"Bad luck, you brutes," she said, merrily.

On the plain, the eye-globes came out of nowhere and circled around and around her. Carialle peered at each one closely, and recorded its burblings to the others through IT. Keff was building up a pretty good Ozran vocabulary and grammar, so she could understand the messages of frustration and fury that they broadcast to one another.

Some time later, Keff's heartbeat slowed down to its resting rate. His brain waves showed he had drifted off to sleep. Carialle occupied herself in the hours before dawn by doing maintenance on her computer systems and keeping an eye on the hunters who had to be wearing themselves out by now.

Carialle gave Keff a decent interval to wipe out sleep toxins, and then switched on again. Her video monitors beside his eyes offered her a most romantic tableau.

On the small bed against the bower wall, the young magiwoman was cuddled up against Keff's body. They were both naked, and his dark-haired, muscular arm was thrown protectively over her narrow, pale waist. Their ankles overlapped and then he started running a toe up and down her calf. Carialle took the opportunity to scan Keff's companion and found her readings of great interest.

Keff snorted softly, the sound he always made when he was on the edge of wakefulness.

"Ahem!" Carialle said, just loudly enough to alert, but not loud enough to startle Keff. "Are you certain this is what Central Worlds means by first contact?"

Keff gave a deep and throaty chuckle. "Ah, but it *was* first contact, my lady," he said, allowing her to infer the double or triple entendre.

"A gentleman never kisses and tells, you muscled ape," Carialle chided him. He laughed softly. The girl stirred slightly in her sleep, and her hand settled upon the hair on his chest. She smiled gently, dreaming. "Keff, I have something I need to tell you about Plennafrey, in fact about all the Ozrans: they're human."

"Very similar, but they're humanity's cousins," Keff corrected her. "And wait until I show the tapes to Xeno. Not of this, of course. They'll go wild."

"She *is* human, Keff. She must be the descendant of some lost colony or military ship that landed here eons ago. Her reactions, both emotional and bodily, let alone blood pressure, structure, systems—she was close enough to your contact implants for me to make sure. And I *am* sure. We have met the Ozrans, and they is us."

"Genetic scan?" Keff was disappointed. Carialle could tell he was still hoping, but he was a good enough exobiologist to realize he knew it himself.

"Bring me a lock of her hair, and I'll prove it."

"Oh, well," he said, gathering Plennafrey closer and tucking her head into his shoulder. "I can still rejoice in having found a mutation of humanity that has such powerful TK abilities."

Carialle sighed. Bless his stubbornness, she thought.

"It's not TK. It's sophisticated tool-using. Take away her toys and see if she can do any of her magic tricks."

Keff reached over the edge of the small bed and picked up the heavy belt by its buckle. He weighed it in his hand, then let it slip on his palm so his fingers were pointing toward the five depressions. "Does that mean I can use these things, too?"

"I should say so."

The links of the belt clanked softly together. The slight noise was enough to wake the young magiwoman in alarm. She sat up, her large eyes scanning the chamber.

"Who is here?" she asked. Keff held out her belt to her and she snatched it protectively.

"Only me," Keff said. "I'm sorry. I wanted to see how it worked. I didn't mean to wake you up."

Plenna looked apologetic for having overreacted to simple curiosity, and offered the belt to him with both hands and a warning. "We mustn't use it here. It is the reason that my bower is secure. We are just on the very edge of the ley lines, so my belt buckle and sash resonate too slightly to be noticed by any other mage." She swept a hand around "Everything in this room was brought here by hand. Or fashioned by hand from new materials, using no power."

"That's in the best magical tradition," Keff noted approvingly. "That means there's no 'vibes' left over from previous users. In this case, tracers or finding spells."

"Or circuits," Carialle said. "How does their magic work?"

Her question went unanswered. Before Keff could relay it to Plenna, he found himself gawking up toward the ceiling. As neatly as a conjurer pulling handkerchiefs out of his sleeve, the air disgorged Chaumel's flying chair, followed by Potria's, then Asedow's. Chaumel swooped low over the bed. The silver mage glared at them through bloodshot eyes.

"What a pretty place," he said, showing all his teeth in a mirthless grin. "I'll want to investigate it later on." He eyed Plennafrey's slender nakedness with an arrogant possessiveness. "Possibly with your . . . close assistance, my lady. You've been having a nice time while we've looked everywhere for you!"

Keff and Plennafrey scrambled for their clothes. One by one, the other hunters appeared, crowding the low bubble of stone.

"Ah, the chase becomes interesting again," Potria said. She didn't look her best. The chiffon of her gown drooped limply like peach-colored lettuce, and her eye makeup had smeared from lines to bruises. "I was getting so *bored* running after shadows."

"Yes, the prey emerges once again," Chaumel said. "But this time the predators are ready."

Plenna glared at Chaumel as she threw her primrose dress over her head.

"We should never have traveled in here by chair," she snarled. Keff stepped into his trousers and yanked on his right boot.

"That is correct," Chaumel said, easily, sitting back with his abnormally long fingers tented on his belly. "It took us some time to find the vein by which the heart of Ozran fed your power, but we have you at last. We will pass judgment on you later, young magess, but at this moment, we wish our prize returned to us."

The two stood transfixed as Nokias, Ferngal, and Omri slid their chairs into line beside their companion.

"Your disobedience will have to be paid for," Nokias said sternly to Plenna.

The young woman bowed her head, clasping her belt and sash in her hands. "I apologize for my disrespect, High Mage," she said, contritely. Keff was shocked by her sudden descent into submissiveness.

Nokias smiled, making Keff want to ram the mage's teeth down his skinny throat. "My child, you were rash. I can forgive."

The golden chair angled slightly, making to set down in the clear space between Plenna's small bed and her table. With lightning reflexes, Plennafrey grabbed Keff's hand, jumped over the lower limb of the chair, and dashed for her own chair. Clutching his armload of clothes and one boot, Keff had a split second to brace himself as Plenna launched the blue-green chariot into the gap left by Nokias and zoomed out into one of the tunnels that led out of the bubble.

Keff threw his legs around the edges of Plennafrey's chariot to brace himself while he shrugged into his tunic. The strap of the IT box was clamped tightly in his teeth. He disengaged it, dragged it out from under his shirt, and put it around his neck where it belonged. His boot would have to wait.

"Well done, my lady," he shouted. His voice echoed off the walls of the small passage that wound, widened, and narrowed about them.

"How *dare* they invade my sanctum!" Plennafrey fumed. Instead of being frightened by the appearance of the other mages, she was furious. "It goes beyond discourtesy. It is—like invading my mind! How *dare* they? Oh, I feel so stupid for teleporting in. I should never have done that."

"I'm responsible again, Plenna," Keff said contritely. He hung on as she negotiated a sharp turn. He pulled his legs up just in time. The edge of the chair almost nipped a stone outcropping. Plennafrey's hand settled softly on his shoulder, and he reached up to squeeze it. "You were saving my life."

"Oh, I do not blame you, Keff," she said. "If only I had been thinking clearly. It is all my fault. You couldn't know what I should have kept in mind, what I have been trained in all my life!" Her hand tightened in his, and he let it go. "It is just that now I don't know where we can go."

The posse was once again in pursuit. Keff heard shouting and bone-chilling scrapes as the hunters organized themselves a single-file line and attempted to follow. This tunnel was narrower than the ones underneath Chaumel's castle. A fallen stalactite aimed a toothlike pike at them, which Plenna dodged with difficulty. She scraped a few shards of wood off the side of her vehicle on the opposite wall. Keff curled his legs up under his chin away from the edge and prayed he wouldn't bounce off.

"Usually I enter on foot," Plenna said apologetically. "A chair was never meant to pass this way."

Keff was sure that Chaumel and the others were figuring that out now. The swearing and crashing sounds were getting louder and more emphatic. If Plenna wasn't such a good pilot, they'd be coming to grief on the rocks, too.

"Can't we teleport out of here?" Keff asked.

"We can't teleport out of a place," Plenna said, staring ahead of them. "Only in. Almost there. Hold on."

Keff, gripping the legs of her chair, got brief impressions of a series of vast caverns and corkscrewing passages as they looped and flitted through a passage that wound in an ever-widening spiral without the walls ever spreading farther apart. To Keff's relief, they emerged into the open air. They were over a steep-sided, narrow, dry riverbed bounded by dun-colored brush and scrub trees. He had a mere glimpse of the partly-concealed stone niche where Plenna almost certainly landed her chair when here by herself, then they were out over the ravine heading into the sunrise. Keff's stomach turned over when he realized how high up they were. He chided himself for a practical coward; he wasn't afraid of heights in vacuum, but where gravity ruled, he was acrophobic.

He turned at the sound of a shout. Through a lucky fluke, Chaumel and Asedow were almost immediately behind them. The others were probably still trying to get out of Plenna's labyrinth, or had crashed into the stone walls. As soon as he was clear, Asedow raised his mace. Red fire lanced out at them. Plenna, apparently intuiting where Asedow would strike, dodged up and down, slewing sideways to let the beams pass. The dry brush of the deep river vale smoldered and caught fire.

Chaumel was more subtle. Keff felt something creep into his mind and take hold. He suddenly thought he was being carried in the jaws of a dragon. Fiery breath crept along his back and into his hair, growing hotter. The fierce, white teeth were about to bite down on him, severing his legs. He groaned, clenching his jaws, as he fought the illusion's hold on his mind. The image vanished in the sweet breeze Keff had come to associate with Plenna, but it was followed immediately by another horrible illusion. She batted it away at once without losing her concentration on the battle. Chaumel was ready with the next sally.

"Don't want them taking my mind!" Keff ground out, battling images of clutching octopi with needle-sharp teeth set in a ring.

"Concentrate, Keff," Carialle said "Those devious bastards can't find a crack if you keep your focus small. Think of an equation. Six to the eighth power is . . . ?"

"Times six is thirty six, times six is two hundred sixteen, times six is . . ." Keff recited.

Plennafrey started forming small balls of gray nothingness between her hands. Her chair wheeled on its own axis, bringing her face-to-face with her pursuers. They peeled off to the sides like expert dog-fighters, but not before she had flung her spells at them. Explosions echoed down the valley. Ferngal's chair tipped over backward, sending him plummeting into the ravine. Keff heard his cry before the magiman vanished in midair. The black chair vanished, too. Nokias zoomed in toward them, his hand laid across his spell-casting ring. Plenna threw up a wall of protection just in time to shield them from the scarlet lightning.

"Divided by fourteen is . . . ? Come on!" Carialle said. "To the nearest integer."

One by one, the last three mages appeared out of the cave mouth and joined in the aerial battle. Keff couldn't watch Plenna weaving spells anymore because the webs made him think of giant spiders, which the illusion-casters made creep toward him, threatening to eat him. He drove them away with numbers.

"How long is a ninety-five kilohertz radio wave?" Carialle pressed him. "Keff, late-breaking headline: a couple hundred chariots just left Chaumel's residence. They're *all* coming for you. Teleporting . . . now!"

"We're too vulnerable," Keff shouted hoarsely. "If they get through to my mind the way they did in the banquet hall, I'll end up their plaything. If they don't shoot us first!"

All six of the remaining mages positioned themselves around Plenna like the sides of a cube, converging on her, throwing their diverse spells and illusions. Hands flying, Plennafrey warded herself and Keff in a translucent globe of energy. Carialle's voice became suffused with static.

Suddenly, the chair under him dropped. Spells and lightning bolts, along with the shield-globe, vanished. The sides of the ravine shot upward like the stone walls in his nightmare.

"What happened?" he shouted. All the other mages were falling, too, their faces frozen with fear. Before his question was completely out of his mouth, the terrifying fall ceased. Keff felt his hair crackle with static electricity, and bright sparks seemed to fly around all the mages' chariots. Unhesitatingly, Plenna angled her chair upward, flying out of the canyon. She crested the ridge and ran flat out toward the east. "What was that?"

"Didn't you pay the power bill?" Carialle asked, in his ear. "That was a full blackout, a tremendous drop along the electromagnetic lines. I think you overloaded the circuits of whatever's powering them, but they're back on line. Fortunately, it got everybody at once, not just you."

"Are you all right?" Keff asked.

The yearning and frustration in the brain's voice was unmistakable. "For that one moment I was free, but unfortunately I was too slow to take off! All the power on the planet is draining toward you—even the plants seem to be losing their color. Everyone is out in full force after you. Keff, get her to bring you here!"

Like a hive of angry hornets, swarms of chariots poured over the ridge in pursuit. Scarlet bolts whipped past Keff's ear. He grabbed Plennafrey's knee, and turned his face up to her.

"Plenna, if you can't teleport out, we have to teleport *into* somewhere—my ship!" She nodded curtly.

Over his head, the girl's arms wove and wove. Keff watched the mass of chairs fill the air behind them. He prayed they wouldn't suffer another magical blackout.

"Great Mother Planet of Paradise, aid me!" Plenna threw up her arms, and the whole scene, angry magicians and all, vanished.

*CHAPTER TEN

Plonk! The chariot was abruptly surrounded by the walls of Carialle's main cabin.

"That was a tight fit," Carialle remarked on her main speaker. "You're nearly close enough to the bulkhead to meld with the paint."

"But we made it," Keff said, scrambling out. Gratefully, he stretched his legs and reached high over his head with joined hands until his back cracked in seven places. "Ahhh . . ."

Plenna rose and stared around her in wonder. "Yes, we made it. So this is what the tower looks like inside. It is like a home, but so many strange things!"

"I think she likes it," Carialle said, approvingly.

"Well, what's not to like?" Keff said. "Are the magimen still coming?"

"They don't know where you've gone. They'll figure it out soon enough, but I'm generating white noise to mask my interior. It's making the spy-eyes crazy, but that's all right with me, the nasty little metal mosquitoes."

"It is *not* you talking," Plennafrey said, watching his lips as Carialle made her latest statement. "There is a second voice, a female's. Your tower can speak?"

Keff, realizing the habits of fourteen years were stronger than discretion, glanced at Carialle's pillar and pulled an apologetic face.

"Oops," Carialle said.

"Er, it's not a tower, Plenna. It's a ship," Keff explained.

"And it's not his. It's mine." Carialle manifested her Myths and Legends image of the Lady Fair on the main screen. With tremendous and admirable self-control, Plennafrey just caught her mouth before it could drop open. She eyed the gorgeous silhouette, evidently contrasting her own disheveled costume unfavorably with the rose-colored gauze and satin of the Lady.

"You're . . . only a picture," Plenna said at last.

"You want me three-dimensional?" Cari said, making her image "step" off the wall and assume a moving holographic image. She held out her hands, making her long sleeves flutter with a whisper of silk. "As you wish. But I am real. I exist inside the walls of this ship. I am the other half of Keff's team. My name is Carialle."

The fierce expression Plenna wore told Carialle that Plenna was jealous of all things pertaining to Keff. That needed to be handled when the crisis had passed. To the magiwoman's credit, she understood that, too.

"I greet you, Carialle," Plenna said politely.

"She's a winner, Keff," Cari said, pitching her statement for Keff's mastoid implant only. "Pretty, too. And just a little taller than you are. That must have made things interesting."

Keff colored satisfactorily. "Now that we're all acquainted, we have to talk seriously before Chaumel and his Wild Hunt catch up with us. What in the name of Daylight Savings Time just happened out there?"

"I have never seen the High Mages so . . . so insane," Plennafrey offered, shaking her head "They have gone beyond reason."

"That's not what I mean," Keff said. "The magic stopped all at once when we were hanging over that riverbed."

"It has happened before," Plenna said, nodding gravely. "But not when I was in the sky. That was terrible."

"The huge drain on power obviously caused some kind of imbalance in the system," Carialle said. She plotted a chair for her image to sit down on and gestured for the other two to seat themselves. "The drop came after the whole grid of what the lady called 'ley lines' bottomed out all over the planet. There was, for an instant, no more power to call. It came back after you all suffered a kind of blackout. Look."

In their midst, Carialle projected a two-meter, three-dimensional image of Ozran, showing the ley lines etched in purple over the dun, green, and blue globe. Geographical features, including individual peaks and valleys on the continents, took shape.

"Oh," Plenna breathed, recognizing some of the terrain. "Is this what Ozran looks like?"

"That's right," Keff said.

"How wonderful," she said, beaming at Carialle for the first time. "To be able to make beautiful pictures like that."

Carialle ducked her head politely, acknowledging the compliment.

"Thank you, miss. Now, this is the normal flow of those mysterious electromagnetic waves. Here's what happened when you got that blast of dust in Chaumel's stronghold."

The translucent globe turned until the large continent in the northern hemisphere was facing Keff and Plennafrey. The dark lines thickened toward a peak on a mountain spine in the southeast region, thinning everywhere else. What remained were small "peaks" on the lines here and there. "I think these are the mages who didn't come to dinner. Now here"—the configurations changed slightly, the bulges shifting southward—"is what happened when you escaped from the dinner party. And this next matches the moment when you teleported to Magess Plennafrey's sanctum sanctorum."

The purple lines performed complicated dances. First, a slight bulge opened out in lines near a river valley in the southernmost mountain range of the continent, corresponding to a slight drop in the forces in the southeast. Chaumel's peak was nearly invisible amidst the power lines, until the mages dispersed to points all over Ozran. Occasionally, they reconverged.

"This big spike indicated when the eight mages found Plennafrey's hidey-hole," Carialle said, narrating, "followed by the big one when everyone came to see the fun. Here comes the chase scene. A huge buildup as the others left Chaumel's peak. And—"

Abruptly, the lines thinned, some even disappearing for a moment.

"That has happened before," Plenna repeated. "Not often, but more often now than before."

"Absolute power corrupts, and I'm not just talking about political." Carialle finished the ley geographic review.

"Can you run that image again, Cari?" Keff said, leaning close to study it. "Magic shouldn't cause imbalances in planetary fields."

"But it does, depending on where it comes from," Carialle said. "What's it for? Why is there a worldwide network of force lines? It must have been put here for a reason." She turned to Plenna. "Where does *your* power come from, Magess?"

"Why, from my belt amulet," Plennafrey explained, displaying the heavy buckle. "The sash is an amulet, too, but it was my father's, and I don't like to use it." She undid her waist cincture and held it out to Carialle.

Carialle had her image shake its head. "I'm not solid, sweetie." Instead, she directed the artifact to Keff. Carialle turned on an intense spotlight in the ceiling and aimed it so she and her brawn could have a better look. Keff turned the belt over in his hands. Carialle zoomed in a camera eye to microscopic focus.

The five indentations were there, as Chaumel had said, part of the original design. The buckle had been adapted for wear by some unknown metal smith at least eight hundred years ago, Carialle judged by a quick analysis. Braces and a tongue had been welded to its sides. The whole thing comprised approximately ninety cubic centimeters, and was plated with fine gold, which accounted for its retaining a noncorroded surface over the centuries. Carialle recorded all data in accessible memory.

"Can you teach me how to use it?" Keff asked, smiling hopefully at her. Plennafrey seemed uneasy, but allowed herself to be persuaded by the fatal Von Scoyk-Larsen charm.

"Well, all right," she said. "I'll trust you." Her expression said that she didn't trust often or easily. Such behavior on this world, Carialle noted, would not be a survival trait.

Plenna stood behind Keff and showed him how to place his fingers in the depressions. "Do not push down, not . . . solidly," she said.

"Physically," Keff corrected IT's translation. He cradled the buckle in his other hand, raising it to eye level.

"Correct," Plenna said, unaware of the box's simultaneous transmission as she spoke. "Imagine your fingers pressing deep into the heart, where they will contact the Core of Ozran."

"Is that why you wear the finger extensions?" Keff asked, after trying to fit his hand into the depressions. His thumb and little finger had to curve unnaturally to touch all five spots, while Plenna, with her pinky prosthesis, could cover them without effort, bending only her thumb.

"Yes. Most mages do not have fingers long enough. It is one way in which we are inferior to the great Ancient Ones who left us these tools," Plenna said with a trace of awe. "Now, think hard. Do you feel the fire inside? It should run up inside your arm to your heart."

"I feel something," Keff said after a while. "Now what?"

She looked around and pointed at the pedometer lying on the console. "Make that box fly," she said.

Keff stared fixedly at the pedometer. His face turned red with effort. To Carialle's satisfaction, the device lifted a few centimeters before clattering back to its resting place.

"There, you see?" she said. "Mechanics."

Plennafrey held out her hand for the belt, and Keff gave it back. "Now, here is how I do it." Barely touching the five depressions, the magiwoman glanced at the box. It shot up to dangle in mid-air. Keff walked over and tried to push down on the hovering device. It didn't budge. He yanked at it with all his strength.

"Its as if you fixed it there," Keff said, sweeping Plenna off her feet and kissing her. "Carialle, we're both right. They do use machines, but it's more than that. I can't duplicate what she just did. I nearly got a hernia raising the pedometer as far as I did. She set it like a point plotted in a three-dimensional grid, and she's not even flushed."

The Lady Fair image didn't show the exasperation that Carialle let creep into her voice.

"All right, so they have natural TK and psi abilities which are amplified by the mechanism. Probably increased by selective breeding over centuries—you see what they've done to the Noble Primitives."

"Sour grapes," Keff said cheerfully. "And this gizmo can work from anywhere on the planet?" he asked Plennafrey.

"Yes," the magiwoman said, "but closer to the Core of Ozran makes it easier."

Keff nodded and sat down next to Plenna so he could examine the buckle once again. "Chaumel mentioned that, but he wouldn't say what it is. Is that the power source? Do you know how it works?"

"I do—or I think I do." Plennafrey's eyes grew dreamy as she raised her hands to sketch in the air. "It is a great, glowing heart of power, somewhere deep beneath the surface of Ozran. It was the Ancient Ones' greatest work." For a moment, the young woman looked sheepish. "My power is weak compared with the others. I have tried to figure out more about the Ancient Ones and the Core to try and increase my power, though not . . . not in the way some did." She glanced uneasily at Carialle.

"I know all about your father, Magess," Carialle said. "Whatever Keff sees and hears, I do, too."

That reminded Plennafrey of what Carialle must have seen and heard that morning, and she blushed from the roots of her hair to her neckline.

"Oh," she said. Carialle kindly tried to take the sting out of the revelation.

"I also agree with everything he said about your situation. You're very brave, Magess."

"Thank you. Hem! As I said, I wished to make my connection to the Core greater with harm to none. I have some ancient documents that I am sure hold the key to the power of the Core, but I cannot read them." She appealed to both brain and brawn. "I dared not ask anyone for help, lest they take away my small advantage. Perhaps you might help me?"

"Documents?" Keff perked up. He rose and paced around the cabin. "Documents possibly written by the Ancients? Will you let me see them? I'm a stranger; I have no reason to rob you. I'm also very good with languages. Will you trust me?" He stopped at Plennafrey's chair and took her hand.

"All right," Plennafrey said. She looked lovingly up into his eyes. "There is no one else I would rather trust."

"She's completely out of her league in this game," Carialle said in Keff's ear. "What a pity there isn't a place on this nasty planet for nice guys. . . . We have one problem," she said aloud. "I can't lift tail from where I'm sitting, and at present, there's a surveillance team of overgrown marbles flying around my hull."

"Where are Chaumel and the others?" Keff asked.

Carialle consulted her monitors, reanimating the globe. The enormous mass of purple had thinned away, leaving single points scattered along the crisscrossing lines. "Everyone's gone home except a few who are hanging around Chaumel's peak."

"I am sure they will be looking for me in my stronghold," Plenna said resignedly. "All is lost."

"We need a conspirator," Keff said. "And I know just the fellow."

"Who? I told you all the others would steal my documents, and then you will be forced to read for them."

Keff's eyes twinkled. "He's not a mage. Cari, can you get me out of here unobserved through the cargo hatch? I'm going to go enlist Brannel."

"Who is Brannel?" Plenna asked, trailing behind Keff and Carialle as they headed toward the cargo hold.

"He's one of the workers who lives in the cave out there," Keff said, pointing vaguely outward.

"A four-finger? You wish to entrust one of Klemay's farmers with secrets of the Core of Ozran?"

"You don't know what's in your files," Carialle said. "Might be a book of recipes from the Dark Ages. Hasten, Magess." Carialle's image stopped in the hold as Keff began to move containers out of the way. Plennafrey trotted to a halt to avoid bumping into her. "We need help. Something very wrong is happening to your world and I think it has been going bad since your ancestors were babies. Your documents are the first piece of real information we've heard about. Brannel can do what none of us can: he can go in and out of your house without being noticed by the other magimen."

"Cari?" Keff gestured at the larger boxes blocking the ladder to the hatch. Service arms detached from the walls and began to stack and move them to other shelves. "I'm also going to have to jump down three meters. You'll have to create a diversion."

"Leave that to me," Carialle said.

She led the magiwoman back toward the main cabin. "Now, we're going to have some fun."

Devoting screens around the main console to three of her external cameras for Plenna's benefit, Carialle tuned into the eye-spheres, the service door, and the main hatchway.

They watched the eyes cluster as Carialle let down her ramp and slid open her airlock to disgorge a servo. The low robot rolled down onto the plateau and trundled off into the bushes with the cluster of spy-eyes in pursuit. The door slid closed.

"Go!" Carialle said, pitching her voice over the speaker in the cargo hold. She slid open the door just a trifle.

Leaving some skin behind, Keff slipped out the narrow opening, and dropped to the ground in a crouch. He ran down the hill and across the field toward where the workers were gathering at the cave mouth for their daily toil.

Trusting Keff to take care of that half of the arrangements on his own, Carialle watched with amusement through one of the servo's guiding cameras as the spies followed. It rumbled downhill into a gully and plunged into a sudden puddle, splashing some of the eyes so they recoiled. Plennafrey laughed.

The servo rumbled forward into the midst of a cluster of globe-frogs, who rolled hastily backward and gesticulated at one another inside their cases, croaking in alarm. They moved into the servo's path, continuing their tirade, as if scolding the machine for scaring them. Cari guided it carefully so it wouldn't bump into any of them and headed it for the deepest part of the swamp.

Low-frequency transmissions buzzed between the spy-eyes. Carialle hooked the IT into the audio monitors. From the look of concentration on her face, Plenna was already listening to them in her own way, and enjoying being in the know for a change.

"Where is it going?" asked Potria's voice. "Do you suppose it's going to where *they* are?"

Plennafrey giggled.

"Is the stranger's house doing this on its own?" Nokias asked. "It is a most powerful artifact."

Carialle huffed. "They still think I'm an object! Oh, well, there's nothing I can do about that yet."

"If they knew you were a living being," Plenna said "they would not treat you as an object. Oh," she said, reality dawning, "they would, wouldn't they? They did with Keff. Oh, my, what has my world become?"

Carialle felt sorry for Plenna. She might be one of the upper class, but she wasn't happy about the status.

On the screen, the spy-eyes were buzzing busily to one another, circling the area, trying to second-guess the servo's mission. Serenely, the robot rolled into a swampy place where pink-flowering weeds grew. Carialle set its parameters to seek out a marsh weed that had exactly fifteen leaves and twelve petals.

"That should keep it busy for a while," Carialle said.

"What does it want in that terrible wet place?" Asedow's voice wailed. "I am getting aches in my bones just watching it!"

"Keep your eyes open," Nokias's voice cautioned them. "There might be a clue in what this box seeks that will lead us to the stranger."

Carialle joined Plennafrey's delighted chuckle.

Keff ran to the far side of the cave mouth so the hill would block the view of him from the spy-eyes' position. The Noble Primitives, still wiping traces of breakfast from their faces and chest fur, were listening to their crew chiefs assigning tasks for the day. Brannel, near Alteis's group, seemed bored with the whole thing. Keff now suspected that there was something in the Noble Primitive's metabolism that rejected the amnesia-inducing drug, or he was cleverer than his masters knew. He was banking on the latter possibility.

"Ssst, Brannel!" he whispered. A child turned around at the slight noise and saw him. Sternly, Keff shook his head and twirled his finger to show the child she should turn around again. Terrified, the youngster clamped her hands together and returned to her original posture, spine rigid. Keff fancied he could see her quivering and regretted the necessity of scaring her. It was easier to frighten the child into submission than make friends. He hissed again.

"Ssst, Brannel! Over here!"

This time Brannel heard him. The Noble Primitive's sheeplike face split into a wide grin as he saw Keff beckoning to him. He rose to hands and knees and crawled away from the work party.

Alteis saw him. "Brannel, return!" he commanded.

Wordlessly, Brannel pointed to his belly, indicating the need to go relieve himself. The leader shook his head, then lost all interest in his maverick worker. Keff admired Brannel's quick mind; the fellow had to be unique among the field workers on Ozran.

"I am so glad to see you safe, Magelord," Brannel said, when they had retreated around the curve of the hill. "I was concerned for your safety."

Keff was touched. "Thank you, Brannel. I was worried for a while, too. But as you see, I'm back safe and sound."

Brannel was impressed. Only yesterday Mage Keff could speak but a little of the Ozran tongue. Overnight, he had learned the language as well as if he had been born there.

"How may I serve, Magelord?"

"I wonder if you would be willing to do me a favor. I need someone with your injenooety," Keff said. Brannel shook his head, not comprehending. "Er, your smart brain and wits."

"Ah," Brannel said, docketing "injenooety" as a word of the linga esoterka he had not previously known. "You are too kind, Mage Keff. I'd do anything you wish."

Inwardly, Brannel was jubilant. The mage had sought him out, Brannel, a worker male! He could serve this mage, and in return, who knew? Keff possessed many great talents and wide knowledge which, perhaps, he might share as a reward for good service. One day, Brannel, too, might be able to achieve his dream and take power as a mage.

Keff looked around. "I don't wish to talk here. We might be overheard. Come with me to the silver tower." When Brannel looked askance at him, he asked, "What's wrong?"

"The noise it made, Mage Keff," Brannel said, and put his fingers in his ears. "It drove me outside."

"Oh," Keff said. "That won't happen again. I want you to come in and stay this time. All right?"

Brannel nodded. The magelord rose to a stoop and began to make his way across the field. None of the workers looked his way. Brannel hurried after him, full of hope.

Instead of entering by the ramp through the open door, Keff directed Brannel around the rear of the tower and pointed upward. A slit as wide as his forearm was long had opened in the smooth silver wall.

"But why . . . ?" he asked.

"The front's being watched," Keff said. He joined his hands together and propped them on one knee. "Put your foot here— that's good. Now, reach for it. Up you go."

Brannel grabbed the edge of the opening and heaved himself into it. Once he was up, he helped pull Mage Keff into a room crowded with boxes. They had to climb down from a high shelf with great care. When Brannel and Keff were inside, the opening in the wall closed. The female voice of the tower spoke in its strange tongue.

"Aha," it said. "Come on through."

"Come with me," Keff said, in Ozran.

They walked down a short corridor. Two figures sat together in front of the great pictures of the outside. One of them rose and stared at him in horror and surprise.

The feeling was mutual.

"Magess Plennafrey!" Brannel, with one fearful glance at Keff, dropped to his knees and stared at the floor.

"It's okay, Brannel," Keff said, reassuringly, plucking at the worker male's upper arm. "We're all working together here."

"Hush, everyone," the other magess said in the tower's voice. "Here comes our diversion. I don't want the spies to pick up any sound from in here."

Carialle turned on a magnetic field in the airlock, strong enough to disable the spy-eyes, should any be bold enough to try to pass inside, but not enough to stop the servo. She slid the door upward. The low-slung robot rumbled imperturbably up the ramp and through the arch. In one slim, black, metal hand it held very carefully a single marsh flower.

Immediately, the spy-eyes thought they had their opportunity to storm the tower and zoomed after the servo. One hit the field before the others and clanked noisily to the ground, disabled. The over-the-air chatter became excited, and the other spheres reversed course at once, speeding away.

"That'll make them crazy," Carialle said. The first spy sphere rolled halfway down the ramp before its owner, on the other side of the continent, was able to take charge of it once again. As soon as it was airborne, it flitted off.

"Good riddance," Carialle said, and returned her attention to the situation inside the cabin.

Keff stood between Plennafrey and Brannel with his hands out. Brannel was on his feet, with his mutilated hands balled into fists by his sides. Plenna had both her long-fingered hands planted protectively on her belt buckle. The Ozrans were glaring at each other.

"Now, now," Keff said. "I need you both. Please, let's make peace here."

"You intend to explain to a worker what we are doing?" Plenna asked, appealing to Keff. "This one only has four fingers! You can give them directions, but they cannot understand detailed instructions or complicated situations."

Brannel, following the secondary dialect with evident difficulty, replied haltingly in that language, which surprised the magiwoman as much as his daring to speak out in her presence. "I *can* understand. Mage Keff has agreed to give me a chance to help. I will do whatever Mage Keff wants," he said staunchly.

Carialle made her image step forward. "Lady Plennafrey, you are suffering from a preconceived notion that all the people who have had the finger amputation are stupid. Brannel is the exception to almost any rule you can think of. He has superior intelligence for someone brought up with the hardships he suffered. I think he's far smarter than the favored few who live in the mountains with you mages. You're not that different. You belong to the same species," she said, reaching for an example, "like . . . like Keff and I do."

"You?" Plennafrey asked.

Almost amazed that such a thought had come from her own speakers, Carialle had to pause to consider the change of attitude she had undergone. Much of it was due to seeing the division of a single people on this world into masters and slaves. She now realized that it was counterproductive to separate herself from her parent community. Yes, she was different, but compared with everything else she and Keff encountered, the similarities were more important. Acknowledging her humanity at last felt right and proper. In spite of the way she always pictured herself, she knew inside the metal shell and the carefully protected nerve center was a human being. She felt warmed by the perception.

"Yes," she said, simply. "Me."

Keff beamed at her pillar. Her Lady Fair image beamed happily back at him. Plennafrey fumed visibly at the interplay. If Carialle was human, then the Ozran had a genuine rival. This, combined with her lover's liberal attitude toward the lower class, obviously dismayed the young woman. As she had proved before, she was resilient and adaptable. Plenna seemed to be considering Keff's point of view, but she thoroughly disapproved of Keff having another woman in his life. To disarm the magiwoman, Carialle made her image step back onto the wall. Plennafrey relaxed visibly.

"So I think you should understand that Brannel deserves an explanation if he is to help us."

"Well . . ." Plennafrey said

"I heard that some of the mages are descended from Brannel's kind of people," Keff said persuasively. "Isn't Asedow's mother one like that? I heard Potria call her a dray-face."

"That's true," Plenna said, nodding. "And he is intelligent. Not good at thinking things through, but intelligent." She smiled rue-fully at Keff. "I don't wish to make things harder for my people or for myself. I will cooperate."

"For what am I risking myself?" Brannel asked hoarsely, look-ing from one mage to another.

"For a sheaf of papers," Keff said. "I need to see them. Magess Plenna will describe them, and Carialle will create an image for you to see."

Brannel seemed unsatisfied. "And for me? For what am I risking myself?" he repeated.

"Ah," Keff said, enlightened. "Well, what's your price? What do you want?"

Plennafrey, losing her newfound liberalism, drew herself up in outrage. "You dare ask for a reward? Do the mages not give you food and shelter? This is just another task we have given you."

"We have those things, Magess, but we want knowledge, too!" Brannel said. Having begun, he was determined to put his case, even in the face of disapproval from an angry overlord though somehow he was begging now. "Mage Keff, I . . . I want to be a mage, too. For a tiny, small item of power I will help you. It does not need to be big, or very powerful, but I know I could be a good mage. I will earn my way along. That is all I have ever desired: to learn. Give me that, and I will give you my life." Keff saw the passion in the Noble Primitives eye and was prepared to agree.

"To give a four-finger power? No!" Plenna protested cutting him off.

"Not good for you, Brannel," Carialle said, emphatically, siding unexpectedly with Plennafrey. "Look what a mess your mages have made of this place using unlimited power. How about a better home, or an opportunity for a real education, instead?"

"What about redressing the balance of power, Cari?" Keff asked under his breath.

"It doesn't need redressing, it needs de-escalating," Carialle replied through her brawns mastoid implant. "Could this planet really cope with one more resentful mage wielding a wand? We still don't know what the power was for originally."

Brannel's long face wore a mulish expression. Carialle could picture him with donkey's ears laid back along his skull. He was not happy to be dictated to by the flat magess, nor was he comfortable being enlisted by a genuine magess.

"No one speaks of what went before this," he said. "The promises of mages to other than themselves always prove false. I served Klemay, and now he is dead. Who killed him? I know whoever kills is not always the newest overlord in a place."

Plenna's mouth dropped open. "How do you know that? You're uneducated. You've never been anywhere but here."

"You talk over our heads as if we aren't there," Brannel said flatly. "But I, *I* understand. Who? I wish to know, for if it was you, I cannot help."

Plennafrey looked stricken at the idea that she could willingly commit murder. Keff parted her hand.

"He doesn't know, Plenna," Keff said soothingly. "How could he? It was Ferngal," he told Brannel. "Chaumel said so last night."

"Yes, then," Brannel said eagerly, "I will do what you want. For my price."

"Impossible," Plenna said. "He is ignorant."

"Ignorance is curable," Keff said emphatically. "It wasn't part of his brain that was removed." He made a chopping motion at his hand. "He can learn. He's already proved that."

Brannel looked jealously at Plenna's long fingers. "But I cannot use the power items without help."

Carialle was immediately sorry Keff had mentioned the amputation. "Brannel, there's nothing that can be done about that now. Some of the other magimen use prosthetics—false fingers. You can, too."

"If we were home," Keff said thoughtfully, "surgery could be done to regrow the fingers." He glanced up to find Plenna gazing at him.

"I must see these wonders," Plenna said, moving closer. "Should I not come back with you? After all, you said you are here to learn about my people on behalf of your own. I can teach you all about Ozran and see your world. Someday we can come back here together." She laid one long hand on his arm.

"Uhhh, one thing at a time, Plenna," Keff said, his smile fixed on his face. Her touch sent tingles up his arm. Her scent and her lovely eyes pulled him toward her like a magnet, but the sudden thought of having a permanent relationship with her had never crossed his mind. Evidently, it had hers. He reproached himself that he should have thought of the consequences before he took her to bed. "Carialle, we may have a problem," he subvocalized.

"We *have* a problem," Carialle said aloud. "The eyes are back. They're circling around outside."

"Oh!" Plenna ran to the screen. "Nokias, Chaumel, and the other high mages. They are trying to decide what to do."

"Have they figured out that we're in here?" Keff asked.

"No," Plenna said, after listening for a moment. "All of their followers are still searching." Carialle confirmed it.

"Then we'd better make our move, pronto, if we want a chance at those papers," Keff said. "All that remains is for our agent here to agree to fetch them for us."

Brannel had been standing beside the console, listening to the three bare-skins talk. He folded his arms over his furry chest.

"I would do anything for you, Mage Keff, but such a chance comes only once to one such as myself. You asked me my price. I told you my heart's desire. Will you pay it?"

Keff appealed to Plennafrey.

"I think he deserves a chance."

Clearly uneasy, Plennafrey eyed the Noble Primitive. "If all goes well, I agree he will be worthy of an opportunity," she said slowly. "I do not know where to find him an object of power yet, but I *will* try."

"All right, Brannel? Magess Plennafrey will teach you how to use a power object. She'll be your teacher, so she will control what you do to a certain extent—but you'll have your chance. She'll also teach you other things an educated man needs to know. Agreed?"

"Agreed," Plennafrey said.

Brannel, his eyes shining, fell to his knees before the magiwoman. "Thank you, Magess."

"There may be no power left for anyone," Carialle reminded them. "If those power drops have been increasing in frequency over time, it may mean that whatever's powering the magic here on Ozran is finally running down."

"What do I look for?" Brannel asked meekly.

Following Plenna's instructions, Carialle created the holographic image of a sheaf of dusty documents, yellow with age, and rotated it so the Noble Primitive could see all sides.

"They are very fragile," Plenna said. "They could shiver to dust if you breathe on them."

"I will be careful, Magess, I promise."

"We're left with only one problem," Keff said. "How do we get Brannel to Plennafrey's stronghold?"

Carialle's Lady Fair image drew an impish smile. "It might be worth a try to count on one of those power drops. If we can attract everyone's attention again, I might be able to break loose when the lights go off. After all, I'm not dependent on the Core of Ozran."

I only need a moment. I can be set to launch at any second, and you'll have your diversion to teleport there in peace."

"How can we do that?" Keff asked, bemused.

"By letting them know where you are," Cari said. "You zoom outside and start the Wild Hunt all over. That will bring everyone here with a view-halloo, and if I'm right, overload the power lines. As soon as the tractor beam on my tail lets go, I'll take off and distract them away from you. I'll lead them on an orbit of Ozran while Brannel is getting your papers."

"Do you have enough fuel?" Keff asked.

"Enough for one try," Carialle said, showing an indicator of her tank levels, "or we may not have the wherewithal to get home. I burned a lot trying to break loose before. Don't fail me."

"Did I burst my heart in the effort I never would, fair lady," Keff said, kissing his hand to her. "We'll rendezvous here in two hours."

With a final reproachful glance at Carialle's image, Plenna took her place on her chariot Keff crouched behind her like the musher on a dogsled, and Brannel, hunched on hands and knees, clung to the back, white knuckles showing through the fur on his fingers.

"Ready, steady, go!" Carialle threw up the airlock door, and the chariot shot out the narrow passage.

"Yeeeee-haaaah!" Keff yelled as they zoomed over the Noble Primitives' cave. The spy-eyes froze in place.

Suddenly, the air was full of chariots. The mages in them looked here and there for Plennafrey, who was already kilometers away from Carialle.

"Look!" shouted Asedow, pointing with his whole arm, and the mob turned to follow them.

Chaumel blinked in, with Nokias and Ferngal alongside him. Like well-trained squadrons, the wings of mages fell in behind. Keff turned and thumbed his nose at them.

"Nyaah!" he shouted.

Two hundred bolts of red lightning shot from two hundred amulets and rods toward their backs. Plennafrey threw up a shield behind them, which deflected the force spectacularly off in all directions.

"If it's coming, its coming now," Carialle said in Keff's ear. "Building . . . building . . . now!"

"Hold tight!" Keff yelled, as the floor dropped out from under them when the power failed. Plennafrey's shoulders tensed under his hands, and Brannel moaned.

Shrieks and shouts echoed off the valley floor as the other mages were deprived of their power and fell helplessly earthward. Some were close enough to the ground to strike it before the blackout ended. One magess ended up sitting dazed, in the midst of broken pieces of chair, staring around in complete bewilderment.

As before, the power-free interval was brief, but it sufficed for Carialle to kick on her engines and break loose from her invisible bonds. With a roar and an elongating mushroom of fire, she was airborne. As one, the hundreds of mages swiveled in midair, ignoring Plennafrey and Keff, to pursue her. Her cameras picked up images of astonished and furious faces. Chaumel was hammering his chair arm.

"Catch me if you can!" she cried, and took off toward planetary north.

Another fifty meters, and Plennafrey transported them from Klemay's valley to an isolated peak. Brannel, a huddled bundle of knees and elbows at her feet, was silent. Keff thought the Noble Primitive was terrified until Brannel turned glowing eyes to them.

"Oh, Magess, I want to do *this*!" he exclaimed. "It would be the greatest moment of my life if I could make myself fly. I could never even imagine this out of a dream. I beg you to teach me *this first*."

Keff grinned at the worker male's enthusiasm. "I hope you'll feel as energetic when you find out how much work it is to do magic," he said.

"Oh, it feels so good to be free again!" said the voice in his ear. Carialle, knowing in advance where they were going, reconnected instantly with Keff's implants. "I have to keep slowing down so I don't lose my audience. They're such quitters! I've almost lost Potria twice."

"Any unwanted watchers out there, Cari?" Keff asked, pointing his finger so the ocular implants could see.

"No spy-eyes here yet," Carialle's voice said after a moment.

Plenna shot in over the balcony, which was a twin to the one at Chaumel's stronghold, and hovered a few centimeters above the gray tiles.

"I mustn't land, or the ley lines will indicate it," she said.

Brannel hopped off and dashed inside.

"Good luck!" Keff called after him. Plenna lifted the chair up and looped over the landing pad's edge to wait beneath the overhang.

Brannel felt the floor humming through his feet and forced himself to ignore it. The discomfort was a small price to pay for associating with mages and having them treat him as a friend, if not an equal. Even a true Ozran magess had been kind to him, and the promise Mage Keff had made him—! The knowledge put a spring in his step all along the corridor walled with painted tiles. At the green-edged door, he turned and put his hand on the latch.

"Ho, there!" Brannel turned. A tall fur-face with five fingers strode toward him. He had a strange, flat-nosed face, and his eyes turned up at the corners, but he was handsome, nearly as handsome as a mage. "You're a stranger. What do you think you're doing?"

"I have been sent by the magess," Brannel said, leaning toward the house servant with all the aggression of a fighter who has survived tough living conditions. The servant backed up a pace.

"Who? Which magess?" the servant demanded. He eyed Brannel's prominent jaw with disdain. "You're not one of us."

"Indeed I am not," Brannel said, drawing himself upward. "I am Magess Plennafrey's pupil."

That statement, and the casual use of the magess's name, shocked the house male rigid. His tilted eyes widened into circles.

Brannel, ignoring him, pushed through the door. The room was lined with hanging cloth pictures. He went to the fourth one from the door and felt behind it at knee level. Gently, he extracted from the hidden pocket a thick bundle. He forced himself to walk, not run, out the door, past the startled house male, down the hallway, and out onto the open balcony.

The chariot appeared suddenly at the edge of the low wall overlooking the precipice, startling him. Keff cheered as Brannel held up the packet and waved him onto the chair's end.

"Good man, Brannel! Where are you, Cari?" Mage Keff asked the air. "We're on our way back to the plain. Yes, I've got them! Cari, I can almost read these!"

The chair swept skyward once more. Now that his task was done and reward at hand, Brannel indulged himself in enjoying the view. One day, he would fly over the mountains like this on his own chariot. Wouldn't Alteis stare?

"Are those what they look like?" Carialle asked, from her position over the south pole.

"Yes! They're technical manuals from a starship," Keff said, gloating. "One of *our* starships. The language is human Standard, but old. Very old. Nine to twelve hundred years is my guess from the syntax. Please run a check through your memory in that time frame for," he held a trembling finger underneath the notation to make sure he was reading it correctly, "the CW-53 TMS *Bigelow*. See when it flew, and when it disappeared, because there certainly was never a record of its landing here."

Keff turned page after page of the fragile, yellowing documents, showing each leaf to the implants for Carialle to scan.

"This is precious and not very sturdy," he said. "If anything happens to it before I get there, at least we'll have a complete recording." The covers and pages had been extruded as a smooth-toothed and flexible but now crackling plastic. In a tribute to technology a thousand years old, the laser print lettering was perfectly black and legible. He wondered, glancing through it, what the original owners would have said if they could see to what purpose their record-keeping was being put.

"Are these documents good?" Plennafrey asked, over the rush of the wind.

"Better than good!" Keff said, leaning over to show her the ship's layout and classification printed on the inside front cover of the first folder. "These prove that you are the descendant of a starship crew from the Central Worlds who landed here a thousand years ago. You're a human, just like me."

"That makes everything wonderful!" Plennafrey said, clasping his wrist. "Then there will be no difficulty with us staying together. We might be able to have children."

Keff goggled. Without being insulting there was nothing he could do at the moment but kiss her shining face, which he did energetically.

"One thing at a time, Plenna," Keff said, going hastily back to his perusal of the folders. "Ah, there's a reference to the Core of Ozran. If I follow this correctly, yes . . . it's a device, passed on to them, not constructed by, the Old Ones, pictured overleaf." Keff turned the page to the solido. "Eyuch! Ug-*ly*!"

The Old Ones were indeed upright creatures of bilateral symmetry who could use the chairs reposing in Chaumel's art collection, but that was where their similarity to humanoids ended. Multi-jointed legs with backward-pointing knees depended from flat, shallow bodies a meter wide. They had five small eyes set in a row across their flat faces, which were dark green. Lank black tendrils on their cylindrical heads were either hair or antennae, Keff wasn't sure which from the description below.

"Erg," Keff said, making a face. "So now we know what the Old Ones looked like."

"Oh, yes," Brannel said, casually standing up on the back to look, as if he flew a hundred kilometers above the ground every day. "My father's father told us about the Old Ones. They lived in the mountains with the overlords many years past."

"How long ago?" Keff asked.

Brannel struggled for specifics, then shrugged. "The wooze-food makes our memories bad," he explained, his tone apologetic but his jaw set with frustration.

"Keff, something has to be done about deliberately retarding half the population," Carialle said seriously. "With the diet they're being forced to subsist on, Brannel's people could actually lose their capacity for rational thought in a few more generations."

"Aha!" Keff crowed triumphantly. "Tapes!" He plucked a sealed spool out of the back cover of one of the folders. "Compressed data, I hope, and maybe footage of our scaly friends. Can you read one of these, Carialle?"

"I can adapt one of my players to fit it, but I have no idea what format it's in," she said. "It could take time."

Keff wasn't listening. He was engrossed in the second folder's contents.

"Fascinating!" he said. "Look at this, Cari. The whole system of remote power manipulation comes from a worldwide weather-control system! So that's what the ley lines are for. They're electromagnetic sensors, reading the temperature and humidity all across Ozran. They were designed to channel energy to help produce rain or mist where it was needed. . . . Ah, but the Old Ones didn't build it. They either found it, or they met the original owners when they came to this planet. Sounds like they were cagey about that. The Old Ones adapted the devices to use the power to make it rain and passed them on to you," he told Plennafrey. "They were made by the Ancient Ones."

"The Ancient Ones," Plenna said, reverently, pulling the folder down so she could see it. "Are there images of them, too? None know what they looked like."

Keff thumbed through the log. "No. Nothing. Drat."

"Rain?" Brannel asked, reverently. "They could make it rain?"

"Weather control," Carialle said. "Now that does smack of an advanced technological civilization. Pity they're not still around. This planet is an incipient dust-bowl. Keff, I'm within fifty klicks of the rendezvous site. Beginning landing procedures . . . Uh-oh, power traces increasing in your general vicinity. Company!"

Keff heard cries of triumph and swiveled his head, looking for their source. A score of magimen, led by Potria and Chaumel, had just jumped in and were homing in on them along a northwest vector.

"They've found us!" Plenna exclaimed, her dark eyes wide. Keff stood upright and grasped the back of her chair.

The magiwoman started to weave her arms in complicated patterns. Brannel, realizing that he was in the firing line of a building spell, dropped flat. Plenna launched her sally and had the satisfaction of seeing three of the magimen clear the way. The rattling hiss of the spell as it missed its mark and vanished jarred Keff's bones.

"Can you teleport?" Keff asked, clinging to the chair's uprights.

"Someone is blocking me," Plenna said, forcing the words through her teeth. "I must fight, instead."

"You'd be a sitting duck in here anyway," Carialle interjected crisply, "because the tractor grabbed me again as soon as I touched down. Keep moving!"

Plenna didn't need Carialle's message relayed to her. She took evasive maneuvers like a veteran fighter, zigzagging over the pursuers' heads and diving between two so their red lightning bolts narrowly missed each other. Keff saw Potria's face as he passed. The golden magiwoman had abandoned her look of elegant boredom for a grim set. If her will or her marksmanship had been up to it, she would have spitted them all.

Contrarily, Chaumel seemed to enjoy toying with them. He shot his bolts, not so much to wound, but more as if he were seeing what Plennafrey would do to avoid them. He seemed to have observed that she wasn't spelling to kill, obviously a novelty among Ozran mages.

Plennafrey dived low into the valleys, defying the magifolk to chase her through the nooks and crannies of her own domain. Keff felt the crackle of dry branches brush his shoulders as she maneuvered her chair through a narrow passage and down into a concealed tunnel. While the others circled overhead squawking like crows, she flew through the mountain. Brannel's keening echoed off the moist stone walls. Just as swiftly, they emerged into day.

Keff thought they might have shaken off their pursuers, but he had reckoned without Chaumel's determination. The moment they cleared the tunnel mouth, the silver magiman was there in midair, winding nothingness around and around his hands. Brannel gasped and threw his hands over his head to protect it.

Plenna flattened her hands on her belt buckle, and a translucent bubble of force appeared around her.

"Oh, child." Chaumel grinned and flicked his fingers. The chair started to sink toward the ground.

"He made the force shield heavy!" Keff said "We're falling!"

Abandoning her defensive tactic at once, Plennafrey popped the sphere and threw a few of her own bolts at Chaumel. Almost lazily, the other gestured, and the lightning split around him, rocketing toward the horizon. He made up another bundle of power, which Plenna averted. She returned fire, sending a handful of toroid shapes that grew and grew until they could surround Chaumel's limbs and neck. Two made contact, then fell away as open arcs, snaring and taking the other rings with them.

A moment later, Potria and Asedow appeared.

"You found them!" Potria called. The pink-gold magess was jubilant. Plenna turned in her seat and fired a double-barrel of white spark lightning at her. Potria shrieked when her fine clothes and skin were burned by some of the hot sparks. At once she retaliated, weaving a web with missiles of force around the edge that propelled it toward the younger magess.

Asedow chose that moment to drive in at them from the other side. His methods were not as smooth as his rival's. He produced a steady stream of smoky puffs that hung in the air like mines until Plennafrey, trying to avoid Potria's web, was forced back into them.

Keff was nearly shaken off when the first exploded against his back. Plennafrey turned her chair in midair, seeking to steer her way clear of the obstacles. No matter how she turned, she collided with another, and another. By then, Potria's web had struck.

All around him Keff felt rolls of silk fabric, invisible and magnetic, drawing him in, surrounding him, then smothering his nose and mouth. As the spell established itself, it threatened to draw every erg of energy out of his body through his skin. He gasped, clawing with difficulty at his throat. He was suffocating in the middle of thin air. Plennafrey, her slender form slumped partway over one chair arm, her skin turning blue, still fought to free them, her hands drawing primrose fire out of her belt buckle. Her will proved mightier than the other female's magic. The sunlight flames consumed the air around her, then caught on the veils of web clinging to Keff and Brannel, turning them into insubstantial black ash. She was about to set them all free when they were overcome by dozens and dozens of bolts of scarlet lightning, striking at them from every direction.

As Keff lost consciousness, he heard Potria and Asedow shrilling at each other again over who would take possession of him and his ship. He vowed he would die before he would let anyone take Carialle.

A sharp scent introduced itself under his nose. Unwittingly, he took a deep breath and recoiled, choking. He batted at the bad smell, but nothing solid was there.

"You're awake," a voice said. "Very good."

With difficulty, Keff opened his eyes. Things around him began to take focus. He lay on his back in the main cabin of his ship. Beside him was Plennafrey, also in the throes of regaining consciousness. Brannel lay in a motionless heap under Plenna's feet. And leaning over Keff with a distorted expression of solicitousness was Chaumel.

✳CHAPTER ELEVEN

Carialle fought against the blackness that abruptly surrounded her, refusing to believe in it. Between one nanopulse and the next, Chaumel had appeared in the main cabin, past the protective magnetic wall she had set up, and stood gloating over the contents of a captive starship. Outraged at the invasion, Carialle set up the same multi-tone shriek she used on Brannel to try and drive him out. Chaumel threw up protective hands, but not over his ears.

Suddenly she could move nothing and all her visual receptors were down. She could still hear, though. The taunting voice boomed hollowly in her aural inputs, continuing his inventory and interjecting an occasional comment of self-congratulation.

She spoke then, pleading with him not to leave her in the dark. The voice paused, surprised, then Carialle felt hands running over her: impossible, insubstantial hands penetrating through her armor, brushing aside her neural connectors and yet not detaching them.

"My, my, what are you?" Chaumel's voice asked.

"Restore my controls!" Carialle insisted. "You don't know what you're doing!"

"How very interesting all of this is," he was saying to someone. "In my wildest dreams I could never have imagined a man who was also a machine. Incredible! But it isn't a man, is it?" The hands drew closer, passed over and *through* her. "Why, no! It is a woman. And what interesting things she has at her command. I must see *that*."

Invisible fingers took her multi-camera controls away from her nerve endings, leaving them teasingly just out of reach. She sensed her life-support system starting and stopping as Chaumel played with it, using his TK. She felt a rush of adrenaline as he upset the balance of her chemical input, and was unable to access the endorphins to counteract them. Then the waste tube began to back up toward the nutrient vat. She felt her delicate nervous system react against pollution by becoming drowsy and logy.

"Stop!" she begged. "You'll kill me!"

"*I* won't kill you, strange woman in a box," Chaumel said, his voice light and airy, "but I will not risk having you break away from my control again as you did when the magic dropped. What a chase you led us! Right around Ozran and back again. You made a worthy quarry, but one grows tired of games."

"Keff!"

"I'm here, Carialle," the brawn's voice came, weak but furious. Carialle could have sung her relief. She heard the shuffling of feet, and a crash. Keff spoke again through soughing pain. "Chaumel, we'll cooperate, but you have to let her alone. You don't understand what you're doing to her."

"Why? She breathes, she eats—she even hears and speaks. I just control what she sees and does."

For a brief flash, Carialle had a glimpse of the control room. Keff and the silver magiman faced one another, the Ozran very much in command. Keff was clutching his side as if cradling bruised ribs. Plenna stood behind Keff, erect and very pale. Brannel, disoriented, huddled in a corner beside Keff's weight bench. Then the image was gone, and she was left with the enveloping darkness. She couldn't restrain a wail of despair.

It was as if she were reliving the memory of her accident again for Inspector Maxwell-Corey. All over again! The helplessness she hoped never again to experience: sensory deprivation, her chemicals systems awry, her controls out of reach or disabled. *This time,* the results would be worse, because *this time* when she went mad, her brawn would be within arm's reach, listening.

Swallowing against the pain in his ribs, Keff threw himself at Chaumel again. With a casual flick of his hand, Chaumel once more sent him flying against the bulkhead. Plennafrey ran to his side and hooked her arm in his to help him stand.

"You might as well stop that, stranger," Chaumel advised him. "The result will be the same any time you try to lay hands on me. You will tire before I do."

"You don't know what you're doing to her!" Keff said, dragging himself upright. He dashed a hand against the side of his mouth. It came away streaked with blood from a split lip.

"Ah, yes, but I do. I see pictures," Chaumel said, with a smile playing about his lips as his eyes followed invisible images. "No, not pictures, *sounds* that haunt her mind, distinct, never far from her conscious thoughts—tapping." The speakers hammered out a distant, slow, sinister cadence.

Carialle screamed, deafeningly. Keff knew what Chaumel was doing, exercising the same power of image-making he had used on Keff to intrude on his consciousness. Against this particular illusion Carialle *had* no mental defenses. To dredge up the long-gone memories of her accident coupled with Chaumel's ability to keep her bound in place and deprive her of normal function might rob her of her sanity.

"Please," Keff begged. "*I* will cooperate. I'll do anything you want. Don't toy with her like that. You're harming her more than you could understand. Release her."

Chaumel sat down in Keff's crash couch, hands folded lightly together. Swathed in his gleaming robes, he looked like the master of ceremonies at some demonic ritual.

"Before I lift a finger and free my prisoner"—he leveled his very long first digit at Keff—"I want to know who you are and why you are here. You didn't make the entire overlordship of this planet fly circuits for amusement. Now, what is your purpose?"

Keff, knowing he had to be quick to save Carialle's sanity, abandoned discretion and started talking. Leaving out names and distances, he gave Chaumel a precis of how they had chosen Ozran, and how they traveled there.

" . . . We came here to study you just as I told you before. That's the truth. In the midst of our investigations we've discovered imbalances in the power grid all of you use," Keff said. "Those imbalances are proving dangerous directly to you, and indirectly to your planet."

"You mean the absences that occur in the ley lines?" Chaumel said, raising his arched eyebrows. "Yes, I noticed how you took advantage of that last lapse. Very, very clever."

"Keff! They're crawling over my skin," Carialle moaned. "Tearing away my nerve endings. Stop them!"

"Chaumel . . ."

"All in good time. She is not at risk."

"You're wrong about that," Keff said sincerely, praying the magiman would listen. "She suffered a long time ago, and you are making her live it over."

"And so loudly, too!" Chaumel flicked his fingers, and Carialle's voice faded. Keff had the urge to run to her pillar, throw himself against it to feel whether she was still alive in there. He wanted to reassure her that he was still out there. She wasn't alone! But he had to fight this battle sitting still, without fists, without epee, hoping his anxiety didn't show on his face, to convince this languid tyrant to free her before she went mad.

"I've discovered something else that I think you should know," Keff said, speaking quickly. "Your people are not native to Ozran."

"Oh, that I knew already," Chaumel said, with his small smile. "I am a historian, the son of historians, as I told you when you . . . visited me. Our legends tell us we came from the stars. As soon as I saw you, I knew that your people are our brothers. What do you call our race?"

"Humans," Keff said quickly, anxious to get the magiman back on track of letting go of Carialle's mind. "The old term for it was 'Homo sapiens' meaning the 'wise man.' Now, about Carialle . . ."

"And you also wish to tell me that our power comes from a mechanical source, not drawn mystically from the air as some superstitious mages may believe. That I also knew already." He looked at Plennafrey. "When I was your age, I followed my power to its source. I know more than the High Mages of the Points about whence our connection comes to the Core, but I kept my knowledge to myself and my eyes low, having no wish to become a target." Modestly, he dropped his gaze to the ground.

If he was looking for applause, he was performing for the wrong audience. Keff lunged toward Chaumel and pinned his shoulders against the chair back.

"While you're sitting here so calmly bragging about yourself," Keff said in a clear, dangerous voice, "my partner is suffering unnecessary and possibly permanent psychic trauma."

"Oh, very well," Chaumel said, imperturbably, closing his hand around the shaft of his wand as Keff let him go. "What you are saying is more amusing. You will tell me more, of course, or I will pen her up again."

Sight and sensation flooded in all at once. Carialle almost sobbed with relief, but managed to regain her composure within seconds. To Keff, whose sympathetic face was close to her pillar camera, she said, "Thank you, sir knight. I'm all right. I promise," but she sensed that her voice quavered. Keff looked skeptical as he caressed her pillar and then resumed his seat.

"Keff says that our power was supposed to be used to make it rain," Plenna said. "Is this why the crops fail? Because we use it for other things?"

"That's right," Keff said. "If you're using the weather technology as you have been, no wonder the system is overloading. Whenever a new mage rises to power, it puts that much more of a strain on the system."

"You have some proof of this?" Chaumel asked, narrowing his eyes.

"We have evidence from your earliest ancestors," Keff said.

"Ah, yes," Chaumel said raising the notebooks from his lap. "These. I have been perusing them while waiting for you to wake up. Except for a picture of the inside of an odd stronghold and an image of the Old Ones, I cannot understand it."

"I can only read portions of it without my equipment," Keff said. "The language in it is very old. Things have changed since your ancestors and mine parted company."

"It's a datafile from the original landing party," Carialle said. "That much we can confirm. Humans came to Ozran on a starship called the TMS *Bigelow* over nine hundred years ago."

"And where did you get this . . . datafile?"

"It's mine!" Plenna said stoutly. She started forward to reclaim her property, but Chaumel held a warning hand toward Carialle's pillar. With a glance at Keff's anxious face, Plenna stopped where she stood.

"Yours?" The silver magiman looked her over with new respect. "I didn't think you had it in you to keep a deep secret, least of magesses. Your father, Rardain, certainly never could have."

Plenna reacted with shame to any mention of her late father. "He didn't know about it. I found it in an old place after he . . . died."

"Does that matter?" Keff said, stepping forward and putting a protective arm around Plenna's waist. The tall girl was quaking. "We're trying to head off what could become a worldwide disaster, and you're preventing us from finding out more about the problem."

"And this 'datafile' will tell you what to do?" Chaumel was delicately skeptical.

Carialle manifested her Lady Fair image on the wall. After a momentary double take, Chaumel accepted it and occasionally made eye contact with it.

"Given time, I can try to read the tapes," Carialle said. "In the meantime, Keff can translate the hard copy."

Chaumel settled back. "Good. We have all the time you wish. The curtain you set about this place will prevent the others from finding us. In a little while they will be tired of chasing shadows and go home. That will leave us without disturbance."

"Can I use my display screens?"

The stiver magiman was gracious. "Use anything you wish. You can't go anywhere."

Grumbling at Chaumel's make-yourself-at-home attitude, Carialle spent a few minutes re-establishing the chemical balances in her system. Two full extra cycles of the waste-disposal processor, and her bloodstream was clear of everything but what belonged there. She increased the flow of nutrients and gratefully felt the adrenaline high fade away.

She assessed the size of the tape cassette Keff held up and noted that there was one place for a spindle on the small, airtight capsule. Two of her input bays were made to take tapes as well as datahedrons. Carialle rolled the capstan and spindle forward from the rear wall of the player, narrowed the niche so the tape wouldn't wobble, then opened the door.

"Ready," she said.

"Here goes nothing at all," Keff said, and slid the tape in.

Carialle closed the door. As she engaged the spindle, the cassette popped open, revealing the tape, and letting go a puff of air. Carialle, who had been expecting just that, captured the trace of the thousand-year-old atmosphere in a lab flask and carried it away through the walls to analyze its contents.

Slowly, she rolled the tape against the heads, comparing the scan pattern produced on her wave-form monitor with thousands of similar patterns.

"Can you read it?" Keff asked.

"We'll see," Carialle said "There are irregularities in the scan, which I attribute to poor maintenance of the recording device that produced it. Of all the lazy skivers, why did one have to be recording this most important piece of history? It would have been no trouble at all to keep their machinery in good repair, damn their eyes."

"Did you want it to be easy, lady fair? Do you know, I just realized I'm hungry," Keff announced, turning to the others. "Plenna, we've had nothing since last night, and damned little then. May I buy you lunch?"

The magiwoman turned her eyes toward him with relief. Her face was beginning to look almost hollow from strain.

"Oh, that would be very nice," she said thinly. A timid croak from the side of the weight bench reminded him Brannel was still with them. He was hungry, too.

"Right. Three coming up. Chaumel?"

"No, very kindly, no," the silver magiman said, waving a hand, although keeping an eye on him that was anything but casual. Keff gave instructions to the synthesizer, and in moments removed a tray with three steaming dishes.

"Very simple: meat, potatoes, vegetables, bread," Keff said, pointing the food out to his guests.

"Hold it, Keff," Carialle said. "I don't trust our captor." Keff aimed his optical implants at each plate in turn. "Uh-huh. Just checking."

"Thank you, lady dear. I count on your assistance," Keff said subvocally. Placing the first plate on its tray in Plenna's lap, he handed the second filled dish and fork to Brannel before he settled on the weight bench to enjoy his own meal.

Brannel was still staring at the divided plate when Keff turned back.

"What's the matter?" Keff asked. "It's good. A little heavy on the carbohydrates, perhaps, but that won't spoil the taste."

Wordlessly, Brannel turned fearful eyes up to him.

"Ah, I see," Keff said, intuiting the problem. "Should I try some first to show you it's all right? We're all eating the same thing. Would you like my dinner instead?"

"No, Mage Keff," Brannel said after a moment, glancing wild-eyed at Chaumel, "I trust you."

If he had any misgivings, one taste later the worker was hunched over his lunch, shoveling in mouthfuls inexpertly with his fork. He probably would have growled at Keff if he had tried to take it away. In no time the dish was empty.

"You packed that away in a hurry. Would you like another plate? It's no trouble."

Eyes wide with hope, Brannel nodded. He looked guilty at being so greedy, but more fascinated that "another plate" was no trouble. As soon as the second helping was in his hands, he began wolfing it down.

"Huh! Crude," Chaumel said, fastidiously disregarding the male. "Well, if you want to keep pets . . ."

Brannel didn't seem to hear the senior mage. He sucked a stray splash of gravy off his hairy fingers and scraped up the last of the potatoes.

"How's my supply of synth, Cari?" Keff asked, teasingly. The worker stopped in the middle of a mouthful. "I'm teasing you, Brannel," he said. "We're carrying enough food to supply one man for two years—or one of you for six months. Don't worry. We're friends."

Plenna ate more sedately. She smiled brightly once at Keff to show she enjoyed the food. Keff patted her hand.

"Bingo!" Carialle said, triumphantly. "Got you. Gentlemen and madam, our feature presentation."

A wow, followed by the hiss of low-level audio, issued from her main cabin speakers. Carialle diverted her main screen to the video portion of the tape. On it, a distant, spinning globe appeared.

"The scan is almost vertical across the width of the tape," Carialle explained. "Very densely packed. You could measure the speed in millimeters per second, so where glitches appear there's no backup scan. Because this was done on a magnetic medium, some is irrevocably lost, though not much. I have filled in where I could. This is not the full, official log. I think it was a personal record kept by a biologist or an engineer. You'll see what I mean in the content."

The tape showed several views of Ozran from space, including technical scans of the continents and seas. Loud static accompanied the glitches between portions. Carialle found the technology was as primitive as stone knives and bearskins compared to her state-of-the-art equipment, but she was able to read between the

lines of scan. She put up her findings on a side screen for the others
to read.

"Looks like a damned fine prospect for a colony," Keff said,
critically assessing the data as if it were a new planet he was
approaching. "Atmosphere very much like that of Old Earth."

"Ureth," Plennafrey breathed, her eyes bright with awe.

Keff smiled. "Uh-huh, I see why they made planetfall. Their
telemetry was too basic. We wouldn't miss above-ground buildings and the signs of agriculture from space, no matter how slight,
but they did. Hence, first contact was made."

The *Bigelow*'s complement had been four hundred and fifty-two,
all human. Keff fancied he could see a family resemblance to the
flamboyant Mage Omri in the dark-skinned captain's face.

Chaumel lost his veneer of sophistication when the first Old
One appeared on screen. He stared at it open-mouthed. Keff, too,
was amazed by the alien being, but he could appreciate that, to
Chaumel, it was analogous to the gods of Mount Olympus visiting Athens.

"I have never seen anything like them. Have you, Carialle?"

"No, and neither has Xeno," Cari said, running a hasty crossmatch through her records. "I wonder where they came from?
Somewhere else in R sector? Tracing an ion trail at this late date
would be impossible."

What could not have been indicated by the still image in the
folders which Keff has seen was that each of the alien's five eyes
could move independently. The flat bodies were faintly amusing,
like the pack of card-men in *Through the Looking-Glass.* The tapes
compressed many of the early meetings with the host species, as
they showed the crew of the *Bigelow* around their homes, introduced them to their offspring, and demonstrated some of the
wonders of their seemingly inexplicable manipulation of power.

The Old Ones had obviously once had a thriving civilization.
By the time the crew of the *Bigelow* arrived, they were reduced
to two small segments of population: the number who lived sin-
gly in the mountains and the communal bands who tilled the valley
soil. Being few, they hadn't put much of a strain on the available
resources, but it wasn't a viable breeding group, either.

Keff listened to the diarist's narration and repeated what he could
understand into IT for the benefit of the Ozrans.

The narrator described the Old Ones and how happy they were

to have the humans come to live with them. He's talking about ugly skills possessed—no, fabulous skills possessed by these ugly aliens, who promised to share what they knew. Whew, that is an old dialect of Standard."

An Old One was persuaded to say a few words for the camera. It pressed its frightful face close to the video pickup and aimed three eyes at it. The other two wandered alarmingly.

"I can understand what it says," Chaumel said, too fascinated to sound boastful. "How it speaks is what we now call the linga esoterka. 'How joy find strangejoy find strange two-eyes folk,' is what this one says."

"He's pleased to meet you," Keff said with a grin. He directed IT to incorporate Chaumel's translation into his running lexicon of the second dialect of Ozran. "It sounds as though a good deal of Old One talk was incorporated into a working language, a gullah, used by the humans and Old Ones to communicate."

The mystical sign language Keff had observed was also in wide usage among the green indigenes, but the narrator of the tape hadn't yet observed its significance. Keff could feel Carialle's video monitors on him, as if to remind him of the times that IT ignored somatic signals. He grinned over his shoulder at her pillar. This time, IT was coming through like the cavalry.

"So that is where the expression 'to look in many directions at once' comes from," Chaumel said excitedly. "We cannot, but the Old Ones could."

In his corner, Brannel was hanging on to every word. Keff realized that his three guests comprehended far more of the alien languages than he could. The two mages chimed in cheerfully when the Old Ones spoke, giving the meaning of gestures and words in the common Ozran tongue, which Keff knew now was nothing more than a dialect of Human Standard blended with the Old Ones' spoken language. Somewhat ruefully, he observed that, with Carialle's enhanced cognitive capacity, he, the xenolinguist, was the one who would retain the least of what was going by on the screen. Carialle signaled for Keff's attention when a handful of schematics flashed by.

"Your engineer identifies those microwave beams that have been puzzling me," she said. "They're the answerback to the command function from the items of power telling the Core of Ozran how much power to send. Each operates on a slightly different frequency, like personal communicators. The Core also feeds the devices themselves. Hmm, slight risk of radioactivity there." One of Carialle's auxiliary screens lit with an exploded view of one of the schematics. "But I haven't seen any signs of cancers. In spite of their faults, Ozrans are a healthy bunch, so it must be low enough to be harmless."

Another compression of time. In the next series of videos, the humans had established homes for themselves and were producing offspring. Some, like the unknown narrator, had entered into apprenticeships to learn the means of using the power items from the Old Ones. The rest lived in underground homes on the plains.

"Hence the division of Ozrans into two peoples," Keff said, nodding. "It's hard to believe this is the same planet."

The video changed to views of burgeoning fields and broad, healthy croplands. Ozran soil evidently suited Terran-based plant life. The narrator aimed his recorder at adapted skips full of grain and vegetables being hauled by domesticated six-packs. The next scene, which made the Ozrans gasp with pleasure, showed the humans and one or two Old Ones hurrying for shelter in a farm cavern as a cloudburst began. Heavy rain pelted down into the fields of young, green crops.

In the next scene, almost an inevitable image, one proud farmer was taped standing next to a prize gourd the size of a small pig. Other humans were congratulating him.

Keff glanced at the Ozrans. All three were spellbound by the images of lush farmland.

"These cannot be pictures of our world," Plenna said, "but those are the Mountains of the South. I've known them since my childhood. I have never seen vegetables that big!"

"It is fiction," Chaumel said, frowning. "Our farms could not possibly produce anything like that giant root."

"They could once," Carialle said, "a thousand years ago. Before you mages started messing up the system you inherited. Please observe."

She showed the full analysis of the puff of air that had been trapped in the tape cassette. Keff read it and nodded. He understood where Carialle was headed.

"This shows that the atmosphere in the early days of human habitation of Ozran had many more nitrogen/oxygen/carbon chains and a far higher moisture content than the current atmosphere

does." Another image overlaid the first. "Here is what you're breathing now. You have an unnaturally high ozone level. It increases
every time there is a massive call for power from the Core of Ozran.
If you want more . . ."

In the middle of the cabin Carialle created a three-dimensional
image of Ozran. "This is how your planet was seen from space
by your ancestors." The globe browned. Icecaps shrank slightly. The
oceans nibbled away at coastline and swamped small islands. The
continents appeared to shrink together slightly in pain. "This is
how it looks now."

Plenna hugged herself in concern as Ozran changed from a
healthy green planet to its present state.

"And what for the future?" she asked, woebegone eyes on
Carialle's image.

"All is not lost, Magess. Let me show you a few other planets
in the Central Worlds cluster," Carialle said, putting up the image
of an ovoid, water-covered globe studded with small, atoll-shaped
land masses. "Kojuni was in poor condition from industrial pollution. It took an effort, but its population reclaimed it." The sky
of Kojuni lightened from leaden gray to a clear, light silver. "Even
planet Earth had to fight to survive." A slightly flattened spher-
oid of blue, green, and violet spun among them. The green masses
on the continents receded and expanded as Carialle compressed
centuries into seconds. For additional examples, she showed several Class-M planets in good health, with normal weather patterns
of wind, rain, and snow scattering across their faces. The three-
dimensional maps faded, leaving the image of present-day Ozran
spinning before them.

Chaumel cleared his throat.

"But what do you say is the solution?" he asked.

"You overlords have got to stop using the power," Keff said. "It's
as simple as that."

"Give up power? Never!" Chaumel said, outraged, with the same
expression he would have worn if Keff had told him to cut off
his right leg. "It is the way we are."

"Mage Keff." Brannel, greatly daring, crept up beside them and
spoke for the first time, addressing his remarks only to the brawn.
"What you showed of the first New Ones and their kind—that
is what the workers of Klemay have been trying to do for as long
as I have lived." He looked at Plenna and Chaumel. "We know

plants can grow bigger. Some years they do. Most die or stay small. But I know—"

"Quiet!" Chaumel roared, springing to his feet. Brannel was driven cowering into the corner. "Why are you letting a fur-face talk?" the silver mage demanded of Keff. "You can see by his face he knows nothing."

"Now, look, Chaumel," Keff said, aiming an admonitory finger at him, "Brannel is intelligent. Listen to him. He has something that no other farmer on your whole world does: a working memory—and that's your fault, you and your fellow overlords. You've mutated them, you've mutilated them, but they're still human. Don't you understand what you saw on the tape? Brannel knows when, and probably *why* your crops have failed, so let the man talk."

Brannel was gratified that Mage Keff stuck up for him. So he gathered courage and tried, haltingly, in the face of Chaumel's disapproval, to describe the failed efforts of years. "We seek to feed the earth so it will burgeon like this—I know it could—but every time, the plants either die or the cold and dryness come back when the mages have battles. The farms could feed us so much better, if there was more water, if it was warmer. Of the crops"—he held up all eight of his digits—"this many do not survive." He folded down five fingers.

"You're losing over sixty percent of your yield because you like to live high," Keff said. "Your superfluous use of power, to show off, to play, to *kill*, is irresponsible. You're killing your world. One day your farms won't be able to sustain themselves. People will die of starvation. No matter what you think of their mental capacity, you couldn't want that because then you'd have no food and no one to do the menial labor you require."

Chaumel looked from Keff's grim face to the spinning globe of Ozran, and sat down heavily in the crash couch.

"We *are* doing that," he said, raising his long hands in surrender. "Everything he says, he knows. But if I lay down my items of power to help, my surrender will not stop all the others, nor will appealing to wisdom. We mages distrust each other too much."

"Then we need to negotiate a mass cease-fire," Carialle said.

"Not without a ready alternative," Chaumel returned promptly. "Our system is steeped in treachery and the counting of coup."

"I found references to that, too," Keff said, consulting a page of the first manual. "Somebody made a bad translation for your forefathers of instructions given to officers seeking promotion. It says 'consideration for continued higher promotion will be given to those individuals who complete the most successful projects in the most efficient manner.' It goes on to say that those projects should benefit the whole community, but I guess that part got lost over time. There's a similar clause in our ship's manual, just in updated language."

Chaumel groaned.

"Then all this time we have been making an enormous mistake." He appealed to Keff and the image of Carialle. "I didn't know that we were acting on bad information. All my life I thought I was following the strictures of the First Ones. I sought to be worthy of my ancestors. I am ashamed."

Keff realized that Chaumel was genuinely horrified. By his own lights, the silver mage was an honorable man.

"Well," Keff said, slowly, "you can start to put things right by helping us."

Chaumel chopped a hand across.

"Your ship is free. What else do you want me to do?"

"Seek out the Core of Ozran and find out what it was really meant to do, what its real capacity is," Carialle said at once. "It's possible, although I think unlikely, that you can retain some of your current lifestyle, but if you are serious about wanting to rescue your planet and future generations—"

"Oh, I am," Chaumel said "I will give no more trouble."

"Then it's time to redirect the power to its original purpose, as conceived by the Ancient Ones: weather control."

"But what shall we do about the other mages?" Plennafrey asked.

"If we can't convince 'em," Carialle said, "I think I can figure out how to disable them, based on what our long-gone chronicler said about answerback frequencies. With a little experimentation, I can block specific signals, no matter how tight a wave band they're broadcast on. The others will learn to live on limited power, or none at all. It's their choice."

"We'd employ that option," Keff said quickly when he saw Chaumel's reaction, "only if there is no other way to persuade them to cooperate."

"And that is where I come in," Chaumel said, smiling for the first time. "I am held in some esteem on Ozran. I will use my influence to negotiate, as you say, a widespread mutual surrender. With the help of the magical pictures you will show us"—he bowed to Carialle's image—"we will persuade the others to see the wisdom in returning to the ways of the Ancient Ones. We must not fail. The size of that gourd . . ." he said shaking his head in gently mocking disbelief.

"I still think you're wrong to leave Brannel behind," Keff argued as Plenna lofted him over the broad plains toward Chaumel's stronghold.

"It is better that only we three, with the aid of Carialle and her illusion-casting, seek to convince the mages," the silver magiman said imperturbably. He sat upright in his chariot, hands folded over his belly.

"But why not Brannel? I'm not a native. I can't explain things in a way your people will understand."

Chaumel shook his head, and pitched his voice to carry over the wind. "My fellows will have enough difficulty to believe in a woman who lives inside a wall. They will not countenance a smart four-finger. Come, we must discuss strategy! Tell me again what it said about promotion in the documents. I must memorize that."

The chariots flew too far away even to be seen on the magic pictures. Brannel, left alone in the main cabin, felt awkward at being left out but dared not, in the face of Chaumel's opposition, protest. He remained behind, haunting the ship like a lonely spirit.

The flat magiwoman appeared on the wall beside him, and paced beside him as he walked up and back.

"I don't know when they'll be coming back," Carialle said very gently, surprising him out of his thoughts. "You should go now. Keff will come and get you when he returns."

"But, Magess," Brannel began, then halted from voicing the argument that sprang to his tongue. After all, this time she was not driving him away with painful sounds, but he was unhappy at being dismissed whenever the overlords had no need of him. After all the talk of equality and the promise of apprenticeship following his great risk-taking in Magess Plennafrey's stronghold, he, the simple worker, was once more ignored and forgotten. He sighed.

"Now, Brannel." The picture of the woman smiled. "You'll be missed in the cavern if you don't go. True?"

"True."

"Then come back when you've finished your work for the day. You can keep me company while I'm running the rest of the tapes." The voice was coaxing. "You'll see them before Magess Plenna and Chaumel. How about that as an apology for not sending you out with the others?"

Brannel brightened slightly. It would be hard to return to daily life after his brush with greatness. But he nodded, head held high. He had much to think about.

"Oh, and Brannel," Carialle said. The flat magess was kind. She gestured toward the food door which opened. A plate lay there. "The bottom layer is soft bread. You can roll the rest up in it. We call it a 'sandwich.'"

He walked down the ship's ramp with the "sandwich" of mage-food cradled protectively between his hands. The savory smell made his mouth water, even though it hadn't been long since he had eaten his most delicious lunch. How he would explain his day's absence to Alteis Brannel didn't yet know, but at least he would do it on a full belly. Associating with mages was most assuredly a mixed blessing.

"Why not relax?" Chaumel said, leaning back at his ease in a deeply carved armchair that bobbed gently up and down in the air. "He will come or he will not. I shall ask the next prospect and we'll collect High Mage Nokias later. Sit down! Relax! I will pour us some wine. I have a very good vintage from the South."

Keff stopped his pacing up and back in the great room of Chaumel's stronghold. Chaumel had decided on the first mage to whom he would appeal, and sent a spy-eye with the discreet invitation. Evening had fallen while the three of them waited to see if Nokias would accept. The holographic projection table from the main cabin was set up in the middle of the room. He went over to touch it, making sure it was all right. Plennafrey watched him. The young magiwoman sat in an upright chair in her favorite place by the curtains, hands folded in her lap.

"It's important to get this right," Keff said.

"I know it," Chaumel said. "I am cognizant of the risks. I may enjoy my life as it is, but I love my world, and I want it to continue after I'm gone. You may find it difficult to convince my fellows of that. I achieve nothing by worrying about what they will say before I have even asked the question. The evidence speaks for itself."

"But what if they don't believe it?'

"You leave the rest to me," Chaumel said. He snapped his fingers and a servitor appeared bearing a tray holding a wine bottle and a glass. He poured out a measure of amber liquid and offered it to Keff. The brawn shook his head and resumed pacing. With a shrug, Chaumel drank the wine himself.

"All clear and ready to go," Carialle said through Keff's implant.

"*Receiving*," Keff said, testing his lingual transmitter, and let it broadcast to the others.

"I have pinpointed the frequencies of all of Chaumel's and Plennafrey's items of power, including their chariots. They're all within a very narrow wave band. Will you ask Plenna to try manipulating something, preferably not dangerous or breakable?"

Plenna, grateful for something to do to interrupt the waiting, was happy to oblige.

"I shall use my belt to make my shoe float," Plenna said, taking off her dainty primrose slipper and holding it aloft. She stepped away, leaving it in place in midair.

"But you're not touching the belt," Keff said. "I've noticed the others do that, too."

Plenna laughed, a little thinly, showing that she, too, was nervous about the coming confrontation. "For such a small thing, concentrating is enough."

"Here goes," Carialle said.

Without fanfare, the shoe dropped to the ground.

"Hurrah!" Keff cheered

"That is impossible," Plenna said. She picked it up and replaced it, this time with her hand under her long sash.

"Do it again, Cari!"

Carialle needed a slightly more emphatic burst of static along the frequency, but it broke the spell. The shoe tumbled to the floor. Plennafrey put it back on her foot.

"No answerback, no power," Carialle said simply, in Keff's ear. "Now all I have to do is be open to monitor the next magiman's power signals and I can interrupt *his* spells, too. I'm only afraid that with such narrow parameters, there might be spillover to another item I don't want to shut off. I'm tightening up tolerances as much as I can."

"Good job, Cari," Keff said. He smacked his palms together and rubbed them.

"You are very cheerful about the fall of a shoe," Chaumel said.

"It may be the solution to any problems with dissenters," Keff said.

A flash of gold against the dark sky drew their attention to the broad balcony visible through the tall doors. Nokias materialized alone above Chaumel's residence and alighted in the nearest spot to the door. As their message had bidden him, he had arrived discreetly, without an entourage. Chaumel rose from his easy chair and strode out to greet his distinguished guest.

"Great Mage Nokias! You honor my poor home. How kind of you to take the trouble to visit. I regret if my message struck you as anything but a humble request."

Nokias's reply was inaudible. Chaumel continued in the same loud voice, heaping compliments on the Mage of the South. Keff and Plenna hid behind the curtained doors and listened. Plenna suppressed a giggle.

"Laying it on thick, isn't he?" Keff whispered. The girl had to cover her mouth with both hands not to let out a trill of amusement.

Nokias mellowed under Chaumel's rain of praise and entered the great hall in expansive good humor.

"Why the insistence on secrecy, old friend?" the high mage asked, slapping Chaumel on the back with one of his huge hands.

"There was a matter that I could discuss only with you, Nokias," Chaumel said. He beckoned toward the others' place of concealment.

Keff stepped out from the curtains, pulling Plenna with him.

"Good evening, High Mage," he said, bowing low. Nokias's narrow face darkened with anger.

"What are they doing here?" Nokias demanded.

Chaumel lost not a beat in his smooth delivery of compliments.

"Keff has a tale to tell you, high one," Chaumel said. "About our ancestors."

Carialle, alone on the night-draped plain a hundred klicks to the east, monitored the conversation through Keff's aural and visual implants. Chaumel was good. Every move, every gesture, was intended to bring his listeners closer to his point of view. If Chaumel ever chose to leave Ozran, he had a place in the Diplomatic Service any time he cared to apply.

She kept one eye on him while running through her archives. Her job was to produce, on cue, the images Chaumel wanted. Certain parameters needed to be met. The selection of holographic video must make their point to a hostile audience. And hostile Nokias would be when Chaumel got to the bottom line.

"You are no doubt curious why I should ask you here, when we spent all day yesterday and all morning together, High Mage," Chaumel said, jovially, "but an important matter has come up and you were the very first person I thought of asking to aid me."

"I?" Nokias asked, clearly flattered. "But what is this matter?"

"Ah," Chaumel said, and spoke to the air. "Carialle, if you please?"

"Carialle?" Nokias asked, looking first at Plennafrey, then at Keff. "Has he two names, then?"

"No, high one. But Keff does come from whence our ancestors came, and his silver tower has another person in it. She cannot come out to see you, but she has many talents."

That was the first signal. Using video effects she cadged from a 3-D program she and Keff watched in port, she spun the image up from the holo-table as a complicated spiral, widening it until it resolved itself as the globe of Ozran, present day.

Nokias was impressed by Keff's "magic," according him a respectful glance before studying the picture before him. Chaumel led him through a discussion of current farming techniques.

At the next cue, Carialle introduced the image of Ozran as it had been in their distant past.

" . . . If more attention were paid to farming and conservation," Chaumel's smooth voice continued.

Maybe a little video of a close-up look at the farms run by the four-fingers would be helpful. Pity the images taken through Keff's contact button were 2-D, but she could coax a pseudo-holograph out of the stereoscopic view from his eye implants. She found the image from the dog-people's commune, and cropped out images of the six-packs hauling a clothful of small roots.

" . . . Higher yield . . . water usage . . . native vegetation . . . advantage in trade . . ."

In the seat of honor, Nokias sat up straighter. Chaumel's sally regarding superior trading power among the regions had struck a chord in the southern magiman's mind.

"My people farm the tropical zone," Nokias noted, nodding toward Plennafrey, who was all large eyes watching her senior. "We harvest a good deal of soft fruit." Chaumel reacted with polite interest as if it were the first time he'd heard that fact. "If the climate were warmer and more humid, I could see a greater yield from my orchards. That does interest me, friend Chaumel."

"I am most honored, High Mage," the silver magiman said smoothly, with a half-bow. "As you see, there has been a deterioration. . . ."

Keeping the holo playing, Carialle ran through the datafile, looking for specific images relating to yield. With some amusement, she discovered the video from her servo's search for the marsh flower. Globe-frogs clunked into one another getting out of the low-slung robot's way. They gestured indignantly at the servo for scaring them.

"Help us save Ozran," Chaumel was saying, using both gesture and word to emphasize his concept. "Help us to stay the destruction of our world by our own hand."

"Help," Carialle repeated to herself, translating the sign language Chaumel used.

"It would also be good to cease dosing the workers with forget-drugs so they will be smart enough to aid us in saving our world," Plennafrey spoke up, timidly.

"That I am not sure I would do," Nokias said.

"Oh, but consider it," Plenna begged. "They are part of our people. With less power, you will need more aid from them. All it would take is giving them the ability to take more responsibility for their tasks. Help us," she said, also making the gesture.

Carialle played the video of the first landing, including the encounters with the Old Ones. Nokias was deeply impressed.

"This proves, as we said, that the workers are of the same stock as we. There is no difference," Chaumel concluded.

"I will think about it," Nokias said at last.

"Help," Carialle said again. "Now, where else have I seen that gesture used?" She ran back through her memory. Well, Potria had used it during the first battle over Keff and the ship, but Carialle was certain she had seen it more recently—wait, the frogs!

She replayed the servo's video, reversing the data string to the moment when the robot surprised the marsh creatures. The frogs weren't reacting out of animal fright.

"They were talking to us!" Carialle said. She put the image through IT. The sign language was an exact match.

Intrigued, Carialle ran an analysis of every image of the amphibioids she had and came out with an amazing conclusion.

"Keff," she sent through Keff's implant. "Keff, the globe-frogs!"

"What about them?" he subvocalized. "I'm trying to concentrate on Nokias."

"To begin with, those globular shells were manufactured."

"Sure, a natural adaptation to survive."

"No, they're artificial. Plastic. Not spit and pond muck. *Plastic*. And they speak the sign language. I think we've found our equal, spacefaring race, Keff. They're the Ancient Ones."

"Oh, come on!" Keff said out loud. Nokias and Chaumel turned to stare at him. He smiled sheepishly. "Come on, High Mage. We want you to be prosperous."

"Thank you, Keff," Nokias said, a little puzzled. Favoring Keff with a disapproving glare, Chaumel reclaimed his guest's attention and went on with his carefully rehearsed speech.

Carialle's voice continued low in his ear. "They're so easy to ignore, we went right past them without thinking. That's why the Old Ones moved up into the mountains—to take the technology they stole out of reach of its rightful owners, who couldn't follow them up there. When the humans came, they didn't know about the frogs, so they inherited the power system, not knowing it belonged to someone else. They thought the globe-frogs were just animals. It would explain why they're so interested in any kind of power emission."

"I think perhaps you're on to something, lady," Keff said. "Let's not mention it now. We're asking for enough concessions, and the going is hazardous. We can test your hypothesis later."

"It's *not* a hypothesis," Carialle said. But she controlled her jubilation and went back to being the audio-video operator for the evening.

"Very well," Nokias said, many hours later. "I see that our world will die unless we conserve power. I will even discuss an exchange of greater self-determination for greater responsibility from my workers. But I will let go of my items only if all the others agree, too. You can scarcely ask me to make myself vulnerable to stray bolts from disaffected . . . ah . . . friends."

"High Mage, I agree with you from my heart," Chaumel said, placing a hand over his. "With your help, we can attain concord among the mages, and Ozran will prosper."

"Yes. I must go now," Nokias said, rising from his chair. "I have much to think about. You will notify me of your progress?"

"Of course, High Mage," Chaumel said. He turned to escort his guest out into the night.

Gasping, Plennafrey pointed toward the curtains. The others spun to see. A handful of spy-spheres hovering there flitted out into the window and disappeared into the night.

"Whose were they?" Chaumel demanded,

"It was too dark to see," Plenna said.

"I am going," Nokias said, alarmed. "These eavesdroppers may be the enemy of your plans, Chaumel. I have no wish to be the target of an assassination attempt."

Escorted by a wary Chaumel, Keff, and Plennafrey, the golden mage hurried out to his chariot. He took off, and teleported when he was only a few feet above the balcony.

"I do not wish to distress you, but Nokias is correct when he says there will be much opposition to our plans," Chaumel said. "You would be safe here tonight. I am warding every entrance to the stronghold."

"No, thank you," Keff said, holding Plennafrey's hand "I'd feel safer in my own cabin."

Chaumel bowed. "As you wish. Tomorrow we continue the good work, eh?" In spite of the danger, he showed a guarded cheerfulness. "Nokias is on our side, friends. I sense it. But he is reasonable to be afraid of the others. If any of us show weakness, it is like baring one's breast to the knife. Good night."

⁂CHAPTER TWELVE

Keff mounted the platform behind Plenna's chair, and put his hands on the back as the blue-green conveyance lifted into the sky. He watched her weave a shield and throw it around them. Chaumel, his duties as a host done, went inside. The great doors closed with a final-sounding *boom*! He suspected the silver mage was sealing every nook and cranny against intrusion.

Nothing was visible ahead of them but a faint jagged one on the horizon marking the tops of mountains. Plenna's chair gave off a dim glow that must have been visible for a hundred klicks in every direction. The thought of danger sent frissons up his legs into the root and spine of his body, but he found to his surprise that he wasn't frightened.

His arms were nudged apart and off the chair back, making him jerk forward, afraid of losing his balance. He glanced down. Plennafrey reached for his hands and drew them down toward her breast, turning her face up toward his for a kiss. The light limned her cheekbones and the delicate line of her jaw. Keff thought he had never seen anything so beautiful in his life.

"Am I always to feel this excited way about you when we are in peril?" Plenna asked impishly. Keff ran his hands caressingly down her smooth shoulders and she shivered with pleasure.

"I hope not," he said, chuckling at her abandon. "I'd never know if the thrill was danger or love. And I do care about the difference."

They didn't speak again for the rest of the journey. Keff listened with new appreciation to the night-birds and the quiet sounds of Ozran sighing in its sleep. In the sky around them was an invisible network of power, but it didn't impinge on the beauty or the silence.

The airlock door lifted, allowing Plennafrey to steer her chair smoothly into the main cabin. This time she was able to choose her landing place and parked the conveyance against the far bulkhead beside Keff's exercise equipment. Keff handed Plenna off the chair and swung her roughly into his arms. Their lips met with fiery urgency. Her hands moved up his back and into his hair.

"Keff, can we talk?" Carialle asked in his ear.

"Not now, Cari," Keff muttered. "Is it an emergency?"

"No. I wanted to discuss my findings of this evening with you."

"Not now, please." Keff breathed out loud as Plenna ran her teeth along the tendon at the side of his neck.

Crossly, Carialle gave him a burst of discordant noise in both aural implants. He winced slightly but refused to let her distract him from Plennafrey. His thumbs ran down into the young woman's bodice, brushed over hard nipples and soft, pliant flesh. He bent his head down to them.

Plennafrey moaned softly. "Carialle won't watch us, will she?"

"No," Keff said reassuringly. He bumped the control with his elbow and the cabin hatch slid aside. "Her domain ends at my door. Pray, lady, enter mine!"

In the circle of his arm, Plenna tiptoed into Keff's cabin.

"It is like you," she said. "Spare, neat, and very handsome. Oh, books!" She picked one off the small shelf by his bed and lightly fingered the pages. "Of course, I cannot read it." She glanced up at Keff with a bewitching dimple at the corner of her mouth. Her eye was caught by the works of art hanging on the walls. "Those are very good. Haunting. Who painted them?"

"You're standing in her," Keff said, grinning. "Carialle is an artist."

"She is wonderfully talented," Plenna said, with a decided nod. "But I like you better."

There was only one answer Keff could give. He kissed her.

At the end of their lovemaking, Keff propped himself up on his elbow to admire Plennafrey. Her unbound hair tumbled around her white shoulders and breast like black lace.

"You're so lovely," Keff said, toying with a stray strand. "I will feel half my heart wrenched away when I have to go."

"But why should I not come with you to your world?" Plenna asked, her fingers tracing an intricate design on his forearm.

"Because I'm in space eighty percent of my life," Keff said, "and when I'm planet-side I'm seldom near civilization. My usual job is first contact with alien species. It's very strange and full of so many dangers I couldn't even describe them all to you. You wouldn't be happy with the way I live."

"But I am not happy here now," Plenna said plaintively, clasping her hands together in appeal. "If you take me with you, I would cede my claim of power to Brannel and keep my promise to him. There is nothing here to hold me; no family, no friends. I would be glad to learn about other people and other worlds."

"Yes, but..."

She touched his face, and her eyes searched his. "We suit one another, do we not?"

"Yes, but..."

She silenced him with a kiss.

"Then please consider it," she said, cuddling into his arms. Keff crushed her close to him, lost in her scent, lost in her.

In the early morning hours, Carialle monitored her exterior movement sensors until she heard sounds of life from the marshy area downhill from her bluff. She let down her ramp and sent her two servo robots forth into the pink light of dawn. The boxy units disappeared through the break in the brush and over the edge of the ridge. Carialle, idly noting a half dozen spy-eyes hovering at a hundred meters distant, heard clunks and high-pitched squawking as they reached their goal. In a little while, the servos returned to view, herding before them a pair of globe-frogs. The amphibioids tried to signal their indignation, but had to keep paddling on the inside of their plastic spheres before the boxes bumped into them from behind. With some effort, the servos got their quarry up the ramp. Carialle shut the airlock door and pulled up her ramp behind them.

As the frogs entered the main cabin, Carialle hooked into the IT, calling up all the examples of sign language that she and Keff had managed to record over the last few days.

"Now, little friends," she said, "we're going to see if that sign you made was a fluke or not." She manifested the picture of another frog on the side screen at their level, like them but with enough differences of color and configuration to make sure they knew it was a stranger. "Let's chat."

A few hours later, Keff's door opened, and the brawn emerged, yawning, wearing only uniform pants. Plenna, wrapped in his bathrobe, followed him, trailing a lazy finger down his neck.

"Good morning, young lovers," Carialle said brightly. "We have guests."

Red lights chased around the walls and formed an arrow pointing down at the two globe-frogs huddled together in the corner nearest the airlock corridor. Keff goggled.

"But how did they get past Plenna's barrier? She told me she warded the area. Any intrusion should have set off an alarm."

"We're protected against magic only," Plenna said, eyeing the marsh creatures with distaste. "Not vermin."

"They aren't vermin and they're aware you don't like them," Carialle said indignantly. "We've been exchanging compliments."

On her main screen she displayed an expanded image of the small creatures staring at a strange-looking frog on the wall.

"That's my computer-generated envoy," Carialle explained. "Now, watch." The image made a gesture, to which the native creatures responded with a similar movement. As the complexity and number of signs increased, the frogs became excited, bumping into one another to respond to their imaginary host.

Keff watched the data string, glancing once in a while at the frogs.

"Monkey see monkey do," Keff said, shaking his head. "They observed the Ozrans making signs and copied them. This little performance is without meaning."

"Beasts Blatisant," Carialle countered. Keff grimaced. "Keff, I didn't make a subjective judgment on the frequency and meaning of these symbols. Check IT's function log. Read the vocabulary list."

When Keff lifted his eyes from the small readout screen, they were shining.

"Who'd have thought it?" he said. "Cari, all praise to your sharp wits and powers of observation."

Plennafrey had been listening carefully to the IT box's translation of Carialle's and Keff's conversation. She pointed to the frogs.

"Do you mean they can talk?" she asked.

"More than that," Keff said. "They may be the founders of your civilization." Plenna's jaw dropped open, and she stared at the two amphibioids. "Your belt buckle—may I borrow it?"

The belt flew out of Keff's room and smacked into Plenna's hands. She started to extend it to him, then withdrew it. "What for?" she asked.

"To see if they know what to do with it. Er, take it off the belt. It's too heavy for them." Obligingly, Plenna detached the buckle and handed it to him.

Very slowly, Keff walked to where the frogs stood. They waited passively within their globes, kicking occasionally at the water to maintain their positions and watching him with their beady black eyes. Keff hunkered down and held out the buckle.

Wearing a startled expression on its peaky face, the larger frog met his eyes. Immediately, the case opened, splitting into two halves, splashing water on the cabin floor, and the frog stretched out for the power item. Its skinny wrist terminated in a long, sensitively fingered hand which outspread was as large as Plennafrey's. The ends of the digits slid into the five apertures. There was a nearly audible *click*.

"It is connected to the Core of Ozran," Plennafrey said softly.

The water that had been inside the plastic ball gathered around the frog's body as if still held in place by the shell. Thus sheltered, the amphibioid rose on surprisingly long, skinny legs and made a tour of the cabin. Its small face was alive with wonder. Keff directed it to the astrogation tank showing the position of Ozran and its sun. The frog looked intelligently into the three-dimensional star map, and studied the surrounding control panels and key-boards. Then it returned to Keff.

"Help us," it signaled.

"You win, lady dear. Here're your Ancient Ones," Keff said, turning to Plennafrey with a flourish. "They were among you all the time." The young magiwoman swallowed.

"I . . ." She seemed to have trouble getting the words out. "I do not think that I can respect *frogs*."

Chaumel was more philosophical when confronted by the facts.

"I refuse to be surprised," he said, shaking his head. "All in the space of a day or so, my whole life is thrown into confusion. The fur-faces turn out to be our long-lost brothers and we have cousins in plenty among the stars ready to search us out. Some of them live inside boxes. Why should we not discover that the Ancient Ones exist under our noses in the swamps?"

"Try talking to one of them," Keff urged him. Doubtfully, Chaumel looked at the three globe-frogs Keff and Plenna had brought to his stronghold. They were rolling around the great room, signing furiously to one another over an artifact or a piece of furniture.

"Well . . ." Chaumel said, uneasily.

"Go on," Keff said. With a few waves of his hands, Keff got their attention and signed to them to return to him. Once or twice the "courtiers" turned all the way over, trying to negotiate over the slick floor, but the biggest maintained admirable control of his sphere.

After the initial attempts at communication, Keff had let Carialle's two subjects go, asking them to send back one of their leaders. Within an hour, a larger frog speckled with yellow to show its great age had come up the ramp, rolling inside a battered case. A pair of smaller, younger frogs, guards or attendants, hurtled up behind it. The first amphibioid rolled directly over to Plenna and demanded her belt buckle. For his imperious manner as well as his great size, Keff and Carialle had dubbed him the Frog Prince. From the two symbols with which he designated his name, Keff decided he was called something like Tall Eyebrow.

"I'm sure it loses something in the translation," he explained.

Chaumel knelt and made a few signs of polite greeting. He was unsure of himself at first, but grew enthusiastic when his courtesies were returned and expanded upon.

"These are not trained creatures," he said with delight. "It really understands me."

"Tall just said the same thing about you," Keff noted, amused.

"It has feet. What are the globes for?"

"Ozran used to have much higher humidity," Keff said. "The frogs' skins are delicate. The shells protect them from the dry air."

"We cannot tell the other mages about them until we have negotiated the 'cease-fire,'" Chaumel told him seriously. "Already Nokias regrets that he said he will cooperate. He suspects Ferngal of sending those spy-eyes the other night and I have no reason

to doubt him. If we present them with speaking animals who need
bubbles to live, they will think we are mad, and the whole accord
will fall apart."

Neither Keff nor Carialle, listening through the implant contacts, argued the point.

"It's too important to get them to stop using power," Keff said
"It goes against my better judgment, but it'll help the frogs' case
if we don't try to make the mages believe too many impossible
things before breakfast."

During the successive weeks, the brawn and the two magifolk
traveled to each mage's stronghold to convince him or her to join
with them in the cause of environmental survival.

Keff spent his free time, such as remained of it, divided between
Plennafrey in the evenings and the frogs in the early morning. He
had to learn another whole new language, but he had never been
so happy. His linguistic skills were getting a good, solid workout.
Carialle's memory banks began to fill with holos of gestures with
different meanings and implications.

Since the mages had always used the signs as sacred or magical communion, Keff had to begin all over again with the frogs
on basic language principles. The mages had employed only a small
quantity of gestures that had been gleaned from the Old Ones in
their everyday lives, giving him a very limited working vocabulary. Chaumel knew only a few hundred signs, Plenna a few dozen.
Keff used those to build toward scientific understanding.

Mathematical principles were easy. These frogs were the five-
hundredth generation since the life-form came to this world. That
verified what Keff had been coming to believe, that none of the
three dominant life-forms who occupied Ozran were native to it.

Knowledge of their past had been handed down by rote through
the generations. The frogs had manufactured the life-support
bubbles with the aid of the one single item of power that remained
to them. The other devices had all been borrowed, and then stolen by the Flat Ones, by whom Keff understood them to mean the
Old Ones.

For a change, IT was working as well as he had always hoped
it would. An optical monitor fed the frogs' gestures into the computer, and the voice of IT repeated the meaning into Keff's implant
and on a small speaker for the benefit of the others. Keff worked

out a simple code for body language that IT used to transcribe the replies he spoke out loud. Having to act out his sentence after he said it made the going slow, but in no time he picked up more and more of the physical language so he could use it to converse directly.

He was however surprised at how few frogs were willing to come forward to meet with the Ozrans and help bridge the language barrier. The Frog Prince assured him it was nothing personal; a matter of safety. After so many years, they found it difficult to trust any of the Big Folk. Keff understood perfectly what he meant. He was careful never to allude to the frogs when on any of his many visits to the mages' strongholds.

On his knees at the end of another dusty row of roots, Brannel observed Keff and Plennafrey returning to the silver ship. Scraping away at the base of a wilted plant as long as he dared, he waited for Keff to keep Carialle's promise and come get him. It seemed funny they couldn't see him, but perhaps they hadn't looked his way when he was standing up. He knew he could go up to the door and be admitted, but he was reluctant to do so until asked as they seemed disinterested in asking him. Weighing the question of waiting or not waiting, he pushed his gathering basket into the next row and started digging through the clay-thick soil for more of the woody vegetables.

His thoughts were driven away by a stunning blow to the side of the head. Brannel fell to the earth in surprise. Alteis stood over him, waving a clump of roots from his basket, spraying dirt all over the place. Some of it was on Brannel's head. A female with light brown fur stood beside the old leader, her eyes flashing angrily.

"You're in the wrong row, Brannel!" Alteis exclaimed. "This is Gonna's row. You should go that way." He pointed to the right and waited while Brannel picked up his gear and moved.

"Your mind in the mountains?" Fralim chortled from his position across the field. What traces of long-term memory the others retained came from rote and repetition, and they had been witness to Brannel's peculiarities and ambitions since he was small. Everyone but his mother scorned the young male's hopes. "We saw the Mage Keff and the Magess Plennafrey fly into the tower. You planning to set yourself up with the mages?" He cackled.

Another worker joined in with the same joke he had been using for twenty years. "Gonna shave your face and call yourself Mage, Brannel?'

Brannel was stung. "If I do, I'll show you what power the overlords wield, Mogag," he said in a voice like a growl. Alteis walked up and slapped him in the head again.

"Work!" the leader said. "The roots won't pull themselves."

The others jeered. Brannel worked by himself until the sun was just a fingertip's width above the mountain rim at the edge of the valley. Any time, food would arrive, and he would be able to sneak away. Perhaps, if no one was looking, he might go *now*.

It was his bad luck that Alteis and his strapping son were almost behind him. Fralim yanked him back by the collar and seat of his garment from the edge of the field, and plunked him sprawling into his half-worked row.

"Stay away from that tower," Alteis ordered him. "You have duties to your own folk."

Moments crept by like years. Brannel, fuming, finished his day's chores with the least possible grace. As soon as the magess kept her promise to teach him, he would never return to this place full of stupid people. He would study all day, and work great works of magic, like the ancestors and the Old Ones.

At the end of the day, he hung back from the crowd hurrying toward the newly materialized food. With Alteis busy doing something else, there was no one watching one discontented worker. Brannel sneaked away through the long shadows on the field and hurried up to the ship.

As he reached the tall door, it slid upward to disgorge Magess Plennafrey and Keff on her floating chair.

"Oh, Brannel!" Mage Keff said, surprised. "I'm glad you came up. I am sorry, but we've got to run now. Carialle will look after you, all right?" Before Brannel could tell him that nothing was "all right," the chair was already wafting them away. "See you later!" Keff called.

Brannel watched them ascend into the sky, then made his way toward the heart of the tower.

Inside, Magess Carialle was doing something with a trio of marsh creatures.

"Oh, Brannel," she said, in an unconscious echo of Keff. "Welcome. Have you eaten yet?" A meal was bubbling in the small

doorway even before he had stopped shaking his head. "I promised you a peep at the tapes. Will you sit down in the big chair?
I've got to keep doing another job at the same time, but I can
handle many tasks at once."

Keff's big chair turned toward him and, at that direct invitation, Brannel came forward, only a little uneasy to be alone in the
great silver cylinder without any other living beings. Marsh creatures didn't count, he thought, as he ate his dinner, and he wasn't
sure what Carialle was.

Though she didn't seem to eat, in deference to his appetite,
Magess Carialle had prepared for him a meal twice the size of the
one he had eaten last time. Each dish was satisfying and most
delicious. With every bite he liked the thought less and less of
returning to raw roots and grains. He was nearly finished eating
when the big picture before him lit up and he found himself
looking into the weird green face of an Old One. He stopped with
a half-chewed mouthful.

"Here's the first of the tapes, starting at the point we left off
last time," Carialle's voice said.

"Ah," Brannel said, recovering his wits.

He couldn't not watch for he was fascinated and her voice kept
supplying translations in his tongue. Brannel asked her the occasional question. She answered, but without offering as much of
her attention as she gave one of Keff's inquiries. He glanced back
over his shoulder, wondering why she had made a picture of the
marsh creatures, and what they found so interesting in it.

" . . . And that's the last of the tapes," Carialle said, sometime
later. "What a fine resource to have turn up."

"What am I to do now?" Brannel asked, looking around him.
Carialle's picture appeared on the wall beside him. The lady smiled.

"You've done so much for us—and for Ozran, by telling us about
farming," she said. "All we can do now is wait to see what the mages
think of our evidence."

"I would tell the mages all I know," Brannel said hopefully. "It
would help convince them to farm better." The flat magess shook
her head.

"Thank you, Brannel. Not yet. It would be better if you didn't
get involved—less dangerous for you," she said. "Now, I don't have
any tasks that need doing. Why don't you go home and sleep? I'm

sure Keff will find you tomorrow, or the next day. As soon as he has any definite news to tell you."

Brannel went away, but Keff didn't *come.*

The worker spent the next day, and the next, waiting for Keff to stop off to see him between his hurried journeys to the far reaches of Ozran on the magess's chair. He never glanced at Brannel. In spite of his promise, he had forgotten the worker existed. He had forgotten their growing friendship.

Worse yet, Brannel now had a head full of information about the ancestors and the Old Ones, and what good did it do him? Nothing to do with teaching him to become a mage, or getting him better food to eat. In time his disappointment grew into a towering rage. How *dare* the strangers build up his hopes and leave him to rot like one of the despised roots of the field! How dare they make him a promise, knowing he never forgot anything, and then pretend it had never been spoken? Brannel swore to himself that he would never trust a mage again.

Ferngal's stronghold stood alone on a high, dentate mountain peak, set apart by diverging river branches from the rest of the eastern range. The obsidian-dark stone of its walls offered little of the open hospitality of Chaumel's home. In the dark, relatively low-ceilinged great hall, Keff had the uncomfortable feeling the walls were closing in on him. Brown-robed Lacia and a yellow-coated mage sat with Ferngal as Chaumel gave his by now familiar talk on preserving and restoring the natural balances of Ozran.

Chaumel, in his bright robes, seemed like a living gas-flame as he hovered behind Carialle's illusions. He appealed to each of his listeners in turn, clearly disliking talking to more than one mage at a time. He had voiced a caution to Keff and Plenna before they had arrived.

"In a group, there is more chance of dissension. Careful manipulation will be required and I do not know if I am equal to it."

Keff had felt a chill. "If you can't do it, we're in trouble," he had said. "But we need to speed up the process. The power blackouts are becoming more frequent. I don't know how long you have until there's a complete failure."

"If that happens," Chaumel told his audience, "then mages will be trapped in the mountains with no means of rescue at hand.

Food distribution will end, causing starvation in many areas. We have made the fur-faces dependent upon our system. We cannot fail them, or ourselves."

Early in the discussion, Lacia had announced that she viewed the whole concept of the Core of Ozran as science to be sacrilege. She frowned at Chaumel whenever the silver magiman made eye contact with her. The mage in yellow robes, an older man named Whilashen, said little and sat through Chaumel's speech pinching his lower lip between thumb and forefinger.

"I do not like this idea of relying more upon the servant class," Ferngal said. "They are mentally limited."

"With respect, High Mage," Keff said, "how would you know? Chaumel tells me that even your house servants are given a low dose of the docility drug in their food. I have done tests on the workers in the late Mage Klemay's province and can show you the results. They are of the same racial stock as you, and their capabilities are the same. All they need is more nurturing and education, and of course for you to stop the ritual mutilation and cranial mutations. In the next generation all the children will return to normal human appearance, with the possible exception of retaining the hirsutism. That may need to be bred out."

"Tosh!" Ferngal's ruddy face suffused further.

"I can't wait to see what happens when we tell him about the Frog Prince," Carialle said through the implants. "He'll have apoplexy."

Keff leaned forward, his hands outstretched, making an appeal. "I can explain the scientific process and show you proof you'll understand."

"Proof you manufacture proves nothing," Ferngal said. "Illusions, that's all, like these pictures."

"But Nokias said . . ." Plennafrey began. Chaumel made one attempt to silence her, but it was too late. "Nokias—"

Ferngal cut her off at once. "You've talked to Nokias? You spoke to him before you came to me?" The black magiman's nostrils flared. "Have you no respect for protocol?"

"He is my liege," Plenna said with quiet dignity. "I was required. You would demand the same from any of the mages of the East."

"Well . . . that is true."

"Will you not consider what we have said?" she pleaded.

"No, I won't give up power and you can stuff your arguments

about making the peasants smarter in a place where a magic item won't fit. You're out of your mind asking something like that. And if Nokias has softened enough to say yes, he will regret it." Ferngal showed his teeth in a vicious grin. "I'll soon add the South to my domain. Chaumel, you ought to know better."

"High Mage, sometimes truth must overcome even common sense."

Abruptly, Ferngal lost interest in them.

"Go," he said, tossing a deceptively casual gesture toward the door behind him. "Go now before I lose my temper."

"Heretics!" screamed Lacia.

With what dignity he could muster, Chaumel led the small procession around Ferngal toward the doors. Keff gathered up the holo-table and opened his stride to catch up without running.

He heard a voice whisper very close to his ear. Not Carialle's: a man's.

"Some of us have honor," the voice said. "Tell your master to contact me later." Startled, Keff turned around. Whilashen nodded to him, his eyes intent.

In spite of Chaumel's pleas for confidentiality, word began to spread to the other mages before he had a chance to speak with them in person. Rumors began to spread that Chaumel and an unknown army of mages wanted to take over the rest by destroying their connection to the Core of Ozran. Chaumel spent a good deal of time on what Keff called "damage control," scotching the gossip, and reassuring the panic-stricken magifolk that he was not planning an Ozran-wide coup.

"No one will be *compelled* to give up all power," Chaumel said, trying to calm an angry Zolaika. He sat in her study in a hovering chair with his head at the level of her knees to show respect. Keff and Plennafrey stood on the floor meters below them, silent and watching. "Each mage needs to be allowed free will in such an important matter. But I think you see, Zolaika, and everyone will see in the end, that inevitably we must be more judicious in our use of power. You, in your great wisdom, will have seen that the Core of Ozran is not infinite in its gifts."

Zolaika was guarded. "Oh, I see the truth of what you *say*, Chaumel, but so far, you have offered us no proof! Pictures, what are they? I make pretty illusions like those for my grandchildren."

"We are working on gathering solid proof," Chaumel said, "proof that will convince everyone that what we say about the Core of Ozran is the truth. But, in the meantime, it is necessary to soften the coming blow, don't you think?"

"I'm an old woman," Zolaika snapped. "I don't want words to 'soften the coming blow.' I want facts. I'm not blind or senile. I will be convinced by evidence." Her eyes lost their hard edge for a moment, and Keff fancied he saw a twinkle there for a moment. "You have never lied to me, Chaumel. You say a thousand words where one will do, but you are not a liar, nor an imaginative man. If you're convinced, so will I be. But bring proof!"

As they flew off Zolaika's balcony, Chaumel sat bolt upright in his chariot, a smug expression on his face. "That was most satisfactory."

"It was? She didn't say she'd support us," Keff said.

"But she believes us. Everyone respects her, even the ones who are spelling for her position." Chaumel made a cursory pass with one hand in the air to show what he meant. "Her belief in us will carry weight. Whether or not she actually says she supports us, she does by not saying she *doesn't*."

"There speaks a diplomat," Carialle said. "He makes pure black and white print into one of those awful moire paintings. Progress report: out of some two hundred and seventeen mages with multiple power items, I now have one hundred fifty-two frequency signatures. It is now theoretically possible for me to selectively intercept and deaden power emissions in each of those items."

"Good going. We might need it," Keff said, "but I hope not."

With Zolaika four of the high mages had given tentative agreement to stand down power at the risk of losing it, but meetings with some of the lesser magifolk had not gone well. Potria had heard the first few sentences of Chaumel's discourse and driven them out of her home with a miniature dust storm. Harvel, the next most junior mage above Plenna, had accused her of trying to climb the social ladder over his head. When Chaumel explained that their traditional structure for promotion was a perversion of the ancestors' system, the insulted Harvel had done his best to kill all of them with a bombardment of lightning. Carialle turned off his two magic items, a rod and a ring, and left him to stew as the others effected a hurried withdrawal. "I think that among the remaining mages we can concentrate on the potential troublemakers," Chaumel said as they materialized above his balcony. "Most of the others will not become involved. A hundred of them barely use their spells except to fetch and carry household items, or to power their flying chairs."

"They'll miss it the most," Keff said, "but at least they aren't the conspicuous consumers."

"Oh, well put!" Chaumel said, chortling, as he docketed the phrase. "The 'conspicuous consumers' have been making us do most of the work for them. I laughed when Howet said he'd agree if we talked to his farm workers for him—Verni, what are you doing out here?"

Below them, clinging to the parapet of Chaumel's landing pad, was his chief servant. As soon as the magiman angled in to touch down, Verni ran toward him, wringing his hands.

"Master, High Mage Nokias is here," he whispered as Chaumel rose from the chariot. "He is in the hall of antiquities. He has warded the ways in and out. I have been trapped out here for hours."

"Nokias?" Chaumel said, sharing a puzzled glance with Keff and Plennafrey. "What does he want here? And warded?"

"Yes, master," the servant said, winding his hands in his apron. "None of us can pass in or out until he lets down the barriers."

"How strange. What can frighten a high mage?"

Chaumel strode through the great hall. The servant, Keff, and Plennafrey hurried after him, having to scoot to avoid the tall glass doors closing on their heels.

The silver mage stood back a pace from the second set of doors and felt the air cautiously. Then he moved forward and pounded with the end of his wand.

"High Mage!" he shouted. "It is Chaumel. Open the door! I have warded the outside ways."

The door opened slightly, only wide enough for a human body to pass through. Chaumel beckoned to the others and slipped in. Keff let Plenna go first, then followed with the servant. No one was behind the door. It snapped shut as soon as they were all inside.

Nokias waited halfway down the hall, seated on the old hover-chair, his hands positioned and ready to activate his bracelet amulet.

Even at a distance, Keff could see the taut skin around the mage's eyes.

"Old friend," Chaumel said, coming forward with his hands open and relaxed. "Why the secrecy?"

"I had to be discreet," Nokias said. "There's been an attempt on me at my citadel already. You've stirred up a fierce gale among the other mages, Chaumel. Many of them want your head. They're upset about your threats of destruction. Most of the others don't believe your data—they do not want to, that is all. I came to tell you that I *cannot* consider giving up my power. Not now."

"Not now?" Keff echoed. "But you see the reasoning behind it. What's changed?"

"I do see the reasoning," the Mage of the South said, "but there's revolt brewing in my farm caverns. I can't let go with violence threatened. People will die. The harvest will be ruined."

"What has happened?" Chaumel asked.

Nokias clenched his big hands. "I have been speaking to village after village of my workers. Oh, many of them were not sure what I meant by my promises of freedom, but I saw sparks of intelligence there. The difficulties began only a day or so ago. My house servants report that, among the peasantry, there is fear and anger. They cry that they will not cooperate. It is stirring up the others. If I lose my ability to govern, there will be riots."

"It's only their fear of the unknown," Chaumel said smoothly. "They should rejoice in what you're offering them, the first high mage in twenty generations to change the way things are to the way things might be."

"They cannot understand abstract thinking," Nokias corrected him sternly.

"I will go and talk to them on your behalf, Nokias," Chaumel said. "I've done so for Zolaika. It's only right I should also do it for you."

"I would be grateful," Nokias said. "But I will not appear in person."

"You don't need to," Chaumel assured him. "I and my friends here will take care of it."

The farm village looked like any of the others Keff had seen, except that it also boasted an elderly but well cared for orchard as well as the usual fields of crops. A few lonely late fruit clung to the uppermost branches of the trees nearest the home cavern. Nokias's farmers were harvesting the next row's yield.

The Noble Primitives glanced warily at the three "magifolk" when they arrived, then went about their business with their heads averted, carefully keeping from making eye contact with them.

"Surely they are wondering what brings three mages here," Keff said.

"They dare not ask," Plenna said. "It isn't their place."

Chaumel looked at the sun above the horizon. "It's close enough to the end of the working day."

He flung his hands over his head and the air around him filled with lights of blue and red. Like will-o'-the-wisps the sparks scattered, surrounding the farmers, dancing at them to make them climb down from the trees, gathering them toward the three waiting by the cavern entrance. Keff, flanking Chaumel on the left, watched it all with the admiration due a consummate showman. Plennafrey stood demure and proud on Chaumel's right.

"Good friends!" Chaumel called out to them when the whole village was assembled. "I have news for you from your overlord Nokias!"

In slow, majestic phrases, Chaumel outlined the events to come when the workers would have greater capacity to think and to do. "You look forward to something unimaginable by your parents and grandparents. You workers will have greater scope than any since the ancestors came to Ozran."

"Uh-oh," Carialle said to Keff. "Someone out there is not at all happy to see you. I'm noting heightened blood pressure and heartbeat in someone in the crowd. Give me a sweep view and I'll try to spot them."

Not knowing quite what he was looking for, Keff gazed slowly around at the crowd. The children were open-mouthed, as usual, to be in the presence of one of the mighty overlords. Most of the older folk still refused to look up at Chaumel. It was the younger ones who were sneaking glances, and in a couple of cases, staring openly at them the way Brannel had.

" . . . Nokias has sent me, Chaumel the Silver, to announce to you that you shall be given greater freedoms than ever in your lifetime!" Chaumel said, sweeping his sleeves up around his head. "We the mages will be more open to you on matters of education and responsibility. On your part, you must continue to do your duty to the magefolk, as your tasks serve all Ozran. These are the last harvests of the season. It is vital to get them in so you will not be hungry in the winter. In the spring, a new world order is coming, and it is for your benefit that changes will be taking place. Embrace them! Rejoice!"

Chaumel waved his arms and the illusion of a flock of small bluebirds fluttered up behind him. The audience gasped.

"No! It's a lie!" A deep male voice echoed over the plainlands. When everyone whirled right and left to see who was talking, a rock came whistling over the heads of the crowd toward Plenna.

With lightning-fast gestures, the magiwoman warded herself. The rock struck an invisible shield and fell to the ground with a heavy *thud.* Keff saw the color drain from her shocked face. She was controlling herself to keep from crying. Keff pushed in front of the two magifolk and glared at the villagers. Some of them had recoiled in terror, wondering what punishment was in store for them, harboring an assailant. The male who had thrown the stone stood at the back, glaring and fists clenched. Keff hurtled through the crowd after him.

The farmer was no match for the honed body of the spacer. Before the panicked worker could do more than turn away and take a couple of steps, Keff cannoned into him. He knocked the male flat with a body blow. The worker struggled, yelling, but Keff shoved a knee into his spine and bent his arms up behind his head.

"What do you want done with him, Chaumel?" Keff called out in the linga esoterka.

"Bring him here."

Using the male's joined wrists as a handle, Keff hauled upward. To avoid having his wrists break, the rest of the worker followed. Keff trotted him along the path that magically opened up among the rest of the workers.

"Who is in charge of this man?" Chaumel asked. A timid graybeard came forward and bowed deeply. "Even if there is to be change, respect toward one another must still be observed. Give him some extra work to do, to soak up this superfluous energy."

"Is this what the new world order will be like? If we allow the workers more freedom of thought, there will be no safe place for me to go," Plenna said to Keff in an undertone with a catch in her voice. He put an arm around her.

"We'd better get out of here," Keff said under his breath to Chaumel.

"It would have been better if you'd pretended nothing had happened," Chaumel said over Keff's shoulder. "We are supposed to be above such petty attacks. But never mind. Follow me." Though he was obviously shaken, too, the magiman negotiated a calm and impressive departure. The three of them flew hastily away from the village.

"I don't understand it," Chaumel said, when they were a hundred meters over the plain. "In every other village, they've been delighted with the idea of learning and being free. Could they enjoy being stupid? No, no," he chided himself.

Keff sighed. "I'm beginning to think I put my hand into a hornet's nest, Cari," he said under his breath. "Have I done wrong trying to set things straight here?"

"Not at all, Sir Galahad," Carialle reassured him. "Think of the frogs and the power blackouts. Not everyone will be delighted with global change, but never lose sight of the facts. The imbalances of power here, both social and physical, could prove fatal to Ozran. You're doing the right thing, whether or not anyone else thinks so."

When they returned to Chaumel's residence, another visitor awaited them. Ferngal, with a mighty entourage of lesser eastern Mages, did not even trouble to wait inside. The underlings covered the landing pad with wardings and minor spells of protection like a presidential security force. Chaumel picked his way carefully toward his own landing strip, passing a hand before him to make sure it wasn't booby-trapped. He set down lightly and approached the black chariot on foot.

"High Mage Ferngal! How nice to see you so soon," Chaumel said, arms wide with welcome. "Come in. Allow me to offer you my hospitality."

Ferngal was in no mood for chitchat. He cut off Chaumel's compliments with an angry sweep of his hand.

"How dare you go spreading sedition among *my* workers? You dare to preach your nonsense in my farmsteads? You have overreached yourself."

"High Mage, I have not been speaking to your farmers. That is for you to do, or not, as *you* choose," Chaumel said, puzzled. "*I* would not presume upon your territories."

"Oh, no. It could only be you. You will cease this nonsense about the Core of Ozran at once, or it will be at your peril."

"It is not nonsense, High Mage," Chaumel said mildly but with steel apparent in his tone. "I tell you these things for your sake, not mine."

Ferngal leveled an angry finger at Chaumel's nose.

"If this is a petty attempt to gain power, you will pay heavily for your deceit," he said. "I hold domain over the East, and your stronghold falls within those boundaries. I order you to cease spreading your lies."

"I am not lying," Chaumel said. "And I cannot cease."

"Then so be it," the black-clad mage snarled.

He and his people lifted off from the balcony, and vanished. Chaumel shook his head, and turned toward Keff and Plenna with a "what can you do?" expression.

"Heads up, Keff!" Carialle said. "Power surge building in your general area—a heavy one. Focusing . . . building . . . Watch out!"

"Carialle says someone is sending a huge burst of power toward us!" Keff shouted.

"An attack," shrieked Plenna. The three of them converged in the center of the balcony. The magiwoman and Chaumel threw their hands up over their heads. A rose-colored shell formed around them like a gigantic soap bubble only a split second before the storm broke.

It was no ordinary storm. Their shield was assailed by forked staves of multicolored lightning and sheets of flaming rain. Hand-sized explosions rocked them, setting off clouds of smoke and shooting jagged debris against the shell. Torrents of clear acid and flame-red lava flowed down the edges and sank into the floor, the ruin separated from their feet only by a fingertip's width.

The deafening noises stopped abruptly. When the smoke cleared, Chaumel waited a moment before dissolving the bubble. He let it pop silently on the air and took a step forward. Part of the floor rocked under his feet. Keff grabbed him. Two paces beyond the place they were standing, the end of the balcony was gone, ripped away by the magical storm as if a giant had taken a bite out of it. The pieces were still crashing with dull echoes into the ravine far below. Plenna mounted her chair to go look. She returned, shaking her head.

"It is . . ." Chaumel began, and had to stop to clear his throat.

"It is considered ill-mannered to notice when someone else is building a spell, especially if that person is of higher rank than oneself. I believe it has now become a matter of life and death for us to behave in an ill-mannered fashion."

"Ferngal," Carialle said. "Using two power objects at once. I have both their frequencies logged." Keff passed along the information.

"Sedition, he said." Chaumel was confused. He appealed to Keff. "What sedition was Ferngal talking about? I have talked to no one in his area. I *would* not."

"Then someone else is talking to them," Keff said. "Nokias mentioned something similar. We'd better investigate."

A quick aerial reconnaissance of the two farmsteads from which Nokias and Ferngal's complaints came revealed that they were very close together, suggesting that whatever set off the riots was somewhere in the area, and on foot, not aloft. Chaumel asked help from a few of the mages who had tentatively given their promise to cooperate. They sent out spy-eyes to all the surrounding villages, looking for anything that seemed threatening.

Nothing appeared during the next day or so. On the third day, a light green spy-eye found Chaumel as he was leaving Carialle's ship.

"Here's your trouble," Kiyottal's mental voice announced.

Plennafrey, sensing the arrival of an eye-sphere from inside the ship, interrupted their attempts at conversation with the Frog Prince to run outside. Keff followed her.

"We've located the troublemaker," Chaumel said, after communing silently with the sphere. "It's your four-finger. He's making speeches."

"Brannel?" Keff said. He glanced out at the farm fields. Wielding heavy forks, the workers were turning over empty rows of earth and bedding them down with straw. He searched their ranks and turned back to Chaumel.

"You're right. I forgot all about him. He's gone."

"Follow me," Kiyottal's voice said. "I have also alerted Ferngal. Nokias is coming, too. It's in his territory."

In the center of the clearing in a southern farm village, Brannel raised his arms for silence. The workers, who had long, pack beast-like faces, were gently worried about this skinny, dirty stranger who had arrived at their farmstead with an exhausted dray beast at his heels.

"*I* tell you the mages are weakening!" Brannel cried "They are not all-powerful. If we have an uprising, every worker together, they will come out to punish us, but they will all fall to the ground helpless!"

"You are mad," a female farmer said, curling back her broad lips in a sneer.

"Why would we want to overthrow the mages?" one of the males asked him. "We have enough to eat."

"But you cannot think for yourselves," Brannel said. He was tired. He had given the same speech at another farmstead only days before, and once a few days before that, with the same stupid faces and the same stupid questions. If not for the flame of revenge that burned within him, the thought of journeying all over Ozran would have daunted him into returning to Alteis. "You do the same things every day of your lives, every year of your lives!"

"Yes? So? What else should we do?" Most of the listeners were more inclined to heckle, but Brannel thought he saw the gleam of comprehension on the faces of a few.

"Change is coming, but it won't be for our sakes—only the mages'. If you want things to change for *you*, don't eat the mage food. Don't eat it tonight, not tomorrow, not any day. Keep roots from your harvest, and eat them. You will *remember*," Brannel insisted, pointing to his temples with both hands. "Tomorrow you will see. It will be like nothing you have ever experienced in your life. You *will* remember. You need to trust me only for one night! Then you will see for yourselves. You grow the food! You have a right to it! We can get rid of the magefolk. On the first day of the next planting when the sun is highest, throw down your tools and refuse to work."

The whirring sound in the air distracted most of the workers, who looked up, then threw themselves flat on the ground. Brannel and his few converts remained standing, staring up at the four chariots descending upon them.

The black and gold chairs touched down first.

"Kill him," Ferngal said heatedly, pointing at the sheep-faced male, "or I will do so myself. His people have been without an overlord too long. They are getting above themselves."

"No," Keff said. He leaped off Plenna's chair, putting himself between the high mage and the peasant. "Don't touch him. Brannel, what are you doing?"

At first Brannel remained mulishly silent, then words burst out of him in a torrent of wounded feelings.

"You promised me, and I risked myself, and Chaumel knocked me out, and you threw me out again with nothing. Nothing!" Brannel spat. "I am as I was before, only worse. The others made fun of me. Why didn't you keep your promise?"

Keff held up his hands. "I promised I'd do what I could for you. Amulets aren't easy to find, you know, and the power is going to end soon anyway. Do you want to fill your head with useless knowledge?"

"Yes! To know is to understand one's life."

Ferngal spat. "If you're going to waste my time by talking nonsense with a servant, I'm away. Just make certain he does not come back to my domain. Never!" The black chair disappeared toward the clouds. Nokias, shaking his head, went off in the opposite direction. The workers, freed from their thrall by the departure of the high mages, went on to eat their supper, which had just appeared in the square of stones. Brannel started away from Keff to divert the villagers. The brawn grabbed him by the arm.

"Don't interfere, Brannel. I won't be able to stop Ferngal next time. Look, man, I guaranteed only that Plenna would teach you."

Brannel was unsatisfied. "Even that did not happen. You sent me away, and I heard nothing for days. When I saw you at last, you were in too much of a hurry to speak to me."

"That was most discourteous of me," Keff agreed. "I'm sorry. But you *know* what we're doing. There's a lot to be done, and mages to convince."

"But we had a bargain," Brannel said stubbornly. "*She* could give me one of her items of power, and I can learn to use it by myself. Then I will have magic as long as anyone."

"Brannel, I want to offer you a different kind of power, the kind that will last. Will you listen to me?"

Reluctantly, but swayed by the sincerity of his first friend ever, the embittered Noble Primitive agreed at last to listen. Keff beckoned him to a broad rock at the end of the field, at a far remove from both the magifolk and the dray-faced farmers.

"If you still want to help," Keff said, "and you're up to continuing your journey, I want you to go on with it. Talk to the workers. Explain what's going to happen."

"But High Mage Ferngal said . . . ?"

"Ferngal doesn't want you to make things more difficult. Help us, don't hinder. Tell them what they stand to gain—in coopera- tion." Keff saw light dawning in the male's eyes. "Yes, you do see. In return, we'll supply you with food. We might even be able to manage transporting you from region to region by chair. Arriv- ing in a chariot will give you immediate high status with the others. You like to fly, don't you?"

"I love to fly," Brannel said, easily enough converted with such a shining prospect. "I will change my message to cooperation."

"Good! Tell them the truth. The workers will get better treat- ment and more input into their own government when the power is diminished. The mages will need you more than ever."

"That I will be happy to tell my fellow workers," Brannel said gravely.

"I have a secret to tell you, but you, and only you," Keff said, leaning toward the worker. "Do you promise? Good. Now listen: the mages are not the true owners of the Core of Ozran. Remember it."

Brannel was goggle-eyed. "I never forget, Mage Keff."

Seven days later, Chaumel returned to his great room dusting his hands together. A quintet of chariots lifted off the balcony and disappeared over the mountaintops. He stood for a moment as if listening, and turned with a smile to Plenna and Keff.

"That is the last of them," he said with satisfaction. "Everyone who has said they will cooperate has also promised to press the ones who haven't agreed. In the meantime, all have said that they will keep voluntarily to the barest minimum of use. On the day you designated two days hence, at sunrise in the eastern province, the great mutual truce will commence."

"Not without grumbling, I'm sure," Keff said, with a grin. "I'm sure there'll be a lot of attempts before that to renegotiate the accord to everyone else's benefit. Once the power levels lessen, it'll give me the last direction I need to find the Core of Ozran."

"Leave the last-minute doubters to me," Chaumel said. "At the appointed moment, you must be ready. Such a treaty was not easily arranged, and may never again be achieved. Do not fail."

✻CHAPTER THIRTEEN

The high mountains looked daunting in their deep, predawn shadow as Plenna and Chaumel flew toward them. Keff, on Plenna's chair, had the ancient manuals spread out on his lap. As he smoothed the plastic pages down, they crackled in the cold.

"The sun's about to rise over Ferngal's turf," Carialle informed him. "You should see a drop in power beginning in thirty seconds."

"Terrific, Cari. Chaumel, any of this looking familiar?"

Chaumel, in charge of three globe-frogs he was restraining from falling off his chair with the use of a mini-containment field generated by his wand, nodded.

"I see the way I came last time," he shouted. His voice was caught by the great mountains and bounced back and forth like a toy. "See, above us, the two sharp peaks together like the tines of a fork? I kept those immediately to my left all the way into the heart. They overlook a narrow passage."

"Now," Carialle said.

Chaumel's and Plenna's chariots shot forward slightly and the "seat belts" around the globe-frogs brightened to a blue glow.

"That's kickback," Keff said. "Every other mage in the world has turned off the lights and the power available to you two is near one hundred percent."

"A heady feeling, to be sure," Chaumel said, jovially. "If it were not that each item of power is not capable of conducting all that there is in the Core. I must tell you how difficult it was to convince

237

all the mages and magesses that they should not each send spy-eyes with us on this journey. Ah, the passageway! Follow me."

He steered to the right and nipped into a fold of stone that seemed to be a dead end. As the two chairs closed the distance, Keff could see that the ledge was composed of gigantic, rough blocks, separated by a good four meters.

The thin air between them was no barrier to communication between Keff and the Frog Prince. Lit weirdly by the chariot light, the amphibioid resembled a grotesque clay gnome. Keff waved to get his attention.

"Do you know where we are going?" he signed.

"Too long for any living to remember," Tall Eyebrow signaled back. "The high fingers—" he pointed up, "mentioned in history."

"What's next?"

"Lip, hole, long cavern."

"Did you get that, Carialle?" Keff asked. Flying into the narrow chasm robbed them of any ambient light to see by. Chaumel increased the silver luminance of his chariot to help him avoid obstructions.

"I did," the crisp voice replied. "My planetary maps show that you're approaching a slightly wider plateau that ends in a high saddle cliff, probably the lip. As for the hole, the low range beyond is full of chimneys."

"That's what the old manuals can tell me," Keff said, reading by the gentle yellow light of Plennafrey's chair. "According to this, the cavern where the power generator is situated is at ninety-three degrees, six minutes, two seconds east; forty-seven degrees, fifteen minutes, seven seconds north." He held up a navigational compass. "Still farther north."

"The lee lines lead straight ahead," Chaumel informed him. "Without interference from the rest of Ozran, I can follow the lines to their heart. You are to be congratulated, Keff. This was not possible without a truce."

"We can't miss it," Keff said, crowing in triumph. "We have too much information."

The sun touched the snow-covered summits high above them with orange light as the pass opened out into the great central cirque. Though scoured by glaciers in ages past, the mountains were clearly of volcanic origin. Shards of black obsidian glass stuck up unexpectedly from the cloudy whiteness of snowbanks under icefalls. The two chairs ran along the moraine until it dropped abruptly out from underneath. Keff had a momentary surge of vertigo as he glanced back at the cliff.

"How high is that thing, Cari?" he asked.

"Eight hundred meters. You wonder how the original humans got here, let alone the globe-frogs who built it."

At his signal, Plenna dropped into the dark, cold valley. Keff shivered in the blackness and hugged himself for warmth. He glanced up at Plenna, who was staring straight ahead in wonder.

"What do you see?" he asked.

"I see a great skein of lines coming together," she said. "I will try to show you." She waved her hands, and the faintest limning of blue fire a fingertip wide started above their heads and ran down before them like a burning fuse. A moment later, a network of similar lines appeared coming over the mountain ridges all around them, converging on a point still ahead. Her glowing gaze met Keff's eyes. "It *is* the most amazing thing I have seen in my life."

"Your point of convergence is roughly in the center of your five high mages' regions," Carialle pointed out. "Everyone shares equal access to the Core."

"Has anyone else ever come here?" Keff asked Chaumel.

"It is considered a No-Mages'-Land," the silver magiman said. "Rumors are that things go out of control within these mountains. I could not come this far in my youth. I became confused by the overabundance of power, lost my way, and nearly lost my life trying to fly away. Here is the path, all marked out before us, as if it was meant to be."

"We should never have lost sight of the source of our power," Plenna said. "Nor the aims of our ancestors." Her own tragedy, Keff guessed, was never far from the surface of her thoughts.

The two chariots began to throw tips of shadows as they ran over the broken ground. Soot-rimmed holes ten meters and more across punctuated the snow-field. Keff followed the indicator on his compass as the numbers came closer and closer to the target coordinates.

All at once, Chaumel, Carialle, and the Frog Prince said, "That one."

"And down!" Keff cried.

✳   ✳   ✳

The tunnel mouth was larger than most of the others in the snow-covered plain. Keff felt a chill creep along his skin as they dropped into the hole, shutting off even the feeble predawn sunlight. Plenna's chariot's soft light kept him from becoming blind as soon as they were underground. Chaumel dropped back to fly alongside them.

They traveled six hundred meters in nearly total darkness. Plenna's hand settled on Keff's shoulder and he squeezed it. Abruptly the way opened out, and they emerged into a huge hemispherical cavern lit by a dull blue luminescence and filled with a soft humming like the purr of a cat.

"You could fit Chaumel's mountain in here," Carialle said, taking a sounding through Keff's implants.

The ceiling of this cavern had been scalloped smooth at some time in the distant past so that it bore only new, tiny stalactites like cilia at the edges of each sound-deadening bubble. Here and there a vast, textured, onyx pillar stretched from floor to roof, glowing with an internal light.

The globe-frogs began to bounce up and down in their cases, pointing excitedly. Keff felt like dancing, too. Ahead, minute in proportion, lay a platform situated on top of a complex array of machinery. It wasn't until he identified it that he realized they had been flying over an expanse of machinery that nearly covered the floor of the entire cavern.

"I have never seen anything like it in my life," Chaumel whispered, the first to break the silence. His voice was captured and tossed about like a ball by the scalloped stone walk.

"Nor has anyone else living," Keff said. "No one has been here in this cavern for at least five hundred years."

"Stepped field generators," Carialle said at once. "Will you look at that beautiful setup? They are huge! This could light a space station for a thousand years."

"It is amazing," Plennafrey breathed.

She and Chaumel leaned forward, urging speed from their chariots, each eager to be the first to land on the platform. Keff clenched his hands on the chair back under his hips until he thought his fingers would indent the wood, but he was laughing. The others were laughing and hooting, and in the frogs' cases, jumping up and down for pure delight.

"The manual says . . ." Keff said, piling off the chair, pushed by

Plenna who wanted to dismount right away and see the wonders up close. "The manual says the system draws from the core below and the surface above to service power demands. It mentions lightning—Cari, this is too cracked to read. I must have lost a piece of it while we were flying."

Carialle found the copy in her memory bank. "It looks like the generators are made to absorb energy from the surface as well to take advantage of natural electrical surges like lightning. Sensible, but I think it got out of hand when the power demands grew beyond its stated capacity. It started drawing from living matter."

Plenna surrendered her belt buckle to the Frog Prince. He left his shell and joined Keff and Chaumel at the low-lying console at the edge of the platform. The brawn, on his knees, displayed the indicator fields to Carialle through the implants while signing with the amphibioids. Stopping frequently to compare notes with his companions, the Frog Prince read the fine scrawl on the face of each, then tried to tell the humans through sign language what they were.

"So that says internal temperature of the Core, eh, Tall?" Keff asked, marking the gauge in Standard with an indelible pen. "And by the way, it's hot in here, did you notice?"

"Residual heat from years of overuse," Carialle said. "I calculate that it would take over two years to heat that cavern to forty degrees centigrade."

"Well, we knew the overuse didn't occur overnight," Keff said. "Ah, he says that one is the power output? Thanks, Chaumel." He made another note on a glass-fronted display as the magiman gesticulated with the amphibioid. "Pity your ancestor didn't have any documentation on the mechanism itself, Plenna."

"Isn't that level rising?" Plennafrey asked, pointing over Keff's shoulder. Keff looked up from the circuit he was examining.

"You're right, it is," he said. Subtly, under their feet, the hum of the engines changed, speeding up slightly. "What's happening? I didn't touch anything. None of us did."

"I'm getting blips in the power grid outside your location," Carialle replied. "I'd say that some of the mages have gotten tired of the truce and are raising their defenses again."

Keff relayed the suggestion to Chaumel, who nodded sadly. "Distrust is too strong for any respite to hold for long," he said.

"I am surprised we had this much time to examine the Core while it was quiescent."

Swiftly, more and more of the power cells kicked on, some of them groaning mightily as their turbines began once again to spin. The gauge crept upward until the indicator was pinned against the right edge, but the generators' roar increased in volume and pitch beyond that until it was painful to hear.

"It's redlining," Keff shouted, tapping the glass with a fingernail. The indicator didn't budge. "Listen to those hesitations! These generators sound like they could go at any moment. We didn't get here any too soon."

"The sound is still rising," Plenna said, her voice constricted to a squeak. She put out her hands and concentrated, then recoiled horrified as the turbines increased their speed slightly in response. "My power comes from here," she said, alarmed. "I'm just making it worse."

The frogs became very excited, bumping their cases against the humans' knees.

"Shut it down," Tall commanded, sweeping his big hands emphatically at Keff. "Shut it down!"

"I would if I could," he said, then repeated it in sign language. "Where is the OFF switch?"

"Is it that?" Chaumel asked, pointing to a large, heavy switch close to the floor.

Keff followed the circuit back to where it joined the rest of the mechanism. "It's a breaker," he said. "If I cut this, it'll stop everything at once. It might destroy the generators altogether. We have to slow it down gradually, not stop it. This is impossible without a technical manual!" he shouted, frustrated, pounding his fist on his knee. "We could be at ground zero for a planet-shattering explosion. And there's nothing we could do about it. Why isn't there a fail-safe? Engineers who were advanced enough to invent something like this must have built one in to keep it from running in the red."

"Perhaps the Old Ones turned it off?" Chaumel suggested. "Or even our poor, deceived ancestors?"

"Off?" Plennafrey tapped him on the shoulder and shouted above the din. "Couldn't Carialle turn off every item of power?"

"Good idea, Plenna! Cari, implement!"

"Yes, sir!" the efficient voice crackled in his ear. "Now, watch the circuits as I lock them out one at a time. The magifolk won't notice—they'll think it's another power failure. You and the globe-frogs should be able to trace down where the transformer steps kick in. See if you can make a permanent lower level adjustment."

The turbines began to slow down gradually as the power demands lessened. The Frog Prince and his assistants were already at the consoles. As the only one with his hands outside a plastic globe, the leader had to monitor the shut-downs and incorporate the readings his assistants took through the controls. His long fingers flicked switches one after another and poked recessed buttons in a sequence that seemed to have meaning to him. The whining of the turbos died down slowly. In a while, the amphibioid raised his big hand over his head with his fingers forming a circle and blinked at Keff in a self-satisfied manner.

"You're in control of it now," Keff signed.

"I am now understanding the lessons handed down," the alien replied, his small face showing pleasure as he signed. "'To the right, on; to the left, off,' it was said. 'The big down is for peril, the small downs like stairs, to your hands comes the power.' Now I control it like this." He held up Plennafrey's belt buckle. His long fingers slid into the depressions. "This one is in much better condition than the single we have, which has done service for our whole population for all these many years."

Tall glanced toward the controls. The switches pressed themselves, dials and levers moved without a hand touching them. The great engines stilled to a barely perceptible hum.

"At last," he gestured, "after five hundred generations we have our property back. We can come forward once again."

He seemed less enthusiastic once the extent of the damage began to emerge. Series of lights showed that several of the turbines were running at half efficiency or less. Some were not functioning at all. At one time, some unknown engineer had tied together a handful of the generators under a single control, but the generators in question were nowhere near one another on the cave floor.

"It'll take a lot of fixing," Keff said, examining the mechanism with the frogs crowded in around him. The indicators in some of the dials hadn't moved in so long they had corroded to their pins. He snapped his fingernail at one of them, trying to jar it loose. "We'll have to figure out if any of the repair parts can be made out of components I have on hand. If they're too esoteric, you might need to send off for them, providing they're still making them on your home planet."

"Home?" one of the globe-frogs signed back, with the fillip that meant an interrogative.

"If you have the coordinates, we have your transportation," Keff offered happily, signing away to the *oops, eeps,* and *ops* of IT's shorthand dictation. "Our job is to make contact with other races, and we're very pleased to meet *you.* My government would be delighted to open communications with yours."

"That is all well, Keff," Chaumel asked, "but do not forget about us. What of the mages? They will be wondering what happened to their items of power. Blackouts normally last only a few moments. There will be pandemonium."

"And what for the future?" Plenna asked.

"Your folk will have to realize that you now coexist with the globe-frogs," Keff said thoughtfully. "And, Tall, she's right. You are going to have to do something about the mages. They're dependent upon the system to a certain extent. Can we negotiate some kind of share agreement?"

"They can have it all," Tall said, with a scornful gesture toward the jury-rigged control board. "All this is ruined. Ruined! You come from the stars. Why do you not take my people back to our homeworld? We are effectively dispossessed. We've been ignored since the day we were robbed by the Flat Ones. No one will notice our absence. Let the thieves who have used our machinery have it and the husk that remains of this planet."

"We'd be happy to do that," Keff said, carefully, "but forgive me, Tall, you won't have much in common with the people of your homeworld anymore, will you? You were born here. Five hundred generations of your people have been native Ozrans. Just when it could start to get better, do you really want to leave?"

"Hear, hear," said Carialle.

One of the amphibioids looked sad and made a gesture that threw the idea away. The Frog Prince looked at him. "I guess we do not. Truth, *I* do not, but what to do?"

"What was your people's mission? Why did you come here?"

"To grow things on this green and fertile planet," Tall signed, almost a dance of graceful gestures, as if repeating a well-learned lesson. He stopped. "But nothing is green and fertile anymore like in the old stories. It is dry, dusty, cold."

"Don't you want to try and bring the planet back to a healthy state?"

"How?"

Keff touched the small amphibioid gently on the back and drew Chaumel closer with the other arm. "The know-how is obviously still in your people's oral tradition. Why not fulfill your ancestors' hopes and dreams? Work together with the humans. Share *with* them. You can fix the machinery. I agree that you should make contact with your homeworld, and we'll help with that, but don't go back to stay. Ask them for technical support and communication. They'll be thrilled to know that any of the colonists are still alive."

The sad frog looked much happier. "Leader, yes!" he signed enthusiastically.

"Help us," Keff urged, raising his hands high. "We'll try to establish mutual respect among the species. If it fails, Carialle and I can always take you back once we've fixed the system here."

Chaumel cleared his throat and spoke, mixing sign language with the spoken linga esoterka. "You have much in common with our lower class," he said. "You'll find much sympathy among the farmers and workers."

"We know them," Tall signed scornfully. "They kick us."

Keff signaled for peace.

"Once they know you're intelligent, that will change. The human civilization on this planet has slid backward to a subsistence farming culture. Only with your help can Ozran join the confederation of intelligent races as a voting member."

"That's a slippery slope you're negotiating there, Keff," Carialle warned, noticing Plenna's shocked expression. Chaumel, on the other hand, was nodding and concealing a grin. He approved of Keff's eliding the truth for the sake of diplomacy.

"For mutual respect and an equal place we might stay," the Frog Prince signed after conferring with his fellows.

"You won't regret it," Keff assured him. "You'll be able to say to your offspring that it was your generation, allied with another great and intelligent race, who completed your ancestors' tasks."

"To go from nothing to everything," the Frog Prince signed, his pop eyes going very wide, which Keff interpreted as a sign of pleasure. "The ages may not have been wasted after all."

"Only if we can keep this planet from blowing up," Carialle reminded them. Keff relayed her statement to the others.

"But what needs to be done to bring the system back to a healthy balance?" Chaumel asked.

"Stop using it," Keff said simply. "Or at least, stop draining the system so profligately as you have been doing. The mages will have to be limited in future to what power remains after the legitimate functions have been supplied: weather control, water conservation, and whatever it takes to stabilize the environment. That's what those devices were originally designed to do. Only the most vital uses should be made of what power's left over. And until the frogs get the system repaired, that's going to be precious little. You saw how much colder and drier Ozran has become over the time human beings have been here. It won't be long until this planet is uninhabitable, and you have nowhere else to go."

"I understand perfectly," Chaumel said. "But the others are not going to like it."

"They must see for themselves." Plenna spoke up unexpectedly. "Let them come here."

"Your girlfriend has a good idea," Carialle told Keff. "Show them this place. The globe-frogs can keep everyone on short power rations. Give them enough to fly their chariots here, but not enough to start a world war."

"*Just* enough," Keff stressed as the Frog Prince went to make the adjustment, "so they don't feel strangled, but let's make it clear that the days of making it snow firecrackers are over."

"Hah!" Chaumel said. "What would impress them most is if you could make it snow *snow*! Everyone will have to see it for themselves, or they will not believe. The meeting must be called at once."

The Frog Prince and his companions paddled back to Keff. "We will stay here to feel out the machinery and learn what is broken."

Keff stood up, stamping to work circulation back into his legs.

"And I'll stay here, too. Since there is no manual or blueprints, Carialle and I will plot schematics of the mechanism, and see what we can help fix. Cari?"

"I'll be there with tools and components before you can say alakazam, Sir Galahad," she replied.

"I had better stay, too, then," Plenna said. "Someone needs to keep others from entering if the silver tower leaves the plain. She attracts too much curiosity."

"Good thinking. Bring Brannel, too," Keff told Carialle. "He deserves to see the end of all his hard work. This will either make or break the accord."

"It will be either the end or the beginning of our world," Chaumel agreed, settling into the silver chair. It lifted off from the platform and skimmed away toward the distant light.

✨CHAPTER FOURTEEN

The vast cavern swallowed up the few hundred mages like gnats in a garden. Each high mage was surrounded by underlings spread out and upward in a wedge to the rim of an imaginary bowl with Keff, Chaumel, Plenna, Brannel, and the three globe-frogs at its center on the platform. All the newcomers were staring down at the machinery on the cave floor and gazing at the high platform with expressions of awe. The Noble Primitive gawked around him at the gathering of the greatest people in his world. All of them were looking at him. Keff aimed a companionable slap at the worker's shoulders and winked up at him.

"You're perfectly safe," he assured Brannel.

"I do not feel safe," Brannel whispered. "I wish they could not see me."

"Whether or not they realize it, they owe you a debt of gratitude. You've been helping them, and you deserve recognition. In a way, this is your reward."

"I would rather not be recognized," Brannel said definitely. "No one will shoot fire at a target that cannot be seen."

"No one is going to shoot fire," Keff said. "There isn't enough power left out there to light a match."

"What is going on here?" Ilnir roared, projecting his voice over the hubbub of voices and the hum of machinery. "I am not accustomed to being summoned, nor to waiting while peasants confer!"

"Why has the silver tower been moved to this place?" a mage called out. "Doesn't it belong to the East?"

"Why will my items of power not function?" a lesser magess of Zolaika's contingent complained. "Chaumel, are you to blame for all this?"

"High Ones, mages and magesses," the silver magiman said smoothly. "Events over the past weeks have culminated in this meeting today. Ozran is changing. You may perhaps be disappointed in some of the changes, but I assure you they are for the better—in fact, they are inexorable, so your liking them will not much matter in the long run. My friend Keff will explain." He turned a hand toward the Central Worlder.

"We have brought you here today to see this," Keff said, pitching his voice to carry to the outermost ranks of mages. "This"—he patted the nearest upthrust piece of conduit—"is the Core of Ozran."

"Ridiculous!" Lacia shouted down at him from well up in the eastern contingent. "The Core is not this thing. This is a toy that makes noise."

"Do not dismiss this toy too quickly, Magess," Chaumel called. "Without it you'd have had to walk here. None of you have ever seen it before, but it has been here, working beneath the crust of Ozran for thousands of years. It is the source of our power, and it is on the edge of breaking down."

"You've been misusing it," Keff said, then raised his hands to still the outcry. "It was never meant to maintain the needs of a mass social order of wizards. It was intended"—he had to shout to be heard over the rising murmurs—"as a weather control device! It's supposed to control the patterns of wind, rain, and sunshine over your fields. We have asked you here so you will understand why you're being asked to stop using your items of power. If you don't, the Core will drain this planet of life faster and faster, and finally blow up, taking at least a third of the planetary surface with it. You'll all die!"

"We're barely using it now," Omri shouted. "We need more than this trickle." A chorus of voices agreed with him.

"This is the time, when everyone can see the direct results, to give up power and save your world. Chaumel has talked to each one of you, shown you pictures. You've all had time to think about it. Now you know the consequences. It isn't whether or not the Core will explode. It's *when!*"

"But how will we govern?" the piping voice of Zolaika asked. The room quieted immediately when she spoke. "How will we keep the farms going? If the workers don't have us in charge of everything they won't work."

"They don't need you in charge of everything, Magess. Stop using the docility drugs and you'll find that you won't need to herd them like sheep," Keff said. "They'll become innovators, and Ozran will see the birth of a civilization like it has never known. You're dumbing down potential sculptors, architects, scientists, doctors, teachers. The only thing you'll have to concentrate on," Keff said with a smile, "is to teach them to cook for themselves. Maybe you can send out some of your kitchen staff, after you build them stoves—geothermal energy is available under every one of those home caverns. You could have communal kitchens in each one of the farmsteads in a week. After that, you can discontinue all the energy you use in food distribution."

Keff urged Brannel to center stage. "Speak up. Go on. You wanted to, before."

"Magess," Brannel began shyly, then bawled louder when several of the mages complained they couldn't hear him. "Magess, we need more rain! We workers could grow more food, bigger, if we have more rain, and if you do not have battles so often." At the angry murmuring, he was frightened and started to retreat, but Keff eased him back to his place.

"Listen to him!" Nokias roared. Brannel swallowed, but continued bravely.

"I . . . the life goes out of the plants when you use much magic near us. We care for the soil, we till it gently and water with much effort, but when magic happens, the plants die."

"Do you understand?" Keff said, letting Brannel retreat at last. The Noble Primitive huddled nervously against an upright of the control platform, and Plennafrey patted his arm. "Your farmers know what's good for the planet—and you're preventing their best efforts from having any results by continuing your petty battles. Let them have more responsibility and more support, and less interference with the energy flow, and I think you'll be pleasantly surprised by the results."

"You go on and on about the peasants," Asedow shouted. "We've heard all about the peasants. But what are *they* doing here?" The green-clad magiman pointed at the frogs.

Keff smiled.

"This is the most important discovery we've made since we started to investigate the problems with the Core. When Carialle and I arrived on Ozran, we hoped to find a sentient species the equal of our own, with superior technological ability. We were disappointed to find that you mages weren't it." He raised his voice above the expected plaint. "No, not that you're backward! We discovered that you are *human* like us. We're the same species. We've found in you a long-lost branch of our own race."

"You are Ozran?"

"No! *You* are Central Worlders. Your people came to Ozran a thousand years ago aboard a ship called the *Bigelow*. That's the reason why I could translate the tapes and papers they left behind. The language is an ancient version of my own. No, Carialle and I still managed to achieve our goal. We have found our equal race."

"Where?" someone shouted. Keff held up his hands.

"You know all about the Ancient Ones and the Old Ones. You know what the Old Ones looked like. There are images of them in many of your strongholds. Your grandparents told you horror stories, and you've seen the holographs Chaumel had me play for you from the record tapes saved by your ancestors. But you've never seen the Ancient Ones. You know they built the Core of Ozran and founded the system on which your power has been based for ten centuries. These," he said, with a triumphant flourish toward the Frog Prince and his assistants, "are the Ancient Ones."

"Never!" Ferngal cried, his red face drawn into a furious mask.

Over shouts of disbelief, Keff blasted from the bottom of his bull-like chest:

"These people have been right here under your nose for ten centuries. These are the Ancient Ones who invented the Core and all the items of power."

The murmuring died away. For a moment there was complete silence, then hysterical laughter built until it filled the vast cavern. Keff maintained a polite expression, not smiling. He gestured to the Frog Prince.

The amphibioid stepped forward and began to sign the discourse he had prepared with Keff's help. It was eloquent, asking for recognition and promising cooperation. The mages recognized the ancient signs, their eyes widening in disbelief. Gradually, the merriment died down. Every face in the circle showed shock. They stared from Tall Eyebrow to Keff.

"You're not serious, are you?" Nokias asked. Keff nodded. "*These* are the Ancient Ones?"

"I am perfectly serious. Chaumel will tell you. They helped me—*directed* me—on how to make temporary repairs to the Core. It was overheating badly. It'll take a long time to get it so it won't blow up if overused. I couldn't do it by myself. I've never seen some of these components before. Friends, this machine is brilliant. Human technology has yet to find a system that can pull electrical energy out of the solid matter around it without creating nuclear waste. What you see here at my side is the descendant of some of the dandiest scientists and engineers in the galaxy, and they've been living in the marshes like animals since before your people came here."

"But they *are* animals," Potria spat.

"They're not," Keff said patiently. "They've just been forced to live that way. When the Old Ones moved to the mountains you call your strongholds, they robbed the frog-folk of access to their own machinery and reduced them to subsistence living. They *are* advanced beings. They're willing to help you fix the system so it works the way it was intended to work. You've all seen the holotapes of the way Ozran was when your ancestors came. Ozran can become a lush, green paradise again, the way it was before the Old Ones appropriated their power devices and made magic items out of them. They passed them on to you, and you expanded the system beyond its capacity to cope and control the weather. It's not your fault. You didn't know, but you have to help make it right now. Your own lives depend upon it."

"Hah! You cannot trick me into believing that these trained marsh-slime are the Ancient Ones!" Potria laughed, a harsh sound edged with hysteria. "Its a poor joke and I have had enough of it." She turned to the others. "Do you believe this tale?"

Most mages were conferring nervously among themselves. Keff was gratified that only a few of them cried out, "No!"

"You say we should share," Asedow said, "but these so-called Ancient Ones might have their own agenda for its use."

"They were here first, and it is their equipment," Keff said. "It is only fair they have access now."

"They could hardly use it worse than we have," Plennafrey shouted daringly.

"What has become of the rest of our power?" Ferngal asked.

"The turbines were overheating. We've turned them down to let them cool off," Keff explained. "There's enough power for normal functions. Nothing fancy. It's either that, or nothing at all, when the system blows up. You'll just have to learn to live with it."

"I won't 'just live with it.' How can you stop me?" Asedow asked obnoxiously.

"Shut up, brat, and listen to your betters," the old woman named Iranika called out.

"Who is with me?" Potria called out, ignoring the crone. "We've been insulted by this stranger. He *claims* he has stopped our power for our benefit, but he is going to give it to *marsh-creatures*. He wants to rule Ozran with that skinny wench at his side and Chaumel as his lackey!"

"Potria!" Nokias thundered, spinning his chariot in midair to face her. "You are out of order. Asedow, back to your place."

"Friends, please," Chaumel began.

"You give more consideration to a fur-face than to one of your own, Nokias," Asedow taunted. "Perhaps you'd rather be one of them—powerless, and fingerless!"

He started to draw up power to form one of his famous smoke clouds. All he could generate was a puff. Keff could see him strain and clench his amulet, trying to find more power. The cloud grew to the size of his head, then dissipated. Asedow panted. Nokias laughed.

"To me, Asedow!" Potria called "We must work together!" Her chariot flew upward, out of its place in the bowl. Asedow, Lacia, Ferngal, and a handful of others joined her in a ring. At once, a lightning bolt rocketed from their midst. It would have struck the edge of the platform but for the thin shield Chaumel threw up.

"This is thin," he said to Keff. "It will not hold."

Nokias, Zolaika, Ilnir, and Iranika flew down from their places toward the platform.

"This means trouble," Nokias called. "How much power is there left?"

"Not much beyond what it takes to run your chariots," Keff said.

"They can pervert that, too," Zolaika warned "See!"

Recognizing the beginnings of a battle royal, many of the other mages turned their chairs and headed for the exit. The chariots started to falter, dipping perilously toward the rows of turbines as the combined will of the dissidents drew power away from them. Many turned back and crowded over the platform, fighting for landing space.

"I will stop them," Tall said his huge hands clenched over the belt-buckle amulet.

"No," Keff said. "If you turn off the power, all these mages will fall."

"I will end this," Zolaika said. "Brothers and sisters, to me." At once, Nokias, Ilnir, and a cluster of other magifolk added their meager strength to that of the senior magess. Accompanied by straining sounds from the generators, she built a spell and threw it with all the force left in her toward the ring of dissidents.

Cries of fear came from the fleeing mages, whose chairs faltered like fledgling birds. The great chamber rumbled, and infant stalactites cracked from the ceiling. Sharp teeth of rock crashed to the platform. The mages warded themselves with shields that barely repelled the missiles. Keff jumped away as a three-foot section of rock struck the standard next to him. It bounced once and fell over the side, clattering down into the midst of the machinery.

In the circle of dissidents high up in the cavern, Potria and her allies held out their hands to one another. Keff could see bonds of colored light forming between them, one ring for each mage or magess that joined them.

"Problem, Keff," Carialle said. "They've reestablished their connection to the Core's controls."

"They are pulling," Plenna said, grabbing Keff's arm. "They're pulling at the Core, trying to break the barrier holding the power down—they've done it!"

"Tall, stop them!" Keff shouted.

"No can," the amphibioid semaphored hastily. "Old, broken."

"Coming on full now," Carialle's voice informed him.

With a mighty roar, the generators revved up to full force. The mages whose chariots were limping toward the exit hurtled out of the cavern as if sling-shot. Keff groaned as he smelled scorched silicon. He and the frogs hadn't been able to do more than patch the fail-safes. Now they were melted and beyond repair.

"As your liege I command you to cease!" Nokias shouted at the dissidents.

"You do not command *me*, brother," Ferngal jeered. He raised his staff and aimed it at Nokias. A bolt of fire, surprising even its creator in its size and intensity, jetted toward Nokias. The golden mage dodged to one side to avoid it. His chair, also oversupplied by the Core, skittered away on the air as if it were on ice. It was a moment before he could control it. In that short time, Ferngal loosed off several more bolts. They all missed but the last, which took off one of Nokias's armrests. Fortunately, the golden mage's arms were raised. He was readying a barrage of his own.

Lacia had engaged Chaumel. The two of them exchanged explosive balls of flame that grew larger and larger as each realized that the Core had resumed transmission. Dissidents dive-bombed the platform. With admirable calm and dead aim, Chaumel managed to keep them all from getting any closer.

"Stop!" Keff yelled. "The more power you use the closer we come to blowing up!"

With an eldritch howl, Potria swooped down at Keff, taloned fingers stretched out before her. He saw the red lightning forming between them and dove under the low console. Brannel and the frogs were already huddled there. Tall Eyebrow stood with his back to his companions, protecting them. Keff wished for a weapon, any kind of weapon. He saw his faux-hide toolkit, hanging precariously near the edge of the platform, anchored only by the edge of a chair that had landed on it. He rose to his hands and knees, and scrambled out of his hiding place, shielded by the cluster of chariots.

With power restored, Brochindel the Scarlet chose that moment to lift off in an attempt to flee the battle going on over his head. Keff threw himself on his belly with one hand out. He managed to grab one centimeter of strap by one joint of one hooked finger. Potria saw him lying there exposed, and screamed, coming around in the air and diving in anew. Wincing at the weight of the tool bag, Keff hoisted it up and dragged it into the lee of the console. He turned out the contents in search of a weapon. Hammers, no. Spanners, no. Aha, the drill! It had a flexible one-meter bit.

"The knight shall have his sword," Carialle said. "Get 'er, Sir Keff."

His fingers scrabbled on the chuck, trying to get the bit loose.

Potria, her power overextended by the immediacy of the Core, threw a ball of fire that left a molten scar in the platform's surface. Keff bounced up as she passed and snapped his erstwhile sword-blade out. He smacked Potria on the back of the hand. She dropped her amulet, but it fell only into her lap.

"You . . . you peasant!" she screamed, for lack of a better epithet. "You struck me!"

Plennafrey hurried to Keff's side. The Frog Prince had her belt buckle, but she still possessed her father's sash. Working the depressions with her long fingers, she formed a thin shell of protection around the two of them and the console. Potria veered upward when her target changed, and retreated, but not until Plennafrey poked a small hole in the shield. She scooped up a chunk of fallen rock and threw it after the pink-gold magess. It struck Potria in the back of the arm, provoking a colorful string of swear words as, this time, the magess lost her grip on her power object. She swooped down to retrieve it before it fell into the machinery.

"Good throw, Plenna!" Keff said, hugging her with one arm.

"Conservation of energy," Plenna said brightly, grinning at Keff.

Asedow zoomed in, his mace at the ready. Keff ducked flat to the floor, avoiding the smoke-bubble bombs, then sprang up. With a flick of his improvised epee, he engaged Asedow and disarmed him, flinging the mace away into the void. Swearing, Asedow reversed. He glanced down at the spinning engines, and felt among the robes at his chest. He uncovered a small amulet and planted his fingers in it.

"Damn!" Carialle said. "I don't have a record for that one."

Fortunately, Asedow didn't use it immediately. Too soon, Potria reappeared over the edge of the platform, her teeth set.

"I just wanted to say farewell," she said, her eyes shining with a mad light. "I'm going on a frog hunt! Are you with me, Asedow!"

"I am, sister!" the green mage chortled. "Our new overlords will be so surprised we came to visit!"

Sounds of alarm erupted from underneath the console. Tall emerged, signaling frantically. Potria, as a parting gesture, threw a handful of scarlet lightning at him. Tall shielded almost automatically, and went on gesturing, panic-stricken.

"My people," he repeated over and over. "My people!"

"We have to stop them!" Keff said. Plennafrey broke the bubble around them, and the three headed for her chair.

"I will guard our friends," Chaumel said, making his way across the platform toward them. Ferngal threw forked lightning, aiming for the silver and golden mages at once. Chaumel ducked, and it sizzled over his head. A second later, he had a thin and shining globe of protection raised around himself and the console, withstanding the attacks of the dissidents.

Plennafrey lifted off the platform. Asedow and Potria were already most of the way to the tunnel. Suddenly, half a dozen chariots loomed over them and dropped into their path, cutting them off. Jaw set grimly, Keff hung on. Tall clutched Plennafrey around the knees as she tried to evade the others, but there were too many of them.

"Traitor!" Lacia screamed, peppering them with thunderbolts.

"Upstart!" Ferngal shouted at Plennafrey. "You don't know your place, but you will learn! Together—*now!*"

The young magiwoman set up a shield, but spells from six or more senior mages tore it apart like tissue paper. Fire of rainbow hues consumed the air around them. An explosion racked the chariot beneath them. Keff, blinded and choking, felt himself falling down and down.

Something springy yet insubstantial caught him just a few meters above the tops of the generators. When his eyes adjusted again, Keff looked around. A net of woven silver and gold bore him and the others upward. Scattered on the surface of the machinery were the pieces of Plennafrey's chariot. It had been blasted to bits. Plenna herself, clutching Tall, was in a similar net controlled by Chaumel and Nokias. Ferngal and the others were halfway down the cavern, turning to come in again for another attack.

"Are you all right?" Chaumel asked them, helping them back onto the platform.

"Yes," Keff said, and saw Plenna's shaky nod. "The generators are running out of control. We have to slow them down."

Tall kicked loose from Plenna's arms and hurried over to the console. Using the amulet, he flicked switches and rolled dials, but Keff could see that his efforts were having little effect. Ferngal and the others were almost upon them. A bolt of blue-white lightning crackled between him and the console, driving him back. Bravely, the little amphibioid threw himself forward. Keff interposed himself between Tall and the dissidents, ready to take the brunt of the next attack.

"That's enough of this!" Carialle declared loudly. Suddenly, the power items stopped working. The dissidents' chariots all slowed down, even dipped. Everyone gasped. Lacia clutched the arms of her chair.

"Stop this attack at once!" Keff roared, flinging his arms up. "The next thing we turn off will be your chairs! If you don't want to fall into the gear-works, cease and desist! This isn't helping your cause or your planet!"

Furious but helpless, Ferngal and the others drew back from the platform. With as much dignity as he could muster, Ferngal led his ragged band out of the cavern.

"Nice work, Cari," Keff said.

"I wasn't sure I could select frequencies that narrow, but it worked," Carialle said triumphantly. "They won't fall out of the air, but that's it for their troublemaking. I'm *not* turning their power items on again. Tall can do it someday, if he ever feels he can trust them." Keff glanced at the globe-frog, who, in spite of the small burns that peppered his hide, was working feverishly over the console. The turbines slowed down with painful groans and screeches, and resumed a peaceful thrum.

"I doubt it will be soon," Keff said. Plennafrey grabbed his arm.

"We have to stop Potria," Plenna said urgently. "She's going to kill the Ancient Ones and she doesn't need power to do it. She's mad. If she can fly to where they are, that's enough."

Keff smote himself in the forehead. "I've been distracted. We have to stop them right away."

"She's gone mad," Nokias said. "*I* will go." The golden chair lifted off the platform.

"*I* will help, Mage Keff," Brannel volunteered, emerging from his hiding place.

"We've got to follow her, Chaumel," Keff said, turning to the silver magiman. "Can you take us, too?"

"Not to worry," Carialle said cosily in Keff's ear. "She's out here. In the snow. Swearing."

"Carialle stopped her," Keff shouted. Nokias turned his head, and Keff nodded vigorously. The others cheered, and Plenna threw herself into his arms. He gave her a huge hug, then dropped to his knees beside Tall. The other two globe-frogs had come out from beneath the console to aid their chief. They all acted alarmed.

"Can I help?" Keff asked.

"Big, *big* power, stored," Tall signed, pointing to the battery indicator. "Made by them," he gestured toward the departed Ferngal and his minions. "Must do something with it, now!"

"A glut in the storage batteries?" Keff said. He could see the dials straining. The others, who knew from long use what the moods of the Core felt like, wore taut expressions. "What can you do? Can you discharge it?"

Tall nodded once, sharply, and bent over the controls with the amulet clutched in his paws.

On the surface, Carialle's fins rested on an exposed outcropping of rock not far from the entrance. She watched with some satisfaction as Potria shook, then pulled, then kicked her useless chariot. Asedow lay unconscious on a snowbank where he'd fallen when his chair stopped. The pink-gold magess hoisted her skirts and tramped through the permafrost to his. It wouldn't function, either. She kicked it, kicked him, and came over to apply the toes of her dainty peach boots to Carialle's fins.

"Hey!" Carialle protested on loudspeaker. "Knock that off."

Potria jumped back. She retreated sulkily to her chair and seated herself in it magnificently, waiting for something to happen.

Something did, but not at all what Potria must have had in mind. Carialle detected a change in the atmosphere. Power crept up from beneath the surface of the planet, almost simmering up through solid matter. Instead of feeling ionized and drained, the air began to feel heavy. Carialle checked her monitors. With interest, she observed that the temperature was rising, and consequently, so was the humidity.

"Keff," she transmitted, "you ought to get everyone out here, pronto."

"What's wrong?" the brawns voice asked, worriedly.

"Nothing's wrong. Just . . . bring everyone topside. You'll want to see this."

She monitored the puzzled conversation as Keff gathered his small party together for the long flight to the surface. By the time they appeared at the chimney entrance, clouds were already forming in the clear blue sky.

Plennafrey rode pillion on Chaumel's chair with the three globefrogs clinging to the back while Keff and Brannel shared the gold chair with Nokias. Nokias's remaining followers straggled behind.

The group settled down beside Carialle's ramp. Potria, her nose in the air, ignored them pointedly.

"What's so important, Cari?" Keff asked after a glance at Asedow to make sure the man was alive.

"Watch them," Carialle suggested. The Ozrans were all staring straight up at the sky. "It's not important to you, but it is to them. In fact, it's vital."

"What's happening?"

"Just wait! You nonshells are so impatient," Carialle chided him playfully.

"The air feels strange," Brannel said after a while, rubbing a pinch of his fur together speculatively with two fingers. "It is not cold now, but it is *thick*."

The crack of thunder startled all of them. Sheet lightning blasted across the sky, and in a moment, rain was pummeling down.

As soon as the first droplets struck their outstretched palms, Chaumel and the others started shrieking and dancing for joy. A few of the mages gathered in handful after handful of the cold, heavy drops and splashed them on their faces. Plennafrey grabbed Keff and Brannel and whirled them around in a circle.

"Rain!" she cried. "Real rain!"

Under his wet, plastered hair, the Noble Primitive's face was glowing.

"Oh, Mage Keff, this is the best thing that has ever happened to me."

In the center of their little circle, the three globe-frogs had abandoned their cases and stood with their hands out, letting the water sluice down their bodies.

"Thank you, friends," Chaumel said, coming over to throw soaked sleeves over their backs. "Look how far the clouds spread! This will be over the South and East regions in an hour. Rain, on my mountaintop! What a treasure!"

"This is what'll happen if you let the Core of Ozran run the way it was meant to," Keff said. Plenna gave him a rib-cracking hug and beamed at Brannel.

"This welcome storm will convince more doubters than any speeches or caves full of machinery," Nokias said, coming to join them. "More of these, especially around planting season, and we will have record crops. My fruit trees," he said proudly, "will bear as never before."

"Ozran will prosper," Chaumel said assuredly. "I make these promises to you now, and especially to you, my furry friend: no more amputations, no more poison in the food, no more lofty magi sitting in their mountain fastnesses. We will act like administrators instead of spoiled patricians, eating the food and beating the farmers. We will come down from the heights and assume the mantle of our . . . humanity with honor."

Brannel was wide-eyed. "I never thought I would live to be talked to as an equal by one of the most important mages in the world."

"You're important yourself," Keff said. "You're the most intelligent worker in the world, isn't he, Chaumel?"

"Yes!" Chaumel spat water and wiped his face. "My friend Nokias and I have a proposition for you. Will you hear it?"

Nokias looked dubious for a moment, then silent communion seemed to reassure him. "Yes, we do."

"I will listen," Brannel said carefully, glancing at Keff for permission.

"Ozran will need an adviser on conservation. Also, we need one who will liaise between the workers and the administrators. It will be a position almost equal to the mages. There will be much hard work involved, but you'll use your very good mind to the benefit of all your world. Will you take it?"

Brannel looked so pleased he needed two tails to wag. "Oh, yes, Mage Chaumel. I will do it with all my heart."

"Shall I tell him now?" Plenna whispered in Keff's ear. "He can have my sash and my other things when I come away with you. Tall Eyebrow already has my belt."

"Um, don't tell him yet, Plenna. Let it be a surprise. *Uh-oh,* Cari," Keff subvocalized. "We still have a problem."

"I'm ready for it, sir knight. Bring her in here."

"Now, friends," Nokias said, wringing out one sleeve at a time. "I am enjoying this rain very much, but I am getting very wet. Come back to my stronghold, where we may watch this fine storm and enjoy it from under a roof." He beckoned to Brannel. "Come with us, fur-face. You have much to learn. Might as well start now."

Brannel, hardly believing his good fortune, mounted the golden chair's back and prepared to enjoy the ride. Nokias gathered his contingent, including the recalcitrant Potria, and Asedow, who was coming to with all the signs of a near-fatal headache.

"Go on ahead," Keff said. "We've got some things to take care of here."

Carialle's Lady Fair image was on the wall as Keff, Plennafrey, Chaumel, and the trio of globe-frogs came into the cabin. At once, she ordered out her servos, one with a heavy-duty sponge-mop, and the other with a shelf-load of towels.

"There, get warmed up," she said sweetly. "I'm making hot drinks. Whether or not you've forgotten, you were still standing on top of a glacier with wet feet."

Keff stepped out of his wet boots and went into his sleeping compartment. "Come on, Chaumel. I bet you wear the same size shoes I do. Everybody make themselves at home."

Plennafrey kissed her hand lovingly to Keff. He kissed his fingers to her and winked.

"Oh, Plenna," Carialle said with deceptive calm. "I've got some data I wanted to show you." Keff's crash-couch swung out to her hospitably as the magiwoman approached. "Sit down. I think you need to see these."

When Keff and Chaumel appeared a few minutes later, freshly shod, Plennafrey was sitting with her head in her hands. The Lady Fair "sat" sympathetically beside her, murmuring in a soothing voice.

"So you see," Carialle was saying, "with the mutation in your DNA, I couldn't guarantee your safety during prolonged space travel. And Keff couldn't settle here. His job is his whole life."

Plenna raised a tear-streaked face to the others.

"Oh, Keff, look!" The young woman pointed to the wall screen. "My DNA has changed over a thousand years, Carialle says. And my blood is too thin—I cannot go with you."

Keff surveyed the DNA charts, trying to make sense of parallel spirals and the data which scrolled up beside them. "Cari, is it true?" he subvocalized.

"I wouldn't lie to her. *No one* can guarantee anyone's complete safety in space."

"Thank you, lady dear, you're the soul of tact—How terrible," he said out loud, kneeling at Plenna's feet. "I'm so sorry, Plenna, but you wouldn't have been happy in space. It's very boring most of the time—when it isn't dangerous. I couldn't ask you to endure a lifetime of it, and truthfully, I wouldn't be happy anywhere else."

"I am glad this is the case," Chaumel said, examining the charts and microscopic analysis on Carialle's main screen. From the look in the mage's eye, Keff guessed that perhaps he had been eavesdropping on their private channel. "You cannot take such a treasure as Magess Plennafrey off Ozran."

Standing before the magiwoman, he took her hand and bowed over it. Plennafrey looked startled, then starry-eyed. She rose, looking up into his eyes tentatively, like an animal that might bolt at any moment. Chaumel spoke softly and put out a gentle hand to smooth the tears from her cheeks.

"I admire your pluck, my dear. You are brave and resourceful as well as beautiful." He favored her with a most ardent look, and she blushed. "I would be greatly honored if you would agree to be my wife."

"Your . . . your wife?" Plenna asked, her big, dark eyes going wide. "I'm honored, Chaumel. I . . . *of course* I will. Oh!" Chaumel raised the hand he was holding to his lips and kissed it. Keff got up off the floor.

"Listen up, sir knight. This fellow could give you some pointers," Carialle said wickedly. Chaumel aimed a small smile toward Carialle's pillar and returned his entire attention to Plennafrey.

"We will share our power, and together we will teach our fellow Ozrans to adapt to our future. Our society will be reduced in influence, but it will be greater in number and scope. The Ancient Ones can teach us much of what we have forgotten."

"And one day, perhaps, our children can go into space," Plenna said, turning to Keff and smiling, "to meet yours." Leaning over, she gave Keff a sisterly peck on the cheek and moved into the circle of Chaumel's arm.

Over the top of her head, Chaumel winked.

"And now, fair magess," he said, "I will fly you home, since your own conveyance has come to grief." Beaming, Plennafrey accompanied her intended down the ramp. He handed her delicately onto his own chariot, and mounted the edge of the back behind her.

"That man never misses a trick," Carialle said through Keff's implant.

"Thank you, Cari," Keff said. "Privately, in a comparison between Plenna and you as a lifelong companion, I'd choose you, every time."

"Why, sir knight, I'm flattered."

"You should be flattered," Keff said with a smirk. "Plenna is intelligent, adaptable, beautiful, desirable, but she knows nothing about my interests, and in the long transits between missions we would drive one another crazy. This is the best possible solution."

Chaumel's well-known gifts for diplomacy and the unexpected treat of the thunderstorm began to bear fruit within the next few days. Mages and magesses began to approach Keff and the globe-frogs in the cavern to ask if there was anything they could do to help speed the miracle to their parts of Ozran. Spy-eyes were everywhere, as everyone wanted to see how the repairs progressed.

The greatest difficulty the repair crew faced was the sheer age of the machinery. Keff and Tall rigged what they could to keep it running, but in the end the Frog Prince ordered a halt.

"We must study more," Tall said. "Given time, and the print-out you have made of the schematic drawings, we will be able to determine what else needs to be done to make all perfect. The repairs we have made will hold," he added proudly. "There is no need to beg the homeworld for aid. I would sooner approach them as equals."

"Good job!" Keff said. "We'll take our report home to the Central Worlds. As soon as we can, we'll come back to help you to finish the job. I expect that by the time we do, between you and the Noble Primitives, you'll teach the mages all there is to know about weather management and high-yield farming."

"The fur-faces will show them how to till the land and take care of it. We do not retain *that* knowledge," Tall said with creditable humility. "Brannel is our friend. We do need each other. Together, we can fulfill the hopes of all our ancestors. Others will take us up and back to the Core after this," the Frog Prince assured them. "Many are protecting us at all times. You've done much in helping us to achieve the respect of the human beings."

"No," Keff said, "you did it. I couldn't convince them. You had to show them your expertise, and you did."

Tall signaled polite disbelief. "Come back soon."

Carialle and Keff delivered Tall and his companions back to Brannel's plain for the last time. The globe-frogs signed them a quick good-bye before disappearing into the brush. Five spy-eyes trailed behind them at a respectful distance.

Chaumel and Plennafrey arrived at the plain in time to see Keff and Carialle off.

"You've certainly stirred things up, strangers," Chaumel said, shaking hands with Keff. "I agree there's nothing else you could have done. My small friends tell me that shortly Ozran would have suffered a catastrophic explosion, and we would all have died without knowing the cause. For that, we thank you."

"We're happy to help," Keff said. "In return, we take home data on a generation ship that was lost hundreds of years ago, and plenty of information on what's going to be one of the most fascinating blended civilizations in the galaxy. I'm looking forward to seeing how you prosper."

"It will be interesting," Chaumel acknowledged. "I am finding that the certain amount of power the Ancient Ones have agreed to leave in our hands will be used as much to protect us from disgruntled workers as it will be to help lead them into self-determination. Not all will be peaceful in this new world. Many of the farmers are afraid that their new memories are hallucinations. But," he sighed, "we brought this on ourselves. We must solve our own problems. Your Brannel is proving to be a great help."

Plennafrey came forward to give Keff a chaste kiss. "Farewell, Keff," she said. "I'm sorry my dream to come with you couldn't come true, but I am happier it turned out this way." She bent her head slightly to whisper in his ear. "I will always treasure the memory of what we had."

"So will I," Keff said softly. Plenna stepped back to stand beside Chaumel, and he smiled at her.

"Farewell, friends," Chaumel said, assisting the tall girl down the ramp and onto his chariot. "We look forward to your return."

"So do we," Keff said, waving. The chair flew to a safe distance and settled down to observe the ship's takeoff.

"They do make rather a handsome couple," Carialle said. "I'd like to paint them a big double portrait as a wedding present. Confound their combination of primrose and silver—that's going to be tricky to balance. Hmm, an amber background, perhaps cognac amber would do it."

Keff turned and walked inside the main cabin. The airlock slid shut behind him, and he heard the groaning of the motor bringing the outer ramp up flush against the bulkhead. The brawn clapped his hands together in glee.

"Wait until we tell Simeon and the Xeno boffins about the Frog Prince and his tadpole courtiers on the Planet of Wizards," Keff gloated, settling into his crash-couch and putting his feet up on the console. He intertwined his hands behind his head. "Ah! We will be the talk of SSS-900, and every other space station for a hundred trillion klicks!"

"I can't wait to spread the word myself," Carialle said with satisfaction as she engaged engines and they lifted off into atmosphere. "We did it! We may be considered the screwball crew, but we're the ones that get the results in the end. . . . Oh damn!"

"What's wrong?" Keff asked, sitting up, alarmed.

Carialle's Lady Fair image appeared on the screen, her face drawn into woeful lines.

"I forgot about the Inspector General!"

The Ship Errant

To Val and Rick
with love

✷PREFACE

To: Dr. Sennet Maxwell-Corey
Inspector General
Central Worlds Administration

From: Commander Lavon Muller-Danes
Alien Outreach Department

A transmission has been received by this office from RNJ-599, known locally as Ozran, requesting transportation of representatives of its government to its homeworld.

I have before me your memo asking me to inform you if such an eventuality arose. While the CK-963 brain/brawn team is, to say the least, unorthodox in its methods, it is effective. Furthermore, they did discover the "globe-frogs," as they call the aliens, and they speak the local language, which none of our other personnel do. Though the CK-963 would not have been my personal choice to undertake this mission, I bow to pressures from above that dictate we should not antagonize the Ozranians in any way, lest that jeopardize future cooperation.

Furthermore, the Ozranians have particularly requested that the same scoutship team convey them to their homeworld. Unfortunately, due to discovery of the Ryxi species a few months later, and the press of budget and time considerations since then, the Ozran file was placed at the bottom of Alien Outreach's agenda. As a result, no secondary contact team had been dispatched to the colony world to make further contact with the amphibioid population as was originally planned. The Ozranians prefer to deal only with humans who are familiar to them, and insist on Carialle and Keff.

I gave orders that the team be pulled from its current assignment. It was a routine courier mission that did not specifically call for the talents of a brainship, and has been reassigned to another available crew.

In reply to your insistence that we immediately remove CK-963 from the Ozran return mission I am taking the opportunity to acquaint you with the details of the original mission. In view of the outstanding success of the first contact, it is AOD's opinion that there is no apparent need to take this action. While I have reviewed the voluminous file you forwarded, there is no event among the forty-six incidents listed that would warrant an immediate recall of the brain/brawn team. If at some future date you produce evidence of instability on a level as to interfere with the mission, we will then follow your recommendation and replace the CK-963 with the group of experts now being assembled for the follow-up mission to Ozran. Those specialists should be on the station designated SSS-900-C within a month. I have simplified the technical material so as to make it understandable by the members of your department.

AOD Mission CK-963 5458.89 OZ0001

Initial observation two years ago of indigenous life on planet RNJ-599 revealed that there were two, possibly three, species of tool-using beings resident there. All three groups were soft-skinned, bilaterally symmetrical upright bipeds. Two of them, very humanoid in appearance, had skin colors in the beige to dark-brown range. One group of these appeared more intelligent and advanced than the others. Their manipulative extremities had five digits, arranged as a human's would be, with four fingers and an opposable thumb. They used a sophisticated system of power manipulation that was so advanced in its technology that it could be used to make the user fly, teleport solid objects, or even change the weather. The second species of humanoid bipeds had only four digits on each manipulaive extremity, and had hairy pelts. These beings served as the first group's trainable workforce. The Ozran "mages and magesses" (gender specific reference) had an extremely complex social hierarchy, and used without comprehension the scientific technology they possessed.

Because it was so easy to use by beings with a high level of telempathy, certain "mage(sse)s" were able to access an amulet's power more readily than others, hence the stratification of society. Because it was easier to use the conductor units than to accomplish a task by hand, over time the humans pushed the gigantic generator almost to destruction. By the time Keff and Carialle landed, the system was disintegrating dangerously, and Ozran society was in a downward spiral.

The third species, observed only casually, was a race of much smaller bipeds with skins in the green part of the spectrum. These lived a marginal existence in the meager swamps and marshlands of the arid continents.

Further observation revealed that both of the larger species were of the same race, and not native to Ozran. In fact, they *were* human beings. The four-fingered hands of the workforce were not the result of mutation, but mutilation. These mages and magesses mutilated the others to prevent the system being used by anyone not considered to belong to the intellectual elite. The servitors were kept tractable with the use of drugs by the five-fingered controllers.

Upon investigation, the humans proved to be a colony of the Central Worlds, who had landed on Ozran ten centuries ago. Ancient records of the initial overfly of the planet showed it to be a plum for settlers, with a fortunate climate, arable land and potable water, nitrox-mix atmosphere, suitably balanced gravity, moons to produce tides, and generally non-toxic plant life. Over time, they entirely lost contact with the Colonization Department. These humans had not invented the power system, but rather had inherited it from a race that had temporarily inhabited the planet. It was this unknown race of aliens that had stolen the power system from its inventors. They passed it on to the human settlers, then died out without telling them its source.

The contact team discovered that the creators of the fabulous power control system turned out to be the small, green creatures (called by the scout team "globe-frogs"), also found not to be native to Ozran. The humans had dismissed the globe-frogs as mere swamp animals, failing to observe the signs of intelligence and civilization the beings displayed. It took special intervention by the brainship team to restore the technology to its inventors before the neglect of centuries caused a planetary cataclysm. Access to the power conductor units was sharply restricted, although not entirely removed from use by the mages and magesses. Before the team left they saw the beginnings of an attempt to establish a system of government shared equally by humans and globe-frogs.

This amphibioid species, while not indigenous to Ozran, is of unusual interest to many sections of the Central Worlds government, not the least of which is this one. Such interest centers mainly around this scientific breakthrough reported by the initial contact team: the device which makes possible the remote manipulation of matter. Empirical observation suggests that those humans who use it have inbred a tendency toward telempathy which is necessary to operate the system. Science Research seems to think that it is possible to develop a variation of the power amulet that will allow anyone to make use of the Ozranian generators. As a result, we are all anxious to cooperate in any way the Ozrans require, to retain access to this important scientific breakthrough. Other departments that have requested more information are Science Research, Linguistics, and Economic Development.

The location of the Cridi (globe-frog) homeworld has been pinpointed as closely as possible by Exploration's astronavigators. Assisted by Carialle, who also translated the globe-frogs' extant charts, a program designed to roll back celestial movement to where the stars lay a thousand years ago, approximately the time the globe-frogs lost touch with their homeworld. Two possibilities have emerged: two dwarf yellow stars in binary combination. The CK-963 team is to try the nearer star first.

We have complied as promptly as possible with the amphibioids' request for the CK-963 to escort them to their homeworld. Central Worlds Administration pictures the globe-frogs as partners not only on the colony world of Ozran, but in the greater task of exploring the universe at large. We regret that the preliminary diplomatic and fact-finding mission to the globe-frogs' homeworld of Cridi also failed to materialize, but it is now too late either for regrets or a hasty dispatch of seasoned ambassadors. We are having to settle for Carialle and Keff going in cold.

I would like to assure you that both Carialle and Keff have been thoroughly briefed on the importance of this assignment, and have been cautioned under penalty to keep the contact on an absolutely professional level.

I again thank you for your interest in this department's function, and suggest that since we have come to terms with the immutable situation you should do so as well. I feel it is unwise to anticipate failure.

Sincerely,

Lavon Muller-Danes, Commander
Alien Outreach

✳CHAPTER ONE

En Route to the Cridi System

"What say you, good Sir Frog?" Keff asked, peering over the head of the small, green, bipedal amphibioid at the pieces of the three-dimensional puzzle spinning in midair at the entrance of the great hall of Castle Aaargh. The green being glanced up at him. He gestured toward the conundrum then flicked the tip of his unnaturally long forefinger against his knobby temple.

"Not difficult," Tall Eyebrow signed. Swiftly, he pointed from one piece to another, indicating which edges fit against one another. As he made each match, the pieces flew together until there was only one object spinning before them. Keff studied it.

"The Mask of Mulhavey," he said, awed.

"What is this Mask of Mulhavey?" the globe-frog asked, combining sign language with the unfamiliar Standard words voiced in the high-pitched peep of his kind. "Is this an important artifact in your culture?"

"Just a pretend artifact, TE," Keff said, as a quick aside. "Carialle made it up for the game. Stay with it."

"Ah, make-believe." Tall Eyebrow nodded, and threw a self-deprecating gesture toward his host. "Forgive me. I forget this is but Myths and Legends." His signs grew more theatrical, in imitation of the human male. "What does this mean?"

"I know not, my lord," Keff said, replying in both frog sign

language and Standard. "Perhaps if we looked through the eyeholes we would see a wonder."

"He's altogether too good at theoretical and combination spatial relations," Carialle said over the central room speaker as the two
"adventurers" bent to see through the apertures of her creation. They
made a curious picture. The man, of medium height for a human,
had a broad chest, muscular arms and legs. He was dressed in a
garment that reached to mid-thigh, not unlike a medieval tunic, over
trousers and boots. His usual gentle countenance wore a watchful,
inquiring scowl. Around his waist, a sword belt held a glow-tipped
epee ready to hand. His companion stood less than a meter high,
had shiny green skin, a short, narrow body and beady black eyes.
His hands and feet were almost as large as those of the human beside
him, the fingers of almost equal length to one another. He wore a
beret, a short cape, and a belt around his small middle, its buckle
a large, gold boss with five indentations in it that looked made for
the fingertips to slide into.

"Better than I am, my lady," Keff laughed, shaking his head. "I
give up, TE. You tell me what you think we need to do with it."

The game they were playing was Myths and Legends. Among
the grounders, who occupied the safe and settled planets, it was
a children's game. Keff had learned it in primary school, and
had introduced it to his brain partner, Carialle, as a means of
occupying the infinitely long intervals of space travel. To Keff
it gave life a certain special meaning, to accomplish points of
honor, to lay successes at the feet of his Lady Fair. He was a
born knight errant. His private aim, ever since he had been a
child, had been to *do good*, a goal that had gotten him into
more than a few playground fights with schoolmates who lacked
his natural devotion to the greater concept of truth. To Carialle,
it provided an outlet for the creative bent that was so often
lacking in the technical jobs given to shellpeople, even brainships. And it was fun. Over time, it had simply worked its way
into their everyday lifestyle, to the despair of the Exploration
arm of Central Worlds. To Exploration and Alien Outreach,
Keff's globe-frog playmate was Tall Eyebrow, ambassador and
representative from a shared colony world known to the humans
who lived there as Ozran. To the knight and his lady, he was
also occasionally the Frog Prince.

Tall Eyebrow gestured to Keff to look through the eyeholes.

Carialle was amused when her brawn had to crouch down on the floor to put his head at the same level as the globe-frog's.

"It should have taken longer for him to solve that jigsaw," she said. "I'm going to have to make the puzzles harder. These little chappies have surprisingly deep minds. I am continually having to reevaluate my judgement of their ability to learn."

"Well, you've already surpassed my understanding, Cari," Keff said cheerfully, rising from his haunches with his hands on his thighs. He turned toward the titanium pillar that contained and protected her physical body, and winked. The two years that had passed since they had first met the globe-frogs had lightened a few more hairs on his curly head, and possibly slowed down his reactions by milliseconds, but hadn't taken a whit off his boundless good nature or enthusiasm. His muscle tone continued to be excellent, Carialle was pleased to note, and the bright blue eyes in his mild, bull-like face were clear and alert. Respiration and pulse, up a little, but that had to do with excitement over the game rather than exertion. He stretched his arms out and rotated his broad torso from side to side to ease his back. "Actually, I'm enjoying being TE's sidekick, if I allow the truth to be known. After adventuring on my own for so many years, a change is nice."

"I, too, am enjoying it," Tall Eyebrow signed quickly. "Too much reality for so long, to strive without fear is high fun."

Keff grinned. "Well, that's why we do it— Yoicks!"

Carialle had chosen that moment to activate the next peril in the ongoing game. The human jumped back as the holographic "stone wall" beside them slid back to reveal four villains, armed with chains and machetes. He felt for the light-tipped sword at his side, and was soon engaged in healthy battle with his computer-generated adversaries.

The enemy was only a holograph, but Carialle made them look utterly real, using a combination of projective cameras like the ones that drove her navigation screentank. The setting, complete with cobwebs and rats, could have been any pre-industrial village, instead of the cabin of a sophisticated starship. The brain behind it was as clever as the swordplay of the villain facing him.

Completely into his part once again, Keff slashed his blade overhand and thwacked the scarred villain in the arm. The man dropped his guard, giving Keff a chance to fling himself forward with a thrust to quarte. The glowing cursor went home, and the

villain collapsed to the floor with a wail. Keff threw back his head
with a feral laugh. "Come on! Who's next? Together we cannot be
beaten!" Another adversary stepped forward over the body of his
fallen chief, saber flashing in the candlelight.

The globe-frog emitted an alarmed squeak. "What are those?"
he signed, pointing at the sparks, like fireflies, that poured out of
the dark hall after the human villains.

"Some foul, unknown peril," Keff called over his shoulder, not
taking time to sign. "Catch them!"

The sparks flitted all over the room. Keff ducked a squadron
of the small glows, then skillfully parried a chop from one of the
hoods wielding a machete.

The globe-frog took a moment, translating Standard human language to his own, then his small brow rose in comprehension. He
bounded up to clap his hand against the wall next to Keff's head,
trapping a "firefly."

"That's one," Carialle said. "Fifteen to go."

"You're letting them get away!" Keff cried. He was cornered
between two of the foe, who stood tossing their weapons from hand
to hand. One of them feinted, and Keff parried, sweating. Tall
Eyebrow ran toward another elusive spark.

"I will assist!" cried Small Spot. He was the more impetuous
of the two aides who had accompanied Tall Eyebrow from Ozran.
Small Spot, in spite of his diminutive sounding name, was large,
as the amphibioids went. The "spot" was a lighter greenish patch
in the center of his forehead. Unlike most of his species, his hide
had a smooth color all over but for that. He sprang up from where
he had been sitting on Keff's weight bench to aid his prince. The
fingers of one hand slid into the five long grooves of his power
amulet, and he rose five meters in the air to capture a "firefly"
that had slipped Tall Eyebrow's grasp.

He floated down from the ceiling, looking sheepishly at his
empty palm. He glanced up at the others shyly.

"I forget, there is nothing there to touch."

His companion, Long Hand, an older and more cautious female,
perched out of the way of the action on the console, emitting the
high-pitched creaking that meant one of their species was laughing.
Small Spot returned to his place, skinny knees bent to show
embarrassment.

"I do not understand human games," he admitted, small face

set in a self-deprecatory grimace. "It is one more cultural oddity to which we must adapt."

"Relax, Small Spot," Carialle said. She made the image of a globe-frog appear on the wall at their level, and addressed him in sign. "There's no disgrace in being fooled by a good illusion. One of my better ones, I must say."

"She . . . gets . . . better . . . all the time," Keff panted, dancing away from an enemy whose skill matched his own.

"I had not been observing properly," Small Spot said.

In shame, he flapped one of his big flat hands away from his face, not looking at her simulacrum. To distract him, Carialle showed him a different hologram, a piece of technological schematic she had adapted from her observation of the Core of Ozran, the gigantic power complex that supplied the amphibioids' amulets. The mechanism connected each user to the Core by means of high frequency transmission. For the journey to the globe-frogs' homeworld, Carialle had installed a similar but much smaller system to serve their needs while they were aboard. Their delicate skins needed to be kept moist. With the amulets they could maintain an electrostatic charge that clothed them with a film of water all over except the palms of their hands and the soles of their feet. It put a tremendous strain on her engines, but she and Keff felt it was necessary to allow them to have freedom of movement and so not everything on this ground-breaking trip would be strange. It was enough that they were the first of their kind to leave their planet for the first time in a thousand years. Carialle felt it was her duty to put the nervous amphibioids at their ease.

"Maybe you can help me," she said to Small Spot. "I felt another odd surge, another sonic feedback, when you used your amulet just now. If I've adjusted the receptors correctly you should be able to draw power from my engines without this much signal noise. I think the problem comes from here." A portion of the diagram enlarged, bulging out from the rest as if under a magnifying glass.

"Let me see," Small Spot signed, gesturing it closer, clearly grateful for the chance to save face. Long Hand bounded down from the console with leggy grace, and trotted over to help. In no time at all, the two were signing away energetically over the faulty circuit diagram. At the other end of the room, Keff and Tall Eyebrow had moved on to the next part of the game, where they had to figure out the mystery that the Mask of Mulhavey was concealing, in spite of other pretend perils that occasionally distracted them. Tall Eyebrow grinned as Carialle responded to his questions, showing some of the hidden map and key as he answered each one correctly. Though make-believe was an unfamiliar concept to his species, Tall Eyebrow was embracing it as if he'd been brought up to it. In fact, the small aliens had adapted with remarkable speed to space travel, too.

The amphibioids, whom Keff and Carialle had dubbed "globe-frogs," for their mode of transportation (clear plastic bubbles partly filled with water) and their resemblance to Earth amphibians, had a very flexible outlook indeed. To ascend as they had from a marginal, swamp-bound existence where computer technology and particle science were taught in theory on clay tablets for lack of equipment in the lonely dream that one day they'd be able to use their handed-down education, to an equal partnership with technically capable but theoretically ignorant humans was a certifiable miracle. To then bring their shared planet forward centuries in only two Standard years was a more than respectable achievement. A human autocracy had been replaced by a republic governed by representatives of both races, human and globe-frog. When conditions had improved to a point where Tall Eyebrow and his conclave decided that the combined society would prosper without constant supervision, they sent a message to the Central Worlds, and asked for transportation to their native planet, Cridi, particularly requesting the CK-963 as their escort.

The team had been called home with a message coded urgent. They were briefed and rebriefed and re-rebriefed as to what to say and how to behave to the homeworld amphibioids. Carialle knew they weren't Alien Outreach Department's favorite team. The upper brass considered them too odd, too idiosyncratic to be good representatives of humanity and the Central Worlds. Still, it had been the CK-963, and not a more traditional team, that had discovered and reinstated the globe-frogs, and it was the CK-963 who must convey the visiting party from Ozran to Cridi. Carialle preferred to call their peculiarity "imagination" rather than "idiosyncracy," but looking at it from the perspective of people who ate pureed mush of unreconstructed proteins and carbs for lunch lest they be troubled by form, color, and texture, she supposed she and Keff must be as strange as . . . well, another alien race.

Several departments of CW had carefully examined all the tapes

Keff and Carialle had made, and they wanted the power control technology. The team had warned that a high level of telepathic ability was necessary to operate it, and that unlimited use was destructive to the environment, but all the brass could see was effortless, remote manipulation of solid objects. Credit balances of high digits followed by endless zeroes danced before their eyes. Whatever obstacles needed to be overcome would be examined after the power control system was in their hands. Surely the Central Worlds had much they could offer in exchange. Carialle and Keff were to bend over backward and whistle if that was what was needed to ensure diplomatic ties with this fully mature, space-ready race of intelligent beings. Nothing must come between humanity and the Cridi, and the Cridi's wonderful scientific advances. The diplomatic arm warned the team to behave themselves, and put dozens of strictures upon them, punishable by fines and penalties too horrible to name. The brass weren't going to be best pleased that the "Odd Couple" had polluted the minds of the visiting party of frogs, teaching them their fantasy game to while away the long voyages. The slack cut for the CK-963 because of their big discovery would only go so far. Silly folderol would not be tolerated.

Carialle didn't care, and she knew Keff didn't, either. All they wanted was the opportunity to revisit Ozran, and they got it. They had been amazed at the difference after only a two-year absence. The almost-desert world of Ozran had become lush. Verdant cropland burgeoned, thousands of young trees sprouted, and the skies rained, rained, rained. Keff had found it dreary, but all Ozrans, shades of green and brown alike, stared up at the gray thunderclouds with expressions of bliss. It all depended upon your outlook, Carialle thought.

Tall Eyebrow had succeeded in trapping all the dragonflies, and Keff was out of swordsmen to kill, so Carialle slowly shifted the holographic view forward, engulfing them in the darkness of "the great hall."

"Great suns, the lights are disappearing," Keff complained. Worried cheeps erupted from the two globe-frogs at the far side of the cabin, whose sole light source now was the hovering circuit diagram.

"Mulhavey," a tiny voice peeped.

Carialle smiled to herself. Tall Eyebrow had amazing powers of observation. On infrared, she watched his skinny form lope towards the spinning mask. He bent to look through it. It allowed you to see in the dark. He followed the floating hologram, grabbing Keff on the way, to three doors concealed behind a tapestry at the end of the room.

"Bend down," TE chirped in Standard, since his sign language was useless in the dark. He prodded Keff to look through the eyeholes at the three doors. They started a low discussion about which door to choose. Carialle left them to it, and made a crosscheck of her systems, and took a look at the long-range monitors. Hmm, number three engine was running a trifle too hot. She damped down the carburetion filter until all five engines were running in harmony.

Tall Eyebrow and his people had been out of touch with their homeworld, ever since the advent of the second alien race. Carialle reviewed the combination sign the Ozran globe-frogs had for these others, one hand with two fingers pointed downward like legs, but with the knees facing backward, and the other stretching the eyelids of one eye wide. No verbal name existed. The Crook-knees learned how the power system worked, commandeered all the power units in one single lightning grab, then moved their population base into the mountains, far out of reach of the Cridi. Without their devices, the globe-frogs were helpless. They couldn't range far from water, and had grown too dependent upon using the amulets to know how to survive without them. But a thousand years of subsistence living had taught them everything there was to know about making use of natural resources. Vulnerable to every hazard and large animal on the planet, sensitive to the atmosphere, and deprived of even basic luxuries they were forced to use the only resource left to them: their intellect. They lived virtually without waste, made use of all available resources, and appreciated every benefit that came their way. Carialle thought that such an admirable attitude would be a better import for the Central Worlds than the amulets.

The adventurers in her cabin passed through the correct doorway, and found themselves in a torchlit corridor, which in normal use was the passageway that led to Keff's quarters, the spare cabin, and the lift down to the storage bay. TE, letting the mask hologram float off, put his hand up flat to his face with the three middle fingers bunched together, and the long pinkie and almost equally long thumb slightly apart from the others so his round

black eyes could peep through. It was his symbol for Carialle, "the
One Who Watches From Behind the Wall."

"Yes?" Carialle asked at once.

"We have succeeded to the next stage. Food and water now?"
the globe-frog asked, his small face plaintive.

"How thoughtless of me! Keff, you can go on for days without sustenance, and I have my own feeding systems, of course.
Certainly, TE!" To keep within the context of the game, she had
a floating globe appear that led the two adventurers toward the
food synthesizer at the end of the cabin near the weight bench
and the other two globe-frogs.

"I'd have just left the castle and gone to find a pub," Keff said
apologetically. "Sorry, TE. You're not familiar with the conventions."

The hatch opened to disgorge in succession a bowl of succulent marsh greens, a glass of water, a glass of beer, some amor-
phous proteins shaped like Ozran grubs, and a plate containing
one of Keff's favorite set lunches. Traveling with the globe-frogs
was good not only for Keff, but for her as well. She had a chance
to stretch her synthesizer's repertoire.

"There is not a strong enough resistor here," Small Spot said,
pointing to the schematic. Carialle, distracted from her musings,
noted his correction, tested it, found it good, and directed her
internal mechanisms to make the adjustment.

"All right, try floating again," she instructed Small Spot. Obediently, the amphibioid put his fingertips into the niches on his
amulet and took to the air.

But monitoring the game, meals, and the schematic took only
a small portion of Carialle's attention. She had an oil painting in
process, a globe-frog paddling its way across the dusty fields of
Ozran, the way they were when she and Keff had first seen them,
two years earlier. The canvas was meant to be a gift to the new
joint government, to remind them of what they had left behind
them. Her custom painting equipment took up as much space at
one end of the cabin as Keff's exerciser did at the other. Critically, she examined each pixel she had done so far of the special
microfiber-cell canvas, and with the greatest of care, flooded ten
more cells of the thin, porous surface with medium green, and
five with dark green, creating a minute stripe and highlight along
a globe-frog's back. The result looked like a brush-stroke with a
very fine sable brush, exactly as she wanted it to. She ought to

be finished with the painting by the time they returned to Ozran. Carialle also gave her own hardware a good going over, to make certain the boffins in the repair bay at SSS-900-C, the last space station they had visited, hadn't left any screws untightened when they had examined her innards to install a ton of new memory. It appeared nothing had shaken loose since her last diagnostic. Their friend Simeon, the shellperson station manager, ran a tight ship. But Carialle liked to look after her own innards.

It was a wonder that the human race hadn't met the amphibioid race at least in passing. The coordinates that TE had given Carialle for his homeworld weren't far from P-sector, where Carialle herself had traveled many years before. Had no bored scientist with a radio-digital telescope ever swung it toward that system and picked up the traces of RF transmission? There could be a thousand explanations for failing to spot Cridi, but the result was, Carialle thought smugly, that she and Keff would be the first to meet the frogs, and the credit would be all theirs. Score two for the screwball crew, Carialle thought, her attention passing lightly over a cluster of unused memory cells. Alien Outreach didn't want a byte of possibly useful information about humankind's newest neighbor sacrificed for lack of space. They'd loaded her with new chips and controllers along every available circuit. Carialle felt that if she coughed she would rattle.

She scanned space around her. P-sector had only begun to be opened up in the last thirty years or so by exploration teams. It contained numerous spatial anomalies that frightened commercial shippers as much as it intrigued them as to what salable wonders might lie upon some of those as yet undiscovered planets circling the only just charted stars. When she herself had visited part of P-sector years ago, it was in the course of an investigation, with her first brawn, Fanine Takajima-Morrow, the mission had ended disastrously. A bomb planted by saboteurs in Carialle's fuel tank exploded, killing Fanine Takajima-Morrow, and leaving Carialle floating derelict, to wait weeks for rescue. She had survived, only narrowly avoiding the madness that haunts sensory deprivation.

It was right near here, in fact. Something long buried in her memory nudged her that she was passing within a few hundred thousand klicks of the exact spot. She did not even need to check the coordinates to know that that was true—how could she not have taken that into her calculations when she was planning the course to the Cridi system? Her thought processes must have been taken up with other things.

Still, her navigation program must have observed details about their route. Undoubtedly, her subconscious had told her she had old business to deal with, and steered her this way. Keff would have warned her to avoid the spot, if he had known. Bad luck, or some other softshell notion. But she wasn't superstitious—shellpeople weren't. Luck had little bearing on their situations. Considerable thought went into every facet of their lives, from pre-natal survival to the last hookup in their shells. Carialle's own disability had been diagnosed while she was still in her mother's womb, and she had been enshelled at once to save her life. So why did she feel, as they said in the old saw Keff had once dug up in his linguistical research, as if a goose had walked over her grave? Could there be leftover psychic vibration in a place where a trauma had occurred? That had to be a myth, and yet she began to experience the anxieties she had suffered when she was marooned here. These—yes, these were the last stars she had seen before the bomb in her fuel tank exploded, destroying her first ship and killing Fanine. Adrenaline surged through her system. Frozen, Carialle felt panic rise, not stopping it as it turned her nerves to barbed wire. It could happen again! Frantically, she ran a safety check on the fuel mix in her tanks, measuring carbon levels, looking for the telltales that might indicate the presence of foreign substances.

"Cari!"

A millisecond passed before she recognized the voice, and responded.

"Keff?"

"Cari, what happened? The game holos are gone. Why did you fire off a message probe? What's wrong?"

That question brought her immediately back to the present. The cabin had indeed lost its veneer of medieval neglect. Keff and Tall Eyebrow stood in the center of the plain, enamel-painted room looking incongruous in tunics and swordbelts. Keff stared at her pillar.

"Are you all right?"

"What message probe?" she demanded, then checked her own telemetry. Sure enough, one of her small emergency rockets was streaking away into endless night, following a vector that would take it toward their last point of contact with the Central Worlds. Carialle searched the chips which supplied her with hard drive storage, found nothing, and extended the search to her other components.

"I didn't do that on purpose," Carialle said, crossly. "It must have been a malfunction caused by a bad connection. Darn it, and I was certain they'd checked everything in dry-dock!" Frantically she traced the circuits leading back from the controller in the rocket port.

"No, wait . . . Somebody planted a post-hypnotic suggestion on me."

Keff shook his head. "You can't be hypnotized, Cari."

"It's the shellperson equivalent," Carialle said, her voice becoming crisp and cold. "Programming has been inserted into my circuits to respond to certain stimuli under certain very precise conditions, with the result you have just observed. There are microfilaments inserted into my nutrient storage tanks. They are probably there to monitor unusual demand for brain chemicals and carbos in a combination that approximates paranoid hysteria with pseudo-psychotic overtones, a condition that I admit I submitted to momentarily just now."

"Who?" Keff asked, his face setting into a grim mask.

"Who do you think?" Carialle countered. "Who's been trying to Section-Eight me for the last twenty years? Who thinks I'm a flying emotional time bomb who should be relegated to controlling traffic on a Central Worlds ground station? Maxwell-Corey, of course. That afterburning, fardling collection of random neural firings Inspector General!"

"Are you sure?" Keff asked.

"Who else would Rube-Goldberg me without my knowledge?" Her blood pressure rose, so she adjusted slightly her intake of saline and gave herself five micrograms of a mood leveler. The panic attack had left behind its debris of epinephrines and excess gastric acids that were fast disappearing down the blood-cleansing apparatus. "He doesn't trust me. He never has."

"This is harassment," Keff said, all his protective tendencies coming out at once. "We should report it to SPRIM and MM." SPRIM was the Society for the Protection of the Rights of Intelligent Minorities, and MM, Mutant Minorities, two agencies that spoke up on behalf of shellpeople who ran into difficulties with unshelled bureaucracy. Dr. Sennet Maxwell-Corey, a psychiatrist by training and a nuisance by avocation, was a particular bugbear to both of them, but he had a special animus toward Carialle. He had never been convinced she had recovered from being marooned. The fact that she and Keff took a lighthearted view toward the naming of the indigenous species they encountered on their missions for Exploration, and their devotion to playing Myths and Legends, made her sanity all the more suspect to the unimaginative bureaucrat.

"I am composing something scathing right now," Carialle said, "while I destroy the implant with extreme prejudice." Her self-repair facilities, micromachines of various designs, crawled along the electronic neural extenders and yanked the filaments out of her tanks and filled in the drillmarks. Others traced down the filaments to the control boxes carefully hidden in deadware like the bottom of her waste tanks.

"Don't send the message without my input," Keff insisted. He got up from his chair and paced back and forth in front of her pillar. "I have something to say about imperiling my partner's well-being. And I want to tell them just what I think of his big-brotherism." He smacked one fist into the other palm. Tall Eyebrow and the other two globe-frogs jumped away from him. He was sorry to frighten them, but he was unspeakably angry.

"Why did it happen?" he asked, stopping short and looking up into her nearest camera eye.

"We're in P-sector," Carialle said flatly.

Keff's eyes went wide. He knew all about her history, and always had been extremely supportive in helping her heal from her traumatic experience. "Are we . . . there?"

"Yes."

Keff noticed the emergency lights on the console board, and went to shut off the alarms. "Are you all right now?"

"Yes." Carialle's voice was thin with anger. "Damn him! I passed my last six psych tests, two of them—two!—since our trip to Ozran. I feel violated. There's a message box in my memory, with all kinds of circumventions to make certain I couldn't detect it. Planted among the microdiodes at the same time as the uninitialized chips. Nowhere near the new stuff, which the wily bastard knew would be the first things I'd suspect. It's a custom job, too . . ."

Keff interrupted. "But why would you have reacted like that? Why would you have set it off at all?"

"I know every inch of this parsec," Carialle said unhappily. "I spent an eternity here, Keff. Not that far from here is where my fuel tanks blew up. There." A holoview of the sector appeared, with their path indicated in blue. A red X blossomed at a distance from their present location and floated toward them, crossing the blue line and passing toward a cluster of stars to their starboard stern. She squared up their current location on the tank, and Keff looked at it solemnly. "I was disabled here for weeks. And just for a moment, I was reliving that experience. I was *counting*, counting the seconds to keep from going insane. Then I remember feeling those footsteps on my hull, feeling those hands dismembering my components, stripping what they must have thought was a wreck, and hearing myself screaming. 'Who are you?'" she wailed.

Keff shuddered and covered his ears. "But it's been almost twenty years, Cari."

"You know what my memory is capable of. The sensation is as clear and intense as if it was just this minute for me! I was desperately afraid those unknowns would break open my shell and leave me to die in space. I was helpless! It affected me so deeply that no matter how well I think I am, subconsciously I have never gotten over it. I never found out who was performing salvage on my skin. The headshrinkers still don't believe that there was anyone there. M-C still must think I had a psychotic episode, dreamed the whole thing. That's why he's has been dogging me all these years. He's been so sure I would flip out. And he made doubly sure I would launch a message probe to him if ever I did, so he could drag me out of my ship and lock me in a padded room. I wonder what else is buried in there," she added bitterly.

"Nothing," Keff said, firmly. "He's not that imaginative. There won't even be a backup mechanism in case that failed. Look, Lady Fair." Sheathing his light sword, he stepped forward to plant both palms earnestly on her pillar. He looked up at the nearest camera eye. "When this is over, we'll find an independent, trustworthy memory doctor and have you scoped for other intruders. I'll stay there the whole time, if you want. I promise."

"I thank you for your courtesy, good Sir Knight."

The lady's face appeared and smiled at him, but the image wavered slightly. Carialle's heart wasn't in it. Keff's insides twisted with sympathy.

"We'll find those bastards one day," he promised her.

"Game is ended?" Tall Eyebrow piped up from behind him. "Enjoy games. Interruptedness?" The little alien stood in the passage opening, looking disappointed. Keff gave his forgotten playmate a rueful grin.

"Sorry, TE," Keff said. He moved away from the pillar, but kept an eye on it, wishing there was something he could do for her.

"I apologize," Carialle said contritely. "I didn't mean to let everything drop. Computer malfunction. Minor. It won't happen again." In a moment, the castle corridor rose around Keff again, and a three-dimensional letter puzzle appeared between them. Tall Eyebrow happily waddled over to it. As he moved his finger through the image of each two- or three-letter piece, it enunciated its sound. Some of them were syllables, and some were just noises, thrown in by Carialle for fun. With a delighted chuckle, the globe-frog began to construct Standard words out of the assorted noises, touching them again and again.

"Ook." "Hind." "Honk!" "Eeuu." "Be." "Aaa-OOO-ga!" "Be." "Loo." Ding!" "Ook." "Loo-ook," emerged from the audible babble as Tall Eyebrow found a match. Keff grinned.

"When all this is over, let's go find the parasites who were hacking you up, Cari," Keff said, making use of the sublingual implant in his jaw so the others couldn't hear him. "What with the bonuses from Ozran still in the bank, and the booty from this trip, we can afford to take even a year off."

"I hope the answers are still there to find," Carialle said in his aural implant.

"Look-be-hind-you," Tall Eyebrow spelled out aloud. "Look behind you," he signed suddenly to Keff. He spun in a circle, clutching his amulet in his long fingers.

"He's good," Carialle said. "Twenty-eight seconds, and it's not his native language."

More villains began to pour into the newly reconstructed great hall. Some were humans, brandishing weapons at Keff. Some were waist-high foes, snarling as they sought to surround Tall Eyebrow. Keff drew his sword, then hesitated, blade in midair. TE stood, gazing curiously at Keff, wondering why the man wasn't charging.

The brawn looked at him, feeling as if he had seen them just now for the first time.

"I just had a horrible thought," Keff said, subvocally to Carialle. "What if it was TE's people, the Cridi, who were the ones stealing your components?"

"Don't think it hasn't occurred to me," Carialle said, her voice crisp in his ear. "I hope not. I'm going to be watching them like a bank guard every minute. But I so hope not."

"I hope not, too. I wouldn't be able to behave the same towards them if they almost killed you, inadvertently or not."

"I refuse to theorize in advance of the facts, as someone once said," Carialle stated firmly. "Right now the important thing is to get TE and his party safely to Cridi. When this is over, we'll go and find out the truth."

"When you will and where you will, my lady," Keff said, swallowing his concern. His partner was under control again. If he pushed for more details he might risk making her relive her ordeal. He raised his sword before his face in salute and, with a gallant bow toward her holographic image, charged into the fray.

"Well, come on, TE!" he shouted at the surprised globe-frog. "You're on the threshold of your first big battle. Hop to it!"

✷CHAPTER TWO

A few days later, Carialle interrupted the game and darkened the room to fill all the walls with views from her external sensors. The bright yellow-white, blue-white, and dull red dots of stars glimmered into view. Subtly, a white grid of low intensity divided the blackness into cubes.

"Gentleman and amphibians," she announced brightly. "Best visuals coming up. You see overhead on Y-vector the border between Sectors P and R. Imaginary, of course, visible only on benchmarking programs, but enhanced for your viewing pleasure. Beside us to starboard is a pentary of five stars known to Central Worlds as The Ring, a source of infernal radio interference to all space travelers hereabout. Below and to port, other constellations, brought in at *treee*mendous expense to the management. No shoving, please move along in an orderly fashion. And the entity ahead of us, frogs and sir, is star PLE-329-JK5, half of a binary otherwise known as your home system. And there, in that spot," she highlighted a single, dim yellow dot, two-thirds of the way around the ecliptic from them, "is your first real view of the planet Cridi. Welcome home, my friends."

"Hallelu!" Keff carolled, picking up datasheets and throwing them in the air.

Tall Eyebrow and Long Hand did a joyous dance together in midair around Keff's head. Small Spot bounded lightly from weight bench to wall to console and to Carialle's rack of paintings and back again, narrowly missing everyone else. They were all laughing in their shrill voices.

"How long until we make planetfall, Cari?" Keff called. He couldn't force himself to stop grinning. The corners of his mouth stayed glued up near his ears. He slapped his small friends on the back and shook their hands.

"A while yet," Carialle said. "I'm dumping velocity so I can drop into orbit at under 1,000 kilometers per hour. In the meantime, take a good look, folks. We made it."

The globe-frogs peeped and chirped to one another in high excitement, gesturing frantically at the holographic display.

"It is different from Ozran," Long Hand signed. "Orbit much wider. Cold?"

"Not recorded. We shall cope," Small Spot said. "See how warm the sun is! How lovely gold red."

"Who shall we meet?"

"Who indeed?"

Tall Eyebrow looked up at Keff in despair.

"What shall we say to one another? How different will we be from them?" he signed. "How will we interact?"

"Well," Carialle said, thoughtfully, "you've had a very small and limited gene pool to work with for ten centuries. I wouldn't be surprised if there hasn't been the beginnings of genetic shift, but it's unlikely to make any real difference. At worst you might need artificial assistance to interbreed with the majority population. We could offer Central Worlds' expertise in that department. Our scientists have no trouble fitting tab A into slot B, particularly with our knowledge of the confluent species that resembles yours in our biosphere. On the other hand, if you're just worried about your past experiences differing, I'd suggest you just be yourselves. They won't be expecting identical lines of development."

"Carialle!" Keff said in exasperation. Once a scientist, always a scientist. He turned to the aliens. "They'll just be glad to see you, TE."

"I do not know," Tall Eyebrow said, seeming dazed, staring at the tank. "It was not real until now."

"Well, it certainly is real," Keff said. He spotted an artifact ahead of them in the holoview. Its surface was too smooth to be natural. "What's that, Cari? Tracking stations? Signal beacon?"

"A little of each, I'd say. I'm getting a scan from it. Lots of subspace transmissions. I am recording them and attempting to translate."

"Feed it to me when you get something, please."

Keff sat down in the crash seat before the console and stared at the screen. He drummed his fingers on the console and tapped his toes in anticipation, feeling perfectly happy. This was a bonus, on top of the payoff for finding the civilizations on Ozran. To be able to observe an anthropological phenomenon heretofore unknown in human history: the first meeting of two different groups of the same race, divided for over a millenium. The linguistic diversity alone would provide him with the material for at least one blockbuster academic paper. Tall Eyebrow waddled over and hopped up to perch on the chair arm to watch with him.

"Anything yet?" Keff asked Carialle. "How about particle scans? How much activity is their spaceport seeing?"

"Patience, please. All I am seeing out there is a little debris, and some very old ion trails," Carialle said. The screen lit up with an overlay of green dust streaks that were scattered and stretched by the orbits of the planets in between. "I'd say no one's come through here in a long while."

"Always underfunded," Tall Eyebrow offered, with his hands turned slightly upward to show apology. "It is in the records. Resources small offered. Metal scarce. Volunteer work never enough, raw materials always short. Mission to Ozran one of three major projects to be funded in ten revolutions around the sun when my many-times ancestors had prepared for the journey to Ozran."

"Bureaucracy never changes anywhere," said Keff, sympathetically. Then he sat up straighter. "You don't mean you have memos dating from a thousand years back?"

"For every day," said the Frog Prince, with a satisfied gesture. "In all our troubles, that was never neglected. We have brought them with us for the perusal of the Cridi government."

Keff felt his jaw drop. The globe-frogs had loaded only a few containers into the cargo hold, and most had contained gifts. "In those little boxes you have a thousand years of records?"

"Communication system is kept frugally," Tall Eyebrow signed.

"I'm impressed with your systems," Carialle said.

"So am I," Keff said, with a whistle, promising himself a good rootle through the boxes when they were offloaded. "Talk about microstorage."

"Aha," Carialle announced. "It's sensed us. I'm receiving a hail from the orbiters."

She ran the data patterns through digital analysis, dividing the sum of on/not-on pulses by a range of prime numbers, formulae and logarithms, until she came up with a coherent 1028-unit wide digital signal. It wasn't a computer program, but a video transmission of an amphibioid wearing a glittering silver collar.

"Take a look at this," she said, and relayed it to the cabin screens. Keff was fascinated, but the three Ozranian globe-frogs were dumb with amazement.

"Not much obvious genetic difference, Cari," Keff said, staring at the image, looking at every detail. "Thank goodness for that."

The camera was centered on the Cridi's hands, rather than its face, which remained expressionless and still, staring at the video pickup with fixed, black eyes. The long hands snapped out signs in a quick sequence, then repeated it over and over again.

"I can read that. 'Identify yourself,'" Keff translated. "'Do not proceed further.'"

"There's a spoken language, too," Carialle said. "Transmitted on either sideband of each copy of this signal on every frequency I tune into: wide band, narrow band, microwave, datasquirt, even a form of tight-beam. Very thorough. They want to make certain you don't miss it. Very musical, too. Listen." She put the sound over the cabin speakers. A pattern of peeps, creaks, chirps, and trills repeated over and over again. Keff squinted with concentration as he listened to the rhythmic squeaking.

"I bet it says exactly the same thing as the hand-jive." Keff's eyes gleamed. "Record it, please, Cari, and run it through the IT."

Keff's Intentional Translator program had been of assistance in learning the Cridi's sign language back on Ozran. He was constantly updating the system, which theoretically contained full grammar and vocabulary for every alien language that the Central Worlds had yet discovered. The program functioned with indifferent success most of the time. It rarely provided them with the key to an alien language *when* an explorer needed it. More often, someone found a key first, then used IT to build up a translation system from collected data. The IT was still full of bugs, Carialle thought cynically, but Keff never seemed to be bothered by them. Still, he *had* been improving its interpretation of the Cridi signs.

"Ah," Tall Eyebrow signed, his black eyes shining, "the language of science! We have all but forgone its use in the arid atmosphere of Ozran. The waters and the globes prevent sound from carrying, and we have had no amulets to broadcast it, so we let it drop except infrequently, in conclave."

"Interesting cultural redundancy," said Keff.

"Not at all. It makes sense for a technologically advanced race to develop some kind of oral language," Carialle said, thoughtfully. "Having to manipulate starship controls while signing home to mission control seemed to me like a difficult combination."

"But they had created remote power control," Keff protested.

Carialle's voice was sugared with sweet and insufferable reason. "What did they do before the amulets came along?"

"Sign is older," Long Hand explained, waving her hands for attention and interrupting the argument. "It was our first true trait of civilization. The small voice," here her hands went to her throat, and indicated diminuition with a finger and thumb, "does not carry as well as long sight. It came useful when science reached us, but not during our earliest years. Silence was essential to hunting together in the earliest days. We have good eyes and poorer ears. The wild food animals had good ears, but bad eyes. We must show silently to one another our intent. To us it meant survival."

"To which condition we were reduced on Ozran," put in Tall Eyebrow. "It has been so many generations since we did anything but survive. I am glad to see in the last year we have not forgotten how to think, how to invent with our hands. I shall not be ashamed to face my ancestors' other descendants." But the Frog Prince looked nervous all the same.

"But can you translate it?" Keff asked, almost bouncing with excitement. He gestured toward the screen where the silver-torqued amphibioid was still signing his message.

"If it has not changed since the mission to settle Ozran," Tall Eyebrow signed, "we may be able to." His hand waggled sideways to show uncertainty.

"This is a job for my all-purpose, handy dandy translating program." Keff flew to his console and opened the file. He sat listening avidly to the excerpt, keying in notes.

"But that trick never works," Carialle protested.

"Sure it does," Keff said with high good humor, purposefully ignoring her insult. "Especially, because this time I can cheat. I have a native speaker with me. TE, will you tell me what each of these sounds means?" He touched a control. "I'll slow it down, and you tell me where each phrase starts and stops, and then translate it for me."

"If I can," TE signed nervously. He slid his hand into his amulet to hover at the human's eye level.

They went through the recorded message together. Keff listened with his teeth clenched as the slowed-down chirrups grated through the speakers like chains being dragged up a gravel road. At the Frog Prince's signal, he tapped a computer key, designating the end of a word or phrase.

"It seems to be linear," he said to Carialle. "The IT is already beginning to crossmatch similarities between phrases on the tape. Multiple overlay of meaning beyond tense or gender would be more difficult to distinguish. Now, TE, what do they mean?"

Tall Eyebrow tried to translate each phrase into sign for them. He listened carefully, signing to Keff to replay each several times.

"The first is formula for diminishing forward velocity to zero, or 'halt,'" he said, holding up a skinny palm. "These next four I do not know. Some familiarity, but not enough. The first three are in command tense, but with certainty I cannot tell you their meanings."

"So there has been some linguistic shift," Keff said, nodding to Carialle's Lady Fair image on the wall. "It moves a lot faster than genetic or geographic alterations. Your ancestors might have used a more complex, extended phrase to mean whatever these do."

The globe-frog nodded, and tilted his head again to listen to the tape. "This is X=N, 'identify.' Three unknowns. This is the formula for no forward motion, 'not-proceed,' a command. More unknowns." Keff watched the small aliens hopefully as the tape ran out.

"Well, that's enough to go on," Carialle said. "It's very much what I comprehended from the visual portion of the signal. 'Stop, tell us who you are before you proceed.' Precisely what you'd expect from one of our own security beacons."

"Expressed entirely in mathematical concepts," Keff said. "Very interesting. TE, will you sing me the numerical sequence, and all the variables for IT?"

"With pleasure," the amphibioid said, still bobbing lightly on the air, "but what to do now about message heard?"

"Well, then, we reply as best we can," Keff said. "TE, do you want to do the honors?" He made way before the communications console, and courteously bowed the globe-frog into his own chair. "It's your home."

"I do not know what to do," the small alien said, looking up at Keff uncertainly. "What does one say to one's cousins after a thousand years?"

"Take one step at a time," Keff said. "Tell them who you are, where you're coming from, and ask permission to land. Mention us as your friends and allies. We don't want to have to explain anything more complicated than that at these long-distance rates. I'll stand behind you so they can see me. We'll answer their other questions when we arrive."

Following Keff's instructions, Tall Eyebrow made a brief translation. Carialle could see on close magnification that the small green male's hands were trembling, but his signing was perfectly clear and precise as he identified himself. The long part, the explanation of his people's long absence from Cridi, he alluded to with some quick symbols and a few chirps, mentioning Keff and Carialle as their rescuers and allies. At the end, he asked for instructions.

"Good, TE, good," Keff said soothingly, patting the globe-frog on the shoulder as soon as the camera went off. Tall Eyebrow's shoulders collapsed inward with relief. His two companions crowded in to comfort him.

"It is difficult," he signed.

"Good job. It's going to be a big day for you," Carialle said, signing through her globe-frog image. "That was just fine."

"And now, what?" Tall Eyebrow asked, stepping out into the air from Keff's chair, which was a meter too high for him.

"And now, we wait," Keff said, reclaiming his seat and throwing himself back with his hands behind his head. "Remember, they said, 'halt and not-proceed.' In the meantime you can sing me the symbols for each number, sign, and modifier."

They didn't have long to wait. Within a few hours, Carialle picked up a new transmission from the beacon. A harried-looking frog, not the silver-torqued one, appeared with a new message, which consisted of a single, short trill, and the screen went blank.

"What was that?" Carialle asked, replaying the transmission. "Welcome? Go away?"

Tall Eyebrow's hands flew. "It means 'proceed to the second planet from the sun, listen on this frequency for beacon, and follow in great-circle, equatorial orbit for landing procedure.' It would seem procedure does not change."

"That little ding-a-lingle meant all that?" Keff laughed.

"No stranger than the 'beep-a, beep-a'," Carialle imitated the communication-line busy signal, "which means, 'the party to whom you wished to speak is engaged on the line. Please disconnect and try again later.'"

"True," Keff said, his eyebrows raised in amusement.

"It is an abbreviation," TE acknowledged. "Such a sign is phonetically recorded in our archives. I am surprised to hear that it really does sound like it is written."

"It's a pity you didn't continue the use of your verbal language on Ozran," Carialle said. "Humans are geared toward spoken dialects. The mages might have realized sooner that you were sentient."

"Things might have gone faster with us, too," Keff agreed. "My IT program is geared more toward aural reception and translation."

"Yet inside our globes," Tall Eyebrow said gravely, "no one could have heard us cry out."

The second planet from the sun, behind a scorched clay rock and an insignificant asteroid belt where an unstable planet used to be, was large and beautiful and wet. As she swept into orbit above the equator, Carialle read her spectroanalysis monitors and discovered high relative humidity, due to a respectably thick and variable cloud cover in a nitrogen/oxygen atmosphere.

"I'll have mold galore, and possibly rust in my drawers when I lift off."

"Don't worry, lady," Keff said, cheerfully. "If TE's cousins have the magic technology, they can keep you as dry as you want."

"Oh, I want, I want," Carialle said. "That's one application of the technology I would look forward to using."

Within minutes, Carialle had picked up the signal from the landing beacon on the largest landmass in the planetary-northern hemisphere. She oriented herself to it, following a great circular route that would pass directly over it.

Beneath them, peeping through the cloud cover, half a dozen

small continents floated on the surface of a vast, blue-green ocean. Small, blue ice caps appeared, then fell off to either side of the globe as Carialle descended. As the clouds parted, they could see how very green the low-lying lands were. Small Spot and Long Hand looked positively awed. They had never imagined the existence of so much water. Hazel-brown islands dotted the seas like freckles. Carialle opened megachip memory to record every detail and gave full visuals to those in the control room.

There was some minor particulate matter in the atmosphere, probably a sign of industrial activity, and creating a beautiful sunset half a world behind them. She caught the occasional sunspark as tiny airborne craft speeding below her reflected the yellow star's light. The whole scene reminded her of any one of hundreds of the Central Worlds, but everything was in such small scale compared to those in a human settlement. Her sensors told her that the flyers were only a meter square by less than two meters in length.

"How could we not have known they were here?" she wondered aloud.

Keff, never moving his eyes from the screen, shook his head slowly from side to side and clicked his tongue in agreement.

"This is the race, all right," Keff said, happily.

The partners' dream had always been to discover a sentient race equal to humanity in technological advancement and social development. There was no doubt about the well-established civilization below them, and their guests were living proof of the culture's prowess in space exploration.

The globe-frogs became agitated as the ship neared the stratosphere. Carialle picked up signals that were almost certainly what was arousing their senses.

"Take a look at the readings for the enormous power source down there," she told Keff. "Much larger than the Core of Ozran. The frequency hash is even greater. I'm reading controller codes in tiny bandwidths that I doubt could sustain what's necessary for one of the older amulets. Your machines will undoubtedly need tuning," she told Tall Eyebrow.

"It is true," he said, placing his long fingers on his belt buckle. "I can feel the great power source, but I cannot focus in on it to draw from it. My amulet frequency is already in use here."

"Well, you can stay on my engines for the time being," Carialle said. "Our hosts should give you a guest frequency when we land."

"But where *are* we going to land?" Keff asked. "The instructions didn't give a location."

As if in answer, the ship shuddered. Carialle felt a forcefield surround her firmly, but gently, like a velvet envelope. She tried to accelerate out of its grasp, but it was everywhere. It swept her out of her orbital path and rerouted her, drawing her into a side-to-side sine-curve path that led toward the surface. Her passengers were thrown off their feet. The surprised globe-frogs missed slamming into the wall only by swift use of their amulets. Keff, without technological assistance, was knocked to the floor. He grabbed for the base of the control chair as he slid towards the bulkhead, and hoisted himself up toward the seat. The three hovering amphibioids looked down at him sympathetically.

"That's why," Carialle said simply. "They're going to put us down on the landing pad themselves. *Damn* it! I hate being man-handled—I mean, froghandled, when I'm perfectly capable of doing this myself."

"Do you mean you didn't make that course adjustment?" Keff asked, hauling himself up to his feet by grasping the arms of his crash couch. He sat down and pulled the impact straps around his body.

"Look, ma, no hands!" Carialle said, feeling somewhat bitter, but at the same time admiring the expertise and technology required to take over her landing. "You know I don't drive that badly. They've taken complete control of my vector and speed. I could shut off my engines right now and probably land very nicely, thank you, but I don't trust strangers that easily."

"They're holding us like an egg," Keff said, looking at the exterior pressure monitors. "It doesn't hurt, does it?"

"No," Carialle admitted, with the sound she used for a sigh. "However much I despise it, I have to admit they're doing a competent job. The Cridi are light-years beyond the skills of the mages of Ozran. It's more like a pillow than pincers. Chaumel the Silver and the other mages could only pin me down with their controllers. They couldn't catch me in flight."

"Lucky for us," Keff said, with a nod.

"And for us," Tall Eyebrow added, staring at the screen that monitored the continents over which they were flying. "Else we would not be returning home now."

"I'm shutting down thrusters," Carialle informed them.

At the same time the force was guiding her downward through the troposphere, Carialle had the sense she was being probed. The "mind" penetrated her hull, through her shielding, into and around her engines, her memory banks, the cabins and cargo hold, and into the shell which held her body. She stilled all life support activity except for respiration, wondering if she would be interfered with by curious technicians, but the touch passed on and out of her ship. She forced her circulatory system to excrete the unnecessary adrenaline produced by her anxiety, and added nutrients and serotonin from her protein and carbohydrate tanks. She disliked being out of control of her functions, but at least this time she could see everything and, to a minor extent, move herself slightly in the soft, invisible grasp.

"I will not panic," she told herself firmly. "I will not panic. I am in control. I can veer upward out of here at any time. I can. I *can*."

Of all the softshells in her cabin, only Keff was unaware of the scan. The frogs, whether through latent telempathic sensitivity or the offices of their amulets, knew someone was examining them. Tall Eyebrow put his hand to his face with his fingers parted: a question to her.

"Yes, I feel it," she said, verbally and with sign through her frog image. "We're being given the look-see to find out who we really are."

"We come in peace," Tall Eyebrow said, worriedly.

"They must know that," Carialle commented, "or they could have dashed us all over the scenery by now."

"They may still," said Long Hand, cynically. "Are they waiting until we are over a certain point to pull us down?"

The velvet envelope absorbed the inertia as it slowed Carialle's velocity down to about a third. Gradually, she dumped more speed as her course destination became more evident. The northern continent appeared over the rim of the planet. The ship was whisked over jungles and rivers and a network of small cities, all looming larger and larger as they dropped. Carialle focused in tightly on the terrain, judging by the angle of descent and speed where the invisible hand would eventually set them down. The datafile she'd gathered of Cridi geography during her spiral told her that ahead on the eastern edge was a broad, flat plain. Most likely the spaceport lay there.

Traveling at only a few thousand kilometers per hour Carialle had time to record more detail of the land below as well as speculate on the welcoming committee. Most definitely the Cridi held all the reins on access and communication. Keff was looking forward to airing his sign language and the smatterings he'd already picked up of cheeps and twitters. Carialle just hoped that she wouldn't have to face one of her worst fears: seeing parts of her original hull being used by humanity's newest allies as chip and dip trays.

The land dished upward into low, rounded, green-backed mountain ranges as a broad river valley spread out beneath her. Carialle's aesthetic sense was pleased by the cities she could see now in greater detail, integrated fully with the rainforests that covered most of the continent. Blue and bronze-metal skyscrapers poked up through clumps of trees that were like giant date palms. Tributaries that eventually led to the great river wound among residential areas, passing under innumerable small bridges. Much of the broad, green plains were uninhabited. Carialle guessed that the Cridi preferred to live in a jungle environment, and leave the open spaces to the ruminants. It was all unimaginably pretty.

"Brace yourselves!" Carialle announced, feeling the restraint around her tighten. Tall Eyebrow and his two companions buckled themselves into the second crash couch, their staring eyes grim as the ship seemed to skim right over the tops of the trees. Carialle widened the view out to give them an accurate picture of their descent. They were actually still hundreds of kilometers above the ground.

Now she could see a landing strip appearing in the extreme range of her sensors. The huge, open field was lined with rows of low buildings. Ragged heaps of undifferentiated junk, half-grown over with vegetation, lay at the edges of the field, but two nearly complete spacecraft stood proudly on the wide, green plain. Perfect miniatures, the graceful spires measured about a sixth of Carialle's height.

"Not much current use," Keff commented. "I guess what Tall Eyebrow said about sparse government funding holds true even ten centuries later."

Their speed lessened again, this time sharply. The passengers surged forward in their crash seats. Keff clutched the arms of his couch and ground his molars together. Forward propulsion was down to a few hundred kilometers per minute, then a few tens, then diminished entirely. Keff had an uncomfortable feeling of weightlessness for a moment.

"I'm upending," Carialle said. And she began to drop. Keff felt his heart slide upward to his throat. He gulped. The frogs, lifted momentarily upward against their straps, exchanged nervous glances among themselves, but none made a sound. The ship fell like a stone.

"If they drop us now, we're scattered components," Carialle said. "I couldn't ignite to full burners in time to save us."

Groaning against the gravity-force upthrust, Keff huddled back in his impact couch against the thrust, his heart racing.

"The question of the day," Carialle said in Keff's ear, her voice sounding sharp with panic regardless of her calm choice of words. "Would a culture with a technology this advanced be reduced to performing manual salvage on a space-marooned hulk?"

"Doubt it," Keff gritted, trying to keep his stomach from forcing its way up his throat and out of his mouth. His heart was in the way, and they'd all come out at once. He tried to sound definite. "Hope not." He closed his eyes and clutched harder, his fingers denting the upholstery of his crash couch, hoping the chair wouldn't have to live up to its name.

The red-painted ship descended gracelessly from high atmosphere onto the junk-strewn Thelerian plain. It landed with a boom that echoed into the surrounding mountains like a bark of divine laughter and sent yellow dust swirling up toward the hot, golden-white sun. Thunderstorm and Sunset waited until the roar of the engines died away, then approached the cylindrical tower.

"Almost a temple," Sunset said, unable to keep the awe out of his voice. He was very young. Thunderstorm smiled, his bifurcated upper lip parting to show the upper row of his fiercely pointed teeth.

"But the godhead is served by strange priests, Sunset," he warned. "Remember that."

A final deafening blast of fire spread out from under the tail of the red ship, making Sunset jump, then the engines shut down. Heat haze spread out from the hull, obscuring the tall cylinder in a shimmer. A tongue-shaped portion of the ship's wall separated and swung down on hinges until the tip touched the ground. A ramp, Sunset thought, trying out the human's word in his mind. Figures appeared in the opening. Sunset would have run ahead to meet the descending aliens, but Thunderstorm rattled a wingtip at him.

"With dignity, youngster!"

Chastened, Sunset dropped behind to follow his elder. Three upright figures walked down the ramp. Two of them stopped a half dozen body-lengths short, but the tallest one came up within a single length.

"Greetings, honored ones," Thunderstorm said. He bowed low, then introduced himself, his assistants, and Sunset. "As always, we are pleased to have you here, Fisman. To what do we owe the pleasure?"

So these were humans! Sunset thought, very excited. The tallest alien, whose V-shaped torso lacked mammary protuberances, meaning that it was a male, grinned, meaning the corners of its mouth lifted, but the lip did not part in the center. What hair it had was mixed black and white. Its bare face was a narrow wedge, point down. Its mouth showed flat, white teeth like those of a rodent. He wore a smooth, slightly shiny tunic over thin covers that concealed his abdomen and limbs. Around his neck was a chain bearing many strange devices, among them a curly piece of metal with a sharpened point mounted at a perpendicular angle on a short stick, a bulbous construction mainly consisting of white glass with a shiny gray metal screw-shaped end, and a rectangular plate with characters on it in the human tongue. Sunset leaned a little closer to read it, and jumped back when the tall male made an impatient sign with his manipulative extremity—his *hand*.

"It's Bisman, damn it, Thunder, but after all these years I ought to know you still can't say your b's. Sunset, glad to meet you. This is Mirina and Zonzalo Don, brother and sister. My partner and her younger sibling. We bring you more parts, Thunder. Is this the apprentice you promised us?"

"Yes, sir."

The younger male approached only a few paces and looked down at Sunset haughtily. "Does he know his stuff?" Zonzalo asked.

Thunderstorm nudged Sunset forward.

He answered in the biped's language, carefully rehearsed for this moment. "I've memorized every component in the manuals. I know how to repair each one according to its rite. I obey orders."

"Very good," Mirina said, with a smile for Sunset. She was slightly wider in frame than her brother, and she had the proper protruberances, both front and side, of a human female. Sunset was glad. He'd been afraid he wouldn't be able to tell, and Thunderstorm had been firm about the etiquette of addressing humans correctly.

"Thank you, ma'am," Sunset said, which won him another smile from Mirina. Sunset noticed with a shock that the human had eyes of two colors arranged concentrically, with the pupil a *round dot* in the center. How incredibly strange. Yet, her eyes were the color of loamy soil: a warm, light brown, with a black ring separating the tan from the white; and her teeth, though flat, were very white. Sunset ducked his head to keep from staring. Humans were not so unattractive after all, even though they lacked proper haunches, tails, and wings.

"Has he taken the Oath?" the younger male asked.

He had. Thunderstorm had adminstered it himself. Sunset remembered all the grand-sounding phrases. They came to his mind as he stood, waiting as his elders discussed him over his head: obedience, silence, competence, humility, striving towards perfection in all things, and always keeping oriented to the Center of Thelerie.

"Yes," he piped up, realizing that Zonzalo expected him to say something.

"Do you know what it means to be a member of the Melange?" Bisman asked Sunset, for the first time looking him square in the eyes. That strange round stare was disconcerting. The younger Thelerie nodded several times to recover himself.

"I do. Humans and Thelerie together form the basis of trust. Since we are different, we may blend together only those things sacred and invisible such as trust and knowledge. But in that partnership we are indissoluble, and must remain loyal to one another throughout all time. Where our travels may lead us is a test of that trust."

It was practically quoting the Manuals, but the human didn't seem to mind. He nodded, bobbing his small round head up and down.

"Good. Well, there's no time like the present. Come on, lad," Bisman said.

"Now?"

Bisman glanced at Thunderstorm with an expression that Sunset could not translate. "Yes, now. We haven't got all day. My people are ready to unload and go as soon as we're refueled. Do you want a chance to serve, or not?"

"Of course I do," Sunset said, realizing he had made a mistake. "I am eager to serve. My skills are ready, and my center is sure."

That must have been the appropriate response, because the adults turned away from him then and chatted low among themselves. Bisman tapped himself on the manipulative extremity and spoke into his wrist. From the red ship, a crew of bipeds emerged. Part of the hull peeled away to reveal a huge storage bay full of containers.

At Thunderstorm's signal, many Thelerie came forward with the heavy lifting equipment they brought from the capital city. The human crew unloaded all the goods onto the pad, well away from where the fire would lick out and consume them when it departed. The cargo consisted of spaceship parts, and Sunset recognized all of them. Only the largest one, which had to be hoisted by derrick onto a flat car, he had never seen except in the manuals. It was a primary space drive, probably the first one on Thelerie in many years. Each one was numbered, he had been told, in over a hundred places, on each of its many components. So interested was he that he didn't hear the final transaction between the elders, Thunderstorm on behalf of the Thelerie, and Bisman, the spokeshuman.

"Come on, lad," Bisman said, coming over to tap Sunset on the wingjoint above his vestigial hand. "As a member of the Melange you've got to prove yourself now. This is your quest. We're looking at another opportunity to build onto your people's space fleet, but it takes time to get to where we're going to get more parts. Can't spend time jawing." He looked at the Thelerie and their wide faces. "You've got plenty of that."

It seemed to be a joke. At least, all the humans laughed. Sunset attempted to emulate the grin, keeping the centers of his lip together. He followed his new captains toward the ship. Sunset stared at it in fascination, seeing the joints of each part interlocked with the ones on every side. And within, the components working together in harmony like . . . like the Melange. All was as he had studied for the last three years.

On the side of the great, red ship were hieroglyphs of the human tongue. Sunset couldn't quite make out all of them, but he recognized the word "Central."He extended his wingtip to Thunderstorm, to ask him what they were, and touched no one. Startled, he looked back over his shoulder to see his elder standing at the side of the field, not moving. Sunset opened his great wings and glided back. It was almost the last time he'd be able to do that for a while, so he enjoyed the sensation of air under his pinions.

"Come on," he urged his mentor.

"I am not coming, youngster," Thunderstorm said, with a shake of his great head.

"Why not?"

The older Thelerie reared back onto his muscular haunches and touched Sunset with a foreclaw. "My reiving days are over, lad. Go with good grace. Come back with honor."

✳CHAPTER THREE

"In ten, everybody. Ten, nine, eight . . ."

When Carialle's tailfins touched the ground, the passengers and Keff felt hardly a bump.

" . . . Two, one. Welcome to Cridi. And thank you for flying Air Carialle. Please wait until the captain has turned off the 'fasten seatbelts' sign before debarking."

Keff, who had been worried about her mental state when the Cridi took control of their flight path, was relieved at her flippancy. He took off his crash straps and stretched.

"Completely painless," Keff said to Tall Eyebrow, who timidly followed his host's lead. "No wonder your people have such a successful space program. No chance of breakup on reentry."

"No chance of missing the launch pad, either," Carialle said, activating one of her exterior cameras and tilting it downward. She had landed exactly in the middle of a round pavement surrounded by a pattern of lights laid out on the ground like a snowflake, illumination marching inward from the points.

Tall Eyebrow saluted Carialle for the safe landing.

"None of my doing, TE," she said. She noticed that his thin hands were still shaking, and made her frog image appear on the wall opposite him.

"Don't worry," she signed to him. "They'll be glad to see you."

"If only I can be certain," the Frog Prince signed back. He shook his head, a gesture of uncertainty that his people shared with humans.

"Here comes security," Keff said. "The party's beginning."

The first sight Keff had of the inhabitants of Tall Eyebrow's homeworld was the tops of helmeted and visored heads sticking out of an open vehicle that was plainly meant as field security. The flattened, molded, bulbous shape of the craft would force any missile, from thrown rocks to laser beams, to bounce upward or outward away from it. If there was anything aloft that looked more like the ancient myth of the flying saucer, Keff had yet to see it. How appropriate when the inhabitants were, verily, little green men. The thin pipes protruding from sockets in the vehicle's upper shell had to be weapons. He couldn't focus quickly enough on the moving craft to estimate whether the pipes shot solid projectiles or some other deterrent.

"I wish we could tell them we're unarmed," Keff said worriedly.

"They know," Carialle said, feeling the light sensation fluttering over all her sensors once more, this time lingering at the ends of her neural synapses. "We're being scanned again. Whew! That was thorough. Good thing I'm not ticklish. They probably also know your age, your shoe size, and how much you weigh."

"If they can do that, then why the heavy armament?" Keff wondered.

Through her audio monitors Carialle also received the frequency signatures of half a dozen frog devices, plus the quasi-telepathic communications that the system both required and made possible. Since the messages were in high-pitched cheeps and arpeggios, she couldn't understand until the IT got more data on the language of Cridi science, but at least she understood the drill. It was carried out on every planet, spaceport and asteroid in the civilized galaxy.

"Trust, but verify," Carialle replied.

Another burst of high-pitched music issued from the speakers, a mathematical sequence that Tall Eyebrow quickly translated for them.

"Sigma is greater than zero. X equals zero. Y equals zero. XY equals infinity."

"Very interesting," Carialle said. "To the rest of us folks, it means, 'Come to a stop; don't move; don't attempt to lift off. Any efforts will result in disintegration into uncountable particles. Not that I can move. They've got me held as tightly as a fly in amber."

The frustration in her voice was not lost on Keff. "Give them a moment to get to know us, Cari. We haven't sent out a herald yet."

Carialle's Lady Fair image appeared on the wall beside him and made a face. Keff grinned.

The security vehicle made one more sweep, zooming close to Carialle's dorsal hull, then there was a hash of static as several controller-based broadcasts collided in mid-frequency. Tall Eyebrow looked at Keff and shook his head. He couldn't translate any of that, either. IT's vocabulary base gathered dozens of new syllables and put them on a hold in the datastream.

From the buildings at the field's edge, a party of frogs emerged and began to make their way across the field. Instead of walking, they glided a few centimeters over most of the beautiful, green sward. Suspicious, Carialle did a scan of her own.

"Do you realize that these landing pads are almost the only dry land in sight?" she said, showing them a map of her soundings. "That bright verdure covers either mud or marsh, depending on where you step."

"I bet only the poor folks on this planet live on dry land," Keff said. "Water is riches around here."

"Then everyone's rich," Carialle said.

The welcoming committee came within half a kilometer and stopped. Keff counted eight frogs he would classify as dignitaries, and twice that many who were hangers-on, aides, and, to judge by the number of devices hovering in the air near them, reporters. Around them and the ship, the hovering security vehicles described slow circles. The three Ozranians stared at the images of their long-lost cousins, hands flying as they speculated on relationships.

"They are just like us," Long Hand said, with great interest.

"That's as far as they're going to come to meet us. You three had better make an appearance," Keff said.

"If . . ." Long Hand said, hands twitching nervously. She held onto her usual composure. "If they do not disapprove our coming."

"You won't know until you try," Carialle said, trying to lighten the situation. "But I know that our government would be thrilled beyond words to rediscover a long-lost colony. Go on."

At once, all three started to make a hasty toilette. Tall Eyebrow divested himself of his beret, sword belt, and cape. Small Spot checked his immaculate hide for dust or smudges. Long Hand dashed for the sonic shower and cleaned herself all over. They resumed their controller units on elastic belts around their chests. Tall Eyebrow already had his on from the game. Keff thought that they did it more for moral support than for use. Once out of the range of Carialle's engines, the ancient amulets would be of little use, even for keeping the skin of water around their bodies. The leader must have sensed Keff's thoughts, for even as he was fitting his long fingers into the five depressions on the bronzed surface of what once had been a lady's belt buckle, he gave a nervous smile.

"For luck only," he signed, crossing his two first fingers, "since they cannot work here. We must go without globes as well as the protective slip of water. I will return to our people's birthplace standing tall and with dignity, ignoring inconvenience and discomfort."

Small Spot looked unhappy about his leader's last statement, but he too stood tall, and strode with what dignity he had toward the airlock.

"If we can do it without losing our pride," Long Hand said, more practically, "I will ask our cousins how to adapt the amulets to their system."

Carialle opened a tiny panel in her outer hull. A balloon pump took a fifteen cubic centimeter sample of the oxygen, which she ran through a barrage of tests for gas density, humidity, and chemical impurities. It confirmed what she had already guessed.

"The atmosphere's safe for all of you," she said. "Good, healthy nitrox mix, few harmful impurities, apart from a trace of predictable industrial pollution. More particulates than you three are used to, but not bad. If you want breathing filters, just ask."

Tall Eyebrow signed a polite refusal. He stared straight ahead of him as Keff moved to the controls for the airlock.

Keff stayed behind and out of sight as the ramp lowered and grounded with a squish. The Ozranians hung back a moment, reluctant to leave the surroundings that were, if not home, then safe and familiar.

"Go on," Keff urged them. "I'll be right behind you."

The amphibioids looked out across the field. Keff tried to picture himself in their place, to be the first to bridge the gap of a thousand years' silence, and was overwhelmed by the urgency of explaining, the enormity of understanding. Keff realized he had forgotten to breathe for a moment. Their feelings must have been shared by the party of dignitaries. The small party of dignitaries had pushed forward ahead of the crowd, and were looking expectantly at the ship's hatch. There was no perceptible physical difference between them and the three Ozran-born Cridi. Seeing no movement, the party surged forward again.

"It's your turn," Keff said, straightening up. "Are you ready?"

"No," Tall Eyebrow signed, "but, yes. Come."

With dignity, the small alien turned and walked out of the main cabin. Long Hand and Small Spot followed his example, straightening their spines and tilting their heads slightly upward. Together, they marched through the corridor and into the airlock. Carialle slid the inner door shut, and the outer door open.

Keff, right behind them in the shadows, heard shrill cheers as the crowd caught the first glimpse of the three Ozranians in the starship's airlock. In silhouette against the bright daylight outside, Keff could see Tall Eyebrow's knees begin to tremble. Small Spot, overwhelmed by the sound, edged backward until he bumped into Keff's legs.

"You can do it," he urged them. "Go on. Take that one last step. Just march forward. Count to a hundred. Don't think about anything but the numbers. Go on."

"One," TE counted out loud in Standard. "Two, three, four . . . " The other two marched behind them, out of the airlock, down the ramp, and into the sunshine. The crowd went wild, throwing flowers and sheaves of green plants into the air. Keff stayed behind to watch. He counted their footsteps. A hundred paces took the three visitors about half the way to the party of dignitaries on the edge of the field. There they hesitated, and the Cridi government officials took their cue at once. Dignified but clearly excited, they glided across the swampy ground, to alight in front of Tall Eyebrow and his companions.

"Go get 'em, frogs! Yeah!" he whispered.

"I'm all choked up," Carialle said in his ear.

Keff squinted, bringing the magnifying lens in his left eye to full telescopy, and listened to Carialle's amplified audio. He could see the expressions on the faces of the dignitaries: bemusement, kindness, curiosity, but no hostility. The globe-frogs had come home.

"Who are you?" signed the leader of the Cridi delegation, an elderly male whose once-smooth skin wrinkled into a million tiny folds around his wide mouth. A narrow cape of ornately braided strips hung to the ground from the nape of his neck. It was held there by a hammered bronze band that stretched across the top of his back and sprouted into filigree coils over his shoulders. "Where do you come from? We have seen the message sent to the beacon, and we do not know what to think."

Another Cridi, a slender female wearing a slim silver torc with matching bracelets and anklets piped an enthusiastic, "B equals B," and signed, "We agree! Since we received your transmission, all has been a flurry of excitement. Where do you come from?"

Tall Eyebrow identified himself and his companions. "We return to you from a colony world known as Ozran." The final name emerged as a buzz and a honk.

"Ozran?" one self-important frog repeated, bellying up to stand before the landing party. Of all the Cridi present, he was the largest: broad, round, and tall. His yellow green skin was mottled, reflecting a choleric nature. "What is this name *Ozran*?" he peeped indignantly. "Not a Cridi name." Keff chuckled to himself. It wasn't easy for a whistle to sound dignified.

"Big Voice is impatient, but he asks a question all of the Conclave have," said the elder. He brushed the palm of one hand lightly over the other and touched a delicate fingertip to his chest. "I am Smooth Hand," he said.

"In our ancestors' records our world is designated as Sky Clear." Tall Eyebrow executed two symbols quickly, and vocalized a long, complex trill. Keff's aural implant barked out a long string of numbers punctuated with signs and symbols. He recognized the resultant formula as spatial coordinates, though naturally not those used by the Central Worlds.

Without changing expression the self-important frog leaned back on his heels and waved a single finger. One of the aides came running up to the leaders with a flat board to show them his notation. The eight leaders gathered around, emitting exclamations of disbelief and amazement. The aide moved back into the crowd, signing in an apparent aside to a friend. Everyone within range observed the gist of his statement, and passed it on. Word went around, catching fire within the group, until everyone was speculating about the data on the screen.

"How is this possible?" the senior Cridi said, looking up from the small board with delight. "We thought that colony had died. It was mourned many hundreds of years past. So many of our world's offshoots have failed, we thought that Sky Clear was just one more."

"We lost touch with Cridi through no fault of our own," Tall Eyebrow said. "It is a story of treachery, survival and, lastly, friendship, with beings like Keff." He turned to look expectantly back at the ship.

"My cue," Keff said, pulling down his tunic hem to make certain it was straight.

"I should say so," Carialle said. "Final subvocal check, please."

"If the folks back at SSS-900-C could see me now," Keff pronounced, into his oral implant as he stepped out into the airlock and walked down the ramp.

"You'd be the handsome prince from the fairy tale," Carialle said, amused. "Don't let anyone kiss you, or you'll turn back into a frog, too. Watch your step."

The high humidity of the air outside slapped him in the face like a wet fish. Keff felt almost as if he were walking through a curtain of water, and highly unsavory swamp water at that. *Phew.* What he'd imagined looked like smooth, rolling fields was a level and endless pool of watery mud with petal-like plants growing on top, giving only an impression of solidity. He'd go floundering if he chanced to step off the solid base of the landing pad. No wonder nothing was ever built out on these open spaces. The atmosphere was breathable and flavored with smelly esters from abundant plant decay. Good photosynthesis action, that meant, resulting in the cyclic exchange of carbon dioxide. No wonder their explorers had chosen Ozran. The Cridi wanted the same things humans did in a colony. The xenobiologists were going to have a picnic here. As long as they didn't spread their cloth out on the green.

Keff moved slowly and cautiously, holding his hands away from his body to show that he was harmless, but there was no way to lessen the impact of his appearance on the crowd. As soon as they saw him, some of the Cridi scattered and ran away, shrieking. The rest stood rigid, staring and pointing, rows upon rows of pairs of beady black eyes, and long, green digits like accusatory asparagus.

He raised his arms to his waist to sign, "We come in peace."

His hands fluttered through the motions, then froze in the air by his belly. He tugged, trying to free himself from the invisible force. Nothing doing. The shock of his appearance had delayed security's reaction, but they were in command again. Cridi amulet power surrounded him with a rock-hard shell of invisible force, clamping him in place and forcing his arms down against his sides. He gasped, but not because of the jungle heat. The forcefield was just a little too tight around his chest. If it closed down any harder, he'd pass out. Giddily, he wondered if he would remain erect.

A host of helmeted frogs all but materialized at his side, preparing to defend against him should he move at all—as if he could.

"TE, tell them I'm your friend!" Keff gritted, willing his lips to move. Black spots danced in front of his eyes at the strain.

He wasn't sure if he could be heard over the screaming, but TE was a superlative lip reader. The Ozranian turned to sign at his hosts.

"Release him! Please!" Tall Eyebrow said, making energetic gestures at the eight leaders. "These are my friends, and the representatives of a great government, here to be our friends." He trotted back across the field and placed himself between Keff and the guards. "You must not treat them like animals or enemies."

The members of the conclave peered at Keff from a safe distance and Keff could feel his restraints ease off slightly. The youngest one took a step forward, thought better of it, and retreated to the far side of the solid platform. Smooth Hand, he of the ribbon cape, tilted his head to one side.

"Well, they are strange to us," he said, apologetically. "So large. Such an odd color in the face. And there is another one onboard the ship. Why will it not come out and show itself?"

"Because she cannot," TE said, emphasizing the feminine pronoun. "She lives within the walls, and never moves. Keff and Carialle are my friends and have been our defenders on the colony world of Ozran."

"Sky Clear!" the self-important one corrected him imperiously. "Why have you changed the name?"

"It is the name by which the joined colony of people like Keff and our own race is known," Long Hand added. "Humans live on the world with us."

"When the homeworld lost touch with Sky Clear there were none but Cridi there," Smooth Hand said, referring to the data pad, which was held for him by a female in a red cloak.

"It would take long to explain by hand," TE said, looking back at his own aides. "We have archives to give you."

Small Spot, smiting himself in the head to show abashment for his forgetfulness, ran back into the ship to get the boxes of records.

Carialle, guessing what he wanted, had thoughtfully rolled out one of her small servo drones, and the excited globe-frog loaded the boxes aboard its flat back. The boxy robot followed him out to the waiting crowd, trundling stoutly over the soggy ground.

"We present to you the complete records for the life of our colony," Tall Eyebrow signed proudly. He stood back from the drone and allowed some of the guards to remove the boxes from its platform. Carialle recalled her robot, ordering it to spin its treads at the bottom of the ramp to avoid trudging mud over her decks.

"A magnificent gift," said the female in silver bangles. She pried open one of the containers and lifted out one of the tightly wound spools of plastic inside. "Unlooked-for treasure. It will make interesting reading. Scholars will vie for the honor of transcribing."

The elder statesman held up his hands to get the attention of the whole crowd. "We welcome you home, cousins, and look forward to writing joint history from now on," said Smooth Hand. "Perhaps together we will discover the well-being of other lost children of Cridi."

The old one stretched out his arms toward Tall Eyebrow, palms out. The Ozranian stepped forward, and laid his large hands against those of the elder. The crowd cheered again, and surrounded the three travelers. The senior Cridi beckoned.

"We all have much to discuss. But come, you are our honored guests. You shall have the finest accommodations, sample the best foods, visit sites of our history and of our future." He put an arm around Tall Eyebrow's back and led him toward the spaceport buildings surrounded by the chirping horde. Suddenly he looked back, an afterthought occuring to him. "Oh, bring the giant, too."

A guard waved his hand, and Keff stumbled forward.

* * *

"Depot in range," said Glashton, the pilot, over his shoulder. "I'm keeping that string of asteroids between us and their sensors."

"Good." Mirina Don paced back and forth behind the pilots' couches, peering at the computer construction of the asteroid-bound repair facility. Old, but well-supplied, if their scout's report was anything to go by. And they'd recently had a delivery that interested the Melange. "Notify Bisman."

The young Thelerie in the co-pilot's seat threw off his straps and arose, prepared to run aft. Mirina caught him by a wing-joint and turned him back. "No, Sunset. Use the intercom."

"Yes, madam," he said, his slit-like pupils wide. He scrambled back into his padded couch and reached out one skinny wing-hand to activate the communications channel, at the same time keeping track of the ship's progress. He lay rather than sat in the couch, his mighty haunches curled up behind, leaving free clawed fore-legs and wing-fingers so that his head was between two agile pairs of hands. The boffins told her that with their long eyes they could watch both sets at once. He glanced back at her eagerly. "He is on his way."

Mirina shook her head. So young. So heartbreakingly anxious to please. Some of the Thelerie never got over their initial awe of humans, never stopped seeing them as benevolent gods, whose bidding must be done no matter how perilous. Not even after their first missions, when the humans proved themselves to be thieves and pirates. The Thelerie just kept on trusting them, even against the evidence. Their ethical culture told them that a person was what he said he was, even if he wasn't. That made them jam for the dishonest beings in the galaxy like the Melange.

Mirina felt responsible for all the Thelerie they enrolled. She suffered nightmares when one of them got injured or killed, and still dreamed about the first time she had had to take the body of an apprentice back to its homeworld. As guilty as she was, the alien family didn't blame her. They trusted humans, not realizing that they were as mortal as Thelerie, with no special powers to save anyone, or any special wisdom to keep them from falling into danger. They thought everything humans did was wonderful. It never occured to them that the ships the humans flew were old, cobbled together out of spare parts and baling wire. They never saw that the couches had been mended a dozen times, nor that the equipment in the control room came from a dozen different derelict ships, and failed as often as it worked.

She'd once been told by a suitor that she had fine eyes. The mirror in her cramped little cabin let her know that the strain of the last years had put a hard quality into them that frightened her, and would have put off that long-gone beau. That tough shell protected what was left of her soul, because business was business. The presence of the Thelerie was essential to the success of her venture. There'd have been far more bloodshed, and much more loss of life if she couldn't rely upon their unique talent. Even to herself she admitted that she minimized the danger in every way possible. She didn't want anyone else to die. Anyone.

"Close in," she said, leaning over Glashton's shoulder. "Plot us in, staying as close to the asteroids as possible till the last minute. I don't want them to have time to push the panic button. Can you see the parts depot?"

"Aye, sir."

Bisman came striding up. He had on an armored pressure suit, the helmet held under one arm. His grizzled hair was hidden under the protective hood, and his sharp, dark eyes were calm.

"Boarding party ready," he said shortly.

"Stand by," Mirina said, turning back to the viewtank. "How long to the drop?"

Sunset ran through one of those instantaneous mental calculations that seemed so effortless for his people.

"Eight minutes, madam."

"Don't call me madam," Mirina snapped, yanked back with annoyance from her planning.

"Sorry again," he said, contritely. "Thunderstorm told me always to use titles of respect."

Mirina felt the corners of her mouth start to turn upward in an unwilling smile. "My name will do. Thank you. Stand by."

"At least he isn't calling you 'holy one,' any more," her brother called from the engineer's seat, where he was waiting to operate the airlock and grapple controls.

Sunset glanced up at the human male, then hastily ducked his head. Bisman smirked at the young Thelerie, his narrow jaws drawn upward. Mirina glared at her co-leader.

"Isn't anyone else here thinking of business?"

"On my way," he said, fending off the evil eye with an uplifted hand.

"Wait a minute, Aldon," Mirina said, as he turned to go. "Remember, just grab those containers and go. No killing."

"That's the idea, lady," he said, offhandedly, holding his helmet up over his head and shaking it to free the hanging tabs. "Strike hard so they don't know where you're coming from, then move out. But I'm not going to stand helpless and let them tickle me. My people will use self-defense as needed." Mirina moved to place herself in his path.

"Disarm and disable only. Those are my orders. Just take the stuff and go!"

He paid no attention as he clamped the headpiece into place. The seals whistled a diminishing scale as he sidestepped her and stalked away down the corridor toward the airlock.

Mirina stared after him, feeling fury rising fit to choke her. There wasn't time to lecture him again, and she was beginning to feel like she was losing control of him. *She'd* turned this operation around into a profit-making enterprise. He and his miserable little group had only three pathetically archaic ships when she met him eight years ago. Now they had sixty, and more under construction. *She'd* been confirmed as the leader by a majority of the vote. But there were some people who couldn't take direction from anyone, especially from not a former government spacer like her. Bisman had been raiding for thirty years, had started under his father, who'd owned the original three ships. Anyone who'd survived that long deserved respect, just for sheer longevity, but damn it, it was bad for crew morale to have him defy her every single order. She snatched up her remote communications headset and clamped it down on her head.

Zonzalo sat in the engineer's seat snickering. Mirina rounded on him.

"What are you laughing at? You couldn't survive in a planetside shopping center."

"Hey," he held up helpless hands. "I didn't say anything. It just reminds me of Mom and Dad, how you two carry on."

"I suppose I asked for that," Mirina said, feeling her cheeks burn. "But I want him to remember what I say."

"It won't help," Zonzalo said. "It never does. I don't know why you keep trying."

Mirina shook her head. She and Bisman had had an affair when she first shipped with them eight Standard years before. He was twenty years older than she. She was attracted by his maturity, by his long, lean looks, daredevil attitude, and hard-driving determination. He liked her clear-sighted organizational bent, and he complimented her on her figure, saying he liked a curvy armful. They'd broken off the physical side of their relationship when they found they couldn't work together *and* be lovers. *He* thought she was compulsive. *She* hated his collections of little knicknacks and his untidy way of thinking. *He'd* said she was too bossy. *She'd* known his recklessness would get them all killed. At almost any cost Mirina wanted to stay in space, but serving under a hot dog who thought he was Jean Lafitte or Xak Milliane Ya was just out of her price range. Bisman was too casual about killing. Mirina wasn't a complete innocent. She had been involved with, or rather felt responsible for, the death of one so dear to her she'd never recovered from it. Mirina never wanted to feel like that again, but she was exposed to the possibility over and over every time their ship went reiving. So, at risk of having Bisman mutiny and strand her and Zonzalo somewhere out of frustration, she kept on his back about safety and minimum use of force.

"You are just like my teacher, Thunderstorm," Sunset said, in his resonant voice, glancing up as his four hands performed his tasks. "He tells and tells, but I make my mistakes all the same."

Zonzalo laughed. He'd become friends with the Thelerie, partly because they were the youngest beings on board and partly because he thought Sunset's innocent pronouncements hilarious.

"She is just exactly like a thunderstorm in space, isn't she?" Zonzalo said. "Uh-oh, the clouds are moving toward me." Mirina advanced upon him and glared down. Zonzalo pretended to cower, his shoulders hunched. Mirina swatted him lightly across the back.

"Act like adults," she snapped. "In case you weren't listening, some of our spacers are going down there. Their safety depends on you, too. Pay attention to your boards." The two young males exchanged humorous glances, then concentrated on their screens.

"Approach final. Attacking speed," Glashton said, not looking up from his console. "Grapples away!"

On the main tank, the background of stars shimmered as the forcefields locked onto five points surrounding the space station. The engines filled the ship with the scream of abused metal as the reiver dumped velocity, using the grapple anchors to halt forward momentum. On external camera, Mirina watched as the flexible white tube shot outward from the side of her ship to cover the airlock of the repair port and sucked closed. Bulbous-headed shadows inside it—Bisman's raiders in armor—bounded downward. There was an actinic flash, from which everyone in the cockpit automatically shielded his or her eyes, then Glashton switched video and audio input to a suit-mounted cam on the uniform of one of the raiders.

The crew plunged ahead into the darkness of the landing bay. Narrow beams of light slashed through the black tunnel, picking out steel-riveted walls, signs and directions etched in enamel next to huge louvered doors and at intersections. Two raiders found a communications circuit box and blasted it with slugs and energy weapons. That should have cut off external communications, but it also caused the inhabitants of the station to take notice. Sirens wailed in the distance. Blurred figures, bleached white by the raiders' searchlights, cannoned into view, weapons leveled. Bisman's people were ready. Mirina watched arms being raised, saw the spark of muzzle-flash. The defenders fell, arms splayed. A few of the raiders ran forward to collect their guns.

Bisman's voice barked hoarsely. "They'll only be out for about twenty minutes. Find the control room. Find the lights! Move it!"

Mirina held her breath as the camera eye followed the bobbing forms deeper into the repair facility. Someone found the control for the lights. The white blurs coalesced into armored backs and armloads of equipment. The siren's discordance chewed away at her nerves until she was tapping her foot with impatience, mentally urging Bisman to hurry and get out of there.

The louvered doors flapped up one by one, revealing empty bays. Suddenly, a door rolled up, and the hoped-for containers were right in front of the video pickup. The inventory numbers for ion-drive engine parts were printed on the side and top of each case. Zonzalo and Glashton cheered. Mirina pointed at the corral of heavy-loaders in the foreground of the screen, and snapped an order into the headset mike. Bisman had seen them, too. His hand appeared in the lens, making an "OK" symbol.

"All right, children, start loading 'em up!" The triumph in Bisman's voice came through the plasteel bubble helmet. Mirina felt smug, too. Even if they only sold half and kept the rest for running repairs and trade with the Thelerie, those engine parts should bring in enough to keep her fleet in space for another six months, at least.

"Hold it! Drop your weapons!" A commanding voice boomed out of the walls. The raiders looked around. His arms held up from the elbows, Mirina's video-carrier turned slowly to face a squad of guards in dark blue uniforms. At their head was a tall, thin woman with silver hair. Her tunic was trimmed with more silver, including rows of medal flashes. From the confident manner with which she held her long-barreled slugthrower, Mirina guessed that some of the medals were for marksmanship. Some of Bisman's crew began to comply, bending over to set their guns on the ground. The raiders were outnumbered at least two to one. Mirina bit her lip. She dreaded what would surely follow.

"Slowly . . ." the woman said, in a calm voice. "Slowly. Good. Now, hands above your heads."

"Now!" Bisman shouted. As one, the raiders dropped flat on the floor. The screen went blank. "Fire!" Mirina could tell by the sounds, they were spraying the defenders with energy bolts. Shouts, then screams erupted, followed by the noise of scuffling. Individual cries rose above the noise.

"What's happening?" Zonzalo asked. He had joined his sister to hang over the viewscreen. Mirina felt her blood drain away toward her feet. She swayed a little.

"It's all going wrong," she said, and turned to Glashton. "Shake 'em up. Give Bisman and the others a chance to get out."

The pilot nodded sharply, the muscles in his jaw twitching. He clawed at a series of controls, activating their secret weapon, the Slime Ball. The ship shuddered under their feet as it lit thrusters and pulled against the grapples. Always steering outward, so the return motion wouldn't yank the asteroid into their hull, Glashton zigzagged from one thruster to another.

The effect as seen on the screen was frightening. The raider wearing the camera was now lying on his back. The ceiling shook, and the giant plates seemed to rub against one another. Mirina wondered if they would crack apart and fall.

The crates of parts were vibrating, too, with every thrust of the ship. Inside their padding, the components were undoubtedly safe from impact damage even if they fell over, but if one landed on a human, there was nothing left to do but hold the funeral.

While those in the ship had suffered a temporary loss of visuals, Bisman and his crew had regained their weapons. Between
surges, the raiders managed to round up most of the defenders.
A few blue-shirts lay, heads a-loll, on the floor; unconscious, Mirina
hoped. Bisman and two of the others, kneeling, held the rest at
gunpoint while the raiders mounted heavy-loaders and lifted stacks
of the valuable crates. The stationmaster made one attempt to
protest. Bisman nodded to one of his gunners, who ratcheted her
weapon to a higher setting, and with one sweep slagged the metal
floor in front of the silver-haired woman. The others gasped as
the woman nearly stumbled forward into the red-hot mass. She
stopped protesting, her hands in the air, but her eyes flashed hatred
at Bisman. The loaders trundled out of the storeroom.

Zonzalo ran to his station to open the cargo bay to receive the
coming crates. He cackled to himself over each load as it passed
the cameras.

"Thruster modules," he said over his shoulder to the others.
"Energy reburner pods! My God, do you know what those are
worth? One new fuel tank, two, three—too bad there aren't a few
more."

"They'll all put oxygen in the tanks," Mirina said distantly. She
was watching Bisman, worrying whether he would make some
violent gesture at the end to keep the defenders from following.
Glashton spoke over the helmet communication link, letting the
raiders know that the violent jerking was over. The ship still swayed
lightly from side to side from inertia, but everyone could stand
up again.

"Mi— Mirina, do not those boxes belong to the humans of the
station-asteroid?"

"They did," Mirina said tersely. "Now they are ours. We need
them more. Your people need them to keep your space program
running. Those humans would have refused to give them to us.
This was the only way." But she had the picture in her mind of
the uniformed men and women on the floor. Something about the
ragdoll quality of the way they lay shouted at her that they were
not unconscious, but dead. Bisman had overdone it again. Instead
of a simple snatch and grab, they had more murders on their souls,
not to mention their growing rap sheets in the Central Worlds
computer bank.

Glashton, responding to a triumphant cry from Zonzalo that

the last of the heavy-loaders was on board and the raiding crew with it, sealed airlocks and blasted away. He gave an OK to Mirina, who yanked off her headset and squeezed herself with difficulty between the pilots' couches against the thrust of the engines. Her flesh flattened against her bones, and she shut her eyes.

God, who'd ever have thought I'd come to this? she mused, wriggling her body down farther to avoid somersaulting out into the corridor. *Fairhaired child of the corps, ace pilot, partner of . . . Damn it, stop thinking of him!* She turned her concentration to the star tank, drilling the hologram with her gaze. The star, around which the asteroid circled, shrank swiftly until it was another undistinguished dot of light on the scope. Just like all the other stars around which orbited facilities, planets, and ships they'd robbed for goods to keep them going.

"Shall I not go out there some day on a gathering mission?" Sunset asked Mirina, once they were clear of the heliopause.

"No," she said shortly, pulling her attention away from the star tank. "Never. You must be kept safe in the ship."

"But . . ."

"But nothing," Mirina interrupted him. She leveled a finger at his weird, striped eyes. "You don't understand your place in the schematic. You're the backup we count on in case of emergency. If we lose every system but drives and life support, you can get us home again, even if our navicomp is a slagged ruin. You're the last line of defense we have. I'm not letting you go out there and risk your neck, not when thirty other lives are depending on you."

"Oh." The young Thelerie pulled himself up, looking important and nervous and proud all at the same time. Mirina bit her tongue at having to tell him a lie, since sooner or later he'd meet up with others of his race who had joined the raiding parties after they'd apprenticed on the navigation board. But he was too young now. He'd be a liability to himself and the raiding crew.

"My center is sure," he told her.

"Good," Mirina sighed. "Keep it that way."

Bisman handed his way into the control room. His armored suit, now dusty, bore the black streak of a laser shot that impacted over the sternum and skidded upward toward his left ear. He grinned triumphantly.

"A megacredit run, at least," he crowed.

"Is everyone back on board?" Mirina asked.

"Yeah. Simborne and Mdeng bought it. They're cooling in the cargo bay with the containers."

"How many injured?"

"Not too many," Bisman said, offhandedly. "Fewer than the blueshirts, that's for sure."

"How many?" Mirina asked, and she knew he knew she wasn't asking for the list of wounded. Bisman pursed his lips and shrugged. "How many?"

"Five? Six or seven at the most."

"What?" she gasped. "What were you doing? Why did there have to be casualties?"

Sunset glanced up, then hurriedly ducked his head behind his wing to avoid the leader's glare. He was shocked at how angry she was.

"But you wanted those parts," Bisman complained. "They wouldn't give them up. What were we supposed to do?"

"That electroshock weapon of yours has more than one setting, doesn't it?" Mirina asked nastily, stepping up to the big male. Bisman retreated a pace out of surprise.

"He was going to pull an alarm! I had to stop him, quick! Damn, I'm tired of your jawing, Miri. We're partners, right? I make some of the decisions, right?"

Mirina's brown-in-white eyes filled with water—tears—and she said huskily, "I had a partner once. He died. I don't want to hear about partners. We're *co-leaders*. They owe us the stuff, *right*?" she said, mocking him. "They owe us, but they don't owe us their lives."

What she said made sense to Sunset, but Bisman appeared ready to disagree with her. Humans' flat faces were full of emotion, easy to read. Bisman's cheeks turned red, and his eyes stood out. Sunset thought for a moment he would strike Mirina, but he clenched his hands and left the room. Mirina's round face was set. She stared after the male, then closed her eyes. Sunset could see a slight vibration shake her body.

"There's enough in this shipment, Miri," Zonzalo spoke up softly from his station. "We could settle down somewhere on our share. CW would never find us. How about the nice place we stopped before we were on Base Fifteen the last time? We're heading back that way. We could scope out a place, buy some land?"

"No," Mirina said, opening her eyes. "I can't *settle*. I hate being groundbound. I prefer to be out here, in the blackness, away from people."

Sunset spread the shoulder pinions of his wings in acknowledgement. He had caught her many times just staring out into the void, communing. Space spoke to her in a way he had always believed it did to the blessed ones. That was no doubt why she was so cross when he interrupted her. Zonzalo was easier to befriend. Mirina turned suddenly to him, and the young Thelerie jumped, wondering if she could read his thoughts.

"Which way's your world, Sunset?" she asked. Without hesitation, he pointed toward his Center, and she sighted along his wing-finger.

"We count on you, you know that," she said, wearily. Sunset nodded. "Good. Go take a rest."

"You should, too, ma— Mirina." Then he dropped on all fours and hurried out of the control room, surprised by his own boldness. The woman stared after him.

Zonzalo waved at his sister, and pointed at a light on his control board.

"Message coming in," he said. Mirina stood over his shoulder and watched the brief transmission.

"Route it to Bisman," she said at once. "He has to hear this."

The co-leader was in the control room almost at once.

"A ship penetrated the other P-sector system near Base Eight? We have to send word to have the others destroy it!"

"We can't," Mirina said. "It's landed on the second planet. It's protected. Listen to this all the way through." She signalled to Zonzalo to play it back again.

"The reptiles," Bisman said, exasperated. "The Slime. Damn it, I thought we had them bottled." He recorded a return message to their base. "Keep an eye out. If anything else happens, take appropriate action and notify us at once. *Appropriate* action," he repeated, with heavy emphasis, and one eye on Mirina. She glared at him, but held her tongue.

✷CHAPTER FOUR

For an interminable third day, Keff sat crosslegged on the floor of the Cridi assembly hall. He sat with his chin braced on one palm, elbow on knee, his wrist held to one side so Carialle could see everything that was going on from the miniaturized video pickup on his shirt front.

"Another day of flapping lips and hands in the Main Bog," Keff murmured behind his hand. "I feel like Gulliver in Lilliput."

The humidity was so uncomfortable that in direct countermand of orders from Central Worlds, Keff had stopped wearing uniforms. Instead, he was clad in his least disreputable exercise clothes, fabric made for sweating in. His hair had wound itself into curls, as it always did when it was damp, and he smelled musty. No one else seemed to notice the odor; perhaps his hosts simply couldn't distinguish it in the swamp miasma that hung over everything on this soggy world. Nor did the Cridi pay any attention to the drops running down his face. Like Tall Eyebrow and the others in the ship, some of them made a practice of wearing a film of water to keep their delicate skins from drying out. Others just counted on the ambient humidity, which, Keff thought, was more than sufficient.

The room's decor reflected the possibility of wet delegates. The ceiling rolled back as easily to allow a passing downpour into the chamber as the view of a sunset or a rainbow. Low, comfortable seats shaped for either sitting upright, crouching, or lounging had soft, water-repellent covers; bright white light came from thick, enclosed bubbles hanging overhead; wooden tables were sealed in plastic, or perhaps made of a naturally resinous wood—Keff hadn't had a chance yet to examine one closely. Every time he approached a sitting group, perforce on hands and knees in the low-ceilinged room, stone-faced security frogs came out of the woodwork and herded him back to his spot.

"At least they're allowing you to stay," Carialle said. "It's a foot in the door. You could be stuck out here with me, watching the swamp gurgle, and listening to the security guards babble formulae at each other."

"I'm getting no forrader in advancing the cause of the Central Worlds," Keff said, forlornly watching Tall Eyebrow and the others, separated among three huge groups of Cridi, answering questions. Long Hand was perched in one of the chairs, waving her hands to get the attention of a pair of natives who were squabbling in high-pitched voices. "All during that muddy tour yesterday and the day before, I kept trying to tell them about the Central Worlds, but Big Voice over there kept saying the conclave hadn't yet discussed whether to allow input from an outworlder that would result in any kind of social engineering, when they've never met an outworlder before. Once they've discussed the topic, we have to wait until they've had input from every other city on the planet before proceeding. The final decision rests with the Council of Eight. I'm not allowed to influence anyone, particularly not with the fact of my being an alien. It's a bureaucracy. Our mission, to encounter strange new holdups and fascinating new ways to tie red tape where no frog has gone before."

"Isn't anyone talking to you?"

"Oh, yes, on and off, but more out of curiosity than diplomatic interest. I think," Keff said, smiling and making a seated bow to a passing delegate, "I'm serving a function all the same. The Cridi are learning not to be afraid of us. That's good. If they see me as a clown, I just have to coddle my own ego. The problem is they treat me rather like a talking dog, a non-sentient that is a wonder because it can pronounce recognizable words. I would be most concerned that they wouldn't take the Central Worlds seriously enough. There's no future alliance possible without respect."

"Respect comes with knowledge. They are getting used to you. They've never seen anything like you—or me. As with humans, it sounds like they've run into very few, if any, sentient species beside their own. It *would* be like one of their dogs starting to talk, if they have dogs. So far I've only seen those blobbies and lizardings they keep for pets. In time, they'll get used to the idea that you do think for yourself. Be thankful that they don't think you're a monster. I was a little worried after that first group took off screaming. They could have burned out Frankenstein *and* his castle with Core power."

"So they could." Keff shifted uncomfortably, pulling the folds of his sweatshirt away from his back. "I'd just prefer to be in the midst of things instead of merely observing. It looks like Tall Eyebrow could use my help." He glanced over at the group surrounding the Ozranian Frog Prince.

"Tch, greedy. Look, they're friendly. You're getting an unprecedented privilege to have the first peep at an entirely new world, something anyone in Xeno would kill for."

Keff brightened, sitting up straighter, ignoring the smell and the sog. "That's true. Alien Outreach chose us. It's us, partner, first and foremost, no matter what. I want to see everything. And I need to look sharp. I keep missing details."

"Well, that's what I'm here for," Carialle said complacently. "My drives haven't stopped humming for the last eighty hours. Just ask your friendly neighborhood shellperson for a free, money-back guaranteed review."

Keff grinned. "If only it was that easy. It has to be in *my* head, too. I wish *I* had extended memory banks." There was so much that was different in the way the Cridi lived on their homeworld than on Ozran. Isolated as he was, he felt as if he was only one more fact away from sensory overload.

At first he had wondered if the Cridian amphibioids had abandoned their amulet power system, since no amulets were in evidence. Carialle had been the first to point out the circuits, like fine gold filigree, that were either worn on, or bonded to the ends of the Cridi's long fingers. It was a tremendous advancement in the technology. To access Core power, the user merely positioned his or her hand, as if inserting the fingertips into the niches on a device, the way humans would use a virtual-reality glove, and they were in touch, so to speak, with the Core. Keff knew that Tall Eyebrow and the other Ozranian visitors were uncomfortable using their antique amulets in front of the homeworlders, but he'd assured them that they should be proud to display them, as symbols, if nothing else. The amulets represented hard-won equality after years of deprivation. Besides, their race had a natural predilection for telekinesis, unlike their newfound allies, the humans. That was an advantage that no archaic equipment could devalue. It didn't dispel the Ozranians' discomfort entirely, but it helped. Keff would have given anything to be able to use an amulet, archaic or no, to be dry just for an hour. His boots were beginning to smell moldy. He considered hiking back to the ship through the rain to get a pair of sandals.

Carialle broke into his reverie.

"Oh, look. Company's coming. One of the 'eight great.'"

Keff glanced up. One of the dignitaries from the Cridi delegation made her way through the crowd and stopped before Keff. She wore a red cloak that was secured at her throat and wrists with gold bands instead of the silver bangles she had worn to meet the ship. Keff guessed from his limited knowledge of Cridi biology that she was fairly young, but still considered an adult. He tried to straighten the crumples out of his shirt.

The hands moved swiftly. "Can your mind reach me?"

Keff responded, "I sign your language, gentle-female."

She gestured a little impatiently. "Why you here?"

"To make a bridge between your world and ours. To make friends with another race who has its own science, its own space system. We have met many new peoples, but have always had to help them develop . . . ."

He would have gone on, but he sensed that the female was getting bored. "What's wrong?" he asked.

"Too long," she replied, emphatically. "*Old.* Like three." She swung around to point at the Ozranian delegates in turn, lingering briefly on Tall Eyebrow. She turned again and fixed her beady gaze on him. "Old."

"Old? How would she know how old I . . ." Keff repeated, bewildered, then was enlightened. "Ah! You mean the language we are using is old. Antiquated." The concept was just out of the reach of his Cridi hand-vocabulary, so he had to reach for it. Encouragingly, the female frog watched him struggle with his explanation, nodding when he made sense to her. "We sound like *ancestors* to you?"

She tipped her little face up and stretched her neck slightly three times, like she was bobbing her head against something from underneath.

"Yes."

"Whew! So that's the problem," Keff said, running his hand back through his hair, and remembering just in time that the gesture wasn't going to offend the Cridi, having a neutral meaning like "low ceiling." "Hey, Cari, that's wonderful!"

"Ah," she said, sardonically. "You're not a monster. You're just dull."

"Yes, but think of it. This would be just the same as if I went back to Old Earth and addressed them in Latin. But you see," he continued, dropping back into Cridi for the female, "that is what I learned from Tall Eyebrow, and his society has had none of the global changes of your people. You must help us to learn the new way of speaking. We are willing."

His visitor launched into a flurry of hand signals that Keff could tell had been abbreviated from the ones he knew, plus complicated overtones in the language of science. He was glad he'd learned the long form first, or he'd never have recognized some of the subtleties. He prayed that his translation program was picking up all of her spoken words. Later he'd commune with the Intentional Translator and see what it would make of all the murmurs, squeaks, chirps and trills.

"Ah. See," she signed in her clipped style. The trills translated to a formula for condensing large numbers into small. "I apologize, but it boring watch the long forms. That is why none speaks you."

"That tells me something," Carialle said quietly in his ear. "It means that the Cridi weren't as dependent upon the power controller system when TE's progenitors left for Ozran. Otherwise they'd have had more voice and less hands then, too, the easier to communicate over remote frequencies. I predict that in another thousand years their language will be all verbal. Hand-sign will just be a topic for some doctoral dissertation."

"I'd love to take you up on a bet, Lady Fair," Keff said, wryly. "You'll just have to remember to check in another millenium for me."

"Ah, Sir Knight, I shall." Carialle's voice was tender.

"Who speak to?" Big Eyes asked.

"To Carialle," he said. "She's my partner. She lives in the ship that brought us here."

"Curious," she said. "Have scanned. Life support absolute?"

"Yes. Very efficient, too."

"Interested in engineering. Degreed."

"Really? What branch?" Keff was starting to get the hang of her abbreviated conversation.

"Aerospace," said her hands, and she added a long vocal trill. IT translated it as a complex navigation formula.

"There's luck," Carialle said in Keff's ear.

"I'll say. You must be the person we've been waiting for. Tell me about Cridi's space program," Keff said eagerly. Big Eyes waved away his request nonchalantly.

"None talk right now," she said.

"Won't she talk about it, or isn't there anything going on?" Carialle asked.

"I don't know," Keff said. "Listen to IT babbling about two potential meanings. Could it be another one of those 'don't tell the alien' subjects?" He broached this suggestion gently to Big Eyes, who openly ignored the question. In fact, she seemed impatient.

"Not now. I worst tell. Father. Much else to see now I know." She pointed at Long Hand, who was giving a dissertation on the farming techniques used on Ozran. "Observe. You asked. I help. Cut middles," she signed to him, lifting an imaginary section out of something with her flattened hands held parallel. Big Eyes repeated key phrases with sign language, and interspersed them with verbal signs that tightened up the long strings of symbolism to the few necessary. Keff had thought the Ozranian version of Cridi sign language was terse and to the point. Big Eyes reduced it still further, to the essence of meaning.

"Very efficient," Keff said, trying to match her gestures. "Cari, I can reprogram IT to give me two choices of expression—dialects, if you will, depending on which planet I'm on, Cridi or Ozran. This is worth at least one paper for *Scientific Galactican* or *Linguistics Today*."

"If Xeno will let you declassify this data so soon. Remember we're the diplomatic advance scout. You'll probably have to teach the combination languages to the reps yet to come."

"All part of the service." He glanced over at Tall Eyebrow again, who was trying to answer questions from three delegates at once, all of whom were clamoring for his sole attention. "He looks as confused as I feel." He turned to Big Eyes. "Excuse me. Talk to my friend."

"Stay," she said, with an urgent gesture and a high-pitched peep that indicated an exponent of urgency. "Elders."

Keff looked around. Two more of the eight, Smooth Hand and Big Voice, were making their way toward him, followed by the usual entourage of aides and flunkeys. Like Big Eyes, they wore modified capes of various colors and lengths attached at throat and wrists.

"You are here already," Smooth Hand said to Big Eyes. "Have you broached discussion with him yet?"

"No," Big Eyes said briefly. "We acquaint."

"Good," Smooth Hand signed. "Here are six of the eight members of the conclave council representatives, so our discussion may be of significance."

"Now's your big chance to impress them," Carialle said.

"Maybe they've made a decision on joining Central Worlds," Keff said, wishing he'd sacrificed comfort for dignity and worn the uniform after all. "How serve, gentle-ones?" he asked, keeping the signs as short as he could. The young female up-nodded encouragingly toward him.

Always a quick study, but unwilling to sacrifice courtesy for speed, Keff tried to incorporate his new friend's lessons in his handspeech. Working from discussions he had had with Tall Eyebrow about traditional protocol, he gave Smooth Hand the respect due the oldest member of the conclave, then greeted the others, ending with Big Eyes. She gave him a quick gesture of approval with joined thumb and long forefinger.

"That was a hash," Keff murmured to Carialle without moving his lips. "The Minute Waltz in eight seconds."

"Looked fine from here," Carialle said. "And they seem happy."

"In return," Smooth Hand said, "we greet you." Keff bowed his head as deeply as he could, and waited.

As usual, Big Voice took the lead in the discussion. The stout amphibioid pushed forward to the center of the group and glared at Keff, who glanced at Smooth Hand for direction. Instead of attempting to overbear the pompous councillor, the old one stood back with an air of indulgence. Keff assumed an air of respectful attention that made Big Eyes's eponymous features twinkle with amusement. Big Voice began his dissertation with exaggerated movements of his elbows designed to clear away anyone standing within half a meter of him. Everyone edged away. Keff carefully pulled in his knees.

"Stranger to this world, we are grateful that you return to us lost descendants of our ancestors," Big Voice gestured hugely. "From the far reaches of the void they come, never thought to have been seen again . . . ." The language of diplomacy appeared to be rooted in both the new and old forms, comprising more sign than was used by Big Eyes—which bored her and the other young members of the council—and more verbiage than Keff's version, which confused the brawn. Keff paused and nodded and smiled in between the flowery statements, waiting for IT to cycle back translations to him utilizing the growing catalog it was picking up of the spoken language. Keff hoped that he would look thoughtful, rather than lost. His brief and polite replies, made when Big Voice stopped for breath, seemed to please his audience.

" . . . And that is how our cousins' journey ended, here on beautiful Cridi."

"We are grateful for your welcome of us."

"You say that you did not know of the Cridi who inhabited Sky Clear?"

"No," Keff said. "We had lost track of some of our own people many hundreds of years ago. They settled on, er, Sky Clear, and thereafter dropped out of communication with us. As it was with your ancestors."

"So, they have been self-governing all this time?" Big Voice asked. "Without the approval of your Central Worlds?"

"Well, not without the approval of the government, but certainly without its knowledge. We lost touch, you see." Keff tried the phrase a couple of ways and hoped they understood.

"So, it is not your Central Worlds who holds the half of Sky Clear?" Big Voice asked.

"Not precisely," Keff said carefully, settling in for a long explanation. "Our people, descendants of *my* ancestors who set out many hundreds of years ago, settled the world alongside yours. To encounter them, we—and they—were as surprised to see one another as you are to meet Tall Eyebrow and his companions."

"But they did not set down upon this world at the same time, nor before the Cridi?"

"He's going somewhere," Carialle said, in between sound bites from IT in Keff's aural implant. "I don't like what I think he's getting at."

"Neither do I. Not to my knowledge," Keff said out loud, sensing he was treading on tricky ground. "The humans who live on Oz—Sky Clear were not as good recordkeepers as the Cridi." Mentally he crossed his fingers, knowing he was eliding the truth. The early settlers had kept good tape archives of their settlement, and none of it included references to the Cridi except as a curious life-form they thought was indigenous to Ozran.

"Are we to understand that you came to our world only to convey our lost children?" Smooth Hand inquired, interrupting Big Voice by standing in front of him.

Keff was grateful to have a respite from Big Voice's pointed questioning. "That and to ask your people to join the great conclave of planets and beings we call the Central Worlds." Keff had worked out a set of handsigns he found symbolic of those concepts of unity and cooperation. The elder picked it up without a demur, and repeated it to the others. "This organization boasts members from many species besides humanity. We are proud of our diversity. I am instructed to convey the compliments of our government and say that they, and we, would be delighted if you would join."

"Beginning to think no intelligent life existed outside our own," Smooth Hand said, with dry humor. "How many are there?"

"Thousands of inhabited planets, hundreds of intelligent species with uncounted subgroups, millions of non-sentient protected species in various stages of development," Keff said, hoping he was placing the exponents correctly in his voiced phrases.

"Most impressive," Smooth Hand gestured, thoughtfully.

The other councillors chattered formulae at one another, speculating on the size of Central Worlds' sphere. Keff waved politely for attention.

"I can give you star charts, if you want."

"Yes! Occasional talk of ships passing through our system," Big Eyes said, describing the decline of an arc across the sky. "Believed to be myths. Not know. You?"

"Maybe," Keff said. "Maybe another race. There are countless others out there that we've never met. You might even have neighbors and not know it."

"Maybe the salvage squad," Carialle sputtered in his ear.

"Not in system," Big Voice protested. "That known of old."

"Meteors or myths," the elder said, indulgently. "If not myths, why not land before now? Why were they not curious? All ground control has ever retrieved is rocks. Fly-by saucers are mythical. System has very strange and strong anomalies."

"You can say that again," Carialle said. "That trash heap at the binary end of the heliopause, whew!"

"Shh, Cari," Keff said softly, nodding and smiling at the delegates.

Big Voice hovered above everyone's head and waved for attention. "The presence of so many other worlds containing humans shall then pose no difficulty in moving those off Sky Clear in favor of Cridi."

"Aha!" Carialle said.

"What?" Keff sputtered. "This is a long-established society, sir. It might have been different if you had made such a demand within say, three years of the discovery. Not after a thousand years. That's like saying that dinosaurs have a permanent claim on Burbank, California, on Old Earth just because some of their relatives are buried in the La Brea tar pits."

Big Voice paid no attention to his simile.

"*Yes*, after a thousand years. If you want the approval of the conclave to join your Central Worlds, you will cede Sky Clear to the Cridi. We have prior landing rights. You have said so yourself." Keff wouldn't have believed it, but Big Voice's shrill cheeping *did* manage to sound menacing. Two of the six council members present, and a few among the entourage bobbed up their heads in agreement.

"That's blackmail," Carialle said. "I wonder how much power he really holds in the conclave. Smooth Hand looks a little shocked at the tactics."

"We can't afford to find out," Keff said sublingually. "If, good sir, you would care to examine the records, you would see that when humans landed on Ozran—or Sky Clear, if you prefer," he corrected himself, seeing that Big Voice was swelling fit to pop, "they were unaware of the presence of the Cridi, owing to the subterfuge of the Others. See here. Do not ask only me. Tall Eyebrow himself will explain that the current generation of Cridi have no objections to sharing the planet with humans. Small Spot is the archivist. He can direct you to the correct records."

Another male, wearing a green cape, pushed forward to get the conclave council's attention. "I withhold approval because I still do not believe in this story of a lost colony. These three Cridi must come from another part of our own world. This is a hoax. A ship built in secret." A chorus of agreement, plus wild signing came from a portion of the group, obviously this male's supporters.

"Uh-oh," Carialle said. "Shades of Ozran."

"Snap Fingers, your data is faulty," Smooth Hand said patiently, shaking his head.

"I would suggest," Keff signed patiently, "that the internal evidence in the archives, added to the fact that we humans are here with the Sky Clear delegation, will prove otherwise."

"Fabricated!"

"But the aliens . . . ?" Smooth Hand began, with a glance at Keff.

"Random chance met!"

"But where?' Big Eyes asked, innocently, "when no whole ship has come in or out of atmosphere for fifty years?"

Big Voice glared fiercely at her.

"Fifty years?" Carialle repeated. "Why hasn't their space program been active for fifty years?"

Keff tried to interrupt the argument to ask, but no one was paying attention to him. The air was full of Cridi. The male in the green cape tapped Smooth Hand's shoulder and flung angry gestures in the old one's face. Big Voice addressed Big Eyes and Snap Fingers alternately, spinning to confront each of them in turn. Creaking broke out all over, making the group sound like a marsh pond in mating season. In spite of the seriousness of the subject, Keff had to try hard not to smile. He hoped fervently that the recording mechanism in IT would be able to distinguish between thirty different Cridi voices when it tried to translate this mess.

Big Voice interrupted with a shrill whistle ordering them to diminish volume. "No decision can be made now! It will take much time for all the archives to be read," he signed.

"Then, please read them," Keff said, sitting up very tall so they had to look up at him. "No decision of any importance should be made in haste."

There was general approval for such a wise suggestion. Big Voice looked upset, as if Keff had stolen his thunder by being reasonable. "We shall read them, you may be assured," he signed, his face grim. "In the meantime, no assurances can be made for or against membership. I shall withhold approval until then myself."

"As you will, gentle-male," Keff said, describing a sitting bow with the flourishes born of long practice.

"Whew!" said Carialle. "At once thrust into the fire and pulled out of it again by the same frog."

"Hot air," signed Big Eyes, merrily. "I am in favor of membership. Many advantages."

"Brash youngster," Smooth Hand said fondly. "Do not decide without all facts."

"Facts dull," Big Eyes said. "Still, should like to see Ozran." She glanced over toward Tall Eyebrow with an approving look. Keff made a mental note to mention the young female's interest to his friend. Then she stood up on her toes and whistled a shrill signal as a tall, thin frog with a mottled skin of a pleasant brownish green entered the big chamber. Keff could tell that he was very old, but he still walked upright. He saw Big Eyes and waved back.

"My father," Big Eyes signed, as the male joined the group. "Narrow Leg I, seventh offspring," Big Eyes offered, presenting the human and the Cridi to one another.

"Seventieth?" Keff asked, singing the number carefully in the highest voice he could muster.

"No," she gestured, and repeated the fluting snatch of song, making sure he saw and heard no decimal multiplier.

"Oops!" Keff exclaimed. "This is an old, thin lad, Big Eyes' dad," he said, playfully to Carialle, noticing the twinkle in the elderly Cridi's eye and deciding at once that he liked him. "No, tad. Tad Pole."

"Oh, Keff," Carialle groaned. Keff snickered. Big Eyes explained Keff to her father with a few gestures, then turned to the human.

"Narrow Leg is head of current space program. Answer questions."

"At last," Keff said, happily. "How do you do, sir?"

"Pleased to meet you," said Narrow Leg. "Wanting to converse on spaceships." He described with a few graceful signs the contours of craft much like Carialle's. Keff stared. Even for a race that had unusually large and long hands, Tad Pole's were extraordinary. When his hand was closed the tips of the fingers seemed to reach partway down the wrist. The gold filigree amulet circuitry looked like an ancient Chinese aristocrat's fingernail stalls. "May I hope for some increment of your time?"

"At some point, I would love to compare our programs with yours," Keff said. "I expect that we'll be discussing the possibility of Cridi joining the Central Worlds for a while longer."

"Ah!" Narrow Leg squeaked. "A unity of many peoples. Will there be a vote?" he asked the councillors.

"No. Nothing will be settled today," Smooth Hand signed.

"Why not?" Narrow Leg asked.

His daughter made an impatient gesture. "They say reading of archives takes time, then the conclave must discuss everything to death. We and Keff shall be hauled back here again and again. Negotiations held up because there are factions who don't believe Tall Eyebrow and Keff are who they say they are. Non-ex-planetary."

"Nonsense!" Narrow Leg gestured definitely. "Of course they are! To what purpose, to what end to create an elaborate charade of this nature? Do you think such a creature as this," he indicated Keff, "arose from primordial ooze without us noticing? He is from beyond atmosphere, and, if you will believe your beacons—and you should—from beyond our system. Human," he turned to the brawn. "Will you take me to your spaceship? I would like to see it."

"I should be honored, gentle-male," Keff replied.

"Bring him," Carialle said. "He's one of the few so far who is making sense."

"And my partner will welcome you, also," Keff added. Narrow Leg looked gratified.

"Not settled yet the questioning about sharing Sky Clear," Big Voice interrupted with an alarming shriek meant to regain the floor. "Do you not realize the offense given by involuntary sharing of Sky Clear?"

"Offense?" Keff asked. "Hadn't you better ask Tall Eyebrow about the cooperative colony? Right now humans and Cridi are coexisting rather well. And without much consultation you could abort an experiment that has the possibility of breaking new ground in interspecies cooperation."

Big Voice wasn't interested. "We explored that sector. It is the first of our colonies we have heard from for fifty years. We want it to revert to Cridi, with no interference."

"Fifty years again," Carialle said urgently. "Ask why it's been so long since there's been contact outside the system."

"Yes," said Keff. "Why isn't space program running?"

All the elders except Narrow Leg turned to glare at Big Eyes.

"I have told nothing," she signed indignantly. "He is not stupid. He sees negative indications."

Smooth Hand shook his head, and turned to Keff. "Too many problems, too little funding."

"Too many natural resources are used up," Snap Fingers added. "We have few heavy metals. Send to colonies in centuries past, get no return." He chattered a complex series of descending notes which Keff didn't need IT's help to translate as a losing program. There were outcries of protest, and the brawn kept turning his head to see everyone who wanted his attention.

"Don't think of it in terms of immediate return," Tad Pole complained, pursing his wide lips distastefully. He turned to the crowd. "See here, my friends, you have no respect for the world as it was fifty years ago, when we had a working program. You're ignorant of your own history. So many strides forward were made as a result over hundreds of years of space study! You forget your past!"

"You do not look to the real future! Program failed. Bad use of funds, of the best minds!" signed Snap Fingers. "I and other members of Cridi Inward see no reason to continue burying good food under the swamp. It's a waste of time. Equipment doesn't work properly."

Big Voice took immediate umbrage. "The equipment is properly made and maintained!"

"Well, we keep seeing anomalies on scopes, like other spacecraft," Snap Fingers said, seeing that he had offended the blustering councillor.

"Well, now we know that those could be true," Smooth Hand signed, with a polite nod to Keff.

"That is true. Yet it does not change facts." With less bombastic gestures, Snap Fingers continued. "Our economy could not support any more failures."

"Yes!" Smooth Hand said. "We would like to recoup losses from space program."

"And that is why laying sole claim to Sky Clear is important to Big Voice," Narrow Leg's daughter said, making a distasteful moue. Big Voice emitted his shriek of protest once again, this time with a five-times multiplier attached. Keff winced.

"There is nothing wrong with honest profit!" Big Voice said.

"If profit does not come at the expense of lives," Snap Fingers retorted.

"Gentles, gentles," Keff said, and held up his hands, "please. Facts? I know nothing of your recent history."

Through the confused mixture of Cridi music and gesture, Keff managed to discover that the last *successful* launch of a spacecraft had been fifty years past. Several tries had been made thereafter, but no vehicle had managed to clear the system since then.

"Have received no messages, no artifacts from other colonies," Narrow Leg added, spreading his hands at shoulder level. "Abandoned? Destroyed? Technological setbacks like Sky Clear? We do not know."

"Three launches, three expensive disasters," indicated Snap Fingers. "I blame the equipment."

"As do I," Narrow Leg said.

"No," Big Voice said emphatically. "Not in the last one! It must be because of radiation or ion storms or some unknown natural menace!"

Narrow Leg turned to Keff. "Our space program is crippled. There is something wrong with the drives, or the shielding, that it cannot carry a craft swiftly enough out of the way of space storms, or protect them well. Once out of range of the Core of Cridi, have to rely upon actual machinery, and it has been shoddy."

"How dare you?" Big Voice demanded, embarrassed.

Narrow Leg pointedly turned his back on the other. "The technicians who built can ignore small faults, like badly fitting seals or insufficiently tightened components. Astronauts don't know about them, can't guard using their own devices because range of power is limited to atmosphere of Cridi. Fault—*boom!* Again and again, just out of atmosphere."

"Storms have become more virulent," Snap Fingers said. "Can we trade with the humans for better technology? We have much to offer."

"There is nothing wrong with the technology!" Big Voice said furiously.

"No," Narrow Leg said, coolly, watching the yellow-brown Cridi swell until he looked as if he might pop. "Only with the construction management."

Keff, ever the diplomat, wanted to follow upon Snap Fingers's suggestion. This was much more of what he hoped would happen in council. "Yes, of course we'd be happy to offer machinery or advice, or whatever you need. I know we'd love to exchange goods and ideas with you. We are fascinated with your power control system. We've never seen anything like it. Our, er, brothers and sisters on Ozran have learned to use it, and I know our government has shown an interest in what we've told them."

"And you?" Big Eyes asked.

"Well, at present I can't use it," Keff said, trying to explain his lack of the necessary telekinetic spark.

"Modification?" One frog signed quickly to another. The topic spread around the room, even superseding the discussions in which the three Ozranians were involved.

The room filled with the cheeping of formulae and wild signing of hands.

"There is virtue in the notion of trade, Core technology for superior Central Worlds spacecraft," Smooth Hand said, stroking his jaw with his long fingers.

Big Voice protested once more, but his argument was losing ferocity as he was ignored by everyone around him. "No, not superior! I tell you, it is the ion storms!"

"Sounds unlikely to me," Carialle told Keff, after running her telemetry. "I didn't notice any undue amounts of radiation, or that much floating debris on the outskirts of this system. I'll contact Central Worlds about ion storms in this area. Warn the council I'm about to launch a message probe. Ask them to let it out of atmosphere. I don't want it returned to sender."

Keff conveyed Carialle's information. At once, there was a fresh flurry of argument, which Smooth Hand quickly put down.

"Of course you may communicate with your government," he said genially. "Convey our compliments, and thank them for their assistance."

Tad Pole perked up. "I should still like to witness the launch of your message rocket," he said. "In fact, may I not have a tour of your ship?"

"Tell him he's very welcome," Carialle said. "I'll tidy up. I might even bake a cake."

"I'll tell him," Keff said. "Cari, do you know what it means that the Cridi have lacked a space program for the last fifty years?"

"Yes," Carialle said with such gusto that Keff winced. "Nothing out of system in all that time. It means the Cridi weren't my salvage squad. I can't tell you how glad that makes me. That only leaves me wondering all the more who they were."

"Don't worry about that now, Cari. We're doing so well with the Cridi. Let's tackle one problem at a time. When this is all shipshape and Bristol fashion, to everyone's satisfaction, I still say we should go out looking for your boojums."

"You bet we will," Carialle said. "But I'm so relieved about the Cridi, I love them all, even that squeaking blowhard, Big Voice."

"I'll tell him so, although I don't think he'll appreciate your description very much."

"Well, think of some diplomatic way to tell him. I'm recording the message to CW now. See you in a few nanos."

✺CHAPTER FIVE

Before he left for the ship with Narrow Leg, Keff collected Tall
Eyebrow and the others. Smooth Hand, seeing that all were now
on fire to discuss exchanges with the Central Worlds, adjourned
the meeting. Tall Eyebrow seemed as if he welcomed the rescue.
All four outworlders were grateful to leave, but had to promise
to appear in the great hall again in the morning to continue the
discussion on citizenship. Narrow Leg led Keff and the Ozranians
out of the damp hall and into what was left of the day. It had
been raining hard. The air still smelled like a gym locker, but Keff
took a deep breath, glad to expand his lungs.

Sunshine glittered on the ornamental paving surrounding the
Main Bog building, picking up light from bright specks of mica
or quartz. The sculpted, multicolored granitelike rock felt rough
and uneven under his boot soles, but the visual effect was one of
undulating ocean waves, most soothing to the eye. Design was
important to the Cridi. Keff appreciated their painstaking attention to detail. Plants sprouted out of pillar tops and along the
guardrails of ramps. Tall buildings containing hundreds of apart-
ment flats poked up through the thick trees, looking as though
they had evolved organically themselves. Since all Cridi had access
to Core power and therefore could fly, entrances to the flats were
as likely to be up as down: on protruding ledges of smooth stone,
in sculpted baskets like giant nests, carved like a child's slide
through a miniature waterfall. Mosaics seemed to have been formed

by stratification in the rock walls instead of being imposed upon them by artistic hands. Huge golden insects with multiple wings like living jewels hovered over V-shaped blossoms in the many planters, sipping nectar. Keff half-expected one of the Cridi to dart out a long tongue and devour one.

Long Hand looked around her, nodding approvingly. Small Spot just sat down on the sidewalk with his long legs collapsing under him, turning his amulet, a long, thin fingertrap, between his hands. Tall Eyebrow seemed drawn and tired. His skin looked dull amid all the bright stonework.

"How has it been going?" Keff asked him in Standard, once they were out of earshot of the other delegates. Clusters of Cridi hung around the pillared entrance, signing to one another, but more than one cast a curious eye toward the strangers.

"I feel lost," the Frog Prince replied in the human tongue, with a glance at Narrow Leg. The elder Cridi up-nodded politely, after understanding that they were having a private conversation, and turned his head the other way. Keff blessed the old one's tact.

"Why?" Keff asked Tall Eyebrow.

"Technology so far beyond ours," he replied, his small face screwed up, searching for the correct words. "I am at disadvantage to show what my people have done."

"Technology isn't everything," Keff said, soothingly. "You have experience and intelligence. You have overcome incredible obstacles to survive. You've rejuvenated a planet."

"And what is that here?" Tall Eyebrow turned his palms upward. "Nothing."

He paused at the edge of the pavement and looked up and down the main thoroughfare passing the Main Bog of Greedeek, the Cridi capital city. It had been raining again, and the lanes ran with multiple streams of muddy water. Around him, delegates were taking leave of one another, gliding out or upward toward their homes. Keff could tell that the Frog Prince wished he wasn't groundbound. The taste of power over the last two years on Ozran had spoiled the globe-frog. On the other hand, the mudflow was daunting even to a human. Keff looked down and took a deep breath before raising a foot over the ooze. Tall Eyebrow, too, paused, reaching for his amulet. When he realized it wouldn't work, he glanced up at Keff with a shamefaced expression. Neither of them wanted to test the depth of the viscous goo.

"Here goes anyhow," he said. "I'd better go first."

"Power surge coming up in your direction," Carialle said. At the same time, Keff felt his feet arrested before they sank into the greeny-black mud. His right foot hovered, supported a few centimeters above the surface. He drew his left foot forward. The invisible floor beneath him held.

A shrill whistle of laughter came from behind them. Big Eyes was lifting them and herself, using her power circuitry.

"Technology *is* something," Tall Eyebrow said, gloomily.

"Go on, go on," the female gestured. "Wish to come to ship."

Her father, who had halted when he found that the others had dropped behind, turned to see what was going on.

"How rude of you, daughter," he said. His enormously long fingers folded together.

"I apologize," Narrow Leg signed quickly. "I forgot. I have not met outworlders before. I forgot you," and he indicated Keff, mainly to save Tall Eyebrow embarrassment, "would not have our advantages."

"Quite all right," Keff said, politely. "Your daughter has resc— offered her kind hospitality."

"You mean she has made herself the center of attention," Narrow Leg signed, with a humorous sigh. "Do you think it is easy, after seven children, to find one who stands out so?"

"I think she would stand out," Tall Eyebrow signed, without looking at either of them, "if there were a million children."

The female let out a tinkling laugh, and put her long fingertips on Tall Eyebrow's arm.

"Gallant one," she said, when he raised his head. They looked deeply at one another for a long moment. Grinning fit to pop his jaw, Keff held his breath. Big Eyes tented her fingertips and thumbtips together and dipped her chin toward them. "You're very kind. I am glad you came home to Cridi. Come, let us see the spaceship."

Tall Eyebrow, buoyed on borrowed power and love, strode proudly in the direction of the landing field with Big Eyes beside him.

"This is most impressive," Tad Pole said over and over again, as he stumped about the main cabin of Carialle's ship. "Most impressive."

Possessed of great height for a Cridi, he was able to see over
the edges of the consoles from the floor. When he had paced from
the food processor to the view tank about a dozen times, he raised
himself on a surge of power and floated. Carialle noted the slight
surges of power that rose around the old frog's form as he levitated. The homeworld Cridi had such a subtle command of their
power system: as different from the Core of Ozran as a scalpel to
a sledgehammer. The Cridi generators were, Carialle estimated, as
much as five times more powerful. Yet with all the use the locals
made of the system, the local environment seemed to show no signs
of deterioration or other ill effects. She would have to question
Narrow Leg on the technology when he was finished with his tour.
She manifested her frog image next to him over the navigation
station to describe what he was looking at.

"Thank you for the compliments, gentle-male. This indicates the
benchmarking codes for this sector," she said, activating the screen
to show Cridi's star in relation to the nearest blue lines. "Sector A is
considered galactic center, and the others radiate outward from it."

Tad Pole had accepted the holograph without question, even
addressing it directly as if it was a new acquaintance. He pointed
at the numerals in the corner of the image.

"So this is where Cridi lies in your reckoning? What does this
designation mean?" he asked.

Keff, with the help of IT, tried to render the musical notes for
the X, Y, and Z axes. Then he whistled it, and shook his head at
himself.

"Oh, fuss and bother," he said. "I can't make an accurate tone
when it's important. Well, that's what IT is for." He rummaged
around in an instrument locker and came out with the small
external speaker that he wore when translation of an alien language was beyond his vocal capabilities. He hooked it into the IT
module he wore on his chest next to Carialle's camera eye. "In
Sector P, X=248.9, Y=1630.23, Z=876."

"This means nine-tenths?" Narrow Leg asked, pointing to one
of the characters, and voiced a very high minor that indicated the
negative logarithm.

That led to a quick lesson in Standard decimal notation, and
the explanation of Arabic versus Roman numerals, which more
closely approximated the Cridi system of written notation. Tad Pole,
a quick learner, nodded his head several times appreciatively.

"It is quick and less cumbersome for a screen of formulae," he said. "Very neat. It may serve as your first import to our world. Although I do not want my spacers to become lazy, having an easy way to express formulae."

"None find it easy to serve Narrow Leg," Big Eyes said, from the weight bench, where she sat curled up with her hands around her thin knees, drawing her red cloak closely against her body. Tall Eyebrow hunched beside her, eyes wide like a wary animal. "He works everyone too hard. Himself, too."

"I do nothing unnecessary," the lean, old male admonished his unruly child. "Should like to have documents on numeric system."

"Gladly," Keff signed.

"I will recommend partnership between human organization and Cridi," Narrow Leg continued. "Among those who are of sense, I carry weight." He thumped his chest proudly.

Turning to Tall Eyebrow, he asked, "What do you call the other?" He circled a forefinger uncertainly. The Ozranian sat up very straight and put his hand before his face.

"The One Who Watches From Behind the Walls," Tall Eyebrow signed, and spoke her name, "Carialle."

"Carialle," Narrow Leg said. "I thank you for my tour. Now we are curious about *you*. You do not really look like one of us, do you, in spite of this flat Cridi which follows me like a friend?"

"No," Carialle said, signing through the image. "I resemble Keff, but I am a female of our species." The white wall beside the visitor displayed images of men and women from infancy to old age. She erased all the others and let the adult female image remain, clothing it in the usual garb worn by her Lady Fair holo. "This is how I usually represent myself, but I am not mobile on two legs as Keff is." Another series of images followed, beginning with a human body, surrounding it in a protective shell, then circuitry and life support tubes, moving outward through every layer until the viewer's eye was outside the titanium pillar beside which Keff was standing. "This ship is my body. I see what is outside with video eyes," she showed some examples of cameras, "and hear with many different kinds of ears." The visitors blinked through a series of images of audio transmitters and receivers, down to the miniaturized implant that Keff wore.

"So different. So very different," Narrow Leg said, awed. "I am glad you have come to our world."

"But you came here for a purpose," Carialle said, resuming her frog image. "I'm sending for data regarding observations on storms and other anomalies in space with special attention to this sector. Keff, I'm piggybacking a message to Simeon to pick up gossip from other ships that have been in this area recently. He'll give us the unofficial scuttle if there's nothing in the records. Watch now."

On the holoview over the main console, Carialle showed the view from the camera over the hatch following the second of her four message rockets. Keff urged Narrow Leg to float as closely as he wanted to the holographic image. The ship's skin peeled back, and the bracket levered the little rocket back, then upright like a child sitting up in bed. An inner hatch closed underneath its tailfins, protecting the other probes from backfire. Carialle sent a command, and the small ring of engines ignited, forming a cushion of fire that elongated into a red tongue as the probe lifted skyward. Carialle changed to another camera view that followed the white-hot dot up through the sky as it gained velocity. It was soon lost from sight.

"It will take a few weeks for the message to get to the outpost of the Central Worlds," Carialle said. "I hope you can put up with us that long."

"It would be our honor, gentle-female. I enjoyed that very much," Narrow Leg said, nodding thoughtfully. "Very much indeed. And now," he said, recovering his good humor and energy. "You must come to see my ship."

"I felt long ago that we must not lose the heritage of ages," Narrow Leg said as he pointed out features of the slender ship on the launch pad. "Space is important. I am old. I remember when the failures began. No one thought anything of it, but when they continued, most gave up all hope. Some saw it as a sign to cease travel into space. Our planet's children, the colonies, had forsaken us, and no project could succeed. Others did not agree. We launched, but the ships exploded just beyond atmosphere, or disappeared before passing the beacons at the edge of our system. I was part of those projects, and I said we should not stop. It has taken me twelve years to achieve funding for this ship, and I will not let anything stop us. The fourth time shall be fortunate."

Keff whistled at the sleek lines of the small ship. As Carialle had said, all the Cridi craft seemed to be about one-sixth to one-third scale to human ships, yet personal quarters were much larger in proportion. Cridi seemed to like a fair bit of headroom. Keff found he was slouching to pass in and out of hatchways, but not actually stooping. Narrow Leg's technology was based upon modular replacements, a notion handed down through the generations to preserve the precious metals and radioactives. Stacks of identical bulkhead panels, numbered in the Cridi way, lay in heaps around the finished craft.

"You have enough here to make another couple of ships," Keff said, kicking one skid.

"One and half," Narrow Leg said. "These plates are designed to fit in over 120 different positions on the craft, both inside and outside. Similar care has been taken with many other components. All circuit boards are the same size, and all plugs, too."

"Are you getting this, Cari?" Keff asked, turning around in a full circle and aiming his transmitter up and down to cover everything.

"Sure am," Carialle said. "It is beautiful. If this is everything it looks like, all hopes Central Worlds has always had for a precisely equal race are achieved. This is as advanced as any CW ship, and it sounds like they've been splitting space for as long as we have, but they've evolved independently. I feel vindicated, and I'm even more glad *we* were the ones to see this. The diplomacy wonks wouldn't give us due credit when they got back from the initial contact mission. When will she be ready to launch?"

Keff relayed the question. Narrow Leg let out a piping laugh.

"When the bureaucrats let me," he said. "They are still arguing about who gets credit for what."

The party reentered the hydroponics section, the first part they had visited upon entering the ship. Small Spot had taken a great fancy to the room, arranged like a jungle garden around a large central bath, and decided he needed to see no more than that. He stood up when Tall Eyebrow appeared.

"How quiet it is in here," Long Hand said, coming in behind. Keff listened. She was right. The incessant peeping and chirping of the technicians could not be heard once the enameled hatch slid shut.

"This is worth recording, senior," Small Spot signed enthusiastically. "Someday, when we are traveling the stars, I should like a room of plants with a pool at its heart."

"Thank you for compliment," Big Eyes signed. "This is my design." Touching Tall Eyebrow's hand, she drew him over to see special details. "It is meant to be quiet during travel. Engine noise absorbed through three layers of paneling. Vibration cut up to 88 percent. Gives mental peace."

"Very impressive," Keff said.

"One has far to go," Narrow Leg added, shaking his old head. "One must be sane when arriving."

"Keff must tell you of the game," Tall Eyebrow said, with enthusiasm. "How humans keep spirit in long transit."

"Uh-oh," Carialle said in Keff's ear. "This is one part I am excising from the record we are bringing back to Xeno. They'll court-martial us, or something, if we spread Myths and Legend to another species. Probably violates a hundred non-interference directives."

Keff, smiling fixedly, bowed to Narrow Leg and his daughter. "I'd be happy to talk about it some time. We have other modifications for comfort that I could offer."

"Gladly received," Narrow Leg said. "I might have forgotten refinements in fifty years."

"Meanwhile, tell me about your propulsion system."

"Gladly," the old one said. He led the way out of the silent chamber with Small Spot reluctantly tagging along behind. The engineering section was the farthest aft, behind cargo storage and more crew quarters.

"I intend this ship to last. It has every fail-safe for survival and ultimate utility. You will see the controls here exactly duplicate those in the command center," he began, but got no farther. A cluster of Cridi security burst into the chamber. Keff froze in place, his muscles held by an invisible suit of armor. Big Voice shouldered his way past the guards and stood with his hands clenched before Narrow Leg.

"The council does not approve of allowing an outworlder on this ship," he signed furiously, interspersing his gestures with angry cheeps of diminishing value equations.

"But it *is* of great worth to have them here," Narrow Leg said, waving a gentle hand. "Until the day we may fly to the Central Worlds in our own ships and show ourselves, this is the only way they can bring back word. Keff is viewing all for Carialle, and she makes a record."

"He's good," Carialle said.

"Yep," Keff murmured. "I'm glad he's on our side."

"Plus," Narrow Leg chirped, having carried on his argument with Big Voice while Keff and Carialle were conferring, "there is undoubtedly little that they do not already know about the theory of space travel. I have requested access to the archives myself. If we preceded them to Sky Clear it was by a few hundred years, that was all. And," he added with fierce stabbings of his remarkably long forefinger in Big Voice's chest, "they have *kept up* their space program, while we have allowed setbacks to keep us confined here. All this is in our own people's writing. You would do well to read the documentation."

"Setbacks?" Big Voice said. "Do you designate the overload of planetary Core 10^3 years ago a setback? Do you call the apocalyptic crash of poorly made colony ship of 85x10 years ago a *setback*?"

"That was first experiment with portable Cores," Big Eyes whispered to Tall Eyebrow and Keff.

"Four x 10^2 years of previously successful space exploration brought to halt by disaster after disaster? Attempts to reconnect with former colonies have only begun in last 10^2 years!" Big Voice stopped, out of breath, to pant angrily.

"We now have open space to meet and interact with a people who were not hampered by constant gaps in space research," Narrow Leg said, without heat.

"This sharing will result in a loss of profit for Cridi industry," Big Voice said, standing his ground. "We will not develop things on our own as we should."

Narrow Leg turned to Keff. "Do all Central Worlds colonies have space travel?"

"Well, no," Keff said. "We require a certain technological and social level to be reached before they can have full membership, but they don't necessarily have to have evolved interstellar travel."

"Don't you see?" Narrow Leg said, turning back to the angry councillor. "This could open up your market to other peoples."

"You'll have to make things larger, though," Keff said, trying out a little exponent humor using IT to describe the proportions between Cridi and humans.

Big Voice was not mollified. "The council will discuss this matter thoroughly and give you their answer." He spun on his flat foot and marched out. The guards, uncertainly, lowered their circuit-covered hands and followed.

"Oh, good," Big Eyes signed behind her fellow councillor's departure. "Then we have *years* to talk about this before he comes back."

Narrow Leg shook his head wearily. "The fellow's a stone—gets set in one place and never moves again."

"What have your people done in space without the Core?" Keff asked.

"Small Core onboard," Narrow Leg said, and his musical whistling described formulae, circuitry, and elemental weights. "It runs on reserve fuel, serves few Cridi intensively for a time until new Core is built on new world. Until then, we walk in mud." His eyes twinkled as a few of the crew-frogs running tests in the engine room caught his signs and shuddered.

"There, you see?" Carialle said, noting their reactions through Keff's body-camera. "Tell Tall Eyebrow he is a hero in spite of his clunky amulet. None of the homeworld Cridi want to go through what his people did."

Keff, careful to make certain Big Eyes saw his signs, relayed Carialle's message to the Frog Prince. The praise made him glow and stand up straighter, especially when the female stared at him with open admiration. Narrow Leg caught Keff's eye behind the two younger Cridi's backs, and up-nodded wisely.

The message rocket streaked out of the system, shedding a burst of glowing electrons as it hurtled through the heliopause. Its passage attracted the attention of a raider ship lying concealed in the asteroid belt just inside the system's invisible barrier.

"Telemetry?" the ship's captain demanded. She was a lean woman with black hair and a thin nose and chin.

"From the reptiles," the navigator confirmed. He stretched out a wing-finger to extrapolate the path of the rocket from its source. He adjusted the computer screen to another view. The second planet had moved along its orbit, but the point of origin based on its current velocity was positive. "Confirmed. It came off the Slime planet."

"Get it," the captain said.

The pilot glanced over his shoulder nervously at her, but he applied thrust while bringing the cranky old drives on-line. The ship decanted from the hollow asteroid and gave chase.

Without looking away from the navigation screen, the captain tilted her head toward the copilot, who acted as communications officer and navigator.

"Send a message to the other ships. Alex is closer, but Autumn's engines are better."

The Thelerie officer nodded. The captain leaned closer, as if willing her ship to greater velocity. They couldn't let the probe get away. The small rocket had a good head start. It would be a miracle if they caught up with it, flying on their rackety old engines. The captain felt the vibration through her feet, sensing each time that connections missed. She was frustrated. There was never time to make the repairs correctly. They never had the right parts. Now, when it was vital for the engines to perform perfectly, they'd lose security in the system because no one had done a tune-up. The ship shuddered and groaned. Suddenly, the cabin went black except for the screens. The captain clutched for something solid to hang on to. The internal stabilizers cut out for a moment, and her wrists were twisted painfully.

"What happened?" she demanded. Her arms hurt, but she didn't let go.

"Cohiro says he's diverting all nonessential power to thrusters," the Thelerie reported.

The captain relaxed, glad her face was hidden by the dark. "Maximum speed, then," she said.

On the screen, the little rocket was a white dot, growing slowly into a dash.

"Can we get near enough to capture it with the tractor?" she asked.

"Not unless we slow it down," her pilot said. Over his shoulder, the captain could see the gauges. They were increasing in speed, but so was the probe.

"Then blast it," the captain said. She braced herself. The whole deck shook as more power was drained away from life support, this time for the weapons.

The white dash ahead of them shuddered slightly, but kept flying. It had slowed down just a bit. The captain urged her ship forward.

"Damaged it slightly," the Thelerie said. "We may catch it now."

The raider homed in on its prey. The captain stared at the streak, feeling her heart pound as it grew larger and larger.

"We're on it," she said. "Prepare to activate tractor."

"Aye, sir," said voices in the dark.

The ship drew up on the probe. The captain watched her screens, seeing the numbers shrink. Closer. Closer.

"Now!" the captain cried. The ship groaned again as power diverted to the tractor ball. "Do you have it?"

"No, sir," the Thelerie said. "I'm trying again."

"Maximum velocity," cried the pilot's voice. "Steady. Steady." The small streak gained detail. The captain could almost count the probe's tail fins.

"Grab it!" the captain ordered.

"I have a lock on it!" the Thelerie announced, just as all the lights went down. Loud grinding echoed through the walls. The captain was thrown to the floor against the backs of the pilot couches. Suddenly, the cabin lights came up again, and a siren wailed under the floors.

"Engines failed," the pilot said apologetically. The crew groaned. The captain pulled herself to her feet.

"Can we catch it?" she said, staring at the screen. The streak had dimmed to a small spot. It gained velocity as it flew, shrinking out of sight.

"No, sir. We've blown half a dozen power connections. Can't go anywhere at all until it's fixed."

"Damn," the captain said, fervently. "Call Alex. Have him come and give us a tow back to the base. Call Autumn to chase . . . never mind. She'd never catch it. We'll have to put out a general message for any crew on its path to intercept it. Can we at least tell Mirina where it's going?"

"It's definitely heading toward Central Worlds, sir," said the pilot, after a glimpse at the navigator's screen. "That's all I can tell you."

The captain sighed heavily. "Give me an open channel. I'd better send right away. Bad news doesn't improve with waiting."

✳ CHAPTER SIX

"See how easy and less cumbersome this is," Tall Eyebrow said, a couple of weeks later, as he and Keff made a quick breakfast in the ship before joining Narrow Legs and Big Eyes at the spaceship facility. Long Hand and Small Spot had left early for meetings with conclave members who wanted clarification of questions they had regarding the archives. Tall Eyebrow had managed to beg off meetings about minutiae, preferring to save himself for constitutional debate and conversations about trade. He was relieved that the council accepted his excuses, allowing him to devote more attention to gaining insights on current Cridi technology and, not incidentally, to spend more time with Big Eyes.

With his knees curled up next to him on the round bench seat, he stretched out his hand and closed his fingers. The food synthesizer turned on, and produced a bowl of greens. As the hatch opened, the bowl flew of its own accord to the table and set itself before Tall Eyebrow with a loud clatter. Some of the contents spattered Keff, who jumped up and brushed at his tunic. The Frog Prince grinned sheepishly.

"Forgive. I am having to refine my heavy touch in order not to crush what I reach for, or send myself flying high up in the air. But, I like it," he said, holding up his hand and turning it so the gold circuitry twinkled in the cabin light. "The council has promised to send sufficient circuitry plus full plans to update the Core of Ozran. It may be possible that all shall have amulets once again, including the mages and magesses."

"Do you think that's a good idea?" Keff asked. "You know most of them will just use it for selfish purposes." He reached for the last of the toast. Carialle was amused by his food choices. Everything he had eaten on the ship for the last several days had contained some stiff fiber. He complained that he'd had enough mush in the Cridi diet, and if he could avoid eating the live insects which were considered a local delicacy, he'd just as soon do so.

"You don't have to give them the new system," Carialle said. "Let the humans keep using the old amulets."

"No!" Tall Eyebrow threw that suggestion away from him with an outthrust hand. "We will all learn responsibility together."

"Attaboy," Keff said, "but long-entrenched privilege is hard to give up."

"True. They have coped well, though further temptation may be hard on them. We will no longer be without oversight from your government, is that not correct?" Tall Eyebrow signed, before picking up his fork. He took one bite, then laid the fork down again to talk. "Nor of mine. I look forward to seeing how well my people can prosper with more Core utility. The transformation of our living quarters will be absolute! More access, more water, better irrigation, less threat from natural pests. We must learn more of the language of science to better communication Ozran-wide. I will give the teachers a current lexicon for teaching the younger generation. We older must pick it up as we go. But we have learned well how to use the amulets. After all these years, our theoretical models proved to be accurate!"

"Good plans, all," Carialle said.

"It's nice to be vindicated, after all your hardship," Keff said. "And now that you're in contact with your homeworld again, the transference of technology will be easier."

"Ah, yes, but what a world we return to! Technology advances beyond our dreams."

"But even we humans have some of these things they're giving you," Keff pointed out.

"It isn't the same," TE said. "These beings look like us. We feel they should be *more* like us, but they are not. It is almost as if we are a different species after so much time. It is confusing that they look like us, but do not think like us. They are more wasteful of resources than we, except in the space program. It is worrying. I do not want our people to become so profligate."

"It'll take more than one generation to do that," Keff assured him.

"The Cridi here do not understand why we have not progressed as they have. I am only able to show that, after a long slide backwards, we are regaining our footing. And that does not impress them."

"It impresses *us*," Carialle said. "You held on to your culture, even your science, with no possibility of relief in sight. That kind of determination is most admirable. Central Worlds certainly was bowled over by our reports."

"But in our own nation we are only *country bumpkins*," TE said, pronouncing the Standard phrase in his high-pitched squeak. Keff blinked his eyes several times. Carialle could see he was controlling his face to keep from bursting out into understandable but inappropriate laughter.

"Don't let them get you down," she said. "After all, how often are you going to see any of them ever again when we take you home?"

"I don't know," TE said. His face was a study in mingled regret and relief. "Big Eyes is . . ." his hands paused briefly, "an interesting person."

"She likes you, too," Keff said.

"But she talks so fast," TE's posture showed despair. "Everyone talks too fast." He settled down dejectedly on the round bench with his legs curled up. "I am a relic."

"You're not a relic," Keff said. "The Cridi have had it easy, and you've virtually lived in a desert war zone. You can't expect most of them to understand what you've been through."

"Besides, you're doing an admirable job," Carialle added. "I've been keeping an ear on the transmissions, and watching the other delegate members whenever I can hook into the mass communication signals. The airwaves are full of interviews with the delegates, portions of the transcripts from the archives, footage from the floor of the Main Bog, color commentators—the full-budget extravaganza. The general consensus is that you are an articulate and strong leader, with an admirable mind. Even the council members who don't agree with you are very impressed with you."

TE studied the floor for a minute while his mobile face went through a series of peculiar grimaces: pride, embarrassment, hope, joy, and shyness. To cover the moment, Keff spoke up eagerly.

"And me?"

"Well, they still think you're a talking dog."

"What?" Keff's face fell.

"I'm joking," Carialle said. "I am joking. You're the flavor of the month. You're the most popular man on Cridi."

"I'm the *only* man on Cridi," Keff pointed out.

"We're lucky there's a free press here. Force of popular opinion will sway the council members who are against us," Carialle said. "You wait and see."

As Carialle had predicted, once word had spread around Cridi of their arrival, the public arena had discussed the situation, dissecting it to its very smallest particles of meaning, and had decided that they believed Tall Eyebrow and his party to be truthful about their odyssey from Ozran. Public opinion was split on whether or not to try and reclaim Sky Clear, but all were in favor of trading with the vast human empire which had been their unknown neighbor for centuries.

As the sole representative of the Central Worlds, Keff was their model. Young Cridi he saw in the streets had begun to wear clothes like his, and adopted his posture, even some of his mannerisms. Some even dyed their skin to match his. The hue was disconcerting on hides normally ranging from yellow-green to brown-green.

But the human trait that spread the fastest and most generally was a smile. Strange Cridi smiled at him in imitation of his own crinkly-eyed, dimpled-cheek grin. It was all the rage. Keff sat in the evenings with Carialle, watching the news programs, including video of himself, usually shot from the knees up so that his face was telescoped into an isosceles triangle. The commentators discussed, with terse movements and much cheeping of navigational and trigonometry, the location and profusion of Central Worlds systems. One even pointed out, to Keff's surprise, the system settled by humans that lay quite close to them on the other side of the R-sector benchmark. That was the original trading post that had been the site of Carialle's disaster. Keff watched Carialle's reactions closely, but she was too involved in the ongoing negotiations and recording gigabytes of data for Xeno to be troubled by her memories.

Keff and the Ozranians were invited all over Greedeek and to the other cities on Cridi by homeworlders eager to meet the long-lost travelers and the alien stranger. Every day there were invitations to visit various societies or venues to talk about Sky Clear, or space travel, or the Central Worlds, or humanity in general. Big Eyes assigned herself the task of social secretary for the four, partly as a courtesy service, but partly, too, to be able to spend as much time as possible with Tall Eyebrow. With a humorous eye, she weeded out the frivolous invitations, or those which she said, "would not be useful or fun." The best of the invitations still made for a very full program. Keff and the three Ozranians spoke to three or more groups per day. He doubted that every civic group wanted to see him or the two junior delegates, but Tall Eyebrow had generously insisted on their inclusion. Privately, Keff thought that the Frog Prince wanted Keff and his two companions nearby for confidence. Tall Eyebrow didn't need anyone to lean on. Once he began speaking about the conditions on Ozran, the agriculture, the people that he led and loved, he was transformed from a nervous, sometimes melancholy figure to a dynamic speaker. Or rather, signer. He stopped asking Keff and Carialle to take him back to Ozran, and began to acknowledge that he deserved his place among his ancestors' people.

Keff and Tall Eyebrow also made a point to spend much of their free time with Narrow Leg at the Cridi space facility. The elder enjoyed talking space with Keff and, by extension with Carialle, exchanging ideas and techniques.

"Human techology is good, very good," Narrow Leg asserted. "Refinements we have forgotten, or never known, worth having."

"There's also a few wiggles that I haven't seen," Carialle said. "I've racked my databases, but I've never before seen a system that allows a planet's worth of temporary power supply to be carried in a cargo hold. If the Cridi government is willing to share that, it'll assuage a lot of hardships for settlers on primitive colony worlds, giving them a pad to work from until they can establish their own systems. The insurmountable trouble is remote control, that's all."

Narrow Leg had the foresight to arrange to have a reporter present at most of the conferences between him and Keff so that all Cridi was party to the discussions.

Over the next weeks, Keff and the others were feted, feasted, and fawned over to exhaustion.

"I'm almost sorry I'm so popular," he confessed to Carialle, as he sat through yet another luncheon where he hunched crosslegged with his meal balanced on his knees. The wooden plate, either a serving platter or a hastily manufactured piece made in proportion to his size, held an unappetizing mess of greens such as Tall Eyebrow and the Ozranians favored, alongside a small clutch of wiggling larvae.

Keff, Tall Eyebrow and his retinue were at the main table in the center of the large room. The Frog Prince, between Smooth Hand and Big Eyes, seemed more relaxed than he had before. Occasionally, Keff felt an invisible hand tap his knee. When he looked up, Tall Eyebrow met his glance, then tilted his head in the direction of this or that conversation. No longer was Sky Clear considered a remote concern. Quite a few local manufacturers and business-frogs were discussing the possibility of setting up shop on the colony.

Long Hand was fielding such a question from an increasingly insistent Big Voice, who had spread before her holographic photo displays and sheets full of graphs and text.

"But all this, exchanges and imports, must wait, gentle-male," Long Hand protested. "We have no hard currency, and our own exports are few and doubtful at present. Wait a few years, until we have more concerns going so we can deal with you on a more equal basis."

Big Voice was undaunted. "I am eager to secure favorable siting for my manufacturing plants. It means jobs and opportunity for Cridi there. Such things should be settled as quickly as possible. Would you approve of investment from outside, an advance of funds, perhaps, against future interests?"

Long Hand let out a peal of laughter. "We have nowhere to spend this imaginary money, gentle-male. All we may do is add your name to the roster of those interested, and we will be sure to speak to you early when we have anything to offer. You must wait."

Keff, missing none of the important details of the conversation because it was all in sign language, smiled to himself. Big Voice wasn't the only one with an eye toward future profit, just the most persistent.

A female in gold torc and bracelets rose to her feet and clicked insistently in her throat for attention.

"Gentle-females and gentle-males," she signed in full formal language, "we are privileged to welcome the stranger from the Central Worlds. Please give him your kind attention."

"Thank you, madam chairfrog," Keff said in Standard, adding the appropriate courtesies in sign language. "I come to you today to offer your people. . . ."

The Cridi media also clamored for interviews. Keff did his share, but he urged the commentators who came to him to take advantage of the returnees instead.

The most important event of all took place several weeks after the CK-963 had made landfall. Ten thousand Cridi were packed into a low room like an amphitheater, hundreds of meters long. The rows of seats were sloped so that the huge audience could see the stage at the bottom, but the ceiling was quite low. Keff lay on his belly to watch, facing downward in one of the side aisles, sweltering in the high humidity. He had been warned to wear his best tunic, and he had done so. To keep from getting it dirty, he'd snaffled a few huge ear-shaped leaves from a handy plant in the lobby, and used them as a ground sheet. Long, reedlike fronds stuck out every which way from the edges of the leaves. Keff had to push them to one side, and finally tuck them under his body to see.

"Just like it was when we first saw you," Tall Eyebrow said, showing his sharp little fangs in a broad grin, his black eyes glinting, pointing to the waving tendrils. "In the high grass on Ozran."

"I was more comfortable then," Keff said, grinning back. He had to prop himself on his elbows to sign. "The blood's rushing to my head. Try to make this one brief, won't you?"

"If I can, friend Keff, if I can."

Smooth Hand, on his way down with Narrow Leg to take their places at the table on the dais, saw this exchange.

"Do not be in such a hurry to bring this meeting to an end," he said, pausing beside the human and patting him on the shoulder. "You will enjoy it more than any other meeting you have attended."

"What do you mean, sir?" Keff asked. But the old amphibioid would say no more. He put his finger to his lips. Keff shook his head, wryly.

"He's got a secret," Keff said, to Narrow Leg. "A human would do exactly the same thing. Interaction between Cridi is so like that of my own people that I'm seeing parallels to our civilization everywhere."

"Some would not like you to say so," Narrow Leg said, with a twinkle in his eye. "But I see it as natural that two such gregarious spacefaring races should ally." As he saw pleased enlightenment dawn in Keff's face, he, too, put a finger to his lips and hurried after Smooth Hand.

"Did you see that, Cari?" Keff said. "What Narrow Leg just said?"

"Unless I read that entirely wrongly, I think we have ourselves an A-class applicant for membership," Carialle said. "Good one, Sir Knight."

"Whew!" Keff breathed out gustily. "For once the brass is going to be pleased with us." He beamed at all of the delegates gathering on the stage, at anyone passing by. His mood was so expansive that he didn't mind moving half a dozen times to accomodate the placement of video pickups and audio cubes. This transmission was going to be beamed worldwide. Keff hoped his view of it was sufficiently good so that his copy could be broadcast throughout the Central Worlds when they got home.

All eight chief councillors, plus the three Ozranians, and Narrow Leg were seated at a long, low table facing the audience. Two small panels of three members of the press sat to either side.

Smooth Hand began in the way that Keff had become used to over many weeks, greeting the visitors and welcoming them to Cridi. He alluded to the sacrifices that all five of them had made to be there, and to the struggles of the Cridi population on Sky Clear. Tactfully, he made no mention of the debate over exclusivity to the colony world. Muttering and surreptitious handsigning in the audience proved that they knew he was leaving it out. Keff knew the question wouldn't be settled quickly. Smooth Hand continued.

"The question was put to the population regarding membership in the Central Worlds. The conclave has been receiving so many favorable votes that the council, even our skeptical members," he up-nodded toward Big Voice and Snap Fingers, "have agreed to hear more about the subject. Will the large stranger Keff come forward and address the full conclave?"

"With pleasure," he signed. He rose to his hands and knees, removed the camera eye he was wearing, and attached it to the wall of the auditorium facing the stage. "Can you see properly, Cari?" he asked.

"Perfectly," she replied. "Recording for posterity. Good luck, my parfait and gentil diplomat."

Keff turned and crawled down the steep slope to the stage amid loud applause mingled with chirps and creaks. Eyes shining, Tall Eyebrow stood up as Keff approached. Big Eyes sprang to her feet. Narrow Leg, moving more slowly, rose next. All the other councillors followed, Big Voice and Snap Fingers reluctantly, until the entire panel, and the audience were slapping out their acclaim. Carefully keeping one hand over his head to avoid bumping into the low ceiling, Keff stood up. He looked out over the audience. Ten thousand Cridi sat before him, but the entire planet was watching or listening. Keff beamed and waved to the ones he knew, feeling like he was standing on the doorstep of destiny. A few young Cridi in the audience, some dressed in human-style tunics, levitated and turned somersaults in midair for joy. Others cheered and cried out Standard phrases they had learned from Keff's media interviews. Smooth Hand signalled for quiet, and signed to Keff to begin his remarks. While the others sat down, Big Eyes remained standing to repeat Keff's speech aloud.

"Thank you for your kind reception," Keff signed, and was amused to hear the phrase reduced to a few notes and trills in the female's high, piping voice. "The Central Worlds is an organization of member states whose purpose is to provide a stable government for the benefit of those planets and stations within its borders. The Central Committee, or CenCom," he enunciated the words and heard Big Eyes repeat it, "is dedicated to reaching out to every people on every planet. To those that have reached a certain level of technological and social advancement, we offer full membership. While my partner, Carialle, and I have found numerous races alien to ourselves in our travels, we always dreamed that one day we would locate that civilization, that people, which had evolved in parallel to ourselves, and were of an equal level in all ways, so that we could be friends and allies, instead of benefactor, patron, or in some cases, a right nuisance."

There was a patter of appreciative laughter. Keff smiled.

"If indeed, you are pleased that the Central Worlds and Cridi have found one another at last, you owe a debt of gratitude to Tall Eyebrow. He, and the leaders who came before him, have preserved Cridi culture on a remote outpost against the most incredible odds, helping it to survive until we discovered it. He is responsible for leading us here so we could be with you today. In the last few weeks I've seen a lot of your planet. I admire your culture. I have seen examples of your art, particularly evident in the architecture and gardens of this beautful city; and strides forward in science. In particular, I want to mention the Core power system, an advance which has never been duplicated in the Central Worlds. You can help us to move into the future. I think we can also help you. And together, we can help support the people of Sky Clear. Thank you very much." He sat down crosslegged next to the dais. Ten thousand pairs of hands pounded together, filling the amphitheater with sound that grew louder and louder until the very walls seemed to shake.

Keff shot a glance at the council. Tall Eyebrow sat proudly erect between Narrow Leg and Big Eyes. Big Voice was conferring energetically with the councillors on either side of him. Smooth Hand let the applause go on, then raised his hands for silence.

"I am sure you have many questions for the tall stranger, now to be called our friend, I hope," he signed, with a slight smile toward Keff. "For now, let your sign be counted. If you approve the approach to Central Worlds, send your vote to your precinct now. Thank you all."

Reporters hurried forward from the side tables and the audience, swamping the panel. Free-floating remote cameras buzzed over their heads and zoomed from face to face, gathering reactions like a species of psychological honey bee. The air was full of flurried gestures and excited Cridi voices. After weeks of intensive training in the spoken language Keff understood more of the verbal exchanges than ever before, and he was delighted with the response.

"Can you hear it, Cari? They want it. They're going to join us."

Carialle sounded amused. "Don't count your chickens in advance, softshell . . . but I think you're right. You should hear some of the scuttlebutt going about on the amulet airwaves. I'm recording the best ones for you to hear later. 'Maximum joy and maximum profit' was the one I heard from Big Voice's media aide."

"And here's the man himself," Keff said, seeing a solemn delegation forcing its way toward them through the crush on the platform. "Good gentle-male."

"Tall stranger," Big Voice signed, *very* politely. "I have exchanged tentative words with Long Hand with regard to the spacecraft concession for Sky Clear. Should this proposition now before us come to pass, I would be concerned that a human delegation might . . . put in a rival bid for choice sites."

"That's the nature of business throughout the universe," Keff signed cheerfully, teasing the pompous amphibioid. Clearly shaken, Big Voice tried again.

"Would not Central Committee consider priority for primary sentient species?" His hands fluttered desperately, trying to gauge Keff's response. "Or partnership?" Keff grinned and relented.

"Central Worlds would not take away the rights from one member species in favor of another," he said. "If you can get an exclusive agreement from the Cridi on Sky Clear, the CenCom won't interfere with that at all."

"Thank you," Big Voice signed, gratefully. "Thank you, tall stranger Keff." He moved away, once again in pursuit of Long Hand. Tall Eyebrow, having observed the whole thing from his place on the dais, grinned to show his sharp white teeth. Keff gave him a wink.

More media types swooped in on him, signing or singing questions from all sides. Keff tried to answer them all in turn, knowing he was getting some of the words wrong in his haste, hoping it wouldn't matter. The IT earned its keep that day, translating his spoken replies into Cridi music, so he could carry on two conversations at once.

"Will other humans come to Cridi?" was among the most frequently asked questions. "Will we be able to visit your worlds?"

"You will be most welcome everywhere you go," Keff said. "In fact, we will expect a return visit, just as soon as Narrow Leg's team finishes constructing their first spaceship." He turned to gesture with an open hand toward the old male who stood half a head taller than every other Cridi in the room. He stiffened with pride.

"That is right, and only right," Narrow Leg said, "that we should make our first visit to our new allies in our own spacecraft. And you may take my words straight to heart. We will be ready."

The reporters chirruped excitedly, obviously adding color commentary.

Smooth Hand moved to the center of the dais then, and held up his long, wrinkled hands.

"The tabulation is finished," he signed, and announced the figures. The numbers were so large that his voice rose almost out of Keff's range of hearing.

"Did I get that right, Cari? Twenty million in favor of membership?"

"Unless your program here split a chip, those in favor of the Central Worlds was 25,697,204. Against: 3,402,110."

Smooth Hand repeated the good news to the crowd, who echoed it as they danced in the aisles. "The measure passes! The measure passes! We join!"

"Sit down, sit down," the elder signed. "There is one thing left to do. *Please*. May we have your attention?"

It took some time until the jubilant Cridi settled back into their seats. The senior councillor turned to Keff.

"This is a great moment for our people. Not only have we rediscovered our lost children, but we make a bond with new friends." He signalled to an aide to come forward.

The silver-torqued frog glided swiftly onto the stage bearing two long rectangles of a high gloss wood. On each was engraved a long screed in an incredibly tiny and intricate script. Beside the Cridi language was the text in Standard. Keff looked up in surprise.

"I helped the engraver with the correct wording," Tall Eyebrow told Keff. "I took it directly from Carialle's file of such documents. You will find it in order, I promise you."

"And I took it from the databanks of your more than unusually helpful IT," Carialle said in his ear.

"You see," Keff said, sublingually. "In no time, you'll look back on the days when you used to laugh at my program."

"I don't see those days receding behind us, Keff," Carialle said, sardonically, "but in this case it came through."

"Is all in order?" Tall Eyebrow asked, concerned.

"I'm absolutely certain it's all right," Keff said, reassuringly. "I have never seen an official government document look so beautiful."

"You honor us," Smooth Hand said, bowing over his moving hands.

At each side of the document were blank blocks enclosed in festoons of scrollwork, images of vines, flowers, insects and birds. Keff figured out that those were the signature blocks when he managed to decipher his name, picked out delicately in filament-thin characters, running in a border around the right-hand block.

The aide floated over the heads of the crowd and laid the squares of wood neatly beside one another in the center of the table. Smooth Hand followed to stand with one long hand touching each.

Smooth Hand nodded to Keff to join him. The crowd of reporters parted, flowing back into the main audience. Keff fumbled at his tunic pocket and drew out two small devices.

"I'm so excited I nearly forgot these," he said. "These are short-run permanent recorders which I would like to use to immortalize this moment for the CenCom. One is a gift to you, to keep in your admirable archives."

"We thank you for your thoughtfulness," Smooth Hand said. "Your request is granted. Set them where they will catch all of this great moment."

"Well," Keff said, picking up the silver scriber the aide handed him. He tested it against his palm and found it sharp-edged enough to skim off a layer of skin. "This is it, Carialle."

"This is it," she agreed. "A moment for all the Central Worlds, and for us as well. Go for it, Sir Galahad."

"I do it all for you, Lady Fair." He grinned to himself and nodded to the senior councillor.

Smooth Hand looked out across the sea of faces. "All of you bear witness to this moment, in which we find we are not alone in this great galaxy, but among friends." He took his scriber and incised his name in the left-hand block on both blocks of wood. The crowd erupted in cheers and applause. He signalled to Keff, who stepped forward and bowed over the first of the documents.

"Hold it," Carialle's voice said sharply in his ear. "Don't do it."

Keff stopped, arrested with his hand centimeters above the wood. "Why not? What's wrong, Carialle?"

"What is it?" Smooth Hand asked, seeing the human's mouth moving almost silently. "Is something wrong?"

"Cari?"

Her voice in his ear was as crisp and sharp as an artificial-intelligence generated construct. "Don't sign a thing. The entire deal is on hold. I have just received a message back from the CenCom. There's a ship at the perimeter of this system, and they are here to take over negotiations. We are off this mission as of now!"

"What?" Keff demanded. "They can't do that!"

"They can, and have! The CenCom sends its *compliments,* but we are ordered to step back to avoid any 'unforeseen difficulties.' It's the Inspector General's doing. I am so mad that I could just flame out!"

Keff didn't like the edge in her voice. "Try and stay calm, Lady Fair. I'll get out of here and come to you. We'll discuss this." He looked up at the crowd, who were fluttering surreptitious messages at one another, and at Smooth Hand, clearly wondering what was going on. Swallowing his concern for Carialle, he forced a smile to his lips. He hoped his growing command of the Cridi language would sufficiently support him through this delicate moment.

"Gentle-males and gentle-females, I sincerely beg your pardon," he said, setting down the scriber. A few in the audience gasped at his action, and he made a gesture intended to show humility. "I have just been informed that, er, that diplomats senior to Carialle and myself have just arrived in your star system. This is such an important matter that they wish to take part in this ceremony themselves. If you will forgive this terrible breach of manners, may I beg a short delay until they may join us?"

Smooth Hand's face, compressed into a frown of concern, opened up in comprehension. "Ah!" he squeaked. "I see. With the greatest of reluctance, friend Keff, I see no reason why not to allow. We know and trust *you,* but we understand the pressures of state."

There was a general murmur, only partly of agreement, from the rest of the council. Keff heard undertones of distrust and dismay beneath it. Big Voice scowled and crossed his arms as if to say he'd assumed all along the humans would back away at the last minute.

"Thank you, Councillor Smooth Hand, and all the rest of the conclave, gentle-females and gentle-males. I must go and prepare for the arrival of our senior delegates. I . . . we'll be back as soon as we can. If you will excuse me?" He barely waited for the council to signal their assent before he was running up the aisles in a crouch.

"Hold on, Lady Fair," he murmured as he ran out of the hall and into the muddy street. "I'll be with you in just a moment. Don't do anything rash."

"I'm not going to do *anything,*" Carialle said, but her voice rose in volume and pitch until he winced. "But Dr. Sennet Maxwell-Corey is going to pay heavily for this. I am *not* crazy!"

✳CHAPTER SEVEN

Tall Eyebrow caught up with Keff about twenty meters outside the door, and swept him up on a wave of Core power.

"I will take you swiftly to 'the One Who Watches From Behind the Walls,' " he said.

The two of them flew up over the jungle-fringed city blocks toward the spacefield. Luckily for Keff's atmospheric acrophobia, he had no attention to spare for looking down. He had enough on his hands trying to calm down his partner, who kept up a steady stream of diatribe in his ears.

" . . . Muck-faced, baby-eating, acephalitic *bastard*," Carialle kept saying. "First, he rigged me with a booby trap, illegally, without my knowledge, and set it to go off without waiting to get full data on the situation. Now he sees to our disgrace before the entire Cridi population. What's next?"

"I'm sure we can work out the mistake," Keff said, over and over again. "Just exactly what did they say?"

With admirable control, Tall Eyebrow brought them to a perfect landing on the ramp of the ship. Keff threw a bare nod over his shoulder for thanks, and ran inside.

"Oh, they were polite," Carialle said. Her voice beat double on his eardrums, coming from the cabin speakers as well as his implant. When he cringed at the sheer power of her vocal volume, she relented and turned it down, deactivating the mastoid bone receiver entirely. "So sorry, but orders are orders."

Keff plumped down in his crash couch. Tall Eyebrow hovered sympathetically near Carialle's titanium pillar.

"Let's see the message," Keff said.

The screen in front of him filled with the hailing graphic used in all Central Worlds Fleet communiques. It vanished, and the image of a man appeared. His long jaws and heavy eyebrows made him look melancholy, but his voice was a pleasantly warm tenor.

"CK-963, this is the DSC-902. Respectful greetings. I am Captain Gavon. I am sending you a tightbeam of messages entrusted to me by the Central Committee. I know the content of these datafiles. I want to assure you in advance that I regret the intrusion as much as you do. Standing by."

The messages followed. As Carialle had dreaded, the first was from the head of Explorations, Dr. Michael Brinker-Levy. His pleasant, dark-skinned face glanced out at them from the screen. He gave them an apologetic smile.

"Carialle and Keff, we have just received communication from the Inspector General for your sectors, Dr. Corey. He had an emergency buoy that you had launched at this point," a star chart overlay his face. "The internal recordings from Telemetry showed you were in no physical peril at the time, but nevertheless show dangerous adrenaline and toxicity levels in your system, Carialle. No updates and no further messages from you were received, except for a routine query for a databank search you sent recently."

"Nonsense," Keff said. "The IG must have heard from SPRIM and MM within microseconds. And what about your complaint for illegal circuit-tapping?"

"*He* oversees all queries about illegalities and improprieties in this sector," Carialle said bitterly. "And who is watching the watchman?"

Brinker-Levy continued. " . . . I have also had a complaint on your behalf from the oversight agencies, SPRIM and MM, citing personal interference from the Inspector General. Under normal circumstances I would be able to take those into account first. Because you're engaged upon such a delicate negotiation that affects matters at the highest levels, if there is anything wrong, and your judgement is in some way impaired . . . you must understand we cannot take chances, and at this distant remove we have no way of judging for ourselves. Please cooperate in every way with Captain Gavon. He's a good man, and will need your help. Your knowledge of the Cridi culture and language are unsurpassed, and I have always been satisfied with the job you do," here he smiled, "even if you are a little unorthodox. I will take up the subject of your complaints while you are on your way back to Central Worlds, and send you updated information in transit."

"On the way back? What is he talking about?" Keff asked.

"There's more," Carialle said. "This was on the sideband." The visual didn't change from the graphic left after the end of Brinker-Levy's message, but a resonant voice broke over the speakers.

"Hi, gal," Simeon said. "Greetings from SSS-900-C. I received your query. I'm at a loss for natural causes that would have destroyed three starships. No abnormal outbreak of ion storms, comets, or other anomalies observed in your pinpoint area. I'm uploading to you all the data I have for the last fifty years. There's not much. Some of it's your own. That spot between P- and R-sector is rarely explored.

"I'm piggybacking on Exploration's message to you because I heard some scuttlebutt you need to know. Maxwell-Corey's out ringing doorbells again. The first probe caused quite a sensation. Pa-lenty unorthodox. He was going to be in deep spacedust with SPRIM, until the second probe arrived. The data on it was garbled, and your voice sounded woozy. That added fire to his insistence that there's still something wrong with your mind, and you need specialized long-term mental care. I sincerely hope not. He's arguing at the least you're severely overwrought. Keep it together, gal. Greetings to Keff."

The graphic faded, and the unwelcome sight of the Inspector General's mustachioed face flicked into being. Keff found himself unable to resist a sneer. Maxwell-Corey's vendetta against his partner had attained foolish proportions over the years, and he was becoming tired of the pompous bureaucrat and his implausible hobbyhorse. A dozen shrinks had proclaimed Carialle sane, but this control freak could not acknowledge the truth, would not acknowledge it. The tragedy was, he might be able to "prove" it by forcing her into unwitting admissions, recording angry outbursts, and twisting data to suit his purpose.

"CK-963 Carialle, in light of your two communications with the Central Worlds I am ordering you to SSF-863 for a full evaluation. You will brief the replacement team in full and return immediately when you have received this message. Maxwell-Corey out."

The screen blanked. Keff relaxed a little, realizing that his hands were ground into tight fists, and he was standing on the balls of his feet, as if ready to meet an attacker.

Captain Gavon's face reappeared, his long face sympathetic.

"I am sorry," Gavon said, and the catch in his voice showed Keff the diplomat was under a tremendous strain. "We'll be with you in a matter of hours. Gavon out."

"They can't do that to us," Keff said. "We'll fight them, Cari. Cari?"

Carialle didn't answer. She ignored the input from her screens, antennae, and camera eyes. For a moment, just for a moment, at the sound of the Inspector General's mocking voice, her long-buried subconscious had flashed back to a memory she thought had been destroyed with her first ship. . . feeling not so much as hearing a slight vibration from the hull above her, as footsteps stopped—as if someone was laughing at her. Laughing at her helplessness!

No, she said to herself, pulling back into the inmost security of her shell. *I will not let myself be forced. I am not mad. I'm cured!* she cried. *I'm cured, I'm cured, I'm cured.* But the tapping and the sounds of her own screams came back to her. She started counting the seconds again. *One, two, three . . .*

Her power levels all dropped for a dizzying, frightening millisecond. Carialle snapped out of her reverie, and went back on full alert. All scopes were back to normal. She wondered what had happened. Then she became aware that Keff was pounding on her titanium pillar and shouting.

"Carialle! Answer me! Cari!"

"What happened?" she demanded. "I felt a blackout."

The brawn staggered backward, limp with relief. "Tall Eyebrow blinked your power, just once. I'm glad it was enough."

"It was," Carialle said, vastly relieved. "I needed the shock. Thank you, TE." She made her frog image appear. It sketched a graceful half-bow and spread out its hands. The Frog Prince swept a self-deprecatory palm across.

"It was nothing. I was worried."

"I was going to pull the fire bell in a moment," Keff said. "We lost you there, lady."

"I'm sorry," she said. "I . . . I was back *there* again. I was *counting.* Maybe in a way that bastard is right."

"He's not right!" Keff shouted. His normally cheerful face was a furious shade of red. Tall Eyebrow, hovering beside the brawn, shook his head vigorously. "If I could teleport in a blink to where he's laired up, I would find the nearest lavatory and stuff his grinning face down the head. Don't you worry. This is all a mistake. We'll show them the flight path and explain to them what happened. Let's tell Gavon the whole story. I'm sure all he knows is the gossip that's floating around, not the facts."

"I'm not giving up my mission," Carialle said. "We have *earned* this. We've earned the trust of the locals. We shouldn't be removed from the mission. I want to see it through."

"So do I. Let's send a message to Gavon and ask him to reconsider. He can keep us here as aides, and then we can go back to CW." Keff threw himself into his crash couch, and scooted it up to be right in front of the video pickup.

Carialle calculated the location of the DSC-902, and put all she had behind the tightbeam message. All they could do until Gavon replied was wait.

During the time that passed, a few of the Cridi who had been in the amphitheater when Keff had to leave drifted by to visit and make their compliments. A few of the councillors were sympathetic. Unexpectedly, Snap Fingers was one of them.

"I am in business," he signed. "I came up from the merest clerk to my position now as second continental chief. I hate it that bureaucrats would take an assignment away from you. That should not happen. It shows a lack of confidence in you, which I wanted you to know was an error on the part of your superiors. If you were Cridi, I would be proud to have you working for me."

"You are very kind," Carialle's amphibioid image said with its hands.

"I mean what I say," Snap Fingers returned. "We are on opposite sides of the expansion question, but that does not mean we cannot be friends."

"Good people," Tall Eyebrow said, as the councillor departed. "I am proud to know them."

"You are one of them," Keff assured them.

Narrow Leg arrived just as Carialle received Gavon's reply. Tall Eyebrow quickly brought him up to date in sign language while Keff and Carialle listened to the message.

Captain Gavon's thin face looked more haggard, and his long jaw was set. "I have received your transmission. I regret that I have no 'slack' to cut you. Very, very sorry. This is not my idea. I have to follow my orders, too, you know. They are unequivocal and absolutely clear. I sent the messages on in advance so you could prepare."

"Damn," Keff said, watching with chin propped on his fist. He saw the record light pop on, and sat up straight.

"I am sorry, too," Carialle said, sending on a reply. "We did appreciate the extra notice, but it doesn't change the situation here. I don't want to put you on the spot, but you must see how this affects us."

"And what about the psychological effect on the native population of replacing a trusted team with strangers?" Keff put in earnestly. "You must let us stay. We can be of inestimable help to you."

Carialle sent the message, all the while muttering. "Rotoscoped, animated bastard from a bad, grade-D, psycho-horror flick—in 2-D! I don't mean Gavon," Carialle said quickly, in Keff's ear. "I mean the IG."

"*What* is he?" Narrow Leg asked, listening with interest but no comprehension to Carialle's stream of invective. Tall Eyebrow attempted to translate, but gave up almost at once as the spare knowledge he had of Standard colloquialisms failed him. Carialle realized belatedly that she had left open the communication channels to the frogs' sign-language image, and swiftly blanked the wall.

"The Inspector General has authority over our department, and he has a personal grudge against Carialle," Keff said, explaining more simply. "He is responsible for having us recalled, and the other team taking our place."

"We have no choice," Carialle broke in. "We'll have to lift sooner or later."

"Maybe I can slow down IT so we have to stay through the negotiations," Keff offered.

Carialle's laugh was bitter. "Hah! IT doesn't need to be slowed down. The holes in it leak data like a screen door."

"That's not fair, lady. IT's been doing a wonderful job here."

She was instantly contrite. "I know. That's true. I'm upset."

"You must not leave," Tall Eyebrow said, gesturing frantically, his black eyes wide. "We may never see you again. How will I and my companions return to Ozran?"

"Gavon will take you," Carialle said. "We have no choice. We're off the mission."

"Or I," Narrow Leg said. "My ship is all but ready to launch. I would be proud to escort you home. Besides," he added, with a shrewd and amused glance, "my daughter would not forgive me if I shortened your time together."

Tall Eyebrow looked somewhat mollified and a little abashed.

"But what about trade between my world and yours?" Narrow Leg asked Keff.

"That won't be affected. Even greater authority for decision-making rests with Gavon. We're not really diplomats. Our usual job is exploration of unknown space. Normally we file the preliminary report on a potentially sentient race. We've never been the follow-up team before."

"We prefer you," Narrow Leg said. "We understand one another, you two and I. A diplomat might not be such a seasoned risk-taker. We may not cooperate with this replacement. I can get the council snarled up for years to delay." The high-pitched voice described a geometric progression.

"Don't. Gavon's a good man," Carialle said. She was pleased by the Cridi's offer to side with them, but disliked the idea of fighting her battles unfairly. "Don't blame him for this. Let's see what he says about letting us stay on to help."

Two hours passed. Keff received more visitors from the conclave, and later served a synthesized meal to the Ozranian delegates, Narrow Leg, and Big Eyes, who turned up again in the late evening to sit with Tall Eyebrow. As he ate, Keff kept his eye on the chronometer, impatiently willing a message to come, to beat the next turn of the number.

"Where is it?" he asked. "Gavon's reply should be on a shorter return loop as the ship nears us. The interval ought to have been no more than half an hour by this time. Isn't he speaking to us?"

"Perhaps Simeon's data is incomplete, and there is a dangerous anomaly in-system," Carialle said, her voice remote from the ceiling speakers. "I'm resending."

Nothing came. Keff cleaned up after dinner, and listlessly did his exercises on the Rotoflex with an interested audience of Cridi commenting on the swell and slide of his muscles.

Carialle found the rhythmic *clang! bump!* of the weighted pulleys a soothing, mindless pattern, then all at once it irritated her. She opened input to all her antennae.

She strained her "ears" for transmissions on the CW ship's frequency, putting the audio of her receivers onto speaker for the others to hear. Keff stopped his deltoid flex and eased the pulleys to a resting position. He looked up hopefully at the sound of static.

"Nothing," Carialle said. "Perhaps Gavon is coming all the way in without speaking to us again."

"Nasty," Keff said. He reached for a towel and wiped his face. "I thought this would be amicable. Maybe I *won't* give him all my files. Let him figure out the subtleties between this and *this*." He made a couple of signs that Carialle, searching the IT database, found to be the symbols for hunger and a mild obscenity regarding mouths and filth. Long Hand looked shocked, Small Spot abashed. Tall Eyebrow and the two Cridi natives grinned widely.

"Wait!" Carialle exclaimed, getting a tickle from her long-distance receiver. "Here's something at last!"

The data-thread was weak and badly garbled. Carialle boosted it, and checked the frequency. It was the same Gavon had been sending on, but the audio portion was mostly static.

" . . . day . . . Intruders . . . May—"

Keff sat up. "Carialle, that sounds bad. Isn't there any more?"

"No."

"Play it again."

Now Carialle strained out a few more of the harmonics and static, and boosted the gain. The message welled up out of the speaker, then faded away again. " . . . ayDAY. INTRUDERS! MAYday . . . ip . . . ." There was no more.

"Something's happened to them," she said. "In the sidebands I'm hearing the ID pulse from their black box, but no ship noise in the low registers, and no more audio messages."

"Intruders!" Keff exclaimed. "They were attacked! How many? Who? Who was it?"

He looked at the Cridi, who shook their heads, signing nervously between one another.

"We've got to help Gavon," Keff said. He shouldered back into his tunic, immediately all business. "Our fellow ship is in trouble. They might need life support assistance." He dared not think of the worst reason the DSC-902 had stopped sending, but concentrated on the possibility of saving the crew.

"I'm starting launch prep now," Carialle snapped out. She activated the control board, and quickly counted green lights. "Tall Eyebrow, Narrow Leg, you'll all have to go. Big Eyes, will you please tell Space Command we request permission to lift. We have an emergency on our hands."

"I will," the young councillor signed, then became still as she squeaked out vocal information through her finger-control transmitters. Carialle heard her voice repeated on first one, then a dozen personal frequencies as the message went out to the command center and members of the conclave via the Core of Cridi.

"I will come with you," Tall Eyebrow said, turning to look from Keff to Carialle's frog image.

Keff shook his head. "Stay here. We could get caught by whatever happened to them, too," he said. "I won't risk you getting hurt. We'll come back as soon as we can."

"I will go now," the Frog Prince insisted. "You may need me." He turned to sign at the local Cridi.

"How long?" Narrow Leg asked Keff. "How long until you go?"

Keff glanced at the board. "Minutes."

"Wait. Give me ten." The old Cridi levitated and flew out of the airlock. He began his high-pitched warbling, too. Big Eyes glanced up, surprised, then followed her father.

They were back within the promised ten minutes, but not alone. Behind them sailed a large crew of Cridi workers, bearing with them tools and a round device the size of a medicine ball, and an impressive tangle of flex, tubes, boxes, and clamps.

Keff peered at it. "It's a ship's Core. But we can't use it, sir." He waggled his fingers loosely.

"I can," Tall Eyebrow said, holding up his hand, on which the new finger-stalls gleamed. "Let me help. You have done so much for me and my people. You may need more than you have."

"Let him come," Carialle said, interrupting her preparations. "Our tractors may not be equal to what we might find out there— and we're unarmed."

Keff's face blanked with shock. "Your salvagers? You think that's who's out there?"

"It's a possibility. There've been several other 'disappearances.' No

space anomalies, Simeon said," Carialle pointed out. "We're in this
sector. I feel there's a connection to my personal disaster. It's just
a guess, Keff. I have no positive data. I couldn't sell it as a certainty."

"I trust your guesses more than other people's certainty," Keff
said. "I've known you these sixteen years."

The miniature Core was installed by Narrow Leg's crew with
remarkable speed and efficiency. Carialle felt its power signature,
and set up a program so it wouldn't feed back on her own systems. It responded well to the technician who tested it, putting
in his own frequency number, and to Tall Eyebrow, whose new
circuitry was tied in as well.

"Its range is 18,000 kilometers," the shipbuilder said, with equal
references to the X, Y, and Z axes. "Enough for a planet plus layers
of atmosphere plus error factor."

"That means getting in right on top of the DSC-902," Carialle
said. "We'd better not miss. I'm calculating their possible location
based on the time signature for their last transmission. I must work
from that assumption."

Keff felt stricken, but he nodded.

Big Eyes waved for attention. "You have permission to lift when
you wish." She looked at Tall Eyebrow. "I go, too?"

"No," Keff and Tall Eyebrow signed at once. "You could be in
danger."

"We don't know what's out there," Carialle snapped out. "No
more arguments. Will you all clear the decks? Keff, TE, secure to
station."

"Go in peace and safety," Narrow Leg said. "Return with honor."
He turned to Carialle's pillar, as he had seen the others do. "We
will assist your launch." The technicians backed away from the
blank panel behind which they had secured the Core. They all flew
out of the airlock as Carialle shut it on their heels.

"Come back," Big Eyes signed simply to Tall Eyebrow. Then, she
was gone.

"Damn M-C," Carialle growled as she lit engines. Flames gathered under her exhaust cones, between the landing fins, wreath-
ing her in light. All her indicators read green and on GO. "This
wouldn't have happened at all if he hadn't decided I was about
to go rogue. He should have believed me! There's something out
there, and it's hostile."

Outside, she observed shadows of Cridi behind the windows of the low buildings at the edge of the field. Farther back, in a great ring around the field, frogs stood, or levitated, or hovered in their saucer-craft, waiting and watching. The infinity of audio broadcast frequencies, both private and public, filled with chatter and speculation, hoping for the first successful launch from their planet in half a Standard century.

"Here goes." She applied thrusters. Carialle felt the invisible hands holding her down to the surface of the planet drop away, and gather at the foot of her ship.

"Ready," Keff said. Tall Eyebrow cheeped an affirmative.

"Brace yourselves," she told the human and the amphibioid as she applied thrust. "Watch your necks."

"Necks?" Keff asked. "Wh—yyyyyyyyy?!"

His question became a strained cry as the g-force pushed his head back. Within a half second of putting on her own engines, Carialle felt the envelope rising under her skirts. It felt like everyone on Cridi was helping to push her into space. The force shoved her hard into the sky like an extra booster rocket, bringing her to breakaway speed in record time. Flames from sheer friction danced down her sides as she cut through the atmosphere and emerged into space, yet her internal temperature remained stable. The Cores, both inside and outside the craft, were protecting her. She felt the exosphere seal behind her, planetary ozone readings returning to normal within milliseconds of her passage. The additional thrust cannoned her forward. She was moving 60% faster than she could have gone unassisted. The shields strained against the additional pressure but were fully capable of holding. She lit her own full engines, corrected course, and opened all her receivers, hoping for word from Gavon's ship. A quick slingshot around Cridi, and she was on her way.

✶CHAPTER EIGHT

"This is the end of the ship's ion trail," Keff said, reading the telemetry monitors. The CK-963 zigzagged the empty space between the orbits of the last planet and the asteroid belt that marked the border of the Cridi system. They were within half a million klicks of the planet, a dusty, battered rock rimed with iron oxide red and nickel oxide blue. The sun was a faint flicker of yellow over Keff's right shoulder.

"And this corresponds to the last coordinates from which they transmitted to us," Carialle said. "But where's the ship?" She scanned space around her. There was a little debris, and a very small amount of residual radiation from the right kind of material, but not enough to tell what had happened. The DSC-902 appeared to have crossed the radiopause and disappeared into thin vacuum.

"If the ship was disabled, it couldn't have drifted far," Keff said, staring at the astrogation tank, searching it for artifacts. "If it was towed, where's the engine trail for the other ship?"

"What if Gavon was remotely pulled away?" Tall Eyebrow asked, showing the circuitry on his long fingers.

"The Cores," Carialle said. Keff let out a low whistle. "The pirates who killed them have Cores!"

"That's why somebody has bottled up the Cridi space program," he said. "The Cores have a limited range, but incredible power inside that radius. That technology alone is worth keeping a secret from the rest of the universe."

"I think you're right about the why," Carialle said. "We still don't know who. And at this moment, I am more concerned with *where.*"

She was silent for so long Keff wondered if she had suffered another memory flashback. He waited for a long time, then cleared his throat.

"Cari? Are you all right?"

"I'm fine," Carialle said, a little too emphatically. "Apart from being burning mad, I'm just on green. I may not like having another ship come in and usurp my mission, but damn it, I will fight my battles myself. Somebody captured or destroyed one of our vessels, and I am damned well going to know who. Nobody messes with a Central Worlds ship on *my turf.*"

"That's the spirit! Evil highway brigands who prey upon the helpless shall not prevail. We will sally forth and beard the miscreants in their den," Keff said, thumping his chest. He kept his voice light, hoping that her train of thought would not lead Carialle back to her memories of isolation. "We shall slay all who do not beg for mercy and swear allegiance to the CenCom."

Carialle was amused in spite of her worries. "Thank you, brave Sir Keff. But seriously, who are they? Not Cridi. They wouldn't be shooting at one another, at least not without giving a reason. And it certainly can't be other humans. There's never been any contact with humanity in this system before."

"That is what Narrow Leg and the others assure me," Tall Eyebrow said.

"And word would have gotten back to Central Worlds about the frogs if someone was ambushing their flights and stealing from them. We'd have begun to see artifacts that no one could explain— little spaceships," Carialle said. "Who could resist the Core technology? All three of the last Cridi missions had Cores on board."

"So what does that leave?" Keff asked, feeling the tingle of excitement. "Another race? Another spacegoing alien race?"

"It might be," Carialle said, cautiously. "It's a big universe. But first we must prove that the disappearance of this ship wasn't mere accident, and that it wasn't bad engineering that slew three Cridi vessels."

They explored the outer reaches of the heliopause. Space was pointedly, echoingly empty. Carialle picked up faint traces of engine trails, some ages old by the pattern of their decay. It seemed that most of the Cridi missions, at least as far back as they'd used an ion drive, had exited the system in this direction. It led, not incidentally, directly toward Ozran and away from the bulk of the Central Worlds. Her entry into the solar system was a quarter of the way anticlockwise around the sun, so the new wake she was forming behind her was clear and undisturbed. She used it to check the strength of the trail she was following.

"Aha," she said, as they arced out toward a group of jagged moonlets dancing along in the asteroid belt. "Now I *am* picking up fresh indications from another kind of space drive. Not Cridi."

Keff stared at the astrogation tank. Tall Eyebrow wriggled up next to him to see. Carialle put the view on full light spectrum analysis. The brawn darted a finger toward the lines that sprang into relief, criss-crossing the holographic display like spider web.

"I see it. There are hundreds of them!" he exclaimed. "Someone else is in this system."

"Very strange," Tall Eyebrow signed. "They've been traveling through here for years, but no one has ever made contact with the second planet. They must have been able to tell someone was living there. The noisy airwaves alone would have told them that, even if they couldn't understand the transmissions."

"They wouldn't exactly come visiting if their only motive was robbery," Keff said. "Wait, these are all cold. They're years old."

"Not these," Carialle said, illuminating three traces that converged on an asteroid cluster. "Those are new."

Keff peered closely at the faint image in the tank, then pounded a hand flat on the console. He had spotted movement.

"Cari, reverse course! Quick!"

Almost before the words were out of his mouth, Carialle had looped the ship around. She was heading for cover behind a pocked moonlet before they could sense her. Three strange ships flew out of crevices and holes in one of the asteroids, and were making straight for them. She kept video cameras aimed aft as she looked for a hiding place. Keff studied their pursuers.

The ships' design looked familiar: long, tapered cones bracketed with emplacements for landing gear, communications, and weaponry, but all were old and in poor repair. Flying junkheaps, he thought, with a sniff. His monitors still didn't show a sensor lock from their pursuers. Their sensors showed radiation leak from two of their engines. One was nearing critical point as it poured on power to catch up with them. They were almost ridiculously undermaintained, but Keff felt no urge to laugh.

"Hurry, Cari!"

By comparison, the CK-963 was an angel on the wing. Carialle cornered wide around two halves of a broken rock ten times her size, then hugged in close behind a flattened sphere, searching for a ravine or a cave she could duck into. The sphere's sides were solid. She tried slipping past it unseen, to another huge rock shaped like a flatiron. One of the intruders was waiting just beyond the great wedge's lip. Carialle grimly turned as sharp an angle as she could in the opposite direction.

A red light, infinitesimally small, bloomed on the pursuer's hull.

"Brace!" Carialle cried out as the energy bolt struck her amidships.

The blast tore straight through her shields as though through cellophane. Painful heat ran along her sensors, which then mercifully shut down. Damage control monitors showed her an elongated oval tear in her dorsal hull. Whoops sounded as the alarm went off in the cabin. Emergency systems kicked into operation at once.

Keff kept himself from being thrown across the control console by gripping the crash couch's armrests and hanging on with all his great strength. Tall Eyebrow, hovering, had nothing to grab onto, but pivoted deliberately in the air and somersaulted into the padding of the other couch. The straps rose up and surrounded him like an octopus seizing prey.

"Wish I could do that," Keff said, between gritted teeth. Tall Eyebrow whistled an apology. The pilot's couch engulfed Keff in safety harness. He expelled his breath in a long sigh and let go his grasp on the armrests.

"Thanks. How bad is it?" Keff asked the air.

"Hull breach, minor. Already being fixed," Carialle said shortly.

The automatic repair system quickly pressurized the sector and filled it with self-hardening polymer/metal compound. Nothing vital had been damaged, but Carialle wondered how many of those hits they could take before being destroyed. Her nerve endings still stung. She fed somatotropins to the injured part, and increased her sugar levels slightly.

Keff shook his hands to help the blood flow to the white and pinched palms, then slammed his fist down on the RECORD button to send a message to CW.

"Mayday. This is the CK-963. We are under attack by three vessels, origin unknown. I am uplinking video of these vessels, plus other data we have gathered regarding the disappearance of a Central Worlds ship in this sector. If we are unable to escape, send fleet ships to the Cridi system at once. We have already taken damage. I repeat, we are under attack—uh-oh!"

The screen caught his attention as the red light on the enemy ship appeared again. "Cari, they're shooting again!"

"I'm moving, I'm moving!" Carialle exclaimed. The ship zigzagged as well as it could to avoid the coming barrage, but she couldn't move far to any side. There was no way to dodge another blast. "Our shields aren't meant to take this."

The Frog Prince once again put his newfound power into operation. His hands whisked back and forth in silent commands. Carialle felt the Core within her walls hum. Suddenly, her hull felt as if it had been dipped in transparent padding. The next bolt of energy, invisible to the naked eye, exploded in a burst of white light against her side. Keff and Tall Eyebrow were jolted around in their couches, but the ship sustained no damage.

"Thanks, TE," Carialle said. "You just earned your keep." The globe-frog signalled a shaky "You're welcome."

The enemy, obviously taken aback that its volley made no impact, sent half a dozen bolts in rapid succession. Carialle attempted to avoid them, but two of them hit her—one in the tail, and one close to the airlock. The white light from their impact momentarily blinded one of her cameras, and the cabin lights faded down for a second. Carialle took the moment of the blast to slide into a narrow alley formed by a winding DNA-strand of floating rocks. The next blast missed them, exploding a meteorite that peppered the hull noisily with sand. Carialle maneuvered through the belt, hoping to keep the distance between her and her pursuer. It vanished among the rocks.

"How long will your shield hold?" she asked Tall Eyebrow.

"I do not know," he said. "Perhaps long enough, but a sustained volley might overstrain it. Especially if they have a Core, too."

"I'm sending that message to Simeon and the CW right now," Carialle said. "If we lose, no one will ever find us. It'll be weeks, if not months before the message gets home. Someone has to know about these people. They've obviously been using the outskirts of this system as a hideout for years, and no one knew about it."

"You did," Keff said, grimly.

"An unhappy surmise, unluckily turning out to be true. At present, that's no satisfaction," she said briskly.

"Are these the ones?" Keff asked, with a concerned look at her pillar. "Are they your salvage squad?"

"*I don't know*," she said. "I was blind then."

"Do the engines match the configuration?" Keff asked. "Did they make physical contact? Can you recognize the vibration? Frequency emissions?"

"I don't know. After the attack I know my sensors went skewiff, so I might have been filtering all I know through bad information. I'll only know if I can get one of them to walk on me again. And I'm damned if I'll ever let that happen."

She recognized that her voice had grown terse, and made an effort to pull herself together. The moment of indecision and resolution took only microseconds, but she knew Keff had noticed the hesitation.

"I'm fine," she said, making the Lady Fair image appear on the wall. The peach-colored veil from her hennin floated softly around her face, which wore an expression of peace. Keff gave it a skeptical glance, but nodded. Both of them had to concentrate right now on survival.

As they wove through the asteroids, two blips appeared ahead on long range scan. Carialle wondered if her new equipment was more sophisticated than theirs; could she see them before they saw her? It might mean the difference between escape and destruction. Carialle studied her telemetry. Where could she turn to avoid them? Nothing truly safe offered itself. A sharp turn in any direction threw her into the teeth of the celestial meat grinder. Suddenly, a gap opened to starboard. She took it, nipping in just before two bolts lanced through the space she'd been occupying.

"This was probably not a good idea," Carialle said. "One lone, unarmed ship doesn't have a chance against a force of three. We've got to get out of here."

"We still have to find the DSC-902," Keff reminded her. "Even if we can just locate it before we get away, that'll be a help. I'd rather rescue them if we can."

"I'm with you, O brave one, but we need to survive this mission to be of any use to them." She broke off to dodge the first ship, which appeared on the other side of a rock full of holes like Swiss cheese. It fired a few times, through one hole then another. Carialle avoided them all, but felt stone shrapnel ping against her hull. The enemy ship spurred after her. She fled, only to find the lone ship had radioed the other two, who appeared on either side of her at the next wide spot. Carialle calculated the period between spiralling rocks, and ducked upward. The three ships, unable to maneuver with her skill, plummeted forward.

Carialle widened the gap between her and the enemy to half a dozen planet-widths by diving down and through the asteroid belt, and coming out "south" of the plane of the ecliptic. She made a note of where the three ships were, and turned back up and into the stone dance at some distance from them. Her sensors indicated that the enemy had figured out what she had done and were coming after her, but she was ahead of them now, scanning for traces of the DSC-902.

"Do you know, they're fast, but their equipment is ancient," Carialle said. "I might be able to outlast them in hide-and-seek, if only we don't get in the way of sustained fire."

"Your engines are better than any of these brutes," Keff said, anxiously watching the aft monitor. One of the ships, blip number two, was outside the belt now, pouring on velocity to catch up. "We can outdistance them. Maybe we can outclass them, too. TE, can we convince them we've got some heavy armament?"

"How?"

"Grab one of those rocks as we go past, and sling it backwards toward this fellow."

The globe-frog looked worried. "It will mean relinquishing control of the shield," he said.

"We'll have to chance it," Carialle said. "My shields are 92% intact, and none of those old pots can match me for maneuverability. Go ahead."

The thick padding around her vanished suddenly, leaving her feeling chilled as if she was exposed to the cold of space. Hastily, she rebuilt her defenses. Carialle felt a momentary drag aft and to port as Tall Eyebrow hitched his power to a rock about three meters across and pulled it out of the dance. It sailed along behind them like a puppy. Carialle turned on all her dorsal thrusters in a sudden burst, and turned on her belly, heading back toward the pursuing ship. Tall Eyebrow made a pushing motion in midair. The rock spiraled up from Carialle's tail and flew in a tightening pattern around her body toward the enemy. With the extra momentum behind it, the missile appeared to elongate in flight.

The enemy ship had only seconds to avoid collision. It veered to up and to starboard. Tall Eyebrow reached out to the end of his range to alter the rock's course to match. It got to within a hundred kilometers of the enemy before the lasers exploded it.

"I missed," Tall Eyebrow complained.

"Whew!" Carialle said. "They *have* got fast reflexes."

"More, TE, more!" Keff shouted, as the pirate recovered itself and fired its weapons at them. The Frog Prince threw the shields back into place just in time. Carialle swept deeper into the asteroid belt, and let a cartwheeling rock take the brunt. In the meantime, Tall Eyebrow picked up more chunks of debris to use as weapons. They circled around Carialle's middle like a planetary ring.

"The other two ships are coming," Carialle warned. "If we can disable this one, I can probably outlast the other two."

"We might be able to rely on psychology," Keff said. "If we're wrong, and they don't have the Cores, seeing us throwing rocks around by remote control might make them back up."

"We can only try it," Carialle said. "I'd better show my pretty face, then."

She dove out of the belt, coming out above ship number two. One and three weren't far behind. Burning her thrusters for an extra burst of speed, she got ahead of Ship Two. Tall Eyebrow used the inertia to help launch a series of stone projectiles, one after another, spiraling them down over Carialle's tail and into the path of the other.

The enemy snaked widely, shooting at the speeding rocks. Tall Eyebrow had chosen a good variety for his missiles. Some burst into gravel; some, with heavy metal content, slagged along the edges but kept spinning. One whirled with sawbladelike inexorability straight into the path of Ship One, which pulled straight up in an acute arc. The molten rock narrowly missed its tail fins.

Ship Two, wound too tightly among the asteroids to flinch, took a pair of fragments amidships. Carialle saw the leak of atmosphere escape from the side of the hull. It streamed out in a haze alongside the exhaust. For the first time she picked up transmissions from the raiders. She couldn't comprehend the language.

"Keff, listen to this," she said. Keff tilted his head as she re-ran the recording and raised his eyebrows at the staccato rhythm of voices. He couldn't understand the deep voices, but he comprehended the urgency.

"That's an SOS," he said definitely. "TE struck something vital."

"Hit them again, TE," Carialle said. "Aim for the engines."

The Ozranian continued his bombardment. Because of the limitations of the Core, he had to depend on a target maintaining its trajectory from the time he let go of a rock. With his superior grasp of spatial relations, Carialle only had to make certain he had a constantly updated overview in the astrogation tank. Keff, a fascinated but helpless bystander, led the cheering section each time one of Tall Eyebrow's missiles found its mark.

Battered and leaking, Ship Two eventually dropped back and out of the race to nurse its damaged hull. Now that Carialle had proved that her ship wasn't helpless, the other two ships became cagey. They flew a wide pattern alongside her, peppering her with laser fire, trying to herd her into planetoids. Carialle's shields fell to 68%. Now they were engaged in what Keff recognized as a true space battle, fought with atlases instead of micrometers.

Carialle focused her telemetry on what lay ahead. The going was more difficult here. If they picked up missiles to throw, she would have to remain on her own shields. Ancient comets had passed through this part of the belt again and again, chopping the asteroids into pieces ranging from those meters across to particles almost as small as dust. She worried that she might sustain a breach. On the good side, the cloud of dust seemed to cut off visuals of her to the other ships. On her scopes she saw them veer around uncertainly. Their medium-range sensors were nowhere near as good as hers.

"We can't get them both at once just tossing boulders," he said. "Can we set up a kind of chain reaction? What if we spin a big rock, the biggest one TE can handle, into one heading the other way? Could we get it to ricochet back toward the Joy Boys back there? Then we can attack the other more directly."

"I don't see why not," she said. She homed in on a set of nearly spherical fragments ahead, and bracketed them for Tall Eyebrow to see. "How are you at playing pool?"

Carialle let herself be "seen" on the enemies' scopes by surfacing out of the dust clouds. The other ships obligingly took the bait, and spurred to catch up with her. All their strategy for keeping their distance from her was dropped. They meant to kill.

"This had better work," Carialle said. "Otherwise, *we'll* have to run, and hope that the Core holds out until we can make Cridi atmosphere."

With almost a casual deflection of power, the Frog Prince set his chain reaction in motion. The cue ball, a stone sphere twelve meters across, was set spinning into its fellows. Most of the rocks it hit split off in a dozen directions, obvious, easy for the ships following to avoid. The eight ball, a rock dark with magnesium oxide, cannoned forward, gaining velocity toward a quarter-planetoid raddled by the eternal passage of fragments. With delightful precision, Tall Eyebrow had aimed his shot toward an obliquely angled "valley." Carialle saw the eight ball hit one angle of the corner shot and deflect onward, and then she was past it.

The other ships paid no attention to a rock that appeared to have missed. Tall Eyebrow had gathered up another stream of small rocks. He shot them at one ship then the other, in twos and threes, with varying degrees of success. It kept the enemy too busy to fire straight at Carialle, or to pay attention to where they were going. Carialle led them around and back along the trajectory she wanted them to follow. To make sure they could keep up, she dropped velocity slightly, daringly. They passed the alley down which the eight ball hurtled. Ship One was too intent upon Carialle, or perhaps its sensors were too confused by the dust and the flashes from its laser barrage, to pick up the huge rock until it rolled almost straight into its aft section.

The two ventral engines imploded, setting off a chain reaction like the lit fuse on a stick of dynamite that destroyed the rest of the ship.

Carialle heard an outcry on its audio frequency, then silence. Ship Three must have picked up that last, futile message, for it broke off its attack.

"What's it doing?" Keff asked, watching the ship veer deeper into the clouds of debris. Within seconds it was out of visual contact. "Is it coming around to sneak up on us?"

"Not unless it's going all the way around the orbit and coming at us from the front," Carialle said. "It's running away." She slowed down, and made her way cautiously out of the asteroid belt. A further check showed Ship Three really was fleeing. It had put the full width of the belt between itself and Carialle. "It's gone. The field's all ours. Congratulations, TE. It was your marksmanship that saved the day for us."

The Ozranian tipped a hand self-deprecatingly.

"Stop being so modest. You're a genuine hero, and I'm going to tell the world when we get back to Cridi. I'm turning around to see if we can pick up traces of the DSC-902." She swung off sunward from the belt, and turned a huge circle. "Call this your victory roll." The frog image repeated the concept with difficulty. Tall Eyebrow ducked his head.

"Cari, we've done it!" Keff said, dusting his hands together. "That'll neutralize the pirates in this system—killing two and scaring off the third. They'll never shoot at a ship in this place again. If they ever troubled you, you've evened it out now. Probably saved the future of the Cridi space program, too."

"I'm not satisfied," Carialle said, firmly. "I want to be certain that they are the ones. *Were* the ones. I want to see them face-to-face. I have to *know*." She paused, waiting until the adrenaline in her system evened out. "And then I want to haul them back to CenCom and prove to that insufferable bureaucrat and his flunkies that I was not hallucinating. Then, I'll be satisfied."

They returned to the asteroid clump where they first saw the raider ships. Carialle searched for the ion traces, now slightly disturbed by their passage and battle.

Behind the cluster of rocks was a confused knot of trails. Carialle and Keff flew back and forth, trying not to destroy the delicate veins, as they read the order of the events that had gone before they arrived.

"Looks like they were here before," Keff said, thoughtfully, sitting at the console with his chin in his hand. "Then they went away and came back again. Where did they go?"

"I think this is where they waited to ambush the DSC-902," Carialle said. "Look at that mass of exhaust particles. Those three ships accelerated to get there, then sat a long time before kicking out. They did it twice, the second time when they came after us. They did grab the ship with a Core—look at the hard thruster emissions from two ships."

"But what happened to the DSC-902's emissions?" Keff asked, studying the starchart.

Tall Eyebrow let out a little gasp and planted both hands firmly over his mouth and nostrils.

"That's it," Carialle said. "Suffocation. They sealed it up in a forcefield like TE's shield, and carried it away."

"But where did it go?"

Carialle bracketed the traces that led away from the cluster. "If I follow the tangle correctly, they went galactic clockwise."

Not far from the original point of contact, the celestial fragments grew larger, until the belt alongside which they were traveling looked like a gigantic string of brown-red pearls. The spider webbing of ions led from every direction to the largest one. Even from a distance, the artificial structures there were apparent.

"A base!" Keff exclaimed. "Give us a closeup, Cari."

The facility looked like a travesty of the spaceport on Cridi. What must have been a small fuel depot huddled beside a prefabricated dome of extreme age. Both were riddled with pockmarks from meteor strikes. Around them lay debris Carialle recognized with a sinking heart as sections from destroyed or dismembered spaceships. The most recent wreck was frosted white. The residual moisture from the life support system of the DSC-902 had not yet had time to leach away in vacuum. Its hatch and all the cargo bay doors stood open, unspeakably lonely and vulnerable. Lights were on inside.

"Oh, no," Keff whispered. Tall Eyebrow murmured a tiny, sympathetic creak.

"The hull shows half a dozen breaches," Carialle said, pulling a closeup of the imploded hull plates, showing black holes partially opaqued by the film of ice. "You can see what happened. They held it in place, and they peppered it with laser fire. See how rough the holes are. They were using a mining laser, not weapons grade. I'm getting no trace of radiation from the engines. It looks like our three friends stripped out the drives. No signs of life."

"Bodies?" Keff asked.

Without a word, Carialle magnified a small section of the asteroid's surface. What Keff had taken for a heap of short lengths of tubing in the faint light from the distant sun were half a dozen human bodies. The expression on the staring faces was that of surprise. Keff swallowed hard.

"Those *bastards*."

"There's more," Carialle said. She shifted focus to another one of her cameras. They were above the base now, able to see the ruins on the other side of the structures. Carialle showed them pieces of tiny ships, strewn like discarded toys.

"Even their Cores couldn't protect them," Carialle said.

"Cridi? They did not crash?" TE asked, smashing one of his long hands down on the other.

"They did not crash," Carialle replied grimly. She showed them the parts of the ships. On extreme magnification the pair in the main cabin could see that the pieces showed little damage, except where the laser holes were evident.

"And the crews?" Keff asked, subvocally.

"Dead," Carialle said, without elaborating, but she made a comprehensive recording of the pathetic scatter of small bodies in protective suits near the landing pad. Carialle wished she could not see them. At least she could spare Keff and TE that, and showed them the bodies from a distance. Keff and TE fell silent.

"I hope we blew up the ones carrying the Cores," Carialle said. "This is what the CenCom should see: what happens when that extraordinary power falls into the wrong hands."

"Four ships," Keff said sadly. "All destroyed."

"More," TE signalled suddenly, pulling handfuls of air towards his chest.

"What do you mean?" Carialle asked.

The Ozranian leader tapped the side of his head. "Observation. Please put the pieces in the air for me. Like the puzzle."

"Ah, I get you." Carialle blew up the parts of the ships and placed them in holograph form before him. With lightning speed the Frog Prince reconstructed three small ships from which pieces were missing, but there were parts left over that could not possibly belong to any Cridi ship. Among the leftovers Carialle recognized a nose cone and landing fins of an obsolete model of a human-made ship. She constructed a hologram of the completed ship around the screen image. Keff gawked at Tall Eyebrow.

"How did you *do* that?" he asked.

The Ozran shrugged modestly. "Observation," he repeated.

"That spatial talent of his," Carialle said. "Extraordinary. I'd like to see his people engaged in engineering design work with ours."

"But, see what is left," TE continued. "It is like yours, but not like."

"It's old," Carialle said. "Do you recognize the model, Keff? It dates from fifty or seventy years back. About the time that Cridi got bottled up."

"So a Central Worlds explorer might have found the Cridi before now," Keff said thoughtfully. "These pirates destroyed them before they could get back to report on their findings."

"Maybe they didn't find *Cridi*," Carialle said.

"What do you mean?"

"These thieves don't live on this rock," she said. "They can't. There's no facilities, no supplies, barely any air. They didn't simply intend to destroy the ship, or they would have left the hulk floating where it died. These unknowns are ambushing and robbing starships. This is a chop shop, a staging area. They come from somewhere else. They *go* somewhere else, with the stolen booty. Doesn't it make sense that it's right here, in the system?"

Keff's teeth showed in a feral grin. "It does. We'll find them. We can't let these brutes get away with mass murder." He poked a finger at the shining strands in the holotank. "Shall we see if those ley lines from the engines lead anywhere?"

✲CHAPTER NINE

"Planet Five," Carialle said, turning all her video screens to the view of the dark hulk silhouetted by the distant sun. "The traitors live right here in the Cridi system."

"Let's take them," Keff said, leaning forward and slamming his fists together. In the navigation tank, strands of ion emission joined hundreds more in a skein around the black sphere, like webs tying up a fly. That was the center. So close, and yet no one knew it was here.

"Have you brushed your teeth and said your prayers?" Carialle asked, interrupting his concentration. "We can't destroy a base by ourselves, let alone a planet."

"No," Keff sighed, sitting back. Reason had been restored. "But we can get data to instruct a CW fleet. Let's see what's down there."

Keeping in the widest possible orbit, the ship circled around to sunside. It looked an inhospitable place, but there were sure signs of habitation, and the three moons, each the size of Old Earth, could have concealed fleets of pirates. Carialle listened on the frequencies she had observed the three assassins using. She picked up a familiar drone.

"Landing beacon," she said, putting the sound on audio for the others. "So far, nothing else. If there are detection devices out there I'm risking having another force come boiling after me, so I'm keeping thrusters ready to run back toward Cridi if necessary."

"What power emissions are you reading?" Keff asked, studying the astrogation tank.

"Not much. If they have any industrial complexes, they must all be underground. Residual decay in a lot of places on the surface, probably power plants from purloined spaceships. Another refueling depot, in the midst of one enormous junkheap. Radioactive dumping ground, ten degrees north of the equator, far from any of the heat vents. Read this spectroanalysis," she said, putting up a chart on one of her screens. "The atmosphere has a hefty ammonia content."

"Our archives say this burns us," Tall Eyebrow signed, looking at the molecular diagram. "Also smells bad."

"Then I'll need a full breather suit," Keff said, perusing the screen with a critical eye. "Oxygen. Grav assist. Maybe take one or both of the servo drones with me in case the gravity is too much."

"What *are* you talking about?" Carialle asked.

"I want to have a close-up look at the people who were just shooting at us," Keff said, but Carialle recognized the gleam in his eye. He'd looked the same way whenever they were sent on assignment to a planet suspected of sustaining life. He pointed at a spot on the planetary map, a field of craters near the refueling depot. "If you set us down there, I can get in and gather data, and be out before they know it."

"Wait a minute, Sir Knight. Yes, we may have encountered a brand new, sentient species, but that doesn't mean you should fling yourself into their midst."

"Cari, think of it—it's unprecedented. Two intelligent life forms evolving in the same solar system—and never meeting. Think of the furor at Alien Outreach. Think of being the only brainship team ever to bring home a prize like that." Keff began to see glory before his eyes, to hear the congratulations in his ears. Carialle interrupted his reverie.

"It's too dangerous! May I point out you just mentioned that these are the same people who were just shooting at us? Who murdered the crews of at least four starships? And who may have tried to kill me twenty years ago? Surely the ships sent messages with our description and video bits to home control on one of these obscure frequencies I've been trying to monitor. We'd be too easy a target landing near their spaceport, and I don't think they'll buy 'I come in peace' from the ship that just destroyed two or three of their craft. If you get caught, they'll kill you. I won't land."

"I haven't forgotten any of that, Cari, but we can accomplish a great deal if I can infiltrate them successfully. We do need data to support a Central Worlds deployment. I'm good at camouflage. All you have to do is land us very quietly in a nice, deep syncline, and give me sufficient data on the terrain. I'll find a bivouac. It'll take time for the CW ships to reach us . . . ." Keff's eye was distracted from the intractable face of Carialle's Lady Fair image. He turned to stare fully at the navigation tank.

"Cari, jump! There's a ship coming up astern. We can hide behind one of those moons, maybe loop around to the nightside. Hurry! Why aren't your proximity alarms going off? Damn it," he said, hammering a fist down on the console. "I thought we scared that third ship into next Tuesday." He scanned the scopes looking for convenient asteroid belts, planetoids, or ion storms in which they could lose themselves. "There's nothing! We'll have to run. Can you read any armament . . . ?"

"Keff!" Carialle shouted, blinking the displays on and off to get his attention. "It isn't the pirates. It's the Cridi. You'll recognize their configuration by the time it gets into range. Tad Pole persuaded the Cridi to launch their new ship in our defense."

"What?" Keff felt his jaw drop open with shock. "Why didn't you tell me?"

"You've been raving so much I didn't have an edgewise to fit in a word. Long Hand is transmitting to me from the other ship. IT is translating her sign language to me, but it's slow going, with their rotten screens. Narrow Leg and the others scrambled as soon as we accomplished a successful takeoff. They want to back us up. Small Spot and Long Hand persuaded them to launch in our defense. They came along, and they brought Big Eyes, among others. I'll play you the audio. It's very amusing. I can hear Big Voice chirruping madly in the background behind everyone else."

"Big Eyes comes?" Tall Eyebrow signed, pleased. Keff looked appalled.

"No! Send them home. This is too dangerous."

"They have better defenses than we do, Sir Knight," Carialle said, patiently. "Besides, they want to help us. I think they recognize the risk they're taking."

"We can't let them, Cari," Keff said. Suddenly the small ship came fully into focus. It looked very small and vulnerable. He dashed a hand through his hair and stared desperately at the screen. "The pirates are armed to their masticatory appendages."

"And a moment ago you wanted me to land in their midst," Carialle said sweetly. Keff had a sudden, heartfelt temptation to kick her pillar.

"I'm trained to take risks," he said. "The Cridi are not. Why did they come?"

"Why? Sir Keff, you spent over a month convincing the Cridi to sign on with Central Worlds as a member nation with full privileges. You did a good job. They've taken the concept of alliance seriously, and they mean to back up what they say. How can they prove they're our equals and allies unless we let them?"

"But not like this!"

"Then, how?"

"I help," Tall Eyebrow put in, with a quick sign, before Keff could object. "They, too."

"See?" Carialle asked. "I'm proud of them."

Keff wasn't convinced, but suddenly the rust-colored planet off Cari's starboard side looked more menacing. It *would* be useful to have backup. CW Fleet ships were months away. If they scrambled tomorrow, it would still take weeks to close the distance. He glanced at Carialle's pillar.

"Was it unanimous?" he asked.

"By no means," Carialle said. "Snap Fingers and his brood think they should mind their own business. But look at the ones who are risking their lives, who *weren't* sure that ship would even break atmosphere safely. But, there they are."

Keff glanced up slyly through his eyelashes. "Big Voice came, too?"

"Believe it or not, he did."

Keff raised his hands in surrender. "All right. But Alien Outreach isn't going to like this."

"Then, they can lump it," Carialle said firmly. "Would they rather have the pirates running around loose? This is the Cridi's necks on the block, too. It's their system, and for the last fifty years, their menace. These pirates took their freedom, and killed who knows how many Cridi astronauts. The Cridi have a right to be here."

"You're correct, as always, Cari. Let me talk to them. I'm going to eat crow." He sat down in his padded seat before the console.

The 1028-square grid appeared on the screen, and coalesced into a rough mosaic of the face of Narrow Leg.

"Captain, Carialle and I welcome you back to space."

"We are successful!" the elderly Cridi squeaked, and IT echoed his tone of triumph. "It flies, it is sound."

"I never doubted it," Keff signed, with a grin. "I've never seen such careful construction. I'm glad you're with us." He cleared his throat, then emitted a short series of chirps. "X equals Y. X plus Y is greater than X. X plus Y is greater than Y. We are equals, and the two of us together are greater than we are alone."

Narrow Leg nodded his head. "That is evident. You honor us. Circling this planet. What must we know about it?"

Carialle spoke up. "We have traced the path of the villains who attacked the diplomatic ship. We have no fleet, no heavy armament, so all we can do is gather information, and send for help from the Central Worlds. We plan to infiltrate the planet's surface."

Narrow Leg's cheeks hollowed, and the faces of the Cridi behind him paled to mint green. They looked terrified, but all of them squeaked up at once.

"Tell us how we may help."

"I didn't want them down here with me," Keff said, sublingually, hunkering himself down further into the crevasse beyond the outskirts of the building they had designated as the spaceport. "I wanted them up there, where they could use their Core to help protect us, and you."

"Nonsense," Carialle said. "There's a delay in response time, even from space. I want them where they can be on the spot if you need them."

Keff didn't protest, but the sound of the plastic globes rolling along the rocky surface of the planet sounded louder than thunder to him. Tall Eyebrow paddled at the head of a party of scouts, heading around toward the other side of the compound. Big Eyes kept up gamely behind him, beside Small Spot and her father, but most of the homeworld Cridi frankly cheated and used their amulet power to levitate their new globes. They bobbed along behind the toiling group, sitting at their ease in the bottom of the transparent spheres.

"Darn it, TE, tell them not to do that," he growled into his helmet's audio pickup. "I know the extra gravity's uncomfortable, but I'd rather take a chance on movement being spotted than extraneous power transmissions." It was bad enough that the Cridi had to use the Core technology to keep the water in the globes from freezing on this cold world. They risked detection of their ship with every deviation from strict survival. "They might at least put down a physical twitch as indigenous wildlife. If there is any. What a bleak place."

A hundred meters away, the lead globe stopped and spun in place. The water inside sloshed upward. Tall Eyebrow made a few signs quickly and with authority toward the other globes. Keff was reminded abruptly that the insecure visitor to the Cridi homeworld was also the leader of the exiled Ozran-born Cridi, who kept his population together, alive, and sane in the most dangerous and deprived of circumstances. He admired the way TE threw in a tactful sign or two that alluded to the difficulty of using a travel globe, but added staccato chops for "absolute necessity." Reluctantly, Big Voice and the others lowered the spheres to the ground. The lead globe rotated 180 degrees, and the party set off again more slowly, but more loudly. Keff flattened himself down so that he could no longer see them. He studied his target.

There appeared to be little activity, but Carialle had detected at least four life-forms in the building. She had a hard time finding body-heat traces. The planet's surface was cold, but it was dotted with hot spots where volcanoes and geothermal vents broke through. Structures placed over these took advantage of the natural heat.

Most of the population had to be below ground, with only a few exits to the open sky. It was impossible to pick out individuals. Ammonia/oxygen flares ignited occasionally, and as swiftly, blew out. Carialle cursed as one trace after another that she was tracking suddenly vanished. Gravity was approximately one and a half times Standard norm; bearable for short periods. The "spaceport" was a ridge, the edge of a huge crater filled in over eons with dust and debris that had solidified into a flat plain. Architects had bored into, or more likely, *out of* the side of the hill overlooking the plain, and built onto it. Carialle reported that heat traces from inside the building registered at least 35 degrees C. That sounded much nicer than the surrounding landscape, which was bare and dusty where it wasn't covered with discarded junk from hijacked spaceships.

"What do these people eat?" Keff wondered out loud, his voice sounding hollow in his survival suit.

"Look at those domes, built to catch every meager ray, even magnify it," Carialle said. "Perhaps our ammonia-breathers photosynthesize, and live on water."

"Or the cities below ground are full of hydroponics," Keff said. "I don't see enough domes to support a breeding population of mitochondroids." In spite of the peril and the anger he felt at the pirates, he and Carialle had dropped back into the game they loved to play, anticipating the facts about an unknown race. "Is it possible this planet was a lot warmer once? Or do you suppose we've discovered silicophages?"

"It wouldn't be the first discovery of mineral-eaters," Carialle said, after running through her memory banks, "but it would be the first one that attained sentience and space travel."

"In stolen ships," Keff said, flatly. "What do we know about them so far?"

"From the emissions of the ship Tall Eyebrow damaged, body temperatures in range tolerable by humans, between twenty degrees C and forty degrees C. Size, from my readings in the structure ahead of you, they are larger than humans, but smaller than lions. Anything else, I must await data from you and our party of rolling frogs."

"Add to that, intelligent and dangerous," Keff said, nodding, but keeping his eyes pinned on the dome. "Well, I can't wait here forever. TE, I'm moving. Watch the building and stop anything that comes in after me."

"I hear," the small voice said in Standard over the helmet speaker.

Staying flat on his belly, Keff crept over the rise. On the other side was a steeply sloping valley. Long-departed rivers or perhaps the celestial pressures of planetary formation had crazed the plain with shallow canals. Keeping low enough to remain out of sight to occupants of the largest structure, Keff crawled on hands and knees. Fine silt, undisturbed for eons, rose briefly around him, then settled out in the heavy gravity, burying his tracks.

Parked a dozen kilometers away beside the Cridi spaceship in a lonely valley, Carialle watched his progress simultaneously on her charts and through the body-cam he wore on his tunic.

"You're coming to a T-intersection," she said, as Keff paused and reared up on his knees so she could see his precise location. "Take the left branch. No, the left one. The right one leads straight into a deep thermal vent."

Keff made his way along the turnings, wrinkling his nose against the clouds of dust even though he knew they couldn't penetrate his protective suit. His heads-up display told him the half-meter-high bank of fog into which he crawled at a low point in a ditch was heavy with ammonia and traces of other gases reduced to liquid. He gulped. One breach in suit integrity, and he was a green icicle. Never mind; he was committed to his mission. In some small way, he was helping Carialle to lay the ghosts of her past, as well as ridding the Cridi of a menace and avenging the deaths of the Central Worlds diplomatic personnel. A moon in its second quarter rose on the horizon and crept up the sky, throwing a little more light on his path. His canal dipped sharply as he crawled another ten meters, then light from the moon was cut off. In the blackness his suit-lights went on. He paused, waiting for the prickle between his shoulder blades that would tell him he was being watched. Nothing.

"You're almost underneath the building now," Carialle was saying. "If you go around to the right, you'll be in front of that hatchway."

Keff's back began to ache from the heavy gravity. He paused with hands on knees.

"It looks a long way up," he panted, staring at the black shape above him, picked out by distant pinpoint stars. His lungs dragged in oxygen.

"What are you building up all of those muscles if not for an effort like that?" Carialle asked dryly.

When she started making ironic comments, Keff could tell she was the most worried. He just shook his head. In an instant the aches in his lower back and thighs went away. "Just oxygen-starved," he said. "Just a moment." He reached into the gauntlet of his right glove for the control pad, and turned up the nitrox mix slightly. The faint hissing sound was a comfort.

In the gloom the building over his head looked ominous. The slab on which it was built had been slagged out of a lip of the ridge, so the people inside had at least stolen, if not evolved, heavy pyroconstruction equipment.

Keff heaved himself up. The domes began at a meter above the platform, giving him an expanse of blank wall against which he could conceal himself. Ahead of him, the platform widened out away from the domed windows to an apron that bore scorch marks from repeated launches and landings. Limp, metal-bound hoses lay on the ground in skeins. They led from the putative fuel tank, which stood on pylons around a fold of the ridge from the domes. *To protect the glass from explosions,* Keff thought, with an approving nod to the designers. A dusty accordion-pleated hood was bunched up around the entrance to the building. It seemed to be long enough to extend all the way to the edge of the platform. Not at all sophisticated, but it would scarcely ever need major repairs. He took the video pickup off his suit and held it up against the bottom margin of the clear wall.

"Can you see anything, Cari?" he whispered.

"Aqua foliage," Carialle replied. "Spiky, like evergreens—no, more like fan coral. I can't see anything moving, even on infrared. My sensors are still picking up those same four body traces. No one much seems to come up to the surface."

"If they're anything like us, it's too cold for them up here. I'm ten meters from the entrance. Where are you, TE?" Keff asked his suit mike.

"We see you, other side of edge," the globe-frog's voice piped. "Under-by tank-container."

"Back me up. I am going to try and enter. If I am not out in fifteen minutes from the time of my entrance, come in and help me. At that point, revealing we have Core technology will be moot."

"Sir Frog waits," the small voice said. Keff grinned.

He crawled the rest of the way to the rough plascrete arch. The entrance resembled an airlock, devoid of any security devices Keff could recognize. The pirates must have been very confident that no one knew they were here.

"Where are the guards, Cari?" he asked.

"All four are deep inside," she said. "It looks like your best chance."

Keff nodded to himself. "Here goes."

He stood up against the inside edge of the arch, hidden momentarily from sight of anyone in the dome. Carefully, he turned around. Inside a metal frame, two flat bars jutted out from the wall.

"I've only got a fifty-fifty chance of cocking up," he said, and a childhood singsong bubbled up from memory. He waggled his finger playfully between the two bars. "My mother said to pick the very best one, and you are *it*." With that, he stabbed the upper bar. It moved easily under his finger, depressing flat to the wall.

Immediately behind him, something heavy and soft dropped to the ground. Keff spun. He was now curtained into the enclosure by a metal and plastic mesh. Hissing erupted from the wall side. In a few moments, a door, large enough to admit a cargo container, slid upward.

Keff listened before he stepped inside, turning up his external mikes to the maximum. No alarms. No one seemed to have heard the airlock open.

"Looks like I'm all right," he whispered.

"For pity's sake, be careful," Carialle said in his aural implant.

He nodded, knowing she would pick up the physiological signs of the small movement. A blinking light on the other side of the threshold urged him forward into another sealed pocket of air. Keff stepped through just as the heavy door slid downward. It closed silently, which surprised him more than a solid bang would have. He heard more hissing, then the curtain and its fender rose, revealing the interior of the dome. A few spotlights stabbed their beams down at the floor, but mostly the arboretum was lit by the faint, distant sun. Bristly growths sprang out of flat, low dishes made of black ceramic on the shiny floor. The plants themselves— if they were plants—were a riot of neon blue, ultramarine, teal, acid yellow, and interplanetary-distress orange. Keff winced.

"Gack," he said quietly. "Their taste in horticulture is nightmarish."

"I told you so," Carialle said. "The colors suggested to me that the atmosphere inside was ammonia-heavy, like the outer atmosphere, but it isn't nearly as saturated as I thought. My spectroanalysis shows that it's much more dilute. Less than one-tenth. You could almost breathe it."

"How'm I doing?"

"You're still alone," Carialle said.

"That's strange," Keff said absently, peering around. "Look, could that be furniture?"

He turned so the video pickup on his chest was facing some metal and fabric constructs in a group amid the riot of spiky, sea-colored plants.

"I would say yes." Carialle studied the forms, and ran projections on an ergonomics program in her memory banks. "Something that prefers a sling to a seat—there's no back—so possibly not upright in carriage. It lies supported. A quadruped? Then why wouldn't it simply lie down on pads on the floor?" She drew image after image of arrangements of torsos and limbs, and rejected them all.

"Here are some divan pillows," Keff said. He turned to face fuzzy, covered pads the size of his bunk. "They're huge!"

"Whew!" Carialle whistled in agreement. "Keff, sit on one so I can see how much a body of your weight compresses the material. I need an estimate on what made those dents."

Keff complied, plumping down on one as if exhausted, which indeed he was beginning to be. He sat and gasped for a moment. The heavy gravity was telling on him. He hoped the Cridi were faring all right.

"Let me see," Carialle said. Keff rose and gave her a good view of his impression from different angles. "My estimate stands. I think they weigh about two hundred kilos apiece."

"I am not staying long," Keff said, positively.

Beyond the seating arrangements was an arched corridor. Like the platform outside, it had been slagged through the mountain with a melter drill of some kind. Down the passageway, Keff spotted the reflected flicker of blue and white lights. It looked familiar. He listened carefully at the entrance for a long time, then tiptoed toward the source of illumination. He passed closed hatchways with the same framed control bars in the wall beside them. At the sudden sound of escaping air, Keff flattened himself into the nearest door frame and held his breath. The noise stopped with a wheeze and a bang.

"Probably a compressor," Carialle commented. "Primitive." Keff nodded, the back of his helmet tapping against the wall. The echo bounded off both ways down the empty hall, sounding like water dripping into a pool.

He waited a moment, then slipped noiselessly into the corridor once again. His heads-up display told him it was three degrees warmer in here than it had been in the atrium. He was undoubtedly already under the lip of the excavated mountain. He looked forward to exploring the labyrinth of caves that underlay this building, but with a suitable escort of CW militia for backup.

"Here's your glow," Carialle said, as he counted the eighth doorway.

"Computer screens," Keff breathed, peering around the frame. On a low table that had once been a galley counter in a Central Worlds ship sat antique CPUs and square monitors. Boxes of jumbled chips and tapes and datasolids sat on the floor beside the table. He edged in so the camera eye on his chest would send the image back to the ship.

"More salvage," Carialle said, severely. "That is a year-old Tambino 90-gig unit. Those are CW special issue screens, and those input peripherals are from half a dozen different systems reaching back a thousand years. And yes, some of that discarded junk is Cridi."

Keff glanced around, wondering how far away the guards were. "Could you crack the data storage system?"

"Sonny, I cut my diodes on tougher stuff than this. Hook me up, and we'll copy everything in the memory. That'll give CenCom plenty to go on."

"What about viruses?"

"Not to worry. I'll isolate the files in a separate section and make them 'read only' outside of that drive base. I have all that spare memory installed for our diplomatic mission. Using it for hacking an enemy system is much more interesting than using it for lists of trade goods and historical texts, wouldn't you say?" There was fierce satisfaction in her voice. "Use the port IT has been attached to. That should be sufficient. You can use the same memory later for language translation."

"Right," Keff said, starting toward the setup. He put one knee on the hanging sling. Suddenly, the computer emitted a loud beep, then a siren wail.

"Oh, no!" he exclaimed, leaping backward. "It's got a proximity alarm. Do they hear me? Are they coming this way?" He stared at the doorway.

"Don't panic," Carialle said, her voice changing to a deep baritone to be heard over the shrill alarms. "I don't hear any high frequencies from motion detectors. It might be a timer."

"It *has* attracted attention. I hear something." Keff's audio pick-ups detected a faint shuffling sound. "They're coming this way!"

He put one eye around the edge of the door and flung himself backward when he saw a huge shadow looming toward him. "I'm trapped. TE, keep out! I'll get free if I can."

"I hear," the Ozranian's voice said, sounding worried.

"Right you are, Sir Knight," Carialle said, suddenly. "All four bodies are moving toward your location. We've got a visitor coming from space, too."

"What?"

"Looks like Ship Three," she said. "It's alone. I'm tracking . . . updates as available. You hide, now!"

The shuffling sounds grew louder. Keff cast about frantically for a place to hide. He threw himself behind stacks of storage containers just as the feet reached the doorway. Stifling groans of pain from the ribs he bruised in his headlong dive, he flattened himself against the wall and hoped the barrier between him and the aliens was stable.

"They're big ones, all right," Carialle's voice said very quietly in his aural canal. "Two hundred fifty, a hundred seventy, and two hundred ten kilos respectively. The fourth one has gone through to the domes. Probably to watch Ship Three land."

"No way out," Keff said.

"Not yet. Your respiration and blood pressure are up. Take a few deep breaths. Take a drink of water. How is your oxygen supply?"

"Okay," Keff muttered sublingually. He heard a slight sound coming toward him and held his breath. He cursed both CW Exploration and Diplomatic for not allowing their ships to carry even defensive weapons. A stun gun would be useful right now in extricating him from this place. The brutes would kill him with the same lack of pity they showed the crew of the DSC-902. The sound continued past him. The next thing he heard was dragging— one of the aliens hauling in a sling from the atrium. They planned to stay in this room, probably until Ship Three landed. It took a mental effort to restart his breathing. He dragged in a gasp of air, then held his breath again.

"They can't hear you," Carialle reminded him, calmly. "Your helmet muffles sound effectively."

"I know," he whispered, "but because *I* can hear me I think they can. I'll relax."

Keff turned up the gain on his audio pickups. The aliens were talking. Their voices were surprisingly musical: deep, resonant, like the call of brass horns. He tried to separate the sounds into words and decided he didn't yet have enough data to go on. The hail from the approaching ship came in over the speakers faintly.

Apparently Tall Eyebrow's improvised missiles had done some damage to the ship, because the transmission kept cutting in and out. He sensed concern in the voices of the ground crew.

Minutes dragged past. His muscles cramped because of the awkward position in which he lay, but he didn't dare shift to ease them. Sweat began to trickle out of his hairline, over his face and neck, and down between his shoulder blades. It itched infuriatingly. He blinked his eyes to clear drops off his lashes. The chatter of voices, both within the room and on the distant ship, reached a crescendo of agitation. Keff thought he heard the words "Central Worlds," in passing, but decided he was trying to read too much into the meaningless multisyllabic babble. Suddenly there was a hush in the room, and he felt the ground shake. The dome made a grand echo chamber for the *boom!* the ship made when it landed.

"Three point five on the Richter scale at the epicenter," Carialle said. "That ship has no boosters left to soften touchdown. TE did good work. It probably won't be able to to take off again."

"We ought to disable it entirely before we leave here," Keff whispered, "just to make sure."

Hissing and groaning from the airlock compressors heralded the arrival of Ship Three's crew. The ground staff greeted them with unmistakable relief. A couple of them hunched past the gap in the boxes behind which Keff was hiding. He heard the hubbub of vocal greeting, and the shifting of feet as they went through their handshake-equivalent ritual, whatever it was. The brawn maneuvered himself so he could peer through, and got his first glimpse of the aliens. He realized with a shock that their faces were just slightly farther from the floor than his. They did walk on all fours! He willed the new arrivals to stay where they were, and as if they could hear him, they did. At first he saw only partially-opaqued helmets and vast protective suits. One by one, the aliens sat back on invisible haunches, took off the helmets and shed gauntlets. Keff vibrated with impatience until one of them moved in front of the gap again.

"Big flat faces," he told Carialle in staccato bursts of narration, "weird eyes. Sleek head, widens to neck. Sandy pelts, slightly fuzzy, like the garden cushions. Claw hands."

One of them moved too close to the cartons and shut off his view with a slick, oversuited shoulder. Keff withdrew his head very slightly, and waited. The body moved away, and the fabric of the coverall slid downward to reveal the creature's back.

"Cari, they have wings!"

Carialle's voice was a businesslike hum in his ear. "Vestigial wings? That says a lot about the devolution of this planet's bios . . ."

"No," he hissed, excitedly. "Full-sized wings. Like bat's wings, but with longer fur."

"Do you know what that means?" Carialle asked, astonished, adding up the facts in a microsecond. "This planet *isn't* hollow. There's no air mass to support flight. Its surface gravity is huge! That means there are no underground passageways, no millions of separately evolved sentients living cheek by jowl with the Cridi. That's why the difference in the air quality between outside and inside. They're strangers. This is an outpost, too! *Where do they come from?*"

"I don't know!" Keff whispered.

He shifted to get a better view, feeling the boxes with his gloved hands to make sure they wouldn't slip. He found another gap, closer to the computer setup, and applied his eye to it.

"I keep seeing flashes of claws and talons. I think there's a pair of vestigial fingers on the wings, where, er, where primary feathers would be, beside that pair of hands on the forelimbs that is used for manipulative as well as locomotive purposes. I'm getting a glimpse of heavy haunches."

"That would explain the slings," Carialle's voice said. "Four hands! Fascinating."

Keff heard the ticking of claws on the smooth floor. One of the aliens paused just on the other side of the containers, giving Keff a good look at it. The brawn peered at the set of the narrow head; the placement of the wings on the broad, golden back; the noble, handsome face. "You know, they look rather like griffins."

Carialle immediately accessed the Myths and Legends handbook, found the cross-reference for Griffins, subhead: Gryphons, then cross-referenced it to encyclopediae and classical works from the European subcontinent of Old Earth. "Those griffins had eagles' beaks and lion's tails."

"These have no nose, but those mouths . . . if they are mouths . . ."

The "griffin," answering a query from one of its unseen fellows, spread the halves of its upper lip, and Keff blanched at the sharp white fangs behind it. "That's a mouth, all right," he said. "We need to file a report with the CenCom, but first I have to get out of here."

"How?"

"I don't know, yet," Keff said.

"We will come to help," said a faint voice in his helmet.

"TE, no," he whispered into his audio pickup. "Stay out. Cari, tell them no. Don't let them."

The sound of his own voice dropped like a pin into the silence of the room. Keff felt the prickles race down his back. He looked up to find a Griffin staring down at him, surprise in its vertically-striped eyes. He scrambled crabwise away from it behind the boxes, but there was nowhere to go. The alien followed on all fours, tracking him on the other side of the crates. Panicking, Keff kicked over stacks of containers. They fell heavily, breaking open to scatter components across the feet of the aliens. He dove across the last stack and rolled an upright position in the corner, hands ready to strike.

"You're right, Sir Knight," Carialle said. "They do look like griffins. Be careful!"

Six of them stood in the room, with the rest crowding the corridor. All of them gawked at him with big, flattish eyes, faces expressionless. None of them moved, but with the advantage of big muscles and wings, they could wait until he was vulnerable. Keeping one hand up in defense, Keff felt his way along the wall, hoping for an escape door, though he'd known this room was a dead end when he had entered. They tracked his progress, calmly, unemotionally, waiting. Their assurance prompted all sorts of horrible scenarios in Keff's imagination. He panted, and his vision swam with blackness around the edges with the difficulty of drawing a deep breath.

One of them moved at last. The lead griffin, the one who had found him, started toward him with wings and spike-like fingers spread. The foreclaws, balancing out the big haunches behind, had fierce talons over ten centimeters long that ticked on the shiny, stone floor. Its big wings obscured the beasts behind so Keff couldn't tell what they were doing. *Mustering for an attack?* Keff flattened himself against the bulkhead, preparing to spring, wondering if his unarmed combat training would help. Where did you pivot to throw something with four legs and an unknown center of gravity? Would tossing it onto its wings disable it long enough for him to escape? The great beast loomed up closer and closer. The top lip split to show the sharp, gleaming fangs and a strip of orange-pink gums above them. The creature was saying something, but Keff could only hear the pounding of blood in his ears.

In the distance, Keff heard the sound of rushing air. The griffins, in a body, turned to look. Keff blessed the distraction. He took his best opportunity, and sprang over their heads.

He had miscalculated the drag of the extra gravity, and fell in the midst of the enemy. Half the aliens were distracted by the noise coming from the domes. The rest turned back to Keff. A couple of them grabbed for his arms with their foreclaws and wing-hands. He rolled away, shaking hard to get loose. The long nails scrabbled on the fabric of his suit. He thought he heard his sleeve rip, and winced. He stood against the wall, panting. More hands reached for him, and his eyes registered a confused blur of wings, claws and eyes. He grabbed a wrist and twisted. One of the griffins cried out. Another added its howl of surprise. Keff, flat on the floor in a jumble of boxes, raised his head as eight globesful of Cridi sailed into the room in midair.

"What takes so long?" Tall Eyebrow's voice said very clearly in Keff's helmet.

"TE, I told you to stay out!" Keff shouted.

To his surprise, the griffins froze in place when they saw the Cridi. Their eyes were wide, not with amazement, Keff thought, but with loathing.

"Slayim!" The word issued with clarion power from one throat, and was echoed by all the others. Every griffin rose to its hind legs and lunged for the Cridi.

Tall Eyebrow stared at the charging griffins for one astonished second, then Big Eyes's globe batted his from behind, sending it careening out of the way just before a griffin landed on it. More of the lithe aliens leaped straight for Big Eyes herself. Narrow Leg's globe shot in front of his daughter's, and the griffins showed their long teeth. The two globes revolved around one another, and bobbed straight upward, with three griffins snapping and clawing for them.

"Hey!" Keff shouted, throwing himself into the fray. "Leave them alone!" He bounded in between two griffins who were on their back toes, giving them almost three meters of reach, clawing for

Narrow Leg's pilot, whose globe had retreated to the safety of the ceiling. One of the griffins spread its wings, knocking Keff sprawling and accidentally batting another griffin in the back. The alien who had been struck turned away from Small Spot. The Ozranian was cowering underneath the computer desk. He scooted out from his hiding place and hurried to hover behind a pile of boxes beside Long Hand, under siege from an alien who reached long wing-fingers around from one side of the stack, then the other. Another griffin dove for the two exiles. Keff gathered himself up and launched, ramming the first griffin under the right wing with his shoulder. It turned, a surprised look on its face, its powerful wings battering at him. Keff felt his helmet skew, and the next breath he inhaled hurt. He coughed painfully. He kicked the griffin in the chest, and to his own amazement, sent it sprawling backwards on its tail. The beasts were bottom-heavy! He assessed and docketed this fact, wondering why he was thinking so slowly, and why he heard a roar coming from under his right ear. He felt sick.

"Keff! Seal that," Carialle ordered in stentorian tones. Keff's head was ringing, from nausea and the volume of her voice. "Keff, can you hear me? Your suit has been breached. You're breathing ammoniated air. Are you all right? Keff!"

"Yes," he gasped shortly, and coughed again. He retched, and caught himself before he threw up. His hands fumbled for the neck of his suit, and he refastened the flapping lip of plastic. Clean, sweet-tasting nitrox flooded his face. Gratefully, he drew in lungfuls. "I'm all right. I. Am. Truly."

Carialle's voice melted with relief. "Thank goodness."

Keff didn't have time to regain his full strength. Two more griffins had joined the pair jumping at Big Voice.

"Aid!" shrieked the plump councillor. "Aid²!"

The other Cridi globes, led by Tall Eyebrow, levitated to assist their compatriot. Swats from claws and wings sent them scattering like a bunch of marbles. Big Eyes' globe hit the wall, and bounced to the floor. The young female lay in her ball of water, her dark eyes staring at nothing. A griffin, spotting her helplessness, tensed its muscular haunches and prepared to spring. A feral grin split its lip.

"Grab them!" Carialle shouted in Keff's ear.

"How?" Keff asked.

"Tell the Cridi! Catch!"

Keff turned and caught Narrow Leg's eye. The human clapped his cupped hands together and pulled the invisible handful toward his body. The elder Cridi nodded sharply.

"Sense!" Narrow Leg's single word echoed through every Cridi amulet. He pointed the fingers of both hands at the griffins, and they froze in place. The springing griffin stiffened in midair, and dropped heavily to the floor on its belly.

The room grew abruptly silent. Ten, ornamental, hexapodal statues in various warlike attitudes glared silent hatred at nothing.

"Nice work," Keff said. He took a deep breath, and sank to the floor. His legs, now aching from lack of oxygen, no longer wished to support him. He felt his sleeve for tears; it was intact. "Good job, everyone. Are you all right?"

"We, yes," Narrow Leg said. "Not used to self-defending. Thank you." Keff only nodded in return. Every other movement hurt.

The Cridi gathered from every corner to assess damage. Tall Eyebrow rolled hastily to his ladyfriend's side. An invisible hand scooped up some of the water in Big Eyes' globe and splashed her cheeks with it. The female blinked. She sat up and turned to smile at him. Tall Eyebrow almost collapsed with relief. Big Eyes clicked her globe gently against his, palm outspread. He opened his hand gently on the inner surface of his sphere, matching hers palm to palm. The two of them floated over to rejoin the others. Keff grinned indulgently.

Big Voice's container was scratched where it had struck the corner of a metal container, but it was not punctured. The stout councillor was voluble in his relief, babbling and waving frantic signs at all of his fellows and Keff. The others, though frightened by the attack, were more curious. Narrow Leg studied the captured aliens closely. He was struck by the hate on each face.

"Their pulses fast," he commented to Keff, near him on the floor. "Anger. Who?"

"I don't know," the human signed. "We've never seen this species before."

"How many?"

"Only ten, what you see here," Keff said.

"Ten?" Big Voice squawked, waving his hands in the confines of his plastic globe. "Thousands! Millions! I thought to be torn alive!"

"Hush!" Big Eyes snapped. She turned to Keff. "Why no more?"

"Because they don't live here," Keff said. "They're invaders. This system is, er, only of Cridi. These come from elsewhere."

"Of course this system is ours," Big Voice said. "Of course." He floated away, muttering about the piles of computer equipment and speculating on their value. "Cridi, alone."

"His mind is clouded," Narrow Leg signed, sympathy on his old face. "Too much to understand at once."

"Most interesting body structure," Carialle said, as Keff looked around at the captives. When the brawn had his breath back again, he hauled himself to his feet. "It feels almost obscene to be able to examine living creatures this way."

"Yes, but it's the only way to study them without getting torn to ribbons," Keff said. "They're strong! Did you see how fast they were moving, even in this gravity? They'd be super-creatures on a Standard planet."

"But they're not natives of this one," Carialle said. "In spite of those magnificent wings they couldn't fly up to get at the Cridi on the ceiling."

"Terrible monsters," Tall Eyebrow signed. He had stayed by Keff as the human took detailed video of the griffins. "More than any in the game we play. Why much hate?"

"I don't know," Keff said. "But I don't think we'd get much of an answer out of them if you released them now."

"What fearsome beings," Long Hand signed, her eyes enormous. Small Spot, color returned to his face, nodded vigorously in agreement.

Narrow Leg rolled in close for a good look, and bumped against Keff's leg for attention. "These are the destroyers of spaceships?"

Keff shook his head. "Ones like them, perhaps. I have no idea if this crew have been around for fifty years."

"We should destroy them," Gap Tooth, one of Tad Pole's crew signed, his small face set. "Killers!"

"We can't do that," Keff said quickly.

"Why not?" Big Eyes demanded. "They killed some of *your* people. Their friends or ancestors killed ours. They die!"

"No!" Keff said. "We don't do things like that. I can't execute anyone. That's against my code of ethics, as well as my instructions."

"Why?" Narrow Leg said, but the question was not for Keff. "Ask them why."

"I can't," Keff said, raising his hands to show helplessness. "I don't speak their language. It would take time to learn theirs. We can't keep these beings like this. I'm frustrated, but any further action is out of my hands. It's up to my superiors to make a decision like this."

"Not our superiors," said Big Voice, catching Keff's sign out of the corner of his eye. "We are superiors."

"But you are under my instructions here," Keff said, signing with strong gestures. "It's always possible that we could be making a mistake. The matter deserves investigation."

All the Cridi broke out in protests. Narrow Leg held up his hands. "Let us be guided by those with experience in such matters. What should we do?"

"We'll disable their spaceship so they can't leave. That will make sure they're here for the CW inspection ships to find. We can search for armaments, and in the meantime, try to discover clues as to where they came from."

"I want to know more about them, too," Carialle said. "This is just an outpost. There is no superior intelligence directing operations from here. I want to hunt them back to their source, find the big fish. I have unanswered questions, too."

Keff repeated Carialle's words to the Cridi. "In the meantime, let's glean what we can from this site."

*CHAPTER TEN

"Move in closer to the face, Keff," Carialle instructed, as he walked slowly around the largest griffin. "I want a good look at that upper lip."

Keff did as he was told, with the Cridi in close attendance. They stayed huddled beside him as if in need of his protection. Keff found it ironic since it was their power that was keeping them safe at that moment. More ironically still, Core power was also keeping the griffins alive. The Cridi had made up their minds that the aliens must be condemned to death. Only through a lot of talking and pleading had Keff argued that one couldn't kill them while they were helplessly frozen in place. The mutterings for revenge abated somewhat. Keff was relieved. With luck, an inspection team could be dispatched quickly from a nearby station, to arrive within a few weeks. The matter needed to be investigated before the Cridi decided to take it upon themselves.

"Very interesting," Carialle said, as Keff shifted the camera eye upward. "I think that those apertures in the gumline are nostrils. Yes. On the infrared level I'm seeing warm gas expelled at regular intervals. Admirable dental sets. Whatever their species evolved eating, it fought back."

"It was nearly us," Keff said. "Docket everything and time-stamp it so we can send word home to Exploration. I don't want anyone else scooping us on the discovery." He walked up behind one being whose long tail was flung up over its back. The tip seemed to twitch, and Keff eyed it suspiciously.

"You are certain that they can't get loose?" he signed to Narrow Leg.

"Held perfectly," the old Cridi said. "Internal pulses may move, but not body."

"Can they see us?" Keff asked.

"Eighty percent probability yes."

"Very interesting," Carialle said, as Keff passed the video pickup around and under the creature's torso. "What beautiful musculature. Look at the evidence of a sophisticated circulatory system. I'm taking internal images to find out whether those organs and orifices around the backside and underside are generative or excretory in function, or a combination. If this was a Terran animal, I'd call it a hermaphrodite. All of this is an educated guess, so far. It's a pity we can't ask them."

"Maybe medical information is in the database," Keff said. "It's time we cracked it."

Tall Eyebrow stayed with Keff. The rest of the Cridi split up to explore the dome structure. Confirming Carialle's guess, they found no access to below-ground excavations, except for heating tunnels that vented to the surface on the ridge high above the domes. The Cridi, recovered from their adventure, were enjoying being the first of their race to explore a new world in fifty years. Keff heard the triumphant chirruping of their high voices echoing in the empty stone corridors. The two councillors, Big Eyes and Big Voice, documented the building and furnishings in their admirably minute shorthand.

Under the baleful auspice of gargoyle wings and fangs, Keff sat down on the sling before the blue-glowing computer screen. He followed Carialle's instructions to disconnect the I/O port for his universal translation device, and hooked it to the computer's small processing unit.

Carialle fidgeted nervously as Keff made the connection. She checked her data security systems over and over again, looking for potential leaks. She had no wish to allow an alien bug to run rampant through her memory banks. Surely the protections in her chips were sophisticated enough to circumvent any intrusions. Just in case, she added a further layer of noise-suppression between her own memory functions and the empty bay she had prepared.

"Ready?" Keff asked.

"Ready," she said.

"You're on-line, Lady Fair." He sat back in the sling, and she saw a flash of gauntlets as he crossed his arms.

Opening the peripheral to the alien computer, Carialle activated the Tambino's hard storage. She allowed first a trickle, then, when nothing bad happened, a flood of memory to upload.

"There's a lot of garbage," Carialle commented, watching bits of data pass or fail to pass through some of her screens. Bad bytes bounced away, disintegrating into sparkle. Now and again she saw a spray of them like a meteor shower when the crystal structure of the disk-matrix was violated. "They've been experimenting with that keyboard, but they didn't know how to purge bad files or compress over bad sectors. I'm dumping them."

"Wait," Keff said. "Keep them. I might get some linguistics clues out of them."

With a sigh, Carialle rescued the data and put it in a separate memory column. "All yours, Sir Knight, and on your own head be it." She began to see graphics and maps appearing in the datastream. "I think I've located the original astrogation program." The Central Worlds Exploration Service logo, as familiar to her as her own engrams, appeared again and again at the head of files. She ran comparisons with her own memory base at half her normal hyperspeed, to make certain she was processing all of the data carefully. Graphics of star systems blinked by rapidly on her optic and neural inputs, in tandem with the screens in her main cabin and in the griffins' control room. The square script that took the place of Standard notation was unreadable, but it was impossible to confuse the starmaps for anything other than what they were.

"Do any of them mean anything to you?" Keff asked. "Is this a record of their own people's exploration? Do they overlap with CW astrogation?"

"Yes, they do overlap," Carialle said, narrating absently as she checked her internal directories. She allowed various diagrams to linger in the tanks in turn long enough for her brawn's slower consciousness to register them. "Too much. *That's* an actual space station, and *that's* a colony system, and *that's* an asteroid belt with a mining center . . . all this stuff is in Central Worlds records. I can't believe in identical exploration patterns, even identical fly-bys of every single system. That would suggest there are thousands of these junk ships flitting all over the galaxy, unnoticed. This information must have been in the database when it was stolen. Hmm. Some of the files have been accessed recently. The Griffins must use it to look for targets, where they pick up their 'merchandise.'"

"The mining lasers they used on us," Keff said grimly, nodding. "They must have forced one of the early victims to show them how the computer system works. What about their own star system—where do *they* live? Does anything stand out? Can you pick out the one that doesn't belong?"

"Of a hundred billion systems? *I* don't keep full files from Exploration—naturally not. They wouldn't fit in my database, and if they did, it wouldn't leave me room for anything else. But I do have an index. It'll just take some time."

"Look at this," Carialle said, about an hour later. Keff stood up from where he'd been doing stretching exercises on the black stone floor and clambered back into the sling. The Cridi, having exhausted the curiosities of the dome, crowded around him. They ignored the griffins.

Carialle accessed Keff's monitor and put up three columns of entries. "All of these match exploration files I possess, but they date from around ten years ago. There's nothing newer, except for a couple of files I *don't* have," Carialle said, highlighting the entries. "I want to see the inside of that ship. Let's cross-reference these with the navicomp onboard. I have an itch in my diodes that says one of these is the lucky number."

"Well, let's spin the wheel and find out," Keff said, rising and laying a hand on the monitor in view of her camera eye. "Cari, does this setup control life support in any way?"

Carialle sent the tiniest filament of a feeler out of the protective shell she had made for herself, and threaded it down through Keff's cable, into the alien database. Beyond the wall, the power fed through a comprehensive filter from a horribly dirty source, probably a thermodynamic-based turbine. She shuddered and backed away from it. This computer had once controlled many other units' systems. The residue of Standard language programming still resided in the CPU, showing titles such as Galley, Engineering, Medical, and Electronic Mail: personal, crew. Carialle felt anger which she quickly extinguished. Retribution for the dead humans and Cridi would come in time, but not at her hands. She let the tendril explore the only other open door that existed in the memory unit, a roughly-hewn portal bristling with bad data. It led to an open communications node and the landing beacon. She guessed by the microseconds it took to reach it that the node lay hundreds of kilometers away on the planet's surface.

"No," she said at last. "Not that I can see. It's a database and ground control, but nothing else."

"Good," Keff said. "I won't kill these people, but I don't want them telling anyone we've been here." He turned to the Cridi, and made a twisting gesture with both hands.

The Cridi responded tentatively at first. Narrow Leg used his amulet to rip the cables from the wall, precipitating a shower of sparks. Tall Eyebrow tore apart the umbilicals joining the peripherals to the main unit with a delicate *pop! pop! pop!* The other Cridi watched. Big Voice, still suffering from shock, put out a tentative hand. He raised the screen a couple of meters in the air, and dropped it. The screen flickered slightly. He picked it up again, and dashed it to the ground, almost under the nose of one of the Griffins. The plastic smashed into particles on the stone floor. Big Voice floated above it, looking triumphant.

"There! There is for my near death!" he exclaimed, his shrill voice rising. "That for the ships who disappeared!" His unholy exultation roused the others. They tore apart the computer components with wrenching gestures, scattering pieces all over the room. Keff, Tall Eyebrow and Narrow Leg watched with dismay and astonishment as civilized engineers and statesmen wreaked destruction with wild eyes and flailing hands.

The outburst was over as quickly as it had begun, and the Cridi stood about in their globes amid the ruins of the computer, looking ashamed of themselves.

"Reaction," Narrow Leg said at last, his hands quivering just a little. "It was bound to come. We must leave before the temptation to further revenge becomes too strong."

Keff agreed. He shepherded the Cridi out of the ruined control room, and into the corridor. He heard no sound but the lonely boom of his own footsteps and the wheeze of the air compressors as he followed the Cridi toward the arboretum. In the corridor, the remaining four aliens who had not participated in the brawl were bunched just outside the door, arrested in the act of leaping forward. Keff felt a shudder. He had been frozen by Core power himself, and felt sympathy for the beasts even if they were killers. Although their faces didn't change, he sensed their reproach—and their anger.

"Let's do this quickly," he said, turning away. "I don't like leaving them like that."

In the arboretum, Keff pushed his way through the spiky, blue foliage to the front of the dome, and looked out. The gangway was still attached to the side of the damaged ship, leaving no gap to the outer atmosphere.

"How did you get in here?" he asked Tall Eyebrow.

The globe-frog pantomimed through the side of his traveling sphere the raising and lowering of a curtain, a door, and another curtain. To demonstrate, he rolled across the glossy floor to the edge of the flexible airlock. Without touching the controls, the Cridi raised the heavy bumper and vanished underneath. Keff heard a faint peeping sound inside. The others floated or rolled after him.

"Aren't you going to raise it enough for me?" he asked through his helmet mike.

"Too thick stiff," Tall Eyebrow's voice said in Standard over Keff's helmet radio, with polite regret.

Shrugging, Keff dropped to his knees, and crawled under the lip. As soon as he was through, the bumper thudded down. Surrounded by round obstructions that caromed into his knees, Keff rose to his feet and used his suit light to find the controls. He hit the framed bar. The great door rose. The Cridi scooted through in a party, with the brawn striding along behind. Keff waited, holding his breath, until the second curtain lifted. Before them, the tube extended out toward a distant light. What illumination there was ran in faint parallel lines along the ceiling. Keff listened, heard nothing, then let himself exhale.

"It *feels* like I'm in a suspense drama," he told Carialle.

"Think of it as another M&L game," she said. "I read no live bodies in the ship. Unless they're capable of telekinesis like the Cridi, they can't trigger any traps on you. Go slow, and I'll look for peculiar chemical or heat traces. Aim the video pickup toward anything suspicious."

The Cridi abandoned any attempt to paddle their globes up the flexible walkway, and levitated a meter above the floor. Big Voice jockeyed his way into point position.

"I shall be the first to go in," he signed, with a self-important cheep over his shoulder at Keff.

"All right," Keff said, with Carialle's reassurance in mind. He caught Big Voice's eye, and signed. "You're an observant man, er, frog. You look out for danger."

The pompous councillor's eyes widened, and he shot back to the group.

"Danger is for humans to detect," he said emphatically. Keff bowed, concealing the grin that poked out both sides of his mouth.

The tube swayed with every step Keff took. The jerking movement made him cough, and he remembered how it felt to take that deep breath of alien atmosphere. Nervously, he checked the right side of his helmet seal every so often to make certain it remained closed.

A clear panel protected the same kind of two-bar control on the spaceship's side. As Keff raised his hand to it, the panel slid away. He punched the top button and waited. Obediently, the hatch slid upward, revealing a plain, square airlock. Keff gasped in recognition.

"This ship is definitely salvage," he said. "I know where the model came from. It's human-made, and half a century old." He felt along the wall with a gloved hand, looking for the small screwplate that should have been just inside the hatchway, but his fingertips found only a couple of small holes where the rivets had been pried out.

"They must have constructed the whole ship part by part," Carialle said, critically. "The controls appear to be retrofitted, but this airlock came off a much larger vessel."

"Appropriate, since they're larger beings," Keff said. Once he and the Cridi were inside, he looked around, turning his body so Carialle could see everything. The airlock closed, pressurized, and released the group into the main cabin of the ship. Keff showed the camera eye the shabby walls, the meager assortment of furniture.

"They haven't redecorated recently," Carialle said.

"No doubt about it, though," Keff said. "They've been shopping at Central Worlds carryout. We're on to something that the CenCom will want to know all about."

The inside of the ship was spartan. Everything was intended for function, with no concession to aesthetics. The slings and benches in the main cabin were worn, and the impact webbing attached to them sported patches in many places. Wall panels, cobbled together from a dozen ships, showed cracks and crazing where the enamel wasn't simply chipped away. Everything Keff saw was old. Even the mismatched floor panels showed worn and dented surfaces. The Cridi emitted small cheeps of interest. Keff let out a low whistle.

"What a lot of junk," he said. "Where's the up-to-date machinery as we saw in the domes?"

"Status?" Carialle guessed. "This ship might be far down the pecking order and gets what's left after the seniors take their pick. Or merely lack of opportunity. Pirates can't maraud through the rich part of space without people noticing, and we'd *know* if anyone reported rapacious griffins."

"Ours is so much nicer," Narrow Leg signed, with pride, gesturing around at the ship. "This lacks continuity. Could not be safe."

"He's right," Carialle said. "I don't know how this thing flies without blowing up. It was leaking high-rad like the proverbial sieve while it was chasing me."

"How quiet it is in here," Keff said, glancing around. The Cridi huddled in a corner, signing to one another. No sound except the burbling and occasional mechanical crunching of machinery broke the silence. "I'd better make sure the griffins didn't leave us any armed surprises."

Two broad doors were set into the walls, one in the wall to Keff's left, leading forward, and the other directly opposite. He signed to the others to wait, and went to the aft door. It opened onto a corridor, narrow only by griffin standards. Tall Eyebrow signed a quick question at him. Keff shook his head.

"I want to take a look before I let anyone else roam around," he said. "It might be dangerous." The Cridi signalled assent, and stayed close together near the airlock.

The rear section was divided into cargo and sleeping quarters. The bunkroom—for it was clearly that—contained more of the divan pillows, plus a few small possessions enclosed in nets on hooks on the walls. Loops of webbing attached to the hull sported frayed fibers.

"Looks like the artificial gravity goes out all the time," Keff commented to Carialle. He fingered one of the bundles, identifying a scarf, some ornamental jewelry, and a soft, fuzzy object that he guessed was a child's toy, almost worn out with love.

"Homey, isn't it?" Carialle said tinnily in his ear. "You'd never guess that these were bloodthirsty pirates, who murder and rob with such efficiency. It took them only hours to strip the DSC-902." Keff shuddered and backed away. Suddenly, the small bundle seemed macabre to him.

The sanitation room bore no resemblance to the one that had been yanked from a CW cargo liner. The facilities were altered to accomodate griffin parts, and the shower had once been two units, welded together. To Keff's surprise, the chamber was spotless. Even the corners had been scrubbed out ruthlessly. He pointed to a residue filling one of the cracks in the enamel.

"Soap," Carialle said, after a moment's analysis. "Or as near as makes never-mind."

"It's all so old," Keff said. "It still strikes me a trifle pathetic."

He went through to the cargo bay. It was full of straps and mounts hanging at all angles from the bulkheads. Keff recognized the configuration. It was used for securing odd-shaped and delicate cargo. He felt naked shock when he saw that some of the artifacts bound into the shockfoam cradles were of recent CW manufacture. He recognized life support equipment, booster engine parts, even coils upon coils of communication cable. One of the containers lashed into place bore the logo of the DSC-902. Something inside him twisted into a solid knot.

"Pathetic?" Carialle said.

"You're right," Keff said, fighting words past the lump. He was angry, and surprised at the intensity of the emotion. "They're not worth my sympathy. I have work to do."

He searched through the cargo area, yanking open bulkhead cabinets, then went back to the dormitory, and poked through every bundle, every drawer and niche. At last, he tried turning over the bed pillows. His gloves slipped on the furry surface, but he seized a fold of the cloth, and wrenched upward. They were remarkably heavy, and he found himself sitting on the floor next to the third one, panting.

"Keff!" Carialle shouted in his ear. Her voice sounded alarmed. "What are you doing?" The brawn glanced up, as if suddenly aware of his surroundings.

"I'm . . . looking around," he said, but he knew his voice didn't sound convincing, and Carialle, from nearly sixteen years of experience, wasn't convinced.

"You're looking for something of mine, aren't you?" she asked, her voice soft. "You want to find proof positive that these are my salvagers."

"Well, yes," he admitted, feeling sheepish. He got to his feet and looked down at the sad, lumpy bedding. He kicked it with a toe.

"Sir Knight, you're my best friend and the finest protector a lady could wish for," she said firmly, "but the frogs are waiting, and it would be cruel to leave those aliens playing statue for much longer, even if they are killers. Let's finish up and get out of here."

"But what if there's something here?"

"Someone else will find it, not us," she said firmly. "My gut-level, as much as I feel anything down there, is that we've seen all there is on this ship. Remember that these might not be the same ones."

"I'd hate to think that there were two bunches of pirates roving around out there," Keff said, but he turned and went back to the main cabin.

"Coincidences have occured before," Carialle said, but now Keff wasn't convinced. "In any case, these are the foot soldiers. I want the top bird."

"What is it *you* want to do?" Keff asked, but he already knew. It was what he wanted as well.

"I want to find their home system," she said. "I have to know what kind of culture fosters a history of mass piracy."

"Right you are, my lady," Keff said, then paused. "You know, Diplomacy and Maxwell-Corey ordered us home. That message they sent with the ship said to relinquish the mission and return."

"Bugger that for a game of soldiers, to quote you," Carialle said at once. "They just want me back under their eye so they can prove me mad. Everything changed when the griffins attacked the DSC-902. Their orders no longer apply. I need to follow this lead up, so I can show them the truth once and for all."

"But if these aren't the ones?" Keff asked.

"Then I'll know. But I'll never find out if we go back. The IG will slap me into protective custody, another highfalutin name for mental confinement. I'll never be satisfied with a remote report. I have to know. I *have* to. In the meantime, we're in pursuit of piratical perpetrators." The P's popped explosively in his ear. "Are you with me?"

"Always and for ever," Keff said. Resolutely, he strode back to the main cabin. With the Cridi in tow, he went into the fore corridor that led to the bridge.

The computer system was substantially like the one in the dome. All parts were of human manufacture. Some showed hard wear, especially the input peripherals. The navicomp, an ancient model of the kind used by vacuum miners, had been augmented by several different and mutually exclusive hard-memory storage units.

"This group knows how to program," Carialle said. "I wonder why a race with the capability to get into space doesn't build its own equipment?"

"Why buy the cow when you can get the milk?" Keff sat down on the sling with Cridi hovering on both sides. "Ready?" he asked Carialle.

"Ready."

He hooked into the information transfer port, and waited anxiously, with one hand on either side of the small screen, staring into its depths, while Carialle sifted the contents of the hard-storage. He could only sense fleeting impressions of individual star system maps as she read the memory and copied it into protected database.

"We have a match." Her voice sounded triumphant. "Three star systems, put in relatively recently."

"What are they?" Keff said, as the graphics appeared in the 2-D display.

"No can tell, Sir Knight. They're in an alien typography. The keyboard must have been altered to create their symbols. There are sixty-eight. Your first clue to their language. Enjoy."

Keff groaned. "Do you mean this is a dead end?"

"Not at all." There was a long pause, and the stars spun by again, accompanied by colored screens full of square letters. "The flight recorder shows that two of them have been visited more than once. And you'll never guess where one of them is!"

"I give up."

"Right next door. The binary mate, PLE-329-JK6—straight across the lowermost boundary of P-sector. I followed the visual log entries, and I could identify half of the visuals from my personal memory."

"That's incredible!" Keff exclaimed, then paused. "No, that's logical. Why else would they go to so much trouble to prevent a lot of traffic in this part of the galaxy?"

"My thinking exactly," Carialle said. "So that's where we go. We try it first, and if it's wrong, we go on to the next one. One of these has to be home base."

"Right. We try them one by one," Keff said.

Tall Eyebrow and Narrow Leg had been watching Keff curiously, hearing half the conversation. Keff looked at them guiltily. He'd forgotten that he was not alone, and his companions were intelligent. And motivated.

"Where to go next? This map?" the Cridi captain asked, pointing at the screen with a long finger.

"You should all go home now," Keff said. "I thank you for your help and support, but I can't ask you to do any more."

"But we would do much more," Narrow Leg signed, his old eyes wise in the wrinkled, green face. "You have done much for us, opening the way. Together, we defeated. You seek a voyage to unknown, to find truth. We wish also. We go with you."

"But your own people need you for defense," Keff said. "It's one thing to have you accompany us in your own system, and quite another to subject you to unknown danger. Your ship is not prepared for a long space voyage. You . . . with respect, you lack training."

"Give us training, then," Narrow Leg said. "We need also to find this truth. Many lives were lost—ships, years, lost also. I want explanations. If you say they are not to be found here, then we go to where they are."

"I will train them," Tall Eyebrow said, tapping himself on the chest. "To survive—I know this."

"Ship is ready interstellar travel," Narrow Leg said, with a throwaway gesture. "All supplies were loaded on board at departure. As for defense, half my crew are assembling two more ships from old ones and new parts. Cridi will be defended in atmosphere and out of atmosphere."

Keff shook his head at the old male's expansive signs.

"Captain, it'll take a long time to reach our destination, and we may not even find what we're looking for at this first stop. It could, no, it *will* be dangerous. I can't let you . . . er, take such important conclave councillors as Big Voice."

Narrow Leg didn't miss the subtlety. He rolled a beady black eye at Keff. "That fat one will be all right. There is no time to waste. We must not divert back to Cridi. You must be after the villains track to source."

"We come, too," Tall Eyebrow said, sweeping his hands to include his two companions and Big Eyes.

"Yes," Big Eyes agreed, with a brilliant glance at him. "We follow Tall Eyebrow. Experienced twice in space."

"Cari? We have to pursue this to the end, but they don't."

"I'm torn," Carialle said. "We could use the backup. It won't come from CW for ages, even providing they know where we are going, which they do not, and we're not armed. The Cridi want to be our allies. On the other hand, I don't like it that they're entirely without experience. Particularly, I do not like flying interplanetary distances with a possibly explosive emotional problem."

"Big Voice?" Keff asked sublingually, without moving his lips.

"He's the only one who's manifested openly so far. Who knows if any of the others will destabilize during a long trip."

Tall Eyebrow had not missed Keff's eye passing from Cridi to Cridi. "I vouch for each," he said in Standard. "They will not fail."

"I think you'd better ask them," Keff said, both in Standard and sign. Tall Eyebrow looked a question at Narrow Leg, who raised his thin shoulders eloquently and let them drop. Big Eyes made a tentative sign, then glanced at Keff. He heard a faint peep as one of the engineers spoke through the amulet link.

"Privacy," Carialle said.

"Right you are," Keff said. He turned his back on them and studied the navigation tank. After a brief conference, punctuated by shrill exclamations and much rolling about the deck, Keff felt a tap against his leg. He looked down at Tall Eyebrow.

"It is decided. We will come with you." He looked at the other seven Cridi. "We are all willing to go. The crew also." Big Voice, at the front of the group nodded vigorously, and favored Keff with a humanlike smile.

"I wish to come. Otherwise this one," he pointed to Narrow Leg, "blames me for spoiling virgin ship flight."

"You will be acclaimed hero, once home," Big Eyes squeaked, with mischief in her eyes. Big Voice relaxed back in his globe, a happy expression on his face. "All will recognize . . . ."

"No," Tall Eyebrow said, stopping her with a downward stroke of his hand. He turned to Keff. "Not for that reason. He will go because he recognizes his fear and uncertainty, as we all do. No one goes just to prevent us from turning back."

"I am selfish," Big Eyes said, her exuberance dimmed slightly by shame. She covered her eyes with her hands, then peeped coyly between her fingers at Keff. She was so cute he couldn't help but smile.

"I go," Big Voice insisted. "Who else will see you do right? Also, I must meet the leaders of"—here he hooked his long thumbs together and spread his hands in imitation of wings—"griffins." I wish to know *why* they hate us. I must ask. We will . . . negotiate." He paused before the last sign and glanced at Narrow Leg as if defying him to laugh. "You must teach us what we do not know." Keff smiled down at him. At last he understood why the plump amphibioid was one of the eight most important frogs on Cridi.

"Thank you," he said. "It'll be good to have you along."

"And we will teach you the joys of Myths and Legends," Tall Eyebrow squeaked happily.

As soon as Keff had disconnected from the ship computer's I/O port, the Cridi destroyed the unit with the same thoroughness that they had the one in the dome. Keff examined the rest of the control board and indicated the communication set and guidance system. Tall Eyebrow delicately disassembled those, taking care to leave life support intact. The lights dimmed briefly, but came up again with a steady glow. At a nod from Narrow Leg, the ship's engineer and two of the crew went aft ahead of the rest of the group. Keff heard clashing and breaking sounds. When the three Cridi rejoined the others in the ship's main cabin, they bore between them a Core unit. It was old, and looked to be in bad shape.

"I'd forgotten about that," Keff said. Narrow Leg looked grim.

"We, never," the commander said. "And this ship will not rise again. We have destroyed the engine. Let us leave now."

Free to use Core power, the Cridi swept their globes and Keff high over the dusty landscape, back toward the small valley where the ships lay hidden. Unwilling to look straight down, Keff turned his gaze back over his shoulder toward the dome, watching it until it vanished among the battered ridges. He signed a question to Narrow Leg.

"What about the griffins?"

"We can hold them all as long as need," the old Cridi replied.

"Good. Release them when we leave orbit," Keff said. "I think we're safe, but I want to make sure."

Narrow Leg sketched a quick OK with his long fingers.

"I want you to hear this, Keff," Carialle said. "I'm shipping this off to the CenCom, and it's the last word they're going to hear from us until we find 'Griffin Central.'"

"You sound so serious, Lady Fair," Keff said. He smiled at the frogs who glanced over when they noticed the movement of his head.

"Never more in my life, but this is plain mutiny. I won't send it unless you give me your all-clear. I want to live to report to the Inspector General. If there's the least chance, I will show him who was crawling over my skin twenty years ago, and that he's been harassing me for nothing, but I refuse to endanger *you*. All I need is a single piece of my first ship for proof or an eyewitness, and if it's anywhere, it's in one of those three systems. Recording:

"'This is the CK-963,'" her voice said, sharp and metallic in intonation in his ear. "'We wish to confirm absolutely that the DSC-902 was the victim of a fatal attack by alien forces. Three ships, carrying stolen Cridi artifacts and CW mining lasers, ambushed the DSC-902 while on its way into this system for a purely peaceful mission. All the crew are dead. Ten of the perpetrators have been marooned on the fifth planet from the Cridi sun. Video accompanying this message will show that this is a life-form with which Central Worlds is unfamiliar. We are following information received, to what we believe to be the aliens' homeworld at once. Coordinates for three potential systems are in the visual portion of this message. We will transmit again with further information when we have reached our final destination. Carialle out.' What do you think?"

"Send it, lady," Keff said, firmly. "I'll be aboard in five minutes."

✨CHAPTER ELEVEN

As if the paralysis had never been, movement returned to the ten Thelerie. Those who had been poised for battle, fell over, and those whose eyes had been frozen open, blinked. No one spoke for a moment. Everyone exercised their muscles, and simply enjoyed the freedom. Then they took heed of their surroundings. The mess was heartbreaking.

"I do not understand, Autumn," Crescent Moon blurted out, pieces of the precious computer clutched in all four of his hands. "Why did the human destroy our equipment? I've done my best to keep this station exactly as the Manual directs. It was neat, it was clean—and now, look!" The ground control commander sounded as near to trilling as a child. "Was he angry with our performance?"

Autumn still kept her eyes closed, waiting for tear fluid to wash away the dust from her large, flat corneas. "You do not understand, Crescent. There are other humans than the Melange. You have never seen them. You showed aptitude for the computer, so it was the wisdom of the Melange that you went here before spending any time reiving. It is a shame."

"It was the wisdom of the Melange," Crescent said, defiantly. The other station crew all dipped their heads and wings in a worshipful manner. "But this human did behave strangely."

Rivulet shook his head. "He did not even speak properly. His hands moved often, but not his mouth. He wasn't like those from whom we receive goods, nor like those for whom we provide."

"I think he is a captive of the Slime," Dawn piped up in his high, musical voice. "He is under their spell. They've directed the Slime Ball," he pronounced the human phrase most carefully, "to alter his mind. You know the power the Ball has. We do not know all its secrets."

"Yes!" Rivulet agreed, holding out a claw. "See how he cowered from us, when he should know we are his to command."

"We are not slaves of Humans," one protested.

"No, no, but they give us all gifts in exchange for our aid," Captain Autumn said, pausing to consider. She lifted a wing claw. "This human needs rescue. My eyes were turned toward the screens when I froze under the monsters' power. I saw which maps he looked at. He wishes to go to Thelerie. Though he could not speak, his signs grew more frantic when he saw that chart. He can receive aid there, and be freed of the Slime. He was trying to tell us."

"Ah!" The soft voices chorused together for a moment as the Thelerie realized the truth in the leader's words.

"We should warn the others the Slime are heading toward the Center," Rivulet insisted.

"How?" Autumn asked. "The Slime tore our communicator to bits." A wing swept over the shattered console. "I am sure they treated our poor ship the same." She turned to Dawn. "See how things stand. Send a message to the Melange if you can."

The second flicked a claw at the rest of the crew. They dragged on their shipsuits and pattered out into the corridor after him. Autumn began to pick up the broken pieces with all her hands. Crescent and the other three ground crew bent to help. Though distressing, the debris was finite. In a short time, the wreckage was all cleared away.

"I feel better," Crescent said, sitting down on his haunches and blowing a puff of air so his upper lip vibrated. "Now I do not feel as though I broke the trust."

Autumn smiled, showing her fangs. Crescent was a simple soul at heart. Once a problem was out of sight, it was gone. "There is wisdom in hard work."

She donned her shipsuit and went out to her craft. Dawn sat amidst the pieces of the control panel, shaking his great head from side to side. The captain looked down at him.

"How bad, my friend?"

"Perhaps the human stayed the Slime's fury," the lieutenant said. "The communication deck is destroyed, but the filtration systems are intact."

Autumn felt the breath leave her body. "We cannot warn the Center in time. The Slime will be ahead of us."

"Very far, I'm afraid," Dawn said, his large eyes worried. "The engine is ruined, but it was in Stage Four breakdown anyway. The landing finished it off."

"The engine?" For the first time Autumn's expression brightened. "Ah." She wheeled on her haunches and trotted down the corridor toward the cargo compartment.

With pleasure she surveyed the secured racks of parts from the CW ship. She was proud that her crew had responded so quickly with the others when the call came from Phyllis that there was a second invader, after the slim ship had escaped them into the atmosphere of the Slime planet. This large ship moved more slowly than the first, so it was easy for the reivers to get into position at the system's perimeter.

As in the three examples in the Manual, the large ship did all the things an enemy would. It signalled them, ordered them to halt, and invoked the authority of the Central Worlds. Verje Bisman, and after him his child, Aldon Bisman, had from the earliest days, reminded the Thelerie that Central Worlds was the enemy. The See-Double-Yew comprised a few planets who stockpiled goods taken from decent beings and refused to allow access to them, even in great need. That was anathema to the Melange, who insisted that all people who could pay, in one coin or another, should have entitlement to all goods. That seemed right and proper.

The Melange had taken goods from this aggressor, to distribute or keep as need dictated. The prize under their feet would have fetched a good price, but Autumn needed it herself now.

At her direction, Dawn and the others knelt to take up the floor plates. Their muscles swelled under their hides as they pulled the heavy metal panels aside to uncover the biggest cargo cradle of all.

Nestled in it a piece of machinery—an engine, a prize, a work of mechanical art. Autumn regarded it with affection and awe. The Central Worlds ship must have been nearly new. Inspection seals etched on the finest metal film were still affixed in the correct places on the engine's surface. The whole unit gleamed. With a claw-finger, Autumn traced the inscription on the largest piece of film: Dee-Ess-See-Nine-Oh-Too.

"Install it in place of our old one. It will give us greater speed and stability for our journey back to Thelerie."

Heartbeat, the youngest of them all, tilted her head up toward her captain, eyes full of despair.

"But the navigation system was destroyed by the Slime."

Autumn tapped the youngster with a wing-finger. "Have you no faith in your own soul? Center. Find your way back to the Center. It may take us many days to reach home, but we shall survive. I regret that we cannot warn Mirina in time. We can only hope she hears the messages we sent when the ship first entered the system."

"Damn that ship," Rivulet said. "I wish they will be lost in the Void forever."

"But it was beautiful, wasn't it?" Heartbeat said, looking at the others with rapture shining from her eyes. "So new." Her hands fumbled on the smooth sides of the engine. "So perfect."

Autumn smiled indulgently. "Someday, such ships will be ours, too. In the meantime, we must tend what we have. Work carefully. Remember all your lessons from the Manual." Heartbeat ducked her head shyly.

Dawn began to sing quietly under his breath. Autumn recognized the anthem: "Thelerie, Heart of the Galaxy." She picked up the melody, her strong baritone joining with his. The others added their voices, their lips spreading with smiles of inner joy. Autumn leaned back on her mighty haunches to help lift the engine. The music helped give the six strength. With a deep breath and a hoist, the unit was out of the cradle and onto the deck.

Sacred orders from the humans dictated that the drive mountings should be made adjustable to take any component that offered itself, though lesser manuals Autumn had seen did not allow for such open tolerances. Their Humans were wiser than those who wrote the books. Hoses, connections, control cables—all were snapped or fastened or sealed into place in very little time. Autumn, taking only a moment to stand back and approve her crew's handiwork, directed the crew into the ship. She guided Heartbeat to the navigator's chair. Dawn took his place in the pilot's sling and engaged the engine. Its soft purr surprised them all. It was so mild, yet so powerful, compared to the old one.

"The Wisdom of the Melange," Dawn said, settling his wings on his back with a satisfied twitch.

"They are wise," Autumn agreed, and turned to Heartbeat. "Now, center, child, *center*. Make the wise ones proud of you."

The youngster bent her attention on the tank full of stars before her. Autumn stood back to watch, half proud and half sad.

They would mourn their lost ones on the way home.

"Cold, damned rock," snarled Bisman from behind the pilot's chair, as the ship swung into an orbit around Coltera. "Why in the hope of paradise would anyone spend more than a minute here?"

"Because it's theirs," Zonzalo Don said, with a surprised look at the leader. "That's what this girl I met said."

"Don't knock the place too hard in front of the inhabitants," Mirina said, turning up a palm in appeal. "I don't want them to kick our base off planet."

"Sacred, high lady," Bisman sneered sarcastically, making her wince, "I was born here. I flew with my father around *those moons* when I was a tot. We brought them their first replacement compressors. Don't tell me how to behave with them."

"I apologize," she said, staring him levelly in the eyes. She was stung, but damned if she'd show it. "I know. The nag was automatic. We have few friends in any part of the galaxy. It's important to me that we keep them, especially if they're kin." The raider straightened up, surprised at Mirina's easy surrender.

"Hell, yes, it's important, Miri," Bisman said, slowly, sounding more reasonable than Mirina had heard him in ages. "That's just sense. And you don't insult 'em if you want 'em to buy what you've got. Loyalty goes only so far. But, spacedust, they'd take what's in our hold if we called their mothers mudworms!" He laughed, and slapped Zonzalo on the shoulder. "Get Leader Fontrose on the line, kiddo. Tell him who we are and what we've got. Then call Twilight and tell her we're coming in for refueling."

"Aye, sir," the youth said, with a humorous glance at his sister.

"Fuel pods, radio-ac insulation, enviro-suits—I smell *profit*," Bisman said, rubbing his hands together in pleasurable anticipation.

"So do I," Mirina said. For a moment they forgot the pressures of the past, and hard times, and smiled at one another the way they used to. It didn't last. In an instant, Bisman reverted back to his normal, harsh self. Mirina hugged herself against imagined cold as the older man turned away with brisk efficiency to the board.

She felt eyes on her. When she glanced up, the young Thelerie, Sunset, was turning his head quickly back to his control board. Mirina had seen sympathy on his face. She walked over and patted him on the wing joint.

"You've got a kind heart, youngster," she said quietly. "And you do good work. Keep it up."

He looked up at her, his huge eyes glowing with worship. "Thank you, Mirina."

"Which way's your homeworld?" she asked.

Sunset put up a wing-finger at once, directed aft and to starboard, tracking Thelerie upward as the ship he rode in transited an orbit around the planetoid. His natural gift was a comfort to her, something constant to hold onto in their chancy travels. She wished she could do that: point to her home, no matter how distant it was. She wished she had a home to point to. The ship on which she had been born was scrapped and recycled before she started primary education. Sunset looked at her with a soft, mournful expression, and Mirina realized she'd let her feelings show on her face. She slapped the Thelerie on the shoulder in unconscious imitation of Bisman.

"Thanks, youngster," she said, then nodded to Zonzalo when he signalled her that the communication link was open.

"Greetings, leader!" she said, pulling a bright face for the screentank. "Will you be glad we visited you today!"

Aldon Bisman kicked the ground and spat. Muddy yellow-brown pebbles scattered against the crates of unimaginably precious air-recirculation valves. Mirina was annoyed, but she contained herself.

"What do you mean, seven thousand apiece?" Bisman said to Mirchu Fontrose, a thin, short, sallow-faced man. "What's this character think he's playing at?"

"All we can afford, Aldon, my old friend," Fontrose said, mournfully. "Unless you'd consider extending us further credit. You know we're good for it."

Mirina folded her arms and watched her partner's face. She was tempted to tell the colony leader to fold his offer into a point of singularity and put it in his eye, but this was Bisman's home, and his show.

"Crap," Bisman said, levelly. "They're worth ten. I know that if I sell them to you at seven, you'll be out of orbit the second we're gone. You'll take them to the bazaar on Phait and sell them yourself for that. I could have done that myself, and you'd be stuck paying eleven or worse to the traders. Ten."

Fontrose and the colonists on Coltera were prone to what Mirina's mother called "poor-mouthing." Even though their gem-mining brought in a good credit, they always made believe they were on the edge of starvation. Nothing could have been a greater lie. Opals, especially ones of the clarity and depth of color that they coaxed out of that impossibly dense matrix, were always in demand, however illicit the market. Coltera wasn't an official CW colony. The independent miners who discovered the strike had checked ownership of this small and marginal world. They hid the signs of success and squatted, staking a homesteading claim through the housing office, as if only one family lived here, registered as subsistence wheat farmers. Ridiculous, Mirina thought, since there was no soil. In the meantime, the opals began to appear on the gray market, traded for fabulous profits that were split up among the whole of the colony. The irony of it all was that the family registered with CenCom government received a subsidy for earning below the poverty level.

A lot of independent thinkers had elected to "disappear" and end up here, falling off the CW tax records much as she and the raiders had. When one didn't pay tax, one had money for a lot of things. Like pressure units.

She glanced around the cul-de-sac at the raised mound that surrounded them on each side. Behind every one of those door-ways was a domicile, half a mansion in size. Their mining equipment, state of the art for extracting delicate opal, was so new the enamel wasn't scratched. Mirina caught a glimpse of their shabby, red ship standing among the rock loaders, and was sufficiently irritated into speaking.

"The price goes up while you stall," she said, tapping her foot, deliberately sounding unreasonable. "When it goes up to twelve, we leave."

Fontrose cringed away from her. "All right, all right. Don't rush me. Don't rush me. That's a lot of money, you know. I suppose you came by it honestly, eh?" He peered from one face to another. Bisman quirked one side of his mouth.

"Salvage," he said simply, flipping a hand up toward space. "Found it out there, somewhere. You know." Fontrose raised his hands in surrender.

"All right, all right, I won't ask."

"Eleven," Mirina said warningly.

"Wait! Wait!" Fontrose turned to her, alarmed. "Please, dear lady, don't raise things until we've had a chance to talk about your first offer. Now, I thought eight and a half . . . ."

A long-legged figure stumbled down the steps of the raiders' ship and ran toward them headlong. Mirina recognized Zonzalo, and wondered why he was so agitated. She stopped him with a fierce glance when he was still half a dozen meters from the group. He gestured with his hands and eyebrows, trying to signal urgency. He stopped waving at her when Fontrose turned to glance at him, but started his semaphoring again as soon as he looked away. Bisman shot her a look of annoyance.

"Go back, Zon," she said at last. "Check and see how they're coming with those containers."

"Miri!" came a choked squawk from Zonzalo. Fontrose swiveled to stare openly. Bisman looked exasperated. Mirina smiled at Fontrose, dangerously, but politely.

"Excuse me just one moment. A matter of crew discipline."

The colony leader nodded, and Bisman took the distraction as an opportunity to move in to close the sale.

"Now, while she's gone, my old friend, let's get the price to where we both like it."

"What is it?" Mirina hissed. Her younger brother was hopping up and down with nerves. "How dare you interrupt a negotiation?"

"It's dire! Twilight's been holding a message for us from Autumn on Base Eight. They've been attacked by a Central Worlds ship. They need help."

"What are we supposed to do about it?" Mirina asked, annoyed. "We're too bloody far away to do anything now. That message will be weeks old!"

"We ought to go and check out Autumn's report," the boy insisted.

"Check out what? If Autumn got word out, then someone was alive to operate the communications board."

"What the hell is going on?" Bisman asked, coming up between them.

"Base Eight's had a run-in with CW ships," Zonzalo said, wide-eyed.

"So what?"

"So, it's been discovered by the authorities," the boy said. "We have to help them."

"Zon, this is not a vid-show. We're ages away from there. Autumn will just have to abandon the place," Mirina said. "She's a survivor. She'll get the rest of the crews out of there."

"Too bad about Base Eight," Bisman said, scratching his unshaven chin. "It lasted a long time. My dad established that one when I was a boy. I spent time there myself."

"But CW might find the Slime," Zonzalo said. "They'll talk."

"Who cares? They don't know who we are," Bisman said, impatient to get back to the negotiations. "Besides, they stopped kicking a long time ago. One ship is no big deal. They'll come, they'll go. In the meantime, we can go back and mine the skies around Planet Two with impact grenades, to make sure no one gets offworld, no matter how many visitors they get from CenCom." His eyes grew dreamy. "Maybe a blanket bombardment, keep kicking them until the whole planet blows up. Always wanted to see how much that Slime Ball defense system could take."

"Stop it, damn you," Mirina said, interrupting. She never knew whether his *enfant terrible* mode was an act or not. "We'll just abandon the base. The Slime don't know where we are or where we went. Zon, send word to Phyllis and Autumn and the others to destroy the equipment, and evacuate. There's no need to cause further loss of life."

Bisman turned on her, one finger thrust upward under her chin, eyes flashing dangerously. "Enough of that, brawn. I'm tired of it. You lost one friend, one brain. I've seen hundreds of friends, family, even lovers die over the thirty years I've been out here. You're here where *my people* live. Do you want to know how many holes there are in my family?"

"I know," Mirina said, staring him straight back in the eye. "You've told me again and again."

"And I know. Charles this. Charles that." His scorn pummeled her, and she gaped at him. He shoved his face close to hers, backing her out of the negotiation circle until she was trapped between him and somebody's front door. "I don't care any more! You don't like death, huh? You don't want to see anyone else die. *It blunts your edge*, woman. You should be able to kill to protect yourself. Why should just one death affect you *so much*?"

"Because I thought he could never die," she shouted, feeling her heart constrict and squeeze the words out of her. Bisman backed away, and Mirina caught her breath. Her eyes stung and she knew she was blinking back tears. Sensing a personal matter, Fontrose had turned delicately away, but he couldn't avoid having heard her. Bisman and Zonzalo stared. Mirina glared back defiantly. She had admitted the truth to herself at last, the secret she'd been keeping locked away for eight years. She felt like screaming some more, but she kept control. Her voice stayed level and low. "Because no one ever understood how much I love being in space. How I *have* to be there. He felt the same way."

"Well, you couldn't sleep with him, couldn't even touch him. What the hell good was he as a partner?"

Bisman spat at the ground, and Mirina hated him. As she looked laser bolts at his back, the co-leader went back to Fontrose, who had moved away. Mirina shook her head, willing her rage to subside. You could *not* explain the brain/brawn relationship to someone who hadn't experienced it. No one else could understand. Bisman never had shown notable signs of sensitivity. She was a fool to expect it.

She turned to Zonzalo. He had stayed alongside them to make sure she was all right, but also a few paces away, well out of the line of verbal fire between his sister and her partner. He fidgeted anxiously, and nodded his head with a slight, hopeful smile. Mirina smiled back, but her eyes were serious.

"We abandon the Slime system, Zon. The Slime don't have a clue who's been out there on Planet Five all those years. We've never left any live captives, so they can't tell Central Worlds authority what we look like. There's not much left on the base. I regret leaving the computer system behind, but it's anonymous. No Standard files anywhere. It's all in Thelerie."

Zonzalo's mouth stretched in a slow smile. "So when CW finds it, they won't be able to read it anyway. Pretty good, Madam Don."

"I didn't do it to please you," she snapped. "I did it so the

Thelerie could use it more easily in emergencies. I hope they can get out."

"Soft in the head, dammit," Bisman said, coming back. He looked pleased with himself. He brandished a plastic card in his hand: the agreement struck with Fontrose, thumbprinted and secured. "Ten. What did I tell you? We'll have to do something about that infiltrator, if it's still hanging around Base Eight space when we're back there. We'll strike hard, and strike fast. One ship shouldn't be so hard to beat, not with our advantage, the Slime Ball."

"I'm not convinced that unit will be of help for much longer," Mirina said, uneasily. It had been getting steadily weaker over the last couple of years. It needed to be fixed, and none of them had the remotest idea how it worked. Only blind chance had led his engineers to discover what it was all those years ago when they took it off the Slime ship. Only sheerest coincidence had allowed them to install the three Balls in reiver ships and gotten them to work without blowing up. Bisman relied too heavily on it, and that concerned Mirina. Their operation shouldn't turn on a single piece of equipment. She'd said so for years.

"It'll be fine. You worry too much," Bisman said, flicking the card between his fingertips.

Zonzalo tried to add a touch of optimism. "We'll probably hear an update from Autumn as we head back in that direction. Another message is probably on its way now. I'm sure they destroyed that ship. It was only one, and we have three on that base."

"Right," said Bisman, grabbing Mirina's arm and leading the way toward the ship. "In the meantime, we've got a delivery for the Thelerie. Don't you like being thought of as a goddess? Bringing aid from the heavens to bring wings to the winged?"

Mirina lay in a bunk in the guest cave and listened to the echoes far down the hall. Bisman and his old cronies had decided to make a night of it in the settlement, and dragged Zonzalo and Sunset along for fun. No matter how hard she pressed to keep the youngsters on the ship, Bisman countered her every argument. He couldn't see any good reason for sequestering them on his home planet. At least he didn't insist on taking them off on strange ports. Mirina was responsible for Zonzalo, and she felt responsible for Sunset. He was the most gormless, innocent creature she'd ever shipped with, even more so than any other Thelerie. He hadn't a guileful cell in his body, and he took everything his precious

humans said as the mathematical truth. Stars knew what a less moral band of humans might have done with him.

Moral, hah!

It had been eight years since she'd shipped on with Bisman. Eight, long, damned years. When she had paired with Charles on the CM-702, she'd only kept in touch in a sporadic fashion with Zonzalo. She was sorry now. She should have been more of an influence in his upbringing, taking more of the role of their deceased parents, instead of trusting it to boarding school counselors. But brainships were on almost constant duty in Exploration. Mirina couldn't get free just to mediate a grades dispute or a behavior violation for her brother. Sometimes she didn't even hear about problems until months after they had occured. She'd failed in her parenting, and that still bothered her.

Not long after Charles died she got a message that Zonzalo had left school and fallen in with Bisman. She hadn't liked the sound of the man at all. Anyone with charm and perseverance could gain influence over her poor, silly, gullible brother, who was still looking for a strong role model to fashion himself after. In this case it could get him killed. Zonzalo hinted deliciously of danger and secret raids accomplished in a fast scout ship. Mirina knew she'd have to go and get her brother away from that crowd. He was the only family she had.

With the reputation of jinx riding her, Mirina couldn't get anyone to help her ship out to find him, nor even get a full hearing on the subject. The authorities paid little attention to a troubled woman babbling about a distant brother and malign influences. The counseling they had given her after Charles' death was inadequate, as if her emotional recovery was of secondary importance to the enormous catastrophe of the death of a brainship. It seemed that no one cared at all about her. She resented that her supervisor in Exploration hadn't intervened more closely in getting her another berth—any berth—when it would have done wonders for her sanity, not to mention her patriotism. Mirina felt that Central Worlds had let her down at every single opportunity. Refusing to untangle the red tape to help her find Zonzalo was the last crumb that upset the scale. Never mind that she thought her brother was in the hands of pirates, and CW might be able to solve robberies in that sector. The official budget wasn't set up to handle "free-lance" missions, her boss had said. Then he'd mined her file with false complaints of

insubordination, so when she went over his head for help, no one would listen to her. She left, cursing Central Worlds and all bureaucracy. Now and forever more, she was on her own.

It took every last credit she had to charter a scout craft to Zonzalo's last known location. Lucky thing it was a base the pirates used all the time. She hadn't intended to stay once she had rescued her brother, but face-to-face, the pirates were a truly pathetic lot. Their equipment was a hundred years outdated, but even bad equipment will work if maintained. Their diet was so unbalanced that crew members were going down sick with fragile-bone disease and scurvy, even the ones who weighed 160 kilos. Mirina needed so badly to be needed that when Zonzalo and a younger, much handsomer Aldon Bisman pressed her to stay, she did. Central Worlds had rejected her, but these people wanted her. They'd pay her anything she asked, just to stay. At the time the offer was hard to resist.

It took two years before she had them whipped into a kind of military order that preserved resources and actually allowed them to build their network outward. She was a good organizer, but for eight years now, it seemed, she'd operated on autopilot. She found it harder every day to break away. The activity kept her from thinking too hard about where she had come from, about Charles, and the horrifying accident that killed him, and what she was doing.

At long last Mirina was thinking again. She needed to take Zonzalo and leave, cease aiding and abetting criminals. She had become one herself. Little niggles and twinges from her conscience told her that she still owed something to Central Worlds. Even after all the wrong CW had done her, she'd never have met Charles and shipped with him if it wasn't for the brainship program. He had been the single most wonderful thing in her life. An old-fashioned but worldly gentleman, Charles himself would have said it was Mirina's duty to turn herself and the others in, and he'd be right. She shouldn't be here. Not that she ought to try and return to the brain/brawn program: she couldn't. She couldn't even go back to the Central Worlds and try to fit into the mainstream. No job would be safe for her. The authorities undoubtedly had a criminal file on her that would cover a small continent, and she would rather die of torture than be locked up groundside. The Don family would have to ship out on their own, skipping from remote outpost to remote outpost forever. Again the sensation of desperate lack of belonging rose out of her belly and clutched her throat until she gasped, sobbing. Mirina sat up in bed and braced herself, elbows akimbo with hands on her knees, just breathing. She was doing good here, too—she was! The work they had done with the Thelerie was benevolent and worthwhile. Look at the advances the winged ones had made in only a few years! She hated to leave that, but she needed to go away and take Zonzalo with her.

A good organizer knows how to organize. She lay back on her bunk, and began to take stock of her assets.

✨CHAPTER TWELVE

The Cridi were green, in every way. They were inexperienced, scared witless, and, well, physically resembled the chorus line for a production of the comedy musical *Frogs In Space*. Keff's natural exuberance and energy were proving to be just shy of what it took to buoy up an entire crew of aliens through their first experience of long-term space travel. Every day brought new anxieties and fears that just proved how quickly a space-going race can forget how it once adapted. He fell into bed at night, completely exhausted.

Things were slightly better now that they had passed the half-way point. Their passage around the trapped magnetic Oort debris, pooled at the balance point between the Cridi system and its sister sun, when all of Carialle's sensors had gone briefly insane, had caused hysteria among the Cridi. It had taken all Keff's tact and patience to keep the other ship's crew from mutinying against Narrow Leg and diving through the anomaly—fatally—back toward their homeworld. Carialle's suggestion, voiced at thunderous volume over all speakers, that both systems must be of identical galactic mass and weight to hold this particular configuration, lured some of the scientists out of their emotional shells to study the phenomenon of twin systems. Narrow Leg and Tall Eyebrow rallied everyone into the project. Keff spent plenty of time answering questions and supplying telemetry scans for their use. An intelligent people, they understood that to occupy their minds fully would help defy the dark. Yet, bogeys crept back nightly, leaving Keff to buoy their hearts up again in the morning.

As he staggered out into the main cabin at the beginning of his shift, in the middle of the second week in space, he glimpsed Cridi from the corner of his eye in half a dozen screens, all staring. They relaxed perceptibly when they saw him. Keff deliberately met each pair of eyes in turn, smiling with confidence. They must have been up since the dot of first shift, waiting for him to appear. Tall Eyebrow, Small Spot, Long Hand, and Big Eyes were in the corner of the cabin near the food synthesizer, the only ones who didn't look nervous.

"I'm not used to this much company," Keff growled under his breath to Carialle. "We've had too many years alone, just the two of us."

"It won't last forever," the brain reminded him, speaking through his aural implant, the lone communication signal that they kept as a private channel. All the others had been left on open broadcast to the Cridi ship so the amphibioids could monitor what was going on, Carialle was also tapped into the frequencies of both functioning Cores. She kept her frog image on the wall of the CK-963 and on one screen of the Cridi ship in case they needed to ask questions while Keff was busy or asleep. "We're doing a public service for them, and they're out to help us with our mission."

"But they're still so scared," Keff said, frustrated.

"They'll get over it once there's something to do."

"I hope so," Keff said. He sat down at the control console, and let out a huge yawn. "They're wearing me out." On the screen over it, two of Narrow Leg's crew stared out. He smiled at them.

"Hello, Gap Tooth and Wide Foot."

"Good mor-ning," they chorused in Standard, faltering only a little over the dipthong.

"That's very good," Keff said, nodding encouragingly. "Have you been studying the drama videos I sent so you could practice listening to colloquial speech?"

"Have," the first one said, then fell back on a combination of sign and numeric squeak. "Interesting, times two—times three! Terror, fire, exciting! N is greater than zero tongue trill sounds. Why?"

Keff stared, baffled. "What do you mean? Which tape were you watching?"

The other Cridi, Wide Foot, held up a card and pronounced the title with great care as she followed the words with a finger. "*Gone With The Wind*," she said, and turned puzzled eyes to him.

"Oh!" Keff smiled, enlightened. "It's a dialect. Trill sounds were sometimes replaced with aspirates in some regional speech patterns on Old Earth."

"Sounds soft," she said, and gave him a timid smile in return. "I like to he-ah such speech. I may adopt it."

"Oh, wonderful," Carialle said, much amused. "A frog with an American Southern accent."

"I think it adds character," Keff said. "I encourage you to experiment," he told Wide Foot.

"I shall."

As Tall Eyebrow and his companions had already proved, the Cridi were rapid learners. They absorbed the *Standard As a Second Language* videos that Carialle dredged out of her memory, and were speaking a form of pidgin by the end of the first week. Keff's own grasp of the Cridi spoken language was increasing every day as a result of answering so many questions. Having no residue of the tongue in his memory, Keff was finding it slower going than the three Ozranians did. Tall Eyebrow was now participating fully in discussions with his long-lost cousins.

Keff was also accumulating a considerable amount of data for the paper he was beginning to write on the evolution of the Cridi languages from a thousand years ago up to the present day.

Language instruction was only part of the program that he, Carialle, Narrow Leg, and Tall Eyebrow had worked out to keep the Cridi sane and functioning throughout the voyage. It also included cultural exchange, elementary space travel, survival techniques, and of course, lessons in how to play Myths and Legends. The new Cridi were about evenly split so far on whether or not they liked the concept of the game, but all agreed it helped to pass the time. Cridi video screens weren't sophisticated enough to produce the quality of holographic images Carialle projected, so they didn't see the same charm in it as the travelers aboard the CK-963. All the Cridi loved her three-D puzzles, which did translate reasonably well.

Carialle also shared the extensive onboard collection of entertainment tapes. Because of the language barrier, she gave them mostly music. The Cridi adored symphonies, folk music, stage musicals, operetta, plainchant, and whatever else she could winkle out of the nooks and crannies of her memory. During one communication period they sang an improvised cantata in the human fashion for her. The shrill quality of their voices sent Keff to his knees with his hands over his ears, but Carialle was touched.

"Only a little in return for all your kindness," Big Eyes had said. "With your help, we are learning not to be afraid of the journey— though all of us wonder what we will find at the end."

Since the Cridi ship ran easily using the remote control manipulation of Core amulets, the crew was able to pursue many activities in the long, empty stretches of space. Narrow Leg had set up a process to manufacture more travel globes. He used the ones Tall Eyebrow had lent them to explore the fifth planet as models, and now the native Cridi had a supply of their own, with plenty of backup units. Tall Eyebrow insisted that part of each day be devoted to learning to use the clear shells, and part for an exercise program to build up the muscles needed to manipulate them easily on a variety of terrains. Though he was aboard the brainship, he monitored exercise periods in both groups of Cridi. He was showing the kind of leadership that had impressed Keff back on the griffins' outpost.

There had been a certain amount of bickering before they'd left the fifth planet over who would travel in which ship. Keff invited any of the Cridi to fly with him and Carialle who wished to, and inadvertantly started a three-tongued argument. Narrow Leg insisted that there was room in his ship for all the Cridi. Tall Eyebrow claimed pride of place with the Central Worlds pair. Big Eyes wanted to travel with Tall Eyebrow. Narrow Leg demanded that his daughter stay with him. Big Voice couldn't decide which one he wanted to travel on, and demanded a vote of confidence. They appealed to Keff to mediate. While on the surface, all Keff's statements had to pass through Tall Eyebrow's globe-pickup. From there, they were translated into the subtleties of the spoken language over the amulet link to the Cridi, and through sign language to Small Spot and Long Hand. It was a lengthy process, sometimes frustrating, sometimes amusing. In the end, Keff had excused himself and let the Cridi battle it out among themselves.

The brainship wound up with only four guests: the original Ozran contingent, plus Big Eyes, who shared the second spare bunk with Long Hand. Narrow Leg wasn't happy having his daughter miles away across the cold void, but he had plenty of responsibilities to keep him occupied. This morning, Keff could see the Cridi commander over the shoulder of one of the crew who was plastered to a viewscreen. Narrow Leg was having one of his daily arguments with Big Voice, this time over the travel globes. The stout councillor stood, arms folded, in the bottom half of his globe. He was up to his knees in water, but still trying to maintain his dignity.

"Why do we do without our amulets?" Big Voice said, in sign and squeak. "I do not like these bubbles. Why must we learn to use them? Technology is so far beyond this already!" Tall Eyebrow automatically turned to translate for Keff in Standard voice and Ozranian sign. Keff sat down, keeping one eye on the screen and one eye on TE. He understood most of this argument. It was an old one.

"Because the ammonia in the atmosphere could burn your skin, and there's not enough oxygen to sustain you, and you may have other things to think of there than breathing," Narrow Leg said, every gesture filled with impatience. "Because the engines of our host ships have only so much energy, most of which must be saved to launch us back home, not to be used by the Core. I have told you before. And again."

Tall Eyebrow relayed the answer, and added, "He does not like discomfort. I would give him a mild sample touch of the gas, to show him what he will not believe."

"It would sting," Keff said, "but you could be right. Prove one point, and he might begin to take your word on others."

"I will suggest it to Narrow Leg when we can speak alone," Tall Eyebrow said. "But I have another notion. Big Voice," he called, interrupting the argument. The councillor used a flick of power to swivel, and stood facing him.

"What?" The impatient question came through loud and clear over both Core frequency and speaker.

"You do not have to learn to use the globe," Tall Eyebrow said, standing up and stretching to the maximum of his great height.

"I do not?" Big Voice asked, with a shrill squeak that went up almost above human hearing.

"Not at all," the Ozranian leader said. "You shall gather information for us. You shall remain safe in the ship at all times while the rest of us make our exploration. We will report back to you what we find."

Big Voice stared and spluttered. "That is not correct! Think of my position. I am a high official of the conclave! I should be in the first rank."

Tall Eyebrow shrugged his thin shoulders, a gesture borrowed from Keff. "If you cannot use a globe, you cannot precede us. The atmosphere is undoubtedly too dangerous. We would not put you in peril of your life. You are, as you say, a high official."

The councillor's eyes narrowed.

"I shall practice," Big Voice said. He glanced at Narrow Leg, whose eyes were wide with amusement. "But only so I may take my rightful place."

Casually, not hurrying at all, Big Voice twisted his hand and curled his fingers. The upper half of his globe lifted, inverted, and fitted itself onto the lower half. Big Voice crouched inside it and resolutely placed his hands on the inside wall. Narrow Leg retreated a few steps as the councillor drove his globe directly at him, heading out into the corridor and away from the video screen.

Tall Eyebrow turned away, chuckling, and rejoined the others. "Every step of the way he fights," he said. "He makes me earn my place."

"You do very well," Keff told him. "I think you're quite a leader. I'd be proud to follow you myself."

Carialle's deep, musical laugh filled the room, and Keff glanced over at her image on the wall. "You should hear him. He's cursing to himself that TE might make him miss out on any of the adventure. In between grunts, that is."

"I am afraid," Big Eyes said, and made a gesture of shame. "I was all excited for adventure; now, prudence."

"It is wise to be afraid, but do not let it paralyze you," Tall Eyebrow signed firmly. He put an arm around her. "You have a healthy body and sharp wits, and the strength of the Core is ours. I may not be a military leader, but I can at least show you how to survive. In terrible conditions we manufactured the globes with which your cousins survive on Sky Clear. You have done that, too. You can learn more. Together we can do better. We can prosper." The young female looked hopeful, encouraging the male to smile. "You teach me more verbal language, I tell you of survival. We exchange as we go."

"Bravo, TE," Carialle whispered over the mastoid implant to Keff.

Big Eyes was obviously impressed, by the way she gazed at Tall

Eyebrow— and other Cridi were listening. Clearly they were nodding wisely to one another, they found encouragement in the Ozranian leader's words.

"I hope you teach me more than that," the female said at last, with a coy look up under her eyelids. Tall Eyebrow looked pleased and a little flustered.

"They don't need us at all," Keff murmured.

In spite of the discomfort of diminished privacy, Keff found the enforced closeness provided him with wonderful opportunities to observe unique sociological interaction. Once the Cridi began to relax, they reverted to their normal personalities.

Tall Eyebrow and the other two Ozranians were also affected by the lack of privacy. TE seemed torn between his desire to spend every waking moment with Big Eyes, and his need to get away by himself for a while.

"It is too crowded," he had said wistfully to Keff in an unguarded moment. Keff sympathized.

Wisely, the young female perceived that not everyone had grown up in a household crowded with dozens of children and other relatives, and left TE several times a day to do other things. She made friends with Long Hand, too. From the occasional eavesdrop, Keff discovered that Big Eyes was asking about life on Ozran. The facts were hard for someone brought up amid plenty and water, but to her credit, the Cridi councillor didn't blanch. She and the elder female also had numerous close conversations in the corner of the large cabin, glancing at the screens showing the Cridi in the other ship and giggling behind their palms. Big Eyes seemed to enjoy Long Hand's sardonic sense of humor.

Some funny moments were universally shared. Big Voice had appointed himself Communications Officer. He solicited messages every day from both ships, and spent about an hour broadcasting back towards Cridi. The transmissions were more amusing than useful. Carialle brought in the frequency so she and Keff could enjoy the pompous administrator practicing self-aggrandizement before the video pickup. Tall Eyebrow and the others watched with interest the first two days. Thereafter they turned off the sound and made rude signs among themselves. Big Voice's tenth transmission made especially good comedy.

"Further advancement has been made. I have observed constellations as mapped by our ancestors in their star charts. I am pleased to let the Council and the constituency of Cridi know that those charts are accurate!"

"Oh, no!" Big Eyes signed merrily, waving her hands at the 3-D image. "Get away."

"I am pleased that he has allowed the poor navigators to trust those maps that have been in place for a thousand years," Long Hand gestured, with a sly look in her eyes.

"Important message from our ship commander, Narrow Leg," Big Voice continued, picking up a minute square of white. "We have approached and passed halfway point of journey, and expect to arrive at our destination soon. This is confirmed by our human companions, Keff and Carialle"—he made the sign of the 'Watcher Within the Walls'—"We are grateful for their input, since they confirm what it is that we learn."

"That's not exactly what you said," Keff said to Carialle. "You told Narrow Leg where we are, and he checked it." Her frog image on the wall made much the same throwing-away gesture that Big Eyes had.

"Let him tell their press whatever he wants," she said. "If it will help public relations, I don't care what he says. Do you think any of them kept listening past the first five minutes?"

"I doubt it," Keff said, sitting down with a thump on the bench of his Rotoflex exercise machine at a good remove from Big Voice's screen. "I don't know why Narrow Leg lets him blather on like that."

The commander, whose face was visible on the screen nearest Keff's bench, must have heard his last remark.

"It serves to unite," the old one said, his wrinkled, pistachio-colored face creasing in a friendly grimace. "It does him no harm, because others have too much tact to tell him he is silly."

"Aren't you afraid all that nonsense will begin to pall? You don't want the folks back home to lose interest in what you're doing because he"—Keff tilted his head toward the main screen—"bores them to death."

Narrow Leg shook his head. "He is too shrewd to allow himself to be boring. And he is not. Every day he finds a new way to make himself ridiculous. It does not matter what the media say, so long as they say something with one's name in it. That is what Big Voice thinks. Most importantly, it keeps our minds off what we are doing. If allowed to brood, I think my folk would go mad. That is why I like your games and puzzles and lessons."

"Thank you," Carialle said. "I wish you'd say that to our administration. They think we are already mad for playing games on long flights."

"I shall," the old one said, with a courtly nod, "at the first available opportunity. How is our progress?"

"Very good," Carialle said. "I was right that the gravity well between the twin systems would destroy the ion trail where it passed closest, but now that we're past it, I'm seeing plenty. I'm also getting traces of low-power radio transmissions from the twin system."

The old one cocked his head to one side and looked pleased. "The fourth planet, yes?"

"Yes. With your people's extensive history of space travel I'm surprised you never explored in the system closest to your own, in spite of the gravity well."

"We did," Narrow Leg said, the pixels in his image updating in waves as he swiveled toward his own computer. "We knew of civilization. Our explorers had images of artifacts, buildings— perhaps houses. Large. See here, now." He waved a hand, and the image that was in front of him superimposed itself on the communication screen between him and Keff. In the Cridi format the view was hard to make out, but on the sides of a rocky, steep gorge, the brawn could make out structures that were clearly artificial.

"Well, I'll be damned," he said, his eyebrows creeping upward into his hairline. "Then why didn't your people ever land there?"

"Already inhabited," the Cridi captain said simply, returning to the screen. "We wished planets for colonization, so we did not pay attention to ones with intelligent life. It was remiss of us," he added grimly. "We should have."

Carialle's frog image looked thoughtful. "Why didn't you make contact with them? They're your nearest neighbors."

Narrow Leg shook his head. "Crude. Too primitive. We knew they were too far behind us to share civilization. Someday, we thought."

Keff snorted. "Well, it looks like they evolved in a hurry."

"If they're our pirates," Carialle said, warningly. "We might just be following the gang from base to base. Narrow Leg, I'd like to copy your data and send it with ours to the CenCom when we transmit next."

"My honor," the captain said, bowing.

"Just a moment!" Big Voice came up behind the commander. While the three of them had been chatting, the councillor had finished his daily tirade. Clearly he had overheard or overseen the last exchange. "I wish to send such a message to your Central Committee. Today!"

"You can't," Keff said, quickly. He glanced at Carialle's frog image, which spread its big mouth in dismay. He knew they shared the same thought. They didn't want to alert the CenCom just yet that they were flying a joint mission with the Cridi. They had already disobeyed a direct order to return. The next time they made contact with CW there'd be a hue and cry out after them, so they'd better have the proof they needed in hand.

Big Voice looked upset. "Why not? You have communication frequencies as we do."

Carialle's frog image suddenly filled the screens. "Honored councillor," she said, waiting while the IT program filtered her Standard speech into Cridi voice-language, "it would confuse matters for our diplomats. Keff and I are the only members of the Central Worlds with a working knowledge of your language. There is no translator in the CenCom who would be able to appreciate your most important words."

"Ah, I see," Big Voice said, leaning back with his long, spidery hands propped proudly on his chest. "Naturally not. I must wait until I may see them face-to-face—which I hope will not be long."

"No," Keff said. "It'll be as soon as we can make it."

Big Voice left, looking very satisfied.

"Well handled," Narrow Leg signed to them, with very small motions obscured from the rest of the room.

Carialle's hand signs were equally discreet. "We have our bores, too."

A soft sound woke Keff in his cabin. He opened his eyes to the darkness.

"Yes? Who's there?"

"Keff?" Carialle's voice came very softly from his aural implant. "Come on forward. I'm getting clearer transmissions from Planet Four. I think you want to hear these."

Keff pulled on a pair of exercise pants and padded out into the cabin. A soft hum, the sound of the frogs breathing, came from behind the closed room across the corridor. Carialle illuminated a faint line of blue along the wall to guide him. He slid into his chair.

"We just came into range where I could pick up those faint radio signals intact. I think it's telephone conversations, words and pictures."

"Really?" Keff asked, interested enough to wake up almost all the way. "And are they the griffins?"

"See for yourself."

"Paydirt!" Keff exclaimed in an excited hiss. He glanced over his shoulder to see if the Cridi had heard him. He turned back for another good look.

In the tank in front of him, a long, narrow image took shape. The being pictured was indeed a griffin. It was younger and slighter than any of the brutes the team had left behind in the Cridi system. It put the tips of its wing-claws together under its chin in a sort of namaste, then let the wings flip around to its back.

"Freihur," it said, the slit upper lip opening and closing breathily. "Solahiaforn. Zsihivonachaella." A burst of static broke up the picture, and it reformed around the speaker saying, " . . . Volpachur."

"You're right," Keff said. "It does sound like half a telephone conversation. I'm surprised you haven't picked up any mass communication channels."

"Maybe they don't have any," Carialle said. "But isn't this better?"

"A thousand times," Keff said, feeling for the keypad to activate IT. The server controlling the translation program beeped softly to tell him it was operating. "I might be able to separate out some appropriate phrases between now and our arrival. Starting with 'hello,' if that's what that first word meant. 'Freihur,'" he said, trying it out with a trill of his tongue. "How close are we?"

"About five days," Carialle said. " . . . Keff, I feel uneasy."

He felt a twinge of anxiety for her, and gazed at her pillar as if it might give him some clue how to help her. "I know how much of a strain this is on you, personally. You know I'm for you, all the way. I simply don't know how much I can help, if we run into—into anybody."

Carialle sighed. "I don't know how *I'll* react. But thank you for your support. This is the best way to lay my personal demons."

"You're right," Keff said, settling himself more comfortably in front of the screen. "And with this I now stand a better chance of cooperation. This is what I was wishing for after the Cridi froze those griffins. How bad is the gain? Can you get me some more?"

"Cued up and waiting for you, Sir Knight," Carialle said, feeling better in the face of Keff's enthusiasm.

At the beginning of day shift, Carialle watched the Cridi on the other ship reacting with surprise to seeing Keff already up before them. Narrow Leg immediately intuited that something important was afoot.

"What is new?" he asked, in Standard, making his way to the screen nearest the console.

"Good morning, captain," Keff said, still staring at the griffin on the screen, a delicate, sable-furred one with a chip on its front left fang. He swiveled toward the screen. "Language lessons."

"The beasts!" Narrow Leg exclaimed, his hands flying.

"We're close enough to pick up their low-power transmissions," Carialle said, forwarding receiver data to the Cridi technical operator. "I think it's a tower-based, amplitude-modulated system."

"Indeed? The monsters have come far," the Cridi captain said. "No electronics were reported many years past."

"How long?" Keff asked. "My own species went from wood stoves to satellite technology in the same generation."

The Cridi opened his large mouth wide, then closed it. "I have forgotten that progress moves tenfold, and tenfold again. It is long since my people discovered non-motor engines."

"Mine, too," Keff said. "It looks like these people made their leap much more recently."

"Have done so without morals," the Cridi said, almost dismissively. "We shall have much to say to them on that subject."

Keff held up his hands. "Slow down a little, Narrow Leg. I've barely learned how to say 'Greetings,' in their language. It is going to take time."

"We shall help you," Narrow Leg said, resolutely. "It is better to work on a project that will advance our understanding than spend time playing puzzles." He shot an impatient glance at his crew, who were now involved in an interactive game with the brainship.

"I'll take care of that," Carialle said cheerfully. She reached into her peripherals for her game function and clicked it off. Screens all over the Cridi ship went blank, and she heard outraged peeps.

Disappointed crew members, suddenly noticing that their captain's eye was upon them, immediately tried to look busy.

"I'll tight-beam them all the linguistic data we have so far," she said.

"Think of it as a new kind of game," Keff said, more lightly than he felt. "We're stalking the wild syntax in its lair."

"No. It is rather another weapon in our hand," the Cridi captain said. "This is the confirmation we have sought, after all: that the marauders are here. That is where retribution begins."

"No!" Carialle interrupted him, with a touch of alarm. "Captain, we are investigating this system to gather information, not start an interstellar war. We're not armed."

"No, you are not, but we are."

"With respect, Captain, we must—and will—stand between you and the griffins if you start a conflict."

"Even though yours have also died at their hands." The old male made it a statement instead of a question.

Keff gulped, the memory of the dead on the asteroid clear in his mind. "That only makes what we have to do that much harder, Narrow Leg. That is the unhappy part of diplomacy."

"In the end such an outcome can only be a tragedy," Narrow Leg said, with a sudden expression of sympathy. "I shall not be the one to sacrifice our friendship. We will help you."

The radio transmissions from the griffin homeworld were primitive and infrequent, but as the two ships neared it, Carialle had no trouble capturing and translating the broadcasts into pictures and sound.

The files they'd gotten from the pirate base computer were put to one side. To Keff and IT those had been no help at all. The overlay of narration in musical horn-call on the astrogation file was unreliable as a point of comparison between the two languages. Where Central Worlds had long commentary on a particular system, there might be a single phrase or two of description in griffin. On a star-chart dismissed by the CW astrogators in four sentences as unimportant, Keff listened to a three-minute horn solo that sounded beautiful, but meant nothing to IT. He couldn't separate the language into words. Here and there, a word in the griffin speech sounded like the CW name for a system: "Farkash," for "Barkus," and so on. The difference was due to the griffin facial physiognomy. Keff wondered what had happened to the human computer operator who had told them how to use the system and pronounced some of the names for them.

In the live transmissions from the planet, Keff saw the creatures speaking in colloquial dialect. After several hours of listening to tape after tape, he was delighted to begin to discern patterns. Each of the messages began with the same word or words of greeting: "Freihur." Keff had his "hello."

"This is my Rosetta stone," he told Tall Eyebrow, with a flourish. "This is the way we can begin to understand the language."

The Frog Prince's eyes shone. He and Big Eyes sat with Keff while he was trying to make some sense out of the griffin tapes during that first day. They imitated the phrases they heard, only two or three octaves higher, flutes playing alongside trombones and trumpets. Keff thought they had reasonably good ears, but it was only music to them. They still lacked any concept of meaning. The Cridi were better at concrete, spatial concepts, rather than abstract, but they retained perfectly what he told them. IT began to pick out sentence patterns, even separating word roots where they were repeated in different combinations. Carialle now had thousands of "telephone conversations" from which Keff could work. He was steadily gleaning vocabulary, where the caller occasionally showed an object to his or her callee. None of it was much help; he doubted he'd have occasion to refer to plants, babies, mixing bowls, or necklaces in a diplomatic conversation, but the use of noun and pronoun patterns was useful. Some of the extra memory that the CW had thoughtfully provided Carialle for the diplomatic mission was coming in very handy. They'd have to see what they could do about keeping it when they returned to base.

Keff stayed at the console, still working on the language question when the Cridi went off for baths and bed. He half-listened to the excited chirps of conversation coming from the spare cabin as the frogs discussed the day's discovery. Soon, the noise died away, and he glimpsed the light go out just before the cabin door slid shut.

He was concerned about what he would find when they made orbit, or landed on the griffin homeworld. Would they have to run for their lives? Were they blundering blindly into a trap? And how would the Cridi react? It would be the end of his and Carialle's careers if they deliberately put the elements together for an interstellar conflict.

And he was concerned about Carialle's state of mind. Their duties as hosts and teachers had taken up much of the personal time they usually spent together. For the first time in years he couldn't guess what she was thinking.

Her determination to pursue the hunt had led her to concentrate most of her attention on it. Her theory that the griffin ship was transiting frequently between the Cridi system and the one next door was borne out by the discovery of the wispy threads of many ion trails. They were delicate, hard to see, and remarkably easy to overshoot. Carialle did a lot of backtracking when the thin traces broke and drifted away where they'd been disturbed by anomalies such as ion storms or comets. Picking up the aud/vid broadcasts and confirming that they were heading for the griffin stronghold should have made her relax, but she seemed more concentrated than ever. Multiplexing astrogation, running the ship, playing M&L with the Cridi, maintaining lines of communication and acting as data librarian pulled her attention in a dozen directions at once. Keff worried that in the midst of it all she was thinking too hard about what lay ahead. What if this turned out to be another dry hole in her search for the beings that once threatened her life and sanity? Where would they go next? The team was risking censure and worse by CenCom, and Maxwell-Corey in particular, by ignoring their orders, and yet they couldn't stay off-line forever. Sooner or later they had to communicate, no matter what that brought in return. True, circumstances had changed a routine mission into an emergency, but would the IG see it that way? M-C already doubted the soundness of Carialle's emotions, enough to jeopardize his own position by rigging her with a telltale missile.

Keff felt his face grow hot, and realized he was still just as mad about M-C's impossible gall as he had been when the message probe had launched. He stood up from the console, commanding IT to save his last hour's progress. Then, he plunked himself down on his exercise bench and started pulling on the weight bars until he began to breathe in rhythm. Soon, the resentment was driven out by the simple beat of the weights clapping together. The tension melted away, replaced by the honest warmth of a good workout. Eyes closed, he smiled at the ceiling.

"Penny for them," Carialle's voice said.

He opened his eyes, but continued to haul on the pulleys. "I was just thinking we haven't talked in a long time. Just the two of us."

"I've been missing that, too," she said, regretfully. "It takes a lot out of a girl, playing hostess nonstop."

"Same here," Keff said, giving one last massive flex of his shoulders that took all the tension out of the part of his back between the scapulae, and let the weights down gently. "Just now I'm tempted to agree with the IG's assessment that we're nuts."

"Still doubt we're doing the right thing?"

"I wonder," Keff said. He stood up and reached for a towel slung over the back of the Rotoflex. "These people trust us enough to accompany them into the great unknown on their very first space-flight, with their very first working ship after being grounded for fifty years. So many things could go wrong!"

"But they haven't, Sir Keff," Carialle said, manifesting her Lady Fair image on the wall. It was outlined in white. Keff smiled at her, feeling as if he was meeting an old and beloved friend again after a long, lonely separation. It occured to him, with characteristic wry humor that it had been a long time since he'd seen a flesh-and-blood woman, either. Time enough for that at mission's end. "Don't overanticipate, my dear friend. I'm not, I promise you. Don't worry about specifics. Just keep on your toes."

"Stand and deliver!" a man's baritone voice barked from beside him. Keff jumped to one side, putting the weight bench between himself and the rude looking villain in a tunic standing in a torchlit doorway. The man was leveling a fearsome sword at his throat. Keff grinned ferociously and edged toward his laser epee, slung handily across the back of one of the crash couches. He realized Carialle had created the aural effect by activating only his left ear implant. The villain paced him with his swordpoint, his black brows lowered over narrow eyes.

"Clever, lady," Keff said. With a quick lift and slide, he unsheathed his sword, and assumed the *en garde* position.

"Put 'em up," she said, in the enemy's deep voice. "We both need a good game, just you and me."

"Right," Keff said, tipping the glowing red point of his blade toward the man's face, and circling it slowly. "Shall we duel with, or without conversation?"

"Oh, with," Carialle said, making the man's image grin ferally. "With, of course."

✴CHAPTER THIRTEEN

The audio channels were full of excited chirping as Carialle and the Cridi ship shifted into orbit over the griffin homeworld.

"We are here!" Tall Eyebrow exclaimed with delight from the crash couch where he was strapped in with Big Eyes. "We have succeeded in reaching this place, all together and with no mishap."

Keff watched as on-screen the clouds parted gently beneath them to reveal a vast and mountainous continent, wedge-shaped, strung from north to south like a harp with silver rivers. On the horizon ahead, a small silver moon rose. Carialle hurtled onward until it passed overhead, and set behind them. A second, larger moon followed, and vanished in turn. A blue ocean swam up, flashed green islands at them, and was replaced by another continent, long and narrow, also mountainous. Keff could see lines of smoke from active volcanoes. Another ocean glided by, this one wider than the first, then the harp reappeared, much closer and larger. Cities showed up in the folds of the mountains, very near the peaks. On extreme magnification, Carialle saw small craft flying, then realized she was seeing griffins on the wing. She showed Keff and the Cridi, who cheeped and peeped over the marvel.

Keff, listening as Carialle monitored active broadcast frequencies for a homing signal, caught Big Voice giving a live play-by-play of the new planet for the benefit of listeners on his homeworld.

"Eleven to the sixth power inhabitants, five oceans, two major continents, but many archipelagoes. Signs are humidity equals point-one atmosphere," Big Voice stated, with great emphasis on the statistics. "It will be uncomfortably dry and hot, but the landing party is prepared for eventualities."

Keff grinned and turned to catch the eyes of the Cridi flying with him.

"Always," Big Eyes said, exasperation evident on her small face. She waved her hands in derisive gesture.

Long Hand watched Carialle's telemetry indicators. "So dry," she said. "It is like Ozran. Some in the other ship will never have experienced such conditions."

"Well, you'll be in water globes," Keff said. "That is, after I make contact and establish parley conditions. I don't want you appearing until I'm sure no one is going to attack us."

"Huh," Small Spot grunted, and raised his hand to show the gleaming finger stalls. "I do not fear. We have the Cores."

"Don't manifest anything that looks like a threat," Keff said.

Tall Eyebrow was studying the astrogation tank carefully, measuring the distance between the two stars that they had just crossed.

"So close. It is a great pity," he said. "These people could have been friends of Cridi and Ozran."

"They still could be," Keff reminded him. "Try to keep an open mind. It may be a fringe group of criminals who've been robbing spaceships. If the government promises to punish the pirates, you could still establish friendly relations—form a Mythological Federation of Planets."

"If they themselves are not involved," Tall Eyebrow said, his small face thoughtful.

The ship rounded the planet twice more at high altitude before beginning to drop. The harp separated into successive bands of tan and blue.

"I've pinpointed the largest population centers," Carialle said, illuminating the planetary map, "but in spite of Keff's suggestions I don't want to land right in the thick of things. Some nice suburban location . . . X marks the spot. I think I detected a flat place I can land."

A blue dot began to glow on the chart about fifty kilometers outside one of the large cities. Narrow Leg's navigator glanced up from her console at the screen nearest him, and nodded to Keff. "Defenses are in place. Yours, too."

"Right," Keff said, taking a deep breath. "Down we go."

* * *

Narrow Leg's ship had dropped back to ride into the lower atmosphere on Carialle's tail. Watching her waveform monitor, she was pleased by the precision that the pilot showed, not getting too close and endangering them both, but staying just far enough back that the end of the elongated oval envelope just nipped his afterburners. You'd think he'd been doing it all his life. The hull sensors went off, indicating Carialle's skin temperature had risen to normal reentry temperatures. She checked the hull for leaks in either the skin plates or in the cooling pods underneath. All was well. The Cridi pilot signalled that he would stay in long orbit, and wished Carialle well.

"We will wait for word to come," he said in creditable Standard.

"See you downstairs," Carialle said, as the Cridi braked, and sailed on above her head.

Her last, long approach was almost entirely over ocean. She descended very quickly, keeping her speed up until the last minute. She hadn't noticed any telemetry beacons, nor radar signals, as if there wasn't a single ear pointed toward space. Strange when you considered that these people were parasites, preying on the isolated Cridi, that they wouldn't be more cautious about invasion of their own airspace. If she'd had functioning saliva glands, she'd have spat.

"All well, Cari?" Keff asked.

"Yes," she said crisply, increasing visual magnification and turning it toward her chosen landing site. "Are you certain we shouldn't land in a covert location? It's possible. Unless that clunky communication system is concealing a much more sophisticated technology underneath, no one can see me."

"No," Keff said. He had prepared his environment suit and kit before strapping in for approach. The light, transparent gloves flapped loose at his wrists as he clutched the ends of his couch arms. "We're not going in to study them. We're entering as envoys of peace, I hope. If nothing else, this will put them on notice that we have observed their people's crimes, and demand cessation of hostilities. What can they do? Attack the entire CW?"

"It looks as if that was just what they have been doing," Carialle said softly. "One ship at a time. Be careful."

"As Big Voice and the other Cridi are always reminding me, lady, we have the Cores. I'll be fine."

Unsatisfied, Carialle returned the greater part of her attention to what lay ahead. Gravity was approximately 1.2 times Standard. That meant those griffin wings had to lift just that much more and stay aloft in very windy skies. They were *strong*. Keff didn't have the advantage he'd had on the base, when they were all fighting that oppressive gravity. He would tire more quickly than they. Carialle maintained respect for the griffins' musculature, having studied the scans all the way from one star to the other. She was trying hard not to admire the fact their bodies, from about the shoulders back looked like a Terran great cat, a species which she was fond of watching for its grace. And those claws and teeth!

Beneath her, the tiny islands flitted by. Volcanic in nature, they had been augmented in size by the growth of a calcifying organism like coral, but less acid sensitive. Her imagination and pattern recognition aptitude saw in the shapes of the most proximate four islets a dragonfly, a chick, an old-fashioned handbag, and a ketchup bottle. Vegetation on the islands was of the same gaudy colors as in the pirate base conservatory; not as vivid, but healthier. That heavy-ammonia atmosphere must not have been good for griffin-world plant life, either. The trace in this air was much, much lower, below half a percent. Keff could almost get along with just eyedrops and nose filters, but she insisted he wear a full envirosuit. She knew she was being too protective, like a mother running after her child with overshoes. Keff meant so much to her she felt an unhealthy twinge of fear at the thought that the griffins might be able to get past the Cridi's impressive shield and harm him. Quickly, she purged toxins from her internal system, and allowed a dose of serotonin and stimulants to enter her bloodstream. She felt better at once. Keff wasn't a child. He had had plenty of experience in worse situations than this. He always sounded as if he was about to do something rash, but he also possessed a healthy sense of self-preservation.

Carialle passed over the sandy coast, parting the tree-oids in her wake. She was low enough now that the fliers had noticed her, and some winged to catch up. With a burst of speed for which she immediately chided herself as arrogant, she lost them over the first mountain range. There she noticed broadcast towers, of a design that hadn't been used by the Central Worlds in a thousand years or more.

"Do you see that, Keff?" she asked. She froze the image, and was ten kilometers past it by the time he responded.

"Antiquities," he said, leaning forward against the straps over his chest. "Are they still using those?"

"My monitors say that's where the broadcasts were coming from."

"Whew!" Keff said.

Trimming slightly to follow the contour of the land, she dipped into a valley and up over the next, higher, mountain range. On the other side she found the first flat terrain. Even in the cultivated fields there were traces of the acid rainbow colors. She looked forward to finding out what those bright red grains were.

"Crops look healthy, but there's very little heavy cover," she said. The Cridi were wide-eyed. She manifested her frog image near Big Eyes.

"Enjoying yourself?" she asked.

"Yes!" the Cridi squeaked, grinning in the human fashion. Clutching Tall Eyebrow with one arm, she signed with the other hand. "A new landscape, the first! Videos of original landings and colonies do not compare to own eyes!"

In the other ship Carialle could see the entire crew glued to the 3-D tanks. She was glad they felt the way she and Keff did about exploration. The Cridi would be a wonderful addition to Central Worlds. When M-C finally allowed the documents to be signed, that was.

"Look, that's a spaceport," Keff said, picking out a distant feature on the horizon after they cleared the next mountain ridge. He peered at the spiky growths poking up from the flat plain on the terrain map. "That is a spaceport, isn't it? Yes! Look, you can fit right in! Just land there."

"I intended to," Carialle said, impatiently, as she was already dumping velocity. She extended visuals to extreme magnification, trying to discern the landing pads, and find herself an empty slot to set down.

"What a collection of derelicts!" she exclaimed in dismay. "I'm never going to pass for one of *those*. I refuse to try. I do have my pride."

Keff leaned up to peer at the screen and signalled for more magnification. Carialle flung up the image she was viewing. The tiny irregular shapes on the cabin screen suddenly took focus.

"Great stars, you're right," Keff exclaimed, looking as if he didn't know whether to laugh or not. "Those look like they've been cobbled together by committees of people who'd once heard a rumor of a story about a spaceship."

"I have no idea how one of those would fly," Carialle said, "but hit me with a hammer if I ever let their ground crew do maintenance on me."

The field reminded them of the scatter of ship remains on the airless asteroid at the edge of the Cridi system. The three craft that stood on the landing pads had been put together with no practical knowledge of the working details. Exhaust vents were ducted to the outside where they would cause the craft to spin in frictionless space. Fuel tanks were exposed, and in one case, the single hatch hung open to show a control room unprotected by anything so pedestrian as an airlock. And yet two of the ships showed clear signs of having launched and returned safely at least once.

"My internal scans show no shielding in half the bulkheads." Carialle said. "The crew must be suffering from fierce radiation poisoning. If they lived."

"These people are suicidal," Keff said flatly. "Or perhaps they're kamikaze pilots, who refuse to be captured alive."

Carialle was silent a long time while she studied the ships. "I think it's buck ignorance," she said at last. "All the pieces necessary are there, but the instructions for assembling them were in a non-native language, so they did the best that they could."

"Like the pedalcycle I had as a boy," Keff said. "No safety backups at all, but it ran."

"Yes, and that's curious, because the ships that were chasing us had full shields."

Someone must have passed the word that Carialle was on her way. By the time she had tipped up and was beginning her descent, the field and the sky above it was full of griffins. Some of them fluttered gracefully to the ground at a respectful distance, but Carialle counted over a hundred in the air alone, with more in sight in the distance. Their followers were catching them up.

"Are they armed, Cari?" Keff asked, surveying the scene with a wary eye.

"Not with anything that carries a heat signature," she said. "Good heavens, but they're big beasts."

"Those teeth!" Tall Eyebrow signed, a-goggle at the screen.

Carialle stepped down magnification to her more immediate

location, and settled neatly toward the landing pad between the taller of the two jalopy spaceships. Measuring her thrust to the minim, Carialle brought her tail to the ground just as her engines shut off.

"Swank," Keff said, grinning. "You look like a candle on a minefield, lady love."

"I intend to outclass the competition right from the start," she said. "All psychological advantage we can gain will be to our benefit, if we ever get to a point where we can negotiate."

"I'm ready," Keff said. "Listen: 'Freihur, co nafri da an colaro, yaro.'" The IT unit on his chest recited in Standard, "Greetings, leader you me take go, please."

"That's fine, if that's what those words mean," Carialle said, skeptically. "Trying to guess from context, it still could mean, 'Greetings, your sister sells rugs in a zoo.'"

Keff didn't bother to defend the honor of his translation program.

"We'll find out," he said, pointing at the short-range screen. "Here come the authorities."

On the field, a white-sided gurney like a medieval siege tower, rolled toward Carialle. The half dozen griffins operating it moved in jerking haste, showing their excitement. An enclosed tunnel with soft bumpers extended and clamped against Carialle's side.

"Ah, so that *was* their design on the remote base," Carialle said. "I'm glad to see they don't steal *everything*."

"Easy, Cari. It's showtime," Keff said.

He stood up and sealed his suit, waiting for the faint hiss as each edge met. With the same care, he put on his helmet, then fastened his gloves. A secure seal. He breathed deeply of the slightly plasticky-tasting air, setting the air-recirculators going. There would be no more sudden breaths of ammonia. He felt excitement warring with nerves in his belly, and told both emotions to quiet down. Another life form, another world on which he would be the first human to step! What an opportunity! It was another notch in his belt, although, technically, Carialle had set foot on the planet first. He pretended to grimace, but he couldn't concentrate on being upset. What would happen to him when he stepped outside the airlock? He wasn't afraid to go, but by the stars, he was wary. On the external screen he could see the crowd of griffins gathered on the landing field. As he was checking his heads-up display, he felt something bump into the back of his legs. He jumped half a meter and spun around in midair.

"What are you doing?" he asked. In the few moments he had his back turned, the four Cridi had climbed into their travel globes, and they were clustered around his feet.

"We are coming with you," Tall Eyebrow signed, rolling back a foot or two so he could look up at Keff's face.

"Oh, no, you're not," Keff said, accompanying his words with firm gestures. "This could be dangerous. Please stay in here and cover me with your amulets. I'm counting on you."

"We would share your peril," Tall Eyebrow said earnestly.

"They tried to kill all of us on that base," Keff pointed out, signalling in exasperation. "Me, they just allowed one of their number to stalk. They went blind mad when they saw *you*."

"They know something of Cridi," Long Hand signed, "having killed three ships with Cridi defenses. It cannot have been easy."

"I do not know why they hate us, since we never did them harm," Big Eyes gestured, her wide mouth pressed into a thin line. "Never in our history have we seen these creatures. We should resent them, but we do not. We only wish to ask why. It is the honor of all Cridi." She added mischievously, "Big Voice would have said so."

"Big Voice wouldn't be diving straight out into their midst! Give me a chance to get this on a friendly footing, then we'll ask them," Keff said, pleadingly. The Cridi conferred for a moment, exchanging signals with the screen on the wall on which Narrow Leg's face appeared.

"Very well," Tall Eyebrow said, turning back to Keff. "We wait."

"Thank you," Keff said formally, with a low bow. He strode into the airlock, and heard the door slide shut and felt the slight drag on his shoulders as Carialle pressurized the cabin around him. His suit inflated slightly around his knees, crotch, elbows, and chest. He braced himself, legs well apart.

"Now, how's that go?" he said out loud. "Hello. Please take me to your leader. 'Freihur, co nafri da an colaro, yaro.'"

"Relax, you've done it a dozen times," Carialle reassured him. "Hold on, they're scanning me." Keff frowned up at the ceiling.

"They are? I didn't think they had anything as sophisticated as scanners."

"I didn't *say* they were sophisticated scanners. It feels like elephants are walking on my hull," Carialle grumbled. She paused, and Keff heard a low hiss beyond the airlock hatch. "Just a moment—if the race we're about to face is hostile, why are they pumping a 90/10 nitrox mix into the airlock?"

"They're *what*?" Keff demanded.

"I swear it by my sainted motherboard," Carialle said. "Look for yourself." The monitor beside him lit up with a specroanalysis of comparative atmospheres. "You'll find the air fragrant, too. Plenty of plant esters."

"Perfume?" Keff felt his jaw drop, and yanked it closed again. "I have to speak to them. Open up." He hurried forward, helmet almost bumping the inner hatch. The door slid partway open, then halted.

Carialle's usually crisp voice was almost tentative. "Be careful, Sir Knight. I'd always rather you return with your shield, than on it."

"So would I, Lady Fair," he said, cheerfully, his voice echoing in his helmet. "But in this case I've got better armor than any dragon. Alert the Cridi to rev up their Core power, and let me go."

The airlock slid open onto a wide flexible tube filled with griffins as far as Keff could see. With one hand flat over his pounding heart, he bowed deeply to them. Two of the great beasts bustled forward, stopping about four paces away, and sat down on their haunches. The narrow clawed hands met under their squared chins in the same gesture of respect he'd seen in a thousand beamed conversations, then the great wings spread as far as they could in the confined space. Then, they waited.

Keff stepped forward, and copied their moves as nearly as he could. "'Freihur, co nafri da an colaro, yaro,'" he said.

"In good time, in good time," the lead griffin said, its upper lip splitting to show the gleaming white fangs beneath. "You are most welcome. Are you in need of refueling? Supplies?"

"Uh . . . no," Keff said, gawking at the being. "Welcome?" His hands were seized and shaken by all the griffins who could reach him. Wings, claws, and faces flashed by him in a blur. "Carialle, did they . . . did they . . . ?"

" . . . speak Standard?" Carialle finished his question. "They sure did. With a respectable accent, too. How in the black hole did they learn it? When? Who from?"

"I don't know! How . . . ?"

"We are so glad to see you, great human," the second griffin said, offering another namaste. "This is a great honor. Never before has one of yours landed in our place."

"Where do they usually land?" Keff asked automatically, struggling to make sense of the situation. "Humans! You know other humans! How? Why—when?" His mental drives were overloaded with the new influx of knowledge. "I never saw any communications with humans in your transmissions." But his greeters did not have a chance to answer. A host of smaller griffins pushed past or sailed over the full-sized beasts, and clustered around him.

"Greetings!" they said, in flutelike voices. "Where do you come from?" "What is this for?"

"This doesn't sound like all the humans they've encountered were captives," Carialle said, pitching her voice low to be heard. "It sounds perhaps as if they were . . . collaborators?"

"Don't jump to any conclusions, Cari."

"I won't, but it sounds pretty suspicious to me," she said.

Keff spoke over the head of the youngsters surrounding him to the adults beyond. "You know humans?"

The leader's lip split again. The expression was clearly the griffin version of a smile.

"Of course, sacred one. You are but testing me. I know of the Melange."

"Sacred ones?" Keff asked.

"The Melange?" Carialle asked, in Keff's ear. He waved a hand in front of the camera eye for silence so he could concentrate on what the lead griffin was saying. "*Who*? I have no entry for any such name in my database."

"What is Melange?" Keff asked. The leader gave him a puzzled glance that narrowed the center stripe in his large eyes.

"The Melange," the second one repeated, as if no explanation was really needed.

"But . . . ?"

"What are you called, human male-man?" one of the children demanded, tugging at his arm. When he looked down, it drew back, giggling at its own boldness.

"My name is Keff," he said, bending down to look into their faces. In spite of their size, and their weight, which must have been around fifty kilos each, they were like any children galaxy-wide:

curious, friendly, bold and shy at the same time, and irresistibly cute. They romped around him on all fours.

"And what does 'Keff' describe?" asked another youngster, pushing in close. Its upper lip opened to show the nares, and it sniffed his hands and knees.

"Me," Keff said, tapping his chest. A couple of the children grabbed his hand with their wingclaws to examine his gauntlet. They exclaimed over the transparent material, running delicate talon-tips up and down his palm. "I, uh, Keff comes from Kefyn, an ancient name of my people."

"Poara, vno!" One of the youngsters had discovered the IT on Keff's chest, and pulled it down for a closer look.

"Uh, please don't touch that," Keff said, pulling his hands free and retaking prossession of IT from the enthusiastic fledglings.

"Vidoro, eha," another child said, and giggled, creeping around behind Keff to feel his clear plastic suit. Keff prided himself on his physical prowess, but these children were effortlessly stronger than he. They butted into his knees, patted his waist and chest. Their affectionate, curious touches had the power of a body blow.

"Kids, please, enough," he said, holding up his hands as he felt for a wall to brace himself against. The floor bobbed up and down under his feet, and he grabbed for the edge of the airlock. One of the children rose up on hind legs to get a good look at the tubes running from the back of his helmet into his suit, and Keff overbalanced completely. Flailing for a handhold, he toppled toward the adults. The first griffin grabbed his arms in both of its strong claw hands and set him upright.

"Forgive, sir-madam," the creature said. "My child is bad-mannered."

"It's sir," Keff said. "He—she?—didn't mean any harm."

"Are you all right?" Carialle's voice erupted in his ear. "Your heart is running the three-minute mile."

"I'm fine, Cari," Keff assured her in an undertone. The children, restrained from physical contact by their parents, were bombarding him with questions.

"Do you wish food, human sir? Good food, at the canteen. Human coo-orn, human broccocoli, human meeeat. All good!"

"Uh, maybe later," Keff said. "Tell me about these humans."

"But, sir, *you* are a human."

"They are rather charming," Carialle said, "and I don't want to like them. Not yet."

"I know what you mean," Keff said. "If they're involved in piracy, they must be the most cold-blooded..."

"What did you say?" One of the youngsters pricked up its fluffy ears. Keff cursed. These beings must have very sharp hearing. "Who are you talking to?"

"To my friend," Keff said, tapping the IT unit. At least they couldn't hear Carialle. "I am asking her questions."

"Who is your friend?" "Can we meet her?" "Your ship is so pretty. Can I go in?" "Ask us questions. We know answers!"

"Excuse me," Keff said, holding up a forefinger to stem the flood, and addressed himself to the first adult. "What is your name, please?"

"I am Cloudy. My friends here are Shower and Moment." The first Griffin indicated the two nearest him. Others began to call out their names, and Keff decided to count on IT remembering them all for him.

"What do you call this beautiful world, Cloudy?" he asked.

"This is Thelerie, at the Center of all things, but you must know that, human sir."

Keff made the namaste, and saw it repeated by every griffin.

"I must assure you I do not know all that. I am pleased to be here. Cloudy, I am here for a most important reason."

The wide smile flashed again. "Ah, so I know. What commodities do you bring to us?"

"Uh, no commodities. I'm just visiting."

Carialle's voice was a siren in his ear canal. "I knew it, piracy! They trade in contraband!"

"Hush, Carialle!" Keff schooled his expression and waited, smiling.

The griffins looked puzzled, and some of the ones further back exchanged glances. "You are not of the Melange?"

"No," Keff said, firmly. "Who are they?"

"You are teasing us," Shower said, shaking its great head.

"How do you know humans?" Keff said, pressing. "How do you all speak Standard so well?"

They looked knowingly at him.

"You *are* teasing us," Cloudy said, his upper lip spreading again. "We did not know of humans to be so merry."

"They are friendly?" asked Tall Eyebrow, rolling out of the open airlock around Keff's feet, with Small Spot and Big Eyes immediately behind. The griffins looked down at the small globes. Tall Eyebrow looked up at them, wearing his best human-type smile. The curious, striped eyes widened.

"Slllaaayiiim!" the aliens shrieked. The large ones grabbed the small ones, and they backpedaled hastily away in the billowing tube. In moments, the long corridor was empty, and bobbing softly. Keff, thrown off his feet by the jouncing, listened to the shrieks outside on the surface as he climbed up again, using the airlock for a handhold, but his gauntlets scrabbled on smooth enamel. As soon as the corridor had broken open to atmosphere, Carialle had slammed the airlock shut.

"Well, that hasn't changed," Carialle said, into the silence. "Your ancestors must have fought hard, TE."

"This isn't the way to start a detente," Keff said severely, looking down at the Ozranian. His back and elbows hurt where he'd slipped against the side of the ship. "I wish you'd waited inside as I asked you. Now they'll probably call out the militia."

"We will protect you," Big Eyes said firmly, showing her finger-stalls.

Keff swallowed his exasperation. "Please wait here. Please." He held up a hand to forbid any of the Cridi to follow him, and threshed clumsily down the tube toward daylight. Two of the globes levitated and started after him, but he held up a warning hand. The plastic balls subsided to the cloth floor. The Cridi inside them sat down crosslegged in the water at the bottom.

"We wait," Tall Eyebrow said, disappointedly.

Lying flat on his belly Keff poked his head out of the end of the corridor. The landing field was deserted. He squinted up into the bright sky, quickly enough to see hundreds of winged shadows fleeing off in all directions.

"Damn," he said.

"At least they aren't calling out the guards," Carialle said in his ear. "No transmissions from this site, and no warm bodies headed in your direction. My, that's a long way down."

Keff glanced at the ground below him. In their haste, the griffins had shoved the gurney away from the ship. The only way down to the pavement was a drop of almost ten meters.

"Do you want me to open my ramp?" Carialle asked.

"No." Keff pulled himself back into the tube and waded back toward the globe-frogs. "I guess you four win, after all. I need an elevator ride to the ground floor."

To his credit, Tall Eyebrow tried not to look triumphant.

"We come with you?"

"Yes, but under conditions," Keff said. "One, you do what I tell you. Two, you stay out of sight until I think it's all right. Three—well, I'll decide on three if I have to. Agreed?"

The Cridi all nodded vigorously.

"This visiting of a new world is fun," Big Eyes said, her dark eyes shining.

"It is," Keff agreed, as they floated out into the sunshine on a wave of Core power. "The worst thing is that we're not the first humans to land here, Cari. After all this, somebody else gets the credit."

"Cheer up, Sir Keff," Carialle said. "We're in this one for another purpose this time."

"I just wish all our witnesses hadn't run away," Keff said. He forced himself to stare straight ahead and not look down as the four Cridi carried him toward the mountain city where most of the natives had fled.

✲CHAPTER FOURTEEN

"Four heat traces inside that one," Carialle said, as Keff obligingly swept his sensors toward the nearest house on the edge of town.

The habitations of the griffins were a peculiar hodgepodge of modern and primitive architecture strewn throughout the ridges of the high mountain reaches. No one seemed to like to live in the valleys. All of the buildings were of stone; unsurprising in a landscape with few trees. Each house had been constructed with considerable physical labor, using handhewn blocks, and yet, on top of this building and the ones visible nearby were delicate metal antennae, the communications transmitters Carialle had detected from space. The houses were roofed and decorated with the local clay, colored blue and green with trace minerals Carialle identified as copper extractives.

"One thing you can say about them, they do landscape nicely," Carialle commented, focusing on various details in the large yard. "Although the preponderance of rock gardens would get old fairly quickly."

"Pee-yew!" Keff said, as the globe frogs floated him over a pit. It was carefully bermed to prevent its strong stench from wafting toward the small blue house, so the only place for the stink to go was straight up, toward him. He gestured with frantic hands.

"Put me down! Now!" He dipped dangerously towards the cesspit, and waved for attention. "No, not in here, over there." He rose through the air once more. Following his signals, the Cridi set him down in the long grass several meters away from the humped construction. Once on the ground, he could see that it was fitted with wide stone steps leading to the lip, and surrounded by handsome gardens that no doubt benefited from the natural fertilizer.

"I see you've found 'the necessary,'" Carialle commented drily.

"You can laugh," Keff said crossly, triggering the stud that controlled air recirculation. "You didn't smell it. It was so bad that it passed the filters in my suit." Grateful to be back on his own feet, he patted the nearest Cridi's globe. Small Spot glanced up at him with large, scared eyes.

"These beasts are not secretly making an attack?" he asked.

"I don't think so," Keff replied. "It does not appear as if we have much to fear from them. They're afraid of *you*."

"Us? They are so many, and we are so few, and yet they do not attack?"

"It would seem not," Keff said. He squeezed his eyes halfway closed to trigger magnification on the house. "Those wires are very new," Keff said. "The contacts have yet to oxidize in spite of the chlorinated atmosphere."

"I am finding it very difficult to believe they continue to live in a semi-primitive state like this after having developed space travel," Carialle said.

"Focused application of technology?" Keff wondered out loud. "Perhaps they have a cultural prohibition against wholesale changes in the environment."

"Yes, but Keff, even sustainable technology could take care of that midden heap in a more aesthetic and less odiferous fashion. Side by side with electric light and telecommunications is that complicated system of water-wheels for ventilation."

"Yes," Big Eyes said. "Why do they not use electricity to run water mills *and* to ventilate? Much more efficient."

"Tradition?" Keff asked, but he wasn't convinced either.

"It's as if all this doesn't belong, as if it has been imposed on the landscape," Carialle said. "Looking at it with an artist's eye, it doesn't make sense. Some scientific advances are used for one purpose, but all other uses are ignored."

Big Eyes, accustomed to luxuries available at the flick of a finger, stared around her at the dry landscape with puzzled eyes. "So barren," she said. "Bleak, primitive."

Tall Eyebrow suddenly looked very sad. "Very much like home on Sky Clear," he gestured. Big Eyes caught the expression on his face, and attempted to apologize.

"It is only that I am not used to it," she said hastily, both in voice and sign. "I do not mean such things cannot be considered attractive."

"I'm going to go speak to the beings in the house," Keff signed, distracting them both from a potentially embarrassing exchange. "Stay close, but don't come out until I signal for you."

With the Cridi in their globes staying low in the tall, crisp grass, Keff circled out of the yard and made his way to the front. A wide but low door, elaborately molded bronze to match the shutters of the wide windows, lay in the exact center of the side of the house, facing a lane.

"Not much in the way of roadbuilders," Carialle said. "But would you be, if you could fly everywhere?"

"Not I," Keff said. He raised his hand to knock, then noticed a cluster of bells hanging just under the eaves. "That's right. They haven't much in the way of knuckles, have they?" He jangled the bells with his fingertips. In a few moments, the door swung wide. A noseless lion face appeared at his chest level.

"Frcihur?" the griffin asked. Its strange eyes darkened as its visitor registered on its consciousness, and it sat back on its haunches. "Za, humancaldifaro!"

"Yes, I'm human. My name is Keff. How do you do? Do you speak Standard?" Keff asked, politely, airing the griffin language he'd elicited from Carialle's telephone tap.

"I . . . yes! Welcome," the griffin said in Standard, in seeming befuddlement. It passed wing-hands over its golden fur, grooming it back into place. "Enter, yaro."

Keff followed his host into the low house. The interior was arranged rather like a nest. All the furniture was made for sinking into or settling on. The big, fluffy pillows looked comfortable. The heavy gravity was wearing on his muscles in spite of the assistance of Core power. Keff would have enjoyed flopping down on the cushion with the silky covering that lay under a sunny window amid potted plants. The windows were unglazed, a blessing in the heat, but were all fitted with screens of a microfine weave to keep out the blowing dust.

Keff was about to ask his host to take him to its leader when he noticed a large square device with a screen on top of it, and a sling shoved hastily to one side. On the screen, another Griffin face was peering out. He'd probably interrupted an important gossip session, then realized that his host was looking at him with fearful anticipation.

"Vaniah? Vaniah, soheoslayim, commeadyoslayim Thelerieya," the caller on the screen said. Thelerie the host didn't know which way to go. At last, it plunged away from Keff and punched a button on the box below the other's image. The screen went black.

"Word spreads," Carialle said. "Better to take the bullfrog by the horns."

"You're quite right," Keff said, and whispered into his helmet. By the time his host turned around, the four Cridi were clustered around his feet on the stone floor. The Thelerie backpedaled, protecting its face with folded wings. Its claws scrabbled, and it felt for a piece of furniture to sink down into.

"It's true, you see," Keff said, standing in the doorway so the griffin couldn't flee. "These are my friends. They are harmless and friendly, and wish to come with me to meet your government. Can you help us?"

"They are not killers?" the griffin asked. Its pupils were spread out across its eyes. "I have children . . . ." It glanced nervously toward the corridor. Keff guessed the young ones were beyond one of the two closed doors he could see.

"No," he hurried to assure the Thelerie. "They are civilized beings, who only wish to speak."

"Greetings," Tall Eyebrow said, rolling up in his globe. The griffin's ears swiveled forward.

"I did not know they can speak."

"They can and do," Keff said.

"This is like . . . toys," the Thelerie said, tipping a wary wing-hand toward the globes.

"Means of conveyance," Keff said. "Your world is too dry for them. They are accustomed to a very wet climate. They are at a disadvantage here."

"Ah." The griffin paused to consider. Its eyes lost some of the expression of terror.

"You can almost hear the wheels turn in its head," Carialle said. "'The monsters are vulnerable.'"

"You will be assisting in the cause of global peace," Keff said, encouragingly, hoping to make the wheels turn in the right direction. "And think of the gossip you'll be able to pass on to your friends."

The Griffin's upper lip split widely, and its pupils narrowed. "I am not forgetting that," it said, with good humor. "What do you want of me?"

"Will you take me to your leader?" Keff asked.

"I thought that griffin would break the sound barrier flying home," Carialle said, as Keff stood on the balcony looking after it.

"And why not?" Keff asked, making sure he had a good grip on the rail while he brushed fine yellow silt from his suit. The broad, stone building about four levels high was the tallest building in the city. This flat parapet appeared to be the landing pad for Theleric visiting the structure, avoiding the dusty plain below. Keff felt at a disadvantage as the only being on the planet, including the Cridi visitors, who had no means of independent aerial propulsion. "He's got the exclusive story of the century, but he couldn't go and tell it until he got us here. Or was it a she?"

"But where is here?" Tall Eyebrow wanted to know. Keff and the Cridi were clustered out of sight of anyone looking up.

"Central government," Keff said, rapping with his knuckles on the light, metal window frame. "Or so our guide said. We ought to be uninterrupted at least until he gets back to his screen. That should be enough time to make our presence known. Ah," he said as the gauze-screened doors opened onto a broad room. Two large griffins in leather harness met his eyes with openmouthed astonishment. "Excuse me. I would like to speak to the being in charge." He threw a glance over his shoulder, but the Cridi globes had hovered up out of sight. "Wait for my signal," he said, with his lips close together.

"We waiting," said a soft voice in his helmet receiver.

"So am I," Carialle said.

Keff marched behind his escort down a wide corridor to a chamber, like a huge eyrie. The outward-slanting walls and square pillars were of a mahogany-colored stone, carved sumptuously in relief, and polished to a gleam. Tiny lamps glimmered in sconces around the walls. Keff saw that they were flames, but of intense brightness for their small size. A dozen Thelerie with white tufts in their golden fur conversed respectfully with one whose coat was nearly entirely white. All of them lounged on embroidered pads before individual carved tables. Near the walls, a dozen or more young and muscular-looking Thelerie sat, holding sharpened bronze weapons that resembled a cross between short jai-alai sticks and back-scratchers. In the corner was a griffin playing on a stringed instrument like a huge dulcimer. The music stopped when the musician spotted Keff. The brawn bowed deeply, and addressed himself to the eldest Thelerie.

"Greetings. I am Keff. My partner, Carialle, and I come in friendship, as a representative of the Central Worlds, to extend the compliments of our government, and to voice grievances brought by some of our member worlds."

"Then you must come in," the elder said, rising from his cushion, and extending his wing-hands toward Keff in a companionable gesture. "You are welcome. I am Noonday, Sayas of Thelerie. These are the Ro-sayo, the assembly of the wise."

Murmurs broke out in the chamber as Keff strode between the guards to the center of the room. He bowed to each of the councillors, centering their faces for his chest camera and Carialle.

"Slayim," he heard repeated over and over again. "Slayim."

"Word has already spread here of our arrival," Carialle said. "Slayim, slayim, slayim."

"Slime," Keff said under his breath, suddenly enlightened. "That's what they've been calling the Cridi."

"For their wet skins," Carialle said. "An uncomplimentary but not unreasonable pejorative. But it's a Standard word."

"It won't remain a mystery long, I hope. May I address this assembly?" Keff asked Noonday. The leader, after looking around at the others and meeting their eyes, nodded his great head.

"Not all speak your tongue, but I shall translate for those of us who do not understand."

"Thank you," Keff said, adjusting IT to pick up the leader's voice. "But first, I must introduce you to your nearest neighbors among the stars."

He stepped past Noonday's cushion and up to the great casement behind him. With a flourish, he threw open the windows, and the four Cridi globes sailed up and in on a wave of wind and dust.

"Slime!"

Brandishing their back-scratchers, the guards at once dove for the four small globes, but they rebounded against another unseen wall of force. They fought and tore at obdurate nothingness with hysterical fury on their big, flat faces.

Gawking, the elderly Ro-sayo leaped off their cushions. They tried to break for the door, the other windows, even out past Keff, who flattened himself against a pillar out of the way. The Thelerie all but rebounded off invisible barriers put there by Cridi Core power, and rushed to the next possible route of escape. Noonday held his place, but he looked aghast.

"You dare to bring our enemy here?" he asked Keff.

Keff hurried to the center of the chaos with his hands out-stretched above his head.

"Please! They are not your enemy! They mean you no harm. My friends are called the Cridi. They are your closest neighbors in this part of the galaxy. Their planet circles the twin of your star. They wish to speak because they feel a great wrong has been done them."

"They?" one of the councillors said. It was backed into a cor-ner, its eyes were huge with fear. Its wings were spread out, claw hands poised to defend. "*They* feel wronged?"

"They do," Keff said. "All they ask of you is that you listen to them. Please!"

It took some more moments of scrabbling at the air to realize that though the Thelerie could not leave the chamber, nothing else ill was happening to them. After many glances over their shoul-ders at the little plastic balls in the middle of the room, they soon stopped hammering on the doors and walls and windows. The small, green aliens sat in the water at the bottom of their travel globes, almost hidden by the circle of guards. The first Thelerie to have spoken closed its big wings, and daringly edged back toward its cushion.

"That's good," Keff said, his voice soothing. Noonday's voice sounded forth one of their multisyllabic sentences like the mel-lowest of brass horns. "Won't everyone else please sit down?"

"They fear us so," Big Eyes signed, her hands shaking. She was almost invisible behind the wings of the guards, but Keff heard her small voice over his helmet speaker. "I guessed nothing of this. For so many years, we pictured the destroyer of spaceships as great unknown."

"And they saw you as unmentionable monsters," Keff said. He moved in and pushed the guards aside. "We must put an end to those misunderstandings now, and discover the truth."

The guards looked to the Sayas for direction. At Noonday's nod, they withdrew to a distance of only three meters and settled onto their haunches. Keff sensed that they were not really relaxed, but ready to pounce again if needed. Slowly, all of the griffins but one resumed their places. The last, a young and slender councillor, found that its pad was closest to the Cridi. It crept close, set a single foot on the cushion, then fled, shrieking, to pound on the door again.

"Jurrelanyaro! Jurrelanyaro, yaro!" it cried. Keff walked between the cushions to the end of the chamber, feeling every head swivel to follow him. He stopped and bowed to put a gentle hand on the Thelerie's back. It jumped a meter in the air, its wings outspread, and landed facing the brawn.

"I am a human," Keff said, softly but clearly. "Your people trust humans. I mean you no harm. I promise you will not be harmed. Will you trust me?"

The beast's striped pupils fluctuated wide to narrow to wide. It may not have understood his words, but it seemed to comprehend his tone. It nodded its head. Keff stepped out a pace or so from the wall, and offered an encouraging hand.

"Come, then, and take your rightful place," he said. It followed him like a tame deer, all the while staring timorously at the Cridi. At Keff's signal, the globe-frogs stayed absolutely still. The young Thelerie settled down on all four legs, but its wings were open halfway, literally ready for flight. Keff turned to find that Noonday was smiling at him.

"You must have young of your own," the Sayas said. "We listen."

"Thank you," Keff said. "I would like to introduce the Cridi. You call them the Slime, but that is not their right name. Cridi." Noonday repeated his words in the musical Thelerie language. Keff smiled to himself as some of the beings around the room tried the foreign word on their tongues. "My companions are Tall Eyebrow, leader of the Cridi of the Sky Clear colony; Big Eyes, one of the eight conclave council members of their homeworld of Cridi; Small Spot and Long Hand, both of Sky Clear. Since, unexpectedly, we share a common tongue, you may hear in their own voices the complaints that they have."

Every eye turned toward the Cridi. Keff sensed how nervous the four were, but they held themselves bravely upright. When one of the globes wavered slightly out of line, Tall Eyebrow brought it back to its place with a sharp gesture from the wrist. Big Eyes rolled closest to him, and matched hands with him on the inside of their globes. Gradually, the assembly was quiet, awaiting.

"But they cannot speak for themselves," a white-headed Thelerie said, breaking the silence. "They are only creatures."

"They are not," Keff said. "In my ship I have video of their homeworld, and I assure you their attainments in art and science are most impressive."

"Impossible. They are dumb animals!"

"We can speak," Tall Eyebrow said, projecting his voice to carry as well as it could from his small plastic bubble. His words caused a sensation. As the hubbub grew louder, his high voice cut through the noise like a cutting torch. "But we choose Sir Keff to speak for us."

"Thank the stars for that," Noonday said, removing the wing-fingers from his ears. "Telling the truth, your voices are painful. We are not aware of any wrong that we have done these . . . people, er, *Sir* Keff, but you may address us as you please." The senior settled himself down, flipping his wings to his back and arranging his haunches like a big cat.

"I will," Keff said, "as soon as the assembly is complete. I await the arrival of the rest of the Cridi delegation. If you will give permission, and the assurance that they will not be harmed, I will ask them to land." He bowed deeply, sweeping an arm around to the rest of the chamber.

"There are more Slime?" one of the Thelerie asked, flinging its wings about it in the protective posture.

An older assembly member scrabbled up. "We are under attack! Guards!"

"Oh, where is the Melange? They should be protecting us," a slender Thelerie said, wringing both pairs of hands at its breast.

"Silence!" Noonday's voice rose over them like a hunting horn's call, though he did not move. "I give the guarantee. Bring them, Sir Keff."

"Cari?"

"On their way," Carialle said. "There's just about room to land on that balcony, but Narrow Leg shouldn't push his luck. He's going to set down on the roof . . . just . . . about . . . NOW!"

There was a *boom!* and the thunder of rocket engines shook the council chamber. The Thelerie assembly looked frightened, but none of them broke for the exits. Keff found himself full of admiration for their bravery. In a moment, the shadows of travel globes appeared outside the woven window screens, and the casements opened wide. Naturally, the plump councillor had jockeyed himself into first place, and entered triumphantly.

"I should have been first, before these others," he signed indignantly at Keff.

"It could have been dangerous," Keff gestured back, in as few gestures as possible.

"No matter!" Big Voice said, punctuating his signs with a squeak, now that all peril was past. "I would have faced it for the sake of my people."

Smiling a little, Keff stood forward, like a court herald, and bowed to the Thelerie.

"Allow me to introduce Big Voice, another one of the Eight, Narrow Leg, captain of the Cridi ship, Gap Tooth, Wide Foot . . . ." As he recited their names, the globes touched down on the polished floor and rolled into an arc around Keff's feet.

"I bid you welcome, Cridi," Noonday said, gravely. "And now, speak. What are these grievances?"

Big Voice rolled out just to one side of Keff, where the human could see and hear his every word.

"I have traveled far and endured many hardships to ask these words," Big Voice said in carefully practiced Standard. His voice quavered when faced with so many griffins, awake and mobile, but he puffed himself up and continued. "Your people have confined us, you have killed us, you have stolen from us. What I must know is *why*? Why do you hate us? Why do you think us monsters?"

The Thelerie stared at him as the assembly resounded with protest. A younger member of the chamber spoke out.

"The Melange told us you were monsters, that you killed innocent beings. You harmed *their* ships, and would kill us, though we only seek to see what is among the stars. We do not harm your kind. It is the other way around."

"We have never seen your people before." Big Voice shrieked, and several of the Thelerie held their ears. "We do not kill others, and we do not destroy or terrorize. Your Melange have lied to you! Keff is the first human we have ever seen, too!"

"Humans don't lie!" a Thelerie howled angrily, a bassoon counterpoint to Big Voice's piccolo. The plump councillor retreated swiftly into the group of his fellows and hunkered down in his globe.

Keff opened his mouth and shut it again. "I can't say anything," he told Carialle. "If I say humans do lie, then I've started one of those conundrums that makes computers break down."

"What have we stolen?" Noonday asked, in a mild tone intended to calm his listeners. "Will you enumerate your losses?"

"Three power sources, known to us as Cores," Big Voice said, counting on his long fingers, "engines and equipment from our ships, the lives of at least three crews, but most of all, our freedom! We have been imprisoned on our world for fifty of our years, because our ships could not pass the barrier you created!"

Keff translated for the Thelerie, who immediately protested.

"We did not set any barrier," Noonday said, earnestly. "Our people have few ships, which have not crossed out of our star's circuit as of yet. The Melange say we are not ready. It must be their barrier you cannot cross. Surely it is for your own good."

Keff shook his head. "Sayas Noonday, the Cridi don't need any protection of that kind. They are accomplished space travelers, with colonies in other systems."

"Are they?" Noonday asked, eyeing the Cridi with new respect. "They seem so helpless, so . . . lacking in a center."

"Once we were not," Narrow Leg said, speaking up. "I am old of my kind. I remember the first time we lost contact with a ship, fifty revolutions ago. The Melange must have destroyed it without warning, for no word ever came back to us. They kill to keep us from leaving our world."

"No!" The Thelerie protested the idea of the Melange killing. Keff held up his hands, pleading for silence.

"The spacecraft we saw when we landed," Keff urged, pointing out of the window in the general direction of the landing pad. "Did you construct these?"

"Yes," said Noonday proudly. "They are made of gifts from the good humans who have visited us in the past."

"But the parts were not given freely to those humans," Keff said. "I recognized some of the components, and my associates recognized others as Cridi technology. Piracy is a great problem in our culture, too."

"It is not piracy. You were *giving* of these objects to us, honored human," one of the younger Ro-sayo said.

Keff shook his head. "I haven't. Many ships were robbed or destroyed to yield those parts."

"It could not be. The Melange is honorable," the first Thelerie protested. The Ro-sayo broke out in hoots and cries of agreement, with the high-pitched whistles of Cridi voices causing many of them to flinch.

"They might have been taking things that didn't belong to them," Keff said.

"Nonsense!" Noonday said. "Some of our most honored citizens have taken ship with the Melange, sworn allegiance, and brought home goods so that we may fly the stars."

"Who are the Melange?" Keff asked, shouting to be heard.

That question provoked the greatest outburst of them all. Noonday gestured for silence, and turned a hard stare on Keff.

"Who *are* you that you do not know of the Melange?"

"We are travelers," Keff said. "We come from the Central Worlds. That means something to you," he added, as some of the Thelerie conferred hastily among themselves. "Central Worlds is a vast confederation of intelligent peoples, governed by common laws to aid life, health, and prosperity. We go from place to place, meeting new people, and sending word of them back to our Central Committee. I promise you, no word of the Thelerie or of the Melange has ever gotten back to the CenCom."

"But how can this be?" Noonday asked, spreading out all four of his hands. "Humans have given us so much, for so many years. They made themselves one with us, gave us helpful innovations. Why, see," he gestured around him with a narrow wing-finger, "these lamps would never be so small or bright without human machines."

"Cari?" Keff said, turning his body full toward the baroque sconce.

He heard a sharp whistle. "It's a dilute form of heavy-water fuel, Keff, very clean and hot-burning, the sort of high-quality stuff I'd use myself if I could get it. If those valves weren't so small, that whole room would go up, blammo!" Keff blanched.

"Where does the fuel come from?" he asked.

"It lies here and there in the deep places," Noonday said, gesturing vaguely with a few of his hands. "The technology to make use of it was brought to us by humans to our mutual benefit, for which we are very grateful. We assumed that all humankind was behind their good intentions."

"Are there more? More innovations?"

"But, of course," Noonday said, with a gentle smile. It was clear he and the others still did not believe Keff's protestations of ignorance. "For everything the Melange takes from Thelerie, they always bring us gifts, more than fair exchange."

"The Thelerie couldn't be using more than a few million barrels a year for light and heat," Keff said, sublingually. "Leaving a source of quality rocket fuel for whoever knows to come and take it."

"I see why now," Carialle said, "but I still don't know who, or if they connect to me."

The youngest Thelerie, Midnight, stood up and placed an indignant wing-hand on its breast. "You have come here with many accusations. You wrong us, and you wrong our friends and benefactors."

"We do not mean to be offensive," Keff said, "but I assure you we tell the truth. You set great store by honesty. I tell you that we left behind in the Cridi system ten of your people, and they were part of a force that lay in ambush for us." Keff continued over the horrified protestations. "That force was responsible for the destruction of a human-run ship from the Central Worlds. The wreckage of that vessel was found near the ruins of at least three Cridi craft, and parts of many others. I swear to you that this account is true. I have video records of this, and of the beings who confronted us on a planetary base. You see why we must find out the truth here and now."

"I would like to see these 'video,' " the young Ro-sayo said.

"You shall," Keff said. "We do not bring these complaints without proof."

"What you are saying is that *Thelerie* have been involved in acts of piracy," Noonday said. His noble face was drawn into lines of pain. Keff felt concern for the leader.

"Cari, is he all right?" he asked under his breath.

"Not a cardiac involvement," Carialle said, after a moment's assessment, "but his pulses are running very fast. He's sustained a shock, which is no surprise, considering how many bombshells you've lobbed in the last few minutes."

"What do you want of us?" the leader asked at last.

"It would seem that most of our questions could be answered by your friends the humans," Keff said. "Can we meet the Melange?"

✷CHAPTER 15

"Where is the other human?" Noonday asked, looking around, over, and under the party as they flew out of the capital city toward the northeast. "I would like to meet it."

"Perhaps later. Carialle stays with the ship at all times," Keff said. "She's . . . very attached to it."

Carialle blew a raspberry in his aural pickup, with the volume turned up just a little higher than was strictly necessary. She observed the neural monitor jump as Keff winced.

"I speak to her by means of small transmitter-receivers on my person," Keff said, pointedly ignoring her. "She hears our words, and sends her greetings to you."

"Ah, thank you and her. I know little of human customs. We in the Sayad do not interact with the Melange ourselves," Noonday admitted, flying ahead of his escort with Keff and Tall Eyebrow for a private word. His great wings beat the air a few times, then spread out to glide on a gusty updraft. "They visit Thelerie only irregularly. I myself only met humans once, very long ago. It was a great honor."

Watching from the camera eye on Keff's chest, Carialle admired the easy play of muscles. Noonday's wings were shaped like those of an eagle, but covered with plushy, golden fur like the body of a bat. The Thelerie were certainly a beautiful folk. She had had plenty of time to go over the anatomical studies and scans they had taken of the griffins left behind on the base, but this was her first time to see them in action, in their own habitat, stress-free. She was attracted to the grace of movement, the artistically right integration of six limbs. Their bodies seemed lithe and smooth, their velvet pelts almost caressing her visual receptors. Should time and circumstances permit, Carialle wanted to ask a few of them to sit, or rather, fly for her, so she could paint them. Carialle's brief glimpse of one of the guards suggested that it was carrying young right now. A scan showed a tiny, six-limbed creature in a thick caul like a soft eggshell inside the uterus. Carialle felt protective of the unborn young. In spite of her worries and misgivings, she was finding herself liking the Thelerie. She chided herself for her sympathies, remembering that these charming beings were responsible for countless deaths, and possibly her own long-ago peril.

"Who, then, is the primary interface with the Melange?" Keff's voice asked. Carialle saw that his pulse rate was up. She checked her telemetry, and found the group was flying at approximately twelve hundred feet, far above his comfort level.

"The Sayas of the Space Program meets with them," Noonday said. "We will ask if it is known when their next appearance is to be."

"Then, why do you all speak our language?" Keff asked, gesturing vaguely.

"Oh, that is in anticipation of when we reach out to the stars," Noonday said, and his eyes widened joyfully. "We want to be ready to communicate at once with the blessed humans who are there."

"Not an unbiased party, is he?" Carialle said, wryly. "I notice he doesn't consider it an honor to meet the Cridi, and they're just as alien as we."

"We're not blessed, Sayas, just another species like you," Keff said.

"Not to us," Noonday said, shaking his head. "It is from a legend that comes from the depths of our history, telling the story about the wingless ones who would come one day and take us where our wings cannot. A most beloved story, by children especially. And one day, you came, and made it true."

"Well, not us. This Melange, whoever they are . . . er, we are honored to have your assistance," Keff said, hesitantly, "and, forgive the discourtesy, but why are *you* taking us to meet this Sayas? Wouldn't this task be easily relegated to a junior Ro-sayo, or a guard?"

The elder's wings tilted back for just a moment, then he flapped hastily to catch up. His forehead was creased, ruffling the plush into furrows.

"Thunderstorm is my child," he said, then said defensively, "Where aptitude exists, should not responsibility follow? If there is any wrongdoing, I wish to know at once. We Thelerie are law-abiding folk. Our . . . *moral* life is strong. As you could see, my assembly was much distressed at the notion that Thelerie were involved with crimes against another people, especially a life-form so physically helpless."

"We are not helpless," Big Voice said indignantly, floating his travel globe close to the Sayas. "You have said that before, but see, we are capable."

Noonday reached out a claw hand to tap the globe. Big Voice ducked automatically. "That is true. By coming along on a flight with those believed to be enemies, I am also demonstrating a measure of trust in you for the assembly. *I* prove you can be friends and allies. As you say, we and the . . . *Cridi* are close neighbors. Neighbors should aid one another in time of need. And in spite of all, even if these charges against Thelerie be true, we must continue to trust in humans. So much of our culture over these last many years is involved intimately with this relationship. They gave us electricity, communication, many things."

"Heat exchangers, humidity controls . . ." Carialle chimed in. "The Thelerie should properly be in a pre-industrial age. The baroque decor is reasonably appropriate to the period, as it was on Earth before electricity. Humans brought all this to them, gave them machines, power, and then space travel, all in the space of fifty years. Strictly against the code of the Central Worlds."

"Well, these humans seem to be doing quite a lot against the code of the Central Worlds," Keff said, under his breath. "We'll know more when we've talked to Thunderstorm. How long until we get there, Noonday?"

"Soon," the Sayas said. The group passed over the ridge of the mountain range separating one great, yellow plain from another. Spare clouds riding the sky above them drew long lines that extended down over the mountaintops in both directions. Noonday directed them down into the narrow shadows between ragged, upthrust monoliths. "This way, for another eighth-arc of the sun at least."

"Plenty of time to get to know one another," Keff said cheerfully, stretching out on his side in the air beside the Thelerie. The Cridi continued to fly him along, and his pulses dropped toward normal as he became more involved in the conversation. Carialle flipped her image of the Sayas from horizontal to vertical to compensate for her brawn's change in position. "You say you're Thunderstorm's parent. Are you his mother or his father? And is he a he or a she?"

"Such differences are not known in our biology," Noonday said, beginning in a lecturer's tone. "Unlike you, we are all made the same way, only changing roles as we mate for offspring. I have borne or sired four children in my life. You would say I am Thunderstorm's mother, for I bore that child sixty-seven turns of the sun ago. We live a long time, here."

Carialle made certain the recording on Keff's signal was perfectly clear. She boxed in auxiliary memory to act as backup, to assure data redundancy. She knew her brawn wouldn't want to let a single erg of information get away.

It was a blow to him that the CK-963 team wasn't really the discoverer of the Thelerie, but he intended at least to be the documentarian whose data made the *Encyclopedia Galactica*, if not the Xeno files. Carialle wished she could have such easy short-term goals, but then, she'd never thought like a softshell. Keff had made her realize her humanity, even made her like it, but she knew they weren't very similar in their outlooks. He was ephemeral. One day, when their twenty-five year assignment was over, she'd be suddenly without him, and it would be a long and sad forever thereafter. It was times like this when she understood how very much she valued him. Keff, with his good humor, optimism, and his enthusiasm for diving into any task no matter how difficult or unsavory, was the best thing that had ever happened to her. He was so fragile, so easily injured, and she was so far away. If the Cridi allowed any harm to come to him . . . !

Realizing she was allowing herself to become melancholy, she gave her system a quick eighth-measure of carbohydrates. If her brain was playing such emotion tricks on her, she must be hungry. She had surely been ignoring the gauges that indicated her blood sugar was unusually low.

Carialle knew she'd been working her system hard. Ever since they hove into this part of space, old memories had been surfacing, giving her flashbacks during her rest-times, and intruding into her conscious mind while she was doing easy tasks like calculations. She saw visions of her first brawn, Fanine, relived the explosion and the rescue, even cast a critical mental eye on the early paintings she had done of space-scapes while in therapy. That should all be behind her, she thought. The interference had made her have to concentrate twice as hard.

Her sensors had been gathering information on the Thelerie ever since they had landed. It was time and past time to send another transmission to the Central Worlds, as a follow-up to the one she had sent from the Cridi system, but she was hesitant. Every event changed their perceptions of the situation. If she and Keff were wrong about the pirates, if the whole construct the two of them had made up about the location and origin of the raiders was incorrect, it was the end of her career, at least. Carialle hoped Keff wouldn't be held responsible—they were *her* incorrect perceptions based on *her* mistakes, arising from *her* disaster. She could always plead guilty to constructive kidnapping, if worst came to worst, to spare Keff an official reprimand. Not that it was likely she would face criminal proceedings, but it was best to be pessimistic where the odious M-C was concerned.

And yet, she found it difficult to believe that this charming and seemingly honest race was involved in piracy and illicit salvage. Of course it wouldn't be illicit for *them* to remove parts from a derelict ship; they wouldn't know it was a legal requirement to post a claim to a wreck with the space agencies. The Sayad had no rules dealing with space salvage yet. And yet, griffins— Thelerie—had been aboard the ships chasing them with mining lasers. Who was fooling whom?

She began to build up a dossier of facts to accompany her message. In it, she stressed the pre-electronic environment in which the Thelerie lived. The most intriguing fact about the modern developments that she and Keff had observed was the limitation of their use. It said clearly that the Thelerie did not understand the mechanisms or the physics behind them. Therefore . . . therefore, another agency was at work. Or was it? Couldn't there simply be a group of griffins who had demanded an education in practical science from spacegoing captives? Then, how had they reached into space in the first place? She and Keff needed that final link in the pattern. With luck, they'd have it before her message reached the CenCom.

On her screen, the Sayas stretched out his beautiful wings and dipped down toward a cluster of buildings on the open plain. Their body-harness glinting in the bright sun, the six guards flew into a protective formation around him. What a picture! Keff and the Cridi dropped back a hundred meters, allowing the Thelerie to approach the installation first.

"My, what a nice little fuel storage facility," Carialle said, just before the image of the square stone building with fluid transfer towers disappeared from Keff's camera eye.

"Isn't it, though?" Keff said. "Now our surmise has another leg to stand on."

Thunderstorm's office was very elegantly furnished, though the structure itself was little more than a stone roof on pillars. The walls consisted of corner-to-corner screens that let in the fresh breezes and bright, yellow sunlight. The cool wind felt so good to Keff after the dusty flight that he opened his filters a little more to allow the circulating air to touch his face. The atmosphere contained really very little ammonia, more of a far-off smell than an all-round stink. It might still harm tender Cridi hides, but exposed human skin might be able to last for longish periods. He thought he could almost take off his envirosuit, but then Carialle would probably go spare. Keff wanted to prevent anything from upsetting her during the investigation of this world. She had trials enough with the entire Mental Sciences division clamoring for brain scans, thanks to the Inspector General. Though it might put him in the brig, Keff would love to relieve the itch in his big toe by burying it halfway up the IG's excretory tract.

Keff occupied himself while they waited for Thunderstorm by studying his surroundings. This installation, at least, was accustomed to receiving humans. The doorframe was over two meters high, instead of the meter and a half that would be adequate for Thelerie to enter on four feet. That seemed to be the only structural consideration. The furniture was all made for griffin comfort—not that Keff would have found it onerous to stretch out on floor pillows, and the sling behind the desk was perfectly adequate as a backless chair. As in the government building, Keff saw very little wood, all of it used as ornament rather than in construction. Some of the small outbuildings around the office seemed to be built of adobe, others of fieldstone and concrete. The

Thelerie might have had only one main building material, but they used it with imagination.

To his surprise, they also had paper. Keff grinned at himself. He'd been looking for computer terminals in a culture that still had open cesspits. The broad-topped desk was heaped with white, squarecut sheets, covered with the same square script he recognized from the attack ship's files. *Those* computers had been the aberration. This setting seemed more in line with their sociological development.

"Cari, there's hardly any trees here. What's this made of?" he whispered, moving close to the deskful of documents. His forefinger pointed at the paper, in clear view of the camera eye.

"Straw fiber," she replied at once. "A combination of rice and some native fiber; hard to tell which one without a closer molecular scan. The ink's a combination of an organic compound and finely ground mineral powder. Like India ink, it'd last for centuries. Here comes someone."

Keff looked around. Carialle must have detected the approach of a flying body on sensors. Yes, there . . . Keff saw a shadow, steadily growing in size as the body that cast it neared the ground. He heard voices, the Sayad guards calling out greetings, and a single mellow reply, as a Thelerie of middle years rounded the corner of a pillar, and entered.

Thunderstorm looked remarkably like his mother, but with a broader head and wider feet that lent him an endearingly awkward gait. His coat had only begun to show flecks of white. His smile, when he saw Keff, was an echo of Noonday's sweet expression. Thunderstorm looked suddenly wary as he came closer, and realized he did not recognize Keff. But the evidence was clear: this being interacted frequently and closely with humans.

"We've found our connection, Cari," Keff muttered under his breath.

"A . . . stranger?" Thunderstorm asked, in very good Standard, attempting to show surprise. "Forgive, I am rude. Parent, to what do I owe the honor of your presence?" He sat back on his haunches and made the gesture of respect to Noonday. The elder returned it. When he raised his eyes, they were worried.

"My child, I come on the gravest of errands," the Sayas said. "This human has told me many things that in— imm—?" he looked up at Keff apologetically, "favrekina Thelerieya."

"Implicate, parent," Thunderstorm said, smoothly, but Keff saw his tailtip switch. He was nervous. "Implicate Thelerie in what?"

"Crimes against other races of feings," Noonday said, so agitated she was unable to keep the upper halves of his lip together to pronounce the "b" in "beings."

"But I beg an explanation," Thunderstorm said, turning his head, to avoid making eye contact with his mother or Keff. He knelt behind the sling and lifted his upper body across it. With his right claw hand, he picked up a pen and made a few marks on a sheet of paper. "Why come to me?"

"I am told you are the head of the Thelerie space program," Keff said. "Is that true?"

"It is," Thunderstorm said. "It is wrong to lie."

"Then my business is with you. I come on a matter of peace. I am not alone. Perhaps you may have heard?"

The younger Sayas looked uneasy. "I have heard rumors."

"I won't conceal anything from you," Keff said. "Allow me to introduce my friends."

The globes sailed one by one out of the side of the pavilion, where they had been waiting out of the hot sun. Thunderstorm's pupils nearly spread to the edges of his eyes, and he sat up on his haunches at bay, his wings batting.

"I cannot believe you would bring them here," he gabbled out, staring. "Parent, what have they done to you?"

"Nothing at all," Noonday said, refusing to let Thunderstorm distract her. "What do you know about them?" She lifted her eyelids warningly.

"I have encountered them," Thunderstorm said at last, his wings wavering. "When I served my apprenticeship with the Melange. They are evil beings."

"Not evil," Tall Eyebrow protested.

"By the temple, it can speak!"

"You didn't know, did you?" Keff asked, leaning across the stone desk. "You never saw one alive. Did you assist in the ambush and destruction of one of their spacecraft?"

A Thelerie might not lie, but evidently it would fight to keep from telling a harmful truth. Thunderstorm stared silently down at the pen in his hand.

"Child, speak," Noonday commanded, sounding like the entire

brass section of an orchestra. It took some time before Thunderstorm could bring himself to open his mouth.

"You recall our first friend, parent? Verje Bisman?" Thunderstorm asked, in a very low voice. Noonday nodded, still watching him carefully. The younger Thelerie turned to Keff. "I was so young, and full of awe for the strangers. Before a formal arrangement had been made between our two peoples, I begged to have him take me in his ship. He apprenticed me and my friend Autumn. He seemed fascinated with the Center, though he could not find it himself, and called us great assets because we could. We flew with him for some years, going from place to place, accomplishing missions for his ship. We gathered things no one wanted, or received them from donors who bargained hard for their goods," Thunderstorm said, looking ashamed. "So I thought. I was naive. On the cusp of the nearest star, we caught a ship that my friend, Verje's child, Aldon, said contained the greatest prize of all, and the Slime would not yield it. We were young and on fire, so we stopped the ship and took it. It was a great battle, for the Slime seemed to have mystic power to attack us without touching us. We were very frightened, but in the end we prevailed."

"How long ago?" Carialle's voice demanded.

"How long ago?" Keff echoed.

"Forty-three Standard years," Thunderstorm said, without looking up. "I knew then we committed crimes. It was the greatest shame of my life."

"Then he wasn't on any ship that touched me," Carialle said. Keff felt some of the tightness in his chest relax, but he grieved for the Cridi, who were only now discovering the truth about their losses.

"The second of our ships," Narrow Leg said, his wide lips flat with disapproval. "Fifteen Cridi lost in that one."

"Why did you never tell?" Noonday asked.

"I had vowed obedience and silence to the Melange," Thunderstorm said, looking up at his parent. "And I knew shame. I begged to be involved in no more assaults, and the humans agreed. After that, I came home to found the space program, finding apprentices for the Melange to train in the art of maintaining and flying craft. They do learn everything they are taught!" he cried, his eyes darting between Keff's and Noonday's. "We are good pupils, and we consider the trust sacred. When we were told these," he gestured at the globes, "were enemies, we believed. We believed, because the humans were the fulfillers of our dearest dream! Those of us who finished with our apprenticeships never speak of it, but some of us *know* we have done wrong. That is why some have left the space program. I stay. I am weak." The Sayas hung his head. "I thought some day when our own ships were spaceworthy, I would go back and see who the Slime were. I was Centered. I knew how to find my way. And now I am too old, and possibly weaker still."

"I am disgraced. What punishment would you demand of this one?" Noonday asked, turning to Tall Eyebrow, who deferred at once to Big Eyes and Narrow Leg. Keff could see the pain in her eyes, but she faced the Cridi without wavering.

"Only weeks ago we might have demanded his life," Narrow Leg said, eyeing his daughter and Big Voice, who rolled forward, bursting to talk. "We want cooperation. Such raiding must stop. We want peace. We want friendship. At what point in our requirements of reparation would such things be impossible?"

"I am the Sayas," Noonday said. "And Sir Keff is of the fourlimbs of the legends. Though Thunderstorm is my child, his life is in my gift. I would prefer to withhold such a gift, if I can. But in the name of peace, we will do anything you ask. We can't keep back one life when you have lost so many."

The two councillors rolled away from the group, followed by Narrow Leg and Tall Eyebrow. Long Hand, glancing over, decided she'd better be part of the discussion, paddled her globe into the circle, leaving Small Spot by himself, staring up at the Thelerie.

"We, too, have recently reconciled with a deadly enemy," the Ozranian said. "I know what I would say about you, but it is not my decision."

Thunderstorm went down on his belly and folded his wing-hands under his chin to the younger Cridi. "I do not deserve the consideration," he said. "I understand my crime, and I have abetted others. Time does not dull my shame."

"What are they doing?" Noonday asked, watching the Cridi sign furiously among themselves. "Is it a ritual? Why do they not talk?"

"They are talking," Keff said, always happy to teach. "They speak both with their mouths and their hands." He spread his arms, palms outward. "This is the first word of theirs I ever learned. It means 'help.'"

"Perhaps we shall learn this tongue, too, child," Noonday said, miming the symbol with his wing-fingers. "It has grace."

"I will do anything I can to make amends," Thunderstorm said earnestly, getting to his feet. "If I am given a chance."

"First, you will stop calling us Slime," Small Spot said, with emphasis.

The conference ended. Big Voice led the group back to the waiting griffins. Narrow Leg confronted Thunderstorm.

"We will not be guilty of spilling more blood," the Cridi captain said, "so we do not want yours. Our council will be made to agree that we are doing the right thing by sparing you. But until you learn what is right, you don't belong among the stars if you cannot respect those you meet there. We will dismember those ships we saw when we landed. They are unsafe anyhow. Your space program is cancelled as of now. One day you will learn right."

Thunderstorm's mouth fell open. "Don't take away my people's dream!" he exclaimed. He again dropped to his belly before the globes. "Take my life, here, now, honored ones, but don't let a foolish few close the door for all the others!"

"And yet, that is what you and your Melange have done to us," Narrow Leg said, severely. "We have colonies we have not visited in revolutions, nor have we been able to explore new systems."

"But the humans gave us this gift," Thunderstorm wailed. "If we had not been intended to fly among the stars, the humans would not have come!"

"Technically speaking," Keff put in unhappily, "the Central Worlds would forbid anyone giving a new species sophisticated systems until their own culture had developed the requisite sciences. Your own development would seem to be rather far below the minimum."

"This is terrible," Noonday said, clenching his hands. "I do not wish to lose the gift of flight, either. What can we do?" Everyone looked at Keff.

"Nothing at all until you've found the humans responsible," Carialle reminded her brawn.

"We need more detail on the Melange," Keff said. "Everything. How to find them, what they do when they're here, what their ships bring in, what they take with them. We need verification, first, for my government's information, whether this is the same group who destroyed the DSC-902 in the Cridi system."

"If it is in the Slime system, it was the Melange, I promise," Thunderstorm assured them, unhappily. "They are jealous of their territory. I am sorry to use the wrong name," he said bowing his head to Small Spot. "But I have known them fifty years, and you only minutes."

"I understand," Small Spot said.

"Do you believe them, Sir Knight?" Carialle asked.

"I think so," Keff said, tapping the desk with his fingers. "We can confirm to CW that those Thelerie that we left behind on the fifth planet were part of a network of pirates. They'll be on the lookout for more ships with the same modus operandi."

"But not all Thelerie are involved," Carialle said, with a sigh of relief. "I'll put that in my message to CW. They'll be very interested to hear about human involvement in this culture."

"Bets on whether the CenCom or Xeno gets back to us first?" Keff asked, playfully.

"Get back to the job," Carialle said, with a wry inflection. "We need data. We still haven't laid hands on the masterminds, and now we only have until the message reaches the CenCom."

"It's incredible that the secret of the Thelerie hasn't leaked to the rest of the Central Worlds in fifty years," Keff said. He settled on one of the spare slings in Thunderstorm's office. The Cridi stayed near him, not yet trusting their new acquaintances, but curious.

"We thought that it had," Noonday said, a little sadly. Thunderstorm could not meet his parent's eyes.

"Would you give up a free source of fuel?" Carialle asked. "This is a remote corner of the sector yet. If it wasn't for the bulk transport difficulties they might have been bootlegging it to exploration ships and miners. And here's an intelligent workforce who do complicated work without asking awkward questions. I think we ought to be amazed they weren't enslaved by this Melange. There's some vestige of morality in there, whatever else is going on."

"That brings me to another question," Keff said, looking from parent to child. "Why did the Melange take you into space in the first place? No offense, but I'd be afraid beings who had never known space travel might be a . . . liability."

Thunderstorm's upper lip parted in a smile. "I think to test a hypothesis. We are at the Center, and they wanted to understand Centering."

"Centering?" Keff asked.

"So you truly do not know," Thunderstorm said in surprise, settling down on a cushion in the sun with his wings on his back and his foreclaws thrust out before him like the Sphinx. "This is the heart of the universe." A wing claw rose to gesture from ground to sky to his own breast. "Its heart is our heart. Where we go, we can always return to here. It draws us. It is a part of us, and we a part of it."

"Extraordinary!" Keff exclaimed. "You mean that if I blindfolded you—covered your eyes—and took you anywhere on this planet, you could get home unaided?"

The sharp teeth showed in a quick smile. "Any child could. All do, to prove adulthood. We are never lost. Our legends of long ago said the Center would lead us home from anywhere, even the stars. But the wise ones of the past didn't provide us with the means to try the theory."

"An internal homing beacon. Whew!" Keff whistled. "But this Melange provided the means."

"Don't lead the witness," Carialle said in his ear. "If we give the CenCom this tape, we want it to be clear he is volunteering this information."

"Yes," Noonday answered, from another divan cushion. Her large eyes lifted skyward and turned dreamy. "One bright day in my youth, the humans came from the stars, and took some of our people away with them, including my child." A wingtip swept toward Thunderstorm. "The legends proved true. Those of our young people who travel far with the Melange learn to go other places with relation to our Center, but always return." The wing-finger twirled around but came to rest in front of Noonday's breast. "The Melange were fascinated by our natural talent, and said we could aid them. They find us worthy to travel with them, to fulfill our dreams of sailing where there is no air to tuck beneath our wings. It is a sacred destiny. One which, alas, has been defiled."

"And in return, you give them things of value," Keff said. "What besides innate navigators?"

"It is only fair to trade value for value," Noonday said with gentle conviction. "They have brought us electricity, useful machines such as distant talkers, knowledge, and the friendship of another race. We are pleased to know them. They have been benefactors to the Thelerie. Metal, ores, handworks, cut stones, smelly fuel-water, the use of a few years of a young Thelerie's time—all seem of little worth in comparison."

"So for fifty years someone's been cashing in on these people and giving them stolen spacecraft parts in return," Carialle said.

"The Interplanetary Revenue is gonna give us a rewaa-ard," Keff chanted in a sing-song under his breath.

"Don't count it yet," Carialle said. "Let's catch these brutes, first. We need the Thelerie to help us."

"I know," Keff said, and looked up at the two griffins, who eyed him curiously every time he stopped to talk to himself. He smiled at them, which seemed to make Noonday relax. Thunderstorm looked even more worried, his wingtips clattering together over his back.

"I represent the Central Worlds, an affiliation of thousands of planets, and many different species," Keff said. "We have rules against the introduction of technology to civilizations that have not yet developed it themselves. Still, there are immense benefits to membership, if you were interested in joining."

"Then we would really become one with humans?" Noonday asked.

"Much more so than with the Melange. From our point of view, they have interfered with your development." Noonday looked puzzled. Keff struggled to explain in Standard, then in pidgin Thelerie, and gave it up as a bad job. "Well, what was it like before the Melange came?"

"Colder at night without house heaters," Noonday said. "Less cohesive among our people."

"The coms," Thunderstorm explained. "Most families have one now."

Keff sighed. "The CW won't actually take something like those away from a people, would they, Cari?"

"Probably not. There's no destructive potential in personal communications or home furnaces. The spaceships, on the other hand, will have to go."

"All these are good things that the Melange shares with us," Noonday said, the beatific smile on her face. "We joined with them, and it has been of benefit to us all. They always assured us that the gifts they brought were traded from outposts, or scavenged from floating space debris."

"I was some of that debris," Carialle screamed.

Keff winced as his aural implant went into overload. "They couldn't know, Cari," he reminded her. It was the first crack in the reserve she'd shown since they had landed.

"How dare the Melange force this lovely people into piracy," Carialle said furiously. "It violates fifty-seven sections of interplanetary law, it's immoral, and it violates the Prime Directive."

"That's fictional," Keff pointed out.

"I don't care. It's still a good idea. I want these people, and I want to be the one who brings them in to Central Worlds. Now there's no excuse for having picked away at my exoskeleton: there isn't a spacer who flies in the Central Worlds who wouldn't recognize a shell capsule."

"We don't know what happened," Keff said, soothingly. "We'll find out. You must understand, Noonday, that spaceship parts don't just become available. Our evidence shows that at least some of them were the fruit of ambush and murder. Thunderstorm will admit he knows about that.

"To my shame," the Space Sayas said, covering his eyes. "Forgive me, parent." His voice was muffled behind the folds of his wings.

"Will you help us to stop such crimes?" Keff asked, looking intently at Noonday.

"We always wish to follow the laws," Noonday said, but the Thelerie was uneasy. Keff was convinced she never really knew that their gifts were stolen merchandise. He waited. He knew the griffins were fascinated by humans, and admired them, so he smiled his most charming smile. It worked. The rectangular pupil widened. "We will do anything we can."

"Thank you," Keff said.

Noonday's sweet smile was sad now. "We dreamed of space travel, and when it was given to us, that dream was fulfilled. But it is wrong to accept technology in advance of our understanding, as you say."

"But you don't understand," said Thunderstorm, rising to his feet. "Some of our greatest triumphs! Some of our most reknowned heroes . . ."

" . . . were flying in stolen ships," Noonday finished gently. "It is over. Sit down, child."

"Fifty years," Keff said, stroking his chin thoughtfully. He shook his head.

"Certainly long enough to be an established concern by the time I came to grief," Carialle said.

"We will stop taking from the traders, but you must convince your own kind to stop bringing it to us," Noonday said. "For as long as it continues to be available, someone will buy it. We cannot police everyone. But so long as there is no source, then no one can buy."

"Then we need to find this Melange, and stop the illicit trade," Keff said. "How do you know when they are coming?"

Thunderstorm rose and opened a low cabinet behind his desk. In it was a communications unit.

"I activate this once a day to receive messages, if there are any."

"Cari!" Keff said, hovering over it.

"Of course, Keff. Tell him to turn it on."

Keff conveyed the order, and the Thelerie tweaked an old-fashioned knob with his claw. He winced at the rising growl that came from the set as its tubes—*tubes*—warmed up. It was of ancient design, possibly of ancient manufacture as well. But it would last nearly forever in this environment, if not subjected to harsh treatment.

"I have the frequency. It's specific, and common, if you happen to hail from Central Worlds. It's in the educational transmissions band."

"Very sly," Keff said. "If a mysterious broadcast comes in over this band, most monitors will think it's kids playing pranks."

"Yes," Carialle said. "In the meantime, I can stay open on that frequency and hear the moment anyone in range uses it."

"Do you ever send a message yourself on this unit?" Keff asked.

"No, never," Thunderstorm said. "I speak to Zonzalo when he calls me, but I do not summon them."

"We have a name," Carialle said. "I can send to the nearest space station for criminal files. Zonzalo what?"

"Don," Thunderstorm said. "He speaks for the leaders, Aldon Fisman and Mirina Don. Mirina is senior sibling of Zonzalo."

"Fisman?" Keff asked. "Related to the first Fisman?"

"Child of that one," Thunderstorm explained. "He is my friend. Strong and fierce, with less warmth than the parent. Mirina embraces the apprentices. She is kindhearted."

"Kindhearted pirates," Carialle said ironically.

"Hush, Cari," Keff said, soothingly. "We have names. Get on to CenCom and let's see how far their records go back."

Carialle opened up her receivers on the frequency she had gleaned from Thunderstorm's unit. With so little on-air traffic on this planet, it should be easy to detect another transmitter. Yes, there it was. Carialle couldn't tell precisely where it was, but she could guess approximately how far away in the direction of the strongest signal, where the antenna lay. She triangulated the location on the maps she had made of Thelerie, and made her best guess. If she had to, she could make a flyover of that region to be certain.

"Got one," she said to Keff, interrupting another information dump from Thunderstorm. From being taciturn and cagey, the Sayas of the space program had become almost too eager to help.

"Only one?" Keff asked. She saw his hand go up in front of his chest with one finger raised, a request for the Thelerie to pause.

"Only one base," Thunderstorm said, as his newfound friend fell silent, communing with the internal voice again. "I will show it to you, if you wish."

"Only one, not too high powered, so our friends count on getting very close to this planet before making contact," Carialle said, running through a quick calculation. "It's north-northeast of you, probably a couple hundred klicks. They're very sure no one will sneak up on them."

"Well, they're wrong," Keff said, smacking one hand into another. "This time, we'll be lying in wait."

"And we freeze them in place," Big Voice said, extending his two fists out in front of him." He rose off the floor above everyone's head, and spun in a circle.

"No, no!" Keff exclaimed, diving for the councillor's globe before it crashed into one of the pavilion's supports. "We need information from them. We can only do that if they're free to move and speak."

"Oh," Big Voice said, looking disappointed as Keff put him back on the floor. "It would be simpler. But how can we do this?"

"I have a cunning plan," Keff said, grinning at the little party in the pavilion. "What do the Melange come here for?"

"To gas up, and to pick up a supply of natural navigators," Carialle said at once.

"Well, to trade," Keff said, clarifying for the others. He sat down in his sling again and held out both hands. "We don't want them to cut and run, we want to talk to them. We're unarmed, and besides, policing is not our job. We gather information. So, what if the next time they come, they find someone here in their particular, secret treasure house, ready to undercut any price they ask for better goods?"

Carialle sounded amused. "They wouldn't automatically identify traders as CW personnel."

"Exactly," Keff said, lifting himself into a pike position with his hands braced on the supports of the sling-chair. "They'd land and try to find out who we are and where we come from.

"They might try to destroy you," Thunderstorm pointed out. "There is no mercy in them."

"It doesn't matter," Keff said. "Once they're out of their ships, they're vulnerable." He plopped back onto the thick, black strap and swung back and forth, pleased with himself.

"We can capture them," Tall Eyebrow said, clamping an imaginary prey between his large hands.

"But you have no trade goods to attract attention," Narrow Leg said. "We have brought nothing."

"That's where you're wrong," Keff said, leaning forward with a grin. "We have some very fine trade goods. Now, listen closely."

✷CHAPTER 16

"No more word from Base Eight," Zonzalo said, slapping an impatient hand down on the console. "That ship must have gotten them. It's too late."

Mirina bowed her head to say a quiet farewell to the lost crews. Some of them had been good friends of hers ever since the beginning of her association with the Melange. Some of them were apprentices she had brought on board and taught the ropes; innocents, like Sunset, who was wide-pupiled at the news.

"Are they all dead?" the Thelerie asked, searching his beloved humans' faces.

"We don't know that," Bisman said nonchalantly, brushing off the youngster's question. "The radios might have broken down, that's all. All the stuff's old."

"All of them?" Mirina asked in a sarcastic tone, taking care to keep her voice low. "Three ships and the master transmitter *and* all the backups broke down at once?"

"What do you want me to say?" Bisman hissed between his teeth. "You want the kid yammering to be taken home because he's scared?"

"He ought to know the truth, Aldon," Mirina hissed back, planting a palm in the middle of his chest and pushing. Bisman, taken by surprise, backed up into the bulkhead with a thump. His necklace of curios jangled. He brushed Mirina's hand away, and she put it on her hip. "The idea is that we let him make his own

515

decisions, based on honest information, so he can function on his own one day in space, just like we promised them. If we don't tell him anything, he's just blundering along."

"Huh. Like the rest of us." Bisman turned away to go aft toward the mess, dismissing her. Suddenly, Mirina felt weary of the constant fighting, the dishonesty, the deaths. She strode after Bisman, finally having to run up the corridor to catch him. He turned around when he heard the hurrying footsteps behind him. Mirina beckoned him under a ventilation duct so the noise would cover their voices to the crew on the bridge.

"What?" Bisman demanded, deliberately standing over her so she had to crane her head back to look at him. She refused to let his tactics dismay her.

"Aldon, I want to quit."

"Quit what?" Bisman asked, acidly.

"I'm tired," Mirina said, standing back a pace and easing her head down. She massaged the back of her neck, and felt the tension in the muscles there. "I've been thinking a lot about this lately. This wasn't supposed to be a permanent arrangement, me staying on with you and the others."

"What's to think about?" Bisman asked, his thick, dark eyebrows tented in a puzzled peak over his nose. "We've got an arrangement. We work together, and we make money. That's what you wanted."

"Well, that's what I wanted for a while. Now, I want to stop."

Bisman scowled at her. "You're not serious."

Mirina let out an exasperated sigh. "Yes, I'm serious."

"Why do you want to leave?" Bisman asked. "We're good together."

"We haven't really been *together* in a long time, Aldon," Mirina said, patiently, trying to make him understand. She searched his face. "You know that. Everyone needs change after a while. I've been here eight years. It's time for me to move on. I *need* to." Then, daringly, "And I'm taking Zon with me."

Bisman was immediately suspicious. "Why?"

Mirina planted her hands on her ample hips. "Because that's what I meant to do eight years ago when I came looking for him," she said, without raising her voice. She could see by his expression that he finally understood her determination, but he still didn't like it. "I meant to take him and go. Then I stayed. Now it's time for us to leave. That's all."

"Miri, honey, you can't go! We need you," Bisman said, bending his knees so he could look directly into her eyes. He clasped her upper arms and shook her gently, a tender look on his face. He rubbed his thumbs back and forth on her shoulders to the indentation under her collarbone. Mirina groaned inwardly as she felt the tingle spread through her body. She knew he was going to try emotional blackmail, and here it came. He hadn't touched her like that in over two years. The contact felt so good, reminding her of the days when they'd been lovers, but she knew it was only a tool he was using on her. Suddenly, she felt angry that she could be so thoroughly manipulated.

"You don't need me," Mirina said, fighting for a clear mind. "You did once, Aldon, but now the operation is running well. It's profitable, and everyone's taking good care of themselves."

"There, you see?" Bisman said, with another friendly shake. "We're in good shape *because* of you. You've done so much for us. We wouldn't have grown like this. Couldn't have. We can't do without you. The Melange needs you."

"You *needed* me," Mirina said, emphatically. "It isn't the same thing any more. As soon as we finish this run to Thelerie, Zon and I are leaving." He heard the hard tone of her voice and let her go, almost pushing her away. Mirina felt cold like the void of space fill the gap between them. Shivers replaced the tingle. No, there hadn't been any residual affection there.

"To hell with you, then," he said, his voice flat. "Go. You've got plenty of money from your shares to go anywhere you want."

"I don't want it." Aha, that surprised him. "I've never taken a thing out of the kitty, Aldon. It's all still there. I'll leave you every credit in exchange for a ship, any ship, even a junker. I can make it run."

"You don't know what you're talking about," Bisman said, making a fist. He held it in midair as if he didn't know what to do with it. For a moment Mirina was afraid he would hit her. Then he slammed his hand against the bulkhead over her shoulder. "You're crazy, the both of you. All right, then. When we make planetfall, you can leave in a ship, and go to hell while you're at it." He threw the last words over his shoulder as he stalked away toward the galley. Always the master of the parting line.

"Thank you, Aldon," Mirina called after him, genuinely grateful. He'd given her his word. Bisman wasn't paying any attention.

Probably planning the next raid to make up for the loss of a ship.

She had to think of her own next move, too, after Thelerie. They were only a day or two away. It was going to take some fancy planning to begin life anew without a credit to her name. At least she could top off the tank of whatever vessel Bisman let her have. Thunderstorm's wrecks were available, but they wouldn't get her a light-year before blowing up. Damn it, she thought. She would have liked to stick around until the Thelerie became spaceworthy on their own. They were coming along so well. It would have been this generation that finally made the last step, and she would've been there to see it. Maybe some day she'd meet one of them in a remote outpost somewhere. Maybe they'd remember her. Mirina sighed, her heart and shoulders equally heavy. Maybe not. She went to tell Zonzalo of her decision.

Mirina woke in the dark and stared up at the ceiling. Yes, she had heard something, a noise on the edge of sound. A hiss.

In the utter blackness of her cabin she couldn't see anything, but she sensed that the shape of the space had changed. She could feel the air blowing on her skin from another angle. The door was open, but the corridor lights had been killed. Mirina's remaining senses roared up to high awareness. The pulses of the ship grew loud, and she felt the thrum of the engines in her flesh. Her sense of smell became enhanced, too. Mirina scented sweat and another, less tangible odor, sharp and thin. Fear. The shape of the darkness changed again, as a body moved between her and the source of air.

"Who's there?" she said out loud. The light hiss stopped, but no one spoke. Mirina felt a cold ball of terror in her stomach. She drew her legs to one side, bracing her muscles to spring to her feet on the bunk. Her balance was bad because her hip couldn't lie flat, forcing her knee to stay up. Damn, she wished she had kept in better shape! Complacency might now be the death of her.

The unseen person drew closer. She was almost certain the intruder was alone. Who was it? Why was it there? Such elaborate preparations boded no good to her.

In a voice so calm it surprised her, she said, "I have a laser pistol in my hand. I don't give a damn if the beam goes through you or the bulkhead. I'll give you to three before I start slagging everything in this cabin. One. Two . . ." She threw back the covers from her arms.

The small sound alarmed the intruder. The footsteps, for the sound *was* feet sliding on the floor, scurried out into the passage. The door ground back into place, and the room regained its proper shape. Mirina clapped her hand to the wall for the lights. After two or three attempts, the switches engaged, flooding the room with white light. Mirina blinked blindly. In a moment, her eyes adjusted, and she scanned the cabin. Nothing looked out of the ordinary. Somebody had disconnected the power to her lights and her door to make his or her work easier, and would join the group expressing shock and outrage in the morning when Mirina would be found conveniently dead. She had foiled the attempt, but the sneak remained at large in the ship, having left no clues as to identity.

She ought to go wake up Bisman, and start an inquiry immediately, and check who, right now, had an elevated pulse. Maybe the sneak left fingerprints on the life-support controls, or footprints on her floor. Then Mirina realized that Bisman couldn't care less any more what happened to her. No clue was worth interrupting sleep.

She beat her hands on her thighs in frustration. How naive of her to think she'd just be allowed to walk away from the Melange! Bisman had gone straight to the mess hall and told everyone the Dons wanted to jump ship. Naturally, the first thought through everyone's mind must have been that she and Zonzalo intended to turn them all in and plead state's evidence. How stupid of her not to take that into account. From now until there was a light-year or so between her and the crew, her life was in danger. She'd better start packing that threatened pistol, and take other precautions. Listening for more footsteps in the hall, Mirina rose and hunted out her toolkit. She disconnected the door's mechanism, so there would be no more surprises, from that source at least.

The next two days were miserable. The raiders shunned even eye contact with the traitor. Mirina had felt lonely before, but she couldn't have anticipated real isolation. Zonzalo was no help. He resented being yanked away from his friends, and what he thought of as a career. He would go with his sister when she left, but he was unhappy, and he let everyone know it, loudly. Mirina was alone in her insistence on their upcoming departure. Fortunately, no one made an attempt on her life during day shift. The atmosphere was growing so hostile that Mirina started wearing the laser pistol on her hip and other weapons concealed about her person. Bisman didn't look at her directly at any time, but she caught sidelong glances when he thought she wasn't paying attention. She wondered what he was thinking.

She anticipated another attack, probably just as she and Zonzalo were ready to leave. They couldn't go, she realized. Not with the knowledge she had of all their operations, all their bases—their identity. By opening her mouth, she'd doomed herself and her brother.

Why hadn't she simply taken Zon and gone away, all those years ago? She'd been a fool. Ignored by the bridge crew, Mirina went back to her cabin and locked herself in.

"Mirina?" Sunset's mellow voice, sweet and sad, came from outside her door on the morning of the third, lonely day.

"Yes?" she asked, without opening it. She checked the monitor camera she had hidden in the bulkhead across from her door during the last dark shift. Nothing there but the back and wings of the young Thelerie. "What do you want?"

"May I see you?" he asked.

"That would be a bad idea right now," she said, keeping her voice flat. She was afraid to show the young Thelerie any warmth, lest Bisman and the others take out their anger on him after the Dons were gone. Or dead.

"Then, when? I must speak."

Mirina sighed. "Come in, but quickly." She reconnected the mechanism and slapped the control. Sunset clattered in on four feet, and stood, his noseless face almost in the works as she pulled the switches apart again.

"You are afraid," he said.

"Yes," she said. Her nervous laugh strangled into a squeak, so she chopped it off. She swung an arm toward the chair at her desk, and lifted one hip onto the edge of her bed. Sunset obediently walked over and slung his midsection across the chair seat. "Don't worry. I can handle it. So, what is it, youngster?"

"The others are talking about you," he said, his wide eyes fixed on her. "I do not wish to question. I am obedient, but you are my friend, and I am concerned."

Mirina was touched. So far even Bisman had failed to corrupt this gentle innocent. If there was anything she could do to make certain he was protected after she was gone, she'd do it.

"Thank you. What did they say?"

"They are afraid you will turn them into the See-Double-Yew," he said. "They fear for their lives."

Mirina laughed bitterly. "Do you think I can go to the authorities?" she asked. "You know what we do, young one. Your eyes are open. They'd lock me up, too. I'd rather die, and they should all know that by now." She flung herself off the bed and paced. "If these idiots want to kill me, all right, let them try! After eight years, if they don't trust me, then I know I stayed too long."

"Don't go," Sunset said, reaching out a claw in a simple gesture that broke her heart. "You are my friend."

"Where's your homeworld?" she asked, her voice suddenly husky. He pointed in the direction of the bridge, his eyes glowing.

"We are very close to the Center now," he said. "Soon, we will be home!"

"You're a good child," she said, coming over to pat his wing joint. "You learn your lessons well. I'm proud of you. Remember that."

"I will," he said. He put his claw hands together under his chin. Mirina repeated the salute. For this one being's sake she felt sorry she was going.

Hungry as she was for personal contact, Mirina sent Sunset back to his post. It would not do for him to remain in her company. After the young Thelerie left, she cursed herself for a poor planner. Why hadn't she thought of his well-being when she decided to leave? The Melange might fall into chaos again after she was gone. This ship could be stranded or captured. That child trusted his sacred humans; that trust should not cost him his life.

Mirina needed a moment alone with Thunderstorm. She would beg him to come up with any pretext at all to pull Sunset off the ship, and forbid any other young Thelerie from going out with the Melange. It was time they all faced the truth of what they were doing.

"No news from Base Eight yet," Zonzalo said over his shoulder to Bisman. Mirina stood in her corner, invisible to the rest of the crew. Bisman, making sure she could see it, walked up and patted the young man on the back. "The last message Thaw heard was the same that we did. An attack, and then nothing." Zonzalo swallowed a couple of times. Bisman shook his head.

"Too bad. What about Thelerie?"

"Thaw reports all is okay planetside. Reports in from some of the other crews with profit statements, particulars when you come by in person. Thaw said they filled the tanks at the landing site. Thunderstorm's been up and back a couple of times."

"Does he have any more apprentices for us?"

Zonzalo shook his head. "Didn't say so."

"Too bad," Bisman repeated in the same expressionless voice, with a glance at Sunset. "This one's doing so well, he might teach another Thelerie what he's learned."

Sunset looked up at Bisman with joy. "I would be honored."

"That's good," Bisman said, amused, and returned to Zonzalo. "Get on to Thunder, and tell him to meet us. We've got some good stuff for him."

"Right," the younger Don said. His eyes turned partway toward his sister, then snapped back to his console. Mirina's cheeks burned. He was distancing himself from her, maybe hoping she'd leave him behind with the others. Well, he was wrong. If she had to knock him unconscious, she was getting him away from Bisman.

"What do you mean, you want to compare values?" Bisman shouted at Thunderstorm over the communication line, waving his arms furiously. The Thelerie pulled back from his video pickup, his wings flat to his back, and his pupils narrowed in distress. "I don't believe what I'm hearing! Compare values? With what?"

"With those brought by the new humans," Thunderstorm said, his upper lip twitching. "I have said that. It is only right, isn't it? To see whether the best deal can be made?"

"*We* give you the best deal, you oversized fuzzy-toy!"

"Who are these other humans with goods to sell?" Mirina asked, pushing in front of Bisman. Zonzalo sat crunched down beside her, staying out of the way. "Thunder, how could you let someone cut in on us? After *we* brought you spaceflight, taught you Standard, and all . . . ."

Bisman rounded on her. "Thought you were out of here," he sneered.

Mirina was not going to let him cow her. "I spent a hell of a lot of time bringing these people up to speed, Aldon. I would think," she turned to the screen again, "they would remember that they owe us something!"

"We do, we do!" Thunderstorm protested, looking from one co-leader to the other in panic. "But you have said we are one with *all* humans. Keff is a human!"

Bisman groaned and slapped his hand to his head. Mirina, in spite of her annoyance, was amused. "That's what you get for feeding them altruistic lines all these years," she said.

"Don't gloat, damn you," Bisman said. "Help me." Mirina, giving Aldon a last, humorous glance, turned back to the screen.

"Who are they, Thunder?" she asked.

"I have spoken with a human named Keff, as I say," Thunderstorm said. "He has many interesting goods. I have seen some of them. He has hull-plates of supreme quality. Thruster pods. Engine conduits. Good equipment, almost new. Some things we have not seen before, a garden that travels in a ship!"

"Who is this guy? What does he look like? Who does he represent?" Bisman demanded.

"He is not as tall as you, Fisman, and broad in the chest, like Mirina. His eyes are the sky, and his hair is the color of good soil," and Thunderstorm described curls by circling a claw next to his head. "He says he represents the Circuit."

"The Circuit?" Mirina echoed, puzzled. "Never heard of them."

"This shouldn't change a thing, Thunder," Bisman said, finally. "We've got goods for you. We'll land 'em, have you look 'em over, and we expect a good exchange for them, as usual. We also need another apprentice or two. Shatz, out by Base 23, needs a navigator for one of his ships. Padwe and Hannah are ready to expand, too."

"I . . . am not sure any are ready to accompany you, honored one," Thunderstorm said. Mirina frowned. Thunder was usually deferential, but he seemed downright scared this time. His wings were pressed hard enough to his sides, Mirina could see the tendons bulge under the fur. "All are too young, too unschooled . . . I hope Sunset is well?"

Mirina signalled to the young Thelerie, who was happy to greet his old mentor. He scrambled over, put his hands under his chin and bowed to the screen.

"I am very well, Thunder," he said. "I look forward to seeing you soon."

"And I you, youngster," Thunderstorm said, with visible relief. The tendons in his wings relaxed.

"There is something wrong down there," Mirina said, when Zonzalo had closed the circuit. "We've got to find out what's going on."

"I'll tell you what's wrong," Bisman snarled, slamming a fist down on the back of Zonzalo's chair. "Somebody's trying to take over our territory. They're going to regret it, damn them."

Thunderstorm turned away from the little console. His wingtips and claws trembled as he tottered back to his desk sling. He collapsed into it. The Cridi, who had stayed well out of range of the communication cabinet's video pickup, clustered around him with concern. Keff raised his eyebrows in a question.

"It is done," the Thelerie said, nodding weakly. "They are coming."

"Good," Keff said. "Tell Noonday. Then we start the ball rolling."

"We are ready," Narrow Leg said, nodding to Tall Eyebrow and Long Hand. "I regret this, in many ways. I do not like being defenseless. I do not like having my ship all to pieces all over a field."

"It won't be for long," Keff assured him. "And you aren't defenseless. You'll all be staying with Carialle in our ship."

"Is not the Watcher nervous, too?" Big Eyes asked.

Carialle answered via helmet speakers, audible to them all. "I certainly am," she said. "But we're on the way to unraveling a lot of mysteries. It'll be worth it, whatever comes."

The crew of the raider ship united instantly against the notion of a stranger's impinging on their domain. Glashton was in favor of killing the intruder on the spot. When the idea began to gather approval from others, Mirina pushed into the midst of them and in spite of the possibility of danger to herself, shouted them down.

"Quiet! What's the matter with you?" she asked, waving a forefinger under all their noses. "There may be a whole *host* of ships behind this one trader. He could be the vanguard for a traveling fleet! Did you think of that? Sooner or later someone was bound to stumble onto Thelerie. Well? Now someone has!"

"I want to know all about this Circuit," Bisman said, forgetting for the moment that Mirina was *persona non grata.* "I've never so much as heard a rumor about them."

"It's a big galaxy," Mirina said, her hands on her hips. "I learned that back in Exploration when we could find whole systems that had been hidden from scans by spatial anomalies. You'd be surprised how easy it is to hide an empire, let alone a rival . . . trading group."

"Send a message to Varvon, Frost, Hannah, and anybody who might have access to a CW news computer station," Bisman ordered. "I want details. Is the scanner working?"

"Intermittently," Glashton said, with a grimace.

"Take a look and see if this character's alone."

"And what are we going to do in the meantime?" It was an automatic question, responsibility kicking in again. Mirina realized it as soon as the phrase left her mouth.

"We?" Bisman glared down at her, also recognizing the incongruity. She saw his face change from annoyance to the old, worn groove of cooperation. It was stupid of her to get involved again when she had so nearly cut the traces, but she owed the Melange some measure of gratitude, too. She nodded. Bisman smiled grimly.

"We're going to pay a visit to this Keff." He glanced up at Zonzalo and Glashton. "He'll be leaving pretty quickly. Prepare to track where he goes. If the scanner's not working, follow him. We've still got the Slime Ball. We can destroy him and his ship if he gets funny."

"What a junker!" Carialle exclaimed. Keff had carefully turned his torso so she could see the huge, red ship land on the field near Thunderstorm's pavilion. It was immediately surrounded by Thelerie of all ages, some flying forward pushing wheeled ramps, others wrestling refueling hoses from the mighty tanks nestled in the crags at the edge of the plain.

"No doubt about it now," Keff said, the consonants blunted because he was speaking sublingually. "The style is all of a piece with the ships we confronted circling Cridi. We have our culprits. The only question is, are these the leaders of the whole shebang, or will we have to go hunting further?"

Carialle conveyed the question to Noonday, who was in her main cabin with two of her bodyguard and the Cridi. The Sayas glanced up from her perch on the weight bench as Carialle zoomed in as the hatch opened.

"This is Aldon Fisman," Noonday said. "I recall him much younger. It is shameful that I and the Ro-sayo did not take closer notice of our involvement with the Melange. But all was so beneficial, and we never questioned their good intentions."

"It is natural to think they would be as morally good as yourself," Long Hand said kindly. In the ammonia-free atmosphere of Carialle's cabin, the Cridi went without their travel globes. The visiting Thelerie were fascinated, and studied their neighbors openly. In particular, they seemed interested in the Cridi's hands, which were nearly the size of their own claws, which in turn were the same size as Keff's hands. It was a sign, Noonday had said, that they all ought to be friends.

"Bisman is their sayas, in cooperation with the female who now descends," Noonday told Carialle.

On the screen, a woman and a younger man who resembled one another followed Bisman down the ramp. Next out of the ship was a young Thelerie, his eyes and jaws wide, taking in gulping breaths as if he could not get enough of the air. He took the ramp at a bound, spread his wings, gathered his mighty haunches under him and sprang into the air for pure joy. All of Carialle's pulses seemed to halt for that one moment as he took flight.

"Beautiful," she said. She checked her datatapes. Yes, that lovely moment was recorded forever in her memory banks.

"Freihur!" the young Thelerie cried. "Fanasta, theleriyagliapalo!"

Thunderstorm, a row or two down from Keff, looked up, and his eyes widened with relief.

"Farantasioyera, shafur," he said, with the booming cough that was a Thelerie chuckle, as the apprentice came to a scrabbling landing beside him. The two embraced warmly, claw hands and wings wrapped around one another's bodies.

"Did you get any of that, Keff?" Carialle asked. IT laboriously sorted through the syllables, and produced "greetings, (unintelligible) homeworld joy your coming." Thunderstorm had said, "Proud (unintelligible) return, young (unintelligible)." Carialle guessed that the missing words were names or endearments. Even days of intensive cramming wasn't enough to fill in the blanks in IT's lexicon and grammar.

Keff turned away to answer her. Carialle was disappointed when her view was cut off, but one couldn't have everything.

"I did," he said. "I'm going to have to rely on the Thelerie speaking Standard. The Cridi will be at a double disadvantage. Standard is new to them, too."

"They're very adaptable," Carialle reminded him. "They're doing just fine. And besides, they are better at reading body language than you are."

"Are you *sure* they won't jump in too soon this time?" Keff asked, a little more forcefully than he intended. "We need information, not statues. The second these people find out we're affiliated with the Cridi, they'll clam up."

"Absolutely," Carialle said. "Tall Eyebrow swore to me he will not act unless your very life is in danger, and he has one of my second-best monitors in that box with him. The others are here with me, watching the scopes. They are all hooked up temporarily with the Core inside my bulkhead. Myths and Legends has found a useful purpose at last outside pure pleasure, my dear. While you've been setting up your trading post over the last few days, they've been role-playing with holos of human beings until they know the difference between simple physical-psychological aggression and actual assault. They're as ready as they can be."

"Hmm," Keff said. "Keep your records of the training sessions; I'd like Dr. Chaudri in Psych on SSS-900-C to take a look at them."

"Already saved and stored," Carialle assured him blithely. "I think you have a customer."

✨CHAPTER 17

The first thing anyone would notice was the poster. Mirina saw it on short-range screens before they had quite landed on the plain. Once she could examine it in detail, she was impressed.

Painted or printed at the top of the huge, white signboard was a pair of silhouetted beings, species indeterminate, exchanging shapeless bundles. Beneath the image of the traders was depicted pictures of certain commodities in various recognizable forms that the trader would accept in exchange for his wares. The first line was an irregular lump of gold, half in and out of quartz matrix; the gold was shown next pressed into an ingot, then as the molecular diagram of the element, and weight at certain gravity, then as various artifacts into which gold could be shaped, such as cups, wire, circuit boards, statues, jewelry. He wishes, Mirina thought. Other lines showed crystals, from simple quartzite sand up through diamond and radioactive crystalline forms; precious metals; radioactives; iron and steel; marble, alabaster, and other decorative heavy stone. Handcrafts were welcome, too. A depiction of weaving and various finished products showed a real familiarity with textile manufacture. Jewelry, pottery, furniture, and practically any type of merchandise approved by the Central Exchange Commission had been pictured in minute detail, but still leaving room for the individual to offer variations. So tidy a mind that could design a sign like this appealed to her. This Keff had a completist's attitude: that everything can be set out so no one misunderstands, and everyone goes away happy. If she'd been staying on with Bisman, she might have suggested such a sign for them.

There were three more lines at the bottom of the signboard, showing various kinds of weapons: guns, lasers, bows, whips, garottes, with a big red X through each. This trader didn't want just anything, Mirina noted. Even if an alien didn't understand what the X or the color red meant at once, it would understand that there was something different about the acceptability of certain things. That showed a kind of morality that she had tried without success to impose on the Melange. No matter. That part of her life would soon be behind her. The signboard was worn and battered, as if it had been in and out of a cargo hold a thousand times. She glanced at the trader in the midst of his wares. Perhaps it had. He certainly looked as if he'd seen a few days himself.

Keff, if it was he, was not a youth. He looked to be about her own age, around forty. A man of middle height with very broad shoulders, trim and fit, he was dressed for comfort in a gaudy tunic and a pair of exercise pants going saggy around the ankle underneath a clear environment suit, the only part of his attire that looked new. The top of the helmet had been opaqued against the hot Thelerie sun. The dark halo threw into prominence his brown, curly hair, and fair skin, made pink by the heat. He was at work straightening piles of goods. Two, little, boxy servo robots rumbled up and down the rows between the stacks, putting things back in order or holding up goods for the Thelerie to see. When the raider crew spread out, the boxies accepted them as customers, and held up on display any item by which anyone stopped for more than a few seconds. And what merchandise!

"He's got half a spaceship scattered on the ground," Mirina whispered to Bisman as they pushed their way along the dusty aisle toward the stranger. "Look at that: hull plates, exhaust locks, life-support circuitry—I don't know what that is." She pointed at a green, pressed-plastic tub about three meters across and two deep that had several protuberances sticking inward over the lip. A couple of locals were looking it over with the aim of making a planter out of it.

Thunderstorm and some of his staff were counting small circuit boards through the plastic of a storage pouch. They stopped to give the respectful greeting to the humans, but went back to their examination. Bisman's face crimsoned with suppressed fury over the whole situation. Mirina thought he might go into an apoplectic fit. She was annoyed, too, at the nonchalance this character showed.

"There must be thirty Thelerie here," Bisman said furiously, shouldering past them. More natives were winging in at every moment, landing at a remove from the scatter of merchandise and loping forward curiously. "What happened to security?"

"Thunderstorm can't control every centimeter of this planet," Mirina said, reasonably, glancing back over her shoulder at the Space Sayas. He looked very nervous, and she patted the air in a calming gesture toward him. "I can't believe this stranger's here all alone."

"Fool evidently has no fear," Bisman said. "Can you believe it? He landed on a strange world and set up shop, never thinking anybody might take a shot at him!"

"There's probably some sophisticated armaments in his ship," Mirina speculated, glancing around. She spotted it at last, and wondered how she had missed it. It stood tall and pure of shape in a niche formed by the natural rock wall at the edge of the plateau, like a classical statue in an alcove. "What a beauty!"

Bisman glanced up in the direction she pointed, and whistled as he made a mental estimate.

"There's money behind him," he said, at last. "We ought to be able to help ourselves to some of it."

"You're Keff?" Bisman asked.

"Who wants to know?" Keff said, stacking white enameled plates. The servo came over and took them away from him with a touch of impatience that was all Carialle's. He let go of the piece of hull and straightened up to greet his new "customer."

His eyes were a vivid blue in the pink-cheeked face. Mirina realized with a shock how attractive he was, and unconsciously thrust out one hip and put a hand on it. Keff grinned at her. Abashed, she stood up straight, folding her arms across her chest.

"Hot day, isn't it, friends?" Keff asked.

"You don't seem surprised to see other human beings," she said.

Keff laughed. "When I landed, these nice people addressed me in my own language," he said. "It didn't take a rocket scientist to figure out that they've known human people for a long, long time.

They didn't get the language from tapes. There were *chairs* in that building over yonder, though none of the locals can sit on them. And your friend here," he pointed to Thunderstorm, "uses colloquialisms."

"Colloq . . . ?" Bisman waved away the unfamiliar word. "So what if he does? If they're in good working order, who cares?" Though Mirina could tell it was costing him something of an effort, he put out a hand to the stranger. "This is Mirina Don. I'm Aldon Bisman."

"Thought it was Fisman," Keff said exasperatingly. "That's what the locals called you. Just call me Keff." He was so damned cheerful, Mirina thought, she might like to strangle him herself. Then he turned the intense blue gaze on her, and she felt her cheeks flame with red. He was very, *very* attractive. He looked her up and down, with a quick, insouciant flick of those eyes. She should have been offended, but instead, she threw back her hair and raised her chin in defiance. He gave her a grin of approval.

"Damned Thelerie can't say their damned b's," Bisman said. "When are you moving on?"

"When I've finished doing business," Keff said. He straightened up and looked Bisman in the eye. He might have been several inches shorter than the raider, but Mirina, with the eye of long experience, thought he'd be a match for him. The way Keff stood so naturally on the balls of his feet instead of flat on the soles suggested he *lived* unarmed combat. Formidable, attractive . . . and smack in the middle of the Melange's patch. She had to remember that. He was an intruder. He represented the outside world. It spelled the end of the Thelerie's sheltered existence, and she couldn't have that.

"What kind of goods do you have here?" Mirina asked.

"Oh, see for yourself. I sell a lot of things. I do a rather good line on state-of-the-art spaceship parts, right out of the heart of the CW," Keff said. Mirina exchanged a glance with Bisman, and saw the light of greed in his eyes. And small wonder, too, with that array on the ground.

"Looks like you have a whole spaceship spread out here," Bisman said, conversationally.

Keff laughed again, but a little nervously. "When you pick things up here and there, they accumulate," he said.

✳   ✳   ✳

"Good guess," Carialle said, auditing the conversation from four hundred meters away. "Good thing he hasn't got the Cridi's skill for abstract puzzle-solving, or he'd see for sure! I'm glad your new design doesn't look like the old ships, Narrow Leg, or these folks would have spotted the resemblance in an instant. Can't have that."

Narrow Leg sat on the console in front of the biggest screentank. In Carialle's protective atmosphere, he and the others were able to move around, free of their travel globes. They watched the screens around the main cabin that were not obscured by the shipbuilder's person.

"I do not like having my ship all to pieces on the ground," he said, wringing his big hands together as on the screen Mirina kicked some of the components. "Do not touch that, silly human!" he wailed shrilly. "That is a delicate power regulator!"

"This stuff is junk," the woman said, turning over a brand-new engine accelerator valve still covered with protective lubricant. "I'll give you fifty credits for it, no more."

"No, thank you," the unseen Keff said, blithely, his hand taking the component away from her and setting it delicately on the top of a servo, who spirited it away. "It's worth a lot more than that."

"Oh, yes? How do you expect me to make a profit on it if I pay you more?" Mirina asked. The woman turned to watch the robot whisk the accelerator valve to the end of a row and set it down on a rickety folding table.

"Aren't we greedy?" Carialle commented.

"I don't expect you to make a profit on it; I expect *me* to make a profit on it," Keff's voice said. "I expect *you* to use it. I prefer to serve the end-user. If you don't want it, someone else will."

She shrugged. "It's junk. Who else would?"

Narrow Leg's black eyes bulged until Carialle thought they would pop.

"How dare she denigrate the components of my ship! They are perfect! I rejected eight to the power of six of that valve before choosing that one! It was the product of ten to the power of sixteen calculations and designs!" His voice rose into almost inaudible registers.

"It's a bargaining ploy," Big Eyes said, floating over from her perch on the round table to try to calm her father. She put a gentle hand on his shoulder, and he shook it off irately. "You exist in the rarefied waters of science too much. You should come to the bazaar, and dig through the mud with me some time. Then you would hear worse than this."

"Bah." Narrow Leg was not appeased. He turned to Carialle's frog image on the near bulkhead. "What if they take some of our parts away?"

"We have many spares," Gap Tooth called to him.

"They are all out there, mains and spares," Narrow Leg gestured angrily.

Big Voice was clearly amused to see his old adversary discomfitted for once. With a tiny flick of his fingers, he drew just enough power from Carialle's engines to glide up from the weight bench and over where the shipbuilder was sitting.

"Keff will protect your ship parts," he said.

"And if he cannot?" Narrow Leg demanded, glaring upward. "How do you expect to get home?"

Big Voice snapped his fingers, making the gold fingerstalls click. "We do not need *your* ship. Carialle will bring us back to Cridi."

"I will, if necessary," Carialle promised the anguished captain. "But your craft will be restored as soon as possible."

"I am not happy," Narrow Leg said. He hunched up his kness and wrapped his skinny arms around them. The small bundle shot off the console and disappeared into the lap of the crash couch behind him.

"Leave him alone," Big Eyes signed, flitting away from the chair like a tadpole swimming in a pond. "It is no use communicating with him when he is like this."

"He should be adaptable, like me," Big Voice said aloud.

From inside the huge chair came a disbelieving "Hah!"

"My child looks nervous," Noonday said, speaking up timidly. "He has shown disrespect to humans, and it weighs upon his conscience." The Sayas and two of her Ro-sayo sat in the corner, out of the way of the Cridi. Noonday occupied Keff's weight bench; and the Ro-sayo, a spare mattress pad from the cargo hold. Carialle switched her monitor away from the conversation Keff was having with the raiders, and zoomed in on Thunderstorm. The Space Sayas went about his shopping as he'd been told to do, but he wasn't happy.

"He's doing fine," Carialle assured his parent, enlarging the view on the screen nearest the weight bench for the sake of the Thelerie visitors. "He did exactly what he was supposed to, to make the

Melange jealous. We don't want them thinking too clearly. People blurt things out when they are angry."

"Flurt?" Noonday asked, her beautiful eyes puzzled.

"Speak forcefully without thinking," Carialle said, slowly.

"These learn," Small Spot said, proudly. He sat as close to the Thelerie as they would allow him. "I teach them more Standard, which I know."

"You're doing fine, too," Carialle assured him, privately amused.

"I cannot believe the beauty of this ship, Carialle," Noonday said. "I see, but my eyes must lie—such things as this and the Cridi ship, they are as dreams."

Narrow Leg was somewhat soothed by the compliments. His wrinkled, green face appeared over the top of the crash couch.

"Not a dream. State-of-the-art for now," he peeped. "We move ahead, always ahead." Carialle transposed the voice to a baritone register and amplified it so Noonday and the others could listen without pain.

"We are getting used to them," Noonday said, to the air. Carialle could tell that she still didn't really understand a human who lived in the walls, nor one who could look like a frog at will, but followed the Cridi's example of behaving as if Carialle was there in the room with them. Shellperson existence was a facet of human experience that had never yet come their way.

She wondered what the CenCom would make of Thelerie, and if they would try to withdraw the technology humans had given them to date, on the grounds that they wouldn't have evolved it yet themselves. She hoped not, but bureaucrats could be so rulebound!

Carialle herself had become completely comfortable with Thelerie. Having had Noonday, Thunderstorm, the Ro-Sayo, and a large number of former members of the Melange tour through her ship during the last several days, she was convinced that none of their gaits matched the footsteps she remembered transiting what was left of her hull after her accident, not even accounting for weightlessness and grav-boots. They were absolved. The question remained: who?

"Well, we might have an offer for you ourselves," Bisman said, rocking back on his heels and staring up at the sun. "We'll take the whole line off your hands, on condition that you take it, and don't come back."

"I can't do that," Keff said. "I have obligations to fulfill."

"The Circuit," Bisman said. Keff nodded. "Where's it based?"

"Oh, here and there," Keff said, too casually.

"Well, it won't be here," Bisman said, not at all fooled. "You have two days, then I want to see your tail-rockets up there." He pointed toward the sky.

"No can do," Keff said, looking pathetically at both leaders. Mirina wasn't moved. "The lady who runs the Circuit would make life miserable for me. You'll understand." And he flashed that insouciant grin once again.

Mirina found that they were getting nowhere with the trader. It stood to reason that a traveler who went around in a fancy ship like that with top-shelf goods like these on the edge of nowhere wouldn't be easy to bluff, but was he too cocky? Bisman might get so frustrated that he would attack him right here. She could stop him, but couldn't prevent the rest of the crew piling in on a fight. At least Zonzalo and Sunset would stay out of it. She'd been very firm in her orders. For whatever reason, neither one argued.

Bisman started some low-level threats on Keff, nothing overt or too nasty, and found his sallies thrown back in his face. Mirina stood by, turning over the odd component or two with her toe. He had some of the damnedest things for sale. Oil paintings? She bent to examine them. A small space-scape caught her eye. She thought she recognized the subject as Dimitri DMK-504-R. Piled anyhow underneath it were the study of a planet she couldn't identify, a lake at sunset, a beautifully detailed portrait of a cat stalking a leaf, and a color sketch of a couple in yellow and silver, holding a baby dressed in deep, burgundy red.

"You've wandered into our patch," Bisman was saying over her head.

"Did you paint these?" Mirina asked, suddenly, interrupting them. She nudged the pile with the side of her foot. "They're good!"

She was rewarded with the warm grin. "No. A friend of mine does them."

"He has talent," Mirina said.

"She. Thank you. I'll pass the compliment along. Maybe you'd like to buy something?" Keff asked, with just the right air of hope.

"Maybe not," Mirina said, crossing her arms again. Good God, he was pushy!

"Oh, then on my next stop here," he said, cheerfully, not at all put off. "You folks get around here much?"

"Now, listen, friend," Bisman said, poking Keff in the chest to get his attention. "There won't be another stop here for you."

"Really?" Keff asked. "I won't ask, 'you and what army,' because I've been watching your toughs gather around me for the last ten minutes, and I promise you I'm just not as green as I am cabbage-looking."

"What?" Mirina demanded, having followed his conversation up until then.

"Save the ancient colloquialisms yourself," Carialle growled in his ear. Keff clicked his tongue in acknowledgement. He had his hand on the top of the red box marked "Medical Waste," where Tall Eyebrow was concealed. One rap, and these brutes would be frozen in place. He hated to show his trump card right away. He would never get what he needed if he was too cocky.

"Sorry," he said, smiling at the woman. "I mean, I was not born yesterday. You don't think for a minute that I don't know how defenseless I *look*." She paused. Keff noticed Bisman's hand sweep down in a gesture that looked casual, but all the other spacers stopped moving toward them.

"So you have some kind of defense in that fancy airplane of yours," Bisman said casually.

"Airplane, hah," Carialle said. "Look at the flying refuse heap he came in."

"Shh!..sssure," Keff said. "My . . . employer wouldn't let me out without adequate protection."

"The Circuit," Bisman said flatly.

"You've heard of us?"

"No, I haven't. You could be a fly-by-night operation with one ship and an attitude. I've seen your kind before."

"Started that way yourself, did you?" Keff asked, and had the satisfaction of seeing the pirate start violently.

"The Melange comes from an old family tradition," Bisman corrected him with a sharp look.

"Ah! Your *father*," Keff translated.

The present-day Bisman breasted up to Keff and glared down at him. "Listen, character, you gather up all your debris, and you lift off of this world within thirty Standard hours."

"My boss will get tetchy if I don't come back with a deal," Keff said, plaintively, his hands spread in appeal. Bisman crossed his arms. Out of the corner of his eye, Keff could see the crew on the move again. "No, eh?"

"Too bad," Bisman was saying. "You tell him he's accidentally impinged on hazardous territory."

"She," Keff corrected him. "You wouldn't believe how tough the broad is at the center of the Circuit. Your threats would make her laugh out loud."

"Oh, Keff, I love it!" Carialle's chuckle sounded in his ear. "Tell him it's a neural-synaptic network, which means we're never far away from the active arm of our organization."

Keff passed on Carialle's words, and enjoyed the puzzled look on the pirates' faces as the two did mental translations. Bisman, at least, came up empty.

"What's this tough broad's name?" the older man asked.

"Carialle."

"Carialle what?"

"None of your business," Keff said, nonchalantly, raising his eyebrows.

"It is if we're going to do business with you," Bisman said.

"And who says you are?" Keff asked. "You want me off what you call your patch. Who in the frosty void do you think you are?"

"Look," Bisman said, suddenly looking bored with him. "I don't talk to underlings. I want to talk to this Carialle."

"Hmmm . . . Might be arranged," Keff said.

"I want a meeting. You can arrange it."

"Well, I'll see what I can do," Keff said, bending down to accept a bag of circuit boards from one of the loader robots. He glanced up at Thunderstorm and the young apprentice from the pirate ship. The older Thelerie had an anxious look on his face.

"Fine, fine," Keff called, waving to the Sayas. "I'll put the value down on a slate for you. Keep looking! You never know if you'll find something else you like." He smiled at Bisman. "It may take some time to get a message through to Carialle, but I'll send one right away and tell her you want to talk with her."

"Face-to-face," Bisman said, tapping Keff painfully in the middle of the chest once for every syllable.

✳   ✳   ✳

While Keff stood there thoughtfully rubbing his chest, Bisman hustled Mirina away . He grabbed Thunderstorm by a claw on the way by.

"Your pavilion," he hissed. "Now!"

Thunderstorm loped unhappily behind them over the stony ground. Mirina could feel the storm of fury growing, but Bisman didn't let fly until they were safely under the roof.

"You're avoiding me," Bisman snapped, rounding at once on the Thelerie. Waving a finger under Thunderstorm's nose, he backed the Sayas up until he bumped into his own desk sling. "Don't try to deny it. I've known you too long. I told you we had stuff for you. You should be buying from us, and only us."

"Tell us about this man," Mirina said, more kindly. The Thelerie looked from one human to the other, clattering his claws together nervously. He settled over the sling and continued tapping his fingertips on the desktop until Bisman glared at him to stop.

"This Keff landed here one day. He said he had goods we might like. And so we do!" Thunderstorm said, miserably. "Things that the Melange has been unable to get for many years, are here! You see the temptation is great. And others saw him before I did, so I could not hide him. They like these goods."

"I understand that," Bisman said. "He's got a few things I might take myself. What I'm talking about is no apprentices. You must have some about ready to ship out. Where are they?"

"I . . . I do not have any I am ready to send. There is more to know."

"Haven't they memorized the Manual?" Mirina asked, puzzled.

"Oh, yes," Thunderstorm said, at once. "In that they are proficient."

"Then what's the hangup?" Bisman asked, banging a fist on the desk. "You know what kind of rewards there are in space travel."

"Yes," Thunderstorm replied, more thoughtfully than usual. "I know."

"So why are you being cagey with us?"

"The air is bad in ships," Thunderstorm said suddenly. "The old ones who I see have weakness in the thorax from lack of elemental acids."

"Chlorine?" Mirina asked.

"Yes," Thunderstorm said.

"Hell, then we'll work out a medical system. Miri . . . no, I'll work something out," Bisman said, dismissing Mirina. She glared, then realized she had no right to complain. He'd accepted her resignation, and he was letting her go.

"It will still take time before any are ready," Thunderstorm said, timidly. "The training continues."

Bisman walked to the entrance of the pavilion. "Next time I won't take no for an answer, Thunder. There are ships out there who need Thelerie apprentices. Just remember who your friends are." With an apologetic glance back at the terrified Thelerie, Mirina followed him out.

Bisman reported the conversation to the others on the ship. The reivers clustered in the galley grumbled about another setback.

"Dammit, this tears the trip out to Sungali," Glashton said. "Hannah had a collection for us. It's not worth burning the fuel if we have to turn around and bring her a navigator on a separate trip."

"At least we can't blame this problem on the trader," Mirina said.

"No, dammit, but he might have said something that set them off," Bisman said, with growing heat. He kicked a battered cabinet door, adding a black bootmark to the damage he'd done it in hundreds of other temper tantrums. Mirina wouldn't miss that part of Aldon Bisman at all.

"Perhaps he's tired of talking to the families of the ones who don't come home again," she said, pointedly.

"Shut up!" Bisman said, rounding on her. "You want out anyhow. This isn't any of your business anymore." He slammed his hand on the countertop. "I've got to find the pressure point, get Thunder back into line, and soon. These Thelerie are a hell of a lot of trouble."

"Well, why are we bothering to go to so much trouble for them, then?" Zonzalo said with disgust.

"Because the soulfrigging flying barnacles can't get lost, that's why," Bisman exploded. "You know that, you young idiot. They always know their way back home, and everywhere in proportion to home. It happened to me once, being lost without a navigator. I never want that to happen again. Wandering lost in eternity may appeal to you, but it scares me juiceless!"

"And there's the fuel," Mirina said thoughtfully. "I didn't see any

Thelerie merchandise out on that field. Did Keff spot the refinery and offer to trade for a tankload?"

"Whatever it is doesn't matter," Bisman said. "We find out what there is to know about this Circuit, and what defenses this Keff is packing in that pretty ship of his. He'll get a meeting set up with this Carialle, and I'll strangle him in front of her as a lesson to stay out of our way."

"And then what?" Mirina asked.

"Then we take care of all of the Circuit," Bisman said. "We've got the Slime Ball, remember?"

"Who knows how many there'll be?" Mirina asked. "The Ball could overheat any day, and then we'll have nothing."

"We've got more than sixty ships and enough armament to carpet a planet," Bisman said offhandedly. "I'll start calling 'em in right away. If he wants to make this system the prize in a blood game, we'll oblige him."

"I don't want the Thelerie hurt!" Mirina said, alarmed at the idea.

"Shut up," Bisman said, facing her down. "Either help, or get out of the way. You're just waiting for an offworld ship now, right?"

It stung, but Mirina had asked for it. "Right," she said. She rose and stalked out of the galley. Zonzalo got up to follow her, but his footsteps stopped at the hatchway. Mirina went back to her cabin alone.

"Are they gone?" Keff asked the air.

"Sealed up in their wretched ship," Carialle said. "They might have a passive scan on you, but it's nothing I'm picking up. Their telemetry equipment is as haphazard as their engines."

"Thank heavens," Keff said. One of the servos rumbled up to him, and he put the Medical Waste box onto its flat top. He slapped the robot's side. "Move it out, quickly. Is the tub full?"

"Big Eyes has it ready and waiting, with an electrolyte shake on the side."

Keff trotted along behind the drone. The sun was setting over the planetary-west horizon, and he glimpsed two moons rising golden above the mountain ranges. Very pretty landscape, he thought, but too, too hot.

"Are you okay in there, TE?" he asked, through his helmet mike.

"Okay," came a faint croak.

"Hurry it up, Cari," Keff said, more concerned. He didn't like the way the globe-frog sounded. Had he stayed outside too long? The servo rumbled around the edge of the stone cliff, and out of sight at last from the pirates' ship. Keff grabbed the crate bodily off its platform and ran with it into the ship. The other Cridi flew around him as soon as he was past the airlock. The lid of the box flew one way, and the little globe lifted straight out.

The sides of the globe were completely misted over with condensation, which broke up as the others moved it. The Frog Prince's body lay at the bottom, immersed in a few liters of water. He roused as Big Eyes wrenched off the upper half of the travel-globe, and sat up. His eyes glistened in an unusually pinched face, but he waved away offers of help to stand. Noonday, who had watched all afternoon with growing admiration, added her concern.

"He will live?" she asked.

"I live," he said, hoarsely. "It is sometimes worse on Sky Clear."

"You're a hero," Keff said. "If you hadn't been there, I couldn't have pulled that off." The Cridi shook his head.

"It is nothing," Tall Eyebrow signed. He licked his lips, which were visibly dry.

"Tchah! Nothing!" Big Eyes flicked her fingers, and the door of the spare cabin flew open. Tall Eyebrow was whisked straight out of the main cabin. Keff ran along behind into the corridor. He heard rather than saw the splash.

"I am all right!" Tall Eyebrow protested in Cridi. "Do not . . . blub!" Big Eyes hands had moved, and Keff suspected she swept a wave of the cool water over her loved one's head. He stuck his head in, and saw gallons of water washing across the floor from the small bathroom.

"He is a hero," Big Eyes said, with a look at Keff and the Thelerie, as she sailed in after him. "He does not complain."

"He does what a leader should," Narrow Leg said, nodding.

"Daddy approves, whether he admits it or not," Carialle said, in Keff's aural receiver. "I do love a love story."

"Seeing him in action, you can't help but admire him," Keff agreed.

"It is true," Noonday said, behind them. "The Cridi are most amazing folk." She gathered her wings about her, avoiding the water flying out of the door of the spare cabin. "Now that night falls I must go back. The Ro-sayo and I have much to discuss. You will accompany us?"

"I'd better not," Keff said. "The Melange will be watching me closely now. The Cridi will go, carrying a receiver so you can hear what Carialle and I say."

Noonday looked up, as if she expected to see the pirates and their surveillance. "But how do I go, if you are watched? They will see me."

"Ah," Keff said. "The extreme cleverness of me! Thunderstorm asked a few of your people to wait on the field. They'll come over and give you cover when we lower the hatch again. You'll be one in a crowd of your people making purchases."

The Thelerie were right on time. When Carialle activated the ramp again, Thunderstorm and a cluster of his apprentices fluttered over, some carrying boxes, some carrying other small items. Using Core power, to the great astonishment of the locals, Narrow Leg and the others unloaded the contents of the boxes, and rolled their globes inside.

Tall Eyebrow emerged from the bath with glistening skin. His face still looked rather peaked, but Carialle checked his vital signs, and found them strong. He showed no weakness as he sealed himself into his travel globe. Big Eyes looked at him with dismay.

"You should not go with us," the young female said. "You should rest."

"I am going," Tall Eyebrow argued. "These people have made many sacrifices for us. This is not a risk at all. I am healthy. I must hear what is said."

"You will all be well-maintained," Noonday assured Big Eyes solemnly. "I will look after Tall Eyebrow myself." Big Eyes relented, but grudgingly, and allowed herself to be shut into a plumbing fixture.

"We will be back soon," Narrow Leg said to Keff, via radio, from inside his crate. Each of the Thelerie took one of the containers gingerly in its claw arms, and flew away with it. Shaking his head, he stepped back into the airlock, and Carialle sealed the door.

"A meeting with this tough broad," Carialle said, still enjoying the sound of the phrase. Her Lady Fair image appeared on the wall armed with morningstar and shield. "You mean a holographic manifestation?"

"Yes, but not like that one," Keff said, smiling. "Whatever would work to get the most information out of them. We have to be careful. I don't want them to leave again if there's the least chance an armed ship is on the way, but I don't want to endanger this population. The Thelerie are vulnerable, and they trust humans implicitly because of these brutes."

"The Melange are a mixed curse," Carialle said, thoughtfully. "On the one hand, I'm glad they discovered this race. They're fascinating. On the other hand, if it had been anyone else, the CW could have nurtured the Thelerie's natural development. Look at this place. Except for the smelly air, it's almost a type-G world."

"Yes," Keff said. "I notice the pirates don't bother with air filters."

Carialle caught the hopeful note in his voice. "No," she said flatly. "There is a cumulative effect on your health. The Cridi have been complaining of the residual ammonia brought into the cabin in the lungs of the Thelerie visitors. You keep your suit on."

"Yes, mother," Keff sighed.

Keff had a grasshopper's eye view of the proceedings in the Sayad, from the camera eye carried on Gaptooth's globe. She was carried in a sack by one of Noonday's guards and released into the Sayad chamber to the horror and protest of the Ro-sayo. She rolled at once into the angle of one of the carved beams as the Thelerie glared down into the camera lens.

"Why are they here?" Midnight demanded, as behind him the Cridi freed themselves from the crates and other containers.

"As witnesses," Narrow Leg said, flying out of a box marked "Art Supplies." "And as a conduit for our good friend Keff."

"But they are enemies!"

"They are not," Noonday said, mildly, settling onto her divan cushion. She coughed, and was surrounded at once by Ro-sayo exclaiming concern for her health. Keff felt pleased that the Sayas was held in such esteem.

"You are unharmed?" Winter asked her.

"All is well," she assured them. "I have spent a day in deficient atmosphere. The effects will pass quickly." With a wing-finger, she signalled for the doors to be secured. "Let no one in or out, and have a patrol hover about the windows on the outside. Our guests must remain hidden from view." The guards sprang out and away, spreading their wings to obey their leader's command. The Ro-sayo settled down on their cushions, casting wary eyes on the cluster of Cridi. Thunderstorm drew their eyes away by stalking into the center of the circle of counselors.

"Before they speak," he said, "I have a speech to make, of apology to our neighbors, for it is true what Keff told you. I will speak in Standard where I can, for the sake of our listeners."

He went on to detail the history of the Melange. Although Keff couldn't understand all of the Space Sayas' words, he could tell that many in the room were shocked at the revelations he had for them.

"Then all of our accomplishments were based on lies!" Midnight said.

Thunderstorm bowed his head. "I deserve that," he said. "But we may rebuild, and beginning now, with the help of legitimate representatives of humanity, we shall."

"And how do we know that Keff and the unseen Carialle are truly from the See-Double-Yew?" another Ro-sayo demanded.

"Does it matter?" Noonday asked. "I saw the Melange show hostility to a stranger human, telling him to leave Thelerie, and never return. That isn't the act of a being who believes we are all one."

Thunderstorm smiled. "I assure you, I know real See-Double-Yew. I spent many years robbing their bases and stations. Also of these, the Cridi. A number of the parts of the ships that stand on our own landing pad come from their ships."

Midnight stood, and solemnly bowed to the Cridi. "We owe you reparation." He held out a claw hand. Narrow Leg and Tall Eyebrow exchanged small, subtle signs that Keff had to squint to see. Together, the Cridi opened their globes and rose to their full, though inconsiderable, heights. Exposing their delicate skins and lungs to the sharp air was a stunning display of trust that moved Keff deeply. The two leaders stepped forward to take the Thelerie's narrow talon, one at a time. The other Ro-sayo grudgingly, fearfully, stepped forward to clasp hands with the shining, water-clad amphibioids.

"We will take aid and assistance instead," Narrow Leg said. "The parts are obsoleted with the new design, the one that is," he added with regret, "lying dismembered on the field."

"What can we do to assist?" the other Ro-sayo asked.

"Be prepared," Keff said, speaking through an audio receiver on

Gaptooth's globe. "Our intention is to obtain recorded confessions from the Melange as to their activities in this sector for use by our judicial arm. I'm concerned that if the Melange becomes suspicious that we are from the CW, your well-being could be at stake."

"A certain amount of *fallout* is inevitable," Thunderstorm said, with a shrug of his magnificent wings. "We have contributed to the galaxy's ills by consorting with criminals. Although I absorb all guilt, my people may suffer. I owe all many lives."

"We will not claim them," Big Voice said, rolling forward and puffing himself up majestically. "The thing we must do is get the information needed by Keff and Carialle."

"It is possible that our military is nearby," Carialle added, amused by Big Voice's self-importance. "They must have received our message by now about the Thelerie we left behind on the Cridi system's fifth planet. They could be here soon to take Bisman and his crew into custody."

"If they leave, what of it?" Noonday said, spreading her upper lip. "My child says that the Melange come here often. They have a friendly bond with our people, whatever they have done to others. A capture will occur, now or in the future. We offer the aid of our guardians, if you need them. At present, we will cooperate to get what it is you seek now."

"I hope so," Carialle said. Keff thought he could detect wistfulness in her tone. He smiled at her pillar.

"With such friends, Lady Fair, how can we fail?"

✳️CHAPTER 18

A few days passed after the Cridi returned safely from the capital city. Keff continued to pretend doing business on the high plain near Thunderstorm's enclave.

The longer the Cridi's ship parts were on display, the more interested the pirates became in buying them. Keff was now in possession of a handful of credit chits whose legitimacy and provenance he very much doubted. Narrow Leg, on duty as Keff's guardian in the Medical Waste box, was less of a success than Tall Eyebrow, because he kept a closer eye on his inventions than he did on the human whose life he was supposed to be protecting.

"I do not like these disappearing," he protested into his radio over and over again during the long, hot day. "They go into the pirates' hold, and they go away toward the city—but they are not *here.*"

"Relax, Tad Pole," Keff said, out of the corner of his mouth. "We'll get everything back just as soon as we're finished here. Thunderstorm promised me that the parts are being well looked after."

"It must be soon," Narrow Leg said. "All this dust, getting into the components! Impair efficiency!"

"Shh! You're exaggerating, I'm sure," Keff hissed, seeing Bisman coming down the ramp of the raider ship. He hoped the Cridi shriek hadn't been audible. The leader was stalking toward him with purpose. Keff stopped pretending to tidy his wares, and waited.

"What have you heard?" Bisman asked, without other preamble.

"Nothing yet," Keff said. "I sent the request for a meeting, as you asked me to. It'll take time for the message to meet her. I had to assure her you're not a small-timer, that it would be worth her while doing business with you. I told her you had sixty ships under your command, is that right?"

Bisman spat into the dust next to Keff's feet. "At least sixty. And I've got other resources. Connections."

Keff raised his eyebrows, but the older man was far too canny to take the questioning look as an opening. He shook his head, and Keff grinned, pretending to look sheepish. "Can't blame a fellow for trying."

"You just tell me when she gets here," Bisman said, poking him in the chest again. "I'll talk a lot more when I hear her bona fides."

"All right," Keff said, but to Bisman's back. As soon as he'd had his say, he'd swung around and stalked off in the direction of Thunderstorm's pavilion.

"I do feel sorry for that griffin," he said into his sublingual pickup. "He's taking all the brunt for us."

"You play the part of the up-and-coming flunky to perfection," Carialle said acidly.

"I've always said I should start at the top and work downward," Keff said, forcing a note of cheer into his voice. "Is there any word today?"

"Not a thing," Carialle's voice said, sounding a little strained. "There has been plenty of time for my first transmissions to have reached the nearest space station. I could have *flown* up and back in the time it's taken them to respond."

A couple of the raiders on the edge of Keff's "bazaar" reached for the same book-chip library at the same time, and started to bicker over it. Keff turned his back on them.

"There's always the question, if there was an armed ship in the vicinity, and whether they could send it," he said.

"They might already have sent it," Carialle pointed out. "If it's behind the anomaly, the ship won't receive any more transmissions from us until it clears Cridi system. By then, the Melange, or at least Bisman, could be long gone. Noonday's guards won't be worth a darn against energy weapons. I wish you could have gotten even one base location out of Bisman. *Any* starting point so I don't have to unravel ion threads again."

"He doesn't like me," Keff said, thoughtfully. "More fool he. But he's starting to lose patience. How long can we stall him before he finally loses his temper?"

"If that happens, he'll attack, in which case our cover, and the Cridi's, is blown; or he'll leave. We'd have to give chase, and I don't fancy our chances. That third Core may still be out there somewhere."

Keff rocked back on his heels and looked up at the sky. He stared at a bank of clouds gathering in the northwest, then realized the novelty of atmospheric condensation in such a dry climate. Looked like a head of stratocumulus building. Did it ever rain here? He must ask Thunderstorm.

"We're not policemen," Keff said, "but we can't just let these people go."

"Not until I get what I want," Carialle said. "Once the CW forces land here, that possibility is gone, and *we're* stewed, too. I'll be in a home for the perpetually bewildered, and you'll be flying a troop carrier."

"We're not making much progress," Keff admitted. "I haven't managed to elicit a single confidence out of those people, not in six days. Not a single detail of where they've been in the past, a single event. You'd think they'd be bursting to brag about their successes, but no!"

"It's a tight ship," Carialle agreed. "They keep themselves to themselves with a vengeance. There are organized minds in charge. I'd admire the Melange, if we weren't trying to break through their defenses."

The air grew heavier, and the sky darkened. Keff checked his chronometer. "Looks like weather," he said. "How far away is it?"

"I've been charting a pattern coming in from planetary northwest," Carialle said. "I've been charting a tropical front in the far west. It hit a cold front a thousand kilometers from here, and I admit it whipped up faster than I estimated. You'd better start getting things under cover. You have about ninety Standard minutes."

"Looks like it could be a gully-washer," Keff said, starting to pick merchandise up at once. He signalled for the servo to come over and help.

"Keff," Carialle said. Her voice sounded tentative. "I've been trying to stifle my natural anxieties, but something needs to happen soon. I've . . . I find I've been *counting*."

Counting, as she had twenty years ago, adrift in space, to keep herself sane. Keff felt an urge to run inside the ship, to be close to Carialle, anything to help her calm down. "Have you had any memory flashes?" He started to pick up piles of circuit boards with a burst of nervous energy, then stopped to look around for the boxes.

"No."

"Good. Hang on, Cari. Nothing's different than it was just a few days ago."

"No, we're *nearer* an answer, Keff. I know it. I'm beginning to feel antsy in anticipation of it."

Aggravated at how slowly he was progressing, he glanced toward the humans browsing through the lanes. The men and women from the Melange had also noticed the lowering sky. They shot glances at him and the tons of merchandise, but moved purposefully toward their own ship. Bisman stood next to the ramp of the raider with his arms crossed and a sneering smile on his face, watching Keff.

"Nice people," he growled, with more force than he'd intended.

"Why?" Narrow Leg asked, hearing Keff's comment.

"Because it's going to rain," he said, in frustration. Movement in the direction of the pavilion caught his eye. "Here comes Thunderstorm, probably to tell me the same thing."

"Rain is rare," Thunderstorm said. "And yet, here is! Do you need assistance?"

"Sure do," Keff said shortly, stacking boxes of components on the robot drone's back. His own worries didn't prevent him from remembering to say, "Thanks."

Thunderstorm started to pick up items with all four of his hands, and gestured to his apprentices with a tilt of his head. The young Thelerie fluttered in at once, and began to help. Across the field, the pirate's ramp ostentatiously clapped shut.

"There's nothing I can do now until the rain's over," Keff said sublingually to Carialle. "Can you last? Otherwise, I'll drag them over to you one by one with my bare hands and torture the truth out of them."

He was rewarded by Carialle's dry chuckle. "No, Sir Keff. That would get you thrown out of the Good Knights Club. I'll make it. Only," she hesitated, "stay by me."

"I'm always here for you, lady love," Keff said, with heartfelt sincerity, "even when I'm ankle deep in dust." He grunted as he hoisted a case of plumbing fixtures over his head, and passed them on to a hovering griffin.

"We will help as soon as the light goes," Narrow Leg's voice squeaked from his concealed post. "The outer shell can wait. Gather the life support and navigation components first!"

"Thanks," Keff said, absently, stopping for a moment to triage the most important items left on the field. He was distracted by his concern for Carialle. Had they set themselves an impossible task, with an implausible deadline?

"Where shall I lay these inside?" a Thelerie voice boomed through the rising wind. Keff sprinted across the darkening field to help her.

Mirina watched on the galley screen as the trader and his two robots scurried to put their merchandise away before the rain came. The small drones rumbled across the rocky plane with impossibly high piles of crates on their backs. It was a credit to AI engineering that not one item fell off all the way across the field and up the ramp of the lovely white ship.

"You're being mean, not letting any of us pitch in and help him," she scolded Bisman, who was watching over her shoulder.

"He's a businessman; he knows the risks," Bisman said, with indecent satisfaction. "Weather's a risk." Mirina shot him a glance filled with disgust. The raindrops were already starting to march across the dusty, tan plain. The Thelerie, who hated getting their fur wet, ran before the wind, hurrying to get undercover before the storm broke in earnest.

Mirina watched for a while, wondering how Keff had ever gotten all that hull plate into his little ship in the first place. He must have been sleeping on containers. You couldn't travel for very long in that kind of discomfort. She guessed he'd probably traded upscale from a much bigger craft, and was now paying the price in smaller quarters. She didn't recognize the design, but it was a honey. She missed being around quality like that. The controls must hum under one's fingers, instead of juddering, clacking, and even breaking loose. Mirina thought she'd like to see her fly.

A crack of thunder erupted and lightning burst like a star splitting apart. Mirina jumped back as the rain began to fall heavily, spikes of silver peppering the golden earth. In moments, the dust turned to mud and began to flow toward them. Mirina had a horrible feeling that the whole ground under them would turn into sticky goo, pulling the ship down into it, drowning them. She hated rain.

"It's a young typhoon," Glashton said, idly, with a glance at the screen. He poured himself a cup of coffee. "Nice to be under cover."

"I wish it would stop," she said, turning away.

"Why? It's just started." Bisman looked at her scornfully. "Nice to get a bit of change. This never happens in space."

"Yes, thank heavens," Mirina said. The others in the galley exchanged pitying looks.

"You weren't born in atmosphere, were you?" Glashton asked.

"Nope," Mirina said, reaching past him toward the replicator and programming herself a combination protein/alcohol cocktail. "They say you don't miss what you never had."

"Like what?" Javoya, the chief engineer jeered. She and Mirina had really never hit it off. Now that Mirina was leaving, the woman had been venting all her saved-up spite.

"Like common sense," Mirina said, coldly. "But then, you wouldn't know, would you?" Zonzalo, and all the others, gawked. Part of Mirina said she was stupid for opening her mouth, but the other part admitted she was human, too.

Grabbing a tool out of her belt, the engineer took a threatening step forward. Mirina found she didn't really care if the woman cut her throat right there, but the other crew members moved between them and made the engineer sit down. Ostentatiously, Mirina took another swig of her drink. Javoya glared. Mirina ignored her, thinking about her own problems. There was no other ship available here on Thelerie for her. She'd have to stay on with Bisman and this increasingly hostile group to the next stop, and maybe the next one after that, until they found a team with one that Bisman could bully, to get rid of the troublesome Dons. The one thing she could depend on was that he would keep his word about a transaction.

Eventually, the engineer tired of her aggressive pose, and threw the spanner down on the table. Everyone relaxed a little.

"Aw, what are we doing still *here*?" Javoya asked, appealing to the others. "It's nice enough. I like Thelerie, but even their hospitality gets to be overwhelming after a while."

"Business," Bisman said shortly.

"Well, let's get on with it already," Glashton said, frowning.

Mirina gestured in the vague direction of the other ship. "We're waiting for word from this Keff's employer about a face-to-face meet. Aldon wants to secure this system for uh—for the Melange."

Glashton made a face at Bisman. "What's the matter, is this guy stalling?"

"I don't know," the leader said, in turn scowling at Mirina. She finished her drink, even the awful coffee-tasting dregs which seemed to be at the bottom of every beverage lately. Everything on the ship was breaking down. A burst of thunder shook the ship. She shut her eyes and told her internal stabilizers to ignore the slight rolling under her seat.

"Spacedust, that's a horror."

"Well, we wouldn't still be here listening to it, if your boyfriend over there wasn't black-holing us," Bisman sneered. Mirina, in spite of her promise to herself not to get involved in any more arguments with him, glowered. He returned the fierce stare, with interest. "You don't want to be with us, madam. Maybe you should go ask Blue Eyes in his new ship to give you a boost offworld."

That reminded everybody of Mirina's upcoming departure. Suddenly, between the rain and the unfriendly glares, the fierce planetary weather felt less threatening.

"Maybe I'll go and see if I can't find out what's holding up the transmission," she said. Very casually, so it didn't look as if she was retreating, Mirina tossed her cup overhand into the disposer, and walked down the corridor. As if they were physical touches, she could feel every eye on her back as she left.

"If you're going, see if you can dicker for the whole load of parts," Bisman called.

"Whew!" Keff said, jumping back out of the way as Carialle closed the cargo bay hatch. "As if there wasn't enough in there with our own things, and your Core."

"It is intact," Narrow Leg said, fussing over the mass of machinery like a mother hen inspecting her chicks. "That is what matters. Oh, *days* lying in all that dust!"

"We have it all safely held in place and dry," Tall Eyebrow said. He closed his small black eyes for a moment. "All is stable. It fits together as neatly as if of a single piece." The Cridi flew or glided nimbly out of Keff's way as he slogged back toward the airlock. Carefully, he removed his environment suit, folding the outside in to keep most of the dust from scattering around the ship. Under the plastic hood, his curls were plastered to his skull with sweat.

"It's a good thing those pirates can't see in there," Keff said to Carialle, pointing down through the floor toward the cargo hold. "They'd wonder how I got the whole shop in here in the first place. Most of the hull and the engine casings are still outside. I'm exhausted!"

The human staggered back into the main cabin and flopped into his crash couch with a sigh. All of his muscles felt as if they were coming unraveled.

"All that weight training has been good for you," Carialle said, manifesting her Lady Fair image on the wall.

Keff was too out of breath to make a suitable rejoinder. He made a quick, one-handed gesture in Cridi that he knew had a slightly rude meaning. The amphibioids tittered.

A faint vibration ran through the body of the ship. Keff glanced up.

"Thunder, almost directly above us," Carialle said. "We are now separated from the rest of the world by a wall of water."

"Rain," Big Eyes signed dreamily, as Carialle directed her cameras to different views outside. The sun had dropped most of the way below the rim of the canyon walls, throwing black shadows across half the plain. The remaining crepuscular rays through the heavy clouds spotlit the distant plain. In the direction of the capital city was a double rainbow in almost 270 degrees of arc.

"This is not such a bad place," Big Voice said. "I would prefer to visit during nice seasons like this."

A slow, very brief, and faint rumble clattered on the hull. Keff glanced idly at the screen, waiting for the brilliant fork of lightning.

"That's outside," Carialle said, suddenly interrupting. She switched one of her screens to show a small, rounded, bipedal figure standing next to the ship's landing fin, holding up one upper limb. "One of the pirates. She's knocking with a rock."

Keff peered much closer, and signalled for magnification. "It's Mirina Don. Wonder what she wants?"

"I don't know," Carialle said. "Let her in. Perhaps one at a time you can get some information out of them about where they were twenty years ago."

"Not a bad notion," Keff said.

"Will it be dangerous to allow her access?" Tall Eyebrow asked.

"I doubt it," Keff replied. "But she can't see you. You'll have to hide."

The Cridi gathered up their belongings with a whisk of Core power. The bowls and cups from their meal flew through the air and sank into the cleaner like pool balls into the corner pocket. Narrow Leg supervised the picking up of travel globes. In a few minutes, the room was as tidy as it had been weeks ago when only Keff inhabited it.

"We will watch to ensure safety for you," Big Eyes assured him. She waved her hand, and the door slid shut.

"I'd better hide, too," Carialle said. She darkened the long slice of the room in front of her pillar, then built an elaborate holographic display of a control panel which she projected from several different angles onto the dark space.

The banging came again.

"I'd better let her in," Keff said. He stepped to the inner airlock hatch as Carialle lowered the ramp. The forlorn figure stumped up the ramp and waited inside as the chamber pressurized. Mirina Don emerged into the corridor and turned back her hood, presenting a sodden face to Keff.

"You left me there standing long enough," she said, resentfully.

"Sorry," he said, smiling an apology. "I was doing a crossword puzzle. What can I do for you?"

The woman shifted uncomfortably. "Er, just visiting. May I come in?"

Keff stepped to one side, and made a slight bow.

"Certainly," he said. "It's nice to have company."

Mirina shed her rain poncho and put it up on a hook next to a selection of protective suits in a closet just beyond the airlock. The Circuit sure supplied their people well. Keff had one of everything. One full environmental suit, one light enviro, an empty hook where the plastic thing should have gone that he'd been wearing, packs, both light and heavy, rebreathers, a thing like a shriveled green skin with a clear-plas helmet that was probably for deep-water environments. Whatever the Circuit was, it had money. Mirina sighed for pure envy.

"This way," Keff said. He led the way into the main cabin.

It may not have been a large craft, but it was new and beautifully appointed. Mirina glanced at the shadowed section where the control panel lay. A complicated holographic screentank filling almost half of that wall showed a long-range view of a slice of sky over Thelerie, with both small moons on the horizon over the cloud mass. A heap of boxes prevented her from getting too close, so Mirina stood back to admire the view. Both main stations had crash couches of generous proportion before them, so Keff could run either in equal comfort.

With no one to please but himself, Keff clearly lived most of his life in this room. She strolled over and examined the complicated-looking exercise station in one corner. On the other side of the console, a couple of worn grommets in the floor showed where a piece of heavy equipment had been removed from the alcove. The food synth looked clean and well-maintained. The round table beside it had an interrupted-ring bench with a dished top. Everything was neat, comfortable, and expensive-looking. Mirina wished for something like this for herself so much she hardly heard her host speaking to her.

"May I offer you something to drink?" he said.

"Certainly," Mirina said, peering at the synthesizer and wondering if the newfangled-looking controls were as easy to operate as they looked.

"Oh, no, not that," Keff laughed, and bent to a cabinet hidden in the wall behind the exercise machines. Behind the touch-open panel lay dusty bottles in shock webbing. Mirina stared at a small fortune in fermented beverages. "I have a nice beer. Not so good as a cask-aged brew that's served where it was laid down, but not bad."

"Mmm," Mirina said, appreciatively, unwilling to demand anything specific from the treasure house. Keff continued to paw through the collection. Now and again, she heard a faint clink as a couple of the fragile containers touched.

"Or—here, how about a drop of this? Red wine, from Denubia. Sixteen years old. No, wait," he said, after a pause during which he stared at the wall thoughtfully. He withdrew his selection. "This is better. Six-year-old Frusti."

"My God," Mirina said, staring as he produced a glass cylinder with a square paper label. The glass was dark, but the fluid within was darker yet. "I haven't had wine, *real* wine in years."

"It's real," Keff said, thumbing the synthesizer control for a couple of empty glasses. "Please, sit down."

Mirina watched him draw the cork carefully. She scented the faint headiness as the wine began to breathe, and drew it in appreciatively.

"You shouldn't be wasting this on me," she said, although she hoped he wouldn't take her at her word and put it away. She watched his hands. Nice hands. Square palms, square fingers, but favored with grace as well as strength. "In these parts that single bottle's worth a quarter of your other stock."

"A thing's only worth what people are willing to pay for it," Keff said, with his engaging grin. "I paid about ten credits for it six years ago when it was grape juice." He tilted the bottle gently to one side. "We ought to chamber the wine for a little while. May I offer you a snack in the meantime?"

✸CHAPTER 19

"She has very nice manners," Carialle commented, as Keff produced biscuits and cheese from the sythesizer and put them in the middle of the small table. "She looked skeptical when you offered her your goulash, as if she wasn't expecting it to taste good, but she didn't say a word. Pleasantly surprised, to judge by her expression, and her pulse."

"She's not like the others," Keff said, smelling the wine. It was ready at last.

He held up the decanter, offering it to Mirina. The woman held her glass up for him to fill, and gave him a luminous smile. Keff smiled back, feeling his pulse pound harder. She had smooth and clear skin, with about a dozen freckles dusted over her nose. Her irises were the color of cognac but were rimmed with sable-brown like her lashes. He guessed her age to be about the same as his. One, no, two silver hairs glinted in her straight, dark-brown hair, but that was the only sign of age. Her round face was youthful, though the expression in her eyes was a sorrowful millenium old. He watched her curiously and wondered. At a big space station, with a thousand women around him, would he have noticed her? And yet she was very attractive, intelligent, and cultured, in spite of the company she kept.

"Am I overreacting, Cari?" he asked, under his breath. "It's been a while since I've seen a pretty woman."

There was a momentary pause, but Carialle's voice was perfectly even, without a hint of sarcasm. "I don't think so, Keff. You're a grown-up. But watch your step, eh?"

Keff smiled at Mirina, and stood up. "Why don't we move over here to finish the wine? The crash couches are much more comfortable." He extended a hand to her and settled her in one reclining chair. He sat down in the other and propped his feet on the console.

"This is delicious," Mirina said, sipping her wine. "And that synthesizer must be absolutely top of the line."

"I think so," Keff said, casually. "I'm not sure. I eat anything. Mostly health shakes." At that, Mirina did make a face, and Keff grinned.

"So," he asked, pouring himself some wine. He set the bottle on the console. "Were you born into the business like your partner? The way the two of you act I assume he's your partner."

Mirina corrected him quickly. "Not really *partners*," she said, with a strong emphasis on the word. "We've worked closely together for about eight years." The woman took a hasty sip of wine, then paused to smile over it. Not long enough to have been involved with Carialle, Keff thought, his heart sinking. She'd hardly have heard tales of a single wreck salvage a dozen years before she came.

"You're not much like him," Keff said, encouragingly. "You've had an education."

"The colloquialisms," she said, with a wicked smile. "You caught that. Yes. He was furious!"

"And some formal training? CW?"

"Good guess, Sir Knight," Carialle said. "Her pulse leaped just then. Dig deeper."

But Mirina had recovered herself quickly.

"That, my dear, was a long time ago," she said, lifting her glass. Only a few drops remained by this time, so she held it out for a refill.

"I'm glad you appreciate it," Keff said. He hoisted himself out of the deep padding, feeling his overtaxed muscles protest, and came over with the bottle. "The wine, I mean. Watch out, or you'll get tipsy. You're not from the same place as Bisman?"

"No. You took the paintings away," Mirina said, pointedly changing the subject. "I wanted to see that spacescape again. I've been to Dimitri."

"Oh, is that where it is?" Keff asked. Mirina nodded. "Never been there myself. Well, it was starting to rain."

"I know," the woman said, and showed a trifle of embarrassment. "Sorry we didn't help you."

Keff shrugged. "Competitors."

"I might like to buy that painting," Mirina said, temptingly.

"No," Carialle said, at once, then relented. " . . . Well, perhaps it wouldn't do any harm. I've had my joy from it. Tell her all right."

"Certainly," Keff said, smiling at his guest. "I'll give you a good price."

Mirina looked very pleased, but suddenly her face fell, and she took another sip of wine. "Never mind," she said. "I can't. I . . . I've run through my budget. I bought . . . something expensive."

"Ah," Keff said, wondering what had suddenly troubled her so deeply. She was staring at a spot on the wall. Keff glanced over his shoulder and wondered if she had seen through the holographic display. No, it was still intact. If anything, Carialle had enhanced the details to make it look even more solid. He cleared his throat, determined to lighten the mood. He went back to his own couch and stretched out luxuriously. "Say, aren't you afraid I might take advantage of your lowered resistance, to send a message to your Melange?"

"Send away," Mirina said, watching him with an amused glint in her eyes. "Couldn't be any worse than what's already happened to me."

"Oh? Confession's good for the soul," Keff said, encouragingly.

Her mind snapped back to whatever had been occupying it, and she stared at nothing again.

"Do I still have a soul?" she asked. Keff opened his mouth, then shut it. The wine had affected her more strongly than he'd guessed. Thunder rumbled, and Keff glanced at the external monitor for the flash of lightning. The storm must be directly overhead. The woman shivered. "I hate rain," she said. "I hate weather. I hate being stuck on a planet. I think I'm only happy out in space. If I had to stay planetbound for the rest of my life I'd kill myself."

"I know what you mean," Keff said, sincerely. "There's nothing like it."

"Yes. I don't want to do anything else," she said. "It's nice enough here, but I want to get out there again." Her eyes tilted up toward the ceiling, and the unseen reaches of space.

"She's a born spacer," Carialle said. "Just a little drunk, I think, but a born spacer."

"Don't you ever get lonely, traveling by yourself?" Mirina asked.

"Not at all," Keff said, sweeping a hand around. "I have . . ." he glanced at where Carialle's pillar should have been visible, and wasn't. " . . . I have all this," he finished.

"It's beautiful," she said, never noticing his hesitation. "You make me wish I had a setup like it."

"Aren't you happy where you are?"

"Are you mad?" she asked, with a pitying scowl. "If it wasn't for the Thelerie, well . . ."

"What about the Thelerie?" Keff asked, quickly.

Mirina looked at him hard. "Are you from Central Worlds?" she asked.

"Reformed," Keff said, with a pious expression that made her laugh, but she was still serious.

"They're a kind, innocent people. I don't want them exploited, do you understand me?"

"Isn't that what you're doing?" Keff asked, very gently.

"No!" Then, more honestly, she added, "Not entirely. We trade with them, but they get value from us, too. My program . . ."

Keff leaned up on one elbow, as if to listen better. Mirina stopped in midsentence, realizing that this dashing, handsome man was pumping her. Keff saw he had gone too far.

"This bottle's empty," he said, swinging himself upright with a casual show of strength that made Mirina's eyes light with appreciation. "Let's see what else is in the cellar. Look at that!" Keff dusted down a squarish container with a glass stopper covered with wax. "I didn't think I had any of this left."

"Your nose ought to be a foot long by now," Carialle said. But Mirina didn't seem to mind. The twenty-five-year-old brandy went down as neatly as the wine had, sip by sip. It loosened up whatever tight grip she'd had on herself, and in time, Keff's careful questions began to elicit answers.

"The program to supply the Thelerie with communication equipment was yours?"

"Yes," she said. "The ones who decided to come home again had seen us using commlinks, thought it was a good idea. No mass communication at all on this planet. Once you were out of sight, you were gone. It was cheap, and they were so grateful! You've got some nice comm circuitry among your merchandise. If the price was right, that is."

"Might knock it down for a friend," Keff said. "I don't have to make anything on it for a good cause."

"I don't care, particularly. The profit's not mine any more anyway. It's the Melange's, and Aldon's. What the hell," Mirina said, expansively, "for the Thelerie, too."

His blue eyes twinkled with understanding. Mirina was reminded of what she used to think Charles looked like. *Careful, girl,* she told herself fiercely. *He's the enemy.* But he was very attractive, she thought, looking at him from under her lashes as she took a sip of the fire-smooth brandy. In return, he gave her a top-to-toe sweep of his eyes that made her gasp for its very insouciance. Unconsciously she shifted position, straightening her shoulders and tilting her head to one side. Great stars, I'm acting like a coquette! And yet, it was so nice to relax for a change.

"How long have you been . . . involved with the griffins?" Keff asked.

She wrinkled her eyebrows, trying to place the reference, then her face cleared as she grinned. "I never thought of that, but they do look like griffins. Did heraldic beasts ever really live?"

"I don't think so," said Keff.

"Not much of a student of history, is she?" Carialle asked.

"Don't be a snob, Cari," Keff muttered. "How'd you come to ship out with Bisman?"

"I came on board eight years ago, right after Charles died. Zonzalo—my brother—fell in with them. He thought flying with reivers was a great adventure. I found him on one of their lousy bases, half-starved, with leaky air-recirculation equipment, no organization. So pathetic, I stayed," Mirina said, staring into the amber liquid in her glass. "Shouldn't have stayed but," her shoulders slumped, "but I had nowhere to go, nowhere to take him *to*."

"Didn't you have to go back to your job, or your school?" Keff asked. "You know your way around ships, I can tell. A valuable employee like you."

"Lost my position," Mirina said, more shortly than she'd intended. "I've been an idiot, but the Thelerie have been wonderful. They're grateful for everything we do. I've had to force Bisman not to lead them into using polluting machinery. They've got plenty of physical strength and simple machines to take care of motive-force needs, plus, dammit! they can fly. No travel problems. The electronics just help with communications."

"She's really thought this out," Carialle said. "*Here's* the organizing mind."

"I'd give anything if she wasn't involved in a pirate ring," Keff murmured under his breath.

Mirina wasn't really paying attention. "What did you say?"

"Very well thought out," Keff said hastily. "You've done good work. You thought of *everything*. You must be some organizer. I, uh, I think there's room in this for both of our groups. I can't say the Circuit won't cut into your parts business, but I'm willing to take it to the Lady over the ethical framework you've built."

She looked grateful and annoyed at the same time. "We'll want a cut," she said. "We've got expenses. Overhead."

"So've we," Keff said, nonchalantly playing the game.

"We'll negotiate it," Mirina said, compromising. "Well, Aldon will. I . . . don't suppose there's room in *your* organization? For a good planner?"

Keff looked surprised. "Thinking of moving on?"

"I have to," she said.

"Being forced out?"

"No. I just can't stand it any longer. The deaths, and all. Now that everything's at about subsistence level Aldon is getting uncontrollable. I never condoned death; I've always tried to prevent it. I hate death. Can't take any more of it in my life."

"How mysterious for someone in her profession," Carialle said.

"Are you going back to what you did before? Were you a pilot?"

"More than that," Mirina said, then thought about it. "Well, and less." The whole accident came back to her, as it did in her nightmares. She had a final, horrible vision of the dock crew trying to spray down the burning ship, the pillar in the control room slagging into molten metal. All the skin on her hands and face were burned, as she tried to fight her way back aboard, to save him if she could. They held her back. They kept her out! Charles!

She let out a cry that brought Keff to his feet in surprise, then fell into heartbroken sobbing. Keff hurried over and sat down next to her on the molded chair's arm. She was beating her fist on her knee. He captured the hand and held it tightly between his own hands.

"I'm sorry," she said, looking up with tears sheeting down her cheeks. "I'm sorry."

"What's the matter?" Keff asked, squeezing her hand. "Why couldn't you have gotten another berth with someone else?"

"Never anyone else like Charles," she sobbed, turning her face into his tunic front. Keff was so nice and sympathetic, but he *wasn't* Charles. Charles remained dead.

"Go on, tell me about it," Keff said. He felt for a handkerchief, and ended up handing her the napkin that was tucked between her hip and the seat cushion.

In between sobs, Mirina managed to tell the story of the accident.

" . . . I guess my supervisor was right—no, I know he was. I was insubordinate, and I should have stayed in therapy, but my brother was in danger! Why couldn't they have understood that?"

Keff's heart melted with sympathy. Over the top of her head, he looked automatically toward Carialle's pillar. He wrapped his arms around the woman and held her tightly.

"Keff, she was a *brawn!*" Carialle said. "What was the brain's name? Charles? Yes, I remember it. You ought to, as well. Charles CM-702. M must have stood for Mirina. It was a freak accident. Combination of a hazardous cargo, an accident on the loading dock, and bad handling by the ground crew. If they hadn't been at a space station, the brawn would have died, too. The last thing that Charles did before his shell melted down was to order one of his servo robots to pull the brawn out of the burning wreckage. There was hardly anything left for the authorities to identify. Now I know why I didn't recognize her name. It's Mirina Velasquez-Donegal. She and her brother must have shortened it when they adopted *noms-de-guerre.*"

"I have heard of the accident," Keff said, out loud. "I knew a brainship had died. Never heard what happened to the brawn."

"Hah!" Mirina said bitterly, into his sleeve. "Exactly."

Keff glanced toward Carialle's pillar.

"They let her down, too," Carialle said, just as bitterly, in Keff's ear. "For all they say we're a valuable, respected resource, the bureaucrats still treat us like animated furniture, shells and softskins alike, damn them."

"Horrible! We have to help her."

"We can't," Carialle said, flatly.

"She's been the only moral influence these people have had," Keff said. "It could have been far worse if she hadn't been here."

"But why was she here at all? Why didn't she take her brother and go?"

"You heard her," Keff whispered urgently. "She was needy. She'd had a mental breakdown—and she had to get over it by herself. You know what that feels like."

"I certainly do," Carialle said, every memory of her own accident coming back to her. "But what would our word do for her? Shorten her prison sentence? But no, she wouldn't last in a prison. She said she would rather die than be groundbound. I think she means it. We should separate her from these people anyhow."

"We'll have to think of something," Keff said, frustratedly. He realized Mirina had been talking.

" . . . Wanted help, just a little help," Mirina was saying, a little incoherently. "They figured I'd ask for it when I needed it. But how would I know when? I was just trying to survive, feeling it was my fault when I knew it wasn't. Hot white explosives. No time. Charles saved my life."

"Shh, I know," Keff said. He was torn between worrying about Carialle's mental state, and the growing concern for a fellow brawn. Mirina seemed as if she had been waiting for somebody to talk to for a long time. He just stayed beside her, stroking her hair, and occasionally dabbing the tears off her cheeks with the edge of his sleeve. Poor Mirina, carrying a weight like this all by herself for eight years. He kissed the top of her head, rocking her gently like a child.

"I knew Charles slightly," Carialle said, solemnly. "He was a stodgy old 700. He thought I was too radical. I thought he was embalmed. I'd never met his brawn."

Keff opened his mouth to reveal their secret, but Carialle, reading his mind, stopped him short.

"Don't," she said. "She's been part of this piracy operation."

"We have to help her," Keff insisted.

"Why? She has no loyalty to the CW."

"But she was one of *us*. A brain chose her as his brawn. That means she had that special something. She's . . . less than half a person now. She's broken. You know what that means."

"I know, oh, I know," Carialle said, her voice rising almost to a keen. She sighed. "You win, Sir Knight. I'll try to think of something we can do for her, some way to help."

Thunder crashed, loudly enough to be heard through the noise insulation. Keff felt Mirina tremble in his arms. He stood up and held out a hand to her. She looked up at him, her caramel eyes drowned with tears, and put her hand in his.

"Perhaps you'd better stay the night," Keff said.

✦CHAPTER 20

He awoke looking up at the ceiling. The shifting of a soft weight on his shoulder made him look down. In her sleep, Mirina cuddled her head just a little cosier against his chest. He tightened the arm around her, fitting his wrist warmly into her opulently curved torso. One of her hands opened on his chest, the fingertips playing delicately on his skin. He remembered the touch of those small but strong hands along his back, and smiled. Two lonely people had found an oasis of peace together for a moment. He was content, and hoped she felt the same.

"Keff? I know you're awake." Carialle's voice came softly through his aural implant.

"Just barely," he said sublingually. "Whasup?" He glanced down at Mirina.

"I've checked her sleep pattern. She's in deep delta. Good morning. The rain stopped just before dawn. I've got a ship on extreme long-range sensors. I've sent a hail out on standard frequency. The cavalry's on its way!"

"Hurrah," Keff said quietly, wishing he could cheer. "About time."

"The Cridi want to get out and around for a while. They're rather bored with being cooped up, and I can't run the water-refresher if you're supposed to be alone."

"Mmm," he said. "Tell them I'll go take a real shower, and they can bathe as long as they like."

He edged himself out of the bunk carefully, lifting Mirina's head

569

from his shoulder onto the pillow. He left the coverlet tucked around her where his arm had been. She let out a small sigh.

"Probably hasn't felt this safe in ages," Keff said quietly to Carialle. He walked silently toward his bathroom. Carialle must condone his sympathy for Mirina. She was perfectly capable of making the humidity or temperature controls in his private quarters go squiffy out of pettiness, but the air was warm on his naked skin, and even the floor had been heated to a comfortable 18 degrees C.

Keff passed up the sonic cleaner for the shower fixture. He fitted the standards into the depressions in the deck, snapped the extendable envelope out into a rectangular booth two meters high and a meter square, and twisted the water spigots on to full. Jets of water shot out of the metal disk at the top, hammering at the booth floor and sides. An answering rush of water across the corridor told him the Cridi had heard his cue. As soon as the water warmed up to a comfortable temperature, he climbed into the booth and sealed it around him. He stood under the shower for a good twenty-five minutes, until his fingers turned into pale prunes.

"Are they finished, Cari?" Keff asked, as loudly as he dared. His voice sounded curiously dead in the heavy plastic tent.

"They are," Carialle chuckled. "Narrow Leg said they wouldn't have had to do this in stages if you hadn't put their swimming pool in the storeroom."

With a thankful sigh, Keff spun the controls off. He shouldered into his toweling robe and walked back into the sleeping room, rubbing his hair dry with a clean cloth. Mirina stirred and opened her eyes at the small sound. Her eyes crinkled as she grinned at him, embarrassed. She sat up, clasping the coverlet to her body.

"Sorry. Have I slept too long?" she asked.

"Not at all," Keff said. "I've just finished. The bath is yours."

She stretched out her arms, throwing her head back with abandon. "Mmm! I haven't had a refreshing sleep like this in ages. Thank you. And, thank you for last evening." The wickedly coy look, through the eyelashes, returned just for a moment. "I was supposed to come and win concessions from you, but I think I gave up as much as I got."

"My pleasure," Keff said, with a twinkle.

"Thank you. I ought to watch my liquor consumption," Mirina said, seriously. "I shouldn't have talked so much."

"Not at all," Keff said. "I understand. Truly, I do." Mirina gave him a skeptical, almost pitying look. He wished again he could tell her the truth, but Carialle was right. He must not blow their cover too soon, even for a fellow brawn in need.

He extended a hand to help Mirina off the bunk, but she smiled a polite refusal, and dropped lightly onto the soles of her feet. She did accept his spare robe, and trailed off into the steamy, tiled bathroom with an easy, spacer's stride. Keff dressed, listening to her hum happily in the shower.

Once they emerged into the main cabin, there were no signs of the Cridi at all, except that the indicator on the food synthesizer was a little lower than it had been the night before. Mirina didn't notice the discrepancy, but then, she'd had the lion's share of brandy and wine. Keff programmed her a nice breakfast, and poured himself a health shake with extra calcium and vitamin E to help chase away the dregs of a headache that loomed behind his eyes. For all her shamed protest, Mirina looked as if she was rather less worse for the wear than he was.

"Mmm, what's that?" Mirina asked, putting down her coffee cup. She pointed at a light blinking on Carialle's imaginary console.

"Communications," Carialle said in his ear.

"Communications," Keff echoed, springing up. "The Lady!" He went to one of the real control boards, and punched a button. That one normally activated the lights in the cargo bay, but Mirina wouldn't know that. One of the screens blanked, then filled with the image of Carialle's Lady Fair. Keff blinked. She wore an up-to-date coiffure, and tunic set of gauzy blue fabric with flowing sleeves, plus plenty of sparkling jewelry. She looked expensive, impatient, and very efficient.

"Keff? Is that you?" Carialle's voice asked impatiently.

"Yes, ma'am," Keff said, speaking with his mouth close to the audio pickup just for effect.

"My ship is in range of this planet, ETA two hours. I want a full report. What's this meeting supposed to be about?" Her eyes flicked past Keff to Mirina. "Who is that woman?"

"She's, uh, she's a representative of the other group," Keff said. "The Melange. Mirina Don, er, Carialle."

"Madam," Mirina said.

"Greetings." The eyes returned to Keff. "I'll expect a full briefing in an hour. The meeting will commence when I make orbit. Do you understand?"

"I do, ma'am," Keff said, humbly. The screen blanked. He turned to Mirina. She looked pleased.

"I'll go tell Bisman," she said.

Carialle had her suit-clad image smile at Bisman and his cronies as they stalked into the central cabin. The half-dozen human raiders shed oily, yellow-brown mud from their boots everywhere. She cast her eyes upward in disgust, and enjoyed the scowl on the leader's face as he slung himself into one of the crash couches.

"Upscale meets bargain basement," she said to Keff over the aural link. "You'll have to tidy that after the meeting's over," she added out loud.

"Yes, ma'am," Keff said, standing obsequiously beside the holographic chair in which her image seated itself. Carialle had set almost all her projective cameras over the end of the room where her painting apparatus usually stood. The rack, and all of her personal paintings, were stowed hastily in the small storeroom behind Keff's cabin. It left her image plenty of room to roam.

"I am Carialle," she said, with a nod of her head. "Greetings, gentlemen, and madam." Carialle nodded to Mirina, clad in a similar shipsuit to the one she'd had on the night before. The ex-brawn seated herself beside her brother at the dining table clear across the cabin. The younger Don was a dark-haired, lanky young man who didn't seem to know what to do with his long arms and legs. Bisman wore a knee-length coat over an open-necked shirt and trousers tucked into his muddy boots. The garments were clean but worn, adding to the impression Mirina had given them of an organization too big for its budget. The only non-human was the young Thelerie, Sunset. "You are all welcome."

"Say, wait a minute," Bisman said, turning his head to the right. He'd made himself comfortable, but something caught his eye. He propelled himself forward to wave a hand through Carialle's midsection. "She's a hologram!" he exclaimed, turning on Keff. "I thought we were meeting with the real thing!"

"You're hearing my real voice," Carialle said, with a trace of haughty annoyance. "And seeing my face. I'm not about to make myself vulnerable to strangers. I'm sure you understand."

"Not being vulnerable, yeah," Bisman said, sitting down again, but not so far back in the couch. He held up one hand and showed them a small commlink on his wrist. "I don't like tricks, either. I want you to know I'm in radio contact with my ship. If something happens, or if my communications are cut off, my people have orders to attack. We are well armed."

Carialle also read the energy trace of a sidearm concealed under the flap of the coat the man wore. She accorded him another gracious nod. "I understand," she said. "We won't shield transmissions. Sounds like they have the third Core," she told Keff privately. "We'll have to get it away from them."

"Yes, ma'am," Keff said, with a respectful bow.

"Why are you here?" Bisman asked Thunderstorm, who sat on his haunches between the airlock and the corridor to the sleeping cabins.

"I represent Thelerie," the Space Sayas said, very nervously. "As I have for many years."

"This was going to be a discussion between our two organizations, wasn't it?" Bisman asked Carialle.

"Of course, but this being makes a valid point," Carialle said, with a polite gesture toward Thunderstorm. "We are occupying his world, after all."

"Okay," Bisman said, crossing his heels on the console. "He can stay."

"Thank you," Carialle said, politely. She made a point of lifting the corner of her lip delicately at his dirty boots, and he grinned. "Shall we begin?"

Keff bowed again. "Shall I serve refreshments?"

"Go ahead. Thank you. Gentles?" Carialle manifested a glass in her image's hand. The visitors declined beverages, and Keff resumed his stand beside his "employer."

"We're here to talk," Bisman said, impatiently. He tilted his head toward Keff. "Your drone here landed on a world we have an exclusive arrangement with."

"Isn't it up to the inhabitants as to whom they do business with?" Carialle asked, with a lift of her eyebrows. "Thunderstorm, what do you say?"

"I . . ." the Thelerie trembled violently and clattered his clawtips together. "I do not say anything just now."

Bisman's blood pressure rose slightly, as did the temperature in his face. He had a bad temper, but he controlled it. His associates were watching their leader closely. Their muscle tension was high: in Mirina's case, almost dangerously so. The former brawn was under a lot of stress.

"The Melange has made a lot of progress with them," Bisman said, with emphasis. "We don't like someone just walking in and benefiting from all our work."

"But when there's profit in it . . . ?" Carialle asked.

"Yeah, but we intend to keep it just the way it's been," Bisman said. His blood pressure drew down to normal again. He was on his own ground here, Carialle thought.

"The resources on this planet are very attractive, *n'est ce pas*? For example, fuel of very high quality."

"Ours. Our refinery, our investment," Bisman said, flatly.

Carialle spread her hands prettily. "But can't we make a bargain?" she asked. "We might like to buy some of this fine fuel. And these people, the Thelerie, are good customers."

"Not a chance," Bisman said. "There's not enough production to supply all of us. The Thelerie need it to run their lamps and heating units. I've got more than sixty ships. How many have you got?"

"Enough," Carialle said. "You'll forgive me not giving out too much information until I know who I'm dealing with."

"We've been around a long time," the older man said, narrowing his eyes at her. He jabbed a finger toward Keff. "I have never heard of you people until we landed and found him here. You come out of nowhere, into established territory, and you act like you've had a mandate from the Invisible Hosts."

Carialle smiled austerely. "Perhaps it does seem as if we've been keeping undercover a little too much."

"Nonexistent, is what I call it." Bisman's voice rose threateningly. Carialle picked up signs of distress from Thunderstorm, who watched the man with wide eyes. He was terrified of Bisman, and Carialle couldn't blame him. He was dangerous.

"And yet, here we are," Carialle said. Her sensors picked up the expected ship orbiting and entering atmosphere. The engine vibration matched patrol ships she'd encountered at many space stations. She listened for an official hail, hoping it was the CW military ship at last. It was curious that there hadn't been any advance instructions for her. She strained her external cameras upward and outward, searching for a glimpse of the descending craft. "Now that we've found one another, we should make arrangements for cooperation where our paths cross."

"Keff!" she said, urgently, while her blandfaced hologram continued a meaningless conversation with the pirate leader. "It's *Ship Three*! They're coming in for a landing. Here!"

"What? Impossible!" Keff muttered to himself, although he was badly shaken. "No, it isn't. The Thelerie are natural navigators. They've Centered their way home."

"But with what? We destroyed their propulsion system."

"We never found the DSC-902's," Keff said glumly. He smiled innocently at Mirina, who was staring at him with open curiosity.

Carialle tried to get the others' attention focused back on herself. "Mr. Bisman, the Circuit is prepared to sell you whatever components and parts you might like, at a good price, but we do believe in coexistence."

"Just a minute," Bisman said, holding up a hand as his pocket unit signalled. He listened to the small speaker. "What?"

Carialle picked up the transmission herself. She listened helplessly to every word the pirate leader heard. She relayed the broadcast so Keff could hear it, too. His eyes widened, and flicked toward her hiding place.

"They saw them on long-range but now they're sure. Autumn says that Keff's ship is the one who attacked them in Slime space," a woman's voice repeated. "Says the human onboard was under Slime control."

"What? Slime? What about the other ship?"

"No one challenged her on the way in. There's nobody in orbit around Thelerie!"

"What? Well, then where's the transmission in here coming from?" Bisman demanded.

"The ship . . ." Carialle could wait to hear no more. She blocked the signal from the pirate.

Bisman jumped for Keff, and backed him up against the nearest bulkhead with a forearm underneath his throat.

"Who is she?" Bisman demanded. "*Where* is she?"

"There's no one else here," Keff said, innocently, pushing the man's arm down enough to gasp in a breath. His windpipe felt half-crushed. "Just me. The Lady's out in space somewhere."

"That's a lie," the pirate leader said, driving home his statement with another bruising push. "One of my ships says there's nobody out there. She's onboard this vessel. Bring her out!"

"You're wrong, friend . . ." Keff began, but he got no more out. The pirate shoved him up against the enameled panel and bore down in earnest. "Hey!" he whispered, battering the man on the back. He saw black spots dance in his vision. Bisman meant to kill him. Dropping all pretense of amiable obsequity, Keff dug both thumbs into pressure points behind the man's ears, and swept a foot back and across Bisman's ankles, sending the older man stumbling. Keff danced out from the wall on the balls of his feet, not turning his back on Bisman. In the close quarters, though, he was at a disadvantage. The pirate, though an older man, had a long reach, and undoubtedly a long, dishonorable history of dirty fighting. He landed a kidney punch before Keff could get by him. Keff staggered, and aimed a slam of his own for the man's gut. Bisman took about half of it, but he slid sideways in the direction of the airlock. Keff closed the distance, and had to dodge back from a dirty kick. He couldn't let Bisman go, not now.

"They'll have backups in a minute," Carialle said. "The rest of the crew is coming. They're armed, and something on that ship is building up energy." Keff nodded but didn't reply. He was concentrating on disabling Bisman without killing him. Mirina and her brother stood beside the table, staring.

"He's CW?" Zonzalo asked, gaping.

"You lied!" Mirina shouted at Keff. She started toward the airlock, but the combatants blocked her way.

"Luring us in here, pretending to be stupid traders," Bisman panted. He evaded a roundhouse kick Keff aimed at him, grabbed Keff's leg, and propelled him backward over the stack of crates toward the image of the third console. Keff fell helplessly among the boxes. The other humans gasped as he disappeared from view into the holographic illusion. Bisman, with a snarl, dove in after him.

"Cari, I can't see!" Keff cried, as a punch came out of nowhere and knocked his head painfully against the deck.

The time for subterfuge was over. Keff's life could be in danger. At once, Carialle dropped the illusion, revealing wall, pillar, and the two men grappling on the floor. The effect on Mirina Don was electric. Her eyes widened, and her mouth fell open.

"Aldon!" she shrieked at the top of her voice. "She's a *brainship!*"

"Central Worlds!" Bisman growled. With a sudden burst of strength, he yanked a hand free, chopped the smaller man in the throat, and scrambled to his feet. He spun and grabbed Thunderstorm, who had been trying to creep unobtrusively toward the airlock.

"You damned traitor," the pirate snarled. "You were in on this." He yanked the Thelerie back on his haunches and drew his sidearm, shoving it under Thunderstorm's throat.

"Help them," Carialle said to Tall Eyebrow and the listening Cridi, activating the door of the spare cabin. "Now!"

Like a barrage of soap-bubbles, the Cridi poured out of the spare room, and surrounded the pirates.

"Slime!" Zonzalo gasped, flattening himself against the wall as Gap Tooth and Small Spot confronted him. Sunset, the young Thelerie clutched Mirina around the waist, and hid behind her, his golden eyes all pupil, while Big Voice, Wide Foot, and Big Eyes edged them backward.

"Stand back," Bisman said, looking up steadily at the floating globes. "I want out of here, now! I want my people out, too. One by one. If we don't, this damned traitor dies. Now!"

"We freeze him!" Small Spot cried, flinging himself forward to save his friend.

"No!" Carialle saw the tiny movement of Bisman's finger closing just as Small Spot's whammy took effect. She sensed the power buildup, an inexorable burst only temporarily halted.

"Small motor control reaction," she said, over all her speakers. The hologram of the Lady vanished, making the human pirates jump. "He's pulled the trigger. If we don't let him go, the gun will fire anyhow in a moment. If we don't try to contain the blast using Core power, it will explode right here in the cabin. If we do, both Bisman and Thunderstorm will die. Sooner or later I will run out of fuel, then the Core won't be able to contain the blast to just the two of them."

"Can he hear us?" Keff asked.

"Yes," said Narrow Leg, hovering in front of the pirate leader's face, watching his pupils.

"Bisman, we'll let you go," Keff said, edging into Bisman's view with his hands out from his sides. "I'm unarmed, and the Cridi will do what I say. Just let Thunderstorm go. You and your people are free." He jerked his head toward the airlock. Carialle slid open both doors, and lowered the ramp. Zonzalo and the other crew dashed out of the door without hesitation. "You're free to go. No one will stop you. TE, ready to pull his hand back?"

"I am ready," the Frog Prince said, his face grim.

"Okay," Keff said to Small Spot. "Let him go!"

The burst of power released five milliseconds after Tall Eyebrow jerked the human's hand back and away from Thunderstorm's neck. Carialle winced as the bolt burned through her ceiling plates and into a fiberoptic conduit. She set a small part of her consciousness to rerouting the functions the severed fibers controlled. She'd have time to repair the ducting later. The Thelerie stood, dazed, the fact that he was alive and unharmed not yet registering in his mind. Like lightning, Bisman ran a few steps, turned, put a bolt straight into Thunderstorm's chest. Sunset fell beside the body of his mentor, crying out shrilly at the black, burned streak in the center of the golden fur. Bisman loosed a few more shots into the cabin, scattering the Cridi, and filling the room with smoke as lights, screens, and upholstery burst and caught fire. Keff dove underneath the crash couch, pulling Mirina down with him.

Carialle dropped her airlock door, intending to trap the pirate inside. Bisman saw the lights activate, and scowled, but he didn't stop running. He raised the energy weapon again, and shot the controls, freezing the doors. She struggled to find another servo that could pull down the door, but the mechanism reacted too slowly. He was able to roll underneath the door. He ran out and down the ramp and out across the field with deliberate, long, heavy steps that ate up the distance. Their rhythm suddenly matched with something Carialle would never, never forget.

"Keff!" she cried. "It's *him*. It's *his* footsteps!"

Keff scrambled out from his hiding place. "Whose?"

"Bisman!" Carialle said, opening all screens to show the pirate leader running across to his own ship. "He was the one, the one who *walked on me.*"

"You're sure?" Keff demanded.

"I couldn't forget it as long as I live. Keff, stop him!" Carialle said desperately. "We have to get him back here. He's the one. He can clear my record, Keff. He can't get away."

Keff dashed for the airlock. He waited impatiently until Carialle had raised it high enough for him to scramble underneath, then dashed down the ramp after Bisman. "Do something about Thunderstorm, for pity's sake," he shouted.

Carialle tried to pull herself together. For once in her life she wished she could go about on two feet, or four, or wings! That man must not get away from her. He held the answers she had been seeking for twenty years. It meant the vindication of her sanity.

But her life was not in danger, and Thunderstorm's was. She pulled herself together and located the nearest transmission tower. With a broad-band sweep, she broke into the thousands and thousands of "phone calls" going on across Thelerie.

"Attention," she said, through the shell of the IT program, wishing that it was up to fluent medical Thelerie. "There is an emergency medical situation on the Melange's plain. Will any healer in the area please come at once?" Hubbub erupted on the open lines as thousands of Thelerie broke into speech all at once, wanting to know more. She repeated her message, shut down the transmission and returned her attention to the inside of her cabin.

"And thus is mass communication born," she said, ironically.

"His heart beats," Big Voice said. He sat on the Thelerie's left, his globe in two pieces behind him. "I know not what else to do, but I can keep that doing."

"I am making him breathe," Small Spot said, clasping one of the Thelerie's claw hands in his own. "Come, friend. Inhale, exhale, inhale, exhale. Am I doing too fast?"

"I don't think so," Carialle said. "He's in pain. I wish I could tell you what nerves to deaden, or what drugs to use, but I don't dare interfere. We might cause permanent damage."

"Don't touch him," Sunset cried, trying to scatter the amphibioids away from his mentor's body. He ran at them, flailing his wings. The Cridi gently pushed him back, mildly using Core power. The wound was serious, but it didn't go all the way through the Thelerie's body, for which Carialle was grateful.

It didn't take long for her message to have an effect. On her screen, Carialle saw a very large Thelerie with a pouch around its neck sail over the plain. Carialle flashed her running lights to attract the griffin's attention. The creature changed direction on a wingtip and landed on the ramp. It galloped on all fours up into the ship.

"I was called," it said. "I heal! How to help?" It saw Thunderstorm and hurried toward him, with concerned horn calls. It spilled herbs, vials, and tools out of its pouch onto the deck, and went to work.

Another Thelerie, and another, appeared behind the first. "I, too! I, too! I am called. I will help!"

"Help is here," Big Voice said, leaning close to Thunderstorm's face. "I told you we did not want your life."

Thunderstorm fluttered his eyelids and wingtips feebly, acknowledging the irony of his old enemies working to save him from the wounds of his allies.

Keff ran, keeping his knees up with an effort. His feet grew more caked with mud at every step. The previous night's rain had made the field a mire. Tall Eyebrow had sailed ahead in his globe, then realized Keff wasn't keeping up with him. He and Big Eyes swept back and pulled him out of the mud with a mighty *pop!* Keff checked to make sure he hadn't left his boots behind, then turned all his attention forward.

The red ship fired slugs and energy beams at the approaching human and his companions. With a single sweep of his fingers, Narrow Leg created a barrier of Core power between them. The missiles ricocheted all over the landscape. A gout of mud kicked up with a *bang!* almost right in Keff's face. Hot steam hissed where the energy bolts sizzled into the mud. Keff hoped fervently that Big Voice and the others were protecting Carialle from attack.

Ahead of them, Bisman reached the ramp, and hurtled up it in a few long strides. The heavy metal door began to slide downward.

"They close the hatch!" Narrow Leg signed, meters ahead of Keff. "What to do?"

"Hold it open! Hold the ship," Keff shouted in Cridi at the top of his lungs. The ammoniated air made him hoarse. "Don't let them launch. Carialle needs them alive, awake!"

"We understand," Gap Tooth and Wide Foot signed. They stretched out their skinny arms as best they could in the confines of the plastic bubbles. The rising ramp halted in mid-arc, and jerked hard a few times. The airlock hatch, manipulated by Long Hand, reversed direction and began to inch upward.

"Good," Keff said, urging his small force forward. "Cari, we have them!"

"Get him," Carialle said, speaking so rapidly he had to listen closely to understand. "You have to bring him to me. He's my proof for Maxwell-Corey. That bastard must listen. This is the man. He will talk. He must talk. It wasn't *aliens*; it was a human being, one who should have known better. He knew a brain pillar when he saw one! He must have known!"

"Almost there, Cari," Keff said, willing her to hang on. Only a few hundred meters to go to the red ship. He heard the screech of tortured servos fighting against the pull of Core power. The ramp had opened almost all the way. He heard shouting from inside the ship, saw men and women in shipsuits fighting to lower the airlock doors by hand.

Suddenly, he and the Cridi were all swept straight through the air into the side of the pirate ship. Keff slammed face first into the hull and slid, dazed, down to the ground. The travel globes split apart, leaving the Cridi dry, gasping, and shocked in the hot, ammonia-laden air. There was no doubt about it: the pirates had the third Core in their ship, and they knew how to use it.

More Thelerie healers, landing on the plain in answer to Carialle's call, swooped in and helped pick the small aliens out of the mud. Two hovering griffins lifted Keff free of the ship's side, and set him on his feet.

"It burns, it burns!" Gap Tooth shrieked, batting at her skin with her hands. "The air is hot!"

The Thelerie, though they understood the small beings were distressed, couldn't understand the language. They fluttered around uncertainly. The Cridi had to help themselves. Tall Eyebrow, with Big Eyes swept up in his arms, cried out to the others. "Pick up globes, purify air!"

Narrow Leg, recovering his wits in a flash, started clapping travel globes together around his crew with waves of his fingerstalls. In a moment, all the Cridi were rallying.

"Are you all right?" Keff wheezed. His ribs were sore and bruised, and one of his eyes felt as if it was swelling shut.

"We have no water," Narrow Leg signed swiftly, "but it is only for a short time."

"Right," Keff said, turning around. "Let's get them." Just as he spoke, the pirate ship lit engines. The distraction had been long enough. Bisman managed to launch. The ship rose swiftly, diminishing to a fiery dot in the sky. "Oh, no!"

More Thelerie winged their way over the plain. Keff recognized

Noonday and her guardians. He waved at them, and pointed at the other ship that had landed.

"More pirates!" Keff had time to shout, as he turned toward Carialle. This time Tall Eyebrow lifted Keff off his feet even before he gave the signal. The wind rushed into his face as they flew back to the ship.

"Ready to lift as soon as you're on board," Carialle said in his aural pickup.

"That one has the last Core," Narrow Leg shouted, his high voice audible even over the sound of Carialle's rockets igniting.

"I know! We'll stop him," Keff said. "Have you got enough fuel for a pursuit, Cari?" he asked.

"Just enough," Carialle said grimly. "If we don't have to use much more Core power ourselves."

The Cridi and Keff swooped in through the door. The Cridi froze their globes to the walls and Keff grabbed the nearest permanent fixture as the airlock slammed shut and Carialle applied full thrust. He was shoved almost all the way to the floor by sheer force, and the roar of the engines threatened to shake his grip.

"Care, care!" Big Voice shrieked. He and half a dozen healers threw their arms across Thunderstorm's body. Their stentorian voices rose in protest, and the patient moaned. Healing impedimenta went flying in every direction, clattering into the bulkheads.

"Sorry," Carialle said over general audio, not taking the time to manifest her frog image on the wall. "It's going to be a rough ride. Cridi, brace everyone and everything that's rolling around loose!"

"We hear!" the shrill voices responded. The external viewscreens swiftly turned from golden to blue to black as Carialle burst out of atmosphere.

As soon as he could move again after the initial push, Keff handed himself toward the crash couch and flung himself into its depths. He started to strap in, when a small human hand reached up and clutched the side of the chair. Keff sat up, and yanked Mirina Don onto his lap. It was a tight fit, but there was just room for both of them. He pulled the straps over her hip and locked them down. She and Keff were pressed almost face to face.

"Oh, please," she said, her soft brown eyes filled with tears. She appealed to Carialle's pillar. "My brother is on that ship. Aldon will kill him. Zon is my only family. Aldon was going to let us leave after we landed here."

"If you can speak to him, do it," Carialle said, concentrating on following the pirate's path precisely. Not one extra centimeter must come between them. "I don't want him dead. I want to talk to him."

"If I help, will you let us go?" Mirina asked. She looked at Carialle's pillar, and back to Keff, who shook his head sadly. "They'll put me in prison. I couldn't stand it."

"I can't," Keff said, helplessly. The desperate look on her face tore at his heart.

"All we can do is try to save lives," Carialle said crisply. "Talk to him. What's the frequency?"

"Reasonable?" Bisman's fierce grimace filled the whole screen. "Reasonable to land and let a CW flunky pick through my brain? They bought you last night, didn't they? You and that sawed-off muscleman."

Mirina had no time for pride. She could see Zonzalo behind Aldon. The boy looked absolutely terrified. She had to do whatever it took to get him to land without harming her brother. He could call her whatever names he wanted to. She clasped her hands. "Please, Aldon. Carialle swears she means you no harm. You have some information she wants. Maybe she'll trade you a favor for it."

"No promises," Carialle cut in. "All I want is a talk. What happens after that is up to the CenCom."

"This is what I say to your CenCom," Bisman sneered. He nodded his head to one side, and Mirina saw Glashton's hands move toward the controls for the Slime Ball. A tremendous jerk rocked the brainship. Mirina was flung backwards. She would have fallen if Keff and the Cridi hadn't caught her. She grabbed the edge of the console and leaned in closer.

"We can't take many of those," Carialle said, grimly. "The Thelerie might have fuel we can use, but no repair facilities."

"Please, Aldon," Mirina begged. "Listen to me. Let Zon go. He's never done you any harm. I'm the one you want. Bring him back, and you can do whatever you want to me."

"Go to hell, Mirina. You're a traitor." Bisman turned away from the screen, but at least he didn't cut off contact.

"We need the Cridi," Keff said, over the top of Mirina's head.

"I will help," one of the little green frogs said, floating away from the Thelerie working on Thunderstorm. "That one is in no danger now."

Mirina was itching to know how the Slime had learned to speak Standard, or why they were so friendly to humans, and she'd give ten years of her life to know how it was flying in midair like that. When Keff gave the order to hang on tight, she dropped back into the crash couch and held onto him. The amphibioid hung like a spider in the air beside the screentank. On it, the image of the reiver ship grew larger and larger.

"All right, Big Voice," Carialle's voice said, softly. "Reach out for the pirate. Gently, but so he knows he's been grappled. Now, hold it, but not hard, like an egg or a piece of fruit. *Now* I wish your landing personnel were here. They know exactly how to do it. Go on. Good."

"So. I see," Big Voice said, gesturing slightly with one surprisingly large hand. The long fingers were coated in a kind of twinkling golden metal. It was a kind of activator. There was a Slime Ball here on this ship. There had been the whole time, and she never knew it!

In the tank, the reiver juddered and hesitated. Mirina was nearly kicked out of the chair by another pull from the Slime Ball aboard the red ship. So this is what it felt like when they used the tractor device on other people: terrifying, inexplicable, intangible, and inexorable. She thrust herself in next to Keff among the padding.

"They must turn back and land at once," another one of the amphibioids ordered, from its place on the wall. "Their Core is overheating! It may explode."

"Mirina," Sunset bleated, from his place on the floor. "Stop the ship jostling! My mentor is injured. This hurts him! How could Bisman do this?"

"He's a bad man, youngster," Mirina said, craning her head over the edge of the chair. Her heart sank at the terrified Thelerie's face. "I should never have let you or any of your people come aboard with him. Heaven knows I shouldn't have done so myself."

"Stop him," Sunset begged Keff.

"I am stopping him," Big Voice said. "Less noise! Must concentrate."

"Bring it back," Narrow Leg interrupted. "That old Core has

reached its end. Can't you hear the frequency?" He followed this with a series of shrill whistles that Keff and Carialle inexplicably seemed to understand.

"Oh, no," Keff said, his face set.

"The Slime will kill them all," Sunset said, trembling.

"No." Thunderstorm stirred and raised a feeble wing-finger to the youth's hand. "They are our friends, too," he whispered. "It is not true they are evil. The humans misled you. I am sorry you learned a lie."

"All I know is broken and lost today," Sunset said, his noble head drooping. Thunderstorm wrapped a wing around him. Mirina felt heartsick.

"I've always cared what happened to you," she said to Sunset.

"That is true," Thunderstorm assured the youngster. Sunset nodded.

"She is my friend. Zonzalo, too."

"Yes," Mirina said, shortly. "He is." Zonzalo must survive. As if she could will him back to safety, she stared at the screen. Bisman's face was shining with sweat. His fingers clutched the navigation controls as Glashton fought to control the Slime Ball. The look on his face told her what the Slime had warned about was happening. Zonzalo had huddled himself into a knot of arms and legs and shock webbing. She was relieved to see that the reivers were too busy trying to manage the ship to think of using him as a negotiating tool. Big Voice tightened his fingers slightly, and the crew on the other ship jerked heavily backward.

"Bisman, land or you'll explode," Keff said urgently. "The Cridi say that you don't have much time before the device you're carrying goes critical! We don't want anyone to die. Turn back at once. Hurry!"

Glashton, visible over Aldon's shoulder, nodded a white-eyed yes to him. Mirina breathed a silent thanksgiving as he backed the engines down.

✦ CHAPTER 21

Carialle timed it so her tailfins touched the ground just before the pirate's did. Keff flung himself up and out of his shock webbing as soon as the altimeter hit zero, not waiting for an all-clear. The Cridi followed him in a stream, except for Big Voice and Small Spot, who elected to stay behind with Thunderstorm and the healers. Tall Eyebrow lifted Keff before he stepped off the ramp, and they sailed lightly over the mud toward the pirate ship. Mirina ran out after them.

"Take me with you!" she shouted. "I have to go to my brother!"

Big Eyes doubled back and picked her up. The woman squeaked in surprise as she was surrounded by an envelope of Core power, then rode in goggling silence the rest of the way.

On the plain near the pavilion, Keff spotted Noonday's white pelt, surrounded by a host of golden backs. Long-eyed like all those of her kind, she saw him long before he'd seen her, and was waving a wing-hand for him to join her. He squinted to bring the artificial lens in his eye to full magnification, and signalled that he was heading toward the newly landed ship. He saw her nod, and go back to talking severely to the others. Keff thought he recognized some of the Thelerie from the remote base in the crowd. The ship behind them was unmistakably Ship Three.

"Hurry!" Narrow Leg cried, flying on ahead as fast as Core power could propel him. "The Core goes critical!"

Tall Eyebrow and the others swept after him. The pirate's ramp lowered, and crew began to pour out of it. Keff and the Cridi flew in over their heads, making for the control room. The pilot stood up. Keff grabbed his wrist and signalled to Wide Foot, who drew him into the air and flew aft toward the exit with him. Zonzalo Don stared up at his sister, hovering in the air with no visible means of support. Keff took him by the shoulders and flung him, with Narrow Leg's help, up into Mirina's arms. Three of the Cridi surrounded Bisman, who cowered down into his chair with his hands above his head. The leader was airborne before he even had a chance to unfold.

"Everybody out!" Keff boomed, pitching his voice over the frightened cries of the crew fleeing for the exit. "Condition red!" He could feel hot gusts of air coming from the aft section. The Core must be back there. No time to remove it. The ship was doomed. "Hurry!"

They emerged into the open air. Waves of heat followed them. The pirates flung themselves out into the mud, gasping for breath.

"It ends," Narrow Leg said. He opened his hands to envelop the group. Keff felt something like a light curtain drop onto his back just before a deafening explosion and a kick of invisible force sent him somersaulting away from the pirates' ship. Plastic globes of Cridi and human bodies hurtled sideways past him. Keff landed with a squashy thud in the yellow mud. He picked himself up on hands and knees, spitting, to watch a plume of fire and smoke rise up from the two halves of the ship, now a hundred meters apart.

"Spacedust," Bisman spat, speaking for the first time. He had landed face first in the mud a dozen meters from Keff. "The hell was that?"

"Something you stole, and never understood," Keff said. "Tad Pole!" he exclaimed, looking up just in time.

"I see," Narrow Leg said. The old Cridi spread his hands again as the debris from the broken ship began to rain down on them. Sections of circuitry, piping, flaming rags, pieces of hull and deck plate, crates of parts, and thousands of little flat pieces of metal pattered down, and bounded off the invisible forcefield ten meters above them like hailstones pinging against a plexiglass dome. The debris splatted down into the mud around them, peppering the landscape. Hundreds of square fragments of metal hammered down on the invisible shield, bouncing off in all directions. Keff realized with a feeling of shock, that he recognized what they were. As soon as Narrow Leg signalled the all-clear, Keff crawled out over the mud, picking through them, searching for one in particular. Suddenly, he spotted the one he was looking for. He pounced on it and put it in his pocket. He turned to his allies and their cowering captives.

"*Now*, let's go back and see Carialle."

Thunderstorm had been settled in Keff's chair like an eagle on its nest, and Noonday occupied the other, so Keff had to stand in the midst of the huge crowd that filled the main cabin. A dozen Thelerie guardians, sitting up on their haunches with their bronze pole-arms ready, surrounded all ten pirates from the hidden base and most of the crew of the now-destroyed raider. The rest were outside, with more of the Sayas's guard. Carialle gazed from a dozen camera eyes at Aldon Bisman, whom Keff had made to stand in front of her pillar. She felt as if she was hammering on a prison door, almost out into the sunshine, if only he would talk! The key was in this obstinate man's mind. He stood with his hands behind him as if on parade rest, staring straight ahead of him, looking at nothing.

"You were in this vicinity twenty years ago, weren't you?" Carialle asked, zooming in on his face with her closest camera eye. Such an ordinary face: human, male, Earth-Indo-European descent, about sixty, confident, choleric. Apart from empirical data, his face gave away no details. "P-sector, not too far from this system."

The man kept his expression blank, though his respiration went up slightly. Keff reached forward and poked him in the shoulder.

"Tell the lady," Keff said, as Bisman turned his head to glare. "She went to a lot of trouble to have you taken alive. The Cridi would cheerfully have split your ship apart in space and left you to die in vacuum. Talk."

"Yeah," Bisman said, at last. His narrow face was coming out in spectacular bruises, whether from the rough landing or Keff's fists, Carialle could not be sure. "I was there. My father's ship. He found this system fifty years ago. It was close to a new CW trading corridor. Easy meat."

"You were stripping wrecks for parts?" Carialle asked. He nodded silently, suspiciously. She almost trembled to ask the next question. "Do you remember one in P-sector that had been destroyed by an explosion in its fuel tanks? It was a Central Worlds Exploration scout. Twenty years ago. Think. You spent about two hours at it. You walked up and back on the hull, four times, two hundred and thirty steps in all." She saw him start, as if she had read his mind.

"I don't have to think," Bisman said, tightlipped. "Yes, I remember one like that. It was hard to tell if anything good was left, it was in such bad shape. Half the tail was missing, all of the control section was slag."

"Would you swear to that?" Carialle asked at once.

"If I had to." His eyes narrowed suspiciously. "Why?"

"Did you know," Carialle asked, feeling her nerves prickle and ordered them under control, "that you were stripping a brainship? A live brainship? *My* ship?"

Bisman's cheeks paled and hollowed as his mouth dropped open. His eyes went wide. "I'd *never*," he choked on the last word and tried again. He looked up straight into her camera eye. "Madam, I would never hurt one of you. Never! What kind of character do you think I am?"

"Did you know?" Carialle asked.

"You've killed a lot of people," Mirina asked, shocked, staring at the man. "Why stop at that?"

"You dumb brawn," Bisman said, whirling to point a finger at her through the crowd of upright Thelerie. "You *fool*! Think of how many people you've bilked out of their savings, Madam Don! You're going to prison, too! You don't get any points for virtue."

Mirina was pale, too, but she confronted him bravely. "You can say a lot of things, Aldon, but you can never accuse me of murder. Did you do it?"

"No! I didn't know," he said, turning back to Carialle's pillar. "It wasn't intentional, madam. I'd never have left a living being in space like that. You don't. Spacer's law. If I'd had any idea . . . if there'd been a sign of life. We monitored for transmissions. There was a beacon going, but what about it? You must have been nearly dead, ma'am. I didn't bomb you."

"I know," Carialle said. "It was sabotage."

"They did the job thoroughly," Bisman said, fervently. "You . . . it was a fused lump. I can't believe you were alive in *that*."

"Oh, I was. I could hear you. You *laughed*. I've been hating you for twenty years," Carialle said, "wondering why you didn't help me get out of there."

"I didn't know," Bisman said, his cool poise shattered. "I swear, none of us did. We saw the hulk, and spotted some components I knew we could boost. We were just trying to make a few credits. But I know the law of space, and I'd hope it would protect me too," he said earnestly. "If I'd had the *least* iota you were alive inside it, I'd have towed you somewhere."

"Somewhere?" Keff asked, shoving his face into the man's and making him back up a pace. "Like that illegal base at the edge of the Cridi system, for example? So you could finish your salvage?"

Bisman faced Keff down with a snarl. "We heard nothing, brawn. That ship was dead, dead, dead so far as I was concerned. If you'd seen how it looked, ma'am, compacted downlike, you would think so, too. There were damaged capacitors firing off now and again nearly blinding us or burning through our gloves, backup batteries imploding up and down the hulk. I'd have put any residual warmth down to those. We didn't have the best equipment, ma'am. That's why we were salvaging. There could've been a heartbeat deep in there, but I swear we checked."

"Not enough," Keff growled.

"Keff, let him alone," Carialle said. "I believe you." The prison door opened, and she saw sunlight beyond it. She felt immeasurably better. "Thank you for the truth." She sighed. "I only wish I had some solid proof to add to your statement."

"I have some," Keff said, pulling the scrap of metal out of his tunic pocket. "I found it in the field when it was raining ship parts." He held it up to the nearest camera eye. Carialle zoomed in on it, but she didn't need magnification. The small titanium square said "963." It was her original number plate.

"I never noticed that one," Mirina said. "He had a whole collection of those from the ships we gutted among the junk he collected. They were his trophies. I'd have recognized it if I'd seen it. They gave me Charles's." She took a square of metal out of her pocket and showed it to Carialle's camera eye over the food synthesizer. On the fragment was etched "702." "I suppose you heard the whole story."

"Yes," Carialle said. "I'm sorry."

"Now we have physical proof and a confession," Keff said,

rubbing his hands together. "We can take this back to the CenCom and shove it up a certain person's nose."

"We have also heard confessions," Noonday said from her nest, looking around for some manifestation of Carialle's to address. Carialle produced the Lady Fair image on the nearest screen over the console, and had it meet the Sayas's golden gaze. "We have those who have shamed us before you now. What will you have us do with them?"

"You'd better ask the Cridi," Carialle said. "I think they have the first claim on reparation."

Big Voice and a few of the others popped up above the crowd. All of the Melange Thelerie protested. The one called Autumn raised her voice.

"Spare us the Slime!" she said desperately, pushing forward to address the image. The guardians crossed their back-scratchers to bar her way. "Only the sacred humans can dictate our fate. I will otherwise kill all my crew."

"Be silent," Noonday said severely.

"We're not sacred," Keff said, shaking his head. "and by the way, I don't think we're your beings of legend. Do you know, Cari, a little idea occured to me. Noonday, let me suggest something to you. Your legend concerns four-limbed, wingless creatures from the stars who were supposed to help you winged ones to fly in the void. Is that right?"

"It is our most beloved story," Noonday said, nodding her great head.

"How old is it?" Keff asked.

"How old? Told for, mmm, one thousand six hundred of our years."

"Narrow Leg," Keff asked, turning to the Cridi captain, "when did the Cridi explore this system and reject it as a possibility for settlement?"

Narrow Leg's eyes twinkled, and he bobbed up and down near the ceiling. The rest of the Cridi looked curious, but he made a few quick hand signals, and they laughed merrily.

"It is possible," he said. "One thousand six hundred revolutions times .88768 equals 1,420 revolutions—yes. It could have been Cridi explorers."

"No!" Autumn said, aghast, gaping at the Cridi. "You assume that all these many years we have revered the *wrong* species?"

"I think that's exactly what you have done," Keff said, rocking back on his heels in satisfaction. "The legend doesn't say how big the beings were, does it?"

"No," Noonday said, peering at him. "It does not."

"Then, it could have been, couldn't it?" Carialle asked, projecting an image of a bipedal being on the wall beside the silhouette of a Thelerie. She made the biped in human proportions, than shrank it to half its original height. "It's more likely they landed here than a stray human ship. They're virtually next door."

"I am disgraced," Autumn said, dropping her gaze to the floor.

The rest of the Thelerie turned to stare at Bisman and the human crew.

"It's not our fault nobody measured your visitors," Bisman said, testily. "Look, we've done a lot for you. "Telephone, gas lights, spaceships . . ."

"You have done much ill, too," Noonday said firmly. "If my child had not admitted the wrongs, if more had been open about their experiences, we would have rejected you long ago." She addressed Carialle. "If you are going back to your Central Worlds, we will keep these bad ones in safe custody until you return."

"There's a lot to do yet," Carialle said. "We can't leave until we . . . I'm receiving an incoming message," she said to Keff. "And this time, it is a CW ship."

"CK-963, this is DSM-344. Remain where you are. Do not lift ship," the uniformed commander said severely from the central screen. "Repeat: do not lift ship. You are under arrest. Any attempts at escape will result in the destruction of your vessel."

"This is the CK-963," Carialle said. "Why are we under arrest?" There was a brief time lag for the distance between the ship and the planet. By the time the screen cleared again, another human had taken the place of the commander in front of the video pickup, a tall, thin man with graying hair and an overwhelming moustache that had been waxed firmly into submission. To Carialle it was the most unwelcome face in the galaxy. Her blood vessels constricted momentarily, but the shock passed quickly.

"This is Dr. Maxwell-Corey, Carialle," he said, in his thin, irritated voice. "You left the Cridi planet strictly against orders."

Keff interposed himself in front of one of her video pickups at once.

"Dr. Maxwell-Corey, how nice to see you," he said. "The circumstances altered the import of your orders. We had to investigate the destruction of the DSC-902, as we transmitted to you, as soon as possible before the perpetrators got too far away. We found them. You did receive our messages?"

"I did," the Inspector General said peevishly. "You conscripted the Cridi for your illegal activity, endangering them on your mad scramble to justify your longstanding mania, Carialle. This will not sit well with Alien Outreach, or Xeno! On my arrival I am insisting that you be placed in protective custody pending a hearing on charges of constructive kidnapping."

"That's ridiculous. We didn't conscript them," Carialle said, feeling the adrenaline in her system increase twofold. "They insisted on accompanying us—their right as an intelligent species. They have saved our lives several times. I am very pleased to have had them as allies."

"They should not be there at all!" The IG's hollow cheeks went red with fury. "An insane brainship and her dupe convincing them to chase off after illusory pirates to a so-called secret base on the fifth planet of the Cridi system? Preposterous! There was a base, if you could call it that," M-C said, disdainfully. "But there were no mysterious 'griffins.' Er . . . griffins," he said, as Noonday moved into range of the video. She smiled at him, and he goggled at her. Carialle knew what it was like for a human the first time a Thelerie smiled, parting its lip to show the needle-sharp fangs underneath, and she enjoyed the effect it had on the Inspector General.

"Thelerie," Carialle said, sweetly. "We know. May I present Noonday, Sayas of Thelerie? She is the head of planetary government. The pirates escaped and came here, sir. They have only just arrived. The commander of that ship is called Autumn, and if you will check the video I sent you, you can see that that is indeed the ship, out there on the landing field." She inserted a view from her external camera of Ship Three, lying abandoned on the plain. "I strongly suspect that if you check their engine compartment, they flew here using components from the DSC-902."

"It is true," Autumn admitted, as Noonday's guards hustled her forward. She wrapped her wings protectively about herself. "Our ship had no propulsion unit left. Nor communications."

Maxwell-Corey stared out of the screen. "They speak Standard." He glared at Keff. "This is undoubtedly *your* doing. You have no right to involve this species in anything. They are not members of the Central Worlds, or if what you say is true in your transmission, possessed of their own technology."

"Breaking the Prime Directive again," Carialle said pertly. "Not guilty on that count either, sir. They spoke Standard when we arrived. That's part of the rest of the story we have to tell you."

"I am glad to encounter you, sir," the Sayas said warmly, opening sincere, striped eyes at the Inspector General. "We wish to apply for membership in the Central Worlds. We wish to be one with all of the blessed humans."

"I . . . I'm not really the one you should speak to about membership," Maxwell-Corey admitted, staring at the golden-eyed beast. "Er, blessed humans?"

"Then, who? We are most eager. We would like to be full members."

"I'm afraid that's impossible. You lack the necessary technology," the Inspector General said. "If the report the CK-963 sent me is accurate, all that you possess is stolen or derelict."

"We are sorry about that," Noonday said, dipping her head slightly. "What you say has recently come to my attention. We're willing to make reparation as we can, but we still wish to fly in space."

"Er, I don't see how." M-C looked bemused.

"*Fait accompli*," Carialle said cheerfully. "They have already been in space numerous times. Plus, they have a viable culture and society. They should be at least given ISS status. The rest will follow."

"We will help them gain access to space," Big Voice piped up, floating close enough to Keff to be included on his camera. Carialle opened up the focus so the IG could see all of the Cridi. "As we began to do many revolutions ago, we will continue. It is only right that we fulfill the promise made so long ago, if such a thing is permitted among the Central Worlds." Behind him, Narrow Leg and the others nodded energetic agreement.

Noonday was very touched. She knelt down onto her belly before the plump councillor. "We accept your offer most gratefully, blessed Cridi."

"Yes," Big Voice said, enjoying himself. "We shall be good patrons to you, and you shall be good customers to us."

✳   ✳   ✳

Mirina stood, feeling dazed, as the conference went on. Autumn and the others were alive! Relief fought in her belly with worry. What would happen to her and her brother now that the Central Worlds authority was coming?

She felt something tap at her knee. She looked down to see one of Keff's—no, Carialle's drone robots beside her. On its platform was the tiny space-scape of Dimitri. She looked up at the wall. An image appeared, the head of the female executive that Carialle had feigned to fool Bisman. It mouthed a single word. "Go."

Mirina dithered for a moment, but only a moment. Everyone's attention was centered on the image of the Inspector General. She grabbed Zonzalo's arm, and began to edge toward the airlock. Sunset glanced up as she sidled behind him. She beckoned hopefully to him, and he nodded, sliding silently backward, away from his spot next to Thunderstorm. The servo made way for them between the guards around the perimeter of the room. At the threshold of the open airlock, the drone offered her the painting with one of its claw hands, and pointed in the direction of Autumn's ship. Mirina needed no further hint. She started running, Zonzalo and Sunset right behind her.

"And in the meantime," Carialle continued, "we've started you off by breaking up a well-established pirate ring with a fifty-year history of theft and murderous raids. That ought to be good for a bonus." M-C turned a fishy eye on Bisman.

"I want to strike a bargain," Bisman said through gritted teeth. "I want legal representation."

"You have nothing we want," Maxwell-Corey said, haughtily.

"Oh, yes?" Bisman asked. "I can give you names, starting with one of your own ex-brawns. How about that, eh?" He scanned the crowd of Thelerie, Cridi, and humans. "She's the real brain behind the operation." He turned around, searching. "Where's Mirina Don?" he demanded.

"Gone," Keff said, pretending to look astonished. "She must have slipped out in all the confusion."

"Her brother's gone, too," Bisman said, angrily. "They can't get far. There's no ship . . ." He turned to look at Autumn.

"Not much fuel, but it flies," Autumn said. "But there is no navigation equipment aboard for humans to use."

"They have Sunset," Thunderstorm said, softly.

The Inspector General rounded on Keff. "You've let a criminal escape!"

"Not me," Keff said, in all innocence. "I've been standing right here the whole time."

Thunderstorm rumbled a phrase in his own language. Carialle whispered the translation into Keff's ear. "My old friend, you have done a good thing." Keff smiled.

Tall Eyebrow stepped forward and addressed the angry human on the screen.

"Think what you do. If you arrest Keff and Carialle, you will jeopardize the fragile alliance between the Cridi and the Central Worlds. If so, we would certainly insist on every human being removed from Sky Clear, which you call Ozran. We could show in a galactic tribunal it was originally a Cridi colony of extreme long standing. I, Tall Eyebrow," he indicated his name in the Ozranian sign language, "speak as the senior representative."

"What?" M-C demanded. Big Voice pushed in close to the camera eye.

"And no access will become possible to our Core technology," the plump councillor insisted. "Such things are to our friends only. We like Keff and Carialle, yet you withdrew . . . what is word, Keff?"

"Portfolio," Keff said, with an angelic expression.

"Portfolio," Big Voice said. "A pity indeed where so much is in common. We would have traded happily for good spacecraft. But no alliance, no ships, no Cores." He shook his head, imitating the human expression of regret, a gesture that was not lost on Maxwell-Corey.

"But—that was part of the agreement sent by the diplomatic service to Cridi," the Inspector General said, looking from brawn to pillar to Cridi with desperation in his eyes.

"Which they were not able to sign," Carialle pointed out. "We delayed having the documents ratified because *you* sent in another team, and they were killed by the Melange."

"My dear Carialle," M-C said, in amazement, "you were withdrawn from the mission because you had a paranoid episode. Your actions were what held diplomacy hostage, not the destruction of the other ship."

"I did *not* have a paranoid episode," Carialle said, coldly. "I had an anxiety attack, brought on by proximity to the location where I once had a near-fatal accident. It is your interpretation of my reaction that caused you to assume paranoia, and to send another ship. You are ultimately responsible for the unnecessary death of the crew of the shuttle."

"Ah, yes," Maxwell-Corey said, maddeningly tenting his fingers together on his narrow belly. "Now we come to it. Your phantom aliens. Your salvage wreckers."

Carialle played the datatape of Bisman's admission on the transmission frequency, and waited. Maxwell-Corey ignored it at first, staring instead straight at his camera eye. Within moments Carialle observed him leaning closer to the screen. A scan sneaked through the sideband of the bandwidth told her he was manifesting anxiety, with increased levels of adrenaline in his system. He spoke at last.

"Yes, well, you could have extorted such a statement from him."

"Bisman!" Keff called. "Is it true?"

The pirate leader looked up. "Yes," he said, through his teeth.

"Do you see?" Carialle said. "And Keff found my old number plate among his effects." Keff displayed it to the video pickup.

"This is very interesting," M-C said, tapping his fingertips together nervously. "Very interesting indeed."

"Indeed," Carialle echoed, icily. "Then you will find it no surprise to hear that I am bringing a second formal complaint against you. Date-coded messages have already gone out to SPRIM and MM as well as my legal counsel regarding the programming you inserted into my message-beacon system. You overstepped reasonable bounds, and I intend to have you taken to task for it!"

"My dear Carialle, it was for your own good!" the IG protested.

"You've had time to absorb the information," Carialle said. "Am I sane? This is official. I am time-coding your reply. Am I?"

"Evidence suggests that the answer might conceivably be . . . yes," the IG said, after a very long pause and a study of the ceiling. "But the evidence only came to light at this juncture, that is to say, now. I was acting on the information of the time. You *could* have imperiled many people, including yourself."

"When your own psychologists said I wasn't a threat," Carialle said. "When we finish this mission, I'll have something to say to the CenCom, *personally*. I assume we are to complete the mission to the Cridi?"

"Yes, yes," M-C said, defeated. His shoulders sagged. "You're reinstated. You are the best team for the job. I've always had the utmost faith in you."

"They have done such a good job," Tall Eyebrow said, floating up to give his words emphasis. "You must tell it to those of CenCom. And teaching us so much about space travel, including such delightful games as Myths and Legends! Such an important cultural gift!"

The Inspector General sputtered, but he managed to hold his tongue. "I will be down presently. We'll talk about the, er, the details of your mission then. I have much to consider before we land. Maxwell-Corey out."

Keff felt a smirk at the corners of his mouth as the screen blanked. "Bravo, Cari!" he said, applauding her. "And bravo, TE. Thank you for rubbing salt in the wound."

"It is not salt," Tall Eyebrow said, puzzled. "It is truth."

At a gesture from the Sayas's wing-finger, the Sayas's guardians assembled the prisoners, both human and Thelerie, and marched out, leaving only the Cridi, Thunderstorm and Noonday.

"The healing really begins now," Carialle said to Keff, who stood close beside her pillar. "He won't dare to persecute me again."

"Which way did she go, Cari?" Keff asked softly.

"I don't know," Carialle said. "I've blanked it out of my memory. But if I were her I'd run for the balance point. Once she's behind the anomaly she can change direction without being detected." Keff looked at Noonday and Thunderstorm.

"If she comes back, will you treat her kindly?"

"As she has always treated us," Thunderstorm said.

"I feel she is already punished somewhat," Noonday said. "And she has killed no one. She will be allowed."

"Thank you," Keff said, sincerely. He turned to the Cridi. "Well, TE, I suppose we'll be taking you home to Ozran soon?"

"Much left to do here, for a while," the Frog Prince said. "Must retrieve all parts of the ship, and hope none are damaged. But once it is reassembled, Narrow Leg wants to take us home himself. He would see where Big Eyes will be living. She is staying with me. It will be difficult . . ."

"It will be fine," Big Eyes interrupted him.

"Congratulations!" Keff said. The young female flirted her eyelids shyly at him as she took Tall Eyebrow's hand and interlaced his long fingers in hers.

"Yes," Big Voice said, waddling forward. "Instead, you shall have the honor of taking *me* home to Cridi, where I shall tell story of great heroism of mine. I captured the evil ship. And see the burns on my back where alien gas touched me, yet I continued with rescue of injured Thelerie!"

Carialle sighed deeply, but it was for pure happiness. "Games are good," she said, "but you can't beat real life. We've never had a game where everyone lived happily ever after."

Keff, thinking of Mirina, hurtling away from the planet in a rickety ship, but free, said, "Or as close as it's possible to be."

Carialle's Lady Fair image appeared on the wall and winked solemnly at him. She knew exactly what he was thinking.

The white and blue ship sank gracefully out of the sky like a diva taking a curtain call. It landed softly but heavily on the plain between Carialle's ship and the smoking hulk of the red pirate, and sank a good three meters in the viscous yellow mud. Keff, hovering among the Cridi centimeters over the surface of the plain, was on hand as the gangplank dropped with a splat. Thelerie, including Noonday and most of the Ro-sayo, swirled in to flit about the ship as soon as the engines shut off. Three security officers in full environment kit and gleaming armored suits trotted out onto the ramp, careful not to step off into the shining goo. They looked up at the gathering crowd, and stared. It only took a moment for them to realize they were looking at three different species of beings. The youngest among them, a thin-faced rating with freckles, stared openmouthed at Cridi and Thelerie until his CO elbowed him. The young man came on guard, his long-barreled gun leveled over his forearm. The CO let out a sharp all-clear whistle, and two more space-suited humans emerged. One, in black armor, must have been the commander of the ship. The other, in official blue and red, was the Inspector General.

"Cari, I'm a little worried," Keff said into his sublingual link as he made a little salute to the ship's crew. The gangplank, under the additional weight of the IG, sank an additional quarter meter into the mud. "Will you be able to handle seeing Maxwell-Corey face-to-face?"

"Oh, don't worry, Keff," Carialle said, confidently. "This time I'm ready for him. Bring him along! And, Keff?"

"Yes?" Keff asked.

"Let him walk!"

~THE END~